READER'S DIGEST
CONDENSED BOOKS

www.readersdigest.co.uk

The Reader's Digest Association
Limited 11 Westferry Circus
Canary Wharf London E14 4HE

For information as to ownership of
copyright in the material of this
book, and acknowledgments, see last
page.

Printed in France
ISBN 0 276 42578 2

READER'S DIGEST CONDENSED BOOKS

*Selected and edited
by Reader's Digest*

CONDENSED BOOKS DIVISION

THE READER'S DIGEST ASSOCIATION LIMITED, LONDON

CONTENTS

SHATTERED

Dick Francis

When jockey Martin Stukely is killed in a
steeplechasing accident, his sudden death
plunges his friend Gerard Logan into a
desperate hunt for a valuable video tape.
Soon, Logan, a glass-blower by trade, is
receiving threats to his life and livelihood.
As he fights for survival, he turns to attractive
local policewoman Catherine Dodd for aid.
Colourful drama and intrigue, from the
much-loved king of British storytelling.

PUBLISHED BY MICHAEL JOSEPH

SILENCE AND SHADOWS

James Long

A team of archaeologists, led by Paddy
Kane, a rock star trying to flee his
misspent past, starts work on a dig in
Oxfordshire. As they uncover the grave
of a remarkable Anglo-Saxon warrior
queen, Paddy crosses paths with her
modern-day lookalike and finds hope,
at last, for his tormented heart. A haunting
story of love and redemption, in which
past and present are deftly interwoven.

PUBLISHED BY HARPERCOLLINS

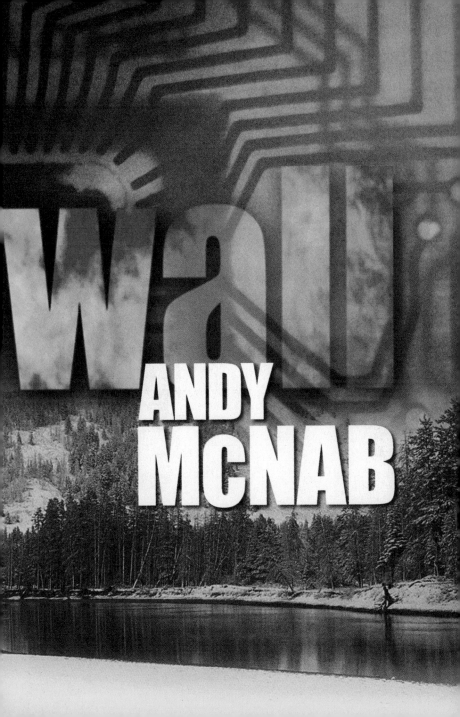

A powerful faction within Russian organised crime is desperate to penetrate the electronic firewall protecting Echelon, a computer database holding some of the West's most valuable intelligence.

Who better to help them than an ex-SAS man who's fallen out of favour with his MI6 bosses, and who's looking for a job?

Enter Nick Stone . . .

One

HELSINKI, FINLAND, Monday, December 6, 1999. The Russians were serious players. If things didn't go as planned, Sergei said, I'd be lucky to be shot dead in the hotel lobby. If they captured me, I'd be taken to a remote bit of wasteland and have my stomach slit open. They'd pull my intestines out and leave me to watch them squirm around on my chest like a bucket of freshly caught eels for the thirty minutes it would take me to die. These things happen, he had explained, when you mess with the main men in ROC—Russian organised crime. But I didn't have a choice; I desperately needed the cash.

'What's it called again, Sergei?' I mimed the disembowelment.

Eyes staring straight ahead, he gave me a brief, sombre smile and muttered, 'Viking's revenge.'

It was just before 7.00pm and it had already been dark for three and a half hours. The air temperature had been well below freezing all day; it hadn't snowed for a while, but there was still a lot of the stuff about, ploughed to the sides of the roads.

The two of us were parked two blocks from the Intercontinental Hotel, in the black Nissan 4x4. The rear seats were down flat to make it easier to bundle the target inside, complete with me wrapped round him like a wrestler to keep him there.

We sat facing Mannerheimintie, 200 yards down the hill from our position. The boulevard was the main drag into the city centre. It carried a constant stream of slow, obedient traffic. Up here it was like a different world. Low-level apartment blocks hugged each side of the quiet street and an inverted 'V' of white Christmas lights sparkled in almost every window.

I kept visualising how, when and where I was going to do my stuff. Once the target has been selected the basic sequence of a kidnap is nearly always the same. First comes reconnaissance; second, abduction; third, detention; fourth, negotiation; fifth, ransom payment; and finally, release. My job was to plan and implement the first three phases; the rest of the task was out of my hands.

Three members of the loud-tie-and-braces brigade from a private bank had approached me in London. They'd been given my name by an ex-Regiment mate who now worked for one of the big security companies, and who'd been nice enough to recommend me when this particular commission had been declined.

'Britain', they said to me as we sat at a window table in the roof bar of the Hilton, 'is facing an explosion in Russian mafia-organised crime. London is a money-laundering haven. ROC is moving as much as twenty billion pounds through the City each year.'

The executives went on to say they'd discovered that millions had been channelled through Valentin Lebed's accounts at their bank in just three years. They were none too keen on the thought of the boys with the blue flashing lights paying him a visit and seeing the name on all his paying-in slips. Their solution was to have Val lifted and taken to St Petersburg, where, I presumed, they had made arrangements to persuade him either to move his account to a different bank or to channel even more through them to make the risk more acceptable.

I looked over at Sergei as he stared at the traffic below. There wasn't anything left to say; we'd done enough talking during the two-week build-up. It was now time to do.

The conference of European Council members was due to start in Helsinki in two days. Like all the high-class hotels, the Intercontinental was housing the exodus from Brussels. Security was tight, and they would certainly have contingency plans for every possible event, especially armed attack.

Sergei had a folding-stock AK assault rifle under his feet. In the old Soviet army body armour he wore under his duvet jacket, he looked like the Michelin man. Late forties, square jaw, high cheekbones and blue eyes that didn't just pierce, they chopped you into tiny pieces. He was a hard, reliable man, and one I felt it was OK to do business with.

I had read about Sergei Lysenkov's freelance activities in Intelligence Service reports. He had been a member of Alpha Group, an elite of special-forces officers within the KGB. When hard-line heads of the KGB led the 1991 coup in Moscow, they ordered Alpha Group to kill Yeltsin, but Sergei and his mates decided that the politicos were all as bad as each other. They disobeyed the order and the coup failed. When Yeltsin learned what had nearly happened he took them under his direct command, cutting their power by turning them into his own bodyguards. Sergei decided to quit and make his experience and knowledge available to the highest bidder, and today that was me.

I needed Russians on the team because I needed to know how Russians think, how Russians do. And when I discovered that Valentin Lebed would be in Helsinki for twenty-four hours of R and R, and not in his fortress in St Petersburg, Sergei was the only one who could organise vehicles, weapons and the bribing of border guards in the time available.

The people who briefed me on the job had done their homework. Valentin Lebed, they told me, had been smart during the fall of communism. His rise was brutal and meteoric: within two years he was one of the dozen heads of the ROC 'mafiocracy'.

Coming from dirt-poor beginnings as a farmer's son in Chechnya, he'd fought against the Russians in the mid-nineties war. His fame was sealed after rallying his men by making them watch *Braveheart* time and again. After the war he'd had other ideas, all involving US dollars, and the place he'd chosen to realise them was St Petersburg.

Much of his money came from arms dealing, extortion and a string of nightclubs in Moscow that served as fronts for prostitution rackets. Jewellery businesses he had 'acquired' in Eastern Europe were used as a front to fence icons stolen from churches and museums. In the Far East, according to the guys who'd briefed me, he'd even bought an airline just so he could ship out heroin without administrative hassle.

Three blocks the other side of the hotel were two more of our six-man team. Carpenter and Nightmare were armed with 9mm mini-Uzi machine guns on harnesses under their overcoats, the same as the bodyguards we were going up against. It was ironic, but Sergei had obtained the team's Uzis and semiautomatic suppressed 7mm pistols from one of Valentin's own dealers.

Carpenter and Nightmare weren't their real names, of course. Sergei—the only one who spoke English—had told me that was how they translated, and that was how he referred to them. Just as well, as I couldn't have pronounced them in Russian anyway.

Nightmare certainly wasn't the sharpest tool in Sergei's shed. Things needed to be demonstrated twenty or thirty times before he got the idea. There was a flatness to his face that, together with his constantly shifting eyes, made him look a bit scary.

Carpenter had a heroin habit that Sergei assured me would not affect his performance, but it certainly had during the build-up. He had lips that were constantly at work, as though he'd swallowed something and was trying to recapture the taste.

The last two on the team I'd christened the Kray twins, and they were in a green Toyota 4x4. Unlike the other two, they didn't have to be told what to do more than twice. They had the trigger on the target's three black Mercedes, which were about a mile away from the hotel. They also had folding-stock AKs, armour-piercing rounds in their magazines and, like Sergei, wore body armour.

The target was well protected and his vehicles were securely parked underground so that no device—explosive from his enemies or surveillance from law enforcement—could be placed. When they finally moved out to pick him up from the hotel with the rest of his bodyguards, the Krays would follow. Carpenter and Nightmare would then take up their positions in the hotel, along with me. Sergei, Reggie and Ronnie would take on the vehicles.

The Krays were both ex-Alpha Group, too. They'd been together since their time as young conscripts in Afghanistan, leaving after the Chechen war, disillusioned with the leadership that had let them lose against the rebels. Both were in their mid-thirties, with dyed blond hair, very clean shaven and well groomed.

I knew I could trust Sergei, but I still wondered about his selection procedure. He obviously wanted to keep most of the wad I'd promised him and had decided not to bring the A team. If they weren't complaining to him about my planning, Sergei said, they were moaning about who was earning what and how they might get ripped off when it came to payday.

The digital display on the dash told me another twenty minutes had passed—time for a radio check. Reaching into my inside jacket pocket, I felt for the SEND button of my Motorola handset. All six of us had one, each connected to an earpiece.

I pressed twice, the squelch sounding off in my ear, then checked with Sergei. He nodded; I was sending. Reggie and Ronnie replied with two squelches, then Carpenter and Nightmare followed with three. There was radio silence for two reasons. One, I couldn't speak the language, and two, EU land security would be listening in.

I was very much the businessman: single-breasted suit, dark-grey overcoat, black woollen scarf and thin leather gloves. Nightmare and Carpenter were dressed in the same style. All three of us were clean shaven, hair washed and well groomed. Detail counts: we had to move about the hotel without anyone giving us a second glance. Across my lap I even had today's *Herald Tribune*.

My overcoat concealed the body armour under my shirt, which consisted of just twelve paper-thin sheets of Kevlar—not enough to stop one of Sergei's armour rounds, but enough to see off the mini-Uzis that might soon be trying to hose me down. Carpenter had refused to wear any because it wasn't manly, and Nightmare had followed suit. Mad.

I was carrying a Z88 pistol and three twenty-round mags. If things went to plan I wouldn't even be drawing down. The lift should be silent and take less than a minute.

I heard six quick squelches in my earpiece. The three pick-up Mercs were mobile towards the hotel. I replied with two squelches, then heard another two from Nightmare and Carpenter, who should now be getting out of their car and heading for the hotel. Sergei just nodded. I got out of the 4x4 and headed up the hill for thirty yards, then took a right turn to the next T-junction. That put me on the road adjacent to the hotel, facing down towards the main drag again.

I could see the large grey concrete building in front of me on the left-hand side of the road. Just short of it were roadworks.

The noise from the main road grew as I walked downhill. The Kray twins would be on it now, following the Mercs. Nightmare and Carpenter should be walking into the hotel from the opposite side and Sergei would be positioning himself at the front. I crossed the road, passing the hotel's rear service and car-park entrance, and continued downhill.

Valentin Lebed's weakest point would be tonight, in Finland, in this hotel, before he left for the theatre to see *Romeo and Juliet*.

About thirty yards short of the main road I hit the semicircular driveway in front of the Intercontinental's entrance and turned left. The ground-floor walls were glass, through which I could see the warm and cosy-looking interior.

The plan was simple. Nightmare and Carpenter were to kill the close bodyguards protecting the target as he came from the lift, then cover me as I took the target towards the main doors. While this was happening, the Kray twins would block off the rear of the Mercs with their 4x4, Sergei would block the front with the Nissan, and all three would be controlling the other bodyguards and drivers with their AKs.

Once outside, I'd head for the back of the Nissan, dragging the target with me. We'd both lie under a blanket, with my pistol rammed in his gob, while Sergei drove to the vehicle drop-off point, where the target would be switched to the boot of a changeover vehicle en route to the border. We'd all RV near the border and get into a truck that was rigged up with hidden compartments. Then it was just a few hours to St Petersburg and payday.

I walked through two sets of automatic tinted-glass doors, then I was in, my face flushed from the downward blast of the heaters above the doorway.

I knew the foyer area well. In front of me, behind a group of noisy Japanese tourists surrounding a mountain of suitcases, was the reception desk. In the far right-hand corner was a corridor that led to the restaurant, toilets and the all-important lifts. Immediately to my right was the Baltic Bar. To my left, bellboys were buzzing around a sprinkling of sofas and coffee tables.

I headed for one of the sofas, sitting so that I had the brass-effect lift doors in view down the corridor. I spread out the *Tribune* on the coffee table and unbuttoned my overcoat.

Three minutes later the headlights of the three Mercs raked the ground-floor windows. Reggie and Ronnie should have pulled up just short of the semicircular driveway where they'd be standing by.

I waited for the inside set of sliding doors to open, keeping my head down, concentrating hard on my newspaper.

In came the bodyguards. Two pairs of shiny Italian shoes and expensive black cashmere overcoats over black trousers. You always avoid eye contact, because they'll be looking for it. If your eyes lock they'll know you aren't there to talk about the beef ban. I watched the two sets of heels make their way over to the far right of the foyer. They paused by the brass lift doors.

The middle door slid open with a gentle *ping*. The shoes went in. The doors closed and the indicator light stopped at the Ambassador Suite. They were going to meet up with the other two bodyguards who were already with Valentin, their principal, my target.

I got up and started to walk towards the main doors. As I moved past them towards the dark-wood Baltic Bar, I could see three black Mercs on the other side of the glass, exhaust fumes condensing in the cold air. The bar was half full. I made my away round the tables and leather chesterfields towards the far door.

I seated myself where I could best see down the corridor to the three lift doors. Beyond them were the reception and foyer. At the other end of the corridor, Carpenter and Nightmare should be in position in the restaurant, with a clear view down to the foyer. Under the table I pulled on my right glove and eased my index finger through the cut I had made in the leather.

Five long minutes went by as lifts came and went, but Val still hadn't made an appearance. My heart was pumping big time.

Another *ping*. The two pairs of expensive Italian shoes emerged from the nearest lift and stopped in the corridor for a second or two, each pair facing in a different direction. Then both moved towards the foyer, disappearing from view.

I gave the Motorola six clicks on the SEND button, hearing the squelch in my earpiece each time. Val would be down any minute.

There was a *ping* from the furthest lift. Another two pairs of black patent-leather shoes, dress-suit trousers under black overcoats. They stepped out on either side of a light grey cashmere coat and the smartest trousers of all, followed by a pair of very long, slim, well-toned, black-stockinged calves, topped off with the world's most luxuriant mink. Val's slapper, keeping him warm on those long lonely nights away from his family.

They turned out of the lift. I stood up slowly.

Carpenter and Nightmare emerged from the restaurant and began to match the purposeful strides of the bodyguards. I fell in behind them as they drew their suppressed weapons.

About five yards ahead of us, the backs and very wide shoulders of the bodyguard pair flanked Val and the slapper as they moved towards the Japanese-filled foyer. We needed to close in on them fast, while they were still in the confines of the corridor.

Three more yards before we were on top of them. There was another *ping* as the lift doors opened and a middle-aged couple began to step out between us and the target.

This was a contingency I had rehearsed. I moved to push the couple back. As I did so, Carpenter's right hand came up. Without taking his eyes off Val, he fired three or four suppressed rounds into the couple as he passed. I could hear the dull thud of the rounds exiting the barrel. Shit, her scream turned the job noisy and we hadn't even taken out the bodyguards.

The couple fell back into the lift, the woman taking all the rounds, her white silk blouse red with blood. Slotting players was one thing, but real people meant big trouble.

The two bodyguards turned and started to draw down their weapons, but Carpenter and Nightmare had closed the gap and gave them both two rounds in the head from less than a foot away.

Carpenter should have moved on, but he continued firing down at the bodies. They were dead. He was wasting time. I saw his glazed eyes. He was high on whatever it was that he used to get through the long winters. Fuck it, I'd kill the maniac myself before this got out of control. I shoved my right hand between my jacket and shirt, towards my 88. Carpenter turned to fire into the other body on the floor. Drawing the 88, I pulled down on the safety catch with my thumb and raised the weapon. But as Carpenter tried to fire again, I could see the top slide of his weapon being held back by the locking lever. He had run out of rounds.

Real life burst into my eardrums once again. It was Nightmare, shouting into his Motorola at the 4x4s to move in on the Mercs as he gripped Carpenter's arm, dragging him towards the foyer.

I was now no more than two steps from Val. He spun round, looking back towards the restaurant, thinking he could make his escape. We had eye-to-eye. He knew I was coming for him, and he knew it was too late to do much about it. He stood there waiting, accepting. He must have known this would happen one day. I put the crook of my left arm round his neck, still moving forward so it jammed tight against his throat. He staggered back as I took another step, forcing his face up. I heard him gag. He was only five foot seven, quite easy to get a grip on. The slapper in the mink didn't react. I expected her to scream, but she just stood to one side, back to the wall, and watched.

With the pistol in my right hand and still moving, I pushed my right arm behind his neck to complete the head lock. At once he started fighting for oxygen; there was no way he wasn't coming with me. There was no need to check him for weapons. He didn't need one tonight; he was a businessman on his way to the theatre.

I continued on into the foyer, heading for the exit. Nightmare came into view by the main doors, doing his stuff to one of the bodyguards, shouting in Russian and kicking his hands away from his body. I was twenty-odd yards away from them.

Through the windows, the blaze of headlights from the three Mercs lit Sergei's 4x4, which had the tailgate open, waiting for me and Val. Beyond the Mercs' roofs, I could see Reggie and Ronnie, AK butts unfolded and in the shoulder, muzzles pointing at the ground. Val's three drivers were face down on the tarmac. Carpenter was to the left of the convoy, his weapon, too, pointing down. He must have been covering the other bodyguard. Sergei would be in the wagon, waiting for me to get out of this lunatic asylum.

With ten yards to go, World War Three broke out. I heard a series of short bursts from a 9mm, the muzzle flashes bouncing off the windows like flash bulbs.

It was Carpenter, giving the bodyguard the best part of a mag.

I couldn't believe it. More muzzle flashes lit up the darkness outside, the heavier 7.62 reports from Reggie and Ronnie echoing through the building. The drivers must have gone for their weapons, thinking they were next. Nightmare was shaking with fear as he stood over the last bodyguard. He stared at me, waiting for direction.

There was no way I was going out of the front door with a firefight in progress. Turning, I moved Val as quickly as I could back to the corner of the corridor. The slapper was still there, well in control of herself. She just stood, watching, not even bothering to wipe the dropped bodyguard's blood off her face.

There was more hysteria as rounds starred the safety glass around the entrance. The bodyguard had obviously seized his chance and got to his feet, firing as he went for freedom. Nightmare took the burst into his unprotected trunk and crumpled.

The bodyguard started towards me, mini-Uzi in his right hand. What was he going to do? He couldn't open up on me without hitting his boss.

Turning Val round to face his bodyguard and protect me, I lifted my 88. I wasn't going to do much against his body armour, even if I could hit a moving target at fifty feet one-handed with a pistol. I had to wait until he was nearer.

I fired at him from about thirty feet, aiming below centre mass. It was pointless aiming at his head at that range.

I'd emptied at least half of the twenty-round mag, not knowing whether it was going to drop him or not, when I heard him scream and he went down, his legs buckling.

Dragging Val, I turned right down a wide corridor, heading for the rear car-park door. I was going it alone now, leaving the contact outside to sort itself out. I knew where I needed to go; time spent in reconnaissance is seldom wasted.

Reaching the bottom of the corridor, I hit the crossbar of the car-park door and burst out of the rear of the building. I could see the car park and loading bays. The only vehicle in sight was a small Hilux van. I tried the door. It was locked. There was no choice but to drag Val up the concrete stairs and onto the loading bay.

Inside was what looked like a minicab office, with a desk. A woman was talking in Finnish on the phone. I shouted and pointed the 88.

'The keys! Give me the vehicle keys. Now!'

She knew what I was saying. She dropped the phone and pointed at the desk. I grabbed them and ran back down the stairs to the van, Val clenching his teeth as he took the pain in his neck.

I ripped off the cardboard that was keeping the windscreen ice-free and opened the passenger door. 'Get in, get in!'

With my pistol stuck into his neck, Val got the drift.

Once I'd finished kicking him into the foot well, I climbed over on top of him, keeping the pistol against his neck as I moved into the driver's seat and put the key in the ignition. Firing the engine, I threw it into gear.

The tyres pounded the cobblestones as I drove downhill to the main road, the demister on full. I got level with the hotel drive. The Nissan was missing. Maybe Sergei had got away. All the other vehicles were still there. Bodies were strewn all over the ground. I couldn't tell who was who from this distance. At the junction with the main road, I turned right and merged with the traffic.

Flashing blue lights streamed past me as I headed in the direction of the city centre.

At the second option I turned right. The 88 was in my right hand, still rammed into Val's neck, forcing me to change gear with my left and hold the wheel in position with my knees.

Plan B was in action now. We'd each make our own way back to the lakeside house where we'd been based for the last two weeks, and wait for twenty-four hours.

I was feeling vulnerable without Sergei. I might have the 'money' curled up in the foot well, but without help there was no way I was going to get it over the border. Sergei was the only one squared away with the world's most corrupt border guards and he had not told anyone else how it was organised. That was his insurance policy.

From all around me came the sound of sirens. I needed to get to the drop-off point as soon as possible and detach myself from the hotel road show. I put my foot down. Four more minutes and I was level with the chain-link fence of a car park. Over towards the hotel, a low-flying helicopter lit up the sky with its Nightsun. The beam bounced around, searching the park and the road.

Car parks are always the best place to lose a car. This one was free—no cameras, no staff and not lit up—which was why Sergei and I had decided to use it. I drove towards the entrance, and as I passed under a height bar it was as if I'd entered a new world, dark and safe.

After driving a circuit to check the area, I found the row of vehicles where the dark blue Volvo saloon was parked with its boot sticking out. I stopped, making a T of the car and the van and leaving my headlights on.

Police sirens wailed in the distance. I looked down at Val and could make out his face in the glow of the dashboard. His eyes showed no fear. He was switched on enough to accept that overreaction at this stage could result in him being killed.

I took the keys out of the ignition. 'Stay.' I sounded as if I was talking to a dog.

I got out of the Hilux and could hear the *thud thud thud* of the heli's rotor blades as it hovered in the distance, raking the ground with its Nightsun. All their attention was still in the vicinity of the hotel, but I knew it wouldn't last.

I walked around the front of the wagon, keeping my eyes on the cab, the weapon down by my side. I felt under the rear right-hand wheel arch of the Volvo and retrieved the key. I hit the fob and the doors unlocked. I inserted the key in the boot lock and pulled it open.

Reggie and Ronnie had glued thick sponge all round the framework of the luggage area, mainly so the target didn't injure himself, but also to subdue any noise if he felt like having a kick and scream while we were in transit. They'd also lined the floor with a thick four-seasons duvet ready to stop him dying of hypothermia. Sitting on top was an orange plastic ball about the size of an egg, a roll of black gaffer tape and several sets of plasticuffs.

I opened the passenger door and Val looked up at me. I didn't have a clue what would happen to him once we hit St Petersburg, and I didn't care. All I was concerned about was the $500,000 on offer, or what was left of it after Sergei got his $200,000.

I brought the 88 up, angled my wrist and rammed the weapon into the space above his waistcoat. Tilting the weapon up so the grip was near his face, I made sure he saw me remove the safety catch with my thumb and heard the click. With my free hand I reached under his waistcoat. 'Up, up, up.'

He came out of the foot well and staggered onto the tarmac.

I turned him so the backs of his thighs were against the boot of the Volvo and leaned onto him. He got the idea and manoeuvred himself in, ending up on his back in the boot.

I got hold of the orange plastic ball and stuffed it into his mouth. Reggie and Ronnie had folded over the last four inches of gaffer tape on the roll so I could do the next bit with one hand. I taped round his mouth and chin, then up around his eyes and ears, leaving just his nose uncovered.

I heard the heli's engine change pitch. It was moving again, its Nightsun now at forty-five degrees, illuminating everything in its path, working its way towards me.

Slamming the boot shut on Val, I jumped back into the Hilux. I sat and waited; there was nothing else I could do. The car and van were flooded with light for a second or two, then the engine note changed and the heli lurched off in the direction of the main route out of town.

I drove the van into an empty space, got out and went to check on Val. He was breathing heavily. I watched him and waited. He might have sinus problems, a blocked nose. I didn't want him to die; I only got paid for meat on the hoof. He snorted loudly to clear his nose.

Headlights veered towards me. I leaned over Val to make it look as if I was sorting out my packages. The problem went. Either the vehicle had found a parking space or left the area. I stood up slowly and had a look around, then rammed the pistol into Val's neck. With my other hand I got hold of his shoulder and started to pull.

He got the drift. I wanted him on his front. The car rocked slightly with his exertions, but there was nobody around to notice. Once he was on his stomach, I got hold of one of the plasticuffs, looped it round his wrists and pulled it tight. Then I wrapped the duvet around him.

The Volvo started first time. I headed left, out onto the main road, away from the hotel, then east out of Helsinki towards the motorway. I only hoped Sergei was doing the same. The RV was at Vaalimaa, about 110 miles away.

I turned on the radio and drove, thinking about everything and nothing. Twice I saw the flashing lights of a heli.

Eventually I passed the Vaalimaa service-station area. This was trucker's heaven, the final stop before Russia. They used it as a meeting point so that they could move on in convoy.

Vaalimaa was just a couple of miles from Sergei's tame checkpoint. Six miles north of the town was the lakeside house.

I checked every lay-by and minor road for police activity. There was nothing. Then my lights hit the marker I was looking for, mailbox 183, a red plastic pedal bin on a white pole. I turned right, onto a deeply rutted track that led into the forest, and switched off the radio.

It was only a matter of hours since we'd last driven up it. About ten yards in, a white-painted chain, suspended between two poles, barred the way. Attached to it was a wooden sign saying PRIVATE PROPERTY, in Finnish.

I left the engine running and got out of the car. I looked carefully at the chain but could see nothing in the shadow cast by the Volvo's headlights. I took the weight of the chain so the first links came loose and pulled gently. I could feel the tension of the cotton that still fastened it to the hook, and then the sudden release as it broke. No one had been through here who shouldn't have.

I drove over the chain, then jumped out and replaced it. To the side, under a pile of stones, the reel of cotton thread was just where I'd left it. I tied the first link to the hook again, replaced the reel and got back in the car.

The pines were tall and close to the track. After 250 yards the trees retreated, leaving a stretch of open ground covered by a blanket of snow three feet deep. The track dipped slightly and the two-storey house was caught in the beam of my headlights. There were no lights on inside, no vehicles outside.

The track led to a wooden lean-to with enough room for three cars. I drove in and killed the engine. A huge stack of firewood filled the whole of the back wall. A door on the left led to the house and the lake on the far side.

The key was hidden in the log pile. I went inside the main building and was hit by wonderful warmth. We'd left all the heaters on. I threw the light switch and went back to the car for Valentin.

After two hours in the boot he was shaking with cold.

'Right, come on. Up, up.' I moved his legs over the sill and pulled him out, then guided him inside and sat him on an old green velour settee next to a radiator.

The decor was functional—bare wooden floors and walls—and the downstairs was one large open space. A stone fireplace stood opposite the door and three evenly spaced wooden pillars, each about a foot in diameter, helped to support the floor above.

I pulled hard on the gaffer tape around Valentin's face. He winced as the adhesive took neck and eyebrow hair with it. He spat out the ball, coughing and spluttering.

'Stay there.' I pointed at the radiator, not that he would be going anywhere plasticuffed up. 'You'll be warm in a minute.'

I went to get a brew on. Standing by the kitchen worktop that stretched along one wall and waiting for the kettle to boil, I watched Val shivering. He'd had a hard life, judging by the lines on his face. But he still had his Slavic good looks: wide cheekbones, green eyes and dark brown hair, grey at the temples.

The water boiled as I opened a packet of crispbread that was on the worktop. I munched a piece and emptied the kettle onto ground beans in a cafetière.

The team's kit had been piled into bags to the left of the main door. Sergei and I had planned to return here after delivering the money to St Petersburg—me to drive to Sweden and then, via ferry, to Germany; him to clean up this place. I picked up a kitbag and threw it on the table. I fished inside for more plasticuffs, putting three together to make one long one.

I dragged Val over towards the central pillar and pushed him down so he was sitting against it. Then I plasticuffed his upper right arm to the support, and with my multipurpose Leatherman tool I cut the original plasticuffs so that his left arm was free.

Returning to the worktop, I pushed the plunger down on the cafetière and filled two mugs with coffee. I threw a handful of sugar lumps into each and gave them a stir with my knife. I didn't know how he took his, but I doubted he was going to complain. I didn't normally take sugar myself, but today was an exception.

I walked over to him and put his mug on the floor. He gave me a brisk nod of thanks.

I took a couple of sips and then it was time to get out of my costume. If I had to start performing, the last thing I wanted to be wearing was a suit and lace-up shoes. Lugging my bag over to the table, I dug out jeans, Timberland boots, T-shirt, sweatshirt and a green fleece. I got changed, and felt much more my old self as I tucked my weapon into the front of my jeans.

I went back to my coffee. Valentin had finished his. I took him the cafetière and packet of crispbread. He nodded as I poured new brews for both of us.

I couldn't stop thinking about Sergei. What if he didn't turn up? I had another thought. What would happen if one of Sergei's boys was still alive? It probably wouldn't take long for the police to get him to talk. I put down my mug. Shit, we had to get out of here.

Getting to my feet, I grabbed Carpenter's bag, took cold-weather gear out and threw it to Val. From my own bag I took a red ski jacket and bottoms and put them on. I put the 88 and the mags in the front pockets.

Leaving Valentin to figure out how he was going to put the clothes on with his arm still secured, I ran upstairs to get two double duvets. Once back downstairs I pulled my weapon, cut him free and stepped back. 'Get dressed!' I shouted, miming putting on a jacket.

He was soon dressed in a pair of yellow salopettes, a green ski jacket, a bobble hat, gloves, a scarf and a pair of cold-weather boots—all of which must have been at least three sizes too big. He looked ready for a stunt as a children's entertainer.

I pointed the pistol back towards the pillar. He went over obediently. I showed him that I wanted him to hug it, an arm either side. Then it was just a matter of making up another set of plasticuffs like a lasso, looping it over his wrists and pulling tight.

Taking my torch I went outside into the lean-to for a couple of shovels. I dumped them on the table and the torch went into my salopette pocket. I downed the last of the coffee, put Valentin's mug in his hand and indicated that he should do the same. Then I took candles and matches from the cupboard under the sink and threw them into one of the bags. Once I'd stuffed the duvets on top and done up the zips, I cut Val free, motioning him to put the bag on his back. He knew what I meant and used the two handles as if they were straps on a backpack.

I put on my black woollen hat and ski gloves, then picked up the shovels from the table and used them to guide him out of the door. I walked behind, hitting the light switch.

Once through the lean-to door we followed the well-worn track in the snow towards the lake shore. It was pitch-black out here and bitterly cold. The wind was strong and swirling snow stung my cheeks as we moved forwards.

A small wooden hut housing a sauna stood about thirty yards away. Beyond it was a wooden jetty, which stood about three feet above the ice.

The Chechen was still ahead of me. He stopped when he got to the sauna. I sent him round to the right. He obediently stepped out a few feet along the jetty.

'Whoa. Stop there,' I shouted. 'Stop, stop, stop.'

He turned round, and I pointed with my pistol down at the frozen lake. He looked at me quizzically.

'Down there. On the ice, on the ice.'

Very slowly, he got down and tentatively prodded the ice to make sure it would take his weight. I knew it would. I'd been messing about on it for the last two weeks.

Once he was standing I got him to move out of reach while I clambered down, in case he decided he'd had enough of this game and wanted to play stealing cars and driving home.

Prodding him along the ice with the shovels, I paralleled the lake shore. By taking this route we wouldn't leave any sign from the house. We covered the 150 yards to the tree line. Once there, we carried on for a bit before I gave him another shout and pointed at the trees to our right. He turned towards them.

The snow was soon up to our waists. He did all the work ploughing through it; I just followed in his wake.

We moved about ten yards inside the tree line—and that was enough. We were in direct line of sight of the house.

Finding what seemed the biggest tree in the forest, I rammed a shovel into the snow just short of where the lowest branches disappeared into it. Moving out of the way so he couldn't hit me with it, I motioned for Val to take off the bag. No problem. Then I gave him the other shovel.

Val didn't need any further encouragement. If we were to stay alive out here we had to find shelter soon. The ambient temperature was low enough as it was, but the wind chill took it to well below freezing.

He worked efficiently, obviously no stranger to physical graft. You can always tell when someone's used to a shovel.

After a while he stopped digging, got on his knees and started to scoop out snow with his gloved hands; then he disappeared into the cave. A few minutes later, he turned and stuck his head out. I thought I could just about make out a proud smile.

I waved him back inside, throwing the bag in with him. Before I joined him I pulled back the index finger of my right-hand glove, pushing my trigger finger through the slit I'd prepared just as I had in the leather pair.

I followed him head first, with the 88 up, hitting the torch button once in cover. The shelter could have taken three people kneeling. Once in, I put the torch in my mouth. For him, it was bondage time again. Pulling a set of plasticuffs from my pocket, I stuck the pistol into his neck.

Snow fell on us as I plasticuffed his left hand to the branch above him. With his arm now strapped above his head, Val sat there as I got out a candle and matches. The candle provided more light than it would normally, thanks to the reflection from the brilliant white walls. I crawled back to the entry point, pulled in the shovels and used one to pile snow across the gap. It would keep out the wind.

I emptied the contents of the bag and started to spread out the duvets on the ground. Contact with the snow would conduct heat from our bodies twenty times faster than if we sat on the bedding. Then I smoothed out the sides of our hole with a gloved hand.

The cave was beginning to look like a steam room as our breath hung in clouds in the confined space. Using the grip end of a shovel, I dug a small tunnel. I needed to be able to see out towards the house, and we needed ventilation. I just had to hope the ambient glow from the candle wasn't bright enough to be seen from the house, because there was no way we could do without it. Even the small amount of heat from a candle can help bring the temperature up to freezing point.

At least two very cold, boring hours must have passed with me listening to the wind and Val constantly fidgeting to get feeling back into his arm, when all of a sudden he said, 'The Maliskia must have offered you quite a sizable amount of money to keep me alive. I am obviously more of a threat to them than I thought.'

I spun round in amazement.

It was a confident, clear voice. He was smiling. He obviously liked my reaction. 'Now that you are alone, I imagine it will be difficult to get me out of the country, to wherever it is the Maliskia want you to take me . . . St Petersburg, perhaps?'

I stayed silent. He was right: I was in the shit.

'You have a name, I presume?'

I shrugged. 'It's Nick.'

'Ah, Nicholas. You're British?'

'Yeah, that's right.' I turned my face back towards the house.

'Tell me, what did the Maliskia offer you? One million US? Let me tell you, I am worth considerably more than that to them.'

I carried on looking out of the hole. 'I don't know who the Maliskia are; they sound Russian, but I was employed in London.'

He laughed. 'London, New York, it doesn't matter. It was them. They would very much like to have a meeting with me.'

'Who are they?'

'The same as me, but infinitely more dangerous, I assure you.'

I couldn't imagine anyone being more dangerous. Russian *Organizatsiya* (ROC) was spreading its operations around the world, growing faster than any crime organisation in human history. The different gangs and splinter groups were infiltrating nearly every country to the tune of billions of dollars. With that much money and power at stake, I was sure there would be the odd disagreement between different groups.

There was silence for a while, then Val spoke again. 'Nick, I have a proposition that I think will appeal to you.'

I didn't respond, just kept my eyes on the house.

'It's a very simple proposition: release me, and I will reward you handsomely.'

I turned to look at him. 'How?'

'Nick, correct me if I'm wrong, but now that your plan has failed, I imagine you would like to get away from this country quickly. Release me, return to London and I will get you the money. One of my apartments is in the name of Mr P. P. Smith. The address is 3a Kensington Palace Gardens. Would you like me to repeat that?'

'No, I've got it.'

'In two days' time, and for the next seven days after that, from noon till four in the afternoon, there will be somebody at that address. Go there and you will receive one hundred thousand dollars US.'

Val knew when to talk and when to shut up and let people think. I went back to watching the house for another hour or so, getting colder and more miserable and slowly convincing myself that if Sergei didn't make an appearance I should take my chances with Valentin in London.

I COULD ONLY HEAR the faint noise of the engine at first. Then headlights appeared out of the tree line, heading towards the house. It was a 4x4. The noise got louder as it moved along the track.

I watched the headlights turn into the lean-to and cut out. I heard one door slam. It wasn't until I blew out the candle so he couldn't use it to burn the cuffs off, and started to push my way out of the snow, that Val sparked up. 'Nick?'

I stopped but didn't turn. 'What?'

'Think about what I said as you go to meet your friends. My offer is infinitely more profitable for you, and, may I say, safer.'

'We'll see.' I pushed myself out into the wind.

As I retraced my route, the wind was blowing head on, making my eyes stream. I tried to focus on the house. The lights were on, but there was no movement inside.

Once on the lake, near the jetty, I pulled my trigger finger from its glove and pulled out the 88, then climbed up onto the bank and moved forward in a semi-crouch until I got to the lean-to door. I stood and listened, not hearing anything apart from the sound of the wind bouncing the door against the lock. Keeping to the right of the frame, I pulled the metal handle down and the wind did the rest, forcing it inwards. On my hands and knees in the snow, I eased my head round the bottom of the door frame.

The Nissan 4x4 was parked the other side of the Volvo, the light from the ground-floor window reflecting off its roof.

I moved into the lean-to and checked that no one was still in the Nissan. Then I pushed the door to behind me and went over to the house. I put my ear against the door. I couldn't hear a thing. I looked in through the window.

My heart sank. Carpenter. Still dressed in his suit, but now without a tie or overcoat, he was taking pills from a small tin and swallowing them, shaking his head violently to force them down. His mini-Uzi was exposed, rigged up over his jacket and dangling under his right arm.

He moved about the room with no apparent purpose, sometimes out of view. Then I saw he had Val's masking tape and ball gag in his hand. He brought them up to his face for a moment, and, realising their significance, hurled them to the ground. Then he started lifting chairs and smashing them against the walls in a tantrum. He'd decided that I had left with Val for the border, leaving him in the lurch.

The table followed the chairs as the combination of narcotics and rage started to mess with his head. He made up my mind for me. I left him to it.

Checking back every ten yards, I crossed the frozen lake. After several minutes I saw headlights in the darkness, heading away from the house. I carried on towards the snow hole.

Once in the tree line I could see the whole of the side of the house. Carpenter had left the lights on, but through the downstairs windows things didn't look right. What the fuck was Carpenter up to? It took me a second or two to realise what was happening.

I moved as fast as I could in a direct line towards the building, stumbling over in snow that sometimes came up to my chest. As I got closer I could see flames flickering and smoke spewing out through a broken pane. Forget the house, it was the Volvo I was worried about.

By the time I reached the lean-to I could already hear the crackling of wood and the screams from the smoke alarms. The door to the house was open, and the inside was a furnace.

I got to the car, the heat searing my back, and reversed out of the lean-to. After a three-point turn I drove fifty yards up the track and killed the engine. Jumping out with the keys, I stumbled back into the cover of the tree line.

By the time I neared the hide I could make out my shadow clearly against the snow. The flames were well and truly taking over.

Sliding into the snow hole, I pulled out my Leatherman, felt for the plasticuffs and cut Val free. I scrambled out again into the wind. He followed and we both stared at the burning building. Bizarrely, he started trying to comfort me. 'It's all right, I knew you weren't abandoning me. I am worth too much to you, no? Particularly now. May I suggest that we leave here, and as soon as possible. Like you, I do not want to encounter the authorities. It would be most inconvenient.'

What was it with this guy? Did his pulse rate ever go above ten beats per minute? He knew that he didn't have to convince me any more to let him go. He knew it was my only sensible option now.

I stopped him short of the car, handed him my Leatherman and carried on to the boot, shouting at him to cut the cord from his jacket. He found the nylon cord that could be adjusted to tighten around his waist, and began cutting.

Val heard the boot open. 'Please, Nick, this time inside the car. It's very cold in there.' It was a request rather than a demand. 'And, of course, I'd prefer your company to that of the spare tyre.'

Responding to my nod, he settled in the Volvo's rear foot well, giving me back the Leatherman and offering his hands. I tied them around the base of the handbrake with the cord.

We drove out. Maybe the fire wasn't such a bad thing; at least there wouldn't be any evidence of me ever having been there.

There was no sign of Carpenter or anyone else as we bumped our way up to the chain gate. I left it on the ground where I found it, as a warning to Sergei. There was still a chance that he'd got away. It was too late now to hope that he might get us over the border. I had lost. I had to accept it. Now I had to take my chances with Val.

'I'll drop you off at a train station,' I said as we headed towards Vaalimaa. 'You sort yourself out from there.'

'Of course. My people will extricate me quite swiftly.' There was no emotion in his voice.

Just over two hours later we reached Puistola, a suburb of Helsinki. Pulling into the station car park, I cut Val free from the handbrake. I got out and stood away from the car, my pistol in the pocket of my jacket.

He crawled out and clapped his gloved hands together to get some circulation going. 'Nick, thank you. You will receive your reward for releasing me. P. P. Smith. Remember the rest?'

Of course I did. My eyes were fixed on his. I considered telling him that if he was lying to me I'd find him and kill him, but it would have been a bit like telling Genghis Khan to watch himself.

He smiled. He'd read my mind again. 'Don't worry. You will see that I am a man of my word.' He turned and walked away.

NORFOLK, ENGLAND. Friday, December 10, 1999. The bedside clock burst into wake-up mode dead on seven. As I rolled over it took me three attempts before I managed to hit the off button with my hand still inside the sleeping-bag.

The instant I poked my head out I could tell that the boiler had packed in again. My house was a bit warmer than a Finnish snow hole, but not much. It was yet another thing I needed to sort out.

I wrapped the unzipped sleeping-bag around me and headed downstairs, trying not to snag the bag on the gripper rod that had been left behind when I'd ripped up the carpet. I'd spent most of my life being wet, cold and hungry for a living, so I hated doing it on my own time. This was the first place I'd owned, and in winter the mornings felt much the same to me as waking up in a hedgerow in South Armagh. It wasn't supposed to work like that.

The place was in the same state as I'd left it just over two weeks ago when I went to RV with Sergei at the lake house, except that the tarpaulin had blown off the hole in the roof, and the FOR SALE sign had been flattened by the wind. There wasn't enough time to sort out any of that today. I had three vitally important meetings in London in a few hours' time.

The trip back to the UK had taken three days. I had driven to southern Norway, and from there had taken the ferry to Newcastle. It was full of Norwegian students. While they got pissed I watched Sky News. There was footage of the Intercontinental, with police searching for evidence, then came pictures of the dead, among them Sergei. A Finnish government spokeswoman declined to confirm it was an ROC shooting.

This house had been a DIY disaster zone ever since I'd bought it after bringing Kelly, my best friend Kev's daughter, back from the States in 1997. In theory it was idyllic, up on the Norfolk coast in the middle of nowhere. There was a small Co-op, and three fishing boats worked out of the tiny harbour.

But the estate agent must have seen me coming. A 1930s three-bedroomed detached mess of pebbledash, just 200 yards from the windy beach, the house had been empty for several years after the previous owners had died. The details said, 'Some renovation required, but with magnificent potential.' In other words, a load of work was needed. My plan was to gut the place and rebuild it. The ripping out was OK; in fact, I'd enjoyed it. But after a while I'd lost interest. So now the house was all bare boards, studwork and entrails of wiring sticking out of the walls.

Now that I was responsible for Kelly, it had seemed the right time to fulfil the fantasy of having a real home. But no sooner had I exchanged contracts than it had started to make me feel confined.

I'd called the place in Hampstead, where she was being looked after, as soon as I'd got back last night. They said she was much the same as when I'd last seen her. I was glad she was sleeping; it meant I didn't have to speak to her. I did want to, but just never knew what to say. I'd gone to see her the day before leaving for Finland. She'd seemed all right, not crying or anything, just quiet and strangely helpless.

I put the kettle on the gas ring and went to check for mail.

There were four envelopes—three bills and a card. The handwriting told me who the card was from. Caroline, who was in her thirties and lived in the village, had started coming here to look in on things now and again, to collect the mail and check the walls hadn't collapsed while I was away working as a travelling salesman. Her husband no longer lived with her—it seemed he took too much whisky with his soda. Things were going great between us; she was kind and attractive, and whenever I was here we would link up for an afternoon or two. But a couple of months earlier she had started to want more of a relationship than I felt able to offer.

I opened the card. No more visits or mail collection. It was a shame; I liked her a lot, but it was probably for the best. A gunshot wound in the stomach, a reconstructed ear lobe and dog-tooth scars along a forearm are hard to explain, whatever you're trying to sell.

Making a lumpy brew with powdered milk, I went upstairs to Kelly's room. The blue two-man tent in the middle of the floor was still holding out. I'd put nails in the floorboards instead of tent pegs and they were rusty now, but I still couldn't bring myself to take it down.

On the mantelpiece were two photos in cheap wooden frames, which I'd promised to bring down to her on my next visit. One was of her with her family—Kev, Marsha and her sister Aida—all smiles round a smoking barbecue. It was taken about a month before I'd found them hosed down in their home in the spring of '97.

The other was of my mate Josh and his kids. He and I still administered Kelly's trust fund, though as her legal guardian, I'd found myself shouldering more and more of the financial responsibility. Josh was aware of her problem, but it was just done via letters now. He was the last real friend I had, and I hoped that maybe one day he would forgive me for nearly getting him and his kids killed.

The order of the day was first the doctor's office at 11.30 to talk about Kelly's progress, then lie to the clinic's accounts department about why I couldn't pay the new invoice just yet. My next visit would be to Colonel Lynn at the Firm. I wasn't looking forward to that, either. I hated having to plead. The third stop was Flat 3a Kensington Palace Gardens. What the hell, I was desperate.

My foray into the freelance market had only reinforced my reluctant dependence on the Firm. I had been weapons-free from the Firm since the foul-up in Washington with Josh eighteen months before. Lynn was right, of course, when he said I should feel lucky I wasn't banged up in some American jail. The Brits were still trying to decide what to do with me—give me a knighthood or make me disappear. I was getting paid two grand a month while they scratched their heads. It was enough to cover Kelly's treatment for about seventy-two hours.

Lynn made it clear that the retainer in no way meant any change in my status; I was still low-life, a K, a deniable operator carrying out jobs that no one else wanted. Nothing would change unless I could get Lynn to put my name forward for permanent cadre, and time was running out. He was taking early retirement in February. I didn't have a clue who was taking over. Contacting the message service last night, I'd heard that Lynn would see me at 13.30.

From inside the bathroom panelling that contained the cistern I retrieved my 9mm USP—universal service pistol—and two thirteen-round mags. I bit open the plastic bag protecting it and loaded the loose rounds, inserting a mag into the pistol grip. I had three USPs in the house, two hidden downstairs when I was here, and one under my bed—a little trick I'd learned from Kelly's dad years ago.

I got into my bike leathers, put the weapon and spare mag in my pocket, slung the daysack over my shoulder and locked up the house.

Waiting for me outside was the bike of my dreams, a red Ducati 966 that I'd treated myself to at the same time as the house. There were times when I reckoned the sound of its engine bursting into life was the only thing that kept me from total despair.

THE LONDON TRAFFIC was chaos. Weaving my way around stationary vehicles, I looked down Oxford Street, where the decorations blazed and twinkled. The season of goodwill was everywhere, it seemed, except behind the steering wheels of gridlocked vehicles and inside my head.

I was dreading this. The house in Hampstead was staffed by two nurses who, under the psychiatrist's supervision, were looking after Kelly twenty-four hours a day. They took her to a clinic in Chelsea several times a week, where Dr Hughes had her consulting rooms. Kelly's round-the-clock attention was costing me just over four grand a week. Most of the £300,000 I'd stolen from the drug cartels in 1997, together with her trust fund, had been spent on her education, the house and now her treatment. There was nothing left.

It had all started about nine months ago. She was an intelligent girl, but her grades since coming to England had been poor. Apart from that, she'd shown no visible after-effects from the trauma. Then, at boarding school, she'd started to complain about pains, but could never explain exactly where they were. Her teachers concluded that she was just attention-seeking. Then it got worse: Kelly gradually withdrew from her friends, her teachers, her grandparents and me. She wouldn't talk or play; she just watched TV, sat in a sulk or sobbed.

About five months ago she'd been with me in Norfolk for the weekend. She was distant and detached, and nothing I did seemed to engage her. I tried playing at camping with her, putting up the tent in her bedroom. That night she woke with terrible nightmares. I tried to calm her, but she just lashed out at me as if she was having a fit. The next morning, I made a few phone calls and found out there was a six-month waiting list for an NHS appointment. I made more calls and later the same day took her to see Dr Hughes, a London psychiatrist who specialised in child trauma and who accepted private patients.

Kelly was admitted to the clinic at once for a temporary assessment, and I'd had to leave her there to go on my first St Petersburg recce, and to recruit Sergei. My worst fears were confirmed when the doctor told me that, besides regular treatment at the clinic as an outpatient, she'd need the sort of constant care that only the unit in Hampstead could provide.

I'd been to visit her there a total of four times now. We usually just sat together and watched TV for the afternoon.

I had some understanding of Kelly's condition, but only some. I'd known men who'd suffered with PTSD—post-traumatic stress disorder—but they were big boys who'd been to war. I wanted to know more about its effects on children. Hughes told me it was natural for a child to go through a grieving process after a loss, but sometimes, after a sudden traumatic event, the feelings can surface weeks, months or even years later. This delayed reaction is PTSD, and the symptoms are similar to those associated with depression: emotional numbness, despair, nightmares.

'The symptoms vary in intensity from case to case,' Hughes had explained, 'but can last for years if untreated. They certainly won't just go away on their own.'

I worked my way in and out of the traffic, heading down towards Chelsea. I eventually got to where I wanted to be and parked. The Moorings was a large town house in a leafy square, with clean bricks, recent repointing and lots of gleaming fresh paint. Everything about it said it specialised in the disorders of the rich.

The receptionist pointed me to the waiting room and I settled down with a magazine about the sort of country house that mine would never be. I was reading about the pros and cons of conventional compared with underfloor heating when the receptionist appeared and ushered me into the consulting room.

Dr Hughes looked as striking as ever. She was in her mid-fifties, and had big grey hair and gold-rimmed half-moon glasses.

Sitting down on the chair facing her desk, I placed the daysack at my feet. 'She hasn't got worse, has she?'

The doctor shook her head, but didn't answer immediately.

'If it's about the money, I—'

She lifted her hand. 'Not my department, Mr Stone. I'm sure the people downstairs have everything under control. I wanted to see you to discuss Kelly's prognosis. I'm afraid to say she is still very passive and preoccupied. Stuck, if you like, or cocooned; either unable or unwilling to relate. I'm afraid the road to recovery is going to be even longer than I at first thought.'

'What sort of time scale are we looking at?'

She pursed her lips. 'It's impossible to say, Mr Stone. I'm afraid that you really must prepare yourself for a long haul.'

'Is there nothing I can do to help?'

Dr Hughes smiled briefly. 'Well,' she said, 'I did ask you here today for a specific reason. Kelly is here, in one of the rooms.'

I started getting up. 'Can I see her?'

She, too, stood up. 'Yes, of course. But I have to say, Mr Stone, that I'd rather she didn't see you.'

'I'm sorry? I—'

The doctor cut in. 'There's something I'd like you to see first.' She opened a drawer in her desk and pulled out several sheets of paper. I wasn't prepared for the shock they gave me. The pictures Kelly had drawn of her dead family looked very different from the happy, smiling photograph I had in my daysack.

The one of her mother showed her kneeling by the bed, her top half spread-eagled on the mattress, the bed cover coloured in red.

In another, her five-year-old sister, Aida, was lying dead between the bath and the toilet, blood everywhere.

Kev, her father and my best friend, was lying on his side in the lounge, his head pulped by the baseball bat that lay next to him.

I looked at the doctor. 'They're the positions I found them in that day—exactly . . . I hadn't realised . . .'

I'd found her in her hidey-hole, the place where Kev wanted the kids to run to if there was ever a drama. She'd never said a word to me about it, and I'd never thought that she'd witnessed the carnage.

Hughes looked over her glasses. 'Kelly has even remembered what was playing on the radio in the kitchen just before the men came. Come with me, if you will, Mr Stone. I'd like you to see her and I'll explain a little more about what I hope we can achieve.'

She led me a short way down the corridor. We stopped outside a door that had a curtain across a small pane of glass. She poked it very slightly aside with a finger and looked through, then moved back and motioned for me to do the same.

I looked through the glass. Kelly was sitting on a chair next to a nurse. The nurse seemed to be chatting away, all smiles. Kelly, however, wasn't replying. She was staring at the window opposite her, head cocked to one side, as if trying to work something out. She had an unnatural kind of stillness.

I'd seen it before.

It was two years ago, but it could have been two minutes. I was on my hands and knees in her family's garage, talking gently as I moved boxes and squeezed through the gap, inching towards the back wall, trying to push the images of the carnage next door behind me.

Then there she was, facing me, eyes wide with terror, sitting curled up in a foetal position, rocking her body backwards and forwards, holding her hands over her ears.

'Hello, Kelly,' I'd said very softly.

She must have recognised me—she'd known me for years—but she hadn't replied. She'd just carried on rocking, staring at me. I'd crawled up beside her, got hold of her hand and guided her gently out into the garage. Then I picked her up and held her tight. She was trembling so much I couldn't tell if her head was nodding or shaking. A few minutes later, when we drove away from the house, she was almost rigid with shock. And that was it, that was the stillness I saw now.

The doctor replaced the curtain and headed back up the corridor. As we walked she said, 'We need to help her deal with all the emotions she's having trouble making sense of at the moment: grief, guilt, anger, depression, anxiety. You notice, Mr Stone, I say "we".'

We had reached her room and went back inside. I sat down again and she went to the other side of her desk.

'Parents are usually the most important emotional protectors for their children, Mr Stone. They can help them talk about their fears, reassure them that Mummy and Daddy will protect them and stay close. Sadly that's not possible for Kelly, but she still needs a responsible adult whom she can depend upon. What it boils down to, Mr Stone, is that Kelly is going to need a trusted adult alongside her during the recovery process, and in my view that person is you.'

She paused to let the implications of what she was saying sink in.

'You see, she trusts you; she speaks of you with the utmost affection, seeing you as the nearest thing she has now to a father. What she needs, far more than just the therapy we professionals can provide, is your acceptance of, and commitment to, that fact. Would you have difficulties with that, Mr Stone?'

'My employers might. I need—'

She held up her hand. 'You have seen the cocoon in which Kelly has placed herself. There is no formula that guarantees breaking through when someone is out of reach. But it is my view that she's decided not to come out until you are an integral part of her life again. I'm sorry to burden you with this responsibility, Mr Stone, but Kelly is my patient and it's her best interests that I have at heart. For that reason, I didn't want her to see you today; I don't want her to build up hopes only to have them dashed.'

I reached into my daysack and pulled out the framed photographs. It was the only thing I could think of. 'I brought these for her. They're pictures of her family. Maybe they'll be some help.'

The doctor took them from me, still waiting for an answer. When she saw she wasn't going to get one—not today, anyway—she ushered me towards the door. 'Please go away and think about it. Now, I believe you have an appointment with the people downstairs?'

I WAS FEELING pretty depressed as I headed east along the north side of the Thames, towards the city centre.

Having a man down was straightforward compared to this. You just got in there, dragged him out and plugged up his holes. Sometimes he lived, sometimes not. The man down always knew that someone would be coming for him; it helped him stay alive. This was different. Kelly was my man down, but it wasn't just a question of plugging up holes; she didn't know whether help was on the way or not. Nor did I.

I knew there was one thing I could do: make money to pay for her treatment. I'd be there for her, but later. Right now I needed to keep busy and produce money.

Working my way through the traffic, I eventually got onto the approach road to Vauxhall Bridge. As I crossed to the southern side, I looked up at Vauxhall Cross, home of the Secret Intelligence Service, a beige and black pyramid with the top cut off, flanked by large towers on either side.

Passing the SIS building, I bumped the pavement, parking up near a motorbike shop—the one I'd bought my Ducati from. I wasn't going in today; it was just an easy place to park. Checking my saddle was secure so no one could nick my USP, I put my helmet in the day-sack, crossed a couple of roads and eventually entered the building.

I headed for the main reception desk, where two women sat behind thick, bulletproof glass.

'I'm here to see Mr Lynn.'

'Can you fill this in please?' The older one passed a ledger through a slot under the glass.

As I signed my name in two boxes she picked up a telephone. 'Who shall I say is here?'

'My name is Nick.' I hadn't even had any cover documentation from them since my foul-up in Washington, just my own cover, which I hoped they'd never know about. I'd organised it in case it was time to disappear, a feeling I had at least once a month.

The ledger held tear-off labels. One half was torn away and put in a plastic sleeve, which I would have to pin on. Mine was blue and said: ESCORTED EVERYWHERE.

The woman came off the phone and pointed to a row of soft chairs. 'Someone will be with you soon.'

I sat and waited with my nice new badge on. After about ten minutes, an old Asian guy in a natty blue pinstripe suit pushed his way through the barrier.

'Nick?'

I nodded and got to my feet.

'If you'd like to follow me.' A swipe of the card that hung round his neck got him back through the barrier; I had to pass the metal detector before we met on the other side and walked to the lifts.

On the fifth floor I followed him along the corridor. Two doors down I saw Lynn's name on the door plate. My escort knocked and was met by the characteristically crisp and immediate call of 'Come!' He ushered me past and I heard the door close gently behind me.

Lynn's bald crown faced me as he wrote at his desk. I stood and waited for him to finish.

'Take a seat. I'll be with you very soon.'

I did, placing my daysack on the floor. I hadn't seen Lynn since the debrief after Washington in 1998. He hadn't changed. Nor had his clothes: the same mustard-coloured corduroy trousers, sports jacket with well-worn leather elbows and Viyella shirt.

He finished writing and looked up with a half-amused smile at my outfit. 'Wot can I do fer yer, Nick?' He was taking the piss out of my accent, but in a sarcastic, not jovial way. He really didn't like me.

'I would like to know if I am ever going to get put forward for permanent cadre,' I said.

He settled back into his leather swivel chair and produced the other half of his smile. 'You know, you are very lucky still to be at liberty, Nick. You already have a lot to be thankful for.'

He was right, of course. I owed the Firm for the fact that I wasn't in some US state penitentiary, even if it was more to do with saving themselves embarrassment than with protecting me.

'I do understand that, and I'm grateful for all that you've done for me, Mr Lynn. But I really need to know.'

'After your total lack of judgment, do you really think you'd ever be considered for permanent cadre?' His face flushed. He was angry. 'Think yourself lucky you're still on a retainer. Do you really think you would be considered for work after you'—his right index finger poked at me—'one, disobey my direct order to kill that damned woman; two, actually believe her preposterous story and assist her assassination attempt in the White House. Your judgment was no better than a lovesick schoolboy's. Do you realise the havoc you've caused, not only in the US but here? Careers have been ruined because of you. The answer is no. Not now, not ever.'

Then I understood. This wasn't just about me, and it wasn't about Lynn taking early retirement at the end of his tour next year; he had been given the sack. He'd been running the Ks at the time of the Washington debacle, and someone had had to pay. Lynn could be replaced; people like me were more difficult to blow out, if only for financial reasons. The government had invested several million in my training as a Special Air Service soldier. They wanted to get their money's worth out of me. It must have killed him to know that I was the one who'd screwed up, but he was the one to carry the can—probably as part of the deal to appease the Americans.

'If not PC, when will I work?'

He had gained a little more composure. 'Nothing is going to happen until the new department head takes over. He will decide what to do with you.'

'Look, Mr Lynn, I need the money. Anything will do. Send me anywhere.'

He didn't even pause. 'No. Now go. Remember, you are still being paid and you will conduct yourself accordingly.'

He pressed his buzzer and the Asian guy came to collect me so fast he must have been listening through the keyhole.

I was still feeling philosophical about the meeting at 3a. If Val had been feeding me a crock, well, there you go, at least I was on my turf rather than his. I'd tucked my USP into my leathers before I left the bike shop, just in case.

Kensington Palace Gardens stretches the whole length of Hyde Park's west side, from Kensington in the south to Notting Hill Gate in the north. At one end a pair of iron gates with a wooden gatehouse positioned between them. Beyond lay a wide tree-lined road and pavements of beige gravel. The large mansion houses were mostly embassies and residences. Flags fluttered and brass plates gleamed.

The gateman looked me up and down when I rode up as if I was something one of the embassy dogs had left on the kerb. 'Yes?'

'Number 3a, mate. Pick up.' I pointed to the daysack on my back.

He pointed up the road. 'Hundred yards up on the left.'

I parked in the line of cars opposite the apartment building. Walking across the road towards its grand gates, I removed my gloves and unbuckled my helmet, then hit the bell and explained to a voice where I wanted to go. The side gate opened with a whirr and a click and I walked through and down the drive.

Pulling off the ski mask that kept the cold off my face, I walked through the main doors into a glittering dark marble and glass reception area. The concierge seemed to view me the same way as his mate down the road. 'Delivery, is it?'

Time to play courier boy again. 'Nah, pick-up. P. P. Smith, mate.'

He picked up the internal telephone and dialled, his voice changing into Mr Nice Guy the moment he got a reply. 'Hello, reception here. You have a courier for a collection. Do you want me to send him up? Certainly. Goodbye.' The phone went down and he pointed to the lift. 'Third floor, fourth door on the left.'

As the lift doors closed behind me I had a check round for closed-circuit cameras, then pulled out my USP. I hit the button for the third floor, folded the ski mask over the USP and placed it in the helmet. The lift slowed. The door slid open with an up-market *ding*, but I stood my ground for a few seconds, listening.

I stepped into the corridor and followed the carpet, looking for the fourth door on the left. It was so quiet that all I could hear as I moved was the creaking of my leathers.

The door didn't have a bell, knocker or even a number. I rapped my knuckles against the heavy wood, then stood off to the side, my right hand on the pistol, thumb easing off the safety catch.

Footsteps echoed on a hard floor and locks were undone. The door started to open, only to be stopped by a security chain. A face, or rather half a face, moved into the four-inch gap. It was enough for me to recognise its owner at once.

Val's slapper from Helsinki was showing me just one very light blue eye and some dark blonde hair. She looked at me without any expression, waiting for me to speak.

'My name is Nick. You have something for me.'

'Yes, I've been expecting you.' The door closed and I heard the chain being undone. The door reopened fully, but instead of standing there and ushering me in, she turned and started to walk back into the flat. 'Close the door behind you, would you please, Nick?'

As I stepped over the threshold, I smelt floor wax. I followed her down the corridor. A couple of doors led off either side, and one at the far end was partly open.

I'd thought it was her high heels that had made Val's slapper look so tall in Finland, but I could see now that her legs did that all on their own. She was maybe just over six foot tall in her cowboy boots. She walked like a supermodel on a catwalk. Her legs were sheathed in a pair of Armani jeans, the logo on the back pocket moving up and down in time with her heels. I couldn't keep my eyes off it.

I walked into the living room where she now stood, a large white space with three dining-room chairs at its centre. The only other objects in the room were four large Harvey Nichols bags.

She bent over one of the shopping bags and pulled out a large buff envelope. 'My name is Liv. Valentin sends his regards,' she said as she brought it over to me. 'And, of course, his gratitude. This is for you. One hundred thousand US dollars.'

Wonderful. That was the slate clean at the clinic, and another four months' treatment in the bank.

She extended a perfectly manicured hand that showed she was no longer a teenager. The skin on her face was crystal clear and had no need of make-up. I reckoned she was in her early thirties.

She wore no jewellery. But then, she needed adorning like the Venus de Milo needed a velvet choker and diamond tiara. I was beginning to see why Val might prefer Finland to Russia.

I hadn't had the time to take much notice of her before. The first time I was aware of her was the day that Val arrived in Finland, three days before the lift. Recces are about planning, not admiring the view. But I did now. Her statuesque body looked like it had been shaped by canoeing or rock climbing rather than jumping up and down to music in a gym.

The feel of the bundles in the envelope brought me back to the real world. I put my helmet at my feet, unzipped my jacket and slipped the envelope inside. I wasn't going to open it there and then. I didn't want to look desperate and untrusting. I was both, but I didn't want her to know that.

She went to sit on one of the chairs, and invited me to take a seat with a wave of her hand. I declined, preferring to stand and be able to react if this encounter turned out to be not entirely friendly.

Liv sat there looking at me the way Mr Spock looks on the bridge of the USS *Enterprise* when he thinks things are illogical. It was the same look she'd given me back at the hotel, penetrating and searching, but somehow managing to give nothing back. It made me uncomfortable and I stooped to pick up my helmet.

She sat back and crossed her long legs. 'Nick, I have a proposition for you, from Valentin.'

I left the helmet where it was, but said nothing.

Her gaze remained cool. 'Are you interested?'

'In principle. What does he want from me?'

'He needs someone to assist a cryptographer—a highly skilled hacker, if you like—to enter a house in Finland. Inside the house are computers that this hacker will use his skills to access. He will then download the contents onto a laptop for removal. The contents, before you ask, are merely some competitive intelligence that Valentin is keen to have in his possession.'

'You mean industrial espionage?'

'More commercial than industrial. Valentin is asking you to assist in the procurement of this data, but without the house owners knowing that you have done so.'

'It's as straightforward as that?'

'There are some minor complications that we will discuss if you are interested.'

I was, but minor complications don't exist. They always turn out to be major. 'How much?'

'Valentin is offering you one point seven million dollars—if you are successful.' She put up a hand. 'Non-negotiable. That is his offer, more than a million pounds. You're a lucky man, Nick; he likes you.'

'Valentin is powerful enough just to take what he wants by force. Why does he need me?'

'This is a job that requires finesse, not muscle. As I said, no one must know that Valentin has this material. It's a delicate matter, and it was obvious in Helsinki that you have a certain skill in this area.'

'What exactly is it I'm trying to lay my hands on?'

'That, Nick, you don't need to know. We just need to be there before the Maliskia.'

I had to cut in. 'You mean steal it before the Maliskia do?'

She smiled. 'Not "steal", copy.'

'I get it. Maliskia must be Russian for "minor complications".'

She smiled again, her lips parting slightly to show perfect white teeth. 'The West call us the Russian Mafia, or simply ROC, as if we were one big group. We're not. We are many groups. The Maliskia are one faction, and Valentin's only real competitor. Whatever you may think about him, he is a man with vision. The Maliskia are not; they are just gangsters. It is very important that they never have access to this information. It would be a disaster for all of us, West as well as East. Now, do you wish me to continue?'

Of course I did. She explained that the target house was still in the process of being prepared to use the 'competitive intelligence' Val wanted. It wouldn't be online for another six or seven days, and only then would I be able to get their man in to copy whatever it was. The problem was that once it was online the Maliskia were likely to trace its location very quickly.

It sounded OK to me. I'd spent years doing this kind of thing for far less than $1.7 million. Maybe this was my chance to sort out my life—and Kelly's—once and for all.

'I'm concerned about going back to Finland,' I said. 'I don't think I'm very popular there.'

She smiled. 'They aren't looking for you, Nick. As far as the Finnish police are concerned it was a purely Russian event. Valentin has already made a statement to that effect to the authorities.'

For the next few minutes I asked questions and she failed to give adequate answers. It didn't sound low risk to me. There were too many questions left unanswered: How many people were in the house? What defences did they have? Where the hell was it? On the other hand, $1.7 million versus £290 a day wasn't the kind of discrepancy I could afford to live with.

She held out a piece of folded paper. 'These are the contact details of the man you will be taking with you, assuming you can persuade him. If you can, the fee goes up to two million dollars, to cover his cut. One other minor complication: neither Valentin nor I can risk being associated with this task, so it's up to you to convince him to do it.'

I read an address and phone number in Notting Hill.

Liv said, 'His name is Tom Mancini. I believe you know him.'

I turned to face her. The name did ring a bell, but that didn't concern me. What did was that she knew things about my past.

She smiled again. 'Naturally Valentin has gone to the trouble of learning a lot about you these last few days. Do you think he would employ someone for such a task otherwise?'

'What does he know?'

'Enough, I'm sure. Also enough about Tom. Valentin is sure you are both the right people for this. Now, Nick, as you will appreciate, there is little time. You need to be in Helsinki by Sunday. All I will require are your travel details. Everything else will be looked after.'

She gave me the remaining contact details. They were very basic, easy to understand. She stood up. Our meeting was obviously over. 'Thank you for coming, Nick.'

I shook her hand, which felt warm and firm. I looked her in the eye, probably for a fraction of a second too long, then bent to pick up my helmet. She followed me to the front door.

I turned to face her; she was so close I could smell her perfume.

'Goodbye, Nick.'

I nodded and the door closed. I heard the locks and chain being put back into position.

I'D JUST GOT PAST the gate and onto the pavement when I heard the noise of an approaching car.

A dark maroon Peugeot 206 was screaming towards me. Behind the wheel was a white-knuckled woman in her early thirties, with a chin-length bob. I waited for her to pass, but as soon as she was about ten yards away she slowed to a more controlled pace.

I watched her reach the barrier, indicate left, then join the stream of traffic. The number plate was R reg, but there was something else more interesting—no sticker on the back window telling me how wonderful the dealership was. I suddenly felt I knew what she was about. Just as quickly, I threw the idea aside. I was getting paranoid.

Pulling my helmet on, I pinged another vehicle about fifty yards up the road—a midnight-blue Golf GTi, two people aboard, both sitting back in their seats with no conversation or movement. The side windows were steamed up but the windscreen had a direct view of the gates to the flats. I took a mental note of their reg. I straddled the bike and pushed it off its stand.

Turning the engine over, I got into first, turned left and made my way down towards the main gates. What made me feel edgy was that the two cars were ideal for city surveillance. Both were very common models in dark, nondescript colours and they were compact, so they could zip in and out of traffic and were easy to park up. And surveillance cars tend not to have the retailer's sticker in the back window because it could become a distinguishing mark.

If they were a surveillance team they would have to be E4, the government's surveillance group that keeps tabs on everybody from terrorists to dodgy politicians in the UK. No one else would be able to stake out anything along this road. There was more security here than at Wormwood Scrubs.

I got to the barrier, headed the opposite way from the Peugeot, and merged with the traffic, trying to be as casual as possible. I looked down at my mirror and saw the reflection of a bike's headlight. I turned left at the next junction, and he followed me.

Looking for a natural stop, I pulled in at a newsagent's. Resting the bike on its side stand, I went through the charade of undoing my helmet and gloves, as an M-reg Yamaha came past.

I took the helmet off but kept the mask on once he'd gone, then got off the bike and walked into the shop. I couldn't just ride straight off again, because that would show I was aware.

I went back to the bike clutching a copy of the *Evening Standard*. I pushed the Ducati into gear and carried on to South Kensington tube station. Parking up in the bike row on the north side, I walked into the packed station, looking as though I was unbuckling my helmet, though I didn't. Instead, I walked straight through to the other exit and crossed the road, still with my helmet on. It was a large, busy and very confusing junction.

I moved with a crowd of pedestrians to the far side and past a row of shops along the Old Brompton Road.

About fifty yards further along, I went into the pub on the corner, took off my helmet and mask, and settled on a bar stool just back from the window. The pub was packed.

I saw the Golf within minutes, but without the passenger. He or she was probably scurrying around in the tube station looking for me. Then I saw the Yamaha and its leather-clad rider.

I sat and watched as the Golf, with a dark-haired male at the wheel, came back round the one-way circuit and pulled in to pick up a short, brown-haired woman. They were off again before her door was even closed. Once they'd failed to pick me up again, their next move would be to stake out the bike. Then some of the team would check out known target locations. There were only two: one was the apartment block, and they'd check with the porter which apartment I'd gone to, for sure. The other was the address where the bike was registered—a PO box just a few shops down from where it was parked.

Nick Davidson was the registered owner of the bike and the real Davidson was going to be incredibly pissed off if he ever came back from Australia, because I'd taken over his life in the UK. He was going to get a hard time from customs, immigration and Special Branch if he ever stepped off a plane here. Now, however, having Nick Davidson as my safety-blanket cover ID was history, and that pissed me off. It had taken painstaking months to get a National Insurance number, passport, bank account, all the things that bring a character to life, and now I had to bin him. Worse still, I'd have to bin the bike. There'd certainly be a trigger on it for the next few hours, depending on how important they thought I was. The only thing that cheered me up was the thought of what would happen to the person who'd eventually steal it after seeing it standing there for a few days. They wouldn't know what had hit them when the E4 team closed in.

I'd nursed a Coke while keeping watch through the large Victorian windows. My glass was nearly empty, and if I didn't want to look out of place I'd need to get a refill. Fighting my way to the bar, I ordered a pint of orange and lemonade, and went and sat in the corner. I just had to sit it out, keeping my eyes on the doors in case they started to check out the pubs. In an hour's time it would be the end of the working day. I'd wait until then and lose myself in the darkness and commuter traffic.

As I sipped my drink, I thought about Tom Mancini. His name was certainly familiar. One of my first jobs as a K in '93 had been to drive him from North Yorkshire, where he worked, down to a naval facility near Gosport, Hampshire. I was told to grip him so hard that he'd beg to be handed over to the Firm's people. It didn't take much, just a few slaps, a scary face and me telling him that if he messed me about the only thing left ticking on his body would be his watch.

Once we'd got him down in one of the 'forts' built along the coast, the Firm's interrogation team explained the facts of life.

Tom had been messing about with the big boys. He worked as a technician at RAF Menwith Hill, on the moors near Harrogate in Yorkshire, one of the largest intelligence-gathering stations on earth. Its massive golf-ball-shaped 'radomes' monitored Europe's and Russia's airwaves. It might be a British base, but in reality it was a little piece of the USA on British soil, run by their all-powerful National Security Agency. Tom had been detected trying to obtain classified information. I wasn't allowed in on the interrogation, but I knew they told him Special Branch would be arresting him the next day for offences against the Official Secrets Act. They couldn't stop that. However, if he didn't get smart, that would be just the start of his problems.

He would shut up in court about what he'd really been tampering with. The Firm didn't want anyone to know about it, even Special Branch, so the charge would be for a lesser offence. He'd serve a short sentence and that would be the end of it. If he ever uttered a word to anyone, however, someone like me would come and pay him a visit.

I finished my drink and headed for the toilets. In a cubicle, I sat down on the lid, unzipped my jacket and pulled out the envelope.

I inspected the nylon-fibre type, bubble-wrap envelope. Then, resting it on my knees and using both hands, I pressed down and started to run my palms over it, fingertips moving up and down the contours of the contents. I turned it over and checked the other side. I couldn't feel any sort of wiring, or anything more solid than what I hoped were the notes, but then again that didn't mean a thing. A wafer-thin battery from a Polaroid film tucked between the bundles would kick out enough power to initiate a letter bomb. It might be Val's special little way of saying thank you.

I picked the envelope up and put the fold to my nose. If they'd used any exotic or older-style explosives, I might be able to smell them. Sometimes it's marzipan, sometimes linseed oil. I was expecting something more sophisticated, but these things have to be tested for.

All I could smell was the urinals.

I decided to open it. It felt like money, weighed like money. If I was wrong, the whole pub would know about it soon. I opened the knife blade of my Leatherman and gently cut down the centre of the envelope, checking for wires. It was looking promising. I started to see green US banknotes. Each bundle of used $100 bills that I carefully pulled out was banded and told me the bundle contained $10,000; there were ten of them.

Staying in the pub for another half-hour, I wondered if the team had been called off yet. By now they'd know that the address for the bike was a PO box arrangement, and that would have set their alarm bells ringing. By tomorrow, they'd also know that Mr Davidson had been to Norway recently. What would they make of that? I doubted that their conclusion would be that it was a skiing trip after Davidson had been seen coming out of a London apartment block where one of the owners was a Russian who'd got hit just days ago in a country a mere day trip away from Norway.

Leaving the helmet under the table, I exited through a door that led out onto a different road.

The priority was to get a hotel for the night, before I contacted Tom in the morning. I also needed clothing: without a bike, there was no way I could walk around looking like Judge Dredd.

I grabbed a taxi to Piccadilly Circus, and changed $1,000 at various bureaux de change, throwing in a couple of hundred at a time. The shopping frenzy was another short cab ride away, in Selfridges, where I bought jeans, Timberland boots, a blue sweatshirt and a dark blue nylon duvet jacket, as well as a washing and shaving kit and a nice little money belt for my new-found wealth.

Then I booked myself into the Selfridges Hotel using my Nick Stone credit card. To have used Davidson's would have invited a knock on the door within hours.

After a bath and a change of clothes I called room service for a club sandwich and coffee.

Five

Saturday, December 11, 1999. I woke up and looked at my wrist-watch. It was just after eight.

I left the duvet jacket with my leathers and went down to breakfast in my new clothes, taking the money belt with me. There was $25,000 left after the clinic had received not only what was owing to them but also a wedge on account. It's strange how finance directors will come in of an evening to collect a payment.

Back in my room, I settled on the bed and called the number on the paper that Liv had given me.

A young woman answered. Her 'Hello' sounded as friendly as if I'd been the fourth wrong number in a row.

'Oh, hi,' I said. 'Is Tom there?'

'No, he's not,' she snapped. 'He'll be in Coins. Who are you?'

'Just a friend. Coins, did you say? What is that, a shop or—'

'It's the caff, off Ledbury Road.' The phone slammed down.

Talking Pages told me that Coins was in Talbot Road, Notting Hill. I put my blue duvet jacket on, buckled on my money belt and jumped into a taxi, borrowing a read of the cabbie's *A–Z* on the way to work out exactly where Tom lived.

The cab stopped at a crossroads and the dividing window opened. 'It's a one-way, mate. I'll drop you off here if that's all right. It's just down there on the left.'

I could see the large awning sticking out over the pavement. I paid him and took a walk. Coins turned out to be double-fronted, with a few empty tables outside.

There was no sign of Tom, so I took a seat in the far corner. The clientele seemed to average late twenties, trying so hard to look individual that they all looked like clones. Everyone was in baggy cargo trousers and body warmers, and must have taken ages to get their hair looking like they'd just got out of bed.

'Hi, sweetie, what can I get you?' An American female voice floated down to me as I studied the menu.

Glancing up, I asked for a latte and toast.

'Sure, sweetie.' She turned and presented the world's second most perfect rear, covered in tight black flares. No wonder Tom came here.

There was nothing else to do but sit and listen to other people's conversations. Rear of the Year came back. 'Here you are, sweetie.' She gave me my glass of latte.

Half an hour later the toast was finished and I was on my second latte when, at last, Tom entered. His greasy hair was now ponytailed just past his shoulders and his cheeks were more hamsterlike than I remembered; maybe the extra pounds he'd put on had changed the contours of his face.

The clothes looked as if they'd come from the same shop as everyone else's here—canvas daps, brown cargoes and a faded green sweatshirt with a T-shirt that had started off white, then gone a few rounds with something blue. He must have been freezing.

Settling his chubby arse on a tall stool by the breakfast bar facing the window, he pulled a magazine out from under his arm—some kind of palmtop computer and games monthly.

A small Puerto Rican-looking woman took his order. I decided to wait until he'd finished eating, then do my 'Hello, Tom. Well well, fancy seeing you here' bit, but my plan got cut short as he suddenly stood up and turned towards the door. Along with a very pissed-off waitress, I watched him cross the road and run up a side street.

He must have seen me.

I got up and paid Rear of the Year, getting an extra-friendly 'Bye, sweetie' when she saw the tip I'd left on my saucer.

Tom had run towards home, so I headed in the direction of All Saints Road. His address—number 4—was a flat in a yellow-painted, stucco-fronted building just off All Saints.

I pressed the button for his flat but there was no answer. I wasn't expecting one from the intercom, but thought there might have been a face at a window. Eventually a curtain twitched on the third floor. I rang again. Nothing.

It was turning out to be more amusing than frustrating. Tom just wasn't cut out for this sort of thing. If you want to do a runner, you don't head straight home.

Looking up again at the dirty window, I made sure that whoever was watching would hear me clunking down the steps, really tearing the arse out of it as if I'd given up.

Walking back the way I'd come, I hung around at the junction with All Saints, knowing that he'd leave sooner or later. It was the wrong thing to do, so he was bound to do it.

Sure enough, twenty cold, boring minutes later, out he came. Still

with no coat on, hands tucked under his armpits, not exactly running but moving towards me quickly.

I stepped out in front of him and his look of horror said it all.

'Hello, Tom.'

At first he just stood there, rooted to the spot, then he half turned
away, screwing up his face and looking down at the pavement, like a
dog that thinks it's going to get hit. 'Please don't hurt me. I didn't say
nothing to no one. On my life. Promise.'

'It's all right, Tom,' I said. 'I have nothing to do with those people
now. That's not why I'm here. Tell you what, let's go back to your
flat, get the kettle on and have a chat.' I was trying to sound nice, but
he knew I wasn't offering him a choice.

I put an arm around his shoulder and he stiffened. 'Come on,
mate, let's have a brew and I'll tell you what this is all about.'

Being only about five foot five, he was easy to get my arm around.
I could feel the softness of his body. He hadn't shaved for a few days
and the result wasn't bristle but the sort of thing you could fill a
duvet with.

I started to make small talk as we walked, trying to make him feel
at ease. Also, this meeting needed to look a bit more normal to any
third party nosing out of their window.

'Hey, I called your flat earlier on, and a woman answered. She
your girlfriend?'

'Janice? Yeah. Look, mate, I have never, ever said nothing to no
one about any of that stuff.'

'Tom, all I want to do is talk. I've got a proposition for you. I think
you'll like what you hear.'

We got to the house and walked up the four stone steps to the
door. Tom fumbled for his key, his hand shaking as he tried to get it
into the keyhole. He still thought he was going to get hammered.

Number 4 had its own small landing, with paint peeling off the
banisters. The door opened into what I supposed was the living room.
The place was in a bad way—damp walls, worn carpet, cold. The
fireplace was boarded up and a gas fire was stuck in its place. An old
TV stood in the corner. To the right of that was a Sony PlayStation,
with a stack of games around it, and the world's oldest PC. Not the
best of equipment for such a high-tech guy, but very good news for
me. It would have been harder to get him to come along if he was
making a fortune.

He walked into a tiny kitchen off the main room and I heard the tap filling the kettle as I lit the fire, clicking the pilot light several times before the gas ignited with a *whoomph*.

'So what are you doing with yourself now, Tom? Still in the computer business?'

He stuck his head into the living room. 'Yeah, I've got a few irons in the fire, know what I mean? Games, that's where the money is, mate. This is just temporary, while I decide who to sell my ideas to. Then it's gravy time. Look for a house to buy, then start my own show. Know what I mean?'

I nodded, knowing exactly what he meant. He had no money, no job and was still full of bullshit. He was going to like what I was about to tell him.

His head disappeared back into the kitchen and things started to be washed up. He stuck his head round the door again. 'Sugar?'

'No, just some milk will be fine.'

He came in with two mugs and passed mine over. His eyes flicked towards the Mickey Mouse alarm clock on top of the fire. Time to get down to business. 'By the looks of it, things aren't that good, are they? I think I can help. I've been offered a job that would earn you enough to buy a flat outright.'

'How much?' He tried to make it sound casual, but didn't quite pull it off.

'Your share would be at least one hundred and thirty thousand— cash. All I need is a week of your time.'

'Is it legal? I ain't doing anything dodgy, mate. I don't want any more trouble. I'm not getting banged up again, know what I mean?'

'It's not illegal. I don't want to go to prison, either. I've just been given this opportunity and I need someone brilliant with computers. I thought of you. You even get a free trip to Finland out of it.'

'Finland? Hey, everyone is online up there. It's the cold, know what I mean, Nick. Too cold, like. Nothing else to do.' He laughed.

I laughed along with him as his eyes moved over to Mickey again. 'Tom, do you need to be somewhere else?'

'Nah, you're all right, it's just that Janice is home soon and the fact is, well, she don't know nothing—you know, my old work, getting banged up, all that stuff. I'm just a bit worried that, you know, if she came in and you said something . . .'

'Hey, no problem. Tell you what, I'll just say I've got a small computer firm and I'm offering you a couple of weeks' work up in Scotland, testing systems. How's that sound?'

'Nice one. But what's the form, what are you after in Finland?'

'It's simple. All we need is to access a system and download some stuff. Until we get there I don't know what, how and when.'

He immediately looked worried. I needed some lies. 'All we're going to do is find out about some new photocopier technology. I can get us into the place, but I need someone who knows what they're looking at once we're in front of one of those things.' I pointed at the computer. 'All you've got to do is access and download. Not steal, mind, just copy. I am going half on the money with you. One hundred and thirty grand, maybe more. Chance of a lifetime, Tom. If you don't take it, someone else will.' I decided I'd give him a bit more incentive. 'Where's your toilet, Tom?'

'Through the kitchen; you'll see the door.'

I stood up and went into the toilet. I sat on the pan, unzipped my money belt and counted out four grand from the dollars. I shoved it in my pocket. Pulling the flush, I came out talking.

'All I know is that it's an easy job. But I need you, Tom.' Reaching into my pocket, I pulled out the cash. 'Here's four grand. Take it. It's a gift. What more can I say? I'm going to do the job anyway. If you're coming with me, though, I need to know today.'

He fingered the money and had to split it in half to get it into his jean pockets. 'Nice one. Thanks, Nick, thanks a lot.'

I needed to make sure he didn't let the money be traced back to me. 'Don't go to the bank to change it or make a deposit, they'll think you're a drug dealer. Take it to a few bureaux de change. Just don't change any more than three hundred dollars at a time.'

He looked up at the sound of a key going into the door lock. 'Shit, it's Janice. Don't say jack. Promise me, Nick.'

She opened the door, felt the heat and looked straight at Tom, ignoring me completely. 'Have you picked up the laundry?'

Tom replied, 'Oh, er nah, I'm going to pick it up in a minute. This is Nick. He's the one that called, you know, this morning.'

It was time for me to leave. 'Thanks for the tea, Tom, I think I'll be off now. Nice to meet you, Janice.'

She nodded, not bothering to look up.

When I turned to leave, he blurted, 'Tell you what, I'll walk down with you, I've got to collect the laundry anyway.'

As we walked back towards All Saints Road, I gave it one more try. 'Tom, think about this seriously. I need you with me, but I must know by tonight if you're up for it.'

He was looking at the pavement, shoulders slumped. 'Yeah. But you know . . .' The cold was starting to get to him.

We got to Westbourne Park Road. I wanted a taxi so I stood on the corner. I put a hand on his shoulder. 'Listen, mate, think about it, and we'll meet up tonight, all right?'

A yellow light appeared in the gloom and I stuck out my hand. The cab pulled up.

Tom was still stooped, hands dug deep in his pockets, shivering. I talked to the top of his head. 'Tom, this is a once-in-a-lifetime chance. Think hard about it.'

The top of his head moved in what I took to be a nod.

I couldn't stand his shivering any more and unzipped my jacket. 'For God's sake, put this thing on, will you?' He protested feebly, then returned my grin as he took the coat.

'Once-in-a-lifetime, mate.' I got into the taxi, asked for Marble Arch and turned to close the door and pull down the window.

Tom was just finishing zipping up. 'Hey, Nick, bollocks to it. Why not, I'm up for it.'

'That's good. I'll call you tonight with the details. We have to leave tomorrow. Is that OK? You got a passport?'

'No probs.'

I put my thumb to my ear and little finger to my mouth to mime a call. 'Tonight at seven. You have a credit card?'

'Er, yeah. Why's that?'

'I haven't got mine. You might have to pay for the tickets, but don't worry, I'll give you the cash before we go.'

The taxi pulled away.

AFTER GIVING THE CAB DRIVER a new drop-off point, I bought myself a blue ski jacket in Oxford Street and went to a chemist's for some bits and pieces I'd need for the dead letterbox so I could leave our details with Liv. Before E4 pinged me at the flat, I'd thought Liv wanting to use a dead letterbox just to hand over some flight details was a bit paranoid. But now I knew it was essential. If E4 were onto her, I didn't want any more contact with her in the UK. I'd never be able to dig myself out of that.

I booked the flights from a phone box, and they held them in Tom's name. I'd get him to pay for them with his credit card at the airport tomorrow; since Davidson was history, I had no choice. I wondered if Tom was still being monitored, now that he was a known subversive, but decided I'd have to take that risk. There wasn't time to do anything about it.

With my new coat to keep me warm I fought my way through the Saturday shopping frenzy to Oxford Circus and headed for the Langham Hilton. About fifty yards short of the hotel were two old-style red telephone boxes. In the windows of each were maybe twenty calling cards, held in position by lumps of Blu-Tack.

I went into the left-hand box and saw Susie Gee's card three-quarters of the way up, facing Oxford Circus. She looked very sultry, on all fours and kissing the air. I peeled her off the glass, got out a large black marker pen and scored a line down the window.

Folding Susie into my pocket I moved on towards the hotel. It was a bit premature to leave the 'dead letterbox loaded' sign, but I wasn't expecting any problems.

I walked through the hotel's revolving doors and into the plush interior. Liv's instructions were perfect. To the left was a bar, to the right was the reception desk and ahead was a restaurant. My destination, however, was the basement.

Down below was every bit as plush as above, air-conditioned and soft-carpeted. Passing two wall phones, I headed for the gents.

Sitting down in one of the cubicles, I took out a little plastic pill box from my wash bag, along with a pack of adhesive-backed Velcro patches. I stuck both a female and a male patch onto the pill box just in case she'd screwed up on what side to use; it would be embarrassing if it didn't stick. Inside the pill box went a small scrap of paper with my message: 'Arriving 15.15 12th.' That was all she needed to know.

I came out of the toilet and went back to the wall phones I'd passed. They were positioned quite low down, for the convenience of users in wheelchairs. I put the wash bag between my legs and shuffled a chair up closer to the phone. Liv had chosen well: not too busy, no video cameras about.

As I sat down, I got out a pound coin and Susie's card, picked up the phone and dialled. I wanted the display to show money being used up; it would look suspicious if anyone passed and saw that I'd been there a few minutes and was only pretending to make a call.

I used my right hand to keep the phone to my ear, waiting for Susie, and felt under the wooden veneer shelf below it with my left. I found what I was looking for in the far corner: it was female Velcro, the soft bit, just as Liv had said.

A husky, middle-aged voice answered the phone. 'Hello, can I help you, love? Would you like me to run through the services?'

I ummed and aahed as the maid named the tariff for spending half an hour with Susie.

'That's great,' I said. 'I'll think about it.'

I put the phone down, picked up the bag, moved the chair back, and headed back the way I'd come. I turned before leaving the basement, checked the box couldn't be seen from that level then went upstairs, through the revolving doors and back onto the street.

All I had to do now was call Tom at seven and tell him the timings for tomorrow morning's flight, then go and dump my leathers in a bin and my weapon in London's biggest armoury, the River Thames.

HELSINKI, FINLAND. Sunday, December 12, 1999. Tom stood in a different queue for immigration. I'd told him he must keep away from me until we were in the arrivals lounge—security and all that. He talked too much and too loudly to sit next to in an aircraft. We'd even checked in separately.

He'd made an effort and smartened himself up a bit for the journey, which was good. I wanted him to resemble an average citizen, not look like food for customs to pull to one side. He was still wearing my jacket, but had swapped the flared jeans for a new, normal pair, and he was also wearing a new red sweatshirt. However, he still had the same canvas daps on, and though he'd finished off by washing and combing his hair, he hadn't shaved.

We got through immigration and customs and there was no need to wait for suitcases. I'd told him that all he needed was a bit of soap and a toothbrush.

The sliding doors opened to admit us into the arrivals hall. No one would be there to meet us yet. We weren't on the flight that arrived at 15.15, as I'd told Liv; we were on the 13.45. I always liked to be early in order to watch who might be waiting for me. Walking into an arrivals lounge to meet people I didn't know gave me the same feeling as knocking on a strange door, not knowing what was on the other side.

We met up in the hall. Tom seemed to be feeling very laddish today, eyeing the women as they moved around the terminal.

'What now, mate? Where we going?'

'We're a bit early for our pick-up. Let's get a brew.'

We followed the signs to the coffee shop and were soon at a table, me with coffee, Tom with a pot of tea. Opposite was a bank of screens, obviously Internet stations.

Tom's eyes lit up. 'I'm gonna have to check that out. You coming?' He did, taking his tea with him. I didn't.

He was back very quickly, before I'd even tasted my coffee. 'You haven't got any coins, have you, mate? I've got no money, well, no Finnish money. Only dollars, know what I mean?'

I hoiked out the change from the drinks.

Fifteen minutes later he was back. He must have run out of money. 'I just emailed Janice and told her I definitely can't get in touch for a while—up in the hills testing kit and all that.'

OUR LIFT WAS EASY to spot, smartly dressed in a grey suit and over-coat, with spiky light brown hair, presenting himself to the people pushing their trolleys through the automatic doors of the customs hall. He was holding up an A4 card with felt-tipped lettering: NICK AND ANOTHER.

We went up and introduced ourselves. As we shook hands he vir-tually stood to attention and clicked his heels together, then offered to take both bags. Tom refused after I did.

The short-term car park was opposite Arrivals. An aircraft roared overhead as we approached a silver Merc. We put the bags in the boot and got in the back. 'Spike' turned the engine on and the Merc started moving.

The airport was quite close to Helsinki and we were soon on the city ring road. We moved onto another motorway, and started to head away from the built-up area.

Tom was resting his head against the seat, eyes closed and Walkman earphones in. I kept my eyes on the road signs. After just under an hour we took the Lahti exit. It was a winter-sports town.

We passed a brightly lit market, then slowed down at a sign telling us we were at the Alexi Hotel. Cutting left, over the pavement, we stopped by a garage door that instantly started to open. We drove down a steep concrete ramp into a large, badly lit underground park-ing area and cruised about looking for a space.

Tom was sitting up now, earphones out and eyes wide. 'It's like one of them spy films, Nick, know what I mean?' His tone changed as he thought about what he'd just said. 'It's all right, innit? I mean, you know what's happening, don't yer?'

I nodded, not really feeling too sure.

Parking in a vacant space, Spike turned off the engine. I got out of the car, and Tom followed just as a black 4x4 Mercedes, the old square shape, moved slowly towards us.

I looked at Spike, who didn't seem remotely concerned. The 4x4 stopped, its engine running. It had blacked-out rear windows and the only occupant I could see was the driver.

She looked very different from the last time I'd seen her. Then, she'd resembled an off-duty Italian; now she was wearing a chunky grey Norwegian-style polo neck which came right up to her chin, decorated with weird and wonderful patterns. A Tibetan hat with ear flaps covered most of the rest of her face, but I could just make out some wisps of blonde hair.

As the front window slid down, I was treated to a very pleasant but businesslike smile. 'Get in the back of the vehicle.' She added something in Finnish to Spike as we climbed into the rear seats. The vehicle was cold; she must have been waiting for us without the engine running or the heater on.

'Please sit well down in your seats and keep away from the windows.'

Tom looked at me for an explanation. I shrugged. 'Later, mate.'

I turned to face the windscreen and saw Liv watching me in the rearview mirror. She smiled. 'Welcome to Finland.' She then tilted her head to look at Tom. 'My name is Liv. I'm very pleased to meet you.'

Tom nodded, looking almost shy. She clearly had the same effect on him as she did on me.

We drove back out onto the road. The lights burned even brighter in the marketplace. It was getting dark.

'We don't have a lot of time,' Liv said. 'Events have moved on from our last conversation. You must carry out the task this Tuesday.'

'I need to see the target,' I said. 'Two nights isn't a lot of time for preparation. You'll have to tell me all you know tonight, and I'll recce the place tomorrow.'

'Of course. I am also concerned that Tom should have enough time to break through the firewall so he can access the system.'

Tom sat up, like a well-behaved child trying to please an adult. 'It'll be OK. Just show me what you've got.'

'I will, Tom. Very soon.'

Eventually we turned onto a tarmac road, tree-lined and cleared of snow, then carried on for another mile or two, down a slight hill, until the trees gave way to a house that was suddenly illuminated by ground lights as the vehicle approached. We must have passed a sensor.

The place was maybe 200 feet long and looked just as if someone had taken an enormous slice out of an apartment block and perched it twenty feet off the ground on two massive concrete supports. Val certainly did things in style.

The driveway took us under the house, where glass panels sealed the area around the pillars to make an internal car park. Two large patio-type doors opened automatically as we approached, then closed behind us.

It was surprisingly warm as I stepped out of the Merc.

Liv hit a key fob and a brown door opened in the left-hand pillar. Tom and I followed her into a hot stairwell.

We entered a vast, high-ceilinged living area, maybe a hundred feet long and sixty wide, and, like the London flat, sparsely furnished. A door to my right led into the kitchen. Two white leather settees faced each other across a glass-and-chrome coffee table, and that was it. No TV, magazines, flowers, pictures on the wall, nothing. White vertical blinds stretched from floor to ceiling where I expected windows to be. It was straight out of a Sunday supplement.

'I'll show you your rooms.' Liv was already walking towards the far right-hand door. We followed into a corridor.

My room was through the first door on the left with a low Japanese-style bed, en suite shower, marble tiling and stacks of brand-new white towels. There was no wardrobe, just small canvas storage spaces suspended from a chrome rail. There were no windows.

Liv said, 'No need for windows. It's always too dark.' She turned away. 'Tom, your room is next door.' She paused in the doorway. 'Would you like some coffee, Nick, and maybe something to eat? Then we must get to work. We don't have much time.'

'Yeah, thanks.'

She nodded and made her way back towards the living area.

A couple of minutes later, Tom and I sat facing each other on the white leather settees. Liv reappeared with a full percolator, milk and mugs on a tray, and a plate of crispbread and sliced cheese. Placing it on the glass table, she sat down next to Tom.

'Let me explain the set-up,' she said. 'I will be staying here with you both. My room is over on the other side.' She pointed to the opposite door. 'The room across from your bedrooms is where the laptop is, for you, Tom, to decrypt the firewall.' She turned to me. 'Nick, also in there are maps of the house you'll be visiting.' She started to pour. 'By Wednesday morning you must have discovered the access sequence, entered the house and copied the files. If not, my instructions are that the deal is off.'

We lapsed into a strained silence. At length I said, 'It will happen.' Tom nodded. 'No drama.'

She stood up. 'Come, bring your drinks. Let's start work.'

We followed her down the corridor. The room on the right was large and rectangular. There were two desks and chairs. One desk had an aluminium briefcase on it, the other, a small, black, sleek-looking IBM laptop, together with the box it had come in, spare leads and a black nylon carry bag with shoulder strap.

Liv pointed at the laptop. 'Tom, that ThinkPad is for you.'

As she and Tom started to talk firewall stuff, I unclipped the aluminium case and lifted the lid. I found several marked maps, all of different scales. It looked as if we were aiming for a town called Lappeenranta, about seventy-five miles to the east of us and close to the Russian border. The target was just over twelve miles north of Lappeenranta. The house was surrounded by forest.

Liv left us to it, and I watched her go. She was unbelievably cool. I realised that I was beginning to like her a lot.

'Hey, Tom?' I turned to face him. He was hunched over the small screen, his back to me.

He turned and looked up. 'What's the matter, mate?'

'I think it would be better if you didn't mention anything to Liv about the money. It's just that she may be getting less than us and will get a bit pissed off. If she asks, just say you don't know, OK?'

'Isn't this her place, then?'

'I doubt it. She's just working on the job, like us. I think it would be best if we kept our cards close to our chests, OK?'

He turned back to the desk. 'If you say so, mate. Whatever.' The keys started to clink away under his dancing fingers.

I returned to the material spread out in front of me and started to memorise the maps. The best way I had learned to do this was by visualising the route I'd take. I sat there, staring at the blank wall, when I noticed a piece of plasterboard that had come loose around a two-pin plug. I got on my knees to look, pulling back the edge of the board to reveal lead sheeting behind, covered with a plastic lining. I glanced back at Tom. He was still hammering on the key-board like a man possessed.

I pushed the plasterboard back in place and walked around the room looking for more holes. Then I realised there weren't any phone jacks. Was it to make the place impossible to communicate with electronically? If so, Val took his work very seriously indeed. It unnerved me a bit.

I walked across to Tom's desk and stood over him, looking at a screen full of numbers and letters. Some of the vertical lines would change every time he hit a key.

'Do you understand what you've got there?'

'No problem; it's all about algorithms and protocols, hardened proxies, stuff like that. I need to find the access sequence among a million or so different sets of characters. That's the firewall between me and the rest of the system. It has a learning program that detects unusual events, like me trying to hack in, and interprets them as an attack. If we were trying to do this on site I wouldn't be able to do it in time. But this set-up is perfect: I have time to play. Once I've hacked into it here, all I have to do is configure the ThinkPad, bring it with me and then I can download all the files she wants.'

'Tom, will you be able to get past this thing?' The screen full of moving numbers and symbols looked like total confusion to me.

'No drama, mate. No drama.'

'I'm going for a brew. You coming?'

'Nah, mate, I'm gonna stay here. Things to do, know what I mean?'

I left him to it and walked to the living area. I wandered around the room, checking for phone points, but didn't find any. I couldn't see any gaps in the wall covering either. Walking over to the ceiling-to-floor blinds I gave one of them a poke. It didn't move, and was extremely hard and heavy.

There was a switch on the wall nearby. When I flicked it, the blinds began to open from the centre.

I turned, hearing bare feet moving towards me. Liv was wearing a blue silk dressing gown which finished just above her knees, exposing each thigh in turn as she moved. Two more steps and she reached past me and hit the switch. She smelt as if she'd just stepped out of the shower.

The blinds began to close again. 'Nick, the blinds must remain closed at all times when Tom is working on the computer.' She waved a palm in the direction of the settees. 'Shall we sit?'

As she crossed the room, I followed. She saw my eyes flick to the blinds. 'Yes, Nick, they are lined with lead. The whole house is. Valentin doesn't like his competitors learning what he's doing.'

'So that's why no phones?'

We sat facing each other on the settees. As she tucked her legs underneath her, the silk followed the contours of her body.

'Please, Nick, will you tell Tom? House rule.'

'No problem. But will you do me a favour in return? It would make things a lot easier for us if you didn't tell Tom anything about the Maliskia, or about the deal we have. He's a worrier and I want him to concentrate on the job.' The last thing I needed was her telling him how much money was really involved.

'Of course.' She smiled, and leaned forward to pick up a book on the coffee table. As she settled back, her silk dressing gown fell down on either side of her legs. I tried not to look, but couldn't help myself. Liv was one of the most beautiful and intelligent women I'd ever met. It was a pity I had champagne tastes and a lemonade budget.

She pulled the gown together as she caught my eye. 'Nick, I need to finalise some dead-letterbox details with you for the information and money exchange. Valentin wants to give you control of the arrangements, as a gesture of good faith. So, we shall all go to Helsinki in the morning, even if Tom hasn't got through the firewall by then. It's important that he isn't kept in the dark.'

I opened my mouth to speak but she seemed to have accessed my own firewall. She seemed to know exactly what I was thinking.

'Once you and Tom have left on Tuesday, you must never return here, whatever happens. That way this place remains secure. In any event, no one will be here, as I am leaving soon after you. I will take anything you want to leave behind, and return it at the exchange. You are to make your way to the dead letterbox on Wednesday morning and leave details for a meeting between just the two of us.'

I nodded. 'What if I don't make the dead letterbox?'

'If you don't, Tom will. That is why he must be with us tomorrow.'

'What time are we leaving in the morning?'

'Eight. Will you tell Tom?' She yawned. 'Time for bed, I think. Good night, Nick.'

I watched her walk towards the door. 'Night, Liv.'

She disappeared into the other half of the house. I couldn't help a smile of regret when I realised that her leaning across me to flick a wall switch was the closest we were ever likely to get.

Seven

Monday, December 13, 1999. We headed south along the motorway towards Helsinki. It was nearly 8.45, and after thirty minutes of staring at headlights it had begun to get light. It was going to be a sunny day; there wasn't a cloud in the sky and the unfolding view of pine trees and glittering snow was straight out of a ski brochure.

Tom hadn't been too keen on coming because, after working much of the night, he was close to breaking the firewall. But I agreed with Liv; he needed to be aware of the game plan. If there was a problem on target and Tom was the only one to get away, she had to know there was still a chance she could get the data to Val.

Another forty minutes and we hit Helsinki city limits. Weaving towards the centre in heavy traffic, we passed a department store called Stockmann. Liv pointed at the window displays as we drove past. 'We'll meet in the coffee shop on the sixth floor. The station is just a couple of minutes' walk away.'

We drove on a couple of blocks before stopping. As I got out, I felt the bitter cold. Every inch of exposed skin prickled. Liv looked at me through the door. 'I'll see you both in two hours. You'll need half an hour to check out the station.'

I nodded and turned to Tom. 'We'll use the rest of the time to get our kit.' I closed the door of the 4x4 and she drove off.

The station was in front of us. The main doors were heavy and wooden, with porthole windows. We pushed through. The interior looked more like a well-kept museum than a station, with stone-paved floors and thick granite pillars.

Liv's dead letterbox was easy to find. We were standing with our backs to the main entrance. In front of us was a wide stairway and escalators that led down into the metro. The three sides of the stair-way surrounded an open square of continuous wooden benches. The dead letterbox was by a rubbish bin on the left-hand side. Tom followed as I walked past it. A teenaged girl in navy-blue salopettes was sitting reading a magazine.

I nodded at Tom just before we got level with her. 'There it is, mate. See the girl in blue?'

He nodded back and we carried on past.

'OK, if you put your hand underneath the bench, where she's sitting, you're going to feel a plastic container attached by Velcro. All you do is make sure no one's looking and pull it off, go away and write a note telling them where they can find you, and they'll come.'

'Isn't this all a bit James Bond, Nick? I don't like it.'

'It's just belt-and-braces stuff. You need to know what to do if it goes wrong. Suppose I break a leg and can't get back here? Then it'll be down to you to hand over the goods and get us our money.'

The girl got up and walked towards us.

'Go on, see if there's anything there yet.'

'What, now?' He looked terrified. 'While everyone's here?'

'It's never going to be empty, Tom. It's a station, for God's sake. All you've got to do is take a stroll over there, sit down, put your hand under the bench and have a feel around. While you're doing that I'll go and change some money for you, all right?'

I went to the bureau de change, exchanged $500, then wandered back. I could see him sitting on the bench, looking very pleased with himself. I sat next to him.

'Piece of cake, mate. Found it first time, look.' He bent down.

'No, no, not now, Tom. Leave it where it is and I'll show you how to tell Liv that you've put a message in there for her.'

I stood up and he followed. We went towards the platform doors and I explained where to leave his 'dead letterbox loaded' marker.

'Just beyond this coffee shop, on the right, is a row of telephones. When the time comes, get yourself a marker pen from one of these shops and draw a line down the booth of the right-hand one, OK?'

It wasn't. 'Why?'

'So Liv doesn't have to sit down and feel under the bench every time to check it. If the loaded sign isn't there, she knows that a message isn't, either. Otherwise she'll look just a bit suspicious on Wednesday, won't she, sitting in the same place every hour on the hour?'

He nodded thoughtfully. 'Tell you what, she could sit next to me every hour on the hour, know what I mean?'

I smiled. Liv would have had him for breakfast.

Thirty feet short of the doors was a bank of four phones fixed to the wall, divided by polished wooden booths. We stood against the nearest one. 'See here?' I said.

'Yeah, you want me to mark . . .' He started to wave his finger.

I pushed his hand down. 'Yes, that's right, mate, a nice thick line. Make sure you pretend to be on the phone.'

'I get it, but you'll tell me what to say in the letter, yeah?'

'Of course. Now let's go and get cold.'

Once on the pavement we cut right in the direction of Stockmann. I handed Tom 2,000 Finnish marks from the wad I'd got from the money changer.

'Tom, I want you to give me your passport and wallet for safe keeping. I've got an idea for a little extra insurance, but listen, this is between you and me. It's not that I don't trust her, but better safe than sorry, eh?'

'Nice one, Nick. Makes me feel better.' He handed them over without questioning.

Tom and I walked into Stockmann. In the luggage department I picked up two weekend bags, one dark green and one black, and two heavy car blankets. Tom had his wad of money clasped firmly in his hand and was looking happy. It was time to say my goodbyes.

'I've got things to do, Tom. Insurance.' I tapped the side of my nose and winked. His big hamster cheeks beamed back. 'I'll see you in the coffee shop in three-quarters of an hour. Get yourself some good warm kit, the sort of stuff I told you about, all right?'

'Yeah, yeah, no drama.'

I clapped his shoulder. 'Remember, get a decent coat and boots.'

Back in the cold, I took out my new holdalls and bulked them out with the blankets. Then I headed for the station again and went into the toilets. It cost me nearly a pound to sit down in one of the cubicles so I could get out the money from my money belt—what was left of the twenty-five grand in $100 bills that I'd brought with me. I removed four grand and then placed the money belt, plus my own documents and Davidson's, into the dark-green holdall. You never know when even a burned ID can come in useful. Tom's documents and $3,000 went into the black bag, and I slipped the remaining grand into my pocket. I then dumped both at left luggage and looked for a hiding place for the receipts and for the two plane tickets—our own little dead letterbox—somewhere Tom would find easy enough to remember.

I went into one of the shops and picked up a computer magazine with a plastic sleeve holding a free CD-ROM. I was queueing at the checkout when I saw her.

Liv was standing by the doors to the trains. The man she was with was very smartly dressed in a long camel-hair coat, shirt and tie.

I ducked out of the queue as if I'd had second thoughts about the magazine, and went back to browsing the racks, watching Liv and her man out of the corner of my eye. They were in each other's arms, their faces just inches apart. They were doing their best to look like two lovers saying their goodbyes but they weren't talking to each other, they were talking *at* each other. I'd done this enough times myself to know what was going on.

They talked for a little while longer, then he pulled slightly away from her. He was in his early thirties, with short brown hair, and looked quite the young trendy businessman.

She turned away, heading for the bus-station exit. There had been no final kiss, no last touch or stroke of the hair.

I let her go past me, then moved quickly to the platform doors, pinging him on platform 6 as he looked at his ticket and checked the coaches. The destination board said the platform 6 train was leaving for St Petersburg in two minutes.

I walked swiftly back to the newsstand and bought the magazine, together with a reel of Sellotape. Taking the plastic sleeve off the magazine, I ripped it into two strips and wrapped the tickets individually. The receipts for the luggage were in with our tickets. Now all I had to do was find a place to hide them that Tom would remember. It wasn't hard. The long banks of left-luggage lockers by the taxi exit were on legs, with a four-inch gap between them and the floor. Pretending to clean the slush off my shoes, I taped Tom's under Number 10 and mine under Number 11. If things went wrong, both of us had a ticket out of Finland.

I made my way back to Stockmann and found Tom in Café Avec. I was pleased to see he'd bought himself a decent pair of boots, and a dark blue, thick, woollen check lumberjack coat.

'Great, Tom. Now listen.' I explained to him where his ticket was hidden. We'd pick them up on Wednesday, but if the shit hit the fan tomorrow night, he should head straight for the station, grab his bag and catch the first flight home.

He started to look a bit more cheerful. 'I just want to get this job done and get back to London with some dosh. I don't really like it here. It must be the cold. That's why I got these for tomorrow.' He bent down and brought out a set of silk leggings and a top then looked anxiously over my shoulder. 'Liv's here.'

She came over and sat down. 'Everything all right?'

I nodded.

'Good. Here are the keys for your car, Nick.' She passed over two keys on a Saab key fob. 'There are maps inside the glove box to get you there, and a detailed one of the area. None of the maps is marked. It will take you more than three hours to get there.'

'There'll probably be things I'll need once I've seen the house.'

'No problem, so long as it's nothing exotic.' She stood up. 'I'll show you where the car is, then go back to the house with Tom.'

THE JOURNEY TO THE TARGET seemed to take longer than she'd told me to expect. It was just after three o'clock and already last light. The reflection from the Saab's headlights twinkled in the snow piled high at the roadside. I used the time to think about Liv's station RV, but didn't come up with any answers. I decided I just had to get on with it.

After taking the exit for Lappeenranta, I counted off the miles until I found the junction I was looking for. With a couple of miles still to go, I changed down to first gear. There wasn't a light to be seen as I checked off each track into the woods on the map. I found the target track, but kept going, looking for somewhere off the road to leave the Saab. About another 300 yards on I found a small cut in the wood line that seemed to be a firebreak. Once tucked in, I switched off the engine.

Putting on the gloves and black woollen hat I'd bought myself at Stockmann, I got out and hit the key fob. Lights flashed as the central locking did its stuff, but I couldn't help that.

Setting off down the gravel road, I made sure the hat didn't cover my ears; I was on a recce, I needed them to be able to work, without fighting to hear through half a lamb's coat.

It was bitterly cold after the snug warmth of the Saab, and there was no noise or light. All I could hear was my own breathing and the snow crunching an inch under my feet before it compressed onto the hard ice beneath. My whole world was trees and snow.

I started slowly down the track. A lot of vehicles had obviously been up and down; there was no snow in the ruts on either side of the small central mound, just compacted ice.

I moved like a tightrope walker along the rut, to cut down ground sign. After about five minutes I began to see weak, intermittent light ahead in the direction of the target. The beams flashed up into the sky or straight at me, disappeared for a while, then bounced towards me again: vehicle lights, coming my way.

I couldn't even hear the engine yet, so it would be impossible for them to see me. There was nothing I could do without leaving sign but dive out of the way. I faced the drift at the trackside, rocked back to try to get some momentum, then leapt. I managed to clear the first few feet of snow, rolling like a high jumper, and landed. The snow lay over solid granite and I hit it hard, knocking the wind out of my lungs.

I started to crawl like an animal, trying to burrow under the branches. The vehicle was getting closer. I dug myself in and waited.

It drew parallel with me and kept going. It was a 4x4 but I couldn't make out how many were inside. All I could see was the light moving slowly along the tree tunnel, followed by a cloud of diesel fumes.

I watched and listened as the light died. They must have reached the top of the track, because I heard the transmission ratios change, then the noise disappeared completely.

I crawled back to my impact site, stood up and launched myself over the bank again. My right shin connected painfully with the central mound, and I lay on my back in one of the ruts, holding my leg, taking the pain and thinking of the money.

After a minute I got up and hobbled on down the track.

What had been concerning me most all along was: how many bayonets? The term dated back to the First World War. How many was I going to have to fight if I was compromised and couldn't run away? If there were, say, four people in the house, two of them might be Tom-type characters who'd never held a gun, but the other two could be hoods who had, and who'd go for it. They were the bayonets.

The track went downhill and began to curve. As I rounded a bend I could see two dim lights directly ahead, maybe 100 yards away.

The trees stopped about five yards from a fence that I could now clearly see in front of me, leaving an empty area running left and right of the track, about two or three feet deep in snow. A large set of double gates was directly ahead. Keeping in the rut, I moved up close. It was made of the same material as the fencing: diamond-shaped work pressed out of quarter-inch steel sheeting.

A large chain fed through both gates and was secured with a heavy steel high-security padlock.

The fence looked about fifty feet high, and was made up of three sections, bolted together and supported by spaced steel poles about a foot in diameter. The house was beyond the fence, about forty yards away. It had a chateau-style tower on the far right-hand side, with a Russian onion-shaped dome that I could just see silhouetted against the night sky. There were no Christmas decorations, just two lights.

One came from a stained-glass panel that I thought was the top half of a door, set back on a verandah. The other was coming from a window further to the left. Beyond that were five satellite dishes, massive things at least ten feet across and set into the ground. This was a proper little Microsoft HQ.

There was a sound behind me. The vehicle was returning. I ran back to the nearest dive point. To clear the bank, which was slightly off the track, before the headlights reached me, I had to throw myself about three feet up and five feet over. I went for it, not quite making the five feet and hitting rock again. It probably hurt, but I wouldn't feel it until later; adrenaline was doing its job, fighting the pain.

I ploughed through the snow to get under branches once more. The vehicle noise increased as it rounded the bend.

A moment later the 4x4 passed. It stopped just short of the gate. I saw the passenger door open and the interior light come on. A very padded body climbed out and started to move towards the gates.

The chain was left dangling as both gates were pushed inwards to let the vehicle pass. The wagon inched forward, its headlights revealing that the snow beyond the gates and inside the target was full of ground sign, feet and tyres. Just as importantly, no alarms or trips appeared to have been turned off before entry.

The chain rattled again, but I wasn't paying much attention to the gate-closer any longer. As the 4x4's headlights swung to the right I saw a covered verandah running along the right half of the house.

The 4x4 rolled to a stop parallel with the verandah. The engine and headlights died. I heard a man's voice as the passenger shouted something to the driver.

The gate man carried on onto the verandah as the driver leaned into the passenger foot well and lifted out some flat boxes. The pair moved together, stamping their feet on the wooden floor of the verandah to clear them of snow.

The driver opened the front door of the house with a key. Light spilled out and I caught a brief glimpse of a hallway before they disappeared inside.

Moving forward, I dived out again, this time taking the hit on my knees. Going back to the gate, I took my glove off and very quickly touched the metal lattice, then leaned over to the left and did the same to the fence. Only then did I turn round and start hobbling back up the track.

Twenty minutes later I was heading back towards Helsinki.

THE DRIVEWAY to the lead-lined house came into sight after just under four, and a half hours. Pulling up outside the big glass shutters, I realised I didn't have a key. There was nothing to do but hit the horn. A few seconds later a light came on and Liv appeared at the door. Thunderbird 3's hangar door opened and I drove in. By the time I joined her she was in the kitchen and I could smell coffee.

'So, Nick,' she said, 'will you be able to get in?'

'No problem. Where's Tom?'

'He's working. He's broken through the firewall, as I hoped.' She said it without excitement, and noticed my surprise. 'You still have to get Tom into the house, Nick. Sit, I'll get the coffee.'

I did, checking my watch. It was just before midnight. I called out, 'You'll need a pen and some paper.'

She came back in with the coffee tray and writing materials, sat on the settee opposite mine and poured two mugs.

I picked one up. 'I'll run through a list of equipment with you,' I said between sips. 'I'm going to need quite a lot of stuff.'

She picked up the pen and pad and wrote as I dictated. She was surprised by my request for six-inch nails—150mm once she had converted them—plus a three-foot length of four-by-two-inch wood, which became a one-metre length of 100 by 50mm.

'Why do you need this, Nick? Aren't lock picks and electronic gadgetry more the sort of thing?'

'Can you get me some?'

She smiled and shook her head.

'I'll show you what it's all for tomorrow. I need the weather forecast, too, for a twenty-four-hour period starting at nine in the morning. I'd also like a weapon—a pistol, preferably silenced.'

She looked genuinely taken aback. 'Why?'

'Better to have it and not need it than the other way round.'

'I'm sorry, Nick, I wouldn't get you one even if I could. I have nothing to do with that sort of thing. Besides, you were employed precisely because Valentin wanted finesse.'

I wanted to tell her it wasn't just finesse that got Val into the boot of the Volvo, but I could see that it was pointless.

She stood up. 'I'm going to bed now, Nick. Please, help yourself to food. I should be back by ten thirty tomorrow with your list.'

Digging out tins of tuna and sweetcorn from a kitchen cupboard, I emptied them into a bowl and went in search of Tom as I mixed it up with a fork and got it down my neck.

He was sitting at the ThinkPad, his head in his hands. He didn't look up as I came in.

'All right?'

'Yeah, all right.' There was a blocked-up nasal sound to his reply. All was not well at Camp Tom.

'Seriously, you OK?'

I wanted to sound surprised at finding him so down, but I could guess at the reason. Being so near the witching hour, reality was grabbing him by the throat.

'I'm really worried, Nick. You know, I . . . I . . .' There was a big sigh from him. 'I want to get home, Nick. I don't wanna do it, mate. No way am I going back inside . . .'

'Tom, I told you, this won't get you put away. No way would I be doing anything that would get me within a thousand miles of a prison. I've done some, too, you know.'

He looked up at me with tears in his eyes. 'I don't wanna go back, Nick. There were some hard boys in there, know what I mean?' His mouth quivered. 'I couldn't hack it, mate.'

'Don't worry, mate. All that's finished with, I guarantee it.'

He sniffed and wiped his nose, embarrassed at his display of vulnerability.

'Best bet is to go have a wash and get your head down. We have a busy night tomorrow.' I tapped his shoulder playfully, leaving him to sort himself out. He didn't need me there to embarrass him even more. Besides, he was coming with me tomorrow night whether he liked it or not.

Back in my room I started to undress, and listened as Tom walked past my door in the direction of the living area, probably in search of a glass of water to replace all the liquid leaking down his face.

I went to bed. I was knackered, but thoughts about the job kept me awake, going over making entry and what to do if there was a foul-up. I must have been lying there for an hour, listening to the hum of the air conditioning, when Tom shuffled past once more towards the living area. He would probably be like this all night now, but he'd live. If he was still wobbly in the morning I'd remind him again about how much money he'd soon have in his pocket. I'd already decided that I would give him the full $300,000. Why not? I wouldn't have got this far without him.

Another half-hour hummed by. I was still thinking about tomorrow night when I realised that Tom hadn't come back.

Yawning, I put on my jeans and shirt and wandered off to have a brew with him, maybe talk him round a bit more.

Crossing the living area, I noticed that the door leading to Liv's side of the house was open, and I knew that she'd closed it behind her. I started to mooch down her corridor. There was noise coming from the first door on the left. I didn't know who was doing what to whom, but the grunts and moans were unmistakably theirs.

I turned back up the corridor, leaving them to it, realising, yet again, that I didn't have a clue when it came to women.

Tuesday, December 14, 1999. By the time I got up, Tom was showered and dressed, hair still wet, sitting on the sofa drinking milk.

I went into the kitchen, poured some coffee and checked out the food. I was dying to ask him about last night, but decided to wait and see if he said anything first.

Fixing myself a plate of crispbread, cheese and cherry jam, I dumped it all on a tray and went and sat opposite him.

'You look a lot better this morning.' I gave him a grin. 'There's nothing like a good night's sleep.'

He avoided the subject. 'It's going to be OK, Nick, isn't it?'

'Of course. I had a good look at the house last night. It's just a big old mansion in the woods, trying to look like Microsoft HQ. Piece of cake. Next stop, the bank.'

He grinned. 'Nice one, mate. Nice one.'

I took a mouthful of coffee. 'Yep, it's good we both got some sleep. We'll certainly be knackered tomorrow morning.'

He sipped his milk, trying to hide his face in his mug.

I couldn't resist any longer. 'I heard you, you know.'

He turned bright red. 'What? What are you on about?'

'Hey, listen, good luck, mate, but keep the noise down in future, will you? Some of us old muckers can't take too much excitement.'

He laughed nervously, embarrassed, but at the same time rather proud. I couldn't blame him.

'What's the secret, Tom? Have you and Miss Nordic Myth met in a past life?'

'Nah, mate. Never met the girl before. But, you know, I was out here getting a drink when she came out. She saw I was worried, and we got talking and that . . . you know.'

I didn't, that was the problem. I gave myself a mental slap. I realised, with a shock, that I was jealous. I needed to concentrate on making money and leave anything else that was going on well alone.

I got up, leaned over and tapped him on the shoulder. 'Just make sure you've got those daps of yours for tonight.'

'Daps?'

'Plimsolls, whatever you call them. Make sure they're clean and dry. Don't wear them today, just keep your new boots on, all right?'

With that I picked up my mug and left.

FRESHLY SHOWERED, I lay on my bed and visualised making entry on target. I always found it easy to run the film in my head, as if my eyes were the camera lens and my ears the recording equipment. I listened to what the snow sounded like as we walked to the verandah, then the creak of the wooden decking, working out how I would deal with it, attacking the lock on the door and then moving Tom around the house until we found what we were looking for. I replayed the footage three or four times, from leaving the car to returning to it; then I started to edit it with different versions: What if Tom and I were on the verandah and the door opened? What if we were compromised in the house? It wouldn't go exactly to script, it never did. But the film was a starting point; it meant I had a plan.

I'd been in my room for about two hours when there was a knock on the door.

'Nick?' Tom poked his head round the corner. 'Liv's back.'

I got off my bed and walked out with him. She was in the living room. There was no exchange of eye contact between them and her whole manner announced there was no time for small talk.

'It's been confirmed,' she said briskly. 'They're now online.'

We followed her downstairs, where the first thing she passed me was a sheet of paper with the weather forecast in Finnish. 'It says there is a possibility of snow showers in the early morning.'

This was bad. We had to get in and out as quickly as possible, otherwise the only footprints left on the ground at first light would be fresh ones, not ours mixed in with the others I'd seen in the compound last night. Unless, that was, the shower kept falling for long enough to cover our tracks once we had left.

Tom was busy opening the rear door of the Merc. He picked up a set of eighteen-inch bolt cutters from the back seat and held them out with a quizzical expression on his face.

I had lifted the tailgate and was holding an armful of bags and boxes. 'Just a bit of standby kit we might need tonight, mate.'

Tom followed me upstairs, the bolt cutters under his arm and his fists full of carrier-bag handles. He dumped it all next to the stuff I'd carried up, on the floor outside the kitchen. Liv was close behind.

'It's pointless you two hanging around,' I said. 'Give me a couple of hours to sort myself out here, and after that I'll explain why I needed all this stuff.'

Liv disappeared into the corridor and the door closed. Tom walked towards our side of the house and I emptied the carrier bags and boxes onto the floor. I sorted the clothing first. The stuff I'd asked Liv for was made of wool and thick cotton. We had to have clothes that weren't going to rustle, and they had to be dark and completely non-reflective—no shiny buttons. I cut out any Velcro holding pockets or flaps with my Leatherman: Velcro makes a noise when pulled apart. Anything dangling, like drawstrings, I also removed. Once in the house, I couldn't afford for them to get caught on something and drag it onto the floor.

Liv had chosen woollen outer gloves for us, as well as thin cotton contact gloves, so I could manipulate the door lock or whatever without my bare hands freezing onto the metal.

I found the bag of six-inch nails and some lengths of thick nylon webbing. The length of wood was exactly as specified. There was a little hacksaw. I used it to cut half a dozen six-inch lengths of wood.

Fifteen minutes later, I had six fist-sized lumps of wood, each with a nail hammered through. The nail had then been bent with pliers into an acute angle about halfway along. The exposed metal of the nail, apart from the bit at the bend and about a quarter of an inch either side of it, had then been covered with rubber bands to eliminate noise when they were used. Tom and I would use one hook in each hand and carry one each as a spare.

I cut four six-foot lengths of the dark green two-inch webbing, knotting together the ends of each so that I ended up with four loops. These I put to one side with the hooks, away from the chaos around me. The climbing kit was ready.

It took me another hour to finish preparing the kit and pack it into a dark blue daysack. Everything was wrapped in my nice white towels, so as not to make a noise or get smashed by the bolt cutters.

Tom wouldn't be needing a daysack. The only kit he'd have with him was the ThinkPad and leads in their carry bag.

Liv emerged from her corridor. By now the jumper was off, and she was in her tight jeans and a white T-shirt—no bra. That would have been interesting a couple of nights ago, but now I was getting on with the job. The circumstances had changed.

She surveyed the mess as coolly as ever. 'Having fun?'

I nodded. 'Want to get Tom in to see what I've made for him?'

She walked past the lead room and I got to my feet. I was still brushing off sawdust when they both reappeared.

'Right, Tom, there's your clothes, mate. You're going to need a bit more on than you bought yesterday.'

He picked up the contact gloves and tried them on, then he pointed at the hooks and straps. 'What are they for?'

When I explained, he looked a bit taken aback. 'What, like Spiderman? Is this the only way, Nick?'

'Listen, this is the only thing you've got to do for yourself. Everything else I'll do for you. I want to leave dead on nine. If the weather's good, we'll be in Helsinki before first light. Then we'll organise the exchange. Now I'm going to get something to eat and then get my head down for a couple of hours. I suggest you do the same.'

I nodded a see-you-later to them both as I went to the kitchen. Tom left for his room.

I started to pull the fridge to bits, throwing all sorts onto a plate. I'd have loved to have left straight away before it had a chance to snow, but we couldn't get in until people were asleep.

I headed for my bedroom with the food, picking at it as I went. Liv had gone. Once on my bed, I started visualising again exactly what I was going to do, except that now in my film it had started to snow. I wasn't happy about the prospect of snow and I wasn't happy about not having a weapon. The vegetable knife I'd used to cut cheese with wasn't much of a substitute.

I GOT UP GROGGILY just after eight and took a shower. I dragged myself to the kitchen for a brew, then took it back to my room and got dressed.

At just before nine I took everything down to the car. Tom was on parade, showered and dressed. Liv didn't follow us down; she would be emptying the house tonight and was busy getting it sterile. She'd take our bags with her, handing them back with the money in them.

Tom and I faced each other as I checked him out, first his pockets to make sure the only stuff in them was the equipment he needed: daps, spare hook, nylon loop, money. He didn't need change rattling around in his pockets, just the paper money in a plastic bag tucked into his boot. Most important was the ThinkPad and leads, jammed into the nylon bag hanging over his shoulder but under his coat.

Tom and I got into the car and wheels turned just after nine o'clock. We got to the drop-off point after three and a half hours, with me flapping every time I had to turn the wipers on to clear the windscreen of muck thrown up by cars in front, thinking that the snowfall had started.

Once in the firebreak near the target I looked over at my passenger. 'You all right, Tom?'

He took a deep breath. 'Ready to roll, mate. Ready to rock'n'roll.' I could sense his apprehension.

'Right then, let's do it.' I got out of the car, closing the door gently. Then I unzipped my flies. Tom was on the other side of the car doing the same, exactly as I'd told him. I could only manage a little dribble.

The daysack went on my back. I pressed the key fob. The car lights flashed. I made sure Tom watched as I placed the key behind the front wheel, covering it with snow.

'We're going to have to keep quiet now. Remember, if you want me, don't call, just touch me, then whisper right in my ear. OK?'

He nodded and I clapped him on the shoulder. 'Let's go then.'

I set off slowly, with Tom two or three paces behind. When we were about five yards down the track I had a check of my watch. It was quarter to one; hopefully they'd gone to bed.

We went down the gentle incline towards the bend that would take us into line of sight of the house. Keeping in the left-hand tyre rut, we slowly rounded the bend. All I could hear was the wind high above us, whipping the tops of the pines, and the sound of Tom moving behind.

Once we were in direct line of sight of the house I stopped. From what I could see at this distance there didn't appear to be any lights on in the house. We were a few yards short of the gap between the tree line and fence when I stopped again. There was a faint glimmer of light coming from the left-hand shutter on the ground floor; it was far weaker than last night. Did that mean everyone was in bed, or crowded round the TV?

I put my hand up in front of his face and signalled Tom to wait where he was. Then my fingers did a little walking-sign motion.

He nodded as I moved off into the darkness, following the wheel rut towards the gate. Nothing much had changed on the other side of the fence; even the 4x4 was parked in the same position.

On the recce there hadn't been any electrical current running through the fence. Biting off my right outer glove, I pulled the touch glove down and quickly felt the gate. As I put the gloves back on I checked the padlocks. They hadn't been left undone—not that I'd expected them to be. That would be too much like good luck.

There was no way I could cut the gate chains or fence, because that would compromise the job. The bolt cutters weighing a ton in my daysack were only to get us out of the compound if we were compromised on target.

I headed back to Tom. Easing the daysack off my shoulders, I knelt down in the wheel rut and tugged on his sleeve.

Tom lowered himself to join me. Getting him to keep the daysack upright by holding the bolt-cutter handles sticking out on either side of the top, I undid the clips and lifted the flap. Then I took out one webbing loop and a hook.

Twisting two turns of the strapping around the nail hook, where it emerged from the wood, I handed the device, now with a three-foot loop hanging from it, to Tom. He gripped the wood in his right hand, as he'd been shown, with the hook angled down and protruding between his index and middle fingers. Attaching a webbing loop to another hook, I handed it over, and he took that in his left hand. I then assembled the other two devices in the same way, reclipped and replaced the daysack on my back, then took one in each hand.

Taking a step closer to Tom, I whispered into his ear, 'Ready?'

I got a slow nod and a couple of short, sharp breaths in return. I started to move the last few yards towards the gate.

I stopped, my nose six inches from the gate, and turned. Tom was two paces behind. Turning back to the gate, I raised my right hand to just above shoulder height, the hook facing the diamond-shaped lattice, and gently eased the bent nail into a gap. The elastic bands around the nail were to eliminate noise, but I'd deliberately left the bend itself exposed: when I heard and felt metal on metal, I'd know it was correctly in position.

The bend in the nail engaged the fencing with the gentlest of scrapes, the bottom of the strapping loop hanging about a foot above the ground. I inserted the left hook about six inches higher, and a shoulder width apart.

It was pointless at this stage worrying about being so exposed to view from the house. All we could do was just get on with it, hoping they didn't see us. At least the front of the house was crisscrossed by footprints and tyre tracks.

Gripping both chunks of wood so the hooks took my body weight, I placed my right foot in the right loop and, using my right leg muscles to push my body upwards and pulling up with my hands and arms, I slowly rose above the ground.

The gate and chains rattled as the structure moved under my weight; I'd expected this to happen, but not so loudly. I froze for a few seconds and watched the house.

Satisfied that the right loop was supporting me, I lifted my left foot into the bottom of the other one, about six inches higher. I was now a foot off the ground, only about another forty-four to go.

I shifted my body weight again until all the pressure was on my left foot and hand. Lifting out the right hook, but keeping my foot in the loop, I reached up and put it back into the fence six inches above the level of the left one, again a shoulder width apart. Tom was right, it was like Spiderman climbing a wall, only instead of suction pads my hands had hooks, and my feet had loops of nylon strapping.

I repeated the process twice more. I wanted first to gain height, then traverse left and continue climbing near a support post. I didn't want us to climb directly above where a vehicle might appear at the gate. I was aiming for the first of the steel poles that the lattice sections were fixed to. If we climbed with our hooks each side of it, it would stop the fence from buckling and lessen the noise.

I now moved vertically and to the left six inches at a time. After three more moves I was off the gate and onto the fence proper, and halfway up the first of the three sections that gave the fence its height. The unmarked snow was six feet or so below me. Stopping, I looked down at Tom and nodded. It was his turn now. He took the weight on his right leg.

The gate moved and the chains rattled loudly. Thankfully the wind carried some of our noise away from the building.

Tom eventually got his left foot into the loop and made his first ascent. He worked hard at it, huffing and grunting as he struggled to sort himself out, then, strangely, he found the traverse a bit easier. I kept my eyes on target while he made his way towards me.

Moving up and across a few more times, my hooks were soon each side of the first support. I waited again for Tom.

Ages later, his head was less than three feet below my boots. Beneath us lay a deep drift of snow. Now that we both had a hook on each side of the support, the going was good and firm. All we had to do from here was climb vertically and get over the top. I moved another six inches, then another, edging my way upwards.

We reached the top of the second of the three sections. A dozen or so more pulls on each side would take us to the top. Tom slapped my leg. I looked down. He was in a frenzy, his free hand waving towards the track as his body swung from side to side.

I looked down. A white-clad body was fighting its way through waist-deep snow in the gap on the other side of the track. Yet more figures were emerging from the tree line and moving onto the track. There must have been at least a dozen. I could tell by the position and swing of their arms that they were carrying weapons. Maliskia.

'Nick! Whatdowedo?'

'Jump!'

Gripping the wood hard and lifting with my arms so the hooks took my body weight, I kicked my feet from the loops and let go with my hands. I just hoped the snow was deep enough to cushion my thirty-foot fall.

I plummeted past Tom, who was still stuck to the fence, and pre-pared myself for the jump instructors' command when the wind is too strong and the drop zone, which should be a nice empty field, has suddenly become the M1: accept the landing.

I plunged into the snow feet first and immediately started a para-chute roll to my right, but crumpled as my ribs banged hard against a tree stump, immediately followed by one of the handles of the bolt cutters hitting me on the back of my head. It was starburst time in my eyes and brain. Pain spread outwards from my chest.

I knew I had to get up and run, but I couldn't do a thing about it: my legs wouldn't play. I moaned to myself as I fought the pain and tried to work out how deep I was buried.

Tom had found the courage to jump. I heard the wind being knocked out of him as he landed to my left, on his back.

He recovered, panting hard. 'Nick, Nick!'

The next thing I knew, he was towering over me, brushing the snow from my face. 'Nick. Come on, mate, come on!'

My head was still spinning, my coordination screwed. I was no good to him and knew it would be only seconds before we were caught. 'Station, Tom! Go, go!'

He made an attempt to pick me up by my arms and drag me, but it would have been hard enough for him in normal conditions, let alone in deep snow. 'Tom, the station. Go, just piss off!'

I opened my eyes to see him pulling the spare hook out of his coat. For a split second I couldn't work out why, and then I heard grunting right behind me. The Maliskia had got to us.

Tom launched himself over me. There was the sound of a thud, and a scream that was too low-pitched to be his.

The next thing I knew, Tom fell beside me, sobbing. There wasn't any time for that, he had to go. I pushed him away from me. Not checking behind him, he left, stumbling over me on the way.

I wanted to follow but couldn't. Rolling over onto my stomach and pushing myself onto my hands and knees I started to drag myself up out of the hole. As I crested the top I saw Tom's victim, just ten feet away and trying to get to his feet. He brought his weapon up, blood oozing from the thigh of his white cold-weather gear around the climbing hook that was embedded in it.

Diving back down into the snow, I heard the unmistakable, low level *click-thud, click-thud, click-thud* of an SD, the suppressed version of the Heckler & Koch MP5 submachine gun. The click was the sound of the working parts as they ejected an empty case and moved forward to pick another from the magazine. The thud was the gas escaping as the subsonic round left the barrel. I wasn't his target, but I lay there not wanting to move and risk getting hit. I wasn't even too sure if he knew I was there.

The firing stopped and I heard short sharp breaths taken in pain. Then I heard a shout. 'OK, buddy, it's OK.'

My pain suddenly disappeared, to be replaced by a feeling of dread. Shit. They were Americans. What the hell was I in here?

The hooked man answered haltingly between anguished gasps. 'Help me to the track, man. Ah, sweet Jesus . . .'

They were swarming all around me, and I knew it wouldn't be long before I got the good news. I turned my head and, as I opened my eyes and looked up, two white-covered figures with black balaclavas under their hoods were nearly on top of me, their breath clouds hanging in the cold night air. Hovering over me, one pointed his weapon soundlessly at my head. Other bodies passed, heading in the same direction as Tom.

I curled up and waited for the first kick to open me up for a search. It didn't happen. Instead, a cold, snow-covered glove pulled my hands from my face and I caught a glimpse of a canister. The moment I felt the ice-cold liquid make contact, my eyes were on fire and I felt as if I was choking.

The flames spread all over my face. I was conscious of what was going on, but was totally incapacitated. As I choked and retched, a hand forced my face into the snow. I struggled for oxygen, trying to move my head against the hand that was holding it down.

A kick aimed at the side of my stomach got between my arms, which were wrapped protectively around it, and I half coughed, half vomited the mucus that had built up in my mouth and nose. As I rolled with the pain, Sprayman pulled me onto my back.

A gloved fist hit me across the head and my jacket was unzipped. Hands ran over my body and squeezed my pockets. They found the spare hook, the vegetable knife. Everything was taken from me. One of them pressed his knee into my stomach with all his weight.

The character kneeling on my stomach was joined by the weapon-pointer on my right-hand side, and his freezing, fat muzzle raked against my face, pushing into the skin. They knew I was wrecked and were just maintaining me in that position. From what I could make out through watery eyes, they looked more concerned with what was going on by the gate.

As I lay passively facing the sky, I felt something wet and cold dissolve on my lips: the first heavy flakes of a snowfall.

There was the crash of the chain as the gate was forced open. Whatever we were trying to get hold of, so were they. It seemed the race wasn't only against the Maliskia.

Things were happening at the house. The front door was being battered. Then I heard screaming cutting through the wind, men's voices that couldn't be from one of the teams. These were the voices that went with high-pitched, big-time flapping.

My two new friends were still looking around, and whatever they were waiting for, they got it. Muzzleman tapped Sprayman on the shoulder and they both stood up. It was obviously time to go. As soon as the pressure on my stomach was released I was thrown over onto my front, face down in the snow while the left-hand strap on my daysack was cut. It was pulled away from my body. Then I was kicked over onto my back again. One of them knelt down, gripping my throat with one wet, cold, gloved hand, putting another round the back of my neck, and started to pull me to my feet. I was frog-marched through the now open gate.

Lights were blazing in the house. There were ransacking noises, furniture being thrown about and glass breaking, but the screaming had stopped. Still not a murmur from the injured guy and his helper.

I was dragged past the 4x4 and onto the wooden verandah. A battering ram had been abandoned on the threshold, a long steel pole with two handles on either side. The top hinge of the door had been pushed in and the bottom one was holding the door at a 45-degree angle inwards, the glass from its windows in shards on the floor.

We crunched over the broken glass and entered the house. A few paces inside I was forced face down onto the hallway floor. To my right were three other people, tied up and face to the floor, two of them in just boxer shorts and T-shirts. They looked about Tom's age, with long blond hair. They looked at me with the same question in their eyes as I had in my head: Who the hell are you?

A boot tapped me on the side of the face and motioned for me to look down. I rested my chin on the floor and my hands were forced in front of me, where they could be seen.

I counted a few seconds, then looked around, trying to gather as much information as possible to help me escape. Everybody seemed to know what they were doing. The pistol that each of them carried was very unusual. It had been a long time since I'd seen a P7, but, if I remembered correctly, it had seven barrels, each about six inches long, and contained within a disposable, Bakelite-type plastic unit. The unit was watertight and clipped into a pistol grip. Once all seven rounds had been fired, you simply removed the barrel unit, threw it away and put on another one. The P7 was originally designed to be fired underwater at close range. I didn't know if they were any good at longer range; all I knew was that they were silent and powerful. Not that it really mattered to me at the moment. What did matter was that these people were uniformed and efficient, and they hadn't been sent here because the computers on site weren't Y2K compliant.

They had to be from a security organisation—CIA, maybe, or NSA—it didn't matter which. It was highly unusual for them to be carrying out such an operation within a friendly nation's territory. That sort of thing was normally left to dickheads like me, so that everything could be denied if it went wrong. They must have desperately wanted something that belonged to them, something so sensitive that they didn't want, or trust, anyone else to go and get it. Had

I been trying to nick American secrets? I hoped not. That was spying, and with no help from HMG I'd be lucky if I got out of prison in time to see Kelly's grandchildren.

I realised what had been causing the dull glow from the left-hand side of the house. Through an open door I could see the glare from banks of TV screens. I made out CNN, CNBC, Bloomberg and some Japanese programme, all with newscasters talking business. Running captions displayed financial information across the bottom of the screen.

In among the TVs were banks of computer monitors, with streams of numbers running vertically down the screen, just like I'd seen Tom messing about with. White-clad figures fiddled with other machines and keyboards in the room. I saw one hand sticking out from its whites and working some keys. It was immaculately manicured, feminine and wore a wedding ring.

The rest of the horizontal surfaces were covered with sweet wrappings, pizza boxes, cans and plastic bottles of Coke. I realised that pizza was what they'd been carrying in last night from the 4x4.

My little recce was cut short when I saw pairs of black boots coming towards me, snow still in the laces. They were Danner boots, an American brand. The US military wore them.

A hood got pulled over my head, the drawstrings were pulled at the bottom and I was in a world of total darkness. My hands were forced together in front of me and a plasticuff was applied.

There was movement next to me and the rustling of clothes. The pizza boys were getting dressed.

The floorboards flexed under the pressure of bodies walking past, heading towards the door. Trailing wires and plugs dragged and clattered across the floor just past my head. I presumed the computers were being lugged out. The roar of engines filled my hood as vehicles drove into the compound. They stopped and handbrakes were pulled up on lock. Engines were left running. Doors opened and closed and stuff was loaded into the wagons; I could hear boots on the vans' metal floors.

The floorboards bent even more as the three lying next to me were hauled to their feet and taken outside amid muffled cries and groans. Then two pairs of large, aggressive hands grabbed each side of me, under my armpits, dragging me upright. I let my boots trail on the floor. I wanted to appear weak and slow.

We crossed the threshold onto the verandah. Stumbling between my escorts down the steps, I was dragged to the right, and I knew I was going into a different wagon. It wasn't a cold metal box; it felt like the back-seat area of a 4x4. There was a climb up to get into it, and it was carpeted and very warm.

The door opposite was opened and hands reached over, gripping my coat and pulling me in. My shins scraped painfully over the door sill, and I was finally pushed down into the foot well.

The vehicle rocked as somebody jumped into the rear seat above me, their heels digging into me, followed by a muzzle jabbed into the side of my face.

Our rear doors were kept open and the loading-bay activity was still audible. A few feet away I heard a door being slammed shut. The vehicle's suspension went into overtime as more bodies piled in. All the doors closed, and it felt as if there were at least three people on the back seat. Boots were all over the place, a couple of pairs digging in their heels to keep me down.

We seemed to be the first vehicle to move out of the compound, windscreen wipers slapping side to side to counter the snow.

We were driving uphill. It wouldn't be far to go now before we hit the road. We moved on for a few more minutes and stopped. There was a clunk as the driver shifted into high ratio, then set off again with a sharp left turn. We had to be on the gravel road.

The front passenger suddenly bounced around in his seat with a shout of 'What the hell?'

The accent was unmistakably New England. 'Jesus! Russians!'

The driver hit the brakes. There was a crash of metal and glass behind us and the sound of heavy-calibre automatic fire.

Our wagon came to a quick, sliding stop, turning sideways on the snow. The doors burst open.

'Cover them, cover them!'

The suspension bounced as everyone leapt down from the wagon, using me as a springboard. I suddenly felt very vulnerable, hooded and plasticuffed here in the foot well—a vehicle is the natural focus of fire. It was time to disappear.

Pulling up my plasticuffed hands, I tried to tug the hood off my face. I heard shouting further down the road. The one advantage of working with Sergei and his gang was that I had learned to recognise some Russian. This had to be the Maliskia.

At last I got the hood off. Pulling myself up, I had just begun to move towards the gap between the seats when I realised it wasn't an option. About five yards away, behind a mound of granite, a white-clad figure was pointing an SD submachine gun at me. The black-covered head screamed at me above the nightmare that was happening down the road: 'Freeze! Down, down, down!'

Change of plan. I got down flat in the foot well. I was feeling even more exposed now I'd seen what was happening. Headlights shone in all directions, illuminating the snowfall. I saw the muzzle flash of the Russian fire, but they were moving back. Wagons screamed past me with skidding wheels. Our vehicle group must have been giving covering fire while they moved out of the danger area.

The New England voice was back in earshot. 'Move on, move on. Come on, let's go, let's go, let's go!'

The guy covering me jumped into the wagon, ramming his heels down into my back and the weapon into my neck. The last thing I had a chance to see was him getting hold of the hood then pulling it back down over my head.

All the others were now jumping back in, making the vehicle rock with their weight. I felt the gearshift being engaged and we started to move off, the tyres slithering and sliding as we turned back on line. I got a heavy slap around the head. 'Goddamn Russians! Who do you think you are, man?'

The front passenger was, without doubt, the commander. His accent sounded as if he should have been standing on an orange box fighting an election for the Democrats in New Hampshire.

There was a short pause, then, 'Bravo Alpha.' He had to be on the net, listening to his earpiece. 'Situation?' He let out a cry. 'Shit! They have Bravo's vehicle. The sons of bitches have some of the hardware!'

He checked through all his call signs. There seemed to be four of them: Bravo, Charlie, Delta and Echo. He must have got a message from Echo.

'OK, roger that, Echo. Roger that.' He turned towards the bodies in the back. 'Bobby has gotten hit in the leg. But everything's fine; it's cool.'

We drove in silence for another twenty minutes, then the Democrat got back on the net. 'Papa One, Alpha. Any news yet on Super Six?' There was a pause while he listened, then, 'Roger that, Super Six call signs are no go. A no go.'

'Papa One' and 'Super Six' didn't sound like ground-call signs. Where possible these are always short and sharp. It stops confusion when the shit hits the fan or comms are bad.

After a pause of two seconds, he announced, 'All stations, all stations. OK, here's the deal. Go to the road plan. Acknowledge.'

Nothing more came from him as he got the acknowledgment from the other call signs. The Super Six call signs must have been aircraft that couldn't fly in these conditions. In better weather we would have been flown out of here to a US base or an American warship in the Baltic, where the computer equipment and its operators would be sorted out and moved on to whoever was so keen to have them.

If I didn't escape soon I'd land up with them in one of the Americans' 'reception centers'. These ranged from cold and wet three-by-nine-foot cells to virtually self-contained suites, depending on what was judged the best way to get information out of people like me. No matter how you looked at it, they were interrogation centres, and it was up to the interrogators—CIA, NSA, whoever they were—whether you got processed the easy way or the hard way.

We drove quite slowly for about another twenty minutes. It was painful lying crammed in the foot well, but that was nothing compared with how depressed I felt about what the future held.

'Papa One, Alpha—blue one.'

The Democrat was back on the net. Papa One must be the operating base. The Democrat was counting down to it, sending a report line so that Papa One knew the group's location.

A minute or so later we turned a sharp right.

'Papa One, Alpha—blue two.'

There was another sharp right turn. Then we were bumping over what felt like a sleeping policeman, and drove another thirty yards or so before the vehicle came to a halt.

The Democrat got out. As the doors opened, other vehicles passed and stopped all around me. The screech of tyres on a dry surface told me we were under cover, and, judging by the echoes, we were somewhere large and cavernous. Then came the echoing clatter of steel roller shutters being pulled down manually with chains.

As soon as the three pairs of feet had used me as a platform to get out of the wagon, a pair of hands gripped my ankles and started to pull me out, feet first. I was dragged over the door sill and had to put my arms out to protect myself as I dropped the two feet or so onto the ground. The dry surface was concrete.

There was lots of movement around me, and the same sort of sound as there had been in the house, the shuffling and dragging of electric plugs. The equipment was being moved out of the vans. I heard the telltale clunk of metal on metal as working parts were brought back and weapons unloaded.

I was turned over onto my back and two pairs of boots walked round to my head. They pulled me up by the armpits and started frog-marching me. My feet scraped along the concrete, through bits of wood, cans and newspapers. Then I was dragged sideways through a heavy door. They steered me round to the right as the door swung back.

The pizza boys were already here: the sound of crying, moans and groans filled what felt like a smaller area than before. The place stank of decay and neglect.

A couple more paces and we stopped, and I realised the others were being kicked; that was why they were screaming. I heard boots making contact with bodies and the grunts of the kickers.

I was pushed down to the ground and given a good kicking as well. I gave a very Russian moan. The sobs seemed to come from my right, and were now somehow muffled one by one. We weren't all in one big room; I guessed we were being put into cupboards or storage spaces.

The moment my head banged against the toilet bowl, I knew where I was. A toilet cubicle. Guided by kicks I crawled into the far-right corner, coming to rest on what felt like years of debris. Still getting kicked, I felt the base of the toilet pan against my stomach. My hands were gripped and pulled up into the air. I felt a knife go into the plasticuffs and they were cut. Pinioning my left arm over the waste pipe at the rear of the toilet bowl, they grabbed hold of the other arm and shoved it underneath so I had a hand on either side.

They gripped my wrists together. I tensed up my forearms, trying to bulk them out as much as possible. The plasticuffs came on and I heard the ratcheting and felt the pressure as they were tightened. They left, slamming the door behind them. Then there was silence.

A couple of seconds later, as if the pizza boys had all been holding their breath waiting for the bogeymen to go away, the moaning began once more. After a while the boys muttered a few words to each other in Finnish.

I shifted my position in an attempt to get some pressure off my wrists. As I stretched my legs, I connected with what sounded like an empty can. It gave me an idea.

I waggled my head past the waste pipe, so that it was resting on my hands. Then, feeling with my teeth through the hood, I got hold of my right outer glove. That came off easily enough and I let it drop to the ground, leaving the touch glove still on.

I reached forward with my head, positioning the bottom of the hood over my fingers, and got to work. I now knew the hoods were done up with a drawstring and ties round the bottom, and it wasn't long before it lay on the ground. It seemed a total waste of effort, however, because the cubicle was in complete darkness.

Leaning as far forward as I could to free up my hands, I started to feel around on the ground through paper cups and all sorts of garbage until I found what I wanted.

I readjusted my body around the pan to make myself comfortable while I pulled off my other outer glove with my teeth. Then, with both touch gloves still on, I squeezed the thin metal of the drinks can between my thumbs and forefingers until the sides touched in the middle. I then started to bend the two parts backwards and forwards. After only six or seven goes the thin metal cracked, and soon the two halves were apart. I felt for the ring-pull end and dropped the other one next to my gloves and hood.

Feeling gently around the broken edge, I looked for a place where I could start to peel the side down like an orange. I found what I wanted and started to pick and tear. My fingers slipped a couple of times, cutting me on the razor-sharp metal, but the pain was nothing to what would be inflicted on me if I didn't get away from here.

Once I'd pared the metal down to under an inch from the ring-pull end, I tried moving my wrists apart. Plasticuffs are designed not to stretch, but there was just enough play to do what I wanted. Cupping the can in my right hand with the sharp edge upwards, I bent it towards my wrist, trying to reach the plastic. If I'd left more tin sticking out it would have gone further, but the edge would have buckled under the pressure. That was also why I used the ring-pull end: the thicker rim gave the cutting edge more strength.

It must have taken a minute or two for the jagged tin to finally bite into the cuffs; then, when I was about three-quarters of the way through, I heard the loud, echoing creak of the swing door opening. Light spilled under the cubicle door.

There was the sound of boots heading in my direction. I started to flap, scrabbling for the hood, and, once it was on, tried to find my gloves, but the footsteps went past.

There was a flurry of muffled pleas in English from the boys as their doors were kicked open and they got dragged out. Within moments, the door swung shut and silence was restored. I felt around for the can end, not bothering to take the hood off. I couldn't have seen anything anyway. I started to work with more of a frenzy; I had to assume that they'd be coming for me next, and soon.

After two or three minutes of frantic sawing, the plastic finally gave. Pulling the hood off, I felt around for the gloves and put them in my pocket, keeping just the touch gloves on.

Next I located the other can end. Getting slowly to my feet, I felt around the cubicle. I found the door handle, opened it and walked carefully out into what I could feel was a narrow corridor with painted brick walls. Picking my feet up and putting them down with infinite care, my left hand supporting me on the wall, I made my way towards a faint glimmer of light about ten feet up on my left.

As I got closer I began to hear a vehicle revving, then starting to move off. Chains rattled as the roller shutter was pulled open. I wondered if the pizza boys were leaving town. Once at the door I couldn't find a keyhole to look through, so I got down flat on the floor and managed to get my eyeball close to the bottom of the door. Reaching into my pocket, I pulled out the bottom half of the can, the one I hadn't worked on. Using the light to find a place in the metal where I could start peeling this time, I got to work and put my eye back against the gap.

It was some sort of hangar or factory space, mostly in darkness, but lit in places by twelve-inch-long fluorescent lighting units.

Several vehicles were parked up in a row on the far left, about forty yards away—saloons, estates, MPVs and SUVs, some of which had roof racks piled with skis.

I looked straight ahead to the exit, my only way out, then at the people who would try to stop me. They were mostly by the two remaining vans, parked haphazardly in the middle of the hangar.

A group of five or six bodies were hurriedly unloading their weapons and taking off their white uniforms and bundling them into what looked like Lacon boxes—aluminium air-freight containers. When one of the bodies did a half turn so that it was in profile, I realised that it was a woman.

Another group of maybe eight were out of their whites and unpacking civilian clothes from holdalls. Others were combing their hair in the wing mirrors, trying to make themselves look like normal citizens.

I caught a glimpse of the 4x4 I'd been transported in: its back-window safety glass was pockmarked with holes where the rounds had passed through. Beyond it were the other vehicles used on the job, which were now probably going to be abandoned. Strike marks from automatic weapons were not the best kind of modification to be sporting at traffic lights.

I couldn't see any evidence of the computer kit. I assumed they'd moved it straight on, along with the pizza boys and the guy with the hook hanging from his thigh. The next destination would be a secure area like the US embassy. From there, the equipment would probably be moved by diplomatic bag back to the USA. The pizza boys would be stuck in the embassy or a safe house until a heli could get in sometime tomorrow and airlift them out of the country, unless there was a US warship in dock.

Everyone was now in jeans, duvet jackets and hats. The woman was organising the loading of the Lacons. Metallic echoes filled the hangar as the boxes were moved into the vans.

One man seemed to be running the whole show. I couldn't see his face from this distance, but he was the tallest of the group, maybe six foot two or three. He gathered everyone around him and seemed to be giving them a brief, but his voice wasn't loud enough for me to understand what he was saying.

While he finished the briefing, the doors of the two vans slammed, both engines revved and they started to leave.

I watched the Democrat's team disperse as they moved off towards the line of vehicles. They were probably going to split up and do their own thing, probably in exactly the same way as they'd come into the country in the first place. They would have cover documents and a perfect cover story, and all they had to do was wander back to their chalets and hotels as if they'd had a good night out, which I supposed they had. None of them was dead.

More engines revved, doors slammed and headlights came on. The people from the embassy would probably take care of the abandoned vehicles. Their priority was to get away from here now that the equipment and pizza boys were safely on their way. Their only problem was that they had a little bonus—me.

It looked like the Democrat and another woman were taking on that responsibility. Soon there was just one car left stationary, its engine running and lights blazing. The Democrat was sitting sideways in the driver's seat, his feet on the concrete, the glow of a cigarette intensifying as he sucked on it. The woman disappeared into the darkness.

At last I'd finished the other half of the can.

Chains started rattling and the shutter closed. The woman emerged from the shadows once again and bent towards the glowing cigarette. They talked for a moment, then he turned back into the car to stub his cigarette in the ashtray. By then she was round the back, pulling open the boot.

The Democrat started walking in my direction. There was a flicker of light, then the fluorescent unit in his left hand burst into life. He'd just finished pulling his balaclava on. I watched his right hand go under his coat and come out again holding a multibarrelled P7, which went into his coat pocket.

My body banged with shock. He was coming to kill me.

The car edged forward with the boot open as he got within about ten yards of the door. I got to my feet and moved to the right of the door, away from the toilets. I wasn't sure how long the corridor was, but I soon found out. I'd only taken four steps when I banged into the end wall. Turning back, I faced the door, fumbling in my pocket for the half can, breathing deeply to oxygenate myself.

The door swung open with a metallic screech of its hinges, momentarily flooding the area with bright white light. I could hear the car whining in reverse. He had turned right, his back to me as he took the first few steps towards my toilet cubicle.

I moved quickly as the door closed, taking long, fast steps to get some speed and momentum, with my right arm raised. With the main door closed and car engine running, there was no way she was going to hear this. He did, though, and started to turn.

I leapt at him. Landing with my left foot forward, I swung my whole body to the left, my right arm crooked and the palm held open. Sometimes a really firm, heavy slap to the face can be more effective than a punch—that's guaranteed if you're wielding a sawn-off drinks can with razor-sharp edges.

It hit his head hard. There was a loud groan. The light danced as the fluorescent unit in his hand clattered to the concrete, and he started to follow it. I swung to the right with my left arm slightly bent, still focusing on his head. I hit the mark; I could feel the softness of his cheek under the can, then felt it scrape round his jaw as he fell. He moaned again, this time with more anguish, and slumped to the ground, hands scrabbling to protect his head.

For a few more frenzied seconds I continued to slash at his hands and head, then his hands fell away and he lay very still. He was never going to get a job modelling for Gillette, but he'd live. There had been no other way out. If you're going to stop somebody, you have to do it as quickly and violently as you can.

The fluorescent unit threw a pool of light across the floor and onto his balaclava. The wool still looked remarkably intact, as it does when a sweater rips and the tear seems to knit itself together, unless you look at it close up. Blood was seeping through the material. Dropping the cans, I rolled him onto his back and pulled out the P7 and a mobile that was also in there. That went into my pocket.

My breathing was now very fast and shallow and just slightly louder than the engine ticking over immediately beyond the swing door. Getting to my feet, I got hold of the top of his balaclava and pulled it off. In places I could see bone through the blood-soaked, hairy mess of his skull.

I pulled the balaclava over my head, trying to cut down on the chances of being recognised later. I checked his body for a radio as he whined weakly to himself. There was nothing; he'd have been planning to be sterile like the rest of them. He'd had to hang on to the P7 to sort me out.

Pushing through the door, I moved into a cloud of red fumes and brake lights. The vehicle was no more than three feet away, engine idling, boot open and waiting for me. I moved to the left-hand side as the swing door banged shut behind me. I pointed the pistol at the woman's face, the muzzle a foot from the glass. If she opened the door, she couldn't knock the pistol out of line quickly enough; if she tried to drive forward, she would die first round.

She stared wide-eyed at the barrel. In the glow from the instrument panel I could see her trying to make sense of what her eyes were telling her. With my left hand I motioned for her to get out. I was supposed to be Russian; I wasn't going to open my mouth unless I had to. She kept staring, transfixed. She was bluffing; she'd drop me at the first opportunity.

Moving back as the door inched open, I decided to put on a Slavic accent. Well, what I thought sounded like one. 'Gun, gun!'

She stared up at me with frightened eyes and said in a little-girl voice, 'Please don't hurt me. Please don't hurt me.'

Then she opened her legs to show me a P7 nestled between her jeaned thighs. I motioned for her to drop it in the foot well.

The moment she'd dropped it I moved in, grabbing her by her shoulder-length, dark-brown hair and heaving her out of the car and onto all fours. Moving back three paces, I pointed at the far wall, and she got up and started walking.

I got into the car, threw it into first gear and screamed towards the closed shutter. She was probably in the corridor by now to find out what had happened to her friend the Democrat.

Stopping alongside the vans and the shot-out 4x4, I got out with a P7 in hand, ready to shoot out some tyres. I took a look behind me; there was nothing happening from the corridor yet.

The P7's signature *thud* was nothing to the high-pitched *dinggg* that echoed round the hangar as the round hit metal. Then there was a hiss as air escaped under pressure. Once all vehicles were taken care of, I jumped back into the driver's seat and aimed for the shutters, though this time in reverse, so the headlights were pointed at the swing door. If she came for me, I wanted to see.

I braked, threw the gearbox into neutral and leapt out. I pulled down the metal chains to open the shutters enough to get the car out, then clambered back in and reversed out into the snowfall.

I left the hangar behind, not knowing whether to feel sorry for the Democrat, relieved at still being alive, or angry with Val and Liv. The mobile went out of the window. No way was such a fantastic tracking device going to stay with me.

The snow was falling heavily. I didn't have a clue where I was, but that didn't really matter as long as I got away. Pulling at the balaclava, I felt the Democrat's blood smear across my face. It finally came off, and I threw it into the foot well along with the P7.

Hitting the interior light, I took a look in the mirror. There was so much red stuff on me I looked like a beetroot.

After maybe an hour I pulled off the road, and had a quick wash in the freezing snow. Then, cleaned up and with the blood-soaked gear buried in a snow drift, I drove through the night, looking for signs that would steer me to Helsinki.

The more I thought about it, the more severely pissed off I became. Whether Liv and Val knew about the Americans wanting to join in the fun, I wasn't sure, but I intended to find out.

Ten

Wednesday, December 15, 1999. I sat on the floor next to a radiator in the corner of the station, facing the telephone booth that displayed the 'dead letterbox loaded' sign. The black-marker strike down the side was clearly visible. I had a copy of the *International Telegraph*, an empty coffee cup and, in my right pocket, a P7 with a full seven-round unit.

As soon as the shops opened that morning I'd bought a complete set of clothes to replace the cold, wet ones I was wearing. I was now in a dark-beige ski jacket, gloves and a blue-fleece pointed hat. I didn't care if I looked a numpty; it covered up my head and most of my face. My pulled-up jacket collar did the rest.

I'd dumped the car at a suburban railway station just after eight that morning and caught a train into the city. On arrival at Helsinki I'd pulled off the left-luggage receipt and airline ticket from under locker number eleven and collected my bag, cash, passports and credit cards. I also checked for Tom's ticket under number ten.

I'd been thinking about him a lot. If the Americans or the Maliskia hadn't killed him last night, the weather would have. Tom had skills, but playing at Grizzly Adams wasn't one of them.

I left his bag ticket where it was. It would be an emergency supply of money and a new passport, once I'd tampered with it, in case what I was about to do went to rat shit.

Despite my best efforts, I found I couldn't help feeling sorry for Tom as I sat and watched a constant flow of travellers moving through the doors. It was my lies and promises that had got him where he was now, face down in the snow or bundled up somewhere in an American body bag.

I looked at my watch. It was 14.17 and I'd been here over four hours already. I was gagging for another brew, but once I drank I would inevitably need the toilet at some stage, and I couldn't afford to miss Liv when and if she arrived.

The longer I'd thought about what happened last night, the more I'd boiled over with hostility towards Liv and Val. So plan B was taking shape in my head. The Maliskia's money would pay for Kelly when I lifted Val and offered him to them for cash. I had no idea how

I was going to do it yet, but the first phase would be to let Liv think I had the ThinkPad with the downloaded information on it, and, because of last night's foul-up, I'd deal only with Val now, and only in Finland. Who knows? If Val turned up with the money, I could just take that and save myself the hassle of getting even.

But that wasn't the message I'd left in the plastic box I'd placed in the dead letterbox. It was empty, just there so that when she came to get it there was something to unload, so as not to arouse suspicion. As she left the station I would grab her and tell her in person, so she made no mistake about what I wanted.

I'd been sitting there for twenty minutes when I saw Liv walk straight past the loaded sign without even turning her head. But I knew she would have seen it. Her long black coat, Tibetan hat and light brown boots were easy to spot among the crowd as she moved through the hall, carrying two large paper Stockmann bags.

I had a good check to make sure she hadn't been followed in, just in case she'd brought any protection with her, or worse, in case the Democrat had a few of the party faithful on her tail.

She disappeared into the ticketing and metro hallway. There was no rush, I knew where she was heading.

Once on my feet I pinged her again, just about to sit on top of the dead letterbox. She sat down. I watched her bend down and mess around with her bags. Her hand moved to pull the empty container from the Velcro. She dropped it into one of the bags; it wouldn't get read here.

I waited for her to leave, positioning myself in a corner so that whatever door she decided to head for I wouldn't be in her line of sight. A few minutes passed before she stood up and headed for the bus-station exit. I fell in behind, waiting for my chance to grab her.

I was about twenty paces behind as she pushed her way through the bus-station doors. Once through them myself, I looked out into the snowfall. All I could see were buses and lines of people trying to get on them. Liv must have turned off as soon as she reached the pavement. I was moving down the steps when there was a shout behind me. 'Nick! Nick!'

I stopped, spun round and looked back up towards the doors.

'Liv! How lovely to see you.'

She was standing by one of the pillars, left of the doors, smiling, arms outstretched, getting ready to greet one of her long-lost friends. I switched on and played the game, letting her kiss me on both cheeks. She smelt great, but what I could see of her hair under her hat wasn't as well groomed as usual.

'I thought I would wait for you. I knew you would be here.'

Still embracing, I looked at her with my wonderful-to-see-you smile. 'Tom is dead,' I said.

The look on her face told me she knew how I felt. She pulled back and smiled. 'Come, walk with me. You have a right to be angry, but all is not lost, Nick.' She invited me to carry her bags. As I bent down I saw that in one of them was a light brown briefcase.

Still smiling at her, I gripped her arm and more or less pulled her down the stairs. Once on the pavement I turned right, towards the town centre. 'What the hell's going on? We got hit by an American team last night. I was lifted. Then the bloody Russians hit them!'

She nodded as I ranted away at her.

I said, 'You already know that, don't you?'

'Of course. Valentin always finds out everything.'

'You and Val have been screwing me over big time. Enough. I want him here tomorrow, with the money.' I increased my grip on her arm and guided her down the road, not caring what passers-by might think. 'Listen, I have the download. But I'll only deal with Val now, not you. There will be no more foul-ups.'

'Yes, Nick. Now tell me, this is very important. Valentin will not do a thing unless he has all the details. Did the Americans take all of the hardware with them from the house?'

'Yes.'

'Did the Americans capture the occupants of the house?'

'Yes. I saw three.'

'Did the Maliskia then manage to take any of the hardware or occupants from the Americans?'

'Not the occupants. They got one of the wagons that contained some hardware, for sure.'

She nodded slowly. We joined a small crowd at a crossing.

I whispered into her ear. 'Liv, I want Val here, with the money, then I'll hand everything over.'

We crossed the main drag, heading for the shopping area.

'That, Nick, will not happen. He will not come, for the simple reason that you haven't anything to trade, have you?' She spoke very evenly. 'Now, please answer my questions. This is very important. For everyone, including you.'

I wasn't waiting for any more questions. 'Why did the Americans hit the house? Whatever we were going in for belongs to them, doesn't it? It's not commercial, it's state.'

'Turn right here.'

I turned the corner. We were on one of the shopping streets.

'The Americans were NSA, Nick.'

My heart sank to hear my suspicion confirmed. I wanted money, but not that badly. Those people were the real government of America. 'Are you sure?'

She nodded. 'They also hit my house last night about two hours after you left.'

'How did you get away?'

She flicked at the ends of her hair. 'By having a very cold and long night out.'

'How did they know to hit you?'

'They must have been guided to the house, but I don't know how. Did you or Tom use email, telephone, fax or anything like that while you were at the house?'

'Of course not, no.' And then I remembered what had happened at the airport. 'Wait. Tom did. Tom—'

She turned her head sharply. 'What? What did Tom do?'

'He used email. He sent an email to someone in the UK.'

The calm, controlled look drained from her face. She stood still, pushing me away as people skipped around what looked like a domestic row about to erupt. 'I told you both not to do that!'

I pulled her back towards me, as if I was in command, leading her down the street. She composed herself, and finally, very calmly, she said, 'So, it was Tom who brought the Americans here.' She pointed, down a cobblestoned street. 'Valentin wants me to show you something, then I am to make you an offer that your pocket and conscience will not let you refuse. Come. Let's get out of the cold, Nick. I think it's time you knew what's really going on.'

THE TEAHOUSE WAS HOT and filled with the aroma of coffee and cigarettes. We bought food and drink from the counter and headed for a vacant table in a corner.

With her hat now removed, it was even more obvious that Liv had had a bad night. We must both have looked pretty rough.

Our table was by a grand piano and partly screened by potted palms. Liv leaned forward and took a sip of tea from her glass while I shoved a salmon sandwich down. She watched me for a while, then asked, 'Nick, what do you know of the UK/USA agreement?'

I took a swig of tea. I knew the bones of it. Set up by Britain and America in the late 1940s, since when Canada, Australia and New Zealand had also become part of the club, the agreement basically covered the pooling of intelligence on mutual enemies.

'Nick, the three men in the house last night were Finns. They were engaged in accessing a technology called Echelon, which is at the very heart of the agreement.'

'You mean you were trying to get Tom and me to access *state secrets* for the Russian mafia?'

She looked calmly around the other tables and took another sip of tea. She shook her head. 'It's not like that, Nick. Valentin wants commercial information, that's all. Believe me, you were not stealing secrets, state or military. Quite the contrary: you were helping to stop others from doing precisely that.'

'So how come the NSA were involved?'

'They simply wanted their toy back. Valentin has no interest in the West's military secrets. He can get those whenever he wants; it's not exactly difficult, as I'll demonstrate to you shortly.' She glanced at the other tables again. 'What do you know of Echelon?'

I knew it was some kind of electronic eavesdropping system run by GCHQ. However, I shrugged as if I knew nothing at all; I was more interested in hearing what she knew.

Liv sounded as if she was reading from the Echelon sales brochure. 'It's a global network of computers, run by all five nations of the UK/USA agreement. Every second of every day, Echelon automatically sifts through millions of intercepted faxes, emails and phone calls, searching for preprogrammed key words. For years Echelon has helped the West shape international treaties and negotiations in their favour, and to know anything from the health status of Boris Yeltsin to the bottom-line position of trading partners. Why do you think we are careful not to use any form of electronic communication? We know that we are tagged by Echelon. From the moment Tom started working at RAF Menwith Hill, every fax and email he sent, as well as phone calls, would have been intercepted and checked.

'Those Finns had designed a system to hack into Echelon. The firewall that Tom breached was their protection around that system. They were online last night for the very first time.'

'Trying to do what? Hack into NSA headquarters?'

She shook her head slowly, as if in disbelief at their naivety. 'Their sole objective was to pick up sensitive market information that they could profit from. All they wanted was to make a few million dollars here and there; they didn't understand the true potential of what they had created.'

'But what has all this got to do with me? What is Val's offer?'

'Nick, it's very important to me that you understand Valentin's motives. He wants the East eventually to be an equal trading partner with the West, and that is never going to happen as long as ambitious men like him do not have access to commercial information that only Echelon can provide.'

'Ambitious?' I laughed. 'I can think of plenty of other words I'd use before that one to describe ROC.'

She shook her head. 'Think of America a hundred and fifty years ago and you have Russia now. Men like Vanderbilt didn't always stay within the law to achieve their aims. But they created wealth, a powerful middle class, and that, in time, creates political stability. That is how you must see Valentin; he's not a Dillinger, he's a Rockefeller.'

'OK, Val is businessman of the year. Why didn't he just strike a deal with the Finns?'

'It doesn't work like that. It would have alerted them to what they had, and then they'd have sold it to the highest bidder. Valentin didn't want to take that chance. He was happy for them to make access and try to play the markets while he found out where they were and got to them before the Maliskia.'

'And the Americans?'

'If you had been successful last night in downloading the programme, Valentin would have told the Americans where the house was. They would then have gone in and closed it down without knowing that he also had access to Echelon . . . Nick, the offer of money still stands, but your task has changed.'

'Of course it has. Tom is dead and the NSA have Echelon back.'

She shook her head. 'Our sources believe the Maliskia have Tom. We believe they also have the ThinkPad. This is very disturbing as it still has the firewall access sequence that—'

I fought to keep my composure. 'Tom's alive? Bloody hell, Liv. I've been sitting here thinking the man was dead.'

Her daughter-of-Spock face never changed. 'The Maliskia think he's working for the Finns. Remember, they also want access to Echelon.'

'So you want me to get Tom back?'

'Before I tell you the objective, Nick, I must explain a complication.'

A complication? This wasn't complicated enough?

She bent down and lifted the briefcase onto the table. She opened it. Inside was a laptop, which she fired up. I watched as she reached into her coat and brought out a dark blue floppy disk in a clear plastic case. She inserted the disk and handed the briefcase over to me.

The disk icon came up on the desktop and I double-clicked it. There were two files on the disk. One said, 'Read Me First'. I opened it and was presented with a web page from the London *Sunday Times*, dated July 25 and displaying an article entitled RUSSIAN HACKERS STEAL US WEAPONS SECRETS.

'American officials believe Russia may have stolen some of the nation's most sensitive military secrets,' the article began, 'in a concerted espionage offensive that investigators have called Operation Moonlight Maze.'

The theft was so sophisticated and well coordinated that security experts believed America might be losing the world's first 'cyber war'. Experts were talking of a 'digital Pearl Harbor', where an enemy exploited the West's reliance on computer technology to steal secrets or spread civil chaos as effectively as any attack using missiles and bombs. With just a few taps on a laptop it seemed anyone could totally screw up any advanced nation. Utilities could be shut down. Telecommunications systems could be jammed. Damn it, these days, who needed armies?

Even top-secret military security installations had been breached. At the Space and Naval Warfare Systems Command (Spawar), a unit in San Diego, California, which specialised in safeguarding naval intelligence codes, an engineer was alerted to the problem when a computer print job took an unusually long time. The file had been removed from the printing queue and transmitted to an Internet server in Moscow before being sent back to San Diego.

I double-clicked the next file. What came up on screen confirmed that the story of the hit against Spawar could be true. The *Sunday Times* might not know what was in the intercepted file, but I did now. The Naval Intelligence crest in front of me headed a list of maybe fifty code words that corresponded to radio frequencies.

As I ejected the disk, Liv leaned over and held out her hand. 'Nick, you can help stop this from happening if you want to.'

I passed the disk over and started to close down the laptop. She was right. If this was the truth, it was an offer my conscience wouldn't let me refuse. The idea of these machines listening to everything we did and said was very Big Brother, but hey, I'd rather have just the UK/USA agreement countries accessing it than every man and his dog with enough cash. As for the leak of military information, that had to be stopped. I had been part of enough foul-ups where friends had died because of insecure information. If I could stop it and come away with a suitcase full of money, it seemed to touch every base.

'So what exactly do you want me to do?'

'You must destroy the Maliskia's Moonlight Maze capabilities and any advance they've made with Echelon. That means, destroy the complete installation—computers, software, the lot. This time, however, you'll be completely on your own.'

I sat back and held up three fingers. 'Sterling. The same arrangements as for the exchange.'

She nodded. 'Three million. You will be paid.'

It worried me slightly that she agreed so easily. 'What guarantees do I have?'

'You don't. But Valentin is well aware of the lengths you went to to track him down before. No doubt you'd do the same again.'

'So tell me, where is the installation?'

'Estonia.'

The only thing I knew about Estonia was that it had been part of the old USSR, and now wanted to be part of NATO and the EU.

'The population is still thirty per cent Russian. The Maliskia find it easier to operate from there.'

She seemed to have overlooked one point. 'If the Maliskia have Tom,' I said, 'I take it he'll be at this installation. Do you want me to bring him back here or just take him back to London?'

She stared at me as if I was an idiot. 'Nick, I thought you understood: Tom must be considered part of their capability. Why else do you think Valentin would pay you three million? Tom must die.'

I was almost lost for words. 'But why? I mean, why don't I just get him out at the same time?'

'That's not an option, Nick. Tom has the ThinkPad and the ability to use it. If you did rescue him he would still be in the country, and the possibility of capture by them is a risk Valentin is not willing to take. It is simply better that Valentin sacrifices Tom and the opportunity to access Echelon himself than risk the Maliskia having it. No one, Nick, can afford for the Maliskia to have Echelon.'

I was still finding this hard to accept. 'But why not just tell the Americans? Val was going to tell them about the Finns' house.'

'Unthinkable. What if they take Tom and he explains what has been going on? Nick, I don't think you would want that. Tom would go back to prison for life and you'd be in the adjoining cell.

'We'll meet tomorrow morning at Stockmann, eleven o'clock in the café. That is the soonest I'll be able to get more information. One thing is certain, after that you must leave as soon as you can. If the Maliskia have got Tom to cooperate, every hour counts.'

Thursday, December 16, 1999. Ten minutes before she was due to arrive, I settled into a corner seat at the Café Avec in Stockmann. On my way over I'd stopped at an Internet café and checked out the Moonlight Maze story on the *Sunday Times* website. It was genuine.

Placing two coffees and two Danishes on the table, I put a saucer over the top of Liv's cup to keep it hot.

The café was as packed as when I'd been there with Tom. I'd spent a lot of time thinking about him last night, lying in my anonymous hotel room. The sad fact was that stopping the Maliskia from combining Echelon with their Moonlight Maze operations, and getting the money for doing it, was more important than Tom's life. But killing him was not going to be easy.

After my tea stop with Liv yesterday I'd gone down to the harbour to check out the ferries to Estonia. Its capital, Tallinn, seemed to be the destination for an array of ferries, catamarans and hydrofoils. The faster craft made the fifty-mile journey in an hour and a half, but there was too much wind for them to make the crossing in the next few days. The only ones that could handle the conditions were the old-fashioned ferries, and they usually took over four hours.

I was going to resuscitate the Davidson passport to go into Estonia, but had booked the ferry ticket in the name of Davies. If stopped for it, I'd just say it was the mistake of the people who did the ticketing. I was sure the Firm would still be looking for Davidson now that he was connected with Liv and Tom.

I had the passports tucked uncomfortably under my foot inside my right boot, and $1,500 in hundreds, twenties and tens in my left. As for Mr Stone, he was well and truly stuffed away in the bag at the station. The P7 would go into the railway bag at the last minute. There was no way I could take the weapon with me to Estonia. I had no idea how heavy the security was on the ferry journeys.

Liv's head appeared first as the escalator brought her up towards me. She was looking around casually, not specifically looking for me. The rest of her body came into view, wearing the black, belted three-quarter-length leather coat over her normal jeans and Timberland-type boots. She had a large black leather bag over her shoulder and a magazine in her right hand.

She spotted me and headed for the table, kissing me on both cheeks. Her hair was back on top form and she smelled of citrus. A copy of *Vogue* landed on the table between us, and we bluffed away with the *How are you?* smiles as she settled into her seat.

I put her cup in front of her and removed the saucer. She lifted it to her lips. It must have been too cold, because it went straight back down on the table.

'The Maliskia are located near Narva. You'll need a Regio one-in-two-hundred-thousand map of Estonia, northeast.' She put her hand on the *Vogue*. 'You'll also need what is inside here. It's from this location that they have been running Moonlight Maze. Now that they have Tom and the ThinkPad, it's where they will be attempting to access Echelon.

'Also inside is an address. You'll meet people there who should help you get explosives and whatever else you need. The best way to Narva is by train. And Nick—these people in Narva, do not trust them. They're totally unreliable. But they're the closest Valentin can offer you to support on the ground. Also in there is a letter. It will ensure you get what you need from these people, but only use it if you need to, Nick. It shouldn't be abused.'

I asked the obvious. 'What's in it?'

'Well, it's a bit like an insurance policy.' She smiled rather bleakly. 'A Chechen insurance policy.'

'How many people are there on site?'

'We don't have that information, but it will be more than last time. This is their most important asset, which is why it's in Estonia—the geography is the best defence system there is.'

Something else needed answering. I leaned closer. 'How do you know Tom?'

'I don't, Valentin does. When Tom was caught at Menwith Hill it was Valentin he was working for. You British never discovered that, however, because your threats to him could never compare with the one Valentin was capable of delivering.'

'And how did you know of my connection with Tom?'

'After your encounter in Helsinki, Valentin wanted to know a little more about you. It was easy enough to order that information from the Maliskia, thanks to Moonlight Maze. Even more incentive to get in there and destroy that capability, don't you think?'

Damn right. I didn't like the sound of any of it.

Liv patted the magazine with her hand. 'I must go now.'

We kissed each other on the cheek and did the farewell routine as she replaced her bag on her shoulder. 'I'll check the station every day, Nick, starting Sunday.'

'One last question. You don't seem too concerned about Tom. I mean, I thought you two were, you know, close.'

She smiled. 'Tom is not someone I'd seek a relationship with. He was weakening, so sleeping with him was . . . insurance. I had to keep him committed to the task. He's the only one who could do this sort of thing. He is a genius with this technology. He had to go with you. That is also why you must carry out your new task as quickly as you can. His capabilities must not be available to the Maliskia.'

She turned and headed for the escalator.

I took a small white envelope from inside the magazine Liv had left behind and made my way to the toilets. Safely in a cubicle, I opened the envelope. Inside were three scraps of paper. The first was a Post-it, on which was an address in Narva—by the look of it I was after a bloke called Konstantin—plus a long-and-lat fix. The Post-it was stuck to half a sheet of thin A4, with about ten lines of Cyrillic script written in ball-point. This had to be the Chechen insurance policy. The third item was a sheet of grease-proof paper on which was a pencilled cross and, towards the bottom left-hand corner of the sheet, a little circle. All I had to do was line up the longs and the lats on the right map and bingo, the circle would be around the location where Tom and the Maliskia were supposed to be.

I folded up the pieces of paper and tucked them into my socks. I flushed the toilet, opened the door and headed for a bookshop where I bought a guidebook to Estonia. I also found the map Liv had specified.

Back at the hotel, it was time to study it. Tallinn, the capital, was in the west, on the Baltic coast. Narva was in the northeastern corner, right next to Russia and just nine miles inland. There was one main road that went from Tallinn to Narva, linking other, smaller towns on the 130 miles between the two. I could also see the black line of the railway that Liv had told me to take, roughly paralleling the road.

Narva was bisected by a river, and the border with Russia was an imaginary line running down the middle of it. There were two crossing points, a rail bridge and a road bridge. On the Russian side, the main road and train line kept going east, with a sign on the edge of the map saying, 'Peterburi 138km'—about eighty-five miles. In other words, Narva was closer to St Petersburg than it was to Tallinn.

I took out the sheet of grease-proof paper and placed the cross over the corresponding longs and lats, then looked at the circle. It ringed a small cluster of buildings a mile or so south of a small town called Tudu, which was about twenty miles southwestish of Narva. Basically, the target was in the middle of nowhere.

I had the Narva contact name and address in my head; an hour of repeating it had sorted that out. I ripped the cross off the grease-proof paper, rolled it in the Post-it and ate it. I kept the map and guidebook because I was going to be a tourist.

There were still a few hours before the five-thirty ferry, so I had a read about the region's immensely rich culture. I couldn't wait.

I FOLLOWED THE HERD out of the terminal waiting room and up the embarkation ramp onto a massive roll-on, roll-off ferry.

Few of my fellow foot passengers appeared anything like as prosperous as the Finns I was used to seeing. I guessed they were Estonians. They all seemed to be wearing fake-fur Cossack-style hats and a lot of leather-effect PVC. They were toting enormous plastic shopping bags, stuffed to the brim with everything from blankets to catering packs of rice.

The crowd thinned as the corridor opened up into a large bar area full of well-dressed Finns who had driven their cars aboard before us. I guessed they were booze cruisers, going over to Tallinn to stock up on duty free.

The currency desk was just the other end of the bar. I lined up and changed $100 US into whatever the real money was called.

Once we were in open sea the boat rocked from side to side and plunged up and down. The Finns, undeterred by the heavy seas, were swigging back Koff beer, or at least trying to. The swell meant there was as much liquid on the floor as there was going down their necks.

I settled on a red, leather-look plastic seat and tried to sleep. Whenever there's a lull, it pays to recharge the batteries.

AN ANNOUNCEMENT over the PA system woke me up and I heard the word Tallinn. The system carried on with its multilingual address. We had about thirty minutes before docking.

I wandered down the corridor. People were walking like drunks because of the swell, and now and again I had to put my hand up on the wall to stop myself falling. I followed the signs to the toilets.

In the gents, there was as much alcohol on the floor as there was on the ground in the bar; the difference was it had been through people's kidneys first. I trod carefully towards the urinals and unzipped.

The toilet door was pushed open and a couple of guys came in. By the look of their Gore-Tex jackets they were Finns. I was sorting myself out, trying to zip up with one hand while using the other to stop me falling over. The boy in black headed for the vacant toilet cubicles behind me, and the other dossed around by the row of basins to my left. His green jacket reflected on the stainless-steel pipes that ran from the water dispenser above my head to the urinals. Whatever he was doing it just looked wrong. At the same time I heard the rustle of Gore-Tex and saw black in the reflection, too.

I turned just in time to see an arm raised, ready to do my back some serious damage with some kind of knife. I screamed, hoping to disorientate him, while charging the two or three steps towards him, focusing on his arm.

Grabbing his raised wrist with my right hand, I kept moving. That turned his body to his left, his natural momentum helping me. My left hand then helped to spin him towards the cubicles so he had his back to me. We stumbled into one of the stalls.

Still gripping his right wrist, I leapt over his back and forced both my knees straight down onto the back of his head. Bone crunched on ceramic. I heard teeth cracking under my weight, mixed with a muffled screaming.

I saw him drop the knife. My right hand scrabbled around on the floor and closed round it. Only it wasn't a knife, but an autojet. I recognised the make and I knew what it did. Gripping the automatic syringe in my right hand, I had my thumb on the injection button, ready to attack the green rustling Gore-Tex behind me.

Too late; the boy was right on top of me. He also had an autojet. I could feel the needle penetrate and then its contents emptying into my buttock; it was like a golf ball growing under my skin. I threw myself backwards, crashing as hard as I could into his body, pushing him towards the urinals.

Once we'd banged against the white ceramic, his fists started to hit the side of my face from behind me as I kept him pinned in position. I couldn't really feel the outcome. The autojet was having its effect on me, depressing my central nervous system. I was sure it was mainly scopolamine, mixed with morphine. When it's injected into a body, the effect produced is a tranquillised state.

Ramming the autojet against the leg that was kicking out on my right, I depressed the button with my thumb. Automatically the needle sprang forward, punctured his jeans and skin, dispensing its juice. Now we were equal; it was just a case of who dropped first.

'Fuck you!' Unmistakably American.

I couldn't get up enough strength to do anything but pin him there, using my legs to push my back against him. His legs were wobbling as much as mine. My head was still trying to bury itself into my chest as he made wild grabs at my face, hoping to get at my eyes.

My legs couldn't hold him in position any more, and I fell, first to my knees, then face down onto the wet floor. The American fell to his knees to my right. He sat back against the urinal, fumbling to get his jacket zip undone. I couldn't let that happen—he could have a weapon—so I started to crawl up him.

His hands tried pushing me off as he growled at me. I managed to get my hand down the top of his jacket, probing with my thumb until I found the collar bone and the soft spot below the Adam's apple, then I pushed in with all my strength.

At once he hit the floor, his legs still under him, bucking to free them as I lay on top of him. He was choking now.

The other boy behind me in the cubicle started moaning and coughing, his boots scuffing the floor as he tried to move. With any luck he was more worried about his dental plan for the next few years than anything else.

Dragging myself to my feet, I staggered on the spot above the American. He was curled up on the soaking floor.

I had to get out of there and hide up until I could get off the ferry. My vision was hazy but I wasn't going to black out: they wouldn't have wanted to carry a deadweight. The drugs would just make it easier to drag me to their car.

Stumbling up the stairs, after about six attempts at pulling the door open I was back in a corridor. Staggering into a seating area, I made my way into the corner, slumping against the back of a seat before falling into it. The Estonian whose big bag had had to be whipped away before I fell on it shook his head knowingly.

Announcements were being made on the PA. My head was swimming. Were they appealing for witnesses?

The man next to me stood up and so did his friend. They started gathering together their bits and pieces. We must have arrived.

There was a sudden migration of people, all going in one direction. I moved off behind them, lurched down a covered gateway and joined the line for immigration. The woman said nothing as she checked my passport. I swayed and smiled as she eyed me, probably in disgust, and stamped one of the pages. Picking it up I staggered on through the arrivals hall.

Outside, the cold wind buffeted my jacket as I staggered across a snow-covered car park. The whole area was brightly lit. Beyond was darkness, then, in the far distance, blurred lighting. That was where I needed to go, to find a hotel.

I got to the end of the car park and hit dark, snow-covered waste ground. There were a number of well-worn tracks heading in the direction of the lights in the distance. Way over to my right, a convoy of headlamps trailing back to the ferry was heading the same way. I started following a track and immediately fell down.

Carrying on as best I could, I was soon in darkness and walking through trees. To my left was a large derelict warehouse.

I didn't even see where the boys came from. All I felt was two lots of arms grabbing me and dragging me towards the decaying building. I put up the fight of a five-year-old.

They threw me against a doorway. I managed to turn so I hit it with my back. I slid down onto my arse. The kicks started to rain in. All I could do was curl up and take it. I felt the daysack being pulled off my back. Then it was a few more kicks and some cursing in Russian or Estonian. They unzipped my jacket and I felt their hands going in, pulling up my sweatshirt and jumper, feeling around my stomach, going into the pockets. These were strange places to be searching for a weapon, and it took a while for it to dawn on me. I wasn't being weapons cleared, I was being mugged.

From that moment on I relaxed. There was no need to mess with these people. I had more important things to do than fight muggers. Besides, in my condition I would lose.

Finally, ripping my watch from my wrist, they were off, their footsteps crunching in the snow.

I felt myself drifting away. The urge to sleep was just too strong.

Friday, December 17, 1999. I came round very slowly. My vision was still blurred and I was feeling groggy. I was numb with cold and shivering, but at least I was aware of it; I was starting to switch on.

Coughing and spluttering, I checked inside my jacket. They'd had the Davidson passport and the money I'd changed. I pressed down inside my boots and made contact with the dollars and the letter. Even more surprisingly, I still had my Leatherman. Maybe they weren't as slick as I'd thought, or maybe it had no resale value unless it came with its case.

I hauled myself to my feet. Feeling in my jacket pockets for my gloves was a stupid idea: they'd taken those too. I needed to get moving and generate some heat.

Freezing air straight off the Baltic blasted my face as I walked out. The loss of my hat and gloves made me bury my head into the collar of my jacket and my hands firmly in the pockets.

Ahead of me in the darkness beyond the trees was the blue glow of a petrol station. I bent down and undid my boot to extract a twenty-dollar bill. After checking that the boot was secure, I staggered towards the glow.

Standing under the bright blue-lit canopy of the petrol station, I tried to make myself look respectable.

As I went through the door, I entered a new world, warm and clean, with plenty of goods laid out in exactly the way they would be in a convenience store anywhere else in Europe. The only thing missing, and which I'd been hoping for, was the smell of coffee.

Two guys in their late teens looked up from behind the counter, then went back to studying their magazines, probably feeling ridiculous in their red and white striped waistcoats and caps.

I wobbled around the shelves, picking up a couple of chocolate bars and some cold cuts from the chilled compartment.

They both stared at me as I dumped my goods on the counter, and it took me a while to realise that I was swaying on my feet. Resting two fingers on the counter to steady myself, I gave them a big smile. 'Speak English?'

The one with the zits saw my twenty dollars. 'American?'

'No, no. Australian.' I always said I was from Australia, New Zealand or Ireland; they're neutral, easy-going and well known as travellers. Tell people you're a Brit or an American and somebody somewhere is bound to be pissed off with you about whatever country you've bombed recently.

He smiled and nodded.

I handed him the bill. 'Can I pay you with this?'

He studied a folder—probably the exchange rates. Behind him, Camel cigarette cartons were neatly arranged around a Camel clock. I tried to focus my eyes on the hands and managed to make out that it was just after three thirty. No wonder I was freezing; I must have spent hours in that doorway.

He exchanged the bill without a second thought. My cold fingers fumbled with the large amount of paper and coins he gave me as change. In the end, I just cupped one hand and scooped the money into it with the other. As he handed me my carrier bag I asked, 'Where is the train station?'

My mate with zits pointed to the right of the forecourt.

I put my hand up in a big Australian thank-you gesture, walked out and turned right as they had directed. Just a quarter of an hour later I was going through heavy glass doors into the dimly lit station. Like any other railway station in the world it offered a full range of drunks, addicts and homeless people.

At least the place was warm. I made my way along the main concourse, looking for a place to curl up and hide. I eventually found an alcove, pulled the food from my pocket, made myself eat the chocolate bars and the meat, then rolled over onto my side, among the dirt and dog-ends. I was past caring. I just wanted to sleep.

I WAS JOLTED AWAKE by a kick in the ribs. My head was still aching, but my eyes were focusing better. I saw a frenzy of men in black, looking like an American police SWAT team, with combat trousers tucked into their boots, baseball caps and nylon bomber jackets festooned with logos. They were shouting and screaming, hitting vagrants indiscriminately with long black night sticks. For the homeless population of Tallinn, this was obviously reveille.

Taking the hint, I pulled myself up and shambled out of the station with the rest of them. The cold early-morning air gripped my face and lungs. It was still pitch-black, but a solitary street light was glimmering. Parked up in a row were five large 4x4s. I waited while the black teams climbed into their wagons and moved off, then I wandered back into the station.

I tried to find out train times. There was plenty of information, all in Estonian or Russian. The ticket office was closed, but a handwritten notice on a piece of cardboard taped to the inside of the glass screen explained that something was happening at 0700, which I took to be the opening time.

My next priority was to get a brew. Nothing was open in the station, but I found a row of aluminium kiosks outside selling everything from coffee to hair bands, but mostly cigarettes and alcohol. I managed to get a paper cup of coffee for a small coin. From the same kiosk I also treated myself to a new watch, a bright orange thing with the Lion King grinning out at me from a face that lit up at the press of a button. His paws rested on a digital display, which the old woman running the kiosk corrected to 06:15.

I bought another bar of chocolate, then I wandered around the kiosks looking for maps. I found a Narva town map. Glancing at Lion King as I paid for it, I realised I had to get a move on.

On the way to the ticket office I brushed the worst of the dirt from my jeans. My body heat was drying them out slowly.

I was first in line when the notice got moved away from the little window to reveal an iron grille behind thick glass, with a small wooden scoop at the bottom where money and tickets were exchanged. A woman glowered at me from behind the fortifications.

I smiled. 'Narva, how much?' I rubbed my fingers together.

She got out a little receipt book and wrote 'Narva' and '707'. The cost was 707 hertigrats, or whatever the money was called.

I handed her a 1,000 note—twenty dollars was going a long way here. She moved away from the glass, rummaged around, came back and dropped my change through the scoop. With it was a slip of paper as thin as tissue. I picked it up.

THE WHEELS RATTLED rhythmically over the rails as I gazed out at the darkness. I couldn't see any of the landscape, just lights from what I supposed were factories and apartment blocks.

I was sitting by the sliding door at the front end of the carriage, next to a window. According to the travel guide I'd be here for at least the next five hours. There were a dozen other passengers spread about the carriage, all of them male, most with carrier bags.

The door slid back with a crash and a woman in her mid-forties came in, wearing a man's overcoat. Draped over her arm were a dozen copies of a tabloid. She started asking me something. I waved my hand politely to say no thanks but she became very animated. She reached into her coat and out came the same sort of book of receipts that Mrs Glum had used in the ticket office. I realised she was the ticket collector, who was obviously running a newspaper concession on the side. I fished out my slip of paper. She inspected it, grunted and gave it back.

The train stopped every ten minutes or so to disgorge a group of workers. After half an hour the lights started to die out and I was looking into darkness again. I decided to follow the lead of the one other passenger left in the carriage and get some sleep.

IT WAS SHORTLY after nine thirty and first light had just passed. The sky, in keeping with everything else, was a gloomy grey. Through the grime on the window I saw snow-heavy trees lining the track. It was time to study my Narva town map, working out exactly where I'd find Konstantin. According to Lion King there was about an hour to go before we arrived.

I looked out of the window. Gone were the trees; instead the view consisted of slag heaps, with massive conveyor belts, factories and forbidding blocks of flats. The scenery didn't change much as the stops became more frequent, except that every spare inch of ground along the track was covered with little vegetable allotments.

The train stopped with a judder and a loud squeal of brakes. We seemed to be in a rail yard. Going by the number of doors opening, it was time to get off. Welcome to Narva.

I looked out of the window and saw people jumping down onto the tracks with their bags. The only other remaining passenger in my carriage was leaving. I did the same, traipsing through the snow, following the others towards an old stone house.

I went through metal double doors into the ticket office. It was closed. A large wooden board was fixed to the wall near the sales window, with plastic sliders upon which were the names of various destinations. I looked for Tallinn. It seemed that the first train back was at 0822 each morning.

I came out of the main entrance and cut across the potholed road, following the map in my head along Puskini, the main street. It wouldn't be far to Konstantin's.

Puskini was lined on either side by high buildings. The newest ones looked as if they dated from the 1970s, and even they were falling apart. This was a miserable, run-down place.

Further along, I came to a minimarket. It was an old building but had the brightest lighting I'd yet seen. I couldn't resist it.

An old man was lying on top of a cardboard box to one side of the main entrance, sheltered by the shop's canopy. His head was wrapped in rags, his hands covered with strips of cardboard.

Inside, the store was laid out exactly like a small-town Spar in the UK. It even had some of the same brands—Colgate toothpaste, KP nuts and Gillette shaving foam—but not much else apart from crates of beer and a large chiller cabinet that had nothing in it except rows of different sausages.

I picked up a family-sized bag of crisps, two packs of sliced, processed cheese and four rolls, and paid for them. I helped myself to two carrier bags, putting one pack of cheese and a couple of rolls into one, the rest in the other. Passing the old guy on the way out, I put the smaller bag down beside him. I knew what it felt like to spend hours outside in the cold.

I came to a giant car park, full of buses and cars. People carrying bags and suitcases were shouting at each other over the noise of air brakes and engines. It looked like news footage of refugees moving through a checkpoint. I realised I was at the border crossing, the road bridge into, or out of, Russia.

Moneychangers plied their trade along the edges of the car park, and kiosks sold all other types of kit. I walked over to a green-painted garden shed with a small sliding window. An old guy showed me his list of exchange rates. It seemed I could get about 12 EEK, whatever they were, to the US dollar.

I didn't want to show that I had money, so I went and sat on a dustbin behind the kiosk, got a warm $100 bill out of my sock and replaced the boot pretty sharpish.

Once he'd carried out about five different checks to make sure the bill wasn't counterfeit, including smelling it, the old guy was very happy indeed with his hard currency, and so was I with my new EEK wedge. I left the refugee camp and headed further up Puskini, towards a roundabout that led to the road I wanted.

I stopped in a doorway by the roundabout, taking the rolls from my carrier bag. Pulling the bread apart, I threw in a few slices of cheese and a handful of crisps. I ate one roll, and started attacking the second as I crossed the roundabout and turned right, towards the river. The address that Liv had given me was on this road, which was known simply as Viru.

Viru wasn't any more uplifting than the rest of town, just grey, miserable blocks of housing and more black snow. Now and again a patched-up Ford Sierra clattered past on the cobblestones, its occupants looking at me as if I was mad to be walking in this neighbourhood. Straight ahead I could see the icy river bank, 500 or 600 yards away. That was Russia.

Number 87 Viru wasn't an apartment block, as I'd been expecting, but a large old house that was now a BAAR. At least, that was what the sign said, in unlit neon lettering above a rotten wooden door. According to the sign next to it saying '8–22', it should have been open. Trying the door handle, I found that it wasn't.

Four cars were parked outside. There was a brand-new, shiny red Audi, and two Cherokee Jeeps that had seen better days, both dark blue and with Russian plates. The fourth vehicle was a red Lada that had been hand-painted and had to belong to a teenager. There were domestic music speakers clamped on the back shelf, from which wires hung like spaghetti.

I looked through the building's grime-covered ground-floor windows. There were no lights on and no sounds. Walking round to the other side, facing the river, I could see a light shining on the third floor, just a single bulb. It was like finding life on Mars.

Back at the wooden door I hit the intercom button near the BAAR sign. There was static and crackling, and a gruff male voice, half aggressive, half bored, quizzed me. I didn't know what the hell he was on about. I said, 'Konstantin. I want to see Konstantin.'

I heard the Russian or Estonian equivalent of 'Eh, what?', then voices in the background. The static ceased. I wasn't sure whether there was going to be some action or not, so I stayed where I was. After about two minutes there was the sound of bolts being thrown on the other side of the door. I moved out of the way as it was pushed open. Behind it was an iron grille door, still closed, and behind that was a guy of maybe seventeen or eighteen, who looked like the style fairy had crept up on him and waved her LA-street-gang wand.

'Do you speak English?' I asked.

'Yo! You want Konstantin?'

'Yeah, Konstantin. Is he here?'

He gave a big smile. 'Yes, he sure is, for that's me, man. You are the England guy, right?'

I nodded and smiled.

He beamed. 'OK, come on in.'

As soon as I'd walked in, both the door and the grille were locked behind me and the keys taken out.

He held up his hands. 'Hey, call me Vorsim.' He wiggled his fingers, the ones that hadn't gone missing, in the air. 'Everyone does. It's Russian for eight. Follow me, England guy.'

I followed Eight up a narrow wooden staircase. He was wearing a pair of blindingly yellow and purple Nike trainers, beneath baggy, blue hip-hop-style jeans and a black PVC leather-look bomber jacket with the LA Raiders pirate logo stitched on the back.

We hit a landing and turned for the next flight. I couldn't see any evidence of a bar, but at least it was warm and dry—almost too dry. It had that dusty smell that places get when the windows are never opened and the heating is on all the time. We passed the second and carried on up to the third floor, then walked along a landing.

Eight opened one of the doors. 'Your name is Nick, right?'

'That's right.' I didn't return eye contact as I walked past him into the room. I was too busy checking what I was walking into.

There was just one bulb in the centre of the very large room. It was boiling hot and a layer of cigarette smoke clung to the high ceiling. There was a glow from the TV to my left, its volume set low, with a body in front of it. Directly in front of me, about fifty feet away, was a single sash window, its shutters open in the hope of letting in a little natural light. To my right, near a large marble fireplace, three men were seated on fancy chairs around what looked like an antique table with ornate legs. They were playing cards and smoking.

The three heads at the table turned and stared as they sucked on their cigarettes. I nodded without any reaction from them at all, then one of the guys said something and the other two guffawed and went back to their game.

The door closed behind me. I looked at Eight, who was bobbing up and down with excitement. 'Well, man'—arms moving around like a rapper—'you hang here, Vorsim won't be long. Things to do.' And with that he placed the grille keys on the table and disappeared through the door near the fireplace.

It was easy to see what went on here. Two sets of electronic display pharmaceutical scales sat under the table at this end of the room. Next to them were stacked maybe ten to twelve large Tupperware boxes, some containing white stuff that definitely wasn't flour, others holding dark-coloured pills that similarly weren't Smarties.

It might be sweltering in here, but I was desperate for a hot brew. The only drink I could see was a bottle of Johnny Walker on the table, which was being emptied by the card players. They all had black leather jackets draped over the backs of their chairs. They'd obviously watched too many gangster movies, because they were all dressed in black, with enough gold dripping off their wrists and fingers to clear Estonia's national debt. It looked like a scene from *GoodFellas*.

The door opened and in came Eight. 'Yo, Nikolai!' The bomber jacket was now off to reveal a Bart Simpson sweatshirt. 'Nick, I've been told to help you. Because, guess what, crazy guy, I'm the only one here who speaks English.' He shifted from trainer to trainer.

'Vorsim, I need a car.'

'Car? Whoa, could be a problem, my man.'

He moved over to the GoodFellas, spoke some very fast stuff and did some mock begging. The oldest one, maybe in his early fifties, didn't look up from his hand but replied really aggressively.

Eight walked back over to me. 'I'll have to give you my car.'

'Is it one of the ones outside?' I'd already guessed, but was hoping I was wrong.

'Yes. But hey, man, I need it for bitches. Will I get it back soon? How long do you need it for? A couple of hours?'

I shrugged. 'Maybe a couple of days.' Before he could react I added, 'I also want to see you later tonight. Will you be here?'

'Cool, I live here, my man.' He pointed up at the loft.

'OK, I'll be back later. Keys?'

'Keys? Oh sure, sure. I'll have to come with you, my man. Show you something cool.' Eight took the keys off the table. We went downstairs and out into the cold.

After locking the door and grille behind us, it turned out that the cool thing he wanted to show me was that I'd have to hit the starter motor with a hammer before it would turn over. He said he liked it busted like this because no one could steal it.

He busied himself showing me what to do. I just wanted to get away and do my job, but Eight wanted to remove his speakers and cassettes first. I was waiting for him to disconnect the speakers when a 5 Series BMW cruised down the road. I looked at the driver.

Carpenter. I couldn't believe it.

He was slowing down as a van approached from the opposite direction, but it wasn't to let him past; he was heading over to where we were, and if he saw me I bet I wouldn't be getting the Russian for 'Hail, good fellow, well met.'

I jumped into the back of the car with Eight and made as if to help him pull out the speakers. The BMW turned into the car park, its tyres crunching louder and louder on the ice the closer it got. I suddenly found the speakers very interesting indeed, and made sure my back faced very definitely towards the BMW.

The engine shut down and the driver's door opened. Eight glanced over my shoulder as Carpenter's door slammed, then turned back to his beloved speakers.

After hearing the wooden door close, I asked, 'Who is he?'

'Oh, just one of the guys. Business, you know.'

He must do a lot of business here to have his own keys.

'Don't say anything about me to anyone, Vorsim,' I said. 'Especially him. I don't want people to know I'm here, OK?'

'Oh sure, my man.' The way he said it was too blasé for my liking, but I didn't want to push the point.

Once the speakers were out I virtually threw the cassettes at him, wanting to get away before Carpenter reappeared. The Lada's bonnet was still open and I gave the starter motor a seeing-to with the hammer. Before Eight had even turned to unlock the door I had the bonnet down, the engine in gear and was away.

My head was churning about Carpenter. What if he was still there when I came back after I'd done the recce? I should have told Eight I wanted to meet elsewhere. Should I even go back and see Eight again? I had no choice: I was going to need help obtaining explosives or whatever else I needed.

I drove out of town, heading west along the Tallinn road for about twenty miles to a place called Kohtla Jarve, home of the giant, brooding slag heaps and long conveyor belts I'd seen from the train. I followed the road west for about another ten miles, then turned left, heading south for a place called Pussi. It was another ten miles further south to the target.

In the Lada's headlights I could see that the road was single track. There were just two tyre ruts worn into the snow. The headlights reached about five to ten yards either side of me, exposing banks of snow and the occasional ice-laden tree.

I drove through Pussi, which looked like a small farming community. The buildings were run-down shacks made of bare, unpainted wood, and surrounded by wrecked cars.

There were no warning signs that I was about to bump over the railway track from Tallinn, and after that I didn't see a single sign of human activity. The road got steadily worse. I checked the odometer, counting down to the only T-junction, which, if I remembered rightly, was a mile or so away.

Once there, I at last got help: a small sign told me it was right to Tudu. I turned left, now knowing that the target would be the first building on the left.

After about a mile, a high concrete wall appeared in my headlights, about ten yards in on the left-hand side. I drove slowly for forty yards or so, past a pair of large metal gates, then for about another forty yards before the wall turned at a right angle into the darkness.

Just a few yards further on was a building resembling a large hangar. It was slightly closer to the road than the wall had been, and wasn't fenced or walled in.

I waited until I'd rounded a bend and was out of sight, then I threw the Lada into a little driveway on my left. It was probably an entrance to a field, but people weren't going to be working on the land for a few more months. I closed the door quietly and used the wipers to secure a sheet of newspaper over the windscreen. I started to walk back down the road, sticking to the ice that had formed on the road to keep footprints to a minimum.

The hangar had been a substantial building, though most of the masonry had collapsed, exposing the steel frame; I could see right through it to the field beyond. It was one storey, lower than the concrete wall further along.

Continuing towards the concrete wall, I crossed the twenty feet or so between the hangar and the target compound. As I approached, I began to make out the dark shape of a normal-sized door set in the concrete wall. I'd have loved to have gone and tried it, but I couldn't risk leaving tracks in the snow.

As I walked on towards the gates the front wall towered above me. I tried looking for CCTV cameras, but it was too dark and the wall was too high and far away. I moved the forty yards or so it took to reach the point where the compound driveway joined the road. The gates were as high as the wall itself—ten to fifteen feet—and made of steel plate. I pushed against them, but they didn't move, and there were no locks I could see holding them in position.

Set into the right gate was a smaller, pedestrian door. It had two locks, one a third of the way up from the bottom and another a third of the way down from the top. I gently pulled the door handle, which of course was also locked.

The gap between gate and ground was four inches. Lying down, and using the length of the tyre rut to avoid making prints in the snow either side of me, I pressed my eye against the gap. There was light on the other side and the gentle hum of machinery, probably a generator. I made out the shapes of two buildings about twenty yards away. The smaller one on the left had two lights shining from ground-floor windows; their patterned curtains were drawn, but light still spilled onto the snow in front of the building.

In the middle of the larger building to the right was a dark area, its rectangular shape, with a semicircular top, suggesting vehicle access.

I lay there visualising how to defeat the wall and get in on target, going through a mental checklist of the kit I'd be needing. Then the cold got to me and I got up and moved back to the road.

I had warmed up by the time I got back to the Lada. Unfortunately, the first thing I had to do after lifting the bonnet was take off my jacket and ram it down onto the starter motor. I didn't want Tom's new friends to hear me when I battered it with the hammer.

Ripping the newspaper from behind the windscreen wipers I got into the driving seat. Keeping the revs low I drove away.

I parked up in the border-crossing car park at 9.24, according to Lion King. There was no way I was going to drive straight to Eight's place; I wanted to check out the area first, in case Carpenter was there.

I locked up the car and headed back to the *baar*, hands in pockets, head down. Approaching, I could see the BMW wasn't there. Only two of the other vehicles were still there and both were covered in ice.

I pressed the intercom button and a crackling male voice answered. I knew the routine now and even a little Russian. 'Vorsim. Vorsim.'

Soon bolts were being pulled on the inside. The door swung open and there stood Eight. As he unlocked the grille, he peered anxiously out into the car park. 'My wheels?'

I walked in and waited as he locked up behind. 'The car's fine. Is the guy with the BMW coming back?'

He shrugged as I started to climb the stairs behind him.

'You'll need a pen and paper, Vorsim.'

We entered the third-floor room. No one was there. He pointed at several cheap ball-point pens and sheets of lined A4 paper scattered among the crap on the table.

'Shall I just say what I need and you write it down?'

He smiled. 'That would be cool, yeah.'

Halfway through dictating the list I had to explain what a detonator was. A few minutes later, he jumped out of his seat, studying his handiwork. 'Wait here, Nikolai, my man.' He disappeared through the door near the fireplace. A few seconds later I heard laughter.

The sound of footsteps echoed from the stairwell, accompanied by volleys of quick, aggressive talking, slowly getting louder as people came up the stairs. I told myself not to worry, even though my heart-beat quickened as I listened for Carpenter.

The door burst open and I watched as the GoodFellas came in and crossed the room towards me. There was no Carpenter. It was the same four card players. The old one kept on his silver-grey fur Cossack-style hat. He was looking at me but talking back to the others. An index finger started pointing at me as he got closer, as if to reinforce whatever he was gobbing off about. I looked down in submission and slightly turned towards the window.

From less than a foot away he began to poke me in the back, shouting very close to my head. I turned and looked at him, then looked down. I wasn't going to react; it might antagonise him even more. I just let him get on with it.

I moved my hand to the window and supported myself, as I was getting the four-finger poke now, my body jerking back with each jab. Glancing across, I could see the other three enjoying the cabaret.

Sounding as frightened as I could I stammered, 'I am here for Eight . . . er . . . V–v–vorsim.'

He mocked me. 'V–v–vorsim.' He mimed injecting his arm, laughing along with the other three.

He turned back and gave me a push with both hands. He was having some fun, maybe taking out some frustration. The others laughed as I rode the pushes, still showing no resistance.

He got more serious. After one particularly hard push I stumbled back towards the television. He followed me, the pushes now punctuated with the odd slap round the head. Then he started gesturing, rubbing fingers and pointing at my boots. Did he want my money and Timberlands? Money I could understand, but boots?

This was getting out of control. I held my hands up in submission. 'Stop! Stop! Stop!'

He did, and waited for his cash.

I slowly reached into the inside pocket of the jacket and pulled out the insurance policy.

He barked a question at me, his eyes narrowing, then grabbed the thin paper, partly tearing it in the process. Opening it, he turned to the table and waved it at them, as if sharing the joke in a Christmas cracker. Bending down into the light given off by the television, he pushed the note in front of the screen.

His laughter subsided as he started to read. Then it stopped completely. Whatever the bit of paper said, it was doing the business. He walked over to the others, muttering, 'Ignaty. Ignaty.'

I hadn't a clue what that meant and I didn't really care. They all had a read, and it had the same effect on everyone. They slowly turned their heads and stared at me across the room. It was good the policy had worked, but I might have to put up with their loss of face. I couldn't afford to fuel that by appearing at all cocky; I still wasn't out of the woods. Walking over to the table, my face full of respect, I put out my left hand and nodded at the sheet of paper. 'Please.'

He handed it back, hating every second of it, and I folded it carefully and put it in my pocket. I turned my back to them and walked to the TV. I could tell that once I was out of earshot there was going to be some very loud shouting, but for now there was just low, disgruntled murmuring behind me.

Five minutes later, Eight came back into the room. I didn't understand what he was saying as he fought with the zip on his leatherette jacket, but by the look of it, we were leaving.

I followed him downstairs at the speed of sound.

'WHERE DO WE GO NOW, Vorsim?'

He already had the Lada's bonnet open. 'An apartment.'

After two metallic bangs, the Lada fired up and he drove us both out of the car park, to the roundabout, then away from the river. We turned left without indicating, then left again down a narrow street, with apartments to the left and a tall wall to the right.

Eight threw the Lada into the side of the road and jumped out. 'Wait here, my man.'

He headed for the main door of one of the blocks. He stopped and checked the stencilling, gave me the thumbs up, then turned back towards the Lada to lock up. I got out and waited.

We entered a narrow hallway. It stank of boiled cabbage. The apartment doors were one-piece sheet metal with three locks and a spy hole. We waited for the lift by rows of wooden letterboxes, listening to the motor groaning inside the shaft.

The machinery stopped with a loud shudder and the doors opened. We entered an aluminium box. Eight hit the button for the fourth floor and we lurched upwards. At the fourth floor the doors opened into semidarkness. I let him step out ahead of me.

We turned left along a corridor, Eight pulling a string of keys from his jacket. Reaching the door right at the end, he messed about, trying to work out which key went where until finally it opened, then he groped for the light switch.

The room we entered definitely wasn't the source of the boiled-cabbage stench. I could smell the heavy odour of wooden crates and gun oil; I would have known that smell anywhere.

The inevitable single bulb lit up a very small hall, no more than six feet square. There were two doors leading off; Eight went through the one on the left and I followed, closing the front door behind me and throwing all the locks.

Only one of the four bulbs in the ceiling cluster worked. The small room was stacked with wooden crates, waxed cardboard boxes and loose explosive ordnance, all stencilled with Cyrillic script. The whole lot looked dangerously past its use-by date.

Nearest was a stack of brown wooden boxes with rope handles. Lifting the lid off the top one, I recognised the dull green bedpan shapes at once. Eight made the noise of an explosion. He seemed to know they were land mines, too.

Piles of other kit lay wrapped in brown military grease-proof paper. Elsewhere, damp cardboard boxes had collapsed, spilling their contents. Lying in a corner were half a dozen electric detonators, aluminium tubes about the size of a quarter-smoked cigarette with two eighteen-inch silver wire leads coming out of one end.

Picking them up one by one, I twisted the leads together to close the circuit, then stored the dets in an empty ammo box. Once I'd finished, I pulled out the policy. 'What does this say, Vorsim?

As he moved under the light, I spotted some dark green detonater cord, a partly used reel with maybe 250 or 300 feet left. I put it to one side and went to check the other rooms. What I was looking for was plastic explosive, but there wasn't any here apart from in the anti-tank mines. These were metal, about a foot in diameter and weighed around twenty pounds, of which over twelve was plastic explosive.

Placing one of them on the bare floorboards, I tried to unscrew the cap, which was in the centre of the top. When it eventually started to move, shifting the years of grime that had formed a seal, I knew at once that it was really old ordnance. The smell of marzipan hit my nostrils—nitroglycerine. The greenish explosive had become obsolete in recent years. It still worked, it did the job, but it fouled up not only armour, but also the head and skin of anyone preparing it. You were guaranteed a fearsome headache if you worked with it in a confined space and extreme pain if you got it on a cut.

Eight sparked up. 'Hey, Nikolai, this paper is really cool.'

'What does it say?'

'First of all, his name is Ignaty. Then it says you are his man. It gets heavy. It says, "If you do not help my friend, I will kill your wife; and then, after you have been crying for two weeks, I will kill your children. Two weeks after that, I will kill you."'

'Who is Ignaty?'

He gave a shrug. 'He's your guy, am I right?'

The card players had certainly recognised the name. I took the policy from Eight and put it back in my jacket pocket.

We carried several boxes down to the car. On the last trip down, Eight locked up the flat and we stood by the Lada. He was going to walk from there as he wanted to go and see a friend.

'Thanks, mate. I'll bring the car back in about two days.'

'Nikolai. Can I . . . can I come to England with you? I can work for you and then I will go to America.'

'I'm sorry, Vorsim, I can't take you to England.'

His shoulders and face slumped. 'Why not, man . . . ?'

'They won't let you in. And even if they do, you won't be able to stay with me. I don't have a house and I haven't got any work I can give you. I'm really sorry but I can't do it.'

And that was it. I gave the starter motor a hammer, fired it up and headed back into town, then found my bearings and headed west.

A filling station appeared. I pulled in, filled up and went to pay. There was a small section in the shop that sold bits and pieces for cars; the rest of the space was given over to beer, chocolate and sausages. I picked up five blue nylon tow ropes—their entire stock—and all eight rolls of black insulation tape on display, together with a cheap multitool set. Finally, I picked up a torch and two sets of batteries, and two of the small rectangular ones with terminals on top. I couldn't think of anything else I needed, apart from some chocolate and meat and a couple of cans of fizzy orange.

The guy who took my money handed me my carrier bags; I wanted some more and pointed. It took a few seconds of miming and a couple of small coins, but I came out with half a dozen spares.

After eating all the food I'd bought, I rejoined the road. My destination was Voka, a coastal town to the north, between Narva and Kohtla Jarve. I had chosen Voka because, since it was on the coast, there was probably a better chance of finding a hotel room.

VOKA TURNED OUT to be a small seaside resort. From what I could see of it in the streetlight, it was now very tired and flaky. There was no one about. I drove slowly along the coast road with the Baltic on my left and eventually found a *hotelli* with a sea view. At first glance it had looked more like a four-storey apartment block, until I saw the small, flickering neon sign to the left of its double glass doors. As I locked the Lada, the wind buffeted my jacket and hair.

The fluorescent lights in the hallway nearly blinded me. A TV blared away in Russian and I walked along the corridor until I found its source. At the bottom of a flight of stairs, a sliding window was set chest high into the wall. Behind it sat an old woman, glued to the screen of an old TV.

She finally noticed me. Nodding and smiling, I pointed at a sheet of paper taped to the window, which I presumed was the tariff.

'Can I have a room, please?' I asked in an Australian accent.

The old woman handed me a towel the size of a teacloth and a set of what had once been white sheets. She wrote down some numbers, which I took to be the price. EEK 150 for the night—about $10. I gave her the money and she put the key on top of the sheets and got back to her TV.

I walked up the stairs and found room 4. I was surprised to find a small fridge in the corner. Next to it was a TV. But the pièce de résistance was a cushioned corner unit and coffee table, set off by a large, triangular thick glass ashtray that any pub would be proud of.

The room was cold and it was obviously up to the guest to put the heaters on. I bent over one of the two electric fires. It was a small, square three-bar thing on the door side of the bed. Plugging it in, I threw the switch and the elements started to heat up. The second heater, nearer the window, was a more elaborate, decorative model, with a black plastic log effect. I plugged it in, too.

To the right of the main door was the bathroom. I checked it out. There was an ancient, oval-shaped gas geyser with a visible pilot light and a long steel tap that swivelled so you could fill either the bath or the basin. I was expecting the worst, but when I turned the tap on the pilot light became a raging flame. The water was instantly hot, which was good news; I'd be needing a lot of that soon. Turning it off, I went back into the bedroom.

I closed the curtains and went down to unload the car, starting with two mines in a box and the bits and pieces from the gas station. The old woman didn't look up once as I came and went.

Once back in the room I started running the bath, slowing the flow to a trickle. I used a screwdriver from the multitool set to help remove the two mine caps. Holding each mine in turn under the tap until it filled with hot water, I then lowered them into the bath, still letting the water run so that it would eventually cover them. Then I went down to the car and collected another two. It took three trips in all to get everything upstairs. On the final trip I took another newspaper from the back seat and covered the windscreen.

I kept unscrewing mine caps until all six were in the bath in two layers, representing a total of over seventy pounds of plastic explosive. Molten explosive would have been injected into the dull green casings at the factory and left to set; I'd have to wait for the hot water to soften it again before I could scrape it out.

Back in the bedroom I got hold of the reel of det cord, which looked just like a green washing line, except that instead of string inside the plastic covering, there was high explosive. I cut off about the first foot of cord with my Leatherman; it was probable that the explosive core had been affected by the climatic conditions and/or age, but, if so, the contamination normally wouldn't have penetrated further than six inches. The reel then went the window side of the bed; only prepared kit would go this side from now on. That way things wouldn't get confusing.

Time to check the batteries. They were normal rectangular nine-volt ones with press-stud tops for the terminals. One of them would be the initiation device, providing the electrical charge that would run along the firing cable, which I still had to obtain. It would then initiate the detonator, which would fire up the det cord and, in turn, the charges. All this could only happen if the power from the battery was strong enough to overcome the resistance from the firing cable and det. You attach the firing cable to a torch bulb; if it lights up when you transmit power along the length of firing cable, you've got enough juice to make the thing go bang.

I pulled the plug off the bedside lamp and ripped the other end of the flex out of the lamp base, ending up with about five feet of firing cable—not enough. I needed to be close to the explosion, but five feet was suicidally close. The fridge flex gave me another five.

I went and checked the bath. All the mines were covered with hot water, so I turned off the tap on the geyser. I couldn't see a toilet brush anywhere, but there was a rubber plunger. Using its handle to prod the explosive in one of the mines, I found it was still too hard.

I connected the two lengths of flex and taped them up. Ten feet of firing cable was still not enough. The trouble was, I wouldn't know how much I needed until I was on target, and I'd have to err on the side of safety. The power line for the TV was quite long; in total I ended up with about eighteen feet of cable. The three lengths were all of different thicknesses and metals, but as long as they conducted electricity that was all I was worried about.

I wrapped the copper wires at one end around the torch bulb and taped it in place. Now all I had to do was complete the circuit with the two steel wires at the other end of the cable on the battery terminals—and bang, perfect, the bulb glowed. I repeated the process with the other battery, and it worked.

Untaping the wire from the bulb, I twisted the two copper wires together, then the two steel wires at the other end, and earthed it against the fridge. That would take away any electricity still in the cable; the last thing I wanted was to connect the wires to a detonator and have the thing explode immediately.

The coil of firing cable joined the det cord on the window side of the bed and I placed the two batteries on top of the TV. You never keep the initiation device with the detonators or the rest of the equipment. The only time all the equipment should come together is when you are going to detonate the charges.

I checked the mines. There was still a while to go before I could start digging out the plastic explosive. To use the time productively, I took a sheet of toilet paper with me, put my jacket back on and walked out into the corridor. I placed a small strip of the toilet paper by the bottom hinge and closed the door on it, checking there was just enough paper to be seen.

I CRUISED SLOWLY around town looking for the materials I needed to construct the explosive charges.

Spotting a row of skips behind a small parade of shops, I pulled in and sifted through them. There was nothing that would do for me, apart from a partly broken wooden pallet. Three sections, each about three feet long, were soon in the back of the car. One section was going to help me get over the wall, the other two were going to prop the charges in place on target.

I left the area in search of more stuff. After ten minutes of patrolling I saw a building that was worth a closer look. Rubbish was piled up outside it, but it was the structure itself that made me curious.

It turned out to be an air-raid shelter. There was a concrete stairwell down to below ground level was full of stuff that had been fly-tipped, and it was in among this that I found some expanded polystyrene packaging. I selected two pieces, each just under three feet square. I now had the frames for the charges.

The last item I needed was a brick, and in a place like this I didn't have to look far for one.

BACK AT THE HOTEL, the old woman had deserted her post.

I walked up the stairs with my finds in my arms. I checked the tell-tale. It hadn't moved. I opened the door and waited for the heat to hit me.

As I took the first step inside, I knew straight away that something wasn't right. The glow from the plastic log-effect fire wasn't dancing round the walls, but it had been when I left.

I stepped back into the corridor. And that was the last thing I did for a while, apart from trying to get off the bedroom floor, only to get a blow to the kidneys that put me back down. I was roughly turned over and a weapon muzzle was pushed hard into my face.

Once I had curled up and played nearly dead, I risked opening my eyes. The oldest of the GoodFellas towered above me, wearing his fur hat and leather coat. I could also see another pair of legs. I looked up and saw Carpenter. Our eyes locked and he spat at me.

They pulled me up by my armpits, one man on each side, and propped me up on the end of the bed. I took a blow on the right side of my face, which took me straight down onto the bed.

Expecting more, I curled up on my side. Starbursts did their best to black me out as pain scorched through my body. I could feel myself starting to lose it, and I worked hard to keep my eyes open. I knew that I had to pull myself together or I'd be dead.

The two of them were arguing. I just lay there keeping my eyes open and coughing blood onto the furry blanket. I probed with my tongue and discovered one of my side teeth moving as a numb, swollen feeling developed on the right side of my face.

With my head on the bed, I was level and in a direct line with the coffee table. My fuzzy vision locked onto the large glass ashtray.

I switched my attention to Carpenter and the old guy. Carpenter had his weapon in a shoulder holster; the other guy had a pistol in his hand. They were both pointing at me. I could also see now what the older guy had hit me with: a leather strop that was probably filled with ball bearings.

The two of them were six feet to one side of me, and the ashtray was three feet to the other. Both men were still more interested in their argument than in me, but would no doubt come to a decision very soon as to how to kill me.

I squinted at the heavy lump of glass on the table that might save my life and, taking a deep breath, sprang off the bed. Keeping my head down, I charged into the two black shapes in front of me and, not waiting to see what happened to them, I swung round and looked for the ashtray. A wheezy gasp came from behind me as they made contact with the wall.

Eyes still fixed on the glass shape on the table, I started to move towards it. Muffled shouts came from behind. Slapping down my palm, I gripped the ashtray and swung round. I took three paces towards the old guy, brandishing the fistful of glass.

I ignored Carpenter as he came towards me from the right. The one I wanted was the old guy, the one with the pistol in his hand.

He pushed himself off the wall and raised his weapon. I swung the ashtray, making contact above his cheekbone. His skin folded over just below his eye, then split open. He fell with a scream, his body banging against my legs on the way down.

I heard, rather than saw, the black shape from the right, almost on top of me. Not even bothering to turn and look at Carpenter, I just lashed out wildly. The thick glass hammered against his skull twice on his way down.

I jumped onto his chest and continued to rain blows onto the top of his head. Somewhere in the back of my mind I knew I'd lost it, but I didn't care. I was just remembering the way this bastard had kept firing rounds into the woman in the lift.

There was a crunching, cracking sound. I stopped. I'd done enough. Thick, almost brown blood oozed from his head wounds. He had lost function in his eyes and had a vacant stare, wide open and dull, pupils fully dilated.

I rested both hands on his chest, not enjoying the fact that I'd lost control. To survive, you sometimes have to get really revved up, but losing it completely, I didn't like that.

I turned to check the old guy. He was alive and that meant he was a threat. There was no other option; he had to die. I wasn't happy about it, but I couldn't leave him here alive when I set off for the Maliskia compound tomorrow. He could compromise everything.

I dragged him into the bathroom and let him slump onto the tiled bathroom floor. I turned on the hot water and the geyser surged into action.

I went back into the bedroom and picked up the old guy's pistol and one of the brown nylon blankets from the bed. I walked back into the bathroom, jammed the muzzle into the blanket and onto his head, quickly wrapped the furry nylon around the weapon and fired.

There was a dull thud and then a crack as the round exited his head and shattered the tile beneath it. I let the blanket fall and cover his face, and listened. There was no apparent reaction to the round from outside the room.

I turned the water off and moved into the bedroom. Carpenter's weapon was still in its shoulder holster. The pistol was a Makharov. I decided to keep it.

I opened the main door into the corridor, checked left and right, then had a look at the telltale. Why was it still in place? I could see the answer at once: it was stuck to the door frame. The sponge-strip draught excluder was brown and gooey with age. Lesson learned. Don't mix telltales with old draught excluders.

Switching the fire back on, I got to work. I used the toilet-plunger handle again to avoid burning my hands, wedging it into a mine cap and fishing the mine out, then turning it upside down to drain. I carried it like that into the bedroom and laid it on the coffee table. Then I opened the window, letting in the cold sea air.

The explosive, which had been more or less rigid plastic, was now soft enough to extract. I began to scoop, having first put a carrier bag over each hand to prevent the nitro from entering my bloodstream via cuts on my hands or straightforward absorption.

By the time I'd finished, the room stank of marzipan, and in front of me on the table was ten pounds of what looked like green plasticine. The remaining two pounds or so were stubbornly sticking to the sides of the mine and were too difficult to get out.

With the bags rustling on my hands, I worked away at the plastic explosive as if kneading dough, trying to keep my head turned so the fumes didn't get to me so quickly. Once I'd got it all nice and malleable in three equal-sized balls, I pulled off the rubber part of the plunger and used the handle as a rolling pin to flatten them out. When the dough was about a quarter of an inch thick and the diameter of a medium pizza, I used the ice scraper to cut strips about two inches wide, getting six per base. That done, I went into the bathroom to refill the bath with more hot water. There were five more mines to be dealt with.

An hour later, with all the explosive in strips, I opened the knife blade of the Leatherman and rested it over the hot bar of the fire. I then laid the first piece of polystyrene foam on the bed, base down.

Using the towel as an oven glove, I lifted the hot Leatherman from the fire and quickly sliced off all the little lumps, bumps and moulded corners from the upper side of the foam. What I was left with was three feet square, one side naturally flat, the other cut more or less level. Next I used the hot blade to mark out a two-inch-wide channel all the way round, following the line of the square and about three inches in from the edge.

Holding the blade at an angle, I started cutting an inverted V in the channel, ending up with what looked like a trench all around the foam square, with four very long bars of Toblerone lying in the bottom of it, peaks upwards. When the frame charge was complete, it would be the flat side that would be placed against the target.

Now all I had to do was lay the explosive along each side of the Toblerone shape and over its peak, making sure the strips were moulded together seamlessly to make one big charge. Once the Toblerone was covered, I got some det cord and cut off two lengths, one about three feet long, the other about five. Putting knots into one end of each length, I pressed these into the explosive that lay over the Toblerone, on two opposite sides of the square.

The reason for having two sites for the det cord was to make the charge more efficient. I tightly taped together, over a distance of about six inches, the two different lengths of det cord so that, from the binding to the charge, they were both of equal length. Trailing from the site of the binding was the two-foot surplus from the longer piece; that bit was called the det tail. I taped over the Toblerone shape to keep it in the foam.

I still had another charge to make, so I put the knife back on the fire. It took me thirty minutes to complete the second charge.

To make them easier to carry, I sandwiched both sets of charges together so the Toblerone peaks were facing each other, storing the attached det cord in between. I wrapped one of the tow ropes around to keep it all together, then slid two of the pallet sections and the reel of unused det cord under the rope. The whole thing looked like a badly packed Boy Scout's rucksack.

I tied the remaining tow ropes together until there was one rope about a hundred feet long, adding extra knots so there was one every three feet. One end was then tied onto the rope that had been wrapped around the charges.

Next I picked up the third length of pallet wood. I cut a groove all round one end, about three inches in from the top, around which I secured the free end of the rope attached to the charges. Holding the brick against the unroped end of the wood, its longest edge parallel to the plank's, I wrapped the towel around both and secured it with yards of insulating tape. All the equipment was now prepared.

Lion King told me it was 3.28, in theory too early to leave, but I didn't know who else knew that Carpenter and the old man had come to visit. I took the charges, draped in a blanket, down to the car.

Fourteen

Saturday, December 18, 1999. In the pitch-dark of the afternoon I headed towards the target.

In the twelve hours since leaving the hotel I'd been cruising around, stopping only a couple of times to fill up with petrol. Anything to keep the heater going. On my way out I'd paid the old woman for another two nights, so with any luck there should be no need for her to come and check the room.

Tented stalls were dotted along the roads like miniature service stations. When I stopped to buy coffee and pastries, it actually helped to have a swollen mouth with visible bruising, because I could get away with just mumbling and pointing.

Now, sliding slowly along the single-track road, my headlights picked up the concrete wall of the target on my left. Nothing appeared to have changed. Parking in the same driveway as before, I turned off the engine.

Forcing myself out into the cold, now wearing the old guy's gloves and fur hat, I took the charges out of the boot. The tow rope wrapped around them made a handy shoulder strap. I hid the key under the rear right wheel. If I got caught by the Maliskia, then at least they wouldn't have my keys if I managed to escape. What was more, I could tell Tom if I linked up with him, and he would also have a means of escape if I didn't make it to the car.

I wasn't going to kill him. I owed him that much after what he'd done by the fence at the Finns' house. I'd been toying with the idea since I lay in my cheap hotel room in Helsinki. That was why I'd brought his passport with me, just in case.

I reached the large steel-plate gates, stopped and listened. I could just make out the generator churning away in the distance. Apart from that, nothing. I tested the gates, but they weren't open. I tried the small door set into the larger right-hand one, but again that was still locked.

Lying down in the right-hand tyre rut, with the charges behind me, I pressed my eye to the gap beneath. Nothing that side of the gate had changed; to the left there were still two lights on the ground floor, and the larger building to the right was just as dark.

Once on my feet again, with the Boy Scout rucksack reshouldered, I started back in the direction of the car, but about seventy or eighty yards past the hangar I stepped left off the road and into the high snow. My aim was to walk out into the fields, turn left and approach the hangar from the rear.

The snow varied in depth from calf to thigh height. I laboured on, my jeans soaking and my legs starting to freeze.

The rear of the hangar loomed in front of me and I climbed inside. The floor was concrete. Moving towards the concrete wall of the compound, after about twenty paces I began to make out the doorway. When I reached the edge of the hangar I stood still and listened. Not a sound, just the gentle moan of the wind.

I waded across the snow to the compound wall, realising as soon as I reached the door that I was going to be disappointed. The door was solid, with no hinges or locks this side of it. I pushed, but there wasn't a hint of movement.

Turning right, I followed the wall and waded fifteen yards further away from the road. Hopefully I was now facing the gable end of the larger building on the other side of the concrete.

Placing the charges on the snow, I unravelled the rope attached to the plank with the brick at the end. With just two or three feet of slack, I started swinging it around me like a hammer thrower, finally letting go with upwards momentum to make the plank clear the wall.

I'd never make the Highland Games. The whole lot fell back down in front of me. I was just sorting out the rope for another try when vehicle lights raked the wall of the compound.

I dropped to my knees, ready to bury myself in the snow. Then I realised that on my knees I *was* buried in it.

The ponderous chug of a big diesel told me that a tractor was heading in my direction. The noise got louder and the light stronger until the tractor burst into view on the road. It looked like some relic from a Soviet collective, with far more silhouettes in the cab than the thing was designed for. Maybe the local pub-quiz team was heading down to the Hammer and Sickle for a few pints of vodka.

The lights and noise faded, and I eventually got the plank to sail over the wall, the charge end firmly anchored in my hands, the plank probably ending up dangling about three or four feet over the target side. Gently, I started pulling it back, waiting for the bit of resistance that would tell me that the point where the rope was wrapped around the plank had connected with the far top edge of the wall. The way this thing worked was that the counterweight of the brick made the top of the plank anchor itself against an angled wall. I slowly let it take my whole body weight. The rope held secure. Using the knots I'd placed along the rope, I started to climb.

It didn't take long to reach the top, and I scrambled up and rested along the wall's three-foot width. The large building blocked most of my view of the target beyond.

I began to pull the charges carefully up the wall. When I'd finally got them up on top with me, I swivelled round and lowered them gently down the target side. It was now simply a question of moving the plank to the other edge in order to reverse the climbing process.

Keeping the tension in the rope, I slowly lowered myself over the edge, then climbed down as quickly as I could. I left the rope in place while I went off and did a quick recce.

The hum of the generator was more than enough to drown the crunch of my feet on virgin snow and ice as I moved towards the side door. I took the torch from my pocket and switched it on. Just a tiny pinprick of light emerged; I'd taped over most of the reflector, leaving just a small hole.

There was work to be done on the door. If I didn't have a better escape route organised than climbing a rope, I'd be in deep shit if I was compromised. I could see that the door was secured by a large bolt, set in the middle, covered in rust and looking as if it hadn't been opened for years. I began to work on the lever with both hands, making a little progress with each movement until the thing finally gave. Pulling the door towards me about three or four inches to confirm that it would open, I then pushed it back into position.

There was no point in risking the rope being spotted now that I had an alternative escape route, so I untied it and let it go. Shouldering the charges, I crunched along the front of the larger building.

The generator noise increased as I reached the large opening. A mass of tyre tracks led in the same direction. Going inside, I moved off to the right so I wasn't silhouetted in the entrance. Taking the torch out of my pocket, I pulled off the tape but kept two fingers over the lens to control its brightness. A quick shine around the cavernous interior revealed a Mercedes van and two saloons.

The torchlight was too weak to reach the generator itself, but thirty paces took me right up to it. Beyond it was the fuel tank, a large, heavy plastic cylinder supported on breeze blocks. Jutting from the front of the generator was a power cable a good three inches thick; it ran through the gable wall, where three or four bricks had been knocked out to accommodate it, and towards the target house.

I dumped my kit at the back of the generator, turned off the torch, and went back out into the compound. Following the many footprints between this building and the target about fifteen yards away, I made my way towards the main door. Directly ahead I saw the triangle of darkness that stretched from just below the ground-floor windowsill to about three feet out into the snow, where the light hit the ground.

Bending down, I edged my way under the first window, as close as possible to the wall. The glass above me was protected by steel bars. The light was shining through yellow floral curtains, too thick to see through. A television was on, and it didn't take me long to work out the channel was MTV. I couldn't hear any talking, just Ricky Martin singing. Bursting in with the chorus was a heavy Eastern European accent trying to give Ricky a hand.

I moved up the two concrete steps to the main door. The steel grille outside wasn't locked but the door was. I stood and listened. The song had ended. From upstairs came shouting. Then I realised it was meant to be singing. The Ricky Martin impressionist was on his way back downstairs.

Moving back down the steps, I followed the tracks towards the far end of the target, ducking under the left-hand window and into its dark triangle. I could hear no sound from inside.

I reached the corner of the small building and cleared it. There were no windows this side. What could easily be seen, however, even in this light, was a large satellite dish. I counted the paces as I moved towards it, in preparation for laying the charges. Seventeen one-yard steps took me to the rear of the building.

Light was shining through curtains from both of the upstairs windows, just enough to cast a dim glow over the satellite dish's two mates. They were on stands, with ice-covered sandbags over the legs to keep them in position. Beyond them, maybe forty yards away, was the dark shape of the rear compound wall.

I turned right and realised that hidden in the shadow of the top windows' dark triangles were two more windows on the ground floor, without light, also barred and boarded over from the inside. To get under the first window took five paces, making it twenty-two in total so far.

It took me another nine paces to the next window to add to the twenty-two. I'd soon know how much det cord to take off the reel. This window was boarded up, but there was a little light spilling out. Two sheets of quarter-inch ply, which should have been flush against the glass, were not, leaving a half-inch gap on the right-hand side.

Pressing my head right up against the iron bars, I got a glimpse of very bright lighting, under which I could see a bank of PC monitors facing away from me, their rear vents black with burnt dust. At least I knew where the kit that had to be destroyed was—all I needed to find now was Tom. I waited for fifteen minutes with my eye to the gap, but nothing happened.

I moved to the next corner of the target, towards the generator. It was another five paces, which made thirty-six in total. I turned right and walked down the small gap between the two buildings, stepping over the generator cable lying in the snow.

I made my way back to the generator building and started to prepare the kit. The first thing I checked was that I still had the batteries in my inside pocket. I'd been keeping them close to my body to stop them getting sluggish in the cold.

Placing the reel of det cord between my feet, I held the loose end in my right hand and stretched out my arm, pushing the cord into my armpit with my left. I did that thirty-six times, plus an extra five to cover what I needed to do this side of the target. I added two more for luck, cutting it with my Leatherman. I then laid it on the floor, next to the charges. This was the main line, and would be used to send the shock wave to all the charges at once.

The next thing I had to sort out was a little brainwave I'd had for the fuel tank. I had in mind the most spectacular explosion this side of Hollywood. When the fuel tank blew it wouldn't be the most productive bang in the world, but the effect would be phenomenal.

I climbed the ladder of the tank with the det cord in my hand, unfeeding it from the reel. When I lifted the flap on the tank, the torch beam hit on the surface of shiny liquid that filled about three-quarters of the cylinder. After tying a double knot on the end of the cord, I pulled the petrol-station carrier bag from my jacket. In it was the spare four-pound ball of plastic explosive that any demolitions man worth his salt always carries to plug up any holes or damage to a charge. I ripped off about half and played with it to warm it up.

Once it was pliable enough, I squashed it around the double knot, and taped the whole thing up to keep the explosive in place. I lowered the green ball into the tank by its string of det cord, stopping when it was dangling about three inches from the surface of the fuel.

I taped the det cord onto the side of the fuel tank, then climbed back down the ladder, carefully unreeling the rest of the cord as I moved towards the hole in the wall. I wanted to cut a long enough length so that, once laid out, it would reach the target house. Nine extra arm's lengths seemed to put me on the safe side. I made the cut, pushed the end of the det cord through the hole in the wall, then cut several eight-inch strips of gaffer tape from the roll and stuck them around both forearms. Finally I shouldered the pack of charges, gripped the coiled-up main line in my left hand and moved back out into the cold.

I cleared the gap between the two buildings and moved towards the rear. Stepping over the generator cable, I checked the det cord was still in the hole, then continued down to the corner. I wanted to make one last check for Tom through the gap in the boards. Maybe I'd be in luck: there's a first time for everything.

Angling my head, I peered through, but couldn't see any movement.

Stepping over the satellite-dish cables, I made my way to the far corner, then turned and counted three paces towards the front of the target. I crouched down and placed the charges and reel of det cord on the snow. The computer room was on the other side of this wall.

Undoing the tow rope that kept the charges together, I placed one of the polystyrene squares against the bricks, the base of the Toblerones facing the target, so the det tail dangled in front of me. Then, ramming the end of one of the wooden pallet slats into the snow at an angle, I used it to keep the foam square in position against the wall.

After a final check, I killed the torch and moved over to the nearest dish. I lifted one of its ice-hard sandbags and placed it halfway along the wall, using it to weigh down the free end of the main line. I then began the process of laying out the cord back towards the charge.

Once I reached the propped-up charge it was gloves-off time. Peeling one of the strips of tape from my forearm, I began to bind the det tail to the main line.

There was a sudden burst of loud music from an upstairs window around the back, stopping as abruptly as it had started. Through the rear windows I could hear various voices shouting. At least three different voices could be heard shouting back.

I began to unreel the rest of the main line round the back and over the satellite cable towards the gap between the two buildings. On the other side of the target house I knelt down and rigged up the second charge so that it was exactly facing the first. Once it was propped and checked, I began taping its det tail to the main line.

I went over to the generator cable hole and gently pulled out the det cord that ran into the fuel tank, taping it to the main line in the same way as I'd done with the other two.

I thought about Tom and hoped he wasn't standing too close to either of the walls.

I pulled the main line for the last few arm's lengths towards the front of the building. Now I just had to attach the electric detonator, which was already fixed to the firing cable, then unreel the cable round the corner and get down below the MTV window before the shit, and everything else in the building, hit the fan.

The main line stopped about six or seven paces short of the corner of the target. Great, at least the firing cable would be long enough for me to be well under the window.

As I gently pulled at the press studs holding the zip flap of my jacket to extract the firing cable, the volume of the music changed again. It was escaping outside. Then I heard the noise of the grille swinging open and the front door slamming shut.

I jammed my hand into my jacket pocket for the Makharov, as I moved towards the corner, taking deep breaths. There was torchlight ahead. I stopped, pushing my thumb down on the safety catch to ensure it was off.

A body appeared, heading towards me. He was looking down at where his torch beam hit the snow. It glinted off his weapon barrel.

I jumped onto him, wrapping my left arm around his neck and pushing the Makharov into his stomach. My legs wrapped around his waist, and as we fell together I pulled the trigger, hoping that our two bodies sandwiching the weapon would suppress its report. No chance. The job had just gone noisy.

Jumping to my feet, I sprinted round to the front of the house, focusing solely on the next corner, heading now for the other end of the main line, leaving a screaming Russian writhing in the snow.

As I neared the main entrance, I scrambled frantically with my left hand for the firing cable and det in my inside pocket.

The door opened, MTV still blasting, and a body, too small to be Tom, emerged. 'Gory? Gory?'

I raised my weapon and fired on the move. I couldn't miss.

I carried straight on past, turned the corner and dived towards the sandbag, dropping my weapon and desperately fishing for the main line coming from under the sandbag.

The wounded man's screams echoed around the compound. I tried to calm myself and slow my frenzied movements. I held the det onto the main line and wrapped a strip of tape around both.

I pulled out the battery and yanked the twisted end leads of the firing cable apart with my teeth. Then, falling to the floor, I squeezed my legs together, opened my jaw and buried my head in the snow as I pushed the two leads onto the terminals.

Less than a single heartbeat later the detonator exploded and initiated the main line. The shock wave of the explosion travelled along it, met the first det tail and then the one leading to the fuel tank. Then the second det tail got the good news.

The two wall charges exploded virtually simultaneously, and the resultant shock waves met in the middle of the room at a combined speed of 52,000 feet per second.

Fifteen

My whole world shuddered, trembled, quaked. It was like being inside a massive bell that had just been given an almighty bang.

The air was sucked from my lungs as hot air blasted over me. Around the compound snow and ice shot upwards a foot or so from the ground. My ears rang. Then the shock wave rebounded off the thick concrete perimeter walls and came back for more.

Crawling forward to the corner of the target, I watched, mesmerised, as an enormous fireball whooshed from the entrance of the generator building and leapt high into the sky. Thick black smoke mixed with bright orange flames. The entire area was bathed in light and I could feel the heat scorching my face.

Chunks of brick, glass and all kinds of other stuff that had been blown sky high started clattering around me. I threw my arms over my head to protect myself and kept close to the wall. The sandstorm of red brick dust had arrived, blanketing the compound; it was just a matter of hanging in there and waiting for the last of the fallout to rain down. I began coughing like a lifelong smoker.

The guy in the gap wasn't screaming any more, but he was still alive, coiled up and holding his stomach. I went over to where he lay trembling in the snow. I picked up his AK and threw it towards the main gate, out of his reach.

When the two shock waves from the opposing explosions had met, they would have wiped out everything in the computer room. The force would then have taken the line of least resistance to escape the confines of the building: the windows and doors. Surging along the hallways, it would have destroyed everything in its path.

The torchlight wasn't much good in the hallway; it just reflected off the wall of dust like a car's headlights in dense fog. I blundered around, stumbling over bricks and other debris, trying to find the gap to the right that would lead to the MTV room.

I found the door, or rather the place where it had been. As I moved through, my feet collided with sticks of furniture, then what was left of the television set and a whole lot more bricks. I could hear no other movement, no sounds of distress.

Tripping over a large bundle on the floor, I switched on my torch

and knelt down to check it. The body was on its side and smouldering, facing away from me. Rolling him towards me, I shone the light
into his dust-covered face. It wasn't Tom.

I continued across the room, kicking out and feeling like a blind
man as I searched for more bodies. There were two, but neither of
them was Tom.

I didn't bother with the computer room: even if there were any
bodies there, they wouldn't be recognisable.

I headed up the stairs. As I reached the top landing I heard a faint
cry. Feeling my way to a door, I pushed, but it wouldn't budge more
than four or five inches. Pushing harder, I got my foot round and
made contact with the body on the other side that was stopping it
going further. I squeezed through and checked. It was just another
poor bastard who wanted his mother.

I heard someone else moaning at my feet. Kneeling down, I got in
there with the torch and turned the body over.

It was Tom, red brick dust over his face and head, red snot running from his nose, but alive.

He was whimpering away in a world of his own. I checked him
over to make sure he had all his limbs. I brushed the crap from his
face so at least he could open his eyes at some stage, then I reached
under his armpits and dragged him out onto the landing.

Still gripping him, I went down the stairs backwards. His feet
bounced from step to step. He was out of it, still bound up in his
own little world of pain and confusion, aware that he was being
moved, but not really conscious enough to help.

We got clear of the brick dust and into the fresh air. I grabbed a
handful of snow and rubbed it over his face. Beginning to recover, he
coughed and spluttered but still couldn't speak.

The flames coming from the generator building illuminated us
quite clearly. Tom was wearing the same sweatshirt as when I last saw
him, but he had no shoes or coat.

I headed back into the dust-filled MTV room. The cries upstairs
were getting louder. I wanted to get away from here before they
sorted themselves out and the police arrived.

I found the first body again. He hadn't been wearing a coat, but it
was his footwear I was after. They weren't exactly walking boots,
more like basketball trainers, but they'd do. Fumbling around, I also
came across a coat among the shredded furniture.

Tom was lying spread-eagled on his back, exactly as I'd left him. I shook the dust out of what turned out to be a parka, and put it around him. The white trainers were about two sizes too big, but he only had to make it as far as the car.

As I began to pull them onto his feet he finally made a noise. He lifted a hand to wipe the shit from his face and saw me.

'Tom, it's Nick.' I shook his head. He would have been deafened by the explosion and I couldn't tell whether his hearing had come back yet. 'It's me—Nick. Get up, Tom. We have to get going.'

'Nick? What the hell are you doing here? What happened?'

I finished tying his laces and helped him up and into the parka. It was like dressing an exhausted child.

I went back to retrieve my gloves. I found them just feet away from the first man I'd shot, who was now clearly dead.

Tom had sat down again in the snow. I got him upright, then helped him move slowly to the gate leading to the hangar.

Turning left on the road, I checked for vehicle lights. I lengthened my stride, keeping a tight grip on Tom. His hearing had recovered a bit by the time we got to where I'd parked the car, but he still didn't know what day it was. Then I realised that the car had gone. My head spun. Maybe I had the wrong place? No, there were the tyre marks. There were other tyre marks, too, from a tractor. And besides my footprints a mass of others. The pub-quiz team must have had the car away. They hadn't even had to break into it, just hitch it up and slide the locked wheels across the ice.

'Tom, change of plan. Follow me.' I started to move down the road, putting distance between us and the target. Tom trailed slowly behind. We'd gone about 400 yards as I sorted out a plan, then stopped and checked for Polaris, the North Star.

As I gazed skyward, Tom muttered, 'It was a nightmare in there, but I knew Liv would get you to come—'

I cut in. 'That's right, Tom. Liv's your fairy godmother.' I didn't tell him what she had planned for midnight.

I confirmed the plan in my head. We'd head north and cross country until we hit the railway line. If we turned left along it we'd be facing west, towards Tallinn. Then we would follow the tracks to a station and catch a train, maybe the first one out of Narva. I wasn't sure, but I thought it left there at about eightish in the morning. So we'd need to be at a station about an hour after that.

According to the Lion King, we had the best part of fourteen hours in which to cover what I guessed would be about twelve miles.

Tom's voice came out of the darkness. 'Are they all dead? You know, that lot back there?'

'I think so. Most of them, anyway.'

His shoulders began to heave and I realised he was laughing. 'How did you know when to set the bomb off? I mean, I could have been killed if I hadn't been upstairs.' It was nervous laughter.

I looked up, searching for the North Star again so he couldn't see my face. 'You've no idea the trouble I went to, mate. Anyway, we'll talk about that later. We have to get a move on now.'

'How far, do you reckon?'

'Not far, Tom. Just a couple of hours. If we play our cards right, we'll be in a nice warm train carriage soon.' Why tell him the truth now? I hadn't bothered to so far. 'You ready then?'

'Yeah, I s'pose so.'

I started down the road and he followed. After a couple of hundred yards we hit a tree line, about fifteen yards off the road on our left. I headed for it. The snow was up to my knees and sometimes waist high.

Tom caught up and I allowed him a minute's rest before we moved on. I wanted to get out into the open fields before starting cross-country, following Polaris. That way we'd give the compound a wide berth as we had to head north, back towards it.

At the end of the tree line, visibility was about fifty yards in the starlight. The landscape was white, fading to black. In the middle distance to my half left I could see the dim glow of the target area. The best way forward seemed to be to keep my feet low and push through the snow. I became the icebreaker and Tom followed in my wake.

Clouds drifted across the sky, intermittently blotting out Polaris. All I could do was keep heading in what I thought was a straight line, only to find we were way off course when the cloud cleared.

I stopped when I found a natural dip and used my back to push a groove in the snow to get us out of the wind. I scraped a channel in the lip to act as my north marker before Polaris disappeared again.

Tom reached me as I dug myself in with my gloved hands. I expected him to follow my example, but when I turned he was having a piss, the steam and liquid disappearing almost immediately in the wind. He should have been retaining his warm body fluids at all costs, but I was too late. Tom was done, and putting his hands back in his pockets he turned and collapsed into the dip.

I slid into the dip beside him. 'Not long now, mate. It's a bit further than I thought, but we'll have a rest here. When you start to get cold, tell me and we'll get moving again, OK?'

The hood moved, which I took to be a nod. He brought his knees up to his chest and lowered his head to meet them.

As I was about to lie down in the dip, I saw Tom lifting some snow to his mouth. I put out a hand. 'That's off the menu, mate.'

I wasn't going to waste energy explaining why. Not only does it use up crucial body heat through melting in your mouth, it also cools the body from the inside, chilling the vital organs. Nevertheless, water *was* going to be a problem. I scooped up a handful of snow, but only passed it over when I'd I worked it into a compressed ball. 'Suck on that. Don't eat it, OK?'

I looked at the sky. The cloud cover was now more or less total.

Now that we'd cleared the danger area, it seemed the right time to ask him a question. I hoped it would help take his mind off the shit we were in. I also needed some answers.

'Why didn't you tell me you knew Valentin?'

'I'm sorry, mate,' he mumbled. 'She's got me by the bollocks.'

'You mean threats? Some kind of threat to you or your family?'

'Mum . . . Dad . . . and I've got a sister with kids, know what I mean? I wanted to tell you, Nick, honest I did, but . . . well, you know. Listen, it ain't Valentin doing this, mate. It's her; she's freelancing. He don't know a thing about it; she's just using his name, letting you think you're working for him.'

'How did you get sucked back into all this?'

'Liv. Well, not her to begin with, but this bloke—Ignaty—he came and saw me in London. The day before you did.'

Where had I heard that name before? Then I realised. It had been his name on the piece of paper in Narva.

'I'm sorry, Nick. I had to do it. She knows everybody's addresses and everything. The bloke showed me pictures of my sister's kids.'

Question after question leapt into my head, but the snowflakes hitting my face made me remember that there were more pressing matters to attend to. We had no shelter, no heat and now no navigation. We had to move, but the marker would only be good for a hundred yards or so; after that, without Polaris, we'd spend the rest of the night walking round in circles.

I looked at Tom shivering in almost uncontrollable bursts. In any other circumstances we should have been digging in for the night and riding out the storm, but we didn't have the luxury of time.

Quite apart from making it to a train, I didn't know what sort of follow-up the Maliskia would go for, and I didn't want to find out. Trying to think of a positive, I finally dredged one up: at least the snow would cover our trail.

Tom mumbled under his hood. 'I'm really cold, Nick.'

I put my arms around him. I felt his body stiffen.

'It's a snow thing,' I said. 'We've got to keep warm.'

He leaned in towards me, shivering. I looked up and saw nothing but blankets of white tumbling down at us out of the blackness. If I'd had access to a genie at that moment, the one thing I'd have wished for was a compass.

A compass! A compass can be made from any ferrous metal. Tom had a faceful of the stuff in the rim of his parka hood.

'Tom, are you still wearing those silk thermals?'

'Nah, just the top.'

I unwrapped my arm from him and removed my glove, holding it in my mouth while I pulled out the Leatherman. Opening the pliers, I put the glove back on before the skin of my hand was exposed for too long.

'Look at me for a sec, would you, mate.'

The parka hood came up. Feeling around the frozen ring of fur with my gloved hand, I located the wire, then trapped it in the jaws of the pliers and squeezed until I felt it give. Teasing apart the material I exposed the metal and pulled. I made another cut and put the two-inch strip inside my glove for safe keeping.

'I need some of that silk, Tom. Unzip your coat.'

His hands fumbled for the zip. I shoved both of my gloves between my teeth so I could help him, then, having battled with numb fingers to open the blade of the Leatherman, I felt under his shirt. I grabbed a handful of the silk vest and started cutting, pulling hard. I wanted to make sure the material ripped, so there were loose threads dangling. The knife made its final cut. I zipped him up.

I lay my gloves in the snow and crouched over to protect myself from the snowstorm. My hands were so numb that I had to pull threads from the silk with my teeth. Once I'd teased out a decent bit—about five inches long—I put it between my lips and fished out the needle-sized length of wire from my glove. Tying the loose end of the silk shakily around the middle of the metal, I finally managed a knot on the fourth attempt.

As I bit on the free end of silk thread with my teeth, it seemed to take for ever to grasp the dangling wire in one hand and the square of silk in the other. At last I began stroking the wire along the silk, repeating the motion over and over, always in the same direction. After about twenty strokes I stopped.

I fished in my pocket for the torch, switched it on and put it in my mouth. Still crouching over it to make sure the wind wouldn't affect the thread and needle, I let go and watched it spin. The short length of wire eventually steadied, just moving slightly from side to side. I knew the direction of the North Star from my snow marker, so all I had to do was identify which end of the wire, magnetised by the silk, was pointing north. I could tell the difference between the ends from the way the Leatherman had cut them.

I shivered and worked out what I was going to do next. I needed roads to make distance, and besides, if Tom started going down with hypothermia, we were more likely to find some form of shelter near a road. My new thought was to go west until we hit one, then head north for the rail track. I realised that the wind was doing its bit to help. It seemed to be prevailing from the west, so as long as I kept it in my face I would be heading the way I wanted.

THE GALE HAD BECOME a blizzard, bringing close to white-out conditions. I still led the way, breaking the trail as we vaguely zigzagged west, still hoping to hit a road. I was having to stop every ten or so paces to get another navigation fix, rubbing the needle again with the silk to reactivate the magnetic effect, and it allowed Tom to catch up. This time I watched him while I waited. I'd been so concerned about navigating that I hadn't noticed how much he was slowing down.

He got level with me as I was trying to stop the wind affecting the compass. I grabbed hold of his parka and pulled him to me, positioning him so he could give the compass some shelter, too.

'You OK, mate?'

He coughed and shivered. 'Yeah, but my legs are really cold, Nick. I can't feel my feet.'

'Just dig deep, mate. It's not going to kill us.' I was lying. 'We'll be on a road soon and the going will get much easier.'

We had a result about twenty minutes later. I couldn't see any tarmac, but I could make out the shape of tyre ruts under the newly fallen snow, and the fact that the snow suddenly wasn't as deep as everywhere else. It was a single-track road.

We started to make distance, huddling together at junctions to protect the compass. Whether a road ran northeast, northwest or even due west, we took it. Anything to get us in the general direction of Tallinn and the rail track.

After about three hours Tom had slowed down dramatically. The fight through the snow and the extreme cold had definitely got to him and he couldn't stop shivering.

He pleaded with me. 'I've had it, Nick. Everything's spinning around me, mate. Please, we have to stop.'

The wind whipped the snow against our faces.

'Tom, look at me!' I pulled his chin up. 'We must keep going. You understand, don't you?' I tried to get eye-to-eye. But it was too dark.

It was pointless trying to get any sense out of him. We were wasting time and losing what little heat we had by just standing still. There was nothing I could do to help him here and now. Our best bet was to get to the railway track and make the final push to a station. I'd know when he'd finally had enough, and that would be the time to stop and take some action.

I grasped his arm and pulled him along. When I stopped to check direction, Tom couldn't help me any more; he just stood on the spot, swaying, as I turned my back to the wind, trying to create shelter for the compass. When I'd finished and turned for him he'd collapsed in the snow. I got him to his feet and dragged him on.

Now and again he would shout out and summon up a burst of energy. It didn't last long before he slowed down or fell back into the snow. His voice had become a whine as he begged to be left where he was, pleading with me to let him sleep. He was in the late stages of hypothermia and I should be doing something about it. But what, and where? I felt sorry for him, but we couldn't rest now. If we stopped for even a few minutes we might not restart.

It was about fifteen minutes later that we stumbled onto the railway line. We'd reached a level crossing and I had tripped over one of the tracks.

I shook him. 'We're here, Tom. We're here.'

No reaction whatsoever. He collapsed on the crossing. I bent down and got my hands under his armpits, heaving him up again. He couldn't control his mouth or teeth and began to make strange snorting noises.

'We have to keep going just a bit further,' I shouted into his ear. 'We have to find a station.' I didn't know any more whether it was him or myself I was talking to.

WE STAGGERED WEST, over the snow-covered hard core at the side of the track. At least the trees on either side gave us some protection from the howling wind. Tom started to go crazy, screaming at the trees, crying, apologising to them, only to fall down again and try to cuddle up in the snow. Each time, I had to pick him up and push on, and each time it got a little bit harder.

We came across a row of small sheds, visible only because of the flatness of the snow on top of their angled roofs. We still couldn't see further than about five yards and I didn't notice them until we were right on top of them.

I fumbled excitedly for the torch, leaving Tom on his knees, shouting at the trees that were coming to get him.

I shone the light around and saw that the sheds were made of wood and built in the form of a terrace, the door of each facing onto the track. Most were clamped shut with old rusty padlocks, but one was unlocked. After kicking the snow away, I pulled it open and turned round for Tom.

He was curled up in the snow on the track.

As I gathered him in my arms, he lashed out with his final reserves of strength. He was having a fit. It was pointless struggling with him; I simply didn't have the energy. I let him drop to the ground and, gripping his hood with both hands, pulled him along like a sledge.

The door was so low that I had to bend down to get in, and the roof wasn't much higher, but the instant I was out of the wind I began to feel warmer. The shed was about eight feet square, and the frozen mud floor was cluttered with bits of wood and brick, old tools and a rusted shovel.

Tom just lay where I dropped him. I put the torch down to give me some light, got my gloves off and dragged over a lump of wood. I then tried to pull out the blade of my Leatherman with shaking hands. Once my soaking gloves were back on I started to scrape at the edge of the wood. I wanted to get to the dry stuff underneath. Then I started to scrape thin shavings onto the shovel face.

Next task was to cut kindling, a stage up from the tinder. I picked up any sticks of wood I could find, then I started to make fire sticks, cutting very thinly into the side of the wood and pushing out the shavings until each piece looked as if it had grown feathers.

Once I'd prepared about five fire sticks I stacked them around the tinder like tepee poles. Then I got out my pistol, taking off the magazine and pulling the topslide to eject the round in the chamber.

Using the pliers of the Leatherman, I pulled the heads off the three rounds and poured the dark grain propellant onto the tinder. I left the third round half full of propellant.

Tom's body had started jerking around in the corner of the hut. His frenzied movements had dislodged his hood. Placing the round carefully on the ground so I wouldn't lose its contents, I got up and crawled over to him. I took hold of his hood and tried to pull it back on. He lashed out with his arms, shrieking stuff I couldn't understand, his hands flailing around.

'It's all right, mate,' I soothed. 'Not long now.' But I was wasting time here. It was heat he needed, not bullshit.

Crawling back to the shovel, I dug inside my glove for the compass silk, held it in my teeth and cut some off with my Leatherman scissors. Then, using the screwdriver, I rammed the cut silk into the half-empty case as wadding on top of the propellant.

I loaded the round into the weapon, pointed it at the ground, and fired. The signature was a dull *oomph*.

There was no reaction from Tom as I knelt on the ground to pick up a glowing, smouldering bit of silk. Once it was in my fingers I waved it about gently to fan the glow, then put it into the tinder. The propellant flared, lighting up the whole hut.

Once the tinder had caught, I started inserting more little bits through the fire sticks into the flame. I got in close and blew gently. The fire sticks started to crackle and hiss as they released their moisture and smoke. I fussed around the flames on my hands and knees, carefully placing wood as the hut filled with smoke.

The flames were now higher. I gathered up as much wood as possible from what was to hand. Once I'd established the fire, I'd be able to venture outside into the howling wind for more.

I kicked the door open slightly to get rid of the smoke. It let some of the wind and snow whistle in, but it had to be done. I'd block up most of the gap as soon as I could.

Tom was much quieter. I crawled over to him, coughing smoke from my lungs. I wanted to see if there was any wood under him. There was; only a few bits and pieces, but it all helped.

I checked the flames and started to feed on some more wood. 'Not long now, mate. We'll be getting our kit off in a minute because we're so hot.'

My next priority would be a hot drink, to get some heat directly to Tom's core. Placing the rest of the wood near the fire to dry it out, I turned and looked at his face. 'Tom, I'm just going to see if I can find something to heat snow in for a—'

He was lying too still. There was something very odd about the way his legs had now curled up to his chest.

'Tom?'

I crawled back to him, pulling him over and getting the hood off his face. Illuminated by the flames it told me all I needed to know. Tilting his head towards the fire, I pulled open his eyelids. There was no reaction to the light. Both pupils stayed fully dilated. It wouldn't be long now before they clouded up.

I could hear the fire sticks collapsing on each other, with glowing embers as well as flame. It was a wonderful sight, but it was too late.

I tried his carotid pulse. Nothing. But that could be just my numb fingers. I listened for breathing and even tried his heart. Nothing. His mouth was still open from when he had taken, or fought for, his last breath. I gently closed his jaw.

It was time to think about me. Pulling off my wet clothes, I wrung them out one by one before putting them back on.

I fed the flames some more, knowing there were still things that I should do to him. I should try to resuscitate and reheat him until I was so exhausted I couldn't carry on, in the million-to-one chance he could be revived. But for what? I knew he was dead.

Maybe if we'd dug in for the night once the weather had closed in he would still be alive. We would have been in a desperate state in the morning, but maybe he would have survived. Maybe if I hadn't pushed him so hard to get here, or had realised what condition he was in and had stopped earlier. All these questions, and the only thing I was certain of was that I had killed him.

I looked at his limp body, his mouth reopened, his long hair wet against his cheeks, the ice crystals now melting down his face. I'd try to remember a gobby but happy Tom, but I knew this image was the one that would stay with me.

Dragging him to the doorway, I sat him up against the gap, leaving a space of a foot or so above him for the smoke to escape. I covered his face with his parka.

Feeling was already starting to come back to my extremities and I knew I was going to be OK. All I had to do was find a station.

I turned back to the flames and watched the steam rise from my drying clothes. There would be no sleep for me tonight. I had to keep the fire going.

Sixteen

LONDON, ENGLAND. Wednesday, January 5, 2000. I was nursing a hot, frothy coffee in the church doorway opposite the Langham Hilton, the only place I could keep a trigger on the hotel and also keep out of the drizzle.

It was breakfast time, and the pavements were packed with over-coated wage slaves and shoppers out early for the sales. I'd seen in the new year aboard an Estonian fishing boat, along with twenty-six cold and seasick illegals from Somalia. Slipping away from a seaside village under cover of darkness, we'd battled across the Baltic in huge seas, heading for a peninsula east of Helsinki.

It was eighteen days since I'd left the hut and set off again into the blizzard. Tom had stayed behind, his body sterile of any item that could ID him. They probably wouldn't find him before the spring.

At first light, and without Tom, I was able to make distance at my own pace, even in the driving snow, and it was only a couple of hours before I hit a station.

A train arrived heading west, towards Tallinn, but I let it go without me. The one after that was heading east, towards Russia, and I climbed aboard. Without a passport it could take weeks to get out of Estonia on my own, but with Eight helping me, maybe it would be a different story. That was why I jumped off at Narva, and that was how I'd ended up on the fishing boat with my new Somalian friends. It had cost me all the dollars in my boot and had meant spending several uncomfortable days and nights hiding in the apartment with the land mines while Eight got things arranged, but it had been worth it.

Eight wasn't too happy about his car becoming history, but he still seemed thrilled to help me, even though he must have been aware of what had happened to Carpenter and the old guy in Voka. He didn't ask me again about helping him to escape to England, but as I stood on the jetty waiting to board the fishing boat, I handed him Tom's passport. From the expression on his face and the tears in his eyes, you'd have thought I'd given him the $3 million.

I knew I was taking a big risk, but I felt I owed him that much. I just hoped he did a good job of doctoring Tom's picture, or that the day he tried to use it immigration weren't checking their computer screens too closely. Otherwise poor Eight would find himself being lifted by a team of heavies and whisked off to a three by nine.

I'd told myself that the passport was part of what I owed him for his help. I knew it was more to do with trying to get over my guilt about Tom. Giving Eight the possibility of a new life was an attempt to make things right.

AT FIRST I THOUGHT it had worked and that things were all right. But I knew they weren't, not with Tom, not with Kelly. She was much the same. I'd phoned the clinic twice since I'd got back. I'd lied both times, telling them I was overseas but would be back soon. I was desperate to see her, but I knew I wasn't going to be able to look her in the eye. Hughes picked up the phone the second time and told me that her plans for Kelly's therapy sessions, which included me, would have to stay on hold until I got back. I still felt confused about it. I knew it had to be done, and I wanted to do it, but . . .

To add to the confusion, I'd also had a call from Lynn. He wanted to see me this afternoon. There seemed to have been a change of heart since our last meeting. He said he had a month's work for me. I'd been tempted to tell him where he could shove his £290 a day, because if all went well with Liv this morning I'd never have to depend on the Firm again. But there was no guarantee that she was going to appear, and though a month's pay wasn't much, at least I would be working instead of thinking.

The exchange was going to be simple. I'd opened a bank account in Luxembourg by telephone as soon as I returned to the UK. The message I'd left Liv in the Helsinki dead letterbox was that she'd be required to move the money electronically. When we met in the hotel in a few minutes' time, she would call her bank with the transfer instructions I would give her, and then we'd both just sit and wait until it happened.

TWENTY MINUTES before the RV time, a taxi pulled up at the hotel's main entrance.

As I watched, the doorman stepped forward and opened the cab door, and I saw the back of Liv's head as she got out and went inside. We had the taxi between us, but I could see she had decided on the jeans today, and her long leather coat, collar up against the cold.

I let her go in and watched for any surveillance or another vehicle pulling up shortly afterwards. Neither happened.

The $3 million was now so close I could almost smell it. As soon as the transfer was confirmed, I'd call the clinic and tell them that Kelly's new treatment could start straight away. It still worried me a bit, but I'd just have to get on with it. Who knows, I might even sort myself out.

Ten minutes to go now. She still had to unload the dead letterbox under the telephone, which held the keycard for the suite I'd booked.

With just two minutes to go, I dodged the traffic and approached the hotel. I pushed past the revolving doors and took the stairs. I climbed to the third floor, opening my leather jacket and checking the position of the USP, tucked centre-front of my jeans; I'd gone back to Norfolk last night specifically to pick up a weapon.

Outside the door of room 316 I stopped and listened. Nothing. I pushed my own keycard into the lock and opened the door.

She was at the far end of the living room, her back to me, looking out of the windows that overlooked the main entrance. The door closed behind me with a gentle click.

'Hello, Liv, it's really good to—'

I went to open my coat to draw down, but knew it was useless. The overcoated body that had moved out from behind the cabinet housing the TV and minibar already had his pistol on me. The other body that sprang from the toilet to my left was no more than four feet away, his weapon at my head.

I released my grip on the leather and let my arms drop.

Liv turned towards me, only it wasn't her.

She spoke in a soft accent that I couldn't identify. 'Step forward and keep your hands high in the air, please.'

I did as I was told. The toilet man moved behind me and started to run his hands over my back and legs. As he removed my USP I couldn't exactly claim I was just delivering room service.

I was pushed from behind towards the settee.

The woman swept past and headed for the door to the corridor. Her blonde hair was dyed; I could see her brown eyebrows.

As she opened the door I could see another overcoated man outside. She left and he came in. He'd been there to block the exit if anything went wrong. It wouldn't have been hard for him to stop me. He more or less matched the dimensions of the door.

Nothing was said as I sat and waited. For what? I remembered Sergei's face when he told me about the Viking's revenge. The pulses in my neck kicked up a gear and I could feel them pumping against my collar. The human door, who was still standing by the real one, must have seen it and recognised the feeling, because he gave me a knowing smile. I did my best to return it. I wasn't going to let them see how much I was flapping inside.

Long minutes that felt like eternity passed, then there was a knock. The human door looked through the peephole, immediately reached for the handle, then stepped reverentially aside.

'Hello, Nick,' Val said as he entered. With him was Liv's train-station contact. They both wore grey suits. 'May I introduce Ignaty?'

Ignaty smiled and bowed his head slightly towards me. 'Hello, Nick. Knowing so much about you, I feel as if we are old friends.'

I nodded back. My best bet was to shut up and play stupid.

Val sat on the settee opposite, while Ignaty stayed on his feet. The Chechen placed a large white envelope on the coffee table that lay between us. He pointed. 'That is for you.'

I reached for it and pulled open the flap. Inside was a sheaf of documents in Cyrillic.

'They are deeds for two apartment blocks in St Petersburg,' he said. 'Their combined worth exceeds three million sterling. I thought you'd prefer an appreciating asset to cash.'

'I'd rather have the cash. That was the arrangement.'

He shook his head. 'But, Nick, there was no arrangement. Liv has been deceiving us both in pursuit of her own greed. Thankfully some are not as disloyal.' He waved his hand behind him.

Ignaty looked smug. 'It is quite complicated, Nick, and you don't need to know the details. Suffice to say, she has now made it virtu-ally impossible for me to access Echelon. The only reason you are still alive is that you thought you were acting on my instructions. Come, work for me in Russia and you can then take advantage of your new property portfolio. The rents are extremely high in that part of the city.'

I shook my head. 'I have things that keep me here.' I hesitated. 'I really could do with the money instead.'

He pointed to the envelope still in my hand as if I hadn't even spoken. 'In there are the details of a contact, here in the United Kingdom, when you wish to come to Russia.'

He stood up, and everyone moved with him.

I had to ask. 'How did you know I was here?'

Val stopped. 'Liv told me, of course. She told me everything.' He paused. 'Before Ignaty . . .' He shrugged.

I bluffed it and looked confused, but in my mind's eye I saw her belly slit open and the eels writhing all around her.

'I hope to see you in St Petersburg soon, Nick.'

As he turned to leave, I said, 'Can I ask one more thing?'

He stopped.

'There's a body. My friend. It's still in Estonia and . . .'

'Of course, of course. We are not barbarians.' Val waved a hand at the envelope. 'The contact. Give him the details.'

I GAVE VAL and his boys twenty minutes before walking downstairs and out of the hotel. Then I went into a phone box and fed in a fist-ful of coins as I picked up the receiver.

'Hello, East Anglian Properties. How may I help you?'

'James Main?'

'Speaking.'

'Nick Stone here. Slight change of plan, James. I want you to sell the house straight away, for anything you can get.'

'But all the offers so far have been well below your purchase price. You'd do much better if you got the roof finished.'

'James?'

'Yes?'

'Which bit of straight away don't you understand?'

I only had to put a twenty-pence piece in for the second call.

'Still abroad, I'm afraid,' I said when I was finally put through to Hughes. 'Looks like I'm going to have to stay here for another month. What effect would that have on Kelly?'

'Well, she won't get any worse, let's put it that way. She'll stay more or less as she is until you can start the sessions with her.'

I closed my eyes and tried so hard to see her smiling, but the only image that came to me was of her on that chair, her head strangely tilted, and sitting so still it was as if she'd stopped breathing, or had been frozen to death in an invisible blizzard.

THE SAME ASIAN GUY ushered me into Lynn's office. Nothing had changed apart from the fact that Lynn had a different shirt on and wasn't writing this time.

'Moonlight Maze,' he said. 'Do you know anything about it?'

'No.' I felt a sharp pain in my chest. He knew what I had been doing. I had to play along. 'Well, not really. Only what I read in the papers a couple of weeks ago.'

'That's about to change. Your job is to assist an NSA officer and his team while in the UK. They will be here for about a month, trying to stop this damned ROC infiltration into Menwith.'

I nodded, as if I assumed it would be a boring bodyguard-cum-escort-cum-tour-guide job, which these things normally are. But I still had the feeling he was playing games with me. 'Why me, Mr Lynn? You said before Christmas that—'

'It has been deemed that the cost of your training and retainer is not being effectively utilised. Now get out.'

I didn't know how he did it, but the door behind me was opened by the Asian guy right on cue. 'Please, sir, follow me.'

I did, and we went up two flights in the lift to the briefing area and into a sparsely furnished office. There were no windows.

'If you wait here, sir, the officer will be with you shortly.'

The door closed behind me. I flapped. I was being set up.

As it opened again, I turned to face the person walking in. My chest pain returned with a vengeance. I had screwed up big time.

'Nick Stone, right?' The Democrat was smiling at me as he held out his hand. His face looked like I'd gone at him with a pastry cutter. The bright-red, scabby scars around his face were held together with black sutures, along with patches of his scalp, where his hair had been shaved before the wounds were treated. His hands were in a bad state, too, but they were all healing nicely.

'There isn't much time, Nick. Me and the team are going to need a lot of help here.' He saw me looking at his scars and dropped the smile. 'Hey, I know. Not good. If I ever find the son of a bitch that did this, I'm gonna be pulling the ring back on one big can of kick-ass . . .'

ANDY McNAB

Realism is the hallmark of Andy McNab's novels, no doubt because in many ways they are inspired by actual experiences. *Firewall*, like his two previous novels featuring Nick Stone, *Remote Control* and *Crisis Four*, draws heavily on knowledge he gained during his years as a soldier. While the techniques and skills he describes in the books are factual, however, the actual events and the character of his hero are the fruits of his vivid imagination. 'The way Nick Stone thinks and the tactical way he deals with situations are based on me, but his emotional character is based on several people,' says McNab. 'I want him to develop and grow as the books go on.'

The book which first catapulted McNab to fame was *Bravo Two Zero*, an account of his extraordinary experiences with the SAS behind Iraqi lines during the Gulf War. He first applied to join the SAS when he was based in England during the Falklands War and realised that he would not be going to the South Atlantic. 'I thought that I'd like to be in the war because that's what soldiers do. And I also thought, Well, when these things happen the SAS are always involved, so if I join them, next time I stand a better chance of going.'

Awarded both the Distinguished Conduct Medal and the Military Medal during his military career, McNab was the British Army's most highly decorated serving soldier when he finally left the SAS in 1993.

He does not miss the army—for one thing, he always knew it was not going to be a career for life. Perhaps, strangely, what he found most difficult in civilian life was that, compared to the mutual trust which is absolutely essential in the armed forces, the outside world was a bit of a 'shark pool'. Nowadays, as well as writing a string of best-selling novels, McNab lectures to security agencies on both sides of the Atlantic.

My Mother's Daughter

JUDITH
HENRY WALL

Ever since we were children, my brother
Buddy and I always wondered what had
suddenly happened to our family. We
seemed to have disappointed our mother in
some deep, profound way. Why did she sigh
so sadly? How had her heart been broken?
When eventually I heard her story, I
began to understand.

Cissy

*My brother, Buddy, never stopped wondering about our birth parents.
He was certain that finding out who they were would give us essential
knowledge about ourselves and somehow change our lives for the better.
We would be happier, more confident. We would have a heritage and
lineage. We would be more comfortable with ourselves. Who were those
other parents, and why had they given us away? Would we ever meet
them? Did they think about us?*

*For many years I wondered along with my brother, who was older
than me by a year and a half. The romance and mystery of birth
parents gave Buddy and me endless hours of shared longing and speculation, mostly spent on a dusty old mattress we'd dragged in front of
the round attic window.*

*When our cousin, Iris, was with us, we would focus instead on the
comings and goings of the neighbours who lived on our tree-lined
street. But when it was just Buddy and me, we focused on mythical,
what-if worlds—on the places where birth parents might dwell.*

*Sometimes we imagined them together, but mostly we dealt with our
birth parents separately, reasoning that a couple who had given away
their children would not still be together. Buddy conjured up scenarios
with our father an undercover CIA agent in Russia or falsely accused
of a crime and locked away in prison. Usually, however, we thought of
him as dead. It was tidier that way. He might have been killed in Korea.
Or swept out to sea during a hurricane. I preferred a scenario in which*

he was killed in a fiery car crash as he raced to be with our mother the night I was born.

Mostly, though, we daydreamed about the woman who had given us birth and tried to find excuses for her. Death worked well here, too. Maybe she had wanted to keep us but died giving me birth. I imagined a woman who looked like Audrey Hepburn, kissing us goodbye and promising to watch over us from heaven. I would cry unashamed tears, seeing all this unfold in my mind's eye. She was young and beautiful, her dark hair spread on a white pillow.

Or maybe she was still alive but suffered from amnesia. Someday she might remember that she was the mother of two children and hire a private detective to find us. She might even be a grand duchess, with Buddy heir to a defunct Russian throne.

At times, I could close my eyes and actually feel our birth mother's presence. She smelt of flowers. Her caress was gentle and her voice sweet. The longing that filled my young breast was quite real.

Of course, up there in the little attic alcove, I felt disloyal succumbing to birth mother daydreams. Our adoptive mother worked very hard at motherhood. She was always saying how lucky she was to have us for her very own children.

Our daddy probably would have understood our need for birth parent daydreams, but Mama would have been hurt. She had earned the right to be first and foremost in our affection. And in my heart I knew our birth mother was probably just some poor, ignorant girl who hadn't the means or courage to raise her own children.

As the years went by, I came to realise that the happiness we yearned for would not come from finding an angelic birth mother but in pleasing the complex woman who was raising us. We seemed to have disappointed her in some profound way. Why did Mama sigh? Had her heart broken when she realised she'd never have children of her own? Or maybe the fear that our aunt, Justine, would swoop into town and reclaim Iris stole away her laughter.

Buddy and I had always known that Iris was the beloved one. Iris was the daughter of our mother's sister and therefore related by blood—not a daughter, but the closest thing our mother would ever have to a blood child. We accepted Iris's special status as rightful. After all, Buddy and I loved her, too. From earliest memory, Iris had been the centre of our lives. She spread joy in her wake. She made our mother happy in a way Buddy and I never could. And more than anything, we wanted our mother to be happy.

One

July 1945—Justine was coming home!

Martha Claire paused in her weeding and sat back on her haunches to relish the thought. At this very minute her sister was on a ship crossing the Atlantic Ocean.

And surely before the year was out, Grayson also would come back to her. Her life could begin anew.

She rubbed at the small of her back before returning to her task. Whether Justine noticed it or not, when she came down the front walk for the first time in two and a half years, she was going to be greeted by a perfectly manicured yard. And inside, the house was well on its way to being spotless. Daddy was putting down new linoleum in the kitchen. Mother had re-covered the seats of the dining-room chairs. Justine's bedroom was freshly painted.

Yesterday Martha Claire had gone across the river to pick wild blackberries so Granny Grace could put up Justine's favourite preserves. Granny Grace already had rows of spiced peaches and pickled okra on the pantry shelf, waiting for her granddaughter's homecoming. Martha Claire would help her grandmother and mother prepare all of Justine's favourite food. Nothing boiled, Justine had written. She was sick of boiled food. And please have a watermelon chilled. She hadn't tasted watermelon for two summers.

Martha Claire decided to cut back the petunias, which had become leggy. The lantanas and periwinkles were in full bloom, though. Across the yard the magnolia tree was laden with huge waxy blossoms, and the freshly painted picket fence around Mother's rose garden shimmered whitely in the sunshine. It was a beautiful yard— one of the finest in Columbus, Texas, as was the house, which had been built by Martha Claire's great-great-grandfather. Had Justine missed it? Martha Claire wondered as she surveyed their childhood home—the place she herself loved best on earth.

What letters her sister had found time to write described the wonder of being in London, of doing her small part for the war effort. If she wrote about the war itself, it was only to complain about the hours spent in bomb shelters. Only at the end would she dash off a few words about missing her family back home.

Grayson's letters, on the other hand, had been mostly about missing her, words Martha Claire read over and over again.

Now that the war was over, however, her husband's letters were more about human tragedy than longing. His unit was involved in the repatriation of prisoners liberated from the concentration camp at Dachau. He was overwhelmed with the horror he found there, overwhelmed with the task at hand but dedicated to it—passionately so. He did not know when he was coming home. Martha Claire tried not to be resentful. She had seen pictures of those poor souls in the newsreels—living skeletons with empty eyes. But her husband had been gone for three endless years, and his father wasn't well. It was time for Grayson to take over the family store, time for him to make a home with his wife and put the war behind him.

Martha Claire wondered what Justine planned to do now that the war was over. Their parents hoped their younger daughter would settle in Columbus or at least someplace not too far away. That's what Martha Claire wanted, too, her sister close by—if not in Columbus, then no further away than Houston, where Justine had worked in a photography studio before enlisting in the Women's Army Corps. Martha Claire had missed her sister as much as she had missed her husband, in some ways more. She was always thinking of things she wanted to tell Justine.

Her body longed for her husband, but she had a hard time imagining conversations with him. Grayson was only a year older than she was, but she felt as though she had been frozen in time while he had grown older. And sadder. More serious.

Martha Claire had been Grayson's wife for three years and one month, but she still lived with her parents. The only time she had shared a bed with her husband had been on their honeymoon and the few weekends they had together before he shipped out.

But surely by next summer she would have her own house and garden, she told herself as she returned to her weeding. And a baby on the way. Oh, yes, definitely a baby on the way.

THE PORTER SHOOK Justine's arm. 'Wake up, miss. Next stop's Columbus.'

Justine struggled to an upright position, her muscles stiff, her stomach churning. Grandpa Mayfield would say she wasn't worth shooting. Her grandpa had died while she was away, she reminded herself. He would not be at the station with the others. Someone else was living in the little house where her daddy had been raised. Granny Grace was the only grandparent she had left.

She sagged back against the seat. She had envisioned a different sort of homecoming, with her smiling and smart in her uniform as she stepped down from the train—not sick and scared, with her future in jeopardy.

On the ship she had tried to convince herself she was suffering from seasickness. And the crossing had been a rough one. Of course, the seas had also been rough two and a half years ago, when Justine made the crossing from New York to Dover as a member of the Women's Army Corps with orders for London, where she would serve as a filing clerk in a military police command. She hadn't been sick then, just scared to death of German submarines.

The cramped quarters she had recently shared with three other WACs were far below deck—in the deepest bowels of the ship, where claustrophobia was at its worst. Justine wondered if any holdout submarines with swastikas on their sides were still swimming around out there, if she could even muster the strength to make it topside to a lifeboat should the ship founder. By the third day, however, she wouldn't have minded going down with the ship. Nothing she ate or drank stayed down. She would retch so hard it felt as though she were turning inside out. When the nausea receded, she would crawl inside a cocoon of semiconsciousness. The third or fourth day out, her darling Billy was inside the cocoon, waiting for her.

She knew he was a hallucination, brought on by serious dehydration and by fear of what awaited her at the end of the voyage. But she needed the comfort of his presence. Billy Baker from Brisbane. An RAF tail gunner. She had called him her Billy Boy. Just a wartime romance. She wasn't about to fall in love with anyone, much less a boy with the life expectancy of a gnat.

Except as the tide of war began to change, she had begun to think that Billy just might make it through, that he just might be alive to celebrate the armistice with her and to wonder what they would mean to each other in a world where there was no war.

In the cave of her bunk bed she would close her eyes and drift with Billy, back to their favourite pub, the Toad in the Hole, in London's West End. At the corner table grizzly old Hugh played the harmonica: 'As Time Goes By', 'Chattanooga Choo Choo', 'Baby Face', 'Danny Boy'. Billy knew the words to all of Hugh's songs, which he sang in a haunting tenor voice, and his laugh was infectious, his grin adorable, his dart game legendary. Maybe a bomb would fall on them tonight, but for now they were absolutely *alive*.

When the air-raid sirens began to wail, they would race towards the Baker Street tube. That last night he grabbed her arm and there in the middle of the pavement drew her into his arms. She could feel his heart pounding, the shock waves from exploding bombs travelling up her legs. The air was filled with the pandemonium of fire sirens, women calling frantically to children. Billy held her so tightly, she could barely breathe. And they kissed. God, how they kissed.

Later, in the belly of a troopship that was transporting Justine to the rest of her life, Billy was with her again—at least a vision of him. And she was grateful. Sometimes she was aware of the other women yelling at her to shut up while she sang pub songs with him and told him that she loved him and that she was sorry she'd never said the words before. She should have that night in London when he'd kissed her in the street. She should have said them then, because she had felt them. All the way to her toes she had felt them.

The last morning of the voyage Justine put on her uniform and walked up the narrow steps to the deck. Under the benign eyes of the Statue of Liberty she filled her lungs with fresh air for the first time in seven days. But as they docked, she was heaving again, leaning over the rail. As she retched, she prayed that it would dislodge the tiny spark of life that had taken up residence inside her and send it floating away to its doom.

In Grand Central Terminal, she sent a telegram to her parents, then sat on her duffle bag and thought of her hometown. She conjured up images of the meandering river that wrapped itself around the north half of the town and of the domed courthouse surrounded by a handsome iron fence. But the fence was gone. Her mother had written that the town donated it to the war effort. Most of Columbus's iron fences had been donated, including the one around the family home on Milam Street.

She thought of her room at the top of the stairs, imagined herself in her bed with smooth white sheets, her mother's cool hand on her forehead. She wanted to go home. But she could not stay. Columbus was her past, not her future. Better to have been killed by a bomb in London than to endure stagnation in a backwater Texas town, no matter how much she loved the people there.

When her train was announced, she climbed on board. The train had been full of returning servicemen, with some passengers forced to sit on luggage stacked in the vestibules. The elderly porter had taken one look at Justine and managed to secure a seat for her.

Now her journey was almost over. She was only minutes from home after being away for a lifetime.

She stumbled into the ladies' lounge to splash water on her face. The reflection in the mirror was ghastly. Her hair was matted, her skin ashen. Her uniform hung on her body like a sack.

She returned to her seat and stared out of the window as the train rolled into town. She could see the roof of the opera house. The station was just ahead. She was *home*.

She could see her family standing on the platform—Mother, Daddy, Martha Claire and Granny Grace—dressed in their Sunday best, their faces anxious and excited as they looked for her in the passing windows. She drew back, not wanting them to see her just yet. Her heart swelled painfully. She did love them. She would always love them, always come back to them.

She collected her things and made her way off the train. Martha Claire arrived first. Her sister. The other half of herself. Her lovely face was registering shock. 'Justine, what happened to you?'

Justine could tell how wasted she was by the feel of her sister's arms around her body and by her daddy's arms engulfing her.

Then her mother took Justine's face between her hands. 'Oh, Justine, what have you done to yourself?' Polly asked. Her arms came around her daughter. Justine leaned into her mother's embrace. She had travelled miles for this moment. 'We'll work it out, my darling,' her mother whispered. 'Somehow we'll work it out.'

POLLY MAYFIELD sat on the side of her daughter's bed and took Justine's hand. 'Feeling better?'

Justine nodded.

She did look better, Polly thought, now that she'd had a bath and slept most of the day. But dark circles rimmed her eyes and her cheeks were as white as her nightgown. Doc Hadley had checked her over and said not to worry. She needed rest.

'Then we'd better discuss what to do,' Polly said, looking down at Justine's ringless fingers. 'I don't suppose you're married?'

Justine rolled her head back and forth on the pillow. No, she wasn't married.

'And no man is going to make an honest woman of you?'

Once again Justine rolled her head.

'And your young man is dead.'

Justine propped herself up on an elbow. 'What young man?'

'The one who flew with the Royal Air Force.'

'How do you know about him?' Justine asked.

'You mentioned him in a letter about six months back. You apologised for not writing and said you'd been sad because a friend in the RAF had been shot down and was killed. You never mentioned him again. Did you love him, Justine?'

Justine fell back on her pillow. 'I don't know. Maybe. It hurt when he was killed. A lot.'

'And then you found someone else?'

'Not someone to love,' Justine said quietly. Then turning her face to the wall, she said, 'I'm sorry, Mother. Don't hate me.'

Polly stroked Justine's shoulders and back, telling her that she could never hate her own daughter, that she would always love her no matter what.

How could this have happened? Polly wondered. She had always assumed that neither one of her daughters would ever disgrace the family in this manner. Martha Claire was the sort of romantic girl who saved herself for marriage. Justine was simply not interested in boys, except as pals. Polly would like to know what happened. Had her daughter's grief over the death of the young airman left her vulnerable? Or had Justine, who had always taken every dare, simply thrown caution to the wind? Polly doubted if she would ever know.

Enough of pondering, though, she decided, adjusting the pillow behind Justine's head. The unthinkable had happened to her daughter, and she had to figure out some way to deal with it. 'Does this man know he is going to be a father?' she asked.

Justine's chapped lips formed the word no.

'Don't you want to give him a chance to do the right thing?'

Justine closed her eyes. 'No,' she whispered.

'He's married, then?'

Justine sighed but didn't answer.

Polly cleared her throat and said the words she had been composing in her mind. 'I have decided that you are married, Justine—to a British soldier you met during the victory celebration when everyone was dancing in the streets and kissing everyone in sight. It was a whirlwind courtship, and you had a simple wedding in a country church with only the minister's wife in attendance. Just weeks later the poor boy was killed trying to defuse one of those undetonated

German bombs still scattered about London. Your husband was an only child, and his parents were killed in the Blitz, so you have no remaining ties with England. You'll have to decide on a last name— for you and the baby.'

Justine struggled to sit up, an astounded look on her face. 'Mother, no one is going to believe a story like that. I would have written to you if I'd gotten married. You would have told the neighbours and put an announcement in the newspaper.'

'It all happened so fast, and then he was dead,' Polly went on, honing her story. 'You had to deal with your grief before you told anyone, and by then you realised you were in the family way. Doc Hadley said he'll put whatever name you want on the birth certificate. You have to think of what's best for the child, Justine. It's better to have a father's name, even if it's a made-up one.'

'What about what is best for me?' Justine demanded.

'And what might that be?'

'Not to have a baby at all.' Justine's chin was lifted in defiance.

'It's a little late for that,' Polly said, smoothing back her daughter's hair—fair hair that couldn't decide if it was supposed to be red or blonde, just like Martha Claire's, just as her own had once been.

'I could get rid of it,' Justine said. 'Doc Hadley won't do it, but there's that coloured woman in Freedmantown.'

'Yes. Aunt Sally Washington. She must be close to ninety now, but I've heard she still does abortions—mostly for coloured girls, but I expect she does a white girl now and then. I imagine that's where poor Sadie Marie Cordell went. You'd probably live through it, but do you really want to take that risk? And do you want to wonder for the rest of your life about the baby you never had?'

'I want a different kind of life,' Justine insisted. 'I'm not like Martha Claire. You know that. I want to be a photographer and make my own way in the world.'

'You should have thought of that back in London,' Polly said, not unkindly. She'd had dreams once herself. She was going to study music and become a concert organist and not just play hymns on Walnut Avenue Methodist's decaying Hammond. But she didn't have the money and life got in the way, and the life she'd ended up with was a good one. She would not change it if she could.

Before the war, Justine had refused to follow her sister to college and had taken a job in Houston as an assistant in a photography studio. People couldn't believe that Polly and Walter Mayfield had allowed their young daughter to live alone in a big city. But Polly knew there was no point in telling Justine she couldn't go. She would have gone anyway.

As it turned out, Justine hated the job. All she did was take pictures of babies and develop film. She probably would have come home and found a nice boy to marry if it weren't for the war. As soon as Justine heard about the Women's Army Corps, she knew she wanted to sign up and begged her sister to join with her. After Pearl Harbor, though, after war became reality, Martha Claire decided to marry Grayson the minute he graduated from Texas A&M, before he began his military service. A&M was a military school; Grayson would graduate as a second lieutenant in the artillery.

Once Martha Claire was married, Justine travelled to Fort Des Moines, Iowa, where she received her military training. She came home the following summer to say goodbye. At the station, when they put a smartly uniformed Justine on the train for her journey to England and the war, Martha Claire had broken down and thrown herself into Justine's arms. 'Promise me you'll come back to Columbus,' she begged. Justine hugged her sister and promised. But she hadn't promised she would come home to stay.

In London, in any spare time she had found, Justine had taken pictures of the war-torn city and the people who lived there with her precious Rolleiflex. One of her photographs had ended up in *Collier's* magazine—almost a full page with Justine's name underneath. It was a picture of two little girls having a tea party with their dolls in the middle of a bomb crater. The local newspaper ran a story about Justine taking pictures in London. 'She'll never come back to Columbus now,' Martha Claire had predicted mournfully.

Poor Martha Claire, Polly thought. If only she'd been able to get pregnant before Grayson left, she would have managed the separation better. That had certainly been her plan. Until the war came along, Martha Claire had been convinced that if she wanted something badly enough, she could make it happen. After all, she had been elected homecoming queen, been named outstanding student at Mary Hardin Baylor College, and had got the boy she wanted to fall in love with her. But she had waited out the war childless, and now her unmarried sister was carrying a misbegotten child. How in the world was Martha Claire going to react to that?

Polly felt a swelling in her breast at the thought of a grandchild in her arms. She had already decided there would be no late-night crossing over the tracks into Freedmantown. She would raise the child herself if she had to. 'You don't have to decide anything now,' Polly told her daughter, 'but keep in mind that you have responsibilities—to the life inside you and to your family, your sister especially. Martha Claire plans to stay in Columbus. Manufacturing a husband would give her a way to hold her head up.'

'It's not *her* problem,' Justine said defiantly.

'You know better than that, Justine Mayfield. Dirty linen is a family matter, especially in a little town like Columbus.'

'Do Martha Claire and Daddy know what's going on?'

'I think they've guessed. I'm going to talk to them now.'

'Oh, Mother, do you have to?' Justine's eyes filled with tears.

'Yes, dear, I do. They have a right to know.' Polly kissed her daughter's forehead. 'I love you, my darling girl.'

Justine put her arms round her mother's neck. 'I love you, too, Mother, but I can't be what you want me to be.'

Polly turned out the lamp. From the doorway she said, 'Don't underestimate the value of a home and a family who will always love you, no matter what. It's your most precious possession.'

'I have to be someone,' Justine said into the darkness.

'Everyone is someone,' Polly said, and closed the door.

THE GLOW OF THE STREETLIGHT silhouetted the branches of the magnolia tree outside the bedroom window. Justine remembered the day Grandpa Hess had planted that tree. She and Martha Claire had watched—two little girls in pigtails, sitting crosslegged in the grass. Their mother's father had died not long after that, and Justine, Martha Claire and their parents had moved from their smaller house on Walnut Street to live with Granny Grace in the big house on Milam Street where their mother had grown up.

And now that tree shaded Justine's bedroom window, a legacy from her long-dead grandfather. She would leave a legacy, too, with her photographs. If there were ever a retrospective of her work, it would include only a few of the pictures she had taken thus far. Only a handful were the kind that evoked a genuine emotional response. The little girls playing in the bomb crater was one such picture. Justine turned on the lamp and looked over at the bookcase. Her old Kodak box camera was there beside a rusty pair of roller skates. She had delivered groceries to earn money for film, and she had got better with each roll. For the rest of her life that was what she wanted—to get better and better while she photographed life, like Dorothea Lange and Margaret Bourke-White.

She rolled onto her side, pulled her knees up to her pregnant belly. 'Go away,' she groaned. 'I don't want you.' If she could have turned back the clock, she never would have got on that train to Dover, never would have fallen into the abyss.

THE NEXT MORNING Justine woke to the sound of her sister whispering from the doorway, 'Justine, are you awake?'

Without opening her eyes, Justine nodded. She felt the bed sag as Martha Claire sat beside her and asked, 'Is it true?'

Justine opened her eyes and regarded her sister's distraught face. 'So it seems,' she said, propping herself up with a second pillow.

'Did some man force himself on you?' Martha Claire asked, her eyes wide. Green eyes—a more startling green than Justine's.

'No, nothing like that.'

'Then if you loved him, why didn't you get married?'

'I never said I loved him.'

'I'm your sister, Justine. I know that you wouldn't have done something like that with a man if you didn't love him.'

'Things were different there. The war changed everything. We had too much to drink, and it just happened. I wish it hadn't. I'm sorry. Very, very sorry. And that's all I'm going to say about it.'

'But we've got to decide what we're going to tell people.'

'I don't want you telling anyone anything,' Justine said. 'Maybe I'll just go off someplace to have it and put it up for adoption.'

'You can't give away a baby,' Martha Claire said. 'We would spend the rest of our lives wondering about it and feeling sorry.'

'And if I don't give it away, I'll spend the rest of my life wishing I had. Actually, I came home with something else in mind. I was going to sneak across the tracks and let that old coloured woman in Freedmantown do whatever it is she does. But Mother knew the instant I got off that train. Can you believe that? Doc Hadley had to poke around, but Mother takes one look at me and knows.'

'You can't do *that*, either, Justine,' Martha Claire said, a hand on her breast, her eyes wide. 'Remember Sadie Marie?'

'Of course I remember Sadie Marie! But at least things got settled for her, didn't they?' Justine felt tears welling and turned her back to her sister. She hated crying. Hated feeling sorry for herself. Maybe she deserved to die like stupid ole Sadie Marie.

Sadie Marie Cordell, whose family lived across the alley, had been made pregnant by her cousin who lived down on Matagorda Bay. Mrs Cordell had taken her daughter someplace—probably to Freedmantown—and that night Sadie Marie had bled to death. When Justine had heard about it she had clutched her sister's hand and marvelled that Sadie Marie could ever have been so stupid.

'I hate you,' Justine whispered to the presence under her outstretched fingers. She wanted to get rid of it but not enough to risk her own death.

Martha Claire began rubbing her sister's back and shoulders and Justine felt herself relaxing. They used to give each other back rubs all the time. And shared all their secrets. But no longer. Life would never be like that again.

'If you stay here,' Martha Claire was saying, 'I'll help you with the baby. But we have to tell people that you got married and your husband died, just like Mother says. He got blown up by a leftover bomb.'

'Go away, Martha Claire,' Justine groaned.

WITHOUT CONSULTING her parents or sister, Martha Claire placed a brief obituary in the next issue of the weekly *Colorado County Citizen*: 'Sergeant Major Philip Benston Dover. Born July 12, 1921, in Liverpool, England. Killed in the service of his country June 4, 1945, in London, England. Survived by his wife, Justine Mayfield Dover, of Columbus.'

Of his own volition, the editor ran a story about the war's last hero. He told how a hometown girl serving as a WAC in London had danced in the streets with a young British soldier during the V-E Day celebrations and married him three days later—only to be widowed soon after when he was killed defusing an undetonated bomb that had fallen in a south London neighbourhood.

Martha Claire thanked God when she saw the story. A story in the newspaper made it true. Her parents were overjoyed. Justine burst into tears.

'I'm sorry, Justine, but I had to do something. Maybe you don't care about this family's reputation. Maybe you think it won't affect us when you get big out to here with no claim to a husband.'

Justine blew her nose and handed the newspaper back to her sister. 'It's OK. You did what you had to do. But why *Dover*?'

'It sounded English,' Martha Claire explained.

Neighbours and friends began showing up at the front door to pay their respects to the grieving family. Reverend Huxley stopped by to ask about a memorial service. A reporter from the *Houston Post*, with a photographer in tow, arrived. He wanted an interview with Mrs Dover and a photograph of the young widow holding her dead husband's picture, but had to settle for a photograph of the Mayfield family's handsome Victorian home with a funeral wreath on the front door. It was printed the following day next to a picture of Justine from a Columbus High School yearbook.

Through it all, Justine stayed in bed. She never should have come back home. She knew that now. She felt as though she were sinking into a quicksand bog from which there was no escape.

I must have been about nine when my aunt Justine and I took a stroll around the town square one evening and stopped in front of the plaques honouring Colorado County's war dead to pay our respects. That was in the years when Justine still came back to us. Justine's visits were more important than Christmas.

'War is so confusing,' Justine said. 'Lots of really sweet boys never came home, and those of us who did will never get over it. Yet, we wouldn't have missed it for the world.'

'I'm glad you didn't miss it,' I told her. 'If you had, you never would have met Sergeant Major Philip Benston Dover, and then there would never have been an Iris.'

Justine smile and nodded.

'It's sad that Iris will never know her father,' I said. 'Of course, Buddy and I don't know our real father, either, but we have Daddy.'

'And so does Iris,' Justine reminded me.

Justine took my hand, and we walked on. I never thought of my aunt Justine as a widow lady, even though that was what she was. Other ladies wore dresses downtown, but Justine—in spite of her widow-lady status—wore slacks, like Katharine Hepburn. In fact, she reminded me of Katharine Hepburn, with her long legs and plain-speaking ways.

I remember wishing I could have been a little like Justine, but the truth was, I didn't have the courage to alienate my mother. I had a need to please her that came from deep inside me. I was, above all, Martha Claire Stewart's adopted daughter. And perhaps, even though I loved Justine, I also shared my mother's disdain for a woman who would leave her daughter for someone else to raise. Justine was able to travel the world and become a famous photographer because my mother was raising her daughter.

Since earliest memory, a picture of my aunt and my mother hung among the gallery of framed family pictures that marched up the stair-case wall. The picture had been taken when the Mayfield sisters, as they were always known, were teenagers. Tall, athletic Justine was wearing a plaid skirt, white blouse and saddle oxfords. My mother was dainty in a ruffled frock and white pumps. After the falling-out between them, Mama burned that picture in the back yard, but in my mind's eye I can see it still. The Mayfield sisters portrayed there were so pretty, their arms linked for ever in sisterly affection. When that picture was taken, they thought they'd have each other for a lifetime.

'I THINK YOU'D MAKE a terrific army wife,' Justine told her sister as she hammered the lid back on the paint can.

'Why do you say that?' Martha Claire demanded.

'Think of all the "finishing" you got at Mary Hardin Baylor College for Women. Officers' wives have to know all about etiquette so their husbands can get promoted.'

'Don't make fun,' Martha Claire said as she worked the paint-brush back and forth on the newspaper that protected the floor.

Justine carefully lowered her pregnant body onto the wooden crate that held the photo enlarger she'd ordered from Sears, Roebuck. 'I'm not making fun of you, Martha Claire,' she said with great earnestness. 'With you managing the home front, Grayson would be a general someday, and a general's wife is like royalty.'

Martha Claire shook her head. 'If Grayson stayed in the army, we'd spend our lives as vagabonds. We'd always be living among strangers, and our children would be born God knows where. I want to live here, and before the war Grayson did, too.'

Even wearing old clothes, with her hair tied up in a bandanna, Martha Claire was lovely. Justine had never known anyone who was so comfortable in her own body, her own face, her own smile. No wonder Grayson had fallen in love with her in high school. Lots of other boys had, too. But Martha Claire had zeroed in on Grayson the first week of her sophomore year, when he marched up onto the stage and sang 'When the Moon Comes Over the Mountain', and she never wavered in her aim.

Justine reached over and stroked her sister's hand. 'I just want you and Grayson to be happy, and I worry that if you make him stay here to do something he doesn't want to do, neither one of you will be. He's not the same man that he was before the war. He's been through hell. He deserves a chance at happiness.'

'Other men have come back home and settled in. What makes Grayson so different?'

'Other men didn't have a military education,' Justine pointed out. 'You know how he took to all the regimental stuff up at College Station. He was the number one cadet. And now he's a captain with medals on his chest. He has a chance for a distinguished military career, and you want him to be a shopkeeper!'

'What's so bad about being a shopkeeper? Daddy has tended his pharmacy for twenty-five years. Grayson's family has always had that dry-goods store. He'll get back here and remember what it was like to grow up in Columbus. He'll want the same for our children. Why would he want to live anyplace else?'

Martha Claire got up and walked around the room, inspecting the walls she'd just painted, signifying the end of the conversation.

Poor Grayson, Justine thought. He would have to hang up his uniform, as his father had done when he came home from the First World War. Grayson would spend his years stocking shelves and selling shirts when he could have had a different sort of life.

And she herself was facing the same sort of prison, here in this very room. Not that it wasn't a nice room, over their father's pharmacy, with two windows in the front that looked out on the square and a storeroom with no windows where she would set up her darkroom. Justine stared down at her belly. She didn't hate the baby any more. It hadn't asked to be conceived. But she did hate what was happening to her life.

She would open a photography studio to support herself and her child. They would live in what once had been servants' quarters over a carriage-house-turned-garage behind the family home. Everyone had pitched in to make it livable.

She stared at her backward name already painted on one of the front windows: JUSTINE MAYFIELD-DOVER, PHOTOGRAPHER. She'd borrowed the hyphen from Margaret Bourke-White.

Dover. Beautiful Dover. Strange that Martha Claire had chosen that name. Justine closed her eyes and saw the castle ruins, the white cliffs. Poor Grayson. She felt for him from the bottom of her heart. His sentence was for life. Hers would not be, she vowed.

MARTHA CLAIRE STOOD with her parents and grandmother at the nursery window, peering through the glass at Justine's newborn baby—an absolutely beautiful baby girl, asleep in a cot. Martha Claire was transfixed. A *baby*—surely the most wondrous thing in the world, what she herself wanted more than anything.

Soon she would have her own baby, but in the meantime she would have her sister's child to fill her heart. Iris was her name. Beautiful little Iris.

Martha Claire wished that Grayson were here to see Iris in the first hours of her life. He had called from New York yesterday. He was accompanying his command to Fort Bragg, North Carolina, and would muster out there. In just a matter of days he would be home.

She felt uneasy about seeing him again. Afraid, even. Grayson had become a stranger to her. His letters talked about the poor souls liberated from Nazi death camps. Broken, diseased people who had no possessions, no family, no spirit; people who had lost everything. His heart was heavy for the suffering of others when she wanted it to be light and filled with hope and love and thoughts of her and the wonderful future that awaited them. Of course, he always wrote how much he loved her, how much he wanted and needed her, but his words seemed rote—a man writing the words a wife might expect to see.

Being with Grayson once had seemed the most natural thing in the world. She had been a virgin when they married, but just barely. They had had their secret place in a riverside grove, where they took off their clothes and did everything short of going all the way. She enjoyed their mutual beauty as much as the touching and kissing.

Justine had wanted Martha Claire to join the Women's Army Corps with her. For a heartbeat Martha Claire had been tempted. They could go off together before she settled down with Grayson. But what if he died over there? If that happened, she wanted him to die as her husband. She wanted his child to love and raise.

She abandoned her plans for a big wedding at some point in the unknown future and decided to marry Grayson in her mother's rose garden the day after he had graduated from Texas A&M. Grayson had been reluctant about the hurry-up wedding. Maybe they should wait until the war was over, he told her.

'But I need to be your wife,' Martha Claire explained. 'I couldn't bear to send you off to war otherwise.'

They worked round the clock to get the house and garden ready for the wedding. Martha Claire had fretted about the weather, but her wedding day arrived fair and blue. Her wedding dress had been worn by her grandmother and her mother before her. Grayson was married in his cadet uniform. In front of family and friends, with her sister at her side, Martha Claire had proudly said the words that bound her to Grayson for a lifetime.

The newlyweds spent their wedding night in a motel outside Sugar Land on the way to a honeymoon on Galveston Island. 'Make me pregnant,' she whispered as Grayson entered her body for the first time. 'Give me a baby, please.'

For one week they walked along Galveston's great empty beaches, gorged themselves on fresh seafood, made love morning and night. Afterwards they would talk about the future with tears and assurances. He would come back to her. They would be happy. Their love was for ever. But Grayson became distant at times, and she knew he was thinking not about their mutual future but his own more immediate one. He tried to hide his excitement, but she could hear it in his voice. He wanted to go, as did Justine. Both of them would rather go to war than stay in Columbus with her. This knowledge ate at her and altered the nature of her love for them.

After she and Grayson returned to Columbus, they spent one night together in her parents' house. The next day Grayson took the train to Fort Sill, Oklahoma, where he would attend the twelve-week battery-officer training course. Three times Martha Claire made the seven-hour train ride into southwestern Oklahoma, getting off in downtown Lawton and walking to a hotel. Grayson would catch a ride into town and meet her there. He would have to be back at the base the next morning, leaving Martha Claire to her long ride home.

She and Grayson had not conceived a child on their honeymoon or during her three visits to Lawton. Their last night together, in the Lawton hotel, she had prayed with fervour. Kneeling beside the bed, she asked Grayson to join her, which he did willingly. He wanted a baby, too. He was thrilled about what lay ahead and scared to the depths of his being. A baby would make facing death easier. As he thrust his way into her body, she floated in a high celestial space. If God loved her at all, He would give her a baby.

Two weeks later Grayson was on his way to war and Martha Claire was staring down at a telltale show of blood on the crotch of her underpants. She wept bitter tears, and a deep-seated fear became embedded in her soul. What if there would be no baby ever? Who would she be if not a mother? Because she was a positive person, though, Martha Claire was able to keep fear at bay. After all, she and Grayson had been married only a short time. He would come home, and she'd have a baby within the year.

For three and a half years she had waited for his return. Waiting became a way of life. And fear became her constant companion, fear that the dreaded military saloon car would pull up in front of the house, with a solemn-faced officer coming to the door.

Grayson had been wounded when a mortar shell hit his Jeep and killed his driver. He had been in southern France then. There had been some worry that he would lose an eye, but he hadn't written about that until the danger had passed.

When Grayson's father had a heart attack, she began helping out at the store. It was only temporary, of course. When Grayson returned, she would become a full-time homemaker and mother.

She had saved all his letters with the heavy black blocks where the censors had made their deletions. Now his letters weren't censored. The war had ended. Yet she almost resented them when they arrived. Other men had already returned. How could she complain, though, when what he was doing was so noble and good? But what if he had volunteered for extended duty to put off his return? Was he punishing her for denying him a military career? He had been gracious in defeat, however, writing that Martha Claire was right—there had been an implied promise on his part that they would make their home in Columbus. He had a responsibility to her and his parents. And he could continue his military service on a part-time basis in the Texas National Guard. It wasn't as though he was hanging up his uniform for ever.

When he'd called last night, she hadn't recognised his voice. 'It's me,' he said. He was calling from the pier in New York City. The ship had just docked. He explained about Fort Bragg. He would call as soon as he knew more.

'I love you, Martha Claire,' he said. 'You are my life.'

His voice broke. He meant what he said. But there had also been resignation in his voice. He wanted her *and* something else, and he was having to settle for just her. She had won, and she had lost.

But they would heal themselves with a family. She wanted three, four, maybe five children. She would bring Grayson here to the hospital to see this precious newborn child. Martha Claire pressed her fingertips against the glass. Iris should be *her* baby. Justine didn't want to be a mother. Maybe she would go off and have her career and leave Iris for her sister and brother-in-law to raise.

THE MINUTE MARTHA CLAIRE saw Grayson step down from the train, she realised that her sister had been right. She was getting back a different man. He had seen horrors she couldn't imagine. She had wanted to believe that once he was home the years would roll back and they would be newlyweds again. However, now that he was actually in her arms, she realised there was a part of him she would never know, when once she had known him completely. But oh, how sweet it was to have his arms around her again.

'All that kept me alive was thinking about you,' he said, burying his face in her hair.

'My darling,' she whispered. 'We'll never be apart again.'

Reluctantly she relinquished him to his parents. His father had suffered two heart attacks and gone from robust to fragile while his son was at war. Martha Claire had tried to warn Grayson in her letters, but there was shock on his face as he embraced his father.

Later, at the hospital, they viewed Justine's baby through the nursery window. 'She's lovely,' was all Grayson said.

They walked silently down to Justine's room, where Grayson politely kissed his sister-in-law's cheek, congratulated her on a beautiful baby, and listened to her rant about being held captive in a hospital for ten days when poor women had babies at home. Then she stopped abruptly. 'Your husband is exhausted, Martha Claire. You need to take him home.'

Martha Claire had rented a two-bedroomed house next door to her in-laws. She had painted every room, restored furniture, and made curtains. Now, during the short ride to their own home, her stomach tied itself in knots. She hadn't been this nervous on their wedding night. Grayson carried her across the threshold.

Martha Claire lit candles and opened a bottle of champagne. 'To my husband,' she said, lifting her glass. He picked up his glass, then put it down again and buried his face in his hands. Martha Claire held him while he cried, unsure of the source of his tears. Finally, the sobs subsided and she felt all the energy drain from his body.

She helped him out of his uniform and drew a bath for him. He was asleep by the time she crawled into bed beside him.

'WHERE ARE WE GOING?' Grayson asked.

'It's a surprise,' Martha Claire said, trying to sound merry when she was so nervous she felt ill. She was taking a risk, something that went against her nature.

Grayson had been home almost two weeks—two very polite weeks. Mealtime was a strain. Sitting in the living room after dinner, they were like two old people, Martha Claire with her sewing basket, Grayson with the newspaper or a book. He was quiet and withdrawn. She wanted him to talk about the war and why he had changed so, but he said he couldn't. 'Will you ever?' she asked.

'I don't know,' he'd answered.

They had made love at dawn that first morning. He cried again and said it wasn't right that he had lived when others had not. Good men. Better than he. Martha Claire stroked his back, kissed his tears. The first time was just something to get over with, she told herself. Next time would be different. And it had been. That evening they came together again, quietly, carefully, without tears. And every night since, it had been so. Martha Claire was left longing for the abandonment of their honeymoon, when their bodies had fused like streams of molten lava.

It was a beautiful evening, with a warm breeze. The river was at its romantic best, all silvery in the moonlight. When she turned down the rutted lane, Grayson sighed. At the end of the lane, in a riverside stand of willow, was their special place, where they had once come to take off their clothes, experience flesh against flesh. Martha Claire wanted to revisit those times of high passion and endless kisses. She stopped the car. 'Please,' she said.

He put his arms around her. 'Ah, sweet Martha Claire. We didn't leave the magic down by the river.'

'Then where is it?' She was crying. Great hiccuping sobs escaped from deep inside of her. *Where had the passion gone?*

'We have to start over,' he said, caressing her hair, her back, her wet cheeks. 'There's no way to go back to that other time.'

'What will happen to us?' she asked.

'We will make our home together, raise a family, run the store. If we make enough money, I'd like to take you to Europe.'

'Do you still want to stay in the army?' she asked, her voice small. 'If it's what you really want . . .'

He buried his face against her neck. 'It's all right. I won't make you leave Columbus. I want more than anything to make you happy. That's all I want out of life—to make you happy.'

And his mouth found hers. The kiss was salty. Deep. Full of need. *Oh, yes*, she thought. *Please.* And they did revisit that other time. At last she could kiss his body with abandon and make him cry out in passion.

Curled in the circle of his arm as he drove them home, hope flowed in her veins. She felt it as never before. Tonight was *the* night. Their first child had been conceived.

POLLY AND GRANNY GRACE kept assuring Justine that the baby was just colicky. She would get over it. And as Justine endured endless nights and miserable days, she felt genuinely sorry for the poor little creature. She didn't doubt that Iris truly was suffering from tummy aches or birth trauma or whatever it was that gave babies colic. Justine was too exhausted to cope, though, too exhausted to care. If asked to choose between a million dollars and an uninterrupted night's sleep, she would take sleep.

Then, during the baby's seventh week of life, Iris smiled at her. Justine was suspicious. Probably it was just wind. Iris did it again. The smile was lopsided, silly, and absolutely precious.

'Does this mean that you are actually a human being?' Justine asked in wonder.

Iris smiled one more time, then promptly closed her eyes and fell asleep.

Justine stared down at her daughter's angelic face, at the tiny hand clutching her finger, and felt something stirring inside her. 'Oh my God,' Justine whispered as understanding dawned. This wasn't supposed to happen, but it had. She was in love.

Falling in love with her baby did not end the colic or cure Justine's exhaustion, but it made her eager to get on with her life. She put an announcement in the newspaper offering an opening-month special on baby pictures and began practising on her daughter. Polly and Granny Grace made sure she had customers that first month—nine in all. The following month Justine photographed her first wedding. Martha Claire organised her life around caring for her husband and her sister's baby. She still wasn't pregnant.

THEY HAD JUST crawled into bed when the phone rang. Grayson hurried down the hall to answer it, with Martha Claire following. No one called after ten o'clock unless there was a problem. Standing behind her husband, she could hear his mother's hysterical voice. Frank couldn't breathe, Lily was shrieking. He was turning blue.

Martha Claire called Doc Hadley while Grayson pulled on trousers and raced out of the door in his bare feet. By the time Martha Claire had thrown on her robe and joined him next door at her in-laws' house, Lily was cradling her husband's body in her arms. Grayson was kneeling beside his mother, sobbing, his face in his hands. They were in the dining room, with an unfinished game of cribbage on the table.

Martha Claire put one hand over her mouth and the other against the wall for support. Frank was dead. She went to stand behind Grayson, to put her hands on his trembling shoulders and kiss the top of his head. 'My poor darling,' she said, 'I'm so sorry. He was such a good, kind man.'

Doc Hadley arrived and called the undertaker. Lily wailed as she watched her husband's body being carried out through the front door. She clung to her son and asked, 'What will I do without him?'

But after Frank's funeral it was Grayson who retreated inside himself. In the weeks that followed, he left early for the store and stayed late. Lily often came to dinner, and he would reminisce with her about his father, but when it was just him and Martha Claire, however, their conversations were perfunctory. He repaired his father's small outboard and fished away Sunday afternoons. He needed time to come to terms, he told his wife; to grieve on his own.

Martha Claire spent as much time as she could with her mother-in-law, who was coming to terms in spite of herself. She didn't like wearing black, and she wasn't about to give up bridge and canasta. Not that she didn't get weepy from time to time, and she was lonely when she woke in the night and Frank wasn't there. But after a time sadness became a bore, and she decided to remember her husband fondly but also to work on her bridge game.

Martha Claire was determined to get Grayson out of his depression. Sometimes he didn't want to make love, and that was upsetting. How could she get pregnant if he didn't reach for her in bed? When she reached for him, he would kiss her and tell her that he loved her, then roll over and fall asleep.

Two months after his father's death she splurged on a rib roast.

She put on a nice dress and set the table with the good china and candles in silver holders. When Grayson arrived, she greeted him with a kiss. 'I don't care what we talk about, but we have to talk about something,' she said. 'I can't stand the silence.'

He held her close for a long time. 'I'm so sorry,' he said.

'No need to be sorry. You had to get through your grief, but now I need my husband back.'

They ate dinner first, making careful conversation. Grayson told her the roast was perfect. She was a fine cook. Over coffee, he began to talk in earnest. It was strange, he explained, to suddenly become his father, to become the Mr Stewart who owned Stewart's Dry Goods, to see the rest of his life laid out in front of him, a replication of his father's and his father's before him. It wasn't such a bad life, he supposed, but Grayson wasn't as comfortable with people as his father was. And he didn't have his father's patience. He got irritated when people couldn't make up their minds after trying on ten pairs of shoes. He had thought he would be better prepared for his father's death. He had known it was coming. After all, it wasn't like it was his first brush with death. But still, Grayson was having a hard time getting used to the idea that he would never see his father again or hear his voice. Just today, down at the store, he had tried to make sense of an invoice from the sewing-accessories supplier. He wasn't sure what buttonhole twist was. And bias tape, bobbins, sharps.

Grayson paused. 'I guess that was just a long way of saying I miss my dad and am having a hard time filling his shoes.'

She took him upstairs without even doing the dishes.

EVERY PASSING MONTH was anguish for Martha Claire as she waited to see if her period would start. It was so unfair. Why couldn't she conceive a child?

With no baby of her own, Martha Claire relished every minute she spent with Iris. She frequently kept the baby at her house while Justine worked, taking pictures of children, high-school beauty queens and football players.

With her first $200 Justine bought a 1936 De Soto and cast her net wider. She photographed prize bulls, weddings, church choirs. In the red glow of her darkroom, as she watched the faces of smiling children and demure brides materialise in the developing tray, she vowed this was just an interim stage in her life. She could not do this for ever.

When she had time, she focused her camera on other subjects—on the sweating bodies of quarry workers and cotton pickers, the children of Freedmantown swimming naked in the river. She displayed these photographs on the walls of her studio. Everyone who came through her door stopped to admire them, but it was the photographs of brides and babies that paid her bills.

Two days before Iris's first birthday, Justine was photographing her first out-of-town wedding, in Texas City, a refinery town on the Gulf Coast. The broad front steps of the church offered a fine view of the harbour and the huge Monsanto chemical refinery. Justine stood at the back of the church, waiting to take a triumphant picture of the newlyweds coming down the aisle. The bride was saying 'I do' when Justine heard an explosion, and instantly the entire building began to shake, the stained-glass windows to implode. Justine was thrown to the floor and rolled under a pew to protect herself from flying glass. People were screaming, calling out in pain. *A bomb*, Justine thought. *Not another war!* She grabbed her camera and ran out of the door with one thought. *Iris.* She had to get home to her child.

But the sight that greeted her was not of war. Not a blitzkrieg. No invading planes flew overhead. But plumes of orange smoke were rising over the harbour, with burning pieces of debris arcing across the heavens like Fourth of July skyrockets. People were running towards the harbour. A ship had blown up.

Justine ran to her car for a different camera, different film, and prepared to join the river of people racing towards the pier for a view of the burning ship. Suddenly she remembered the small airfield she had passed on the way into town. An aerial photo would be more dramatic. She drove fast, hoping to get to the airfield before the roads were clogged with emergency vehicles.

A pilot who looked too old to drive a car, much less fly an aeroplane, took her up in an open-cockpit biplane. He flew so close to the burning ship that Justine choked on the smoke. They had just finished a flyby of the shore, which allowed her to photograph the crowds of people watching the spectacle, when she realised the chemical plant was on fire. She yelled at the pilot and was pointing in that direction when the Monsanto refinery exploded.

An instant later the concussion reached the plane. Justine held on for dear life as the plane rocked about wildly. As soon as the pilot got it under control, she raised the viewfinder to her eye and photographed the huge fireball rising over the refinery. The people on the pier had been incinerated. They hadn't had a chance. Hundreds of them. As her mind tried to deal with the horror, her hands automatically inserted another roll of film into her camera. She kept on snapping the shutter, frame after frame of profound tragedy worse than anything she had witnessed in London.

Finally, her film exhausted, the pilot flew Justine to the Houston airport. By then she knew her pictures were too important for a state newspaper. She arranged to have the film on the first flight to New York and called the *New York Times*'s newsroom to say that film documenting the Texas City disaster was on its way. It was only then that she thought to call home. Her mother answered the phone and began weeping hysterically. 'My God, Justine, when we didn't hear from you, we thought you were dead.'

If she had run down to the pier to take her pictures, she would be, Justine realised.

The following day her photographs of the Texas City explosion, which killed more than 500 people and injured more than 3,000, were on the front page of the *New York Times*. The ship had been a French freighter. The company that owned the freighter insisted it had been carrying fertiliser, not explosives. Already a controversy was brewing. Could fertiliser explode?

A Mr Silverstein at the *Times* wanted Justine to stay on the scene as more and more dead were pulled from the rubble. And he wanted pictures of the mass funeral at the high-school football stadium. 'You're doing a great job,' he told her.

She willed herself to stay dry-eyed throughout the service. After the film was on its way, she would cry.

Her pictures had gone out over the wire, which meant they were in newspapers all over the world. She hadn't felt this alive since London. Her postwar life had finally begun.

Three

My aunt Justine used to tell how people back east always thought she came from Alabama or Georgia. 'You sound Southern,' they would insist. Justine would explain that east Texas was right next to Louisiana, and our drawl—and our ways—were more Southern than Western. Not that we had ante-bellum plantations with white-columned verandahs where we lounged about sipping mint juleps. But most of Columbus's original settlers had come from Louisiana and Arkansas, and they had grown cotton and owned slaves.

The Columbus of my childhood hasn't changed greatly from the days when my parents were young. An antiques store occupies the building where my grandfather once operated his pharmacy. A dress shop is in the building that once housed Stewart's Dry Goods. Other businesses are gone, too—the Orphic Theater, Smitty's Sandwich Shop, the depot—but many of the old buildings that housed them are still standing, occupied by tearooms, gift shops, even an art gallery. The courthouse, Stafford's Opera House and the Stafford Mansion next door look pretty much the same.

Sometimes at twilight I turn my back on the ugly new bank building north of Courthouse Square, so that only the courthouse and the old buildings on the west and south sides of the square are in my line of vision, and I can almost see us three kids—Buddy, Iris and me—on our bicycles, a nickel in our pockets for a cherry soda at the Sandwich Shop.

After our sodas we would turn our bikes down Milam Street, towards the big old Victorian house where our mothers, Grandma Polly and Granny Grace had all grown up. In spite of its cracking paint and sagging front porch, living in such a house had given our family a certain prestige. Our family was 'old Columbus', our parents descended from original settlers. Since Buddy and I were both adopted, we didn't actually have old Columbus blood flowing in our veins, but I felt proud that we lived in such a wonderful house, with its gingerbread trim, high peaked roof, round gable window, and—best of all—the broad front porch where we spent at least a part of every summer evening. The house would someday belong to Iris, but at that point in our lives it belonged to Buddy and me just as much as it did to her.

'THERE IS NO PLACE on earth I would rather live than this house,' Martha Claire announced as she and Grayson stood back to admire the newly refurbished parlour. For weeks now they had been refinishing the floors, papering the walls, reupholstering the side chairs. They had just finished rehanging the pictures and replacing her mother's upright piano.

'Well, that's one room down and ten to go,' Grayson said with less enthusiasm than his wife. He wished his mother-in-law had sold the house when her husband died rather than invite him and Martha Claire to move in with her and Granny Grace. What at first seemed a way to save money was in reality a financial albatross. He hadn't realised the extent of the decay and termite damage to hundred-year-old timber, hadn't understood the problems that came with antiquated wiring and corroded pipes.

Martha Claire wanted the house to look the way it had when her great-great-grandfather built it. But Grayson had inherited a dry-goods store that was barely able to pay their bills and those of his widowed mother. He and Martha Claire would have a difficult time if it wasn't for the government cheque he received every three months for his service in the Texas National Guard and the generous cheque that Justine sent every month to cover Iris's keep.

For the past few years Martha Claire and Grayson had been taking care of Iris. Justine was now in Korea covering the end of the war. Her pictures of the first-released American POWs crossing the bridge over the Imjin River had been on all the front pages.

Martha Claire had decided that there was a man in Justine's life—based on what, Grayson was unsure. As a result, his wife worried constantly that her sister would settle down and take Iris from them. He feared that, too. Iris was the most delightful child imaginable. She was the light of their lives. Already Grayson was anticipating her delight over the finished parlour. He glanced at his watch. Granny Grace and Polly had taken her with them to make Sunday afternoon calls on the housebound. 'All it needs now is an oriental rug for the floor,' Martha Claire was saying. 'Then the room will be complete.'

'Don't hold your breath on that one,' he said as they walked down the hall towards the kitchen.

They sat at the big round table drinking lemonade and munching on cookies. Martha Claire was full of plans for modernising the kitchen. Grayson only half listened, occasionally reminding her that they couldn't afford this or that. But dreaming about the house was good for her, he supposed. It distracted her from the other problem. Grayson always knew when his wife's period came. She would become quiet and wouldn't let him share her sadness. Then, a few days later, she would become hopeful again.

She was asking him if they could put down new linoleum them-selves or needed to hire someone, when there was a knock at the front door. Grayson wondered who could be calling on this quiet Sunday afternoon. He hoped it wasn't Reverend Huxley soliciting for the building fund or enquiring about Grayson's sporadic atten-dance at church.

When he opened the door, it was Doc Hadley standing on the front porch, holding a baby in his arms—a very small baby wrapped in a faded green shawl. 'Hello, Grayson,' the doctor said. 'I've got someone here I want you and Martha Claire to meet.'

Grayson heard Martha Claire call, 'Who is it?' But he couldn't seem to answer.

'It's Doc Hadley, Martha Claire,' the physician called back. 'You got a minute?'

Grayson stepped to one side and allowed the physician into the entrance hall. He could hear Martha Claire's footsteps coming from the kitchen. When she arrived at her husband's side, Doc Hadley pulled the corner of the shawl from the infant's face. 'It's a girl,' he said. 'She was born this morning.'

Martha Claire took a hesitant step closer. 'Whose baby is it?'

'Yours, if you want her,' the doctor said.

Grayson stared down at the tiny newborn face. *Their baby if they wanted her?* As the words sunk in, he had to grab the newel post to steady himself.

'But where did she come from?' Martha Claire asked.

'Can't tell you,' Doc Hadley said in his usual brusque way. 'All I can tell you is that she's a love child—there wasn't a rape or anything like that—and her parents are not from hereabouts. That's all you're ever going to know about this little girl's history. If you take her, it's with a clean slate.'

'Grayson and I will have to talk it over,' Martha Claire said.

'I don't have time for talking over. This baby needs someone now. If you're not interested, I'm driving her over to the Baptist Children's Home in San Antonio.'

'But something as important as taking in a child needs to be discussed,' she insisted.

'I don't see it that way, Martha Claire,' Doc Hadley said, his voice stern. 'You either want a baby or you don't.'

Then the doctor fell silent. The two men watched Martha Claire, trying to take a reading from her frowning face, and waited.

His wife was lovely still, Grayson thought, even in a faded housedress. Her skin was as satiny smooth as a girl's, the line of her jaw as young and lovely as before. But she had changed in other ways. She seldom laughed out loud, was seldom spontaneous. Only when she was playing with Iris could Grayson glimpse the vivacious girl with whom he had fallen so completely in love. But in spite of Martha

Claire's diminished spirit, he still loved his wife, still wanted to spend his life with her at his side. And if that life was to be forever lived in this small town, he knew it would be more fulfilling if they took in this little nameless child with her secret history.

Tears were making their way down Martha Claire's cheeks. She looked at Grayson. All he could offer was the smallest of nods. It was Martha Claire's decision. He couldn't ask her to become the mother of a child she could not fully accept as her own.

Martha Claire took a step closer to the doctor. She reached out and touched the baby's cheek, and a whimper escaped from her lips. Suddenly she was gathering the baby into her arms. Grayson's knees gave way, and he sank to the bottom step. *At last, a baby for Martha Claire.* This wasn't the way he would have chosen for her prayers to be answered, but it would do. Yes, it would do.

They would get a call about the legal stuff from the secretary in the county judge's office, Doc Hadley said before leaving them.

Then they were alone with a baby, *their* baby, suddenly parents after years of longing. 'Oh, Grayson, isn't she beautiful?' Martha Claire said, her voice filled with such reverence.

Grayson was aware that in the years to follow he would look back on this day as one of the most joyous of his life, and the source of that joy was the look on his wife's face. He already loved his nameless daughter because she was theirs. Later he would come to love her for herself. But today he loved her because she had done something he had not been able to do. She had made Martha Claire happy.

They were laughing and crying at the same time now. With their baby between them, they shared salty kisses and stared with adoration at her newborn face. 'What do we do now?' he asked.

His question sent Martha Claire into action. She sent Grayson to borrow enough baby milk formula from the neighbours to last until the store opened in the morning. Then she dispatched him to the attic for Iris's crib, baby clothes, baby bottles and a steriliser.

Granny Grace, Polly and Iris had already heard the news by the time they came rushing up the front path.

Iris never left the baby's side. 'Is she going to be my sister?' the four-year-old asked.

'No, honey, she is your cousin,' Granny Grace said.

'I'd rather have her be my sister,' Iris insisted.

'She will be just like your sister,' Granny Grace explained.

Grayson set up the crib in the corner of their bedroom, and Iris insisted on placing a mattress on the floor beside it so she could sleep next to the baby. Already she was calling her new cousin Sissy.

In bed that night, Grayson curled his body against Martha Claire's. He wanted to celebrate their good fortune by making love, but with Iris in the room that was out of the question.

'As soon as Iris is asleep, you can carry her to bed,' Martha Claire whispered. While they waited for Iris to fall asleep, they surreptitiously kissed and caressed.

Their lovemaking that night was so infinitely sweet, it made Grayson weep. He loved and was loved in return. He was a husband and father. Life was good. He was just drifting off to sleep when the baby whimpered. 'Let me,' Grayson told Martha Claire.

He carried the baby downstairs and warmed her bottle, then sat in the rocking chair. 'Thank you, sweet child,' he told her with tears in his eyes. He kissed his baby's forehead. 'I will be the very best father I can possibly be,' he promised his daughter.

The following Sunday the baby was christened Cecelia Claire Stewart, but Iris's name for her cousin stuck, only they would spell it with a C, Martha Claire decided. Their baby would be Cissy.

NO ONE UNDERSTOOD what Martha Claire had gone through in the minutes after Doc Hadley offered her a baby, and she could never explain it, not even to her mother or husband.

She immediately realised that adopting the baby would ease the anguish of Justine's visits, when Justine took Iris to stay with her in the garage apartment for days or weeks on end. Last fall, after Justine announced she was taking Iris to Dallas for an entire week, Martha Claire found herself wishing that something would happen to make Justine cancel the trip. Maybe she'd come down with pneumonia or influenza. Sometimes Martha Claire had thoughts even more troubling than wishing her sister came down with the flu.

Although truce talks were under way in Korea, the fighting continued, and Martha Claire had found herself guiltily imagining a phone call informing the family that Justine had been killed there—a phone call that would make Iris irrevocably hers.

That morning, as she had looked down at the newborn child in Doc Hadley's arms, Martha Claire thought, If I take this baby, maybe I can be a better person; maybe I can stop wishing my sister would die. When she took the baby in her arms, she vowed to pray every night that her sister lived a long and healthy life.

In the months that followed, Martha Claire realised that her husband assumed the baby had put an end to her monthly lapses into depression. And maybe Cissy did help some, but mostly Martha Claire did a better job of concealing them. Because of this child she was supposed to be a whole woman now. She knew, however, that nothing on this earth would ever cure the emptiness inside her except a baby conceived in her own body.

SIX MONTHS AFTER CISSY joined their family, Doc Hadley returned with a two-year-old boy in his arms. 'This little boy is Cissy's older brother,' he announced. By this time Cissy was a sweet, easy baby who delighted in patty-cake and peekaboo.

Holding Cissy on her hip, Martha Claire watched Grayson approach the little boy carefully, his hand outstretched, his expression gentle. The boy was a pretty child, with dark eyes and hair like Cissy's. Without taking his eyes from the boy's face, Grayson asked Doc Hadley, 'What's his name?'

'They call him Buddy. He needs a home, too.'

'Hello there, Buddy,' Grayson said, taking the boy's small hand and shaking it formally. Then he took the child from the doctor's arms. 'My, what a nice big boy you are,' he said. 'Do you like cookies? I'll bet this nice lady here might have a cookie for you.'

In the kitchen, Martha Claire gave the doctor a piece of pie and the boy a cookie, which he nibbled while sitting on Grayson's lap.

'Who's been taking care of him?' Martha Claire demanded.

The doctor shook his head. 'No questions. This one comes with a clean slate, too. I just thought it would be nice for a brother and sister to be raised together.'

Martha Claire was leaning against the sink, her arms folded across her chest. 'Why didn't you tell us Cissy had a brother?'

''Cause if there'd been two kids, you wouldn't have taken either one of 'em,' the doctor said.

Martha Claire sighed. He was right, of course. And she wasn't sure she was going to take a second one now. She was only thirty-one. What if she took this little boy and got pregnant? She already had her hands full with Cissy and Iris, and Granny Grace had had a stroke and needed help doing the simplest tasks. Her mother and Grayson's mother were both helping out down at the store now, leaving her to look after her grandmother and the children and manage all the cooking and cleaning. And she was beginning to think their money problems were never going away. Grayson worked hard at the store, but he wasn't a born businessman like his father. She didn't see how they could afford to take in another child. But there was such longing in Grayson's eyes. A boy to play catch with and take fishing—every man wanted that, she supposed.

She took the child from Grayson's lap. The boy was looking at her with big dark eyes. Then he offered her a bite of his cookie. Martha Claire took a small nibble and told him, 'Thank you.'

What kind of woman would she be if she said no? Did she really have a choice? 'Oh, I suppose,' she said. 'But no more, you hear? Don't bring me another brother or sister in six months.'

'You can count on that,' Doc Hadley said. 'Mighty fine pie, Martha Claire.'

FROM EARLIEST MEMORY Buddy and I loved to hear the story about how Doc Hadley brought us to Mama and Daddy, and how happy our arrival in their lives had made them.

On our birthdays Mama always said that our birth mother would be thinking of us on our special day. Even now, on my birthday, I still wonder if there is a woman out there someplace thinking of the day she gave birth to a baby girl and gave her away, but it is only a passing thought. Mostly I think about Mama and all those celebrations around our dining-room table. Back then, kids didn't have major birthday parties with clowns and balloons, but we could invite a friend or two to dinner, and sit in Daddy's chair at the head of the table. I remember how special it was sitting in my daddy's chair and how silly it seemed to have him sitting in mine. And I remember Mama standing beside me, smiling as I blew out the candles, telling me how proud she was to have such a fine big girl as her daughter.

Mama was an intense mother, often grabbing us children in the middle of a sentence to smother us with kisses and hugs. And she was always grooming us—combing, straightening, sending us back upstairs to rewash faces and scrub fingernails. She always had a Band-Aid in her bag. She never forgot to hand out vitamin pills in the morning. My daddy sometimes accused her of mothering him along with us kids. And she did, reminding him to drink his juice and feeling his forehead if he looked feverish. That was who she was—a mother.

And my cousin Iris was a fiercely devoted niece to her mothering aunt. Iris taught Buddy and me from an early age that our job in life was to please our mother. That's what good children did. We were to rub her neck when she was tired and brush her hair in the evening when the family gathered to watch television. We were to make our beds every morning and never, ever leave clothes on the floor. Pleasing Mama was something I took very seriously. I thought that if I could be a good enough girl and show my mother how much I loved her, it wouldn't matter to her so much that she really wasn't Iris's mother and that Buddy and I were adopted.

We didn't need to worry about pleasing Justine, who periodically swooped into our lives with hugs and gifts and enchanting photographs of faraway places. She was now living in New York City, but her visits to Columbus were magical times for us kids. Everyone in town knew Justine, and when we walked downtown, people stopped her on the sidewalk to say how much they enjoyed her photographs. If Justine had not been famous, she surely would have faced censure for not raising her own daughter. But famous people were allowed to play by different rules; after all, how could Justine take all those pictures if she never went anyplace? Folks were proud to know Justine, proud that she still called Columbus home, proud when a picture of their town made its way into one of her magazine spreads. Our bridge had been in Life *our county fair in the* Saturday Evening Post.

Every day was an adventure when Justine was with us. She would turn somersaults and cartwheels on the lawn. She would sit cross-legged on the old mattress in the attic and tell us ghost stories by candlelight. She took us on the train to Houston, where she would buy us new shoes at Krupp and Tuffly's and take us to lunch at the wondrous Forum Cafeteria. She took us to the beach at Galveston and to the Brenham creamery to eat the richest ice cream in Texas.

When she had the chance, Mama went along on our excursions, but not often. First Granny Grace was sick and shouldn't be left alone. And in the last years Justine came to us, it was Grandma Polly who needed looking after. And there was always the housework. We kids helped with the chores, but still there was a lot for Mama to do, and she wasn't one of those people who could leave things until later. Never once do I remember leaving the dishes undone so we could rush off to a ball game or the drive-in movie.

As much as I adored the time we spent with Justine, I sometimes stayed home with Mama while Justine took Buddy and Iris on the adventure of the day. And it wasn't just that I felt sorry for my mother and all the work she had to do; I cherished the times with just her and

*me and enjoyed being my mother's little helper. I didn't want her ever
to doubt that I loved her.*

*When Granny Grace began what my mother referred to as 'slipping
away', I helped her to the bathroom and up and down the stairs and
constantly tried to bring a smile to her inattentive face. I loved my
great-grandmother very much, but looking back, I'm sure a great deal
of my motivation for looking after Granny Grace was that it brought
words of praise from my mother.*

*One morning I couldn't make Granny Grace wake up. I don't think I
ever had thought through the term 'slipping away' to its inevitable conclusion, for her death came as a terrible shock to me. Afterwards I had a
difficult time re-entering the world of childish pursuits. I couldn't bring
myself to jump rope or play jacks when my Granny Grace was dead in
the cemetery. Mama took me to see Doc Hadley, who took my face in
his hands and told me that I was a little girl and it wasn't good for a little
girl to ride her bicycle out to the cemetery every day. He said that from
then on I could go to the cemetery only once a week, on Sunday afternoon, and if he heard I was going more often, he would have to give me
an anti-cemetery shot right in the butt, with a fat needle. Then, like
always, he let me listen to my heart with his stethoscope and gave me a
roll of gauze so I could play doctor with my dolls. Even back then I
knew I wanted to be a doctor when I grew up, just like Doc Hadley.*

WHEN JUSTINE wasn't around, Martha Claire sometimes would go
on and on about what a negligent mother her sister was and how
phone calls and visits didn't take the place of someone who was with
the child every day and took care of her when she was sick, and who
crawled into bed with her when she had bad dreams.

The irony of it was, of course, that because Justine wasn't a full-
time mother, Martha Claire had the privilege of filling in for her.
She absolutely doted on Iris, and Iris loved her aunt and wasn't shy
about showing it. She hovered around Martha Claire, fixing her
cups of tea, helping with Buddy and Cissy. But the pure and simple
truth was that Martha Claire was jealous of the love Iris also had
for her mother. Iris was always overjoyed when Justine called on the
telephone, and would count the days until her mother's next visit.
Martha Claire refused to understand that she and Justine weren't
competing for Iris's love. The child loved them both, but in different
ways. Martha Claire was for every day, Justine for fun and trips. Iris
didn't think in terms of whom she loved more. She simply loved.

'No, sweetheart, think now—nine times seven?'

Buddy looked down at his lap and shrugged. 'I don't remember, Mummy,' he said, his voice an agonised whisper.

Martha Claire reached over to caress his soft cheek. Such a beautiful child. At eight years old Buddy had a wonderful head of thick, curly black hair, huge dark eyes, and perpetually rosy cheeks that stood out against fair skin. Buddy was more beautiful than his sister, but he had none of Cissy's quick intelligence.

But Buddy could learn, and he would learn. Martha Claire would see to that. Grayson said she pushed the boy too hard, that he needed more time to run and play, but she couldn't bear the thought that their son might be held back a grade, that people might think he was a dummy, so she drilled him endlessly on his spelling lists and multiplication tables. Grayson helped some, too, and Iris when she was finished with her own homework. Even Cissy, who was a precocious second grader, would help her brother with his reading. Together they would get him through all the grades.

'I'm sorry, Mama,' Buddy said.

'Why, sweetie?'

'That I can't remember things.'

She opened her arms, and he came to sit on her lap. Soon he would be too big for this, she realised, and she held him tighter, kissing his neck and hair. 'Life isn't fair, my darling boy. Some children just have to work harder in school than others.'

'I love you, Mama,' he said.

'And I love you, Buddy.'

'I'm sorry, Mrs Richardson, but I can't give your money back on a dress pattern that you've already opened and used.'

'But I didn't use it,' she protested. 'It was too complicated.'

'But the pieces are all wadded up,' Grayson pointed out. 'No one else would buy the pattern now.'

'They can be ironed flat,' she insisted. 'I'm certainly not going to keep a pattern I can't use.'

Grayson took a breath to compose himself. He wanted to tell this annoying woman that she could take her piddling purchase and go elsewhere. But he couldn't do that. He couldn't afford to lose even one customer, piddling or otherwise. In the end, he gave Mrs Richardson her money back on the pattern.

He was no good at dealing with the Mrs Richardsons of the

world. Maybe if his mother or mother-in-law had been there, they might have fared better. But Polly wasn't well, and Lily mostly worked mornings, leaving her afternoons free for bridge.

Grayson's New Year's resolution for 1960 had been to be more innovative at the store. His mother kept telling him that doing things the same old way wasn't working. He should add a small sports goods department, she suggested, and sell only men's and boys' shoes and clothes, since he'd never been any good at selling dresses and ladies' underthings. He had laughed at first, but now he was considering her idea. He could partition off the back and carry shotgun shells, decoys, fishing lures and line, bats and balls. Not full lines. Just the stuff that people had to replace from time to time.

But would it be worth the effort? He would still be a shopkeeper, and a mediocre one at best. He was never going to be able to fix up the house for Martha Claire or pay for Buddy's and Cissy's college education. Maybe a few changes would make a difference, though. He would discuss it with Martha Claire when he got back from guard camp, he decided. Tomorrow he would be travelling with his unit to North Fort Hood for two weeks of manoeuvres, and he looked forward to the time away from the store.

After two weeks he was generally ready to come home, though, ready to see the children, ready to make love to his wife. The centre of his universe was still Martha Claire, even though he wasn't sure why. Youthful ardour was pretty much a memory, and at times he still wondered what life would have been like if he'd never come back to Columbus after the war. Whenever he thought of his wife, though, it was with tenderness.

'HEY, MARTHA CLAIRE, are you high on something?' Justine asked as she stretched out on the blanket.

'What do you mean?' Martha Claire asked.

'You seem so up. I haven't seen you run around and play with the kids in ages. You were actually *frolicking* out there in the surf. And you've laughed more in the past two days than you have in years. You even look younger. What's going on?'

'It's just nice to have you home for two whole weeks. And Grayson's sports corner at the store is beginning to turn a profit. Buddy passed fifth grade. And it's a beautiful day to be with my sister and our children on Galveston Island.'

Justine raised herself on her elbow and regarded her sister. 'If I didn't know you so well, I'd swear you were having an affair.'

Martha Claire gasped. 'How dare you say such a thing!'

'Sorry,' Justine said. 'I know you wouldn't do that. It's just that women I've known get all silly like you are when they're in love.' She lay back down. Yes, something was definitely going on with Martha Claire. She hadn't protested that she was too busy for a day at Jamaica Beach, and she'd even dug out a bathing suit to put on, much to the children's amazement.

'Can you keep a secret?' Martha Claire asked.

Justine regarded her. With knees hugged to her chest, Martha Claire was staring dreamily out to sea. The wind was teasing her hair, which shone golden in the sunlight. Her profile was as pure as a Raphael Madonna. Justine reached for her camera and snapped the shutter before Martha Claire was aware what she was doing.

'Of course I can keep a secret,' Justine said. 'Did I ever tell anyone that it was you who stole that jug of homemade brew off old Mr Logan's back porch?'

Martha Claire groaned. 'That was the sickest I've ever been in my life. Mother thought we had food poisoning.'

Justine sat up. 'So what's the secret?'

'I'm almost five weeks late with my period.'

'You think that you're *pregnant*?'

'Yeah. Wouldn't that be something, after all these years? I have an appointment with Doc Hadley tomorrow.'

Justine regarded her sister's slim figure. Her breasts were as small as ever, and obviously she wasn't suffering from morning sickness. She'd been up at dawn, devilling eggs for the picnic. 'Well, I hope you're right, if that's what you really want.'

'I know it's difficult for you to understand, but I've never stopped hoping,' Martha Claire said. 'Motherhood is no big deal for you, but it's the most important thing in the world for me.'

Not trusting herself to respond, Justine rose and started walking towards the surf, then broke into a run. She raced into the water and began swimming. She swam past the breaking waves until she could look back and her sister was only a speck on the distant beach. But Martha Claire's words followed her. *Motherhood is no big deal for you.* The words had stabbed like a knife.

MARTHA CLAIRE regarded Doc Hadley's cluttered office, with medical journals stacked on the table, desk and floor. Pictures of babies he had delivered over the years covered one wall in a random, thumbtacked montage. Every time Martha Claire saw that wall, she wished that a picture of her baby would be up there someday. Maybe now her wish would finally come true.

Doc Hadley had seemed impressed when Martha Claire told him she was thirty-four days late with her period. He had conducted her pelvic examination with his usual briskness, then told her to get dressed; he would talk with her in his office.

Martha Claire could hear voices coming from an adjacent examining room and hoped the doctor wouldn't take too long.

But then she heard his footsteps on the wooden floor and the door to his office opened. 'Sorry to keep you waiting, Martha Claire,' he said, lowering himself into his desk chair. She held her breath while the doctor took off his glasses and cleaned them with his pocket handkerchief. When he put them back on, he looked across the desk at her. 'You're entering menopause, Martha Claire.'

'*Menopause?* But I'm only thirty-nine years old.'

'That's young, but not abnormal,' he said.

'Are you saying that I'm not pregnant?'

'Yes. I'm sorry to disappoint you again, but at least you won't have to worry about it any more. Looks like you're never going to have a baby, Martha Claire. But you've got Iris and Buddy and Cissy. Surely getting pregnant is not as important as it once was.'

'Couldn't you be mistaken? Maybe I should see a specialist.'

He shrugged. 'You can see all the doctors you want, but it isn't going to make you pregnant. Now go on home and count your blessings. You've got a fine husband and three lively young'uns to raise.'

Martha Claire knew she was supposed to leave now, but she felt as though her body had turned to lead. *Menopause.* No baby, ever.

She didn't realise she was crying until Doc Hadley was thrusting a handful of tissue at her. She sobbed on and on, painful sobs that came from deep inside of her, from a broken heart and a womb that would be forever empty. Finally Doc Hadley called out to his nurse, who brought him a hypodermic needle to inject in Martha Claire's hip. Even as the nurse was leading her to a bed in the back room, Martha Claire could feel blessed oblivion flowing through her veins.

It was night when she awoke, and she was in her own bed with Grayson at her side. He immediately took her in his arms and told her it didn't matter, that she was more precious to him than anything in the world, that he loved their life just the way it was.

'Do Mother and Justine know what happened?'

'Yes, but not the children. When Doc Hadley called, I closed the store and went to bring you home. Tell me, my darling, what can I do or say to make you feel better?'

Martha Claire considered his request. And she thought of Doc Hadley's words—that at least the monthly torment was over. 'Just keep loving me,' she said. Then she kissed him. She found that she needed the reassurance of passion to reaffirm her womanhood. And this night his love filled her more completely than it had in a long time. She wondered, Could it be a new beginning, with loving just for loving's sake? She clung to him for a long time afterwards, relishing the scent and feel of him, this husband for a lifetime.

'Are you sure everything is all right?' Martha Claire asked.

'My goodness, Martha Claire, you've only been gone since this morning,' Polly said. 'The children are home from school. Cissy is across the street playing with the Williams girls. Iris put a roast in the oven and is out in the yard playing catch with Buddy. Now stop worrying and go make yourself pretty for your husband. Grayson's been looking forward to this reunion for ever so long, and the man deserves a weekend away with his wife.'

Martha Claire hung up the phone and sat on the bed, staring at her reflection in the dresser mirror. Yes, she worried too much. But her mother wasn't well. Doc Hadley said her heart was worn out and it was a miracle she had lasted this long. If it weren't for Iris, Martha Claire wouldn't even have considered leaving town. At sixteen Iris was as responsible as any adult and would take good care of her grandmother and fourteen- and twelve-year-old cousins. Martha Claire smiled. Yes, she would relax and have a great time.

Hanging on the closet door was Grayson's dress uniform, silver oak leaves on the shoulders. He was now a lieutenant-colonel in the National Guard, and a battalion commander. Tonight they were attending the twentieth reunion of his class at Texas A&M. Tomorrow there was a football game against Texas Tech, with the men being honoured during half time.

Grayson was singing the school War Hymn in the shower, which brought another smile to Martha Claire's face. She wanted to look pretty tonight and was glad she'd let Iris talk her into buying a black velvet sheath that showed she still had a decent figure.

When she finished getting ready, Martha Claire did a little pirouette for Grayson's benefit. There was admiration in his eyes as he came to attention and offered her a snappy salute. Martha Claire hadn't seen him in dress blues for years. He looked so handsome, it took her breath away.

She remembered many of the men and their wives from the military balls she'd attended during Grayson's undergraduate years. At dinner they sat with Bobby and Ruth Mitchell, who now lived in Fairbanks, Alaska. Bobby and Grayson had shared rooms during their senior year and served in the same artillery battalion in France. This was the first time they had seen each other since the war. Martha Claire and Ruth chatted about their children, but mostly they sat quietly while the men reminisced about the war years.

After dinner she and Ruth headed for the ladies' room. When they returned, Bobby was commenting about how good Grayson looked, with not even a scar from his wound. 'He would have lost an eye for sure if we hadn't been able to get him on a medevac flight to England,' Bobby told his wife.

A flight to England? Martha Claire replayed the words in her head. Grayson had never been to England. She waited for her husband to correct Bobby's statement. But Bobby was still talking, explaining to his wife how Grayson had been wounded during the battle for Le Luc. The Germans had massed a strong defence of the town. Their battalion had been moved in as reinforcements. They were low on fuel, so they walked fifty minutes and rode ten. Grayson was just getting back into the Jeep for his ten-minute ride when the Jeep took a hit. The driver was killed. Grayson had taken some shrapnel in his right eye and was given emergency treatment at a field hospital, then evacuated to a hospital north of London, where he could be seen by an eye surgeon.

Martha Claire tugged on Grayson's sleeve, but he didn't meet her gaze, didn't say that Bobby was mistaken.

Suddenly the band was playing, and Grayson was pulling her onto the dance floor. The music was from their era—'Falling in Love with Love'—music they had danced to when they were young and filled with sweet longing. Their bodies fitted together as perfectly as they had back then. Martha Claire closed her eyes and let the music take her, mentally pushing puzzlement aside.

Martha Claire waited until the weekend was over, when she and Grayson were on their way home, to ask him why he'd never told her about going to England during the war.

'I'm sure I wrote to you about it.'

'The letter probably got lost,' Martha Claire acknowledged.

The next day, while the children were at school, her mother was resting, and Grayson was at work, she went up to the attic and looked in the trunk where his wartime letters were stored. She found the letter telling her about having to wear a patch over his eye after having a piece of shrapnel removed, but nothing was said about treatment in England, which seemed odd. England was where Justine had been stationed. Wouldn't he have called his sister-in-law? Wouldn't she have gone to see him? Surely a wounded brother-in-law would have warranted a short train ride.

The following morning, without analysing the reason why, Martha Claire climbed the stairs to Justine's apartment. The walls were covered with photographs she had taken, mostly of family, but also ones of Columbus—the bridges, the courthouse, Stewart's Dry Goods. Having no idea what she was looking for, Martha Claire looked in every drawer, opened every cupboard, shook every book for what might be hidden between its pages. Finally she went through a shoebox that held pictures Justine had taken in London during the war—photographs of people digging through bombed-out buildings, medics carrying the injured on stretchers.

One picture in particular captured her attention—of a soldier and little boy kneeling beside a dead dog, with bombed-out terraced houses in the background. Justine had written on the back: *Charlwood Street, 150 houses destroyed by parachute mines*. The focus was on the grief-stricken face of the boy. If Martha Claire's perusal had been a more casual one, she might have passed right over it, taking it for a candid picture of two unknown people—an American soldier comforting a grieving child in war-torn London.

But this American soldier had a bandaged right eye, and she recognised the familiar line of his cheek and jaw. It was a picture of her husband, and her sister had taken it.

THAT NIGHT, after Grayson had turned out the light and he and Martha Claire had gone to bed, she told him that she had found a picture of him that Justine had taken in London. He had been comforting a boy whose dog had been killed.

Grayson didn't speak for long, silent minutes; then his voice said into the darkness, 'I met her for a drink at a pub.'

'That picture wasn't taken in a pub.'

'No, it was taken the next day, after an air raid.'

'Why did neither of you mention something as remarkable as seeing a relative from back home in London during the war? What reason could you possibly have for not mentioning it?'

'It all happened so suddenly,' he said. 'Just hours after I was injured, I was on my way to London. Probably I decided to wait until I knew the outcome of the surgery before I wrote. My driver's chest was blown open. I tried to help him, but blood was gushing out of my eye. I thought I was dying, too. It wasn't something I could put in a letter home to my wife.'

'So you told Justine?'

'Yes. She was there; you weren't.'

Their arms were so close she could feel the warmth from his flesh. She shifted her weight, eliminating the risk of an accidental touch. 'Did something happen between you and my sister?' she asked.

'Not in the way you mean. Air-raid sirens were going off. Justine helped me figure out how many shillings to leave for our tab. We were putting on our coats; then suddenly the building was caving in. We managed to crawl down to the cellar and ended up trapped down there. Buildings were burning around us, people screaming. She made me promise I would kill her rather than let her burn to death. It wasn't something either one of us wanted to talk about afterwards.'

'And nothing else happened? Do you swear on the lives of the children that you didn't have a last fling before the flames got you?'

'No, we didn't, but would it have been so terrible to want that sort of human comfort in the face of death? Hearing Justine's soft Texas voice made me think of you. Before the bombing started, I remember thinking how I wanted to sit in that pub all night and listen to her sound just like my wife.'

Martha Claire allowed him to take her in his arms, to assure her of his love. But the seeds of suspicion had been planted. She believed him, and she didn't. But she would probably never know if her doubt was justified, so she decided to ignore it.

For a time it worked. Life went on. She took care of her children and nursed her mother.

Then one summer evening, while she was sitting at the table paying bills and half watching an episode of *I Love Lucy*, the cloud of doubt began to lift, leaving sickening realisation in its stead.

Polly was lying on the sofa propped up with pillows. Buddy and Cissy were stretched out on the floor in front of the television. Grayson was in his easy chair, with Iris sitting on the floor in front of him, using his legs as a backrest. Martha Claire paused a minute in her cheque writing to admire her niece's profile. Iris's hair was pulled back into a ponytail, her knees drawn up to her chest. She was slimmer than Justine had been at that age, but Iris had Justine's long legs and her dimpled chin, her widely spaced eyes and full mouth.

Now, however, Martha Claire noticed something about Iris she'd never realised before, something that made her put her hand to her heart and catch her breath. *Iris had Grayson's nose.*

Iris's nose was shaped exactly like his and matched its tilt, matched the way it curved into his forehead, the flare of the nostrils, the slight indentation at its tip.

Martha Claire studied Cissy's and Buddy's noses, her mother's nose. She reached up and touched her own nose. Everyone's was different. Only Grayson and Iris had noses that were exactly the same.

She realised her mother was watching her. Martha Claire met her gaze, and Polly shook her head slowly back and forth, her message clear. *Whatever it is that you are thinking, let it go. Don't ask questions that are best left unanswered.*

Martha Claire pushed back her chair and walked out to the porch, where she stared into the night. Should she have seen it before? Other ways in which her husband and her sister's child were alike began to crowd into her mind. Their perfect teeth. Their laugh. Their beautiful singing voices. But what she was thinking could not be so. Grayson's injury had happened in late summer in 1944. Iris was born in March 1946, which meant she hadn't been conceived until after the war had ended, not until the summer of 1945. Had Grayson gone back after the armistice?

Later, after she had helped her mother into bed, Martha Claire sat on the edge of the bed and said, 'Talk to me, Mother.'

Polly placed her hands across her chest before she took a breath and said, 'You have created a beautiful family and allowed me to be a part of it. I've felt so blessed to spend my last years with you and Grayson and the children in the house where I have lived most of my life. In all those years there has never been anything but love in this house. Don't change that now, Martha Claire.'

'I am such a fool that I didn't see it before.'

Polly said, 'You haven't *seen* anything.'

'Come on, Mother. I saw the look on your face. You've wondered, too, haven't you? Wondered if Grayson were Iris's father?'

'If such a thought had ever crossed my mind,' Polly said, her voice firm, 'I would have put it right out of my head.'

Martha Claire stared down at her mother, who had once been plump and pretty and was now little more than wrinkled skin over bones—a woman nearing the end of her days. After a lifetime of caring for those she loved, she wanted a tidy ending for her life.

'So you want me to sweep it under the rug?' Martha Claire asked.

'Yes, that is what I want you to do, what I beg you to do.'

'I'm not sure I can.'

Polly squeezed her daughter's hand. 'Yes, you can, Martha Claire Mayfield Stewart. For your family, you can do that.'

ONCE THE FLOODGATE had been opened, however, Martha Claire could not look at Iris and Grayson without seeing some new way in which they were alike. Their ear lobes. Their bearing. They both drank tea without sugar.

And there was something else that occurred to her. Before the war Justine and Grayson had been great friends, always kidding and horsing around. In the years since the war her husband and sister had had very little to do with one another, she realised. She couldn't remember a single time that just the two of them had gone anyplace together, not even for a walk around the block. They saw each other only in the presence of other family members.

Finally one night, after the lights were out, when the silence in their darkened bedroom grew too heavy to bear, Martha Claire stared up at the ceiling shadows and asked, 'Did you go back to England after the war and have an affair with my sister?'

'No,' he said.

'Just *no*?' she challenged. 'Not, "My God, Martha Claire, how on earth can you say such a thing?"'

When he didn't respond, she asked, 'Did Justine come to you?'

'No.'

'You swore on the lives of the children that nothing happened between you and Justine during the war. Now I want you to swear on their lives that after the war you did not have an affair with her.'

'You have to stop this, Martha Claire,' he said.

'Then you won't swear.'

'No, I won't swear.'

'Then I don't want to sleep in the same bed with you.'

Silently he rose from the bed and crossed the hall to Granny Grace's old room.

The next day Martha Claire avoided him. That night he went straight to the spare room. And the night after that.

Martha Claire moved his clothes into the spare room, and his stack of books and magazines from the bedside table.

More and more Polly stayed in her bed, the sickness in her heart taking on an added dimension. The children realised, of course, that all was not well with Martha Claire and Grayson, and tried to be better children. Buddy kept promising he would work harder at school. Cissy kept her bedroom as immaculate as a nun's cell. Iris baked more pies and cakes than they could eat.

For weeks Martha Claire kept her silence, until she could stand it no longer. After the house was dark and quiet, she crept across the hall to the room where her husband now slept and knelt beside the bed. Grayson didn't move, but she could tell he was awake, and she began telling him the ways in which he and Iris were alike. And how, when he came back from the war, he and Justine acted like strangers. 'Maybe the reason you never wrote me about going to England was because you knew you would be going back there to be unfaithful to me with my own sister.'

'I'm not sure why I didn't write you about it,' Grayson said. 'Maybe I felt guilty because I had told Justine things I had never been able to tell you. I told her that I didn't want to come back to Columbus, that I didn't want the same things out of life that you did, that I had tried to tell you we shouldn't get married but suddenly you were inviting people and painting the gazebo.'

'And you went back after the war to finish the conversation?'

He said nothing for the longest time. A freight train's lonely whistle pierced the humid darkness as Martha Claire waited, whatever love was left in her heart for this man ebbing slowly away. *He hadn't wanted to marry her when she thought he loved her more than anything.*

'Well?' she demanded, her voice harsh. 'You went back after the war to discuss *the Martha Claire problem*.'

'Something like that,' he said.

Martha Claire fell back on her haunches. Grayson rolled to a sitting position, his feet on the floor, his forehead in his hands. 'I wasn't sure what to do,' he said. 'I didn't want to come back here, but I didn't want to hurt you. It was tearing me apart. Justine and I had a lot to drink. It just happened. I never planned for it, and I've regretted it ever since. God, how I've regretted it.'

Martha Claire put a hand on the bedpost and pulled herself up.

'I don't know if Iris is my child,' he went on, the wetness on his face shining in the moonlight. 'Justine told me that she'd slept around after her boyfriend was killed. When you wrote that she was pregnant, it was easy to convince myself it had nothing to do with me. I never asked her who the baby's father was. Justine never said. After a while I stopped thinking about it.'

Martha Claire slapped him hard across his face, the sound reverberating in the silent house. 'I hate you with all my heart and soul. I want you to leave this house and never come back.'

'I would rather die,' he told her, falling to his knees in front of her. 'If you will let me stay here with our children, I will do so on whatever terms you set. Please, Martha Claire, for their sake. They shouldn't suffer for something I did. This will be our secret for ever. Iris need never know, or Cissy and Buddy.'

MARTHA CLAIRE WONDERED how she could face the rest of her life with the knowledge she now possessed. *Her husband and her sister*. She had no doubt that Iris was *their* child. The child she and Grayson had loved as their own was in fact *his* daughter—his and Justine's. She could no longer bear to look at Iris, knowing what she now knew. It was too much to endure. The knowledge poisoned her insides and made food taste foul. It stole away her sleep. She was tormented with indecision. She did not want to subject herself and her children to a divorce, yet she could not live under the same roof with Grayson. She wished he would die. Then she could be a respectable widow and get on with her life.

And then, in the middle of all this anguish, on an overcast November day, with the children at school and Grayson at the store, she took her mother a lunch tray and found her gasping for breath. Even as she dialled Doc Hadley's number, she knew it was too late. She raced back down the hall and knelt beside Polly's bed. 'Don't go, Mother. I need you. I love you so.'

Her mother's last words were, 'Grayson loves you.'

MARTHA CLAIRE PUT thoughts of her crumbling marriage on hold and went about the business of planning a funeral.

Justine was travelling throughout the South, photographing demonstrations against school segregation, and did not arrive until the day before the funeral. The children waited up for her and greeted her with hugs and tears.

'Mama and Daddy don't talk to each other any more,' Cissy told her. 'Daddy sleeps in Granny Grace's old bedroom.'

Justine looked at Iris. 'Do you know why?'

Iris shook her head.

While the children fixed her a snack, Justine went upstairs and opened the door to the room where her sister now slept alone.

'I don't want to talk to you,' Martha Claire said from the bed.

Justine turned on the lamp. Martha Claire was leaning against the headboard, her arms folded across her chest. 'I need for you to tell me about Mother,' Justine said.

'I don't think she suffered much.'

'The last time I talked to her, she kept telling me how much she loved me. I'm so sorry I didn't drop everything and come then.'

'Oh, but you have your *career*,' Martha Claire said, 'and that's always been more important to you than family.'

Justine regarded her sister's face and was shocked by the hatred she saw there. 'Tell me what's going on. What's happened?'

'We will talk about it after the funeral.'

Icy fingers of dread tickled Justine's neck as she backed out of her sister's room, closing the door behind her. She hesitated outside the room where Grayson now slept. She and Grayson hadn't had a private conversation in seventeen years. She needed to talk to him now. She was aware of Martha Claire's listening ears, though, and went back down to the children. Somehow Martha Claire had figured out her deepest, darkest secret.

AFTER THE FUNERAL Martha Claire asked Justine to come to her room. She sat on the window seat. Justine sat on the dressing-table stool. The door was closed. The children had gone home for the evening with Grayson's mother. Justine didn't know where Grayson was. He had been like a shadow all day, saying nothing.

'You are no longer welcome in my home,' Martha Claire announced. 'I will always love your daughter, but I hope I never have to see you again.' Martha Claire held up her hand when Justine started to speak. 'And don't tell me I can't know how it was during the war. Grayson has already done that. He told me about the bombs and about the two of you almost dying. Well, I wish you *had* died. Everyone has had close calls in their life. A close call didn't give you the right to have an affair with my husband. How could you? You might as well have plunged a knife in my back.'

'You are right to blame me,' Justine said. 'Grayson was in a fog. I could have stopped it, but I didn't. And I told him if he had any sense, he'd tell his father to sell the store and give you an ultimatum.'

Justine began to pace, fighting down the need to lash back at Martha Claire, but the words came out anyway. 'You were always so god-damned self-righteous. You never did anything wrong. I wanted to be just like my sister. I played by the rules and never made love to a man I loved very much. And then his plane was shot down. He was dead. Just like that. I didn't have the memory of lying naked in his arms. I wish he were Iris's father, but he's not. You know what Grayson and I talked about? We talked about you, about how much we loved you, about how in the hell we were going to convince you to take a risk, to at least give military life a try. We didn't plan for anything to happen. We got drunk and maudlin, and it just did. It wasn't a love affair. It was just two lonely, confused people who needed to touch another human being. I closed my eyes and turned him into an Aussie named Billy. And he turned me into you. I know it was wrong, but it wasn't wrong enough for you to throw away a good man and ruin your wonderful family.'

But Justine could tell by the hard, ugly look on her sister's face that she wasn't listening. Suddenly Martha Claire began to shriek. 'How dare you come back here year after year! It makes my flesh crawl to think of it. What kind of a monster are you?'

'But I gave you my daughter,' Justine protested. 'Do you think I wanted to? When you didn't have a baby of your own, I knew that was my penance. I had to let you raise Iris. But now that's changed. I'm taking her with me. I wish I could take Buddy and Cissy, too. This house isn't a fit place for children.'

Martha Claire went white. 'You will not take her,' she said through clenched teeth. 'Iris is *mine*!' Then she marched out of the room and down the stairs. She picked up the telephone and called Iris home from her grandmother Lily's house.

Justine watched from the upstairs railing as Martha Claire paced back and forth across the entrance hall. When Justine heard footsteps on the front porch, she hurried down the stairs. The door flew open, and there she was—Iris, the child they would both die for.

Martha Claire presented an ultimatum. 'You are the child closest to my heart. I have loved you and cared for you since you were born. But now my sister wants to take you away from me. If you go with her, you will never be welcome in this house again.'

Justine felt as though her heart were being twisted from its moorings as she watched her daughter look from her to her aunt. She would have to choose. She could no longer have them both. For an instant Justine wavered. Maybe she should back off. Maybe she should make the noble gesture. She knew, however, that every time Martha Claire looked at Iris, she would think of who she was. Her love for Iris would be tainted.

Iris had no answer, of course. Not then. She ran upstairs to her room and slammed the door.

In the night, Grayson went to Iris's room. She was still dressed, lying on top of the spread. He sat on the side of her bed and held her hand. 'You must leave,' he told her.

'But what about you and Martha Claire?' Iris said, sobbing. 'What about Cissy and Buddy? Why did everything change?'

'It's my fault and no one else's. You must never blame Martha Claire or your mother. You have a right to be happy, and I don't think anyone who stays on in this house will ever be happy again.'

He had brought a suitcase and helped her gather the things from her room that were most precious. Then the two of them crept down the stairs and across the yard. He carried the suitcase up the stairs to the landing. He heard the door open. He knew that Justine was watching as he hugged Iris's slim body against his chest.

Dearest Iris. He could not imagine life without her.

When Martha Claire emerged from her room the next morning and realised that Iris and Justine were gone, she crawled into bed with Cissy and wept. Buddy came to sit on the floor beside the bed and hold his mother's hand and tell her not to cry.

Never had Martha Claire felt so alone. Her mother was dead. Her sister and husband had betrayed her. Iris, the child she loved more than anything, was gone. All she had left were these two frightened children who counted on her to mother them. And she would do that. But first she had to deal with other things.

She decided Buddy and Cissy were too upset to go to school. Later she realised she should have sent them anyway, as they watched with fearful eyes as she carried all of Justine's memorabilia down from the garage apartment and burned it in the back yard—yearbooks, clothes, albums, toys, letters, books. She also burned the portrait of the Mayfield sisters that hung on the stairwell wall.

Then she prepared lunch and left the children to clean up the kitchen. 'I'll be all right,' she said, 'but I have to be alone for a time.'

She stayed in her room for three weeks.

IN THE DAYS after Justine took Iris away, we learned that the Russians had installed missile bases in Cuba.

While the outside world hovered on the brink of war and other Columbus families were planning evacuation routes in case a missile armed with a nuclear warhead hit the refineries that surrounded Houston, what was left of our family was dealing with its own more immediate crisis. Three times a day I would put Mama's meal tray in front of her door, then knock and tell her it was there. Not a hint of life would come from behind that door except the occasional sound of the shower running or the toilet flushing.

Daddy, Buddy and I spoke in whispers and kept the volume on the television turned on low while we watched spyplane photographs of missile silos in Cuba and President Kennedy giving an ultimatum to the Russians. All the while I kept thinking of Mama up in her room. Did she know that any minute we all could die?

After I was in bed, Buddy would sit on the floor beside the bed and we would speculate about what happened to adopted children if their parents got a divorce. Whom would we belong to then? Often Buddy fell asleep on the floor, and I would slip a pillow under his head and cover him with a blanket. The Russians eventually backed down, but our mother was still upstairs.

Then one afternoon we arrived home from school to the heavenly aroma of baking bread. To this day, the smell of baking bread makes me think of the time my mother came out of her room.

At dinner that first evening, and ever after, not one word was said about Mama's three-week retreat from the family. In fact, words about anything at all were painfully scarce. I remember staring at my plate, desperately trying to think of something to say. Iris could have got us talking, but I was not Iris.

The week after Mama came downstairs, Buddy and I got our first letter from Iris. She was going to an all-girl high school where the students wore navy blazers and pleated skirts. Her French teacher was taking the entire class to Paris in the spring. But she was terribly lonely for Columbus. Her mother had promised she could visit next summer if that was all right with Martha Claire.

'Do you think Mama will let her come?' Buddy asked.

'I hope so,' I answered, but I wasn't sure. I knew that in Mama's mind Iris had betrayed her by leaving with Justine.

As those first days of the post-Iris era turned into weeks and then months, Buddy and I began to relax a bit. Our parents never kissed, never smiled at one another, but Daddy returned to what I had come to think of as my mother's bedroom. They couldn't still hate each other if they were sleeping in the same bed.

As the school year drew to a close, we waited anxiously while Mama decided if Iris could come and visit us. In the end, she decided that no, Iris could not come. Buddy and I could correspond with her, but she wasn't to call on the telephone. I don't think I had ever before talked back to my mother, but that night I told her she was mean. Before she had time to reply, I rushed to my room and slammed the door. I cried so hard, I got sick and threw up on the floor. Daddy found me trying to clean it up and held me while I cried some more. When I had calmed down, he told me to go and tell Mama I was sorry. 'But it's the truth,' I insisted. 'She is mean.'

'Go,' he said, pointing to the door.

I did as he asked, but had my fingers crossed behind my back. Mama said there were things I didn't understand. I wish now that I had known the reason why Mama wouldn't let Iris come, because even at the age of twelve I think I would have found some understanding for her decision. Buddy and I did not know, however, and we came close to hating our mother for denying us a visit from someone we loved so much.

Iris wrote to say how disappointed she was about Martha Claire's decision and proposed a plan 'to keep us close'. I was to call her on the first Sunday night of the following month, reversing the charge—after Mama and Daddy were asleep—and she would explain.

And so, on the appointed night, with a pounding heart, I crept down the stairs after midnight and carried the phone into the hall closet, where I burrowed behind the coats. Iris answered on the first ring. 'Hi, sweetie,' she said, and immediately I began to sob as all that missing overflowed. In a soothing voice Iris started telling me what once had been my favourite bedtime story—about the day that Doc Hadley gave *me to Mama and Daddy and how Iris decided that I was her sissy and she would take care of me and love me for ever and ever. 'I love you, Iris,' I was finally able to say. 'I love you, too, my little Cissy,' she said. We talked for more than an hour—a magical hour. Her plan, she explained, was for me to call her on the first Sunday night of every month, reverse charge. She had her own phone, right by her bed. Justine said that we could talk all night if we wanted to.*

After that I kept an ongoing file in my head of all the things I would tell Iris the next time we talked. She wasn't always home on the first Sunday night of the month. Sometimes she and Justine would be travelling, and I would have to wait until the following month. But that was OK because I knew there would be a next time. My cousin, who had been like a sister to me, had been reduced to a voice in a dark closet, but that voice served as an amulet to soften the pain brought by warring parents and an unsure future.

With the monthly cheques no longer arriving from Justine, money was tighter than ever, and Daddy took a job as area sales representative for a company that made children's shoes. He was gone from early Monday morning until late Friday evening, and Mama took over at the store. She didn't talk about fixing the house up any more. The best she could do was keep the place painted and patch the leaks.

Every afternoon after school I worked at the store—Buddy, too, sometimes. But usually he had practice—baseball, basketball, football. Academically Buddy struggled, but he was a wonderful athlete. In the fall Daddy always made it home on Friday nights in time for Buddy's football games. Buddy played defensive end, and already people were saying he might be good enough to get a college scholarship. Those evenings, as we cheered together for our Buddy, it felt almost like before, when Mama and Daddy still loved each other.

Daddy took over at the store on Saturday morning. After he closed up, he would work through the list of chores Mama always had waiting for him, spending the rest of the day washing windows, cleaning out the rain gutters, painting whatever. He always did her bidding, even if her request was an irrational one—like crawling up onto the roof to check the television antenna when the TV was working just fine. She never said thank you, but was quick to point out something she considered less than satisfactory. Buddy thought Daddy should stand up to her, tell her he had the right to relax at the weekend, but he never did.

Every Sunday evening I baked cookies for Daddy to take on the road. On Monday morning I would wake up early to fix him breakfast and walk him out to the car. I knew that with his college degree from Texas A&M he could have found a job in town, but he drove away every Monday morning and spent four evenings a week alone in run-down motels, because that was what my mother wanted. I could not understand how our beautiful family had come to this.

I didn't want to love one parent more than the other, but my feelings for my daddy became more and more tender. Even if he had once done some terrible, hurtful thing to Mama, he had a good heart and had by now surely earned the right to be forgiven.

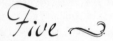

Five

He had always wanted to travel, Grayson would remind himself as he drove up and down the state highways and county roads of his sales territory, which stretched across southern and eastern Texas. And he did try to find satisfaction in what had become his lot in life, as he went from one small town to the next. After he had made his calls on local merchants, giving his spiel about the perfect fit for growing feet, he would explore the surrounding countryside. But after a time everything took on a sameness.

The day President Kennedy was shot, he was in Navasota. He closed up his sample cases and went to his motel to keep the vigil in front of the television, hoping against hope the President would live. When Walter Cronkite made his fateful announcement, he called Martha Claire, who was beside herself to the point of hysteria. But she didn't want to console or be consoled. She needed to get back to the television. Not even in a foxhole in France had he felt this lonely.

He hated all the jokes about travelling salesmen, but did consider taking up with a woman in Tucker. Pretty, plump Loretta ran a homely little café with chequered curtains, and her pies rivalled Martha Claire's. He looked forward to Loretta's welcoming smile, but he couldn't bring himself to deceive Martha Claire a second time. His hope was that if he did Martha Claire's bidding without question, she would someday find it in her heart to forgive him. But Grayson hated to see his children watching silently from the sidelines while their mother constantly carped at him. What sort of memories would they have of this awful time?

'REMEMBER THOSE TIMES up in the attic when we used to daydream about finding our birth mother?' Buddy asked.

'Of course I remember,' Cissy said.

They were waxing the station wagon, which Buddy had permission to use tonight—for a date, Cissy suspected. Buddy refused to admit he was going on a date, even though he had polished his shoes, had a haircut, and talked Cissy into helping him make the ten-year-old vehicle more presentable. Buddy didn't go on many dates. Girls started being busy when Buddy asked them out. Cissy knew it was because he didn't treat girls very well. Buddy didn't want to be like their father. He didn't want any girl to treat him the way Mama treated Daddy.

'I'd like us to do that,' he said, dabbing wax on a faded fender.

'Do what? You're not talking about searching for her?'

'Why not?' he asked.

Cissy sat on the open tailgate. 'Buddy, we don't have a single clue to go on. We don't even know where we were born.'

'You must have been born close by, since you were only a couple of hours old when Doc Hadley brought you to Mom and Dad.' He sat down beside her and said, 'We could put a personal ad in the newspaper: "Seeking information about a white woman who gave birth to a baby girl October 17, 1950."'

'What if Mama found out? It would break her heart.'

'But we have a right to know.'

'Not really. The law protects the identity of women who put their babies up for adoption.'

'I asked Doc Hadley about her,' Buddy admitted.

'What did he say?' Cissy asked.

Buddy shrugged. 'That part of his job was knowing when to keep his mouth shut. He said doctors take an oath about that. I asked him to at least tell me why she gave us away, if she was sick or in prison or something like that. He just shook his head.'

'Let it drop, Buddy. All you're going to do is hurt Mama.' Cissy scooted off the tailgate and went back to polishing.

'I need to know if she loved us,' he said stubbornly.

Cissy turned, startled to realise he was crying. She put down her rags and went over to him. 'We have a mother who loves us.' She rubbed a soothing hand up and down his arm. 'And a daddy.'

'You were just a newborn, but I was a year and a half when you were born. I was old enough to walk around and hug her neck, and *she gave me away.* Why would she do that? I need to ask her why. Maybe she's sitting someplace hoping more than anything that we will find her. Please help me find her, Cissy. Please.'

'Buddy, you're not making sense. What if you found her and discovered she's an awful woman? Maybe the police took us away from her because she wasn't a fit mother. Did you ever think of that? No, I will not help you. It would be going against Mama.'

'I WISH THEY WEREN'T making such a fuss,' Buddy said as his mother smoothed down his hair and straightened his collar.

'The whole town is proud of you, son,' Martha Claire said.

From their backstage vantage point Buddy could see the lectern onstage, a row of chairs behind it. The audience was filled to overflowing. The band was playing 'King of the Road'.

When the coach told him there would be a public announcement, he had no idea it would be like this. His father had even come home midweek to attend. Dad hadn't come home in the middle of the week since last year when Grandma Stewart fell and broke her hip. Buddy glanced over at his grandmother in her wheelchair. She lived with them now, in the downstairs room that had been Grandma Polly's after she got too weak to go up and down stairs.

His mother looked slim and pretty in a flowery yellow dress. She was talking to his dad and straightening his tie, even smiling at him.

The principal was lining them up to march onto the stage. Cissy was to wheel Grandma Stewart out last and sit with her on the end of the row. Cissy looked pretty, too, with her dark, curly hair worn down for a change and not in its usual ponytail. She was smiling at him, offering a thumbs up from her position behind the wheelchair. Buddy returned the gesture and felt a lump in his throat. This should be Cissy's day, too. He never would have passed anything except PE if she hadn't coached him all the way.

The band played the school song as they marched to their places. Buddy felt his neck turning red. He couldn't believe it. Half the town must be out there. He bowed his head while Reverend Huxley offered a prayer that made it sound as though Buddy had won a football scholarship to Texas A&M because he was a God-fearing boy. He squirmed a bit at that. Buddy only went to church because his mother made him. He stared down at his large hands. His birth father was probably some dumb farm boy with hands just like these, not someone who was expected to go to college.

Buddy kept staring at his hands while his high-school coach had his turn at the lectern, offering a lengthy chronology of Buddy's high-school football career, ending with his triumphant senior season, when he was recruited by every college in Texas.

Then it was Mr Lemkey's turn. Lemkey was the A&M assistant coach who had recruited Buddy. His words were less glowing. He called Buddy a solid player who had a lot of potential if he worked hard and made his grades. Then he called Buddy to the lectern. 'And now, it gives me great pleasure to announce on behalf of the Texas A&M Athletic Department that Buddy Stewart of Columbus High School has accepted our offer of an athletic scholarship and will be playing for the finest football programme in the entire nation.' The band struck up the school War Hymn, and the audience rose to its feet, clapping and singing.

When everyone once again was seated, Buddy was left alone at the lectern. In a quivering voice he thanked Mr Lemkey and said the words he had rehearsed with Cissy the night before. He had chosen A&M because of its great traditions and because it was his father's alma mater. He promised to work hard and do his best. He thanked his coach, the school, his team, the town. Then he surprised himself by adding words that had not been rehearsed.

'My mother always said that Columbus, Texas, is the best place in the world for kids to grow up, and I think she's right. I guess all of you know that my sister and I are adopted. We grew up in Columbus because two good people took us in and raised us. Cissy and I are the luckiest kids in the world to have ended up in this town with Grayson and Martha Claire Stewart as our parents. We owe them everything, and I love them very much.' Then he hugged his parents, who both had tears in their eyes. Buddy was crying, too. And Cissy. His words about his parents had been heartfelt. He did love them and was grateful to them for the life they had given him. Maybe they weren't perfect, but then neither was he.

After the assembly Cissy said, 'You were wonderful,' as he held her close.

'Cissy, what if I'm not good enough for this?' And suddenly he wished he had signed on at one of the small state schools where they didn't expect football players to do much more than show up for class. But everyone told him he'd have a better chance of a professional career if he went to a Division I school. And Mr Lemkey had promised he would have tutors who would make sure he enrolled in classes taught by professors who understood the importance of football to the school. Mr Lemkey didn't know, however, that Buddy never would have got through high school without his sister's help. If only Cissy could come with him to College Station, but she wouldn't graduate from high school for another year, and she was hoping for an academic scholarship to the women's college in Denton, where she could study nursing.

'What if I can't hack it at college?' he whispered to his sister. 'Everyone will hate me if I screw up.'

Cissy put a finger to his lips. 'Just do the best you can. No one can hate you for that.'

During Buddy's three semesters at Texas A&M, I came to realise that I had not done my brother any favour during those nightly study sessions at the dining-room table. I'm not sure he ever would have graduated from high school without my help, but maybe that would have been for the best. A big strong boy like him could have joined the army or got a job on the docks in Baytown or Texas City.

After he left for college, I did what I could over the telephone, but Buddy simply was no good at memorising things—historical dates, the Gettysburg Address, multiplication tables. He did modestly well on the freshman football team, but he was beginning to worry that he didn't have a prayer of completing college, no matter how many tutors the athletic department provided. I think he wanted to quit school then, but the whole town was expecting him to become a football legend.

In his sophomore year he played in most of the games and was cited in newspaper articles as a 'promising' defensive player. I was at college in Denton by then, with studies of my own. I told myself that as long as Buddy went to class, he'd be all right. And maybe he would have been, but he frequently cut classes. I suspected his cutting had to do with all the beer he drank. His room-mate bragged to me that Buddy had the team record for consuming the most six-packs at one sitting.

I spent my childhood watching over my brother and being my mother's little helper. The time had come for me to find other purposes in life, but it was difficult. It felt as though I was succeeding at my brother's expense.

Texas A&M won the Southwest Conference in 1967, earning the right to face Alabama in the Cotton Bowl on New Year's Day. Buddy went home for Christmas, but the team was required to return to College Station the day after to prepare for the bowl game. *The Cotton Bowl.* His family and all his friends would be there. Millions of people would be watching on television.

In the locker room before the game he received a telegram from Justine and Iris. They wished him luck, said they loved him and would be watching and cheering for him and the Aggies. Buddy got tears in his eyes. They loved him. In his mind he dedicated the game to Justine and Iris. And to Cissy. Always to Cissy.

The game was a close one, and Buddy didn't get to play as much as he thought he would. By the fourth quarter, however, there were injuries. Buddy knew he would play the rest of the game.

With the Aggies ahead 20 to 14 in the waning minutes of the game, all the defence had to do was hold the Crimson Tide for one last possession. But on fourth down, the Alabama quarterback broke loose. Buddy realised that he was the only Aggie with a chance of catching him. He ran like he had never run before, closing on the Alabama player as he crossed the thirty, then the forty.

Buddy's lungs were bursting, but it didn't matter. This was going to be his moment. He was aware of crossing the midfield stripe. *Now*, he told himself, before the guy reached field goal territory. Buddy reached deep within himself for a final burst and flew at the guy, knocking his feet out from under him.

Almost instantly, Buddy was engulfed by his fellow players. Hugs that lifted him off his feet. Backslapping. Cheers. All around him yelling and cheering. The cheering from the stands was deafening. All for him. All for Buddy Stewart of Columbus, Texas. He thought of his parents and Cissy watching in the stands, of Justine and Iris watching in New York. He hadn't let them down.

After the game, in the shower, with hot water washing over his bruised body, he cried with the emotion of it all. It was a day he would never forget. A beginning. From now on he was *someone.*

The next day his picture was on the front page of the *Colorado County Citizen.* When he walked downtown, people stopped him on the sidewalk to shake his hand. His mother had a picture of him in his Texas A&M football uniform framed and put in the store window. His dad and sister were proud, too, but they reminded him that finals were coming up, that he needed to spend the rest of the Christmas break studying. Cissy had exams of her own to prepare for, but she made out a study schedule for him and outlined the main points that would be covered in his finals. Buddy never ceased to marvel at his sister. How could she know what would be covered in the final exam in a class she had never taken? But she would look over the course syllabus, run her finger down the textbook's table of contents, and start writing. He should learn the major muscle groups and the basic food groups. He needed to review the rules for field hockey, badminton and rugby. She wrote out a number of maths problems for him to solve.

Buddy promised himself that he would spend at least three hours a day studying, but whenever he opened a book he would find himself replaying the Cotton Bowl game. He would stare down at the Southwest Conference championship ring on his finger and thank God he hadn't gone to a smaller school. Playing football for Texas A&M was a dream come true. After a time he would give up on studying. Surely none of his professors would flunk a player who had made the game-saving tackle in the Cotton Bowl.

He was wrong. The first week of the second semester the coach called Buddy into his office. 'Stewart, we told you that you had to at least show up for your classes,' he said in disgust, shaking the grade report for the first semester in Buddy's face.

'But I only missed Monday morning classes,' Buddy insisted.

'You only had classes on Monday, Wednesday and Friday mornings. That's *one-third* of your classes you didn't show up for.'

'I thought all my professors supported football.'

'Yeah, they're supporters. They could have flunked you, but they didn't. Each one of your professors gave you a D. You made straight D's! Your grade-point average is a goddamn one point, Stewart! That means you are now academically ineligible.' The coach took a breath. 'I'm sorry, Stewart, but you're finished here. If you still want to play football, you'll have to raise your GPA and apply at a Division II school. I wish you well.'

Buddy shook the coach's extended hand and walked back to the athletic dorm in a daze. This couldn't be happening to him. Not after last season, not after the Cotton Bowl.

What was he going to do now? How would he ever be able to face his parents?

He threw himself onto his bed, where he stayed for three days, getting up only to go to the bathroom and stumble down the hall to get a candy bar and soda pop from the vending machine.

Finally he packed his bags and went to the bus station.

He didn't go home, though. He travelled to Denton. To Cissy.

DENTON WAS A LONG way from College Station, almost to the Oklahoma border. He looked out of the window at the passing landscape and thought about Cissy. Staring at the ceiling the past three nights, a major truth had evolved. He and Cissy were not related. When night fell, Buddy studied his own reflection in the bus window and found reinforcement for this theory. Other than the fact that they both had dark hair and brown eyes, he and Cissy weren't alike at all. He was built like a refrigerator, and she was as slim as a reed. He was good-looking, he supposed, in a big, rawboned kind of way, but Cissy had a look of quality about her. She was as delicate as the china figurine that graced his mother's parlour. Cissy was an angel. A princess. She was as dear to him as life itself.

The phone at Cissy's dormitory rang and rang before a sleepy-voiced housemother finally answered. Was this an emergency? she wanted to know. 'This is her brother,' Buddy said.

The woman let out a 'Humph', not believing him. He would have to call back in the morning.

'Please, just tell her that Buddy is at the Denton bus station.'

Yes, she would do that—*in the morning.*

Using his duffle bag as a pillow, Buddy stretched out on a bench and fell asleep. When he awoke, Cissy was standing over him. He leapt up and hugged her. 'Am I glad to see you.'

'Buddy, what's going on? What are you doing here?'

He led her to a corner booth in a nearby coffee shop and explained that he was finished at A&M.

She cried a little and told him she was sorry. 'What will you do?'

'Get a job here in Denton to be near you. I thought maybe we could rent an apartment and live together.' He reached across the table and grabbed her hands. 'I can't go back to Columbus with my tail between my legs.'

Cissy frowned and shook her head. 'Undergraduates aren't allowed to live off-campus,' she said. 'I'd be kicked out of school.'

'Then come away with me,' he blurted out.

'Buddy, what are you talking about?'

'We don't have the same parents, Cissy. I don't know why it took me so long to figure that out. I'm oversized and stupid. You're little and smart. I'll take care of you. I love you more than anyone.'

More tears welled in Cissy's eyes. 'Oh, Buddy, whether we're related by blood or not, we were raised as brother and sister. I love you like a brother. I'll always love you like a brother.'

'Then just let me be with you. I need to be with you.'

She covered her mouth with her hands and slowly shook her head back and forth.

Buddy wondered if his life was over, if it would be better to die. Numbly, he allowed her to buy him a ticket to Columbus.

'I'll call Mama and explain everything,' she said, hugging him goodbye. 'It's just as well. Mama needs you at the store.'

As Cissy watched the bus roll out of the station, she wondered if it was a mistake for him to go back home. Maybe she could have got special permission to live off-campus. After all, Buddy was her brother. She had not been totally surprised by his words, however. She had sensed that something like this might happen. Sometimes her feelings for her brother were confusing. There had been moments when she was deeply aware of his big, strong body. And yes, she, too, had wondered if they were truly brother and sister. But all that wondering and adolescent attraction was just a phase she had passed through. Now she was genuinely in love. Randy Calhoune was a senior premed student across town at North Texas State. She'd met him at church. Yesterday, after the eleven o'clock service, he'd asked her out, and she'd been floating ever since.

For the first time in her life she was turning her back on her brother. But Buddy was twenty years old, she reminded herself. He needed to start solving his own problems.

Cissy went to a payphone. When her mother answered, she said, 'Buddy is on his way home, Mama. He's flunked out of school.'

Martha Claire drew in her breath. 'Oh, Cissy, are you certain?'

'Yes. He was just here. I put him on a bus for Columbus.'

'What was he doing in Denton?'

'He was afraid to come home. I told him you and Daddy would be OK about it. Tell him how much you need him, Mama. He needs to feel important. Tell him you want to make him assistant manager of Stewart's Dry Goods.' Cissy fished around in her pockets for a tissue. She was crying hard. 'Oh, Mama, it just breaks my heart. He's like a lost little boy.'

She could hear her mother blow her nose. 'It will be all right, dear. Thank you for letting me know.'

'His bus is scheduled to arrive at four fifteen.'

'I'll be there.'

'I love you, Mama.'

'I love you, too, Cissy. You are the greatest blessing of my life.'

MARTHA CLAIRE hung up the phone and cried for her little boy. Her poor Buddy. She understood well the message of Cissy's call. Buddy needed to be built up, not torn down, which she might very well have done if Cissy hadn't prepared her.

She dried her tears on her apron, then walked across the back yard to the garage and climbed the stairs. Buddy would live here, she decided as she inspected the empty apartment. He needed both the comfort of his home and the dignity of a place of his own. As she ran her finger across the dusty table, she remembered that awful day when she'd carried Justine's possessions down to the back-yard incinerator and burned them. Justine and Iris had been gone for almost seven years now, and Martha Claire still didn't want to ever see her sister again, unless maybe it was her dead body in a casket. She hated her that much.

When Iris wanted to come back for a visit that first summer, Martha Claire had not allowed it. Iris never asked again. Martha Claire knew that Cissy and Iris had middle-of-the-night phone calls. When she first realised what was going on, she had wanted to jerk open the closet door and pull Cissy out of there, but she hadn't. In reality she was glad they had each other. She herself had no one to talk to. She had invested all in family. Her best friends had been her husband, her mother and her sister. Now all she had left was two children who were careful in her presence.

Martha Claire longed to tell them what their father had done and see some understanding in their eyes. But she and Grayson and Justine had sworn they would never tell anyone. No one was ever to know that Grayson was Iris's father.

Grayson's mother had died last spring. Martha Claire hadn't wanted her to come to live with them, for she had never really liked Lily, but what could she say? Her own mother and grandmother had lived with them for years. Maybe if Martha Claire had still loved the woman's son, she might have felt differently. When Grayson told her how much he appreciated what she was doing for his mother, she simply shrugged.

After Lily died, they moved the bed back upstairs and put the television, sofa and easy chairs back in the morning room. Most nights she sat there by herself, her dinner on a tray. She didn't hate Grayson like she used to, but she didn't love him, either. She missed her children and didn't like being alone at night. As a result, she looked forward to Grayson's being home at weekends and wasn't such a slave driver any more. Sometimes they would cook hamburgers on the grill and walk downtown for a movie.

She glanced at her watch. It was time to go to the store. *Assistant manager*, she thought with a smile. Her Cissy was a clever girl, no question about that. Grayson was going to be disappointed about A&M, but they'd always known the boy was no student. Surely Grayson would see that home was the best place for him.

ON FRIDAY EVENING, when he arrived home, Grayson was surprised to see a light on in the garage apartment. He got his suitcase from the truck and started across the yard. The back door opened. 'Buddy's home,' Martha Claire said through the screen door.

'Is he OK?' Grayson asked.

'He was expelled because of his grades,' Martha Claire said, holding the door open for her husband. 'He's telling people he has a bad knee and decided not to stay in school if he couldn't play football. He's going to work for me at the store.'

Grayson went into the bathroom to wash, and he stayed for a while to grieve in private for the death of a dream. Grayson knew that Buddy was a marginal student at best, but after three semesters he'd convinced himself that the school would look the other way and let him play ball. Maybe he could even earn a degree. With a degree, even if he didn't play professional ball, he could have coached high-school kids, could have held his head up for the rest of his life. Grayson splashed water on his face, then went to have dinner with his wife.

'You look tired,' Martha Claire said.

'I'm just hungry, and if I'm not mistaken, that's pot roast I smell. Isn't Buddy eating with us?' he asked, nodding at the kitchen table which was set for two.

'Some of his friends came by. They went to a basketball game.'

'Is he OK?' Grayson asked again.

'I think he will be,' Martha Claire said as she lifted the Dutch oven from the stove and set it on a trivet.

'I don't think having him work at the store is a good idea,' Grayson said, and watched Martha Claire's spine stiffen. He should have sounded more tentative, Grayson realised. Now Martha Claire would dig in whether she had reservations about his working at the store or not. Grayson tried to backtrack. 'It's not the store, really. It's the town.'

'What's the matter with the town?' Martha Claire demanded.

'There's not much opportunity here. Buddy needs to learn a trade. He can't stay here for ever and let his parents support him.'

'We won't support him. I'll *pay* him for working in the store.'

Grayson shook his head. 'He's never shown any interest in that store. We practically had to threaten him to get him to wash the windows or help take inventory. You work hard, but Buddy won't. He'll put a sign on the door and go fishing.'

'I didn't realise you had such a low opinion of your son.'

'Not low, just realistic. A storekeeper he is not.'

'Like father, like son. Is that what you're telling me?'

'Wouldn't you like our children to be happier than we have been?'

'It wasn't the store that made us unhappy. Now, are you going to eat this food or not?'

Suddenly more angry than tired, Grayson glanced towards the door. He didn't want to sit here in this unhappy home with his unhappy wife no matter how fine the food might be. Maybe he should just leave.

She put her hand on his arm. 'Please don't go.'

He looked at her for a long moment. In a way, the store was the root of their unhappiness, he thought. It represented the preordained life that he had not wanted. But then he put his hand over hers. And nodded. He would stay.

'POOR BUDDY,' Iris said. 'School was always such a struggle for him, but football made him proud. Is he just devastated?'

Iris was twenty-three now, in her second year of medical school. She had had lots of boyfriends over the years and had even been engaged once in college, but the young man had second thoughts about her plans for medical school.

'Yes,' Cissy was saying. 'He wanted to move to Denton and rent an apartment for us to share. I told him I'd be kicked out of school if I moved out of the dorm, but maybe I could have got special permission to live with my brother,' she admitted. She was sitting at a desk by the second-floor dorm's only telephone. 'Do you think I should have him move up here?' she asked.

'No, sweetie, I don't think you should do any such thing. You'd end up cooking his food, washing his clothes, picking up after him. You'd turn into his little mother when you should be having fun and enjoying college life.'

'He's decided that we're not really brother and sister,' Cissy said softly, checking to be sure no one was within earshot. 'He thinks he's in love with me.'

Iris said nothing for a long minute. 'Buddy adores you, Cissy, because you're a sweet, precious girl who has made life easier for him. But the only kind of love you owe him is that of a sister for her brother. He'll find some other girl to take care of him.'

'I'm not so sure. He's not very nice to other girls. He doesn't trust them. He's afraid of ending up browbeaten like Daddy.'

Iris sighed. 'Buddy has to work out his problems on his own. If you don't let him, he'll end up ruining both of your lives.'

After the cousins said goodbye, Cissy wondered why she hadn't told Iris about Randy Calhoune. She hadn't told anyone else, either, in case he turned out to be not as nice as she thought he was. Still, Iris's words gave her courage. She had done the right thing for both herself and Buddy. Randy Calhoune had come along at just the right time. Thinking about him gave her resolve.

Was Randy thinking about her? Had he already begun to imagine a future with her? She wasn't sure she wanted to be a doctor's wife, though. Doctors' wives didn't practise nursing. Yet the idea of marrying Randy and living a comfortable life filled with children and a lovely home was not altogether unattractive.

Randy was tall and slender with wavy brown hair and matching brown eyes. He had a sensitive face and elegant hands—like a piano player's or a surgeon's, Cissy thought.

After her freshman year in Denton she planned to take the remaining three years of her nurse's training at Parkland Hospital in Dallas. Randy would be in Dallas, too. He had grown up in Dallas and planned to go to medical school there.

Dallas. A real city with skyscrapers. The thought of living there both scared and excited Cissy. She wanted to visit museums, libraries, even the fabled Neiman Marcus store. Now she wondered if she would do those things with Randy Calhoune at her side.

IT WAS ONLY three in the afternoon when Martha Claire returned earlier than expected from a funeral in Rosenberg for her father's cousin Trudy. Arriving at the store, she found the lights off and the door locked. With a sigh of disappointment she fished around for her key and went inside. The merchandise on the sale table was in a jumble, and the cash register drawer was open.

How much had Buddy taken? Martha Claire wondered. She couldn't get it into his head that she paid him what she could afford and he absolutely could not help himself to more money whenever he felt like it. He didn't pay rent and ate most meals at home, so he should have enough money to make payments on his used Ford pick-up and to manage his few other expenses. But she knew he was already behind on the truck payments.

Buddy went out with his friends almost every night and didn't come back until all hours. Sometimes he didn't show up at the store until noon or later. He was a good salesman, however, when he put his mind to it. Male customers would linger after they had made their purchase to talk sports, often thinking of something else they needed to buy while they rehashed Dallas's victory over the Dolphins in the Superbowl or Buddy's game-saving tackle in the 1968 Cotton Bowl game.

It was just going to take time, Martha Claire told herself as she folded the sweaters on the sale table. Buddy still wasn't over the disappointment of being dismissed from A&M. Eventually he would settle down and assume more responsibility for the store.

Grayson didn't agree. He insisted that Buddy was going to have to leave Columbus. 'If he stays, he'll never amount to anything.'

Grayson thought Buddy should join the army or learn a trade, like welding or auto mechanics. Only last week he'd told Buddy that he was going to kick him out if he came home drunk again.

'This is my property,' Martha Claire reminded her husband.

Buddy had smirked at his father. 'Hear that, Dad? Guess we know who wears the pants around here, don't we?'

This weekend Martha Claire didn't want to fight about Buddy. She planned to tell Grayson that. There wasn't anything he could say that would make her send Buddy away, so there was no point in discussing it. She would cook a pork roast for dinner.

Grayson phoned Friday morning to say he was making a call in nearby Sealy and should be home by six. 'Tell Buddy that I expect him to have dinner with us. If you go to the trouble to cook a meal, he should be there to eat it. And I thought we could sit down after dinner and look at some of the brochures I've sent for. There are some excellent vocational programmes around the state.'

Martha Claire started to say she had no intention of sending Buddy away, but she held back. She wanted a nice evening. Besides, Buddy wouldn't show up for dinner. He never did when Grayson was at home. He didn't want to hear his father's lectures.

Sure enough, right before closing time, Buddy left the store. Martha Claire knew she wouldn't see him until he dragged himself out of bed on Saturday morning.

The first thing Grayson said when he walked in the door was, 'Where's Buddy?'

Martha Claire couldn't help herself. She put her hands on her hips and told her husband that Buddy was having a hard time adjusting. Yes, he drank too much, but he just needed time to get himself straightened out. Maybe someday he would learn to drive sixteen-wheelers or become a welder, but it had to be something the boy decided and not something his father dictated. And she didn't want to hear another word about sending him away.

'It probably doesn't matter anyway,' Grayson said, tossing a packet of brochures in the trash. 'He's probably going to be drafted. He'll end up crawling around a jungle in Southeast Asia.'

BUDDY'S DRAFT NOTICE came in the spring. After basic training at Fort Hood, he came home for one last weekend before he left for Vietnam. I drove down from Dallas to say goodbye to him. I cried and told him to take care of himself. I wondered if I would ever see him again. I prayed I would, and that the army would make a man of him. Something sure needed to. If that war didn't destroy him, I feared he would end up doing the job himself.

My father had now moved back into Granny Grace's old bedroom, and I suspected he would never again be welcome in my mother's bed. Their war over Buddy seemed to have eroded whatever goodwill they had reconstructed in the years since Iris left.

My dad had inherited forty acres of low-lying land from his mother and sold off most of it to a cotton farmer, saving a river-hugging sliver for himself. He used the money from the sale to bulldoze a narrow lane, buy construction materials, and dig a well and an outdoor toilet. After Buddy left for Vietnam, Daddy built a one-room cabin with a porch that overlooked the river. I knew he wanted a retreat, someplace to which he could escape from Mama.

Buddy was assigned to a quartermaster unit in Saigon. He never wrote, but he did call home every couple of weeks. Mama said that he liked it there and actually seemed to be enjoying himself. No one shot at people in the quartermaster corps.

After a year and a half he returned to Columbus and the rent-free garage apartment, seemingly unchanged from his time in a war zone. He was as irresponsible as ever. I suspected that my brother had become an alcoholic or worse. I knew I should go home and confront him, make him see a doctor or join Alcoholics Anonymous, but I didn't. As I finished my last year of nurse's training and spent as much time with Randy Calhoune as our schedules allowed, Columbus and the problems there seemed very far away.

Randy wanted to give me an engagement ring, but I told him I wasn't ready. I loved him, and for two years now I had lived for his phone calls, his presence. True love was supposed to be for ever, but the lesson I had learned from my parents told me that was not always so. I wondered how I might feel about Randy in fifteen or twenty years—and how he would feel about me.

THE LAST SUNDAY *in May my parents and Buddy drove up to Denton for the Texas University for Women commencement ceremony. I graduated with highest honours and even won the Florence Nightingale Award for most exemplifying the highest ideals of nursing. I had worked hard to make my parents proud.*

Randy sat with them. He had given me a birthstone ring as a graduation present. A friendship ring, he called it, because I still wasn't ready to be engaged. He had not protested greatly. There was plenty of time, he supposed. He still had years of training ahead of him.

Eventually my foot-dragging turned into a decision of sorts, and he found someone else. Even as I suffered the pain of rejection and the genuine sadness that comes at the end of a relationship, I felt as though a burden had been lifted from my shoulders. My future was no longer laid out in front of me like a road map.

I was a better nurse after that. I became a professional, not just a girl biding her time until the wedding bells rang. I began to think about maybe training to become a nurse-anaesthetist. With Randy out of my life, I could do it in Houston. With the interstate highway, Columbus and Houston were now just an hour apart.

I actually looked forward to being the dutiful daughter again. My parents needed me, and I needed them. They were a part of me as nothing else in my life.

If Buddy had been a more devoted son, if Iris wasn't lost to them, if Justine still came to visit, if they had a joyous marriage and hordes of close friends and money in the bank, I might have felt less connected to them. As it was, I was needed.

Six

Bob Anderson regarded Martha Claire from behind his large, very cluttered desk. 'What does Grayson think about this?' he asked.

Martha Claire shifted in her chair. Grayson wanted to sell the house. He called it an albatross. 'He's not crazy about the idea,' she admitted. 'But it is my house.'

The portly bank officer picked up Martha Claire's loan application. 'This is a lot of money you're asking for.'

'That's what it will take to fix up the house,' she said. 'The plumbing has to be replaced, the kitchen modernised. I'll want to finish out the attic and put two bedrooms, a bathroom and a sitting room up there. The estimates are attached.'

'A lot of money,' Bob said again. 'And what if this bed-and-breakfast idea catches on? Other folks might rent rooms. The town could end up with more guest rooms than it can support.'

'Mine would be the best,' Martha Claire said with a lift of her chin. 'I can make the house pay its way, Bob. I know I can.'

'Maybe so, maybe not,' he said, leaning back in his chair. 'But if the bank does agree to finance this project, I'll have to have a mortgage on the house, Martha Claire. And I will need Grayson to sign the note.'

'But the property belongs to me,' she protested.

'Yes, but it's going to take both of you to make this project work, and we've got to have a co-signer. If you really want to do this, you'd better sit down and talk it over with Grayson. It's a big undertaking and a big debt to assume. Unless you both are completely behind it, I think you'd better forget about this loan.'

She felt hot anger rise to her cheeks. She had mentioned it on and off to Grayson for a couple of years, but he always changed the subject. Martha Claire wanted to tell Bob Anderson never mind, that she would take her business elsewhere. But if her hometown bank wouldn't loan her the money, how could she expect anyone else to? She stood. 'I'll talk to Grayson,' she said.

MARTHA CLAIRE and Grayson still had their Friday evening dinners—just the two of them. Buddy was seldom around. Strange how she looked forward to them. Martha Claire doubted if she and

Grayson would ever again sleep in the same bed. They never kissed, never touched. But Friday morning she would wash her hair, and Friday evening she would prepare something nice for dinner. Over dinner they would share any conversations they'd had with Cissy. Martha Claire would give Grayson a report on the store and catch him up on town gossip. He would tell her about his week on the road. Buddy was mentioned only in passing. If they talked about Buddy or spending money on the house, they argued. And they tried not to argue on Friday evenings.

This Friday night, however, Martha Claire couldn't wait. She passed Grayson the bowl of mashed potatoes and told him all in a rush that she needed for him to co-sign a mortgage so she could turn the house into a bed-and-breakfast establishment.

'Right now we are without debt, Martha Claire,' he said, putting down the bowl. 'That is one of the few things we have going for us. I know how much you love the house, but we're too old to take on a debt like that. I'd never be able to retire. If we sold the house, we could buy a smaller place and maybe go to Europe. Just think of how tied down you would be with a bed and breakfast.'

'I want it more than anything,' she told him. 'And you owe me this, Grayson.'

He met her gaze. 'So if I sign this note, does my penance end?'

Martha Claire regarded her husband of more than thirty years. All she had ever wanted was to marry this man and have his children. If she had never discovered the truth about Iris's birth, she could have lived the rest of her life in blissful ignorance. Then maybe this dilapidated old house wouldn't be so important to her. As it was, however, all her dreams were invested in it. Her only chance for happiness was to turn her family home into a bed and breakfast.

But Grayson wanted to strike a bargain. He would sign the papers at the bank if she would agree to renew their marriage. How remarkable to think that he still cared about her enough to want that. She should be flattered, she supposed. She could tell him yes, that she would wipe the slate clean if he would only sign that note. He could return to her bed and her arms.

But he had made love to her sister, and for ten years she had had to live with that image. The two of them meeting someplace, kissing, undressing one another, exploring each other's bodies. She could see it all. She could see the act that had given her sister a baby when she herself would never have one. She could never forgive him.

CISSY'S ELDERLY LANDLADY stood in the middle of the tiny apartment and clasped her hands to her meagre bosom. 'You have made it very pretty,' Mrs Tran said in her very precise English.

Cissy looked around, seeing it through Mrs Tran's eyes. In the past week she had painted the walls and ceiling, installed a ceiling fan, and sanded and varnished the floors. It did look nice, she decided. A garage apartment, no less, just like back home. It was only a ten-minute drive to Houston's Baylor Medical Center and cheap enough that she didn't have to have a room-mate.

She had disappointed her mother terribly when she accepted a position in the intensive-care unit at Baylor. It was nursing at its most intense, triumph and loss on a daily basis. Maybe someday she would be satisfied with working in a small-town hospital, but right now she wanted challenges. She yearned to grow in her profession and learn all that she could.

The dynamics of her parents' marriage had shifted once again since her father had refused to mortgage the house and let Mama start a bed and breakfast. Her father no longer automatically did everything her mother asked, and spent more and more time in his fishing cabin. He had bought an old generator, and now the place had electric lights and even a television. He had visited Cissy in September, and she had taken him through the intensive-care unit where she worked. Later they had toured the Houston Museum of Fine Art, where he had lingered in front of the paintings by European masters and told her how, after the war, he had spent many afternoons in the Louvre and travelled to Rome to see the Vatican art treasures.

'You always said you were going to go back to Europe someday,' Cissy said, and immediately wished she hadn't. The look of pain on her father's face made her look away.

'Yes. I always wanted to take your mother there, but I don't think she really wants to go. Once maybe, but not any more.'

'I'll go with you,' Cissy said. 'Maybe Iris could come with us.'

'Do you still talk to Iris?'

'Yes, but not like before. She's doing her residency, so she's as busy as I am. We're lucky to catch each other every other month.'

'Please tell her that I think about her every single day.'

Cissy realised her father had tears in his eyes and reached for his hand. 'I will,' she promised. Then she added, 'I love you, Daddy. Iris does, too. She says you are the finest man she's ever known.'

CISSY DIDN'T ARRIVE home for Thanksgiving until almost eleven o'clock on the Wednesday evening, but her parents came out to greet her as always. Her father carried her bags up to her room, and her mother insisted on putting out milk and cookies. Buddy was out. He had left directions to a roadhouse on the Brenham highway if Cissy wanted to drive over and meet his friends. Saturday night she would go, Cissy promised herself. Tonight she was tired.

Her parents sat with her at the kitchen table, quizzing her about work, the performance of the used Volkswagen she had bought, Houston traffic. As she watched them, she thought how handsome they were. Life had disappointed them, but as they sat here talking to her, their faces were filled with the pleasure of her company. Cissy felt guilty that she didn't come home more often.

That night Cissy awoke to the sound of the phone ringing. She rolled over and stared at the clock. Three fifty-seven. Then she looked out of the window to see if Buddy's truck was parked by the garage. It was not. She rushed into the hall. Her father was already hurrying down the stairs, an anxious expression on his face. Her mother had come out of her room. Cissy stood with her mother at the banister rail. *Let it be a wrong number*, Cissy prayed. *Please.*

When he hung up the phone, Grayson looked up at them. 'There's been an accident. Buddy was coming back from Brenham. They're taking him to the hospital there.'

'Was he badly hurt?' Martha Claire asked, her voice trembling.

Grayson nodded.

Cissy drove, with her mother in the front seat and her dad in the back, heading up Highway 109. Near Kearney they passed a breakdown van towing Buddy's hideously twisted pick-up. Martha Claire cried out, 'Oh my God!' and began to sob.

Cissy clutched the steering wheel and prayed with all her might that her brother would survive. She should have driven to Brenham last night to meet him, no matter how late it was. She should have let him move to Denton. Insisted he come to live with her in Houston. Buddy wasn't strong like she was. He needed her to take care of him. Yes, she would do that. She would nurse him back to health, help him get himself straightened out.

The nurse looked up as they rushed into the emergency room, and she paged the doctor. Cissy knew at once that Buddy was dead. It was too quiet. There was no activity, no ER staff racing around.

The slim young doctor introduced herself and explained that

Buddy had been dead on arrival. He had been thrown from the car, his neck broken. He had not suffered.

'Where is he?' Martha Claire demanded.

The doctor walked over to a door and opened it for them. 'I'm sorry,' she said, and stood aside to let Martha Claire and Grayson enter the room.

Watching from the doorway, Cissy gasped as her mother pulled back the sheet, exposing the face of her dead brother.

Martha Claire caressed Buddy's lifeless features, kissed his brow, and called him the dearest little boy in the world. Then suddenly she whirled to face her husband. 'Go ahead. Say it's my fault. I should have sent him away before it came to this.'

Tears streaming down his face, Grayson shook his head. 'No, it's my fault. I saw this coming and didn't stop it.' He approached the body of his son with halting steps and kissed his lips. 'Oh God, my poor Buddy. My poor Buddy. We didn't do you any favour when we made you a member of this family. No favour at all.'

Then, with sobs that felt as though they were ripping open her chest, feeling the worst pain she had ever felt in her life, Cissy approached her brother's body and lay her own across it. She was so sorry. So very, very sorry. And there was no way to make amends.

AFTER THEY SAID their farewells to Buddy, Cissy told the nurse at the Brenham hospital the name of the funeral home in Columbus. Then there was nothing else to do but go back home.

Once there, her mother said she wanted to be alone. Cissy helped her into bed. While she covered her with a quilt, she heard her father's footsteps on the stairs. The door to his room closed.

Cissy went downstairs and picked up the phone. It wasn't Sunday. She didn't hide in the closet. She didn't reverse the call charge.

Iris answered at once with a crisp 'Dr Dover'.

Cissy began to cry. 'It's Buddy, Iris. Buddy is dead.' She heard her mother's door open, then her father's. She knew they were looking down at her as she told Iris, the banished child, what had happened to their Buddy, heard her pour out her heart, how she could have saved him, taken him in and watched over him.

'Yes, you could have become his little wife,' Iris said, 'but would that have turned him into a man? You need to remember all the reasons why you love him and bury the rest.'

When Cissy hung up, she heard her mother's door close, then her father's. She sat there in the hallway of her childhood home, where three happy children once had lived. She could almost hear their voices, their laughter. Why had it all changed?

THE MORNING of the funeral arrived bright and fair. Cissy insisted that her parents come downstairs and eat breakfast. When the funeral-home limousine arrived, they were ready.

Cissy wanted her parents to hold hands or walk arm in arm, but there was no touching between them, not as they walked down the front walk, not in the limousine. Not a word passed between them as they travelled to their son's funeral.

The sunlight was intense and, once inside the church, it took Cissy's eyes a minute to adjust to the dusky interior, to realise the smart-looking young woman standing in the vestibule was Iris. Stunned, Cissy's hands flew to her mouth. *Iris!* She took a few halting steps; then suddenly they were embracing. It was really Iris, after all those years. Tears flowed once again, her sadness mingling with joy. Iris had come to help them bury Buddy.

Then Cissy felt Iris pull away, and she stood to one side so Iris could approach Martha Claire and Grayson—the aunt and uncle who had raised her. Martha Claire was standing erect. Grayson looked as though he was about to faint. 'I had to come,' Iris explained. 'Buddy was like my little brother. Mother and I cried together. I know how you both must hurt.' Martha Claire nodded and allowed Iris to kiss her cheek. Grayson stood like a statue while she embraced him, but tears were running down his cheeks.

They sat together in front of Buddy's open casket. Cissy clung to her cousin's hand on one side, her mother's on the other. Behind them every seat was taken, and men were standing at the back. They had come to bury the boy who helped give them some of the best years of football Columbus High School had ever had.

At the graveside Martha Claire grew faint and almost fell off her chair. Grayson grabbed her and held her close, but she pulled away. Reverend Huxley hurried to the end of his prayer.

The ladies of the church brought lunch to the house, and people came throughout the afternoon to offer their condolences.

'I remembered them all,' Iris said later as she sat with Cissy at the kitchen table, drinking first coffee, then bourbon. 'Some of them asked about Mother, but only when Martha Claire wasn't listening. They must wonder what the hell happened.'

'Don't we all?' Cissy commented.

They sat into the night, reminiscing about Buddy, about life as it once had been. 'I used to think this was the best house in the whole town,' Iris said, looking around the kitchen—at the worn linoleum, the cracks in the ceiling. 'It makes me sad to see it like this. Maybe they should sell it and move someplace smaller.'

'That's what Daddy says, but I don't think Mama will ever sell it. She was going to leave it to you someday, since you're blood kin, but then you went away.'

'And you don't want it?' Iris asked.

'Probably not. I don't really know what I want. Sometimes I think I should move back home.'

'Don't sacrifice the rest of your life for them, Cissy.'

Cissy sighed. She didn't try to explain her need for atonement. Iris would not understand. She had failed her brother, and now he was dead. She didn't want to fail her parents, too.

They listened while the clock on the mantelpiece struck twice. Then Iris pushed an envelope across the table. 'What's this?' Cissy asked.

'An open-ended plane ticket to New York. You can use it any time. I'm not leaving here until you promise that you will.'

Cissy picked up the envelope. 'I always wanted to come and visit, but I knew how it would upset Mama.'

'I realise that, but I'm tired of only phone calls. Martha Claire's not going to disown you, honey. You're all she has.'

'Don't I know it,' Cissy said. 'I *will* come, though. I promise.'

BUDDY HAD BEEN *dead more than two years when Iris called to say it was time for me to see if that plane ticket was still good. If it wasn't, she would send another. She was getting married.*

I was shocked. I knew she kept company with a German physician who had been one of her teachers in medical school, but I had envisioned a kindly old soul who took a fatherly interest in her.

'Isn't he the man who was in a concentration camp?' I asked.

'Yes. Hillel lost his wife and baby. His parents, brothers, everyone. He was the only one of his family to survive. He finished his medical education here. He's quite brilliant—a neurologist.'

'So he's Jewish?'

'Yes, but our beliefs are more alike than different.'

'Are you in love with him?'

'In a romantic way? Not really. But I do have tender feelings for him. He's a good person, and I respect him terribly.'

'Why did you decide to get married?' I asked.

'Because we need each other. We'll make a baby or two. He hasn't had a home and family for a long time. You have to come, Cissy. It will be just a small wedding at Mother's apartment. You will be my only attendant—my maid of honour.'

I agreed to go, of course. But I dreaded telling Mama.

We were having coffee at the kitchen table when I explained that Iris was getting married and I was going to be her only attendant. She looked out of the window for a long time. 'I used to dream about her getting married in the rose garden—as I had done.'

I wanted to ask if she had ever thought of me getting married in the rose garden, but I didn't. Instead I asked the larger question. 'What happened, Mama? Why did it all end?'

She pushed her chair back and took her cup to the sink. 'Go to New York if you must. But don't come back with wedding pictures for me to look at. I don't want you to speak of it at all.'

Two WEEKS before Iris's wedding Cissy boarded a plane for New York. Justine, Iris and Hillel greeted her at the airport.

Justine was an older version of herself—long, lean, greying hair, wrinkled white shirt tucked into expensive brown slacks. She engulfed her niece in a huge hug. 'You didn't grow much, honey. You're still little Cissy.' Then she reached into her bag for a handkerchief, and the three women shed tears.

Hillel looked like her idea of a typical professor, with a tidy beard and a baggy brown suit and tie. His hair and beard were sprinkled with grey. He told Cissy he was honoured to know her.

They had dinner at Justine's apartment. With its high ceilings and wooden floors, it reminded Cissy of her mother's house. Justine's photographs covered the walls of the long hallway, but the walls of the living room were covered with watercolours, obviously all by the same person. A friend of Justine's, Iris said.

Over coffee, Hillel explained to Cissy the high regard he had for her cousin. 'I want you to know that I would have been content the rest of my life simply to be her good friend.'

'Getting married was my idea,' Iris interjected. 'I was looking for a nice man to have children with, and one night we were at our favourite Chinese restaurant. I looked across the table at him and thought, Why not Hillel? He came to America with nothing. The neighbourhoods where he grew up no longer exist. He needs a family, too. Our kids will be smart. I'm going to insist he speak only German to them. And when they are old enough to understand, we will tell them what happened to this whole other family in Europe they will never know but must never forget.'

'And what about the family in Texas they will never know?' Cissy asked. 'What will you tell them about Columbus?'

Iris said nothing for a minute, then looked at her mother.

Justine said, 'I will tell my grandchildren about two sisters who didn't get along and spent the rest of their lives being sorry. Or at least one of them was sorry.'

Then she opened a bottle of brandy, and they sat out on her little balcony, which overlooked Central Park. Cissy listened to the street sounds. She was actually here, actually in New York. With Justine and Iris. It seemed a miracle.

The next week passed in a blur for Cissy as Iris showed her the sights. They went to the Metropolitan Museum of Art, the Empire State Building, the Statue of Liberty. They prowled through Greenwich Village; they toured the UN and saw the Mets play the Phillies.

Cissy spent the second week of her visit at a women's clinic Iris had helped establish in a poor section of Brooklyn. The clientele was mostly immigrant, some from countries Cissy had never heard of. The clinic was located in a former grocery, with shelves still on the wall. Curtains hung from the ceiling to create examination rooms. The first day, Iris and two other female obstetricians saw more than a hundred pre- and postnatal patients and forty-seven sick children. They desperately needed a paediatrician, Iris said. 'Our problem is low birth weight,' she explained. 'Women who have had prenatal care and adequate nutrition throughout their pregnancies deliver healthy babies more than ninety per cent of the time.'

The wedding was simple. An elderly judge officiated. Iris and Hillel vowed to be honest and treat each other with respect. A friend of Justine's played the cello. The woman who had painted the water-colours in Justine's living room made the luncheon. Astrid was her name. She looked like Ingrid Bergman—Scandinavian, large-boned, incredibly beautiful.

The apartment filled as the evening went by—people coming to offer their congratulations. It was the most eclectic group Cissy had ever seen—artists, rabbis, professors, physicians, students, nuns, social workers. As the evening went on, Cissy saw Hillel begin to weary. Iris saw it, too, and began telling people good night. She and Hillel needed to get some sleep before they left for a brief honeymoon in Toronto, and Cissy had an early flight in the morning.

Finally it was time for the cousins to say goodbye. 'I'll pay your way through medical school,' Iris whispered as she hugged Cissy.

'Don't be ridiculous,' Cissy said, wondering how many years it would be until she saw Iris again.

Seven

'With your grades and experience, any medical school would have to accept you,' Iris insisted.

'But what would I tell Mama?' Cissy said. She stared down at the four-page application form that Iris had had sent to her.

'Just tell Martha Claire that you won a scholarship,' Iris said.

'I never said I wanted to go to medical school,' Cissy said. She carried the application form and the phone to her bed and wearily propped herself against the headboard. She had worked a double shift. She often worked double shifts to keep her weekends free for trips home. Tonight she'd barely had the energy to climb the stairs to her apartment, which was in sad need of cleaning. She couldn't remember the last time she'd dusted. Or changed the sheets. She really should have her car serviced before she drove another mile. And she had promised her mother she'd be at the church in Columbus by six for the covered-dish supper honouring Reverend Huxley, who was finally retiring to his books and fishing. He had a standing invitation out at her father's place on the river as long as he didn't bring up the issue of Grayson's immortal soul.

'You always said you wanted to be a doctor when you grew up,' Iris reminded her. 'When you were in high school, you told me you'd like to be a paediatrician, but it would cost too much. You settled on nursing because you had a scholarship to Denton. Well, here's your chance, with no strings attached. I just want you to have what I have, Cissy. It's really quite selfish of me. I can't enjoy my life until I get yours straightened out.'

'I wasn't aware that my life was crooked,' Cissy said drily. 'Look, Iris, I truly appreciate your offer, but I don't have the time or energy for medical school.'

'You would if you didn't go home every weekend,' Iris pointed out. 'Martha Claire and Grayson are never going to be happy, Cissy. You need to look after yourself. That's why I decided on a school in Dallas instead of Houston. Dallas is far enough away that Martha Claire and Grayson can't expect you home all the time.'

Cissy stretched out her aching legs. 'At least when I'm home, Mama and Daddy sleep under the same roof and sit down at the same table. It's really quite selfish of me. I can't enjoy my life until I get theirs straightened out,' she said, parroting Iris's words.

'Well, aren't you cute!' Iris said sarcastically. 'Martha Claire and Grayson have forgotten how to be anything but miserable. And you're not doing much better. If you want, specialise in psychiatry and dedicate your life to healing alcoholic young men before they kill themselves behind the wheel of a car. And make enough money to fix up Martha Claire's house. So many more things are possible if you have MD after your name.'

'Why isn't it good enough that I stay a nurse?' Cissy demanded. After all, most of the time she loved what she did. At times, of course, she got tired of following orders and wondered what it would be like to be the person giving them, and to know more about the diseases that affected her patients.

'I've already told you—I want you to have what I have. I feel guilty, too, sweetie. We all are suffocating under piles of guilt. I could have told Mother that I didn't want to leave Columbus. After all, Martha Claire and Grayson raised me and loved me as though I was their own. I don't know why our mothers started hating each other, but maybe if I had stayed, things would have turned out differently. As it was, I left you and Buddy there to deal with all that misery by yourselves.'

Cissy closed her eyes and rubbed her forehead. 'I'm too tired to talk about this now. I'll call you in a few days, OK?'

'At least tell the folks that you've been thinking about medical school, that you've been offered a scholarship.'

'It's not a scholarship.'

'Yes, it is. I am awarding a one-time-only scholarship to a practising nurse who graduated from Columbus High School and Texas University for Women. Fill out the application, Cissy.'

TELLING HERSELF that it was more to appease her cousin than because of any pressing desire on her part to enrol in medical school, Cissy filled out the application form. But writing the required one-page essay made her realise just how much she wanted to be a doctor. She hadn't had the money or the courage to go down that long and difficult road before, but now she was older, less fearful, and Iris had offered to pay her tuition. As a nurse, she could find part-time employment to help meet her living expenses. She still hadn't told her parents. Maybe it wouldn't be necessary. Maybe her application would be denied.

The letter from the dean's office arrived four weeks later. Cissy tore it open and read that she had been accepted for the fall of 1977. Enclosed was orientation information and her class schedule.

Iris was delivering a baby at the clinic when Cissy called. She left a message and called her mother. 'I thought I'd drive over for dinner,' she said. 'I've got something I want to tell you.'

'Are you engaged?' Martha Claire said hopefully.

'No, Mama, nothing like that. Is Daddy there?'

'No, he's out at that place on the river.'

'Would you drive out and ask him to come home for dinner? I'll pick up a pizza. I want to talk to both of you together.'

Her parents seemed almost relieved when she told them her news, even when they realised she would be moving to Dallas. Apparently they had been worried that she had become too dependent on them since Buddy's death. A young woman needed a social life and friends her own age, they said.

'Our little Cissy is going to be a doctor,' Grayson said with pride. For an instant she thought he was going to reach for Mama's hand, but Martha Claire got very busy closing up the pizza box. 'How did you find out about this scholarship?' he asked.

'A doctor told me about it. It's for a practising nurse.'

They sat on the porch for a while. Several neighbours called out hellos, and Martha Claire had them come over to hear their news.

Before she left town, Cissy stopped by her brother's grave. In the moonlight she knelt on the damp grass and touched his tombstone. If she had taken care of Buddy, she probably wouldn't be going to medical school. Nothing made any sense.

As she drove east on the interstate, the euphoria rose in her breast. Her parents were pleased! Everything was going to be all right. She was going to be a physician. *Cecelia Claire Stewart, MD.*

'WELL, WELL, WELL, if it isn't our soon-to-be Dr Cissy Stewart,' Doc Hadley said a week or two later, holding open the screen door for her.

Cissy was stunned at the sight of him. The man who had looked after the health of their town for half a century was himself wasted and ill. She hadn't seen him for years but had found herself thinking about him more now that medical school was in her future.

He led her past the parlour, where his daughter Trudy's collection of Chinese porcelain was displayed, and down the hall to the kitchen. He now lived with Trudy, the oldest of his three daughters.

'Trudy said you'd called,' he said. 'She's off at one of her meetings, but she left lemonade and cookies.'

'Well, well, well,' he said again as he poured the lemonade. 'Your folks are certainly busting their buttons over you. You know, over the years, lots of youngsters told me they were going to be a doctor when they grew up, but you're the only one to actually do it. 'Course, you were always the most inquisitive. Just listening to your own heart wasn't enough. You wanted to listen to mine and your mama's. You had to watch when I lanced your brother's boil and cut out his ingrown toenail.'

Cissy smiled. 'You remember all that?'

He nodded. 'You and your brother weren't just any other patients. I had a hand in your family like no other and always felt a special responsibility towards the Stewarts. I was almost glad when you kids got colds and measles, so I had a chance to hover.'

'Did you always want to be a doctor?' Cissy asked.

'No. I had grown up thinking I would be a vet. Then I worked for one and got kicked in the head by a sick mule. I figured it was a sign and decided I'd better find something else to do.'

'But why medicine?'

'Same reason as you, I suppose. You want to do something more than just make money.'

'What about when people died, though?' she asked. 'Didn't that bother you?'

'Depends. Sometimes letting people go ahead and die is the only cure you can offer. You welcome death like an old friend and wonder what in the hell took the old buzzard so damned long. Other times you'll wonder if you couldn't have done something differently that would have saved a patient, specially the young ones. After I'd have a mama bleed to death during childbirth, I'd swear I was going to move to a city where there was a real hospital with fancy machines and specialists, but I never did. People in little towns need someone to look after them.'

They talked for a while. Then she got him settled in front of the television. She thanked him for everything he'd done for her and her family, and walked down the hall to the front door.

Her life had been set when Doc Hadley bundled her up and found her a home. Now he was at the end of his life. She might never see him again. She retraced her steps. He was waiting for her. 'If you're going to ask me about your birth parents, don't,' he said.

'I'm not even sure I want to know,' Cissy said from the doorway. 'Buddy wondered about them more than I did. But sometimes I wonder if my birth mother knows about us or if she even cares.'

'Buddy got to where he asked me every time he saw me. The last few years he kept trying to get me to say that you two weren't related by blood. But secrets are the one thing I get to take with me. Physicians usually end up with lots of them, specially docs like me with a small-town practice. Hippocrates even put keeping secrets in his oath for us docs. We all have to promise not to divulge the things we see or hear in the lives of men.'

'But have you ever talked to her over the years?' Cissy persisted. 'Does she know that Buddy died? Will you tell her that I'm going to medical school?'

He shook his finger at her. 'You go on now, Cissy, and make the parents who raised you proud. You'll be a fine physician.'

DOC HADLEY died the following month. The funeral was held in the high-school gymnasium, the benches filled to overflowing.

Everyone cried, of course. Cissy had come prepared with pockets full of Kleenex. She cried for the loss of the man himself and for the thread he represented to her beginnings, to her birth mother. That thread was now forever broken.

WITH HER PARENTS' help and a rented truck, Cissy moved her possessions to Dallas, back to the city where she had lived during the three clinical years of her nurse's training. She rented a three-room apartment in a shabby neighbourhood near the medical centre campus. Martha Claire cooked their meals in the tiny kitchen. Grayson installed chain locks on the door.

Her parents stayed for three days, with Martha Claire sleeping with Cissy in the bedroom and Grayson on the sofa. When they finished cleaning and painting, the place looked livable.

The three of them agreed that Cissy would not come home until Thanksgiving. It was a six-hour drive from Dallas to Columbus, and Cissy would need weekends for her studies and nursing.

They all blinked back tears when it came time to say goodbye. Grayson insisted on giving her a wad of bills. 'I don't want you skipping meals,' he said.

Cissy stood on the kerb and watched her parents drive away. How she loved them. If only she could fix whatever was broken between them and make them happy once again.

With her parents gone, her new home seemed deafeningly quiet. Cissy turned on the radio and stared at the clothes her mother had hung in her closet, pondering what to wear to tomorrow's orientation. She decided on a sleeveless black dress and sandals.

Cissy washed her hair, shined her shoes, filed her nails. And felt as if she had gone backwards in time, preparing for the first day of school. New books. New teachers. A new beginning.

The first-year class was welcomed by the dean, who told them they could expect to work harder over the next four years than they had ever worked in their lives. Then he gave a run-down of the class demographics. Of the 120 class members, 102 were men and 110 were residents of the state of Texas. Ninety-eight had come directly from an undergraduate programme. The remainder included six military veterans, two accountants, a commercial pilot, five paramedics, four pharmacists, two schoolteachers, a Presbyterian minister and one nurse.

'Are you the nurse?' one of Cissy's classmates asked during the break. She had noticed him earlier—the good-looking guy wearing a sports jacket, jeans and well-worn cowboy boots.

'Does it show that much?' she asked, reaching up to pat the top of her head. 'I could have sworn I left my white cap at home.'

'Just a guess. The other females look too young and affluent.'

He looked to be about thirty, with white teeth, a square jaw and close-cropped blond hair. With his lean, tanned body and west Texas drawl, she would cast him as a cowboy, but there weren't any cowboys on the dean's list. 'Are you a veteran or the pilot?' she asked.

He saluted. 'Captain Joe McCormack, at your service.'

At lunch they ate in the cafeteria together. He had grown up on a cattle ranch outside Lampasas and gone into the army after college.

Cissy gave a perfunctory run-down on herself, including the part about her cousin paying her tuition. 'I am definitely not one of the affluent,' she said. 'I put my name on the special-duty roster at every hospital in the area. I'll be doing most of my studying at the bedside of the comatose and dying.'

That afternoon they were introduced to their cadavers in the gross-anatomy lab. Cissy and her three lab partners were assigned the body of an elderly black woman. Her lab partners were the pilot and two young men freshly graduated from the University of Texas. It was disquieting for Cissy to see the cadaver's emaciated body exposed for all to see. She was as flat-chested as a boy, and the formaldehyde had turned her skin a leathery grey. One of the young graduates laughed nervously. 'This old gal looks like she's been rode hard and put up wet.'

'Shall we name her?' the pilot asked.

'What's a good name for a teacher?' Cissy asked. 'We will need to learn a great deal from her.'

'What about Grandmother?' the other young student asked.

The rest nodded. Grandmother it would be.

At the end of the day Joe McCormack caught up with Cissy and invited her out for a hamburger. They sat on the outdoor deck at a west Dallas restaurant and talked the evening away. His group had named their cadaver Teddy Roosevelt. 'The old guy must have weighed three hundred pounds,' Joe said.

Over their second beer they talked about aspirations. Joe wanted to be a family doctor back in Lampasas or some other west Texas town. He would run a few cattle, raise a few horses and kids, have family dinners at a big round table in a kitchen with wooden floors. And laugh a lot. 'I forgot how to laugh for a while,' he said.

'Vietnam?'

He nodded and called for the bill. 'I'm in the middle of a divorce. She said I changed too much in Nam. She didn't care for the nightmares, I guess.'

'I'm sorry. That must have been difficult for you.'

'Still is. What about you?'

'Almost engaged once—to a medical student. Sometimes I have regrets. I hope I'm more suited to being a doctor than a doctor's wife.'

Joe drove her to her car. 'Good night, Cissy Stewart from Columbus. I hope we're both still around four years from now.'

'Me, too.'

It had been a good day, Cissy thought as she drove home, in part because of Joe McCormack.

Cissy was surprised at the ease with which she made friends with her classmates—especially her three anatomy-lab partners. But then, they saw each other several hours a day as they slowly dissected Grandmother. Their evening sessions in the lab were frequently followed by a beer, often with Joe and his room-mate, another Vietnam vet. When she lifted the glass to her lips, the aroma of beer mingled with the smell of formaldehyde.

Cissy often studied with Joe. They quizzed each other constantly. Name the ligaments of the hand. The nerves of the axilla. Cissy hadn't known there was room in her brain for all the things she learned in just that semester. She never listened to the radio or watched television, never read a book that wasn't a textbook. She didn't see *Rocky*. Sports, politics, current events all but ceased to exist for her as she immersed herself in anatomy, physiology, biochemistry and genetics.

It wasn't until she was on the highway, driving to Columbus for Thanksgiving, that she came up for air. Her mother was preparing a traditional Thanksgiving feast for the first time since they lost Buddy. Tomorrow was the fifth anniversary of his death.

'It's good to be home,' she said when she arrived just before eleven. In spite of the hour, the three of them lingered at the kitchen table, drinking milk and nibbling on cookies. Cissy enjoyed telling her parents about Grandmother and Teddy Roosevelt, about her classes and friends. She didn't mention Joe.

The next day her father carved the turkey as always, but there weren't enough people at the table, not enough words and laughter to fill the room. Cissy knew her parents, too, were remembering other Thanksgivings with family all around—good memories that made the present poignant and sad.

SHE DIDN'T START sleeping with Joe until after the spring break.

They had talked about it off and on all through that first year. They both confessed to being horny. Joe said he had been all but asexual since he and his wife split up. But as consumed as he was by school and studying, he was always having sexual thoughts.

Cissy was tired of her virginal state, tired of being the only one who hadn't done it. Back in college she and Randy Calhoune had petted for hours but never went all the way. Initially she thought she would save herself for marriage, but now she wondered if she would ever be any man's wife. She certainly didn't want to be the sort of wife Joe said he wanted—a chief-cook-and-bottle-washer sort of wife. And at the moment she didn't want courtship, either. She didn't have time for 'dating', but she would have to do something to deal with the distracting, turned-on state in which she found herself. Joe was the first guy she had met in medical school, and she had spent more time with him than anyone else. She liked it when he grinned at her and she felt herself responding whenever he touched her arm or their thighs touched under the table. It seemed only right that he do the honours.

She got a prescription for birth-control pills. But instead of solving their mutual problem, soon they were having sex at every possible opportunity. They would meet in his van for a quickie between classes. He spent nights at her house, going to his own place only to change clothes.

'We have created a monster,' Cissy said finally. 'I fell asleep in class again today.'

They rationed themselves. They'd have sex on Wednesday and Saturday nights only. Cissy missed his presence in her bed but was relieved. She didn't want to think about him all the time. She was here to make a physician of herself. But when she wasn't with Joe, she still thought about him, and the thoughts began to take a different turn. She imagined herself in a wedding dress.

Yet when they were studying for their embryology final and Joe asked if she thought they should get married, Cissy didn't know if she should feel hopeful or unbearably sad. She would marry Joe in a flash if she thought it would work, but she feared she was no more the right woman for Joe McCormack than she had been for Randy Calhoune. She liked Joe better, loved him more, resented him just as much—resented the fact that he wanted a traditional wife who would look after him and the kids. If she had to choose between Joe and becoming a physician, she would choose the latter. But what she truly wanted was to practise medicine *and* for Joe to change his expectations for marriage.

On the morning of their embryology final she parked her car and was crossing the street to the basic sciences building when she saw Joe being dropped off by a young woman driving a new Mercedes. He pretended that he didn't see Cissy, but she knew he had.

She didn't realise she had stopped in the middle of the street until a car honked at her. Very carefully she walked to the kerb, then to the steps. She lowered herself to the bottom step, put her head between her knees, took several deep breaths, and convinced herself she wasn't going to die, that she was going to get herself up the steps and to the nearest ladies' room.

The cold water felt almost erotic on her hot face. Again and again she splashed her face. Then she looked in the mirror. 'OK, Cissy Stewart, you get your ass down that hall and make a better grade on that test than Joe McCormack.' She was the last one in the room before the invigilator closed the door.

It was almost midnight when he called. He spoke so softly that at first she thought it was an obscene phone call. He wasn't alone, she realised. *She* was there, asleep or in the bathroom. 'Coward,' she said. 'You could at least come and tell me in person.'

'My wife wants us to get back together,' he whispered. 'She's moving up here.'

'With some of Daddy's money, I take it. How nice for you—home cooking *and* a Mercedes. You can't beat a deal like that.'

'Don't, Cissy. I am really sorry, but I guess I never stopped caring about her. She's a good person. She will devote herself to me and our children. Maybe I'm selfish to want that, but I do.'

Cissy hung up and threw her coffee cup against the wall.

Eight

When the first year of medical school ended, Cissy ranked fourth in her class. By the end of the second year she had slipped a few notches but was still in the top ten. Her classmates and professors all knew who she was—Cecelia Stewart, the nurse from Columbus who had made top ten two years running.

With the two years of basic sciences out of the way, the time had come to leave the classroom. For the next two years Cissy would follow attending physicians around, learning from them at the bedsides of actual patients. Her first clinical rotation was surgery. The first day, she and another third-year student scrubbed up for the amputation of a fifty-five-year-old diabetic male's left leg, just above the knee. The sound of the saw and the putrid smell that rose from the gangrenous limb were too much for the other medical student. He started weaving back and forth, then grabbed hold of a nurse's arm for support. The surgeon yelled at him to get the hell out of there.

The operation lasted more than two hours. Cissy concentrated on the hot shower she would take as soon as she got home—a very long shower that would wash away the smell of rotting tissue and the tension that pressed like a vice across her shoulders and neck. But she also felt satisfaction. Because of her nurse's training, she knew that she was better prepared than her classmates for the experiences that awaited her over the next two years.

Her second rotation was internal medicine, which was run by the first and only female department chair in the history of the medical school. Daisy Cunningham was barely five foot tall, pushing sixty, and formidable. The first day of the rotation Dr Cunningham marched her new crop of students from bedside to bedside as she examined patients.

At the conclusion of rounds she encouraged the students to speculate about the patients and describe any significant symptoms they had noticed. When one hapless young man referred to a patient as the fat lady at the end of the hall, she told him in a frosty voice that the woman had a name. 'On my service, *all* patients have names. They are human beings and will be treated and spoken of with dignity. Now, does anyone remember this patient's name?'

When no one answered, Dr Cunningham looked in Cissy's direction. 'Dr Stewart?'

'Mary Sinclair,' Cissy answered.

'What else can you tell me about Mrs Sinclair?'

'Her diagnosis is acute pulmonary oedema brought on by congestive heart failure.'

'No, no, no,' Dr Cunningham said impatiently. 'I mean, what else can you tell me about her as a person?'

'She is a retired secretary, married, and has three children.'

Dr Cunningham nodded. 'How do you know these things?'

'They were on her chart.'

'Did you learn anything else about this patient at her bedside?'

'She has the beginning of a bedsore on her right elbow, and I suspect that she is lonely,' Cissy said.

'What makes you think that?' Dr Cunningham asked.

'She was admitted last Monday, and there are no get-well cards on her cabinet, no magazines that people have brought by.'

'Thank you, Dr Stewart,' Dr Cunningham said. 'Would you please come to see me this afternoon?'

It was after three when Cissy was escorted into Dr Cunningham's cluttered office. The first thing Cissy noticed was the quilt that hung on the wall. Another was draped over the worn leather sofa. 'The wedding-ring pattern,' Cissy said, indicating the quilt on the wall. 'It's beautiful. My mother has one. My great-grandmother made it for her as a wedding present. Who made this one?' she asked, examining the fine stitches.

'I bought it at an estate sale. I have more at home. They comfort me, especially the old ones made from feed sacks and old clothes. When I think of the women who made them to warm their children and beautify their homes, even if the home had a dirt floor, I am reminded that people are more than simply systems and symptoms.' She waved Cissy to the sofa, then poured water from an electric kettle into two waiting china cups and bobbed tea bags up and down. Dr Cunningham placed the cups on a wicker tray next to a plate of cookies. She set the tray on a small table, pulled her chair from behind her desk, and sat down opposite Cissy. 'I've been waiting for you, Cecelia Claire Stewart.'

'I'm sorry,' Cissy said. 'I didn't think you had specified a time for me to come.'

Dr Cunningham shook her head. 'I wasn't talking about today. I've been waiting for you for two years.'

'I don't understand.'

'I was a nurse, too. I went through a three-year hospital programme when I got out of high school, and I put myself through medical school, like you're doing.'

Cissy nodded. 'I earn most of my living expenses. My physician cousin paid for my tuition and books the first two years. Now I've got a scholarship.'

'How many hours a week do you nurse?'

'It varies. Usually about twenty, mostly night shifts, obviously.'

'Is that why you never joined the Women's Student Medical Association here?'

Cissy knew that Daisy Cunningham was the founder of the local chapter. Still, she answered honestly, 'Not really. I prefer to think of myself as a medical student, not a *woman* medical student. And I've never been much of a joiner.'

'There are too few women in medicine,' Dr Cunningham pointed out. 'We have to band together. If we don't, we're overlooked. Women aren't elected president of their medical school class. They don't serve as medical school deans. The best residencies go to men. That has to change. If you don't learn anything else from me, I want to teach you to look after other women and not be one of those nasty creatures who claws her way across the drawbridge, then pulls it up behind her.'

After that first meeting the two women became friends. Cissy joined the Women's Student Medical Association, and she dined in her mentor's home many times.

Daisy Cunningham lived in a period house in a lovely neighbourhood. The rooms were spacious and filled with American antiques. The back yard was shared in equal parts by a swimming pool and a vegetable garden.

'Are you happy living alone?' Cissy asked her one Sunday evening over sherry. She had often wondered why Daisy had never married.

'No, but I wasn't happy living with a man, either. A man wants a woman to fuss over him. I never fussed.'

'My mother liked doing that for Daddy and us kids,' Cissy said. 'I always thought I would grow up and be just like her.'

'Why didn't you?'

'I almost did. I came very close to marrying a medical student back in my nursing-school days,' Cissy said. 'I would have put my nursing degree in a drawer and devoted myself to being a good doctor's wife and a good mother to his children. It might have been OK. It might even have been wonderful.'

'Do you still think about him?' Daisy asked.

'No. I think about the man who came after him,' Cissy answered. Randy Calhoune was history. She would go for weeks without thinking about him. But she still thought about Joe McCormack.

After dinner that evening Cissy took a short detour on the way home, driving by Joe's house, then circling the block and parking across the street. Light came from a side window and pooled itself on the lawn. A dining-room window, perhaps. They could be having dinner right now, she thought.

Such a pretty house with a steeply pitched roof and diamond-paned windows. Jose and his wife were probably deliriously happy.

Cissy put her head against the steering wheel. What if there was never another Joe in her life?

THE NEXT DAY she began dialling Joe's phone number. Every time Cissy had a chance, she dialled—to see if *she* answered. Cissy didn't even know the woman's name. She was simply Joe's wife. With her finger hovering above the disconnect button, Cissy would listen as the ringing went on and on.

All day Tuesday, even though she had promised herself that she wouldn't, Cissy once again repeatedly dialled Joe's house. His phone number became a litany, replaying itself endlessly in her brain. She was out of control. She had to get a grip on herself. Because she knew that even if Joe's wife had truly gone back to Lampasas, that didn't mean she had left for good.

After the fourth day of such insanity she bought a bottle of cheap wine on her way home. Sitting on the back step, she drank from the bottle and watched thunderheads form overhead. When the rain began, she carried the bottle inside and watched from the kitchen window as hail beat down on her tiny back yard.

With the noise of the storm, it took her a minute to realise the phone was ringing. It was Joe. He was just round the corner. Could he drop by?

Cissy didn't know what to do first. Comb her hair? Pick up the clutter? She just stood there clutching an empty wine bottle until he came to the door. He was drenched, his hair plastered to his head, a puddle forming around him on the floor.

'How's your wife?' Cissy asked.

'She's pregnant and throwing up every fifteen minutes. She went home so her mother could look after her.'

'Then what the hell are you doing here?' she screamed at him.

'I can't stop thinking about you.'

'Just leave, will you, before I throw this bottle at you.'

'Are you sure that's what you really want? I saw you sitting out in front of the house the other night. I haven't been able to think about anything else since.'

Of course she didn't want him to leave. What she wanted was for him to stay for ever. 'I hate you,' she said as he grabbed her and wrapped his wet arms round her. It felt so good to say those words that she said them again and again. She did hate him. But her body didn't know that. Her body felt as though she had just come home after a long and perilous journey.

Afterwards he told her she was beautiful.

'No, I'm not. I'm ordinary.'

He propped himself up on one elbow and looked down at her. 'No, you are not ordinary. You are the most extraordinary woman I have ever known. You are lovely and brilliant.'

'So why did you leave me? Is *she* so extraordinary?'

'No, she's not. But I knew if I survived the war, all I wanted was a sweet wife who would look after me and our kids. A pretty house. Financial security. That's not the way it would be with you and me. Lynette needs me, Cissy. You don't need anyone.'

Lynette. She had not wanted to know that name. 'So you get what you want, and I don't? Do you love her that much?'

'I love her,' he said, 'but not like I love you.'

'I hate you,' she said again, trying to push him out of the bed, but he began touching her again, pushing his face against her belly.

Finally they both lay paralysed, a sheet pulled over their damp bodies. She knew he wouldn't be there when she woke up. 'Don't come back,' she told him. 'Not ever.'

In the night she heard him leave and knew she was supposed to feel sad. But the pain of too much wine throbbing behind her eyeballs precluded other feelings. She needed to sleep some more; then she would feel sad or angry or whatever.

Towards morning she awoke again, and it occurred to her to wonder when her last period had been. She had stopped taking birth-control pills, but she wasn't mid-cycle. Close, maybe, but days off. Surely she was in the clear. But a shiver of fear shot through her body. She should have at least insisted on a condom.

She stood under the shower for a long time, symbolically and literally washing away Joe. 'No baby, please,' she whispered.

CISSY WAITED three weeks before giving up hope. And then, in spite of morning nausea, tacked on another week just in case. She wanted to hate Joe, to blame him, but when he called that fateful night, she had allowed him to come over.

An early abortion was the only way out of this mess. It was legal now, in the wake of *Roe* v. *Wade*. But what if she never married? What if this was the only time her body would ever be pregnant?

Cissy thought about her own origins. She wondered if her birth mother had considered abortion. Maybe this pregnancy was an opportunity for Cissy to come full circle with her own life—a paying back of sorts for her mother's not ending the pregnancy that resulted in her own birth. Cissy could carry the child and give it up for adoption as her birth mother had done before her.

Cissy also thought about Justine and Iris. If Justine had given Iris away, how different her own life would have been. Iris had been the most joyous part of her childhood. Iris was the reason she was in medical school. If Cissy screwed up medical school because she had got herself pregnant, she would be letting Iris down.

Iris was pregnant now—and deliriously happy, as pregnant women should be.

Cissy's thoughts led her round and round in an endless confusing circle. There was no easy answer. No answer to be found by re-examining the past. The past was a maze of secrets and unhappiness. So much unhappiness, and she didn't even know why. It had killed Buddy. It had made Justine take Iris away. It made her too afraid to make this all-important decision about her own life.

Her mother would never explain the past. Martha Claire would insist that nothing had happened, that marriages wear out like cars, that hers and Grayson's was simply an old, tired marriage.

Finally Cissy made the six-hour drive to Columbus—not to the house on Milam Street, but to her father's cabin by the river.

WHEN GRAYSON HEARD the crunching of car tyres on gravel, he thought that Paul Huxley had been able to get away after all. The retired minister came most Sunday afternoons to fish. And to sip a bit of Jack Daniel's—their little secret. Paul always brought a lemon to suck on while he drove home. His wife, Amanda, was a past state president of the Women's Christian Temperance Union. If Amanda thought he'd had so much as a sip of demon whisky, she would probably kick him out of the house.

Last week, however, Amanda had fallen and broken her hip. She was in hospital in Houston, and Paul had planned to visit her this afternoon. Grayson hadn't been expecting him.

He put down his book and walked through the cabin to greet his visitor. The cabin was less primitive now, with interior walls, a second-hand refrigerator, and a pump mounted over a metal sink.

Monday, Wednesday and Friday were now his days to tend the store. Grayson and Martha Claire kept the store open more because it imposed a needed structure on their days and weeks than for the modest income it produced. Grayson was surprised that they had any customers at all. Martha Claire insisted on keeping clothing on the racks long after it should have been sold at the sidewalk sale at

50 per cent off the last marked-down price. Not even the sports corner attracted much business these days.

Grayson was surprised to see Cissy's battered Volkswagen rolling to a stop behind his own elderly pick-up. He smiled and waved, but apprehension prickled its way across his forehead. He hadn't expected to see his daughter until Thanksgiving. 'This is an unexpected surprise,' he told her, wrapping her slight body in his arms, laying his cheek against her soft hair. How he loved this darling girl—the only child he had left to love.

She touched his hair. 'A few more grey ones, I see,' she said, teasing. 'You look very distinguished.'

He looked down at his ragged T-shirt and laughed. 'Yes, Grayson Francis Stewart, Esquire, at home on his country estate.' He linked arms with her, walking up the gravel path. 'If I'd known you were coming,' he said, 'I would have had fish to fry.'

'I can't stay long. I just drove down for a few hours.'

He opened two cans of beer to take out on the porch. 'You didn't spend the night with your mother?'

She shook her head. 'No. I came to see you.'

Grayson felt a heaviness settle in his chest. *Something was wrong.*

'It really is pretty here,' Cissy said, staring out at the river.

'Sit down and tell me what's on your mind,' he said.

Cissy leaned back in the dilapidated wicker rocker and closed her eyes for a long minute. When she opened them, she said, 'I came to ask what happened to our family.'

Grayson opened his mouth to speak, then closed it for lack of words. He tried to clear his throat but could not. He just sat there, feeling like a fool. Had he actually thought he might live out his life without his daughter's asking that particular question of him? Maybe he should have left years ago to prevent just such a moment. Or died. To have been spared this. And Buddy's death. 'Have you talked to your mother about this?' he managed to ask.

'No, but she wouldn't tell me if I did.'

'No, I suppose not.'

'I've reached an impasse, Daddy. I need to know what happened before I can get on with things.'

Grayson sucked in his breath, then let it out slowly. A heron, with a silvery fish in his mouth, rose gracefully from a stand of cat's-tails. From across the river a crow cawed noisily. A perfect day. In the summer it was too hot for comfort and the mosquitoes were ferocious, but even then he stayed out here to avoid the pain and censure that still resided in his wife's eyes. For so long he had hoped that he would be able to work his way back into Martha Claire's heart, but he had hurt her too deeply for any hope of redemption. Maybe if he'd known that forgiveness would never be forthcoming he would have driven away and never come back. But he never could bring himself to abandon Cissy and Buddy to a mother whose spirit he had shattered.

Slowly he rose from his chair and went inside. Such a cliché, to keep money hidden under a floorboard. His secret cache. He tucked away bills now and then, telling himself he was going to take that trip to Europe someday, a pilgrimage to the battlefields and cemeteries of his war. But there would be no trip to Europe, no trip to anyplace.

He didn't know what had happened in Cissy's life to precipitate her question, but the need in her eyes was real. He only hoped when she had her answer she could forgive him. He had lost Iris and Buddy. The prospect of living the rest of his years cut off from Cissy was too sad to contemplate. He handed her a wad of bills. 'Go see Justine,' he said. 'I'll let her know you're coming.'

'Is it that difficult for you?' Cissy asked.

He nodded. He had got medals for bravery, but he didn't have the courage for this.

AT THE AIRPORT Justine almost didn't recognise Cissy. She seemed deflated, older, and so thin. Justine opened her arms and wondered if this would be the last time she would embrace her niece. How would Cissy feel about her when she knew the truth?

'Are you all right, honey?' Justine asked, reaching for Cissy's bag.

Cissy smiled. 'Sure. Just tired.'

As they headed for the car, Justine explained that they were going to spend the weekend at her friend Astrid's house on Shelter Island. 'It's not a long drive,' she promised, glancing at her niece.

'I'm fine. Really,' Cissy insisted.

Justine found herself talking about Iris, of course. She was thrilled about the baby and worried about Iris—four months pregnant and taking a trip to Europe. Hillel had sworn he would never return to Germany, but last year he located an elderly male cousin who had survived the Holocaust. The man was in failing health; if Hillel was ever going to see a member of his family again, he would have to journey back to the place where they all had died. Iris wasn't about to let him face that emotional journey alone.

It began to rain, and Justine became preoccupied with finding the right turnoff. Cissy sat with her hands in her lap, her face blanched an unnatural white in the light from oncoming traffic.

Justine had begged Grayson not to send her up here. Cissy was *his* child. *He* could explain their sordid history himself. Or lie to her. They had taken a vow with Martha Claire that their children were never to know the secret that had destroyed their family.

'I know,' Grayson said. 'But Buddy is dead, and Iris escaped. Cissy is bearing the burden of the past on her own, and it's become too much for her.'

'What if she never speaks to you again?' Justine was in her dark-room, bathed in the red glow of the safelight. She almost hadn't picked up the phone, but it might have been Iris calling from Europe. Grayson's was the last voice she expected to hear, but she had recognised it almost at once.

'I can live with that if it helps Cissy get on with her life. Please, Justine, talk to her. I don't have the courage.'

'Then let Martha Claire do it.'

'Martha Claire's version would be vindictive.'

'And my version?' Justine demanded. 'How will it be?'

'Kinder, I hope, than Martha Claire's.'

Justine sank onto a high stool and stared down at an enlargement of one of her wartime London photographs as it slowly materialised in the developing tray. A Manhattan gallery had scheduled a retro-spective exhibition of her work: 'Justine Mayfield-Dover—Thirty-Five Years of Photojournalism.' For months now she had been spending hours in her darkroom reliving her career.

She didn't want to do this thing Grayson was asking of her, didn't want to relive those confusing two days when she had tarnished her soul and created the daughter who had given her life meaning.

'Will you talk to Cissy if I send her to you?'

Justine sighed deeply. 'No promises,' she said. 'I don't know that I have the courage, either.'

On the ferry, Justine babbled on a bit about the island. How prop-erty values had soared. Astrid had spent summers here when she was growing up. 'I come here a lot these days. I take pictures and Astrid paints.'

After they had carried in the suitcases and groceries, they pre-pared a simple meal. Justine lit candles and poured wine. 'We'll eat first and save the serious stuff for later,' she said. She had several glasses of wine to calm her nerves.

Cissy only took tiny sips of wine but ate a bowl of pasta and two slices of the chewy French bread. She looked fragile, Justine decided, with weariness in her eyes. She wondered where her niece found the stamina in that small body to face the rigours of medical school and long hours of special-duty nursing.

'Tell me about my sister,' Justine said. 'What are her days like now? What gives her joy?'

'Well, she has the church, of course,' Cissy began, 'but it's less important to her now that Reverend Huxley has retired. And she still loves her garden. She was never able to turn the house into a show-place, but the yard is on the annual Garden Club tour.'

'Iris tells me your father spends most of his time by the river.'

Cissy nodded. 'Yes. He and Mama see each other, though. They trade off days at the store. And he has dinner at home on Friday nights and stays over—in his own room.'

'Does she ever go out there—to the river?'

'Not that I know of.'

'They got married out by the rose garden,' Justine recalled. 'When I saw them together, Martha Claire in Grandma Polly's wedding dress, Grayson in his uniform, with such hope in their eyes, I thought my heart was going to burst inside my chest. They were so beautiful and so much in love. I wish they could rekindle some of what they were feeling that day.'

'Me, too,' Cissy said, 'but I don't think they ever will. Mama is not one to forgive.'

Justine nodded. Yes, her sister was not the forgiving sort. But Justine wasn't so sure if she herself would have been able to forgive such a crime if their positions were reversed. And now the time had come for her to confess that crime to her sister's child.

THE RAIN HAD PUT a chill in the air, so after they tidied up the kitchen Justine built a small fire in the stone fireplace. She brought a cup of tea for Cissy and more wine for herself.

They pulled their chairs close and stared at the flames for a time. If she were a praying woman, Justine would ask that Cissy change her mind and let sleeping dogs lie. But Cissy was gathering herself to speak, and Justine waited with a heavy heart.

'Since I was twelve years old,' Cissy began, still staring at the fire,

'I've been navigating a maze without knowing how I got there. I have tried to heal my parents without knowing why they're the way they are. I have tried to make up for not being Iris and tried to help us all come to terms with Buddy's death, all the while wondering whether if I had been a real daughter and not an adopted one if things would be better. What happened to us, Justine? I need to know. I'm pregnant, and I have to decide what to do about it.'

Then she burst into tears. Justine knelt beside her and held her, smoothed her hair. 'Precious little Cissy,' she said, her voice soothing. She handed Cissy a napkin and watched while she wiped her eyes. 'What about the man who got you this way?' she asked, her knees creaking as she rose and returned to her chair.

'I got myself this way,' Cissy said wearily. 'It was so dumb. But to answer your question, he's married. He doesn't have a clue about what's going on, and I intend to keep it that way.'

Justine sighed. 'I had this same conversation with my mother when I came back from the war. Does Martha Claire know?'

'You're the first person I've told,' Cissy said. 'Before I decide what to do, I want to know what happened to our family. Why has Mama never been able to forgive Daddy for whatever it was that he did? I spent my whole life trying to make my mother love me, but she was more dedicated to *not* loving Daddy and you and Iris than she was to loving Buddy and me. Now, I wonder, if I have this baby, would Mama think it is yet another way that one of us had failed her, that I was a misbegotten child bringing another misbegotten child into the world for her to deal with?'

Cissy stopped talking, and with her hands folded in her lap, waited for Justine's response.

Justine took a sip of wine. 'I don't know where to begin.'

Cissy began for her. 'I grew up believing that you were a widow, that a British soldier named Philip Benston Dover was Iris's father. But since there was never one shred of information about this man, I decided that you had to get married and didn't really love him. Now I wonder if he ever existed at all.'

'He didn't,' Justine said softly. 'Your grandma Polly made him up, and Martha Claire put his obituary in the newspaper.'

'Does Iris know?'

Justine shook her head. 'No.'

'I also thought for many years that Daddy was my birth father,' Cissy continued.

'What made you think that?' Justine asked.

Cissy shrugged. 'I was casting about for a damning secret. That one seemed to fit the bill. I decided that Doc Hadley knew all about it. Maybe Daddy even asked him to give me to them so he could raise me. Probably it was Doc Hadley's idea to tack Buddy onto the deal. Then in those last weeks of Grandma Polly's life, Mama somehow found out. When you came home for the funeral, you stuck up for Daddy and told Mama she should forgive him. The older I got, however, the more difficult it became to believe that story. I couldn't imagine Daddy sneaking off behind Mama's back. And no one could hide a pregnancy all the way to term in Columbus.'

'So now what do you think?' Justine asked, her fingers curling around the arm of the chair, waiting for the axe to fall.

Cissy hesitated. 'It wasn't until Daddy told me to come to see you that the pieces began to fall into place. Now I think my daddy fathered a child, but it wasn't me. I think he is Iris's father.'

'Why do you think that?' Justine asked.

'Mama has never forgiven him,' Cissy explained. 'If he'd had an affair with anyone else, she would have given him a hard time but eventually got over it.' There were other things, too, she went on. 'Iris and Daddy both got hiccups when they laughed too hard, both chewed on their thumbnails when they were puzzled. Did you ever hear them sing "La Vie en Rose"? Their voices blended so perfectly, like syrup and melted butter.'

Cissy paused, waiting for Justine to confirm or deny. Justine sat motionless, saying nothing.

Finally Cissy broke the silence. 'How did Mama find out?'

Justine took a deep breath. 'I think the same way you did. She realised how alike they were. Then she looked for proof.'

Cissy lifted her chin. 'Were you in love with my father?'

Justine wondered, if she had been in love with Grayson, would that mitigate her sin or worsen it? The night they sought shelter from the bombs, in the cellar under her favourite pub, as she clung to him for what she thought was the last bit of human comfort she would ever feel, maybe then she understood that Grayson Stewart was a man she could have loved if he wasn't married to her sister. But did such feelings have any relevance now?

Then Justine began to speak in a great outpouring of words, trying to explain how it was during the war, how she revelled in the intensity of that other time and place. But when the young Aussie airman she had fallen in love with was killed, everything changed. She told Cissy about that awful night, waiting in the pub for Billy to come through the door as he always did, with his hat at a jaunty angle and a grin on his darling face. Instead, two mates from his wing came to give her the news. Her Billy Boy was dead.

'I never made love with him,' Justine said. 'In the middle of a world war, with planes being shot out of the sky on a daily basis, I had clung to my virtue like it was the most important thing in the world. My sister had been a virgin on her wedding night, and I would be, too, by golly. But when Billy died, I slept with every man who came along. For months I did that. Then I picked up my camera and took pictures instead.'

She had her camera with her the evening she saw Grayson in London, she explained. He was in England for medical treatment. He had a bandaged eye when they met for a drink. Then the bombs started falling and they were trapped, clinging to each other as the fire from burning buildings crept closer. She told Grayson about the boy she had loved and the men she had slept with. He told her he didn't want to go back to Columbus, that he wanted a different sort of life, but knew Martha Claire would never agree to it.

When finally they were rescued, they spent the rest of the night and the next day walking through the ruins. She took pictures until she ran out of film. Then they found a pub where they could talk until it was time for him to leave.

'It was an extraordinary twenty-four hours,' Justine said. 'We had faced death together and shared our innermost secrets. After the armistice Grayson came back. I took a train to Dover and met him there. The war was over, but we were still scared. I was scared that after all my bravado about wanting to live a different kind of life, I didn't have the guts. And Grayson was afraid of going home to spend the rest of his life tending the family store. He wanted to stay in the army, and he wanted me to tell him that he had a right to do that even if it meant not going home to his wife.'

Justine turned her face towards the fire. 'I told Grayson he would never find anyone who loved him as much as my sister, but he had to make her understand how he felt. Then I went home and realised how determined she was to stay in Columbus.'

'Did you go to Dover knowing that you would make love with him?' Cissy asked.

'I'm sure I didn't. We planned to go just for the day but missed the last train back. The innkeeper assumed we were married. We downed one too many pints. But excuses don't count. It was the worst thing I could have done—my own sister's husband.'

'When you discovered you were pregnant, did you think about not having the baby?'

Ah, so now they had arrived at the heart of things, Justine thought. She would have to go carefully into those deep waters.

'Of course I thought about it,' she said. 'That was my plan. I wasn't about to have my brother-in-law's child. As soon as I got home, I would go to Freedmantown for a kitchen-table abortion, but my mother decided otherwise. And I must admit it was a relief to have her take charge. When I was in high school, a neighbour girl died after having an abortion. I didn't want a baby, but I didn't want to die, either. Eventually I resigned myself to having it, but I never intended to love it. Strange how things turn out. Being Iris's mother has been the best part of my life.' Justine leaned forward. 'Before you decide on an abortion, you need to ask yourself why. Would you be doing it because it's what you want or because you are afraid to tell your mother?'

'Both, I guess. I don't want a baby unless I have a husband and my mother can hold her head up. I'm all that Mama and Daddy have left. How can I disappoint them like that?' Cissy stood up abruptly, putting an end to the discussion. Justine rose to her feet, and the two women stood facing each other. 'Thank you for talking to me,' Cissy said, her tone formal. 'I know this has not been easy for you.'

'Your parents and I swore that you children would never know who Iris's father was,' Justine said. 'I still don't want Iris to know. And please, don't tell your mother that you know. She hates me enough the way it is.' She paused. 'Do you hate me, too?'

'A little,' Cissy admitted. 'Just like I hate myself. But I have loved you for my entire life. And Daddy. I can't go back and change that. My mother did that, and look what happened to her.'

At the door to the guest room, Justine wasn't sure if a hug was in order, so she kept her distance. 'Let me know what you decide. Either way, I'll pay your expenses.' Cissy started to protest, but Justine wouldn't let her. Whether she had the baby or not, she would need money. 'Should I tell Iris?' Justine asked.

'No. She would want a say. I need to decide this on my own.'

'I love you, Cissy,' Justine said. 'I haven't told you that in years, but I do, and I've always felt guilty about taking Iris away from you.

I know how you suffered for what your father and I did.'

'Yes, but what you and Daddy did gave me Iris in the first place. I don't so much forgive you as accept that it happened. OK?'

'May I hug you?'

Cissy slid into Justine's arms. Justine had always loved her niece but probably never more than at that moment.

I WENT TO NEW YORK thinking I was entitled to have the sins of the past revealed to me so that I could find some justification for the mess I had made of my own life. I learned that my father and my aunt made love while my mother was anxiously waiting for their return. I ached for my poor mother but wished she had been valiant enough to rise above what had been done to her, to either send my father packing or help him earn her forgiveness. My father had stayed on in their loveless marriage out of remorse, and because of his love for me and my brother. Together, our parents condemned us to bear silent witness to their rotting marriage.

I tried to imagine how it might have been for Justine and my father in Dover. Had they simply allowed liquor to push Martha Claire out of their minds? Or had they acted out of anger at my mother's unwillingness to go forth with them into the larger world?

I had not asked those questions of Justine. But then, I'm sure she would not have been able to recall her exact feelings and motivations. Just as I had no earthly notion of why I had had sex with a man who I knew loved his wife and was committed to living the rest of his life with her. But at some level, though, my father and aunt had knowingly committed a vengeful act against my mother, just as Joe and I had figuratively screwed his wife. We had been raging against the person who represented limits for what had been seemingly limitless lives.

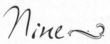

Nine

Cissy took the middle road. She would have the baby and give it up for adoption. Her parents must never know. Nor should Joe. Or Iris. Anyone who might try to change her mind.

The thought that Joe would find out filled her with dread. What if he saw her pregnant and realised how she had got that way? She imagined him demanding that she have an abortion, thrusting money into her hands. Their shared secret. A secret that would bind them for life.

One evening she heard two residents talking about the baby of a third-year medical student one of them had delivered and realised they were talking about Joe's baby. A live birth, but at only twenty-three weeks. The infant wasn't expected to live.

Suddenly a new fear struck arrowlike through Cissy's heart. With the death of this infant, Joe might hire a lawyer and lay claim to the one she carried. If Cissy wasn't going to raise it, he and his saintly wife would. Cissy placed her hands on her abdomen. No, they could not have her child. She did not want this baby raised by a mother who would always have a reason not to love it.

DAILY, CISSY INSPECTED her body from all angles, trying to decide if anyone might guess. She could make it to the end of the semester, she decided, then go someplace else before she began to show. Other than Justine, the only person she would tell was Daisy Cunningham, and only because Cissy needed her help in salvaging the second half of the academic year.

Over dinner one evening with Daisy, she confessed.

'I wondered when you were going to tell me,' Daisy said.

'How did you know?'

'All of a sudden you stopped wanting a glass of wine with dinner.'

'Yeah, my stomach doesn't like alcohol any more.'

'So what happens now?' Daisy asked.

'I don't want anyone to know, including my parents. Can I transfer to an out-of-state school for just one semester?'

'It would be unusual, but I'll see what I can work out.'

'You must be terribly disappointed in me,' Cissy said.

'Not so disappointed as shocked,' Daisy said. 'You're not some dumb little high-school girl, Cissy. You know better than to have unprotected sex. What were you thinking?'

'I wasn't,' Cissy said.

'And the baby?' Daisy asked.

'I'll give it up for adoption.'

'You're sure?'

'Yes, quite sure.'

Daisy nodded her agreement. 'You won't have time for motherhood—not for years,' she said.

'No time or money,' Cissy added. 'I have to work at a paying job to pay my rent and eat. Already there are twenty-four-hour stretches when the only time I'm at home is to shower and change clothes. I've gone too far to just give up on medical school.'

'I would think that went without saying,' Daisy said.

Daisy poured herself a glass of wine and Cissy a glass of iced tea. From her perch on a barstool Cissy sipped the tea and watched Daisy bustle around her kitchen. Cissy loved the room. Maybe someday she would have a lovely home herself. She hoped that she would be able to fill it with people on occasion as Daisy did. Not a bad life. A worthy profession. A lovely home. A safe existence. No great joy, but no agonising pain, either. And maybe, Cissy thought wistfully, she would enjoy this good, safe life more knowing that somewhere out there was a child to whom she had given birth.

THE FOLLOWING THURSDAY afternoon Cissy received a summons from Daisy. When she arrived at her office, Daisy closed the door. 'You will spend a semester of clinical training in Tulsa. The University of Oklahoma medical school has opened a branch campus there. You're being offered a special one-semester fellowship. You will have to pay out-of-state tuition, though.'

'My aunt has offered to help me financially.'

'Well, let me know if you need any additional help,' Daisy said.

'I hope I can do something wonderful for you someday.'

Daisy waved her away. 'Go home and get some sleep. You look like a scarecrow with two black eyes.'

CISSY HAD WORRIED needlessly about what she would wear when she went home for Christmas. Other than snug waistbands, her clothes still fitted fine. She warned her mother that she'd had an intestinal virus and didn't have much of an appetite. Actually, though, with the nausea of early pregnancy fading, Cissy arrived home feeling reasonably well. Her mother's pork roast and mashed potatoes had never tasted better.

On Christmas morning her parents emerged from their separate rooms. Grayson fixed waffles and sausage for breakfast and then they gathered round the tree. Just the three of them. Cissy remembered when their family had filled the room. Her mother sighed and said, 'What this house needs is children.'

The next morning, before leaving for Dallas, Cissy explained about Tulsa. It was a wonderful opportunity—a fellowship. Her expenses would be paid. She planned to sublet her duplex.

'Tulsa is so far away,' Martha Claire protested. 'We'll never get to see you.'

'It's just for a few months,' Cissy told them.

CISSY ENJOYED her solitary journey to Tulsa. With each mile that rolled by, she felt calmer. Tulsa was six hours from Dallas and twelve hours from Columbus. Her secret would be safe there.

She arrived before dark and had no trouble finding the rooming house where Daisy had arranged for her to live. Her room was spartan, with a tiny bathroom and a window that overlooked a church parking lot. She spent the evening putting away her things and mentally declaring herself at home.

By the end of the first week she had settled into a routine, spending her days at a family clinic on Utica Avenue and at sprawling St Francis Hospital. She was able to conceal her pregnancy much longer than she would have thought possible. The mandatory white jackets that all medical students wore helped.

It wasn't until her seventh month that women started asking when the baby was due, whether she wanted a boy or a girl, if she had selected names. Men seldom commented.

Justine had insisted that Cissy should not do any special-duty nursing in Tulsa, and sent more money than Cissy really needed. Cissy was grateful. She felt well enough but was always so very tired.

Justine called often. Was she all right? Had she talked to Martha Claire this week? Did she need more money?

'You don't have to feel responsible for me,' Cissy told her.

'Yes, I do. I abandoned you once. I'm not doing it again.'

Justine called from the hospital after Iris had her baby—a beautiful little girl with big eyes. Cissy talked to Iris, who sounded exhausted but happy. 'You'll have a baby one of these days,' she told Cissy. 'Our children will grow up together.'

For the first time Cissy felt the sting of regret. But she dismissed it. The infant she was carrying would have another family.

Now that she was in her last trimester, she went to the women's clinic every two weeks. At seven and a half months the physician who examined her also delivered a lecture. She needed to take better care of herself. She was anaemic. Her blood pressure was elevated. She hadn't gained enough weight. Getting enough rest? Drinking milk and eating plenty of fruit and vegetables? Just popping a prenatal vitamin every day was not enough.

Cissy used the leftover money from Justine's cheques to buy a tiny refrigerator and stopped by the grocery for juice, milk, carrots, apples. When she got home, she fell across her bed, exhausted. She knew she had a responsibility to the life she carried. She had failed to keep her brother alive. She would not fail this child, too.

THE FOLLOWING FRIDAY afternoon Cissy began experiencing intermittent contractions. The obstetrician who examined her said she was threatening to go into premature labour. He gave her a shot of terbutaline and prescribed bed rest with bathroom privileges for the rest of the pregnancy.

Cissy protested. She couldn't just go to bed. She needed to finish the semester.

'Try bed rest for a week, and we'll see how you're doing,' the physician said, compromising.

How much time could she miss without losing credit for the semester? Cissy wondered as she headed for her car. On the way home she stopped at the convenience store for a quart of milk and a ham sandwich. Later she would go to the grocery.

She dozed through the evening news, then ate part of the sandwich with a glass of milk. She drifted back to sleep, then awoke a couple of hours later and nibbled on the rest of the sandwich. She tried to study a bit.

The next time she awoke, she felt a bit queasy and chewed on a couple of antacid tablets. She tried to go back to sleep but lay there feeling her stomach grow progressively more rebellious. She was relieved when she finally threw up.

When next she awoke, she threw up again. It was the sandwich, she realised—either the mayonnaise or the ham had gone bad. Maybe both. By tomorrow she would be fine. Salmonella, probably. It shouldn't hurt the baby at all. She just needed to stay hydrated. She drank half a glass of water and went back to bed.

The water stayed down less than five minutes. She rinsed out her mouth, then carried the glass to her bedside table.

She awoke the next morning to her neighbour tapping on her door. She had a phone call.

'What took you so long?' Justine's voice asked.

'I was in bed,' Cissy said.

'Why? Are you sick? You don't sound like yourself.'

'I ate a sandwich that made me sick. The worst is over.'

'You sure?'

'Yeah. I just need to drink water and sleep.'

Cissy listened while Justine spoke rapturously about Iris's baby. She had mailed Cissy the latest pictures. Then she stopped mid-sentence. 'Would you rather I didn't talk about the baby?'

'Of course not, but right now I need to get to the bathroom.'

'Call me tomorrow,' Justine demanded.

Cissy barely made it to the toilet.

Before she went back to bed, she dutifully took several tiny sips of water. She hoped some of it would stay down. If it didn't, she would have to go to the emergency room for IV fluids. She woke several times during the day, going to the bathroom, sipping water, throwing it up in the metal wastebasket beside her bed, but not all of it. She was sure of that.

When she woke to darkness, she turned on the lamp and looked at the alarm clock, but she couldn't focus her eyes. Reaching for the glass of water, she knocked it over. Her head hurt like hell. Her stomach, too—high on the right, under her ribs. Really bad pain.

She half crawled from her bed to the desk chair and used it to pull herself to her feet. She took three shaky steps to the door but collapsed against it. She knew exactly what the trouble was. After all, she was a third-year medical student. She was suffering from serious dehydration. Food poisoning. But her main problem was the toxaemia of pregnancy. She had all the symptoms. Lights were even flashing in front of her eyes, and her legs were beginning to twitch—just like the textbook said. She put her hands on her belly. 'I think we're in trouble,' she said.

'Help! Will someone please help me?' she called out. She could barely hear her own voice, though. How was anyone else supposed to hear her?

SOMETHING WAS HURTING her left arm. Cissy reached down to pull it out. But whatever it was, it was covered by a piece of tape.

She opened her eyes and stared up at a bag of IV fluids. She was in a hospital. A patient. She'd never been a patient in a hospital before. It was good she was here, she thought as her eyes closed again. But what about the baby? She reached down and touched her stomach. It was soft. Like a pillow without its stuffing.

'It's a boy,' a voice said. Her father's voice.

Cissy opened her eyes. 'Daddy?'

'I'm here, sweetheart. You gave us quite a scare.'

'How long have you been here?'

'Since yesterday.'

'How did you know? What happened? When—'

'Justine tried to call you. She made the landlady unlock your door and check on you.'

Cissy touched her stomach again.

'Yes, you had the baby. He's a tiny little thing but moving about. They have him in an incubator, but he's breathing on his own.'

'Does Mama know?'

'Yes, Cissy, your mother knows.'

THE RING OF THE PHONE in the middle of the night had cut through Martha Claire's chest like a dagger. She rushed downstairs, thinking of the last time the phone had rung in the night—the night that Buddy died. Her hello was breathless. Then she listened while a woman explained that she was Cissy's landlady in Tulsa and Cissy had been taken to the hospital in an ambulance.

'Why?' Martha Claire demanded. 'What happened to her?'

'I'm not sure,' the woman said. 'She was unconscious. Her aunt insisted that I look in on her when she didn't answer my knock.'

'Her *aunt*?'

'Yes. She had called several times, but Miss Stewart never seemed to be in her room. Finally the aunt asked to speak to me and said she was worried about her niece and asked me to check on her. Miss Stewart was unconscious, lying on the floor right next to the door. I thought she was dead. Scared me half to death. We called the police. When I called the aunt back, she asked me to call you and gave me your number. They took your daughter to St Francis Hospital. I hope she's all right.' The woman paused. 'And the baby, too.'

'The *baby*?'

'Yes. Her aunt said you didn't know. Your daughter was pregnant, Mrs Stewart. She was planning to put the baby up for adoption. She's a lovely young woman, your daughter. So polite. Not the type at all you'd think would get herself in a situation like that.'

Martha Claire hung up and immediately called New York information for the number of Justine Mayfield-Dover. With a trembling hand she punched in the numbers. Justine answered immediately.

'What is going on with my daughter?' Martha Claire demanded without identifying herself.

For two heartbeats there was no sound. Then Justine said, 'I talked to her the day before yesterday and thought she sounded shaky. Then I kept calling back to check on her. Finally I convinced the landlady to unlock the door and see if she was in there.'

'How come you know about my daughter's situation and I don't?'

Justine sighed. 'She came here last November, wanting to know the family secrets. She told me she was pregnant.'

'The family secrets?' Martha Claire's throat was dry. It was suddenly hard to speak. 'What did you tell her?'

'She had pretty much figured things out on her own. All I did was confirm them. She seemed to think that understanding what had happened between you and Grayson would help her decide if she wanted an abortion or not. The only thing she knew for sure was that she didn't want you to know. She couldn't bear the thought of disappointing you.'

'You had no right to tell her,' Martha Claire said. 'We swore those children would never know.'

'Cissy asked me. I wish I had told her years ago. She has suffered because of what happened. She has a right to know why her mother hates her father, why her brother turned into a drunken bum who ultimately managed to kill himself, why I ripped Iris out of her life. She has a right to know why no matter how hard she tries she will never be able to make you happy. How could I not tell her?'

'If the past was so important to her, she should have asked me.'

'She knew you wouldn't tell her. She went to her father, but poor Grayson didn't have the guts to go against you and tell Cissy what she wanted to know, so he asked me to do it.'

'You have talked to Grayson?'

Once again Justine sighed. 'Yes, I talked to him. It was the first real conversation I'd had with him since England. He was all torn apart inside back then, and he still is. You've really done a number on that man. I'd think you'd be tired of it after all this time.'

'Don't you go heaping blame at my doorstep. You were the one who took the axe and chopped this family in half.'

Martha Claire heard Justine draw in her breath. 'Yes, you have every right to hate me. But you should forgive Grayson.'

'Why?' Martha Claire demanded, spitting out the word.

'Because, God help him, the man still loves you. Are you going to

Tulsa and see about Cissy? Because if you're not, I will.'

'You leave my family alone!' Martha Claire said. 'I will look after my daughter.'

'Goodbye,' Justine said, and the phone went dead.

Martha Claire slammed down the receiver. 'I hate you!' she screamed, her voice echoing in her big empty house. 'I hate you!'

GRAYSON AWOKE to the beam of headlights shining through his curtainless window. He pulled on his trousers and grabbed his shotgun. A couple of weeks ago he'd had to scare off some teenage boys intent on pushing over his outhouse.

Martha Claire was standing in the beam of her headlights. 'Cissy's in the hospital,' she called. 'We have to go to Tulsa.'

'What happened?' he asked, stepping down from the porch.

'I'll explain on the way. Pack some things and let's go. Hurry.'

Grayson stumbled up the steps, then stood in the middle of the room trying to think of what he should do first. But his only thoughts were of Cissy. *Please don't let anything happen to her*, he silently implored to a god he had not addressed in years.

He didn't have a suitcase out here, so he emptied a box of magazines and threw in some underwear, a few shirts, a pair of khaki trousers, his shaving things and toothbrush. Then he put on shoes and a shirt, picked up the box and went back outside.

Martha Claire had moved to the car's passenger side. Grayson put his box in the trunk and got in. 'Tell me,' he said as he backed down the rutted lane.

'Did you know she was pregnant?'

Grayson shook his head. 'No, I didn't.'

'She went to Tulsa to have the baby and put it up for adoption. I called the hospital. She was unconscious when they brought her in. She had an emergency Caesarean section and is in intensive care.'

'Will she be all right?'

'The doctor wouldn't say.'

'And the baby?'

'Alive.'

'A boy or girl?'

'I didn't ask.'

He heard the rest of the story in bits and pieces. About Justine getting worried. The landlady checking Cissy's room. Martha Claire had called Justine—not a good conversation apparently. His wife was angry with him for sending Cissy to Justine. But her anger was tinged with weariness. And fear.

Whenever they stopped, Martha Claire would call the hospital. 'No change,' she would tell him.

Grayson wanted desperately to talk about the baby, but he didn't dare. Why had Cissy kept it a secret? Had some boy hurt her? Grayson's hands tightened on the steering wheel at the thought. He would want to kill anyone who hurt Cissy. Finally he had to ask.

'How do you feel about the baby?'

'Angry that she got herself that way. Angry that she didn't tell me. Angry that she told Justine instead.'

'But the baby itself. How do you feel about it?'

'I don't know.'

It was late afternoon when they reached the hospital in Tulsa. Cissy was still unconscious. They stood by her bedside, weeping, begging her to live. 'We need you so,' Martha Claire said, clinging to her daughter's limp hand.

Then they went to the nursery. Martha Claire tapped on the door next to the viewing window. Five cots were lined up in front of the window. Grayson stared at a baby in an incubator that was pushed into a corner, separated from the other babies. The word 'confidential' was written across the name card. When the nurse opened the door, Martha Claire explained that they were Cissy Stewart's parents, that they wanted to see their daughter's baby.

'It was a confidential delivery,' the nurse said, glancing at the lone infant in the corner. 'I can't let you see the baby.'

'Our daughter is in a coma. We need to see this baby,' Martha Claire said. Then she added a soft, imploring 'please'.

'Stand in front of the window,' the nurse said. 'I may need to move the babies around. His incubator might pass by the window.'

'Then it's a boy?' Grayson asked.

'Yes. A boy. A scrawny little thing, but holding his own.'

She closed the door, and they watched while she rearranged her charges. Then she looked around furtively and pushed the incubator to centre stage.

Grayson watched his wife. He knew that any future he might have with this infant depended on what happened in the next few seconds. He watched his wife standing in front of the window, watched as tears began streaming down her cheeks, as her face took on a look of such rapture he had to look away. Only then did he focus his attention on his grandson, who was stretching, clenching tiny little fists over his head. Martha Claire was weeping now, holding on to Grayson's arm for support.

THEY WAITED through the evening. At about ten o'clock Martha Claire went downstairs to find them some coffee. When she got back, Grayson was standing by the bed. Cissy's eyes were open.

'Mama, I'm sorry. I didn't want you to know,' Cissy said.

'Shhhh,' Martha Claire said. 'We saw him. He's a beautiful baby.'

'Oh God,' Cissy whispered.

'You go back to sleep, honey,' Martha Claire said. 'We'll talk about it in the morning.'

They waited till one of the nurses checked her vital signs and assured them that Cissy was out of the woods. Then she urged them to get some sleep and directed them to a nearby motel.

'Do you want me to get two rooms?' Grayson asked as he pulled up in front of the motel office.

'Two beds will be fine,' Martha Claire said.

She waited until she was sure Grayson was asleep, then put on her robe and went to sit by the window. She parted the drapes and stared across the highway at the hospital, where Cissy was. And the baby.

Martha Claire hadn't wanted to leave her daughter's side, but Grayson looked as though he could sleep standing up. She needed to get some sleep, too. She had to be clear-headed when they talked to Cissy in the morning. And Grayson—she would need to talk to him first. He had to be a part of this. Yes, she had to decide exactly how she would present her plan to both of them.

Her hands were resting on her belly. Even after all this time she could feel her barrenness as surely as she felt hunger or thirst.

'Please,' she prayed into the dank darkness of the cheap motel room. 'I'll forgive Grayson if You'll let us have that baby.'

A baby could heal them, could make them happy again.

GRAYSON WATCHED while Martha Claire explained. She was standing at Cissy's bedside, holding her hand. 'Your father and I have it all worked out,' she said. 'We will take care of the baby while you finish school and serve your residency.'

Cissy was frowning, trying to work through this new option in her life. 'But what would you tell people?' she asked her mother.

'That you had a baby,' Martha Claire said with a shrug.

'When Justine had Iris, you made up a story,' Cissy challenged.

'Times were different then,' Martha Claire said. 'If a girl had a baby out of wedlock, her family could never hold their heads up again. Bea and Jim Hawkins's daughter isn't married, and they're all there at church on Sunday morning, proud as peacocks, with their granddaughter all dressed in ruffles and bows.'

Cissy sighed. 'I don't know, Mama. That baby connects me to a man I'd just as soon forget. I'd worry that he'd find out and that someday the baby would demand to know who his father was.'

'Neither the child nor the man will find out unless you tell them,' Martha Claire said. 'Don't forget, the baby would be living in Columbus, at least until you've finished your medical training.'

Cissy stared out of the window. 'Do I have to decide right now?'

'No, of course not,' Martha Claire said too brightly. 'You take your time, honey. This is a very important decision.'

Grayson stood. 'We should leave. Cissy needs her rest.'

A peeved look descended onto Martha Claire's face. She didn't want to leave until Cissy promised not to give away that baby.

'Are you sure you and Daddy want to take on a baby?' Cissy asked. 'You're not as young as you used to be. What about night feedings and all that?'

'We've had a great deal of experience,' Martha Claire said softly, hopefully.

'And the expense. We're poor as church mice.'

'I'll sell the house if I need to,' Martha Claire announced.

Cissy let out a little gasp. 'You'd do that?'

Martha Claire pulled back her shoulders. 'In a flash.'

Silence settled over the room. Then Cissy looked at her father. 'What about you, Daddy? You haven't said a word.'

Grayson took his daughter's hand. 'I think you should listen to your heart. It might help for you to see the baby, but that's up to you.' Then he half pulled Martha Claire from the room.

'We can't just leave her,' Martha Claire spluttered as he guided her towards the elevator. 'What if someone from the adoption agency comes? If Cissy gives that baby away, I'll hire a lawyer, Grayson. I'll fight her with every breath in my body.'

'I know you will, Martha Claire. And that might even be the right thing to do. But let's see how things play out first.'

They went to Cissy's rooming house. Martha Claire had called the landlady and arranged for them to stay there while Cissy was in the hospital. A fold-up cot was already waiting in the corner.

Martha Claire was a caged lion for the rest of the afternoon. Keeping the door ajar so she could hear the phone, she paced about the small room. Grayson had made a deal with her that they could return to the hospital after dinner if they hadn't heard from Cissy. At five thirty Martha Claire prepared some sandwiches. Silently she ate hers and pretended to watch the evening news on television, then went into the bathroom to groom herself for what lay ahead.

Cissy was out of bed, sitting in a chair, the IV line still in her arm. 'Is it all right for you to be out of bed?' Martha Claire asked.

Cissy smiled. 'I'm fine, Mama. Did you have a nice afternoon?'

Martha Claire glanced at Grayson. 'We rested.'

'Good,' Cissy said. 'Me, too. And I saw the baby.'

Grayson held his breath. Martha Claire's hand flew to her breast.

'He's a skinny little thing, isn't he?' Cissy paused, as though she expected them to say something.

Grayson was afraid to speak. Martha Claire, too, apparently.

Cissy's expression softened. 'You poor darlings. You really want this baby, don't you?'

Like two puppets, they both nodded.

'I guess it will be OK, then.'

'Thank God,' Martha Claire said, sinking onto the bed.

Grayson knelt in front of his daughter and put his hands on her shoulders. 'I hope you're not doing this just for us.'

'I'm not, Daddy. I promise that I'm not.'

'Well,' Martha Claire said, 'we need to think of a name.'

Cissy actually laughed. 'Mama, something tells me you have a name already picked out.'

'He's such a little angel,' Martha Claire said, clutching her folded hands in her lap. 'I was thinking about Gabriel. We could call him Gabe.'

GRAYSON DROVE BACK to Columbus to tend the store and prepare for the arrival of his grandson, with Martha Claire staying behind to look after Cissy and the baby. It was with much pleasure that he restored the crib, Polly's rocking chair and a chest of drawers. He chose Buddy's room for a nursery.

Clearing it out had been heart-wrenching. This had been Buddy's room throughout his childhood, and his possessions remained pretty much as he had left them. As he boxed up trophies, athletic paraphernalia, yearbooks, photographs, model planes, baseball hats, Grayson talked out loud to his dead son, telling him how much he had loved him, apologising for not being a stronger father, for not keeping him alive.

Once the room was empty, he painted the walls a soft white. He put the crib by the window so Gabe could see the trees and the sky. In the store's back room he found the picture of Buddy in his Texas A&M uniform, which Martha Claire once had displayed in the store window. Grayson carried it home and hung it over the chest of drawers. He didn't think Martha Claire would mind.

When Gabe was four weeks old, Grayson drove to Tulsa to bring him and Martha Claire home. Cissy had already returned to her duties. On the drive back, they had just crossed the Red River when Martha Claire asked him to move back into the house. 'The boy will be needing his grandfather,' she pointed out.

'Yes. I'd like that,' he said.

They drove straight through, pulling into the driveway in the middle of the night. While Martha Claire fed Gabe, he was all eyes, looking around. Such an alert little guy. After he had been fed and changed, Grayson carried him upstairs and rocked him to sleep in his great-grandmother Polly's rocking chair.

Martha Claire seemed pleased with the baby's room. She watched while Grayson carefully lowered Gabe into the crib and covered him with a baby blanket. 'It was hard going through all of Buddy's things,' he admitted. 'Is the picture all right?'

'It's perfect.'

They stayed there for a time, side by side, staring worshipfully down at the tiny boy who already filled their hearts.

Later, Grayson stood under the shower for a long time, trying to bring some ease to his aching muscles. In his room, he gingerly stretched out on the bed. *Home*, he thought. He was home to stay. He closed his eyes, wondering how long the baby would sleep, and felt his own body ease into slumber. He was surprised when the bedroom door opened. Martha Claire stood in the doorway, the light from the hall backlighting her body in her nightgown. 'You don't need to sleep in here,' she said.

MARTHA CLAIRE'S DECISION to invite Grayson back home had been carefully thought out. She needed his help with Gabe, and a fatherless boy needed a close relationship with his grandfather.

She had not planned, however, to invite Grayson back into her bed. The sweet moments they had shared putting the baby to bed had softened her, she supposed. She had watched while Grayson stroked Gabe's tiny back until he fell asleep. Grayson had always had all the patience in the world with children. She wanted to touch Grayson's arm and tell him she was remembering their first night with Cissy. She didn't, though. She had stopped touching her husband during the years they warred over Buddy's future, had not reminisced with him since they lost Iris.

From her room she had heard Grayson come out of the bathroom, heard the sound of the door to his room closing behind him. Martha Claire had left her own door ajar, to hear the baby. She had bragged to Cissy about their experience tending babies, but she was out of practice. When her children were small, she heard every whimper in the night. But that was a long time ago. Iris was almost thirty-four. Cissy would soon be thirty. What if she had lost her knack? What if she didn't wake up when Gabe cried? But if both she and Grayson left their doors open, one of them would surely hear the baby when he woke for his feeding. She got out of bed, padded across the hall, tapped on the door. 'Grayson,' she said, turning the knob.

The light from the hall fell across his bed. He had propped himself up on an elbow and was waiting to see what she wanted. She meant to tell him to leave his door open, but those other words had come out. *You don't need to sleep in here.* Words that indicated she wanted him to sleep in her bed. Did she? Martha Claire no longer thought about sex, no longer needed or wanted it. How could a grandchild change that? It was crazy. Grayson was still Iris's father. That would never change. Still, she felt giddy. Feverish, even.

She went back to her bed with her heart pounding. *What had she done?* She heard him coming across the hall, felt his weight on the side of the bed—the wrong side, she realised. In the past, when they shared this bed, their positions had been reversed.

'Good night,' she said.

'Good night,' he responded.

She wished she had her robe on. She was naked under the thin fabric of her nightgown. She lay motionless, hardly daring to breathe. Maybe she dozed a little. Then she heard the sound of muffled sobs. Grayson was crying into his pillow. She sat up and touched his arm.

'I'm sorry,' he said into the pillow. 'Oh God, Martha Claire, I've missed you so. God, how I've missed you.' He grabbed her hand and kissed her palm. 'I wish I had died in the war,' he whispered. 'Then I wouldn't have hurt you like that.' He said her name again. Softly. As though it were the most beautiful two words in the world. Then he asked if he could hold her in his arms.

She said yes. There were no more words after that. They kissed for an incredibly long time, as they had back in their courting days. She felt beautiful, like that girl back then, like she had been on their honeymoon on Galveston Island before her husband went to war, before he went to England to be with Justine. Yes, she was on Galveston Island, with the sound of the waves, the night breeze coming through the open window and cooling her warm young flesh as she made love with the only man she had ever loved.

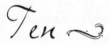

Ten

Martha Claire bent over to pull an offending shoot of nut grass from the lawn, then climbed the front steps, put her pruning shears and straw hat on the table, and seated herself in her favourite wicker rocker. She picked up her hat and began to fan herself, trying to decide if she should go inside and start breakfast or just wait out here for Gabe and Grayson.

Martha Claire rocked back and forth. She loved this porch. When Gabe was a baby, Grayson would sit out here rocking him, often singing the old songs they once had sung around the piano: 'Jacob's Ladder', 'On Top of Old Smoky', 'She'll Be Coming 'Round the Mountain'. It was only in the past year that the boy had finally learned to fall asleep on his own, without his grandfather rocking and singing or stretched out with him on his bed, and then only because Martha Claire reneged on a previous ruling and let Puppy Dog sleep with him.

Puppy Dog had been a tiny little thing when they found him near Grayson's shack. The poor animal had been half dead, with every rib showing, but he made a beeline for Gabe and started licking his face. Puppy Dog was now a big, ungainly creature who left a trail of slobber everywhere he went, but Martha Claire had often wished she'd let Buddy have a dog and wasn't going to repeat her mistake.

She paused a minute in her rocking, studying an overgrown branch on a holly bush. But she resisted the urge to take up her shears and snip it off. The offending branch would still be there tomorrow. Cissy liked to say that she and her mother both made rounds in the morning. Cissy marched up and down hospital halls with a stethoscope, and her mother marched round the yard with her pruning shears. It was true, Martha Claire thought. That was how she started every day, grooming her yard.

And such a wonderful yard it was. The crape myrtle were in full bloom now, and the rose of Sharon. The beds of coleus, caladium and impatiens were in full foliage under the trees. Cissy said that one of these days, when she had finished her residency and she was finally in practice and making all that money everyone said she was going to make, the first thing she was going to do was replace the handsome iron fence that had marched its way round the yard in all those old photographs. Cissy wanted to do all the things to the house that they had never been able to afford, and sometimes Martha Claire let herself revive the old dream of restoring the house to its former glory, but mostly she lived from day to day, enjoying what blessings came her way. When the time came, she would probably tell Cissy to put on a new roof and forget about the fence.

Martha Claire lifted her apron and wiped the sweat from her brow. Already, at eight in the morning, it was muggy and still. But what else could one expect in south Texas in July?

Soon she saw them coming up the street—grandfather and grandson. Grayson had their fishing poles over his shoulder. Gabe saw her sitting there and began to run, holding up the morning catch. 'I caught two, Grandma! I caught two!'

At four, Gabe was an undersized little boy. He had started life small and would always be small, like his mother. Small but mighty, his grandfather liked to say. Mighty curious, for one thing. Gabe was a boy with a million questions. He kept his grandfather constantly going to the encyclopedias to find out what was the largest bug in the world, why Texas was named Texas, why worms didn't have legs. He was the exact opposite of Buddy, who had been a big athletic boy with few questions.

Gabe came running up the steps holding his catch in the air. 'Can we take the fishes to Houston and show them to Mommy?'

'They would smell up the car, honey, but we could take her some vegetables, though. Why don't you and I go round the back and pick some things for her. I bet she'd like some okra.'

'My mommy likes okra a lot,' he said.

Martha Claire had to take his dirty little face between her hands and kiss it. Such a dear boy. Her love for this child filled her up and made her a better person. If only she could have allowed herself to love her children this way. 'Yes, your mommy likes okra,' she agreed. 'But do you know what she likes even better?'

His face broke into a big silly grin. 'She likes me better than anything,' he said proudly.

'Oh, indeed she does. That mommy of yours is looking at the clock right this very minute and thinking that in only three more hours her Gabe will be there to spend two days with her.'

'And after two days she's going to put me in the car and drive us back to Columbus, and she'll stay here for five whole days. We'll pick blackberries, visit Reverend Huxley at the nursing home, and put on a show for you and Granddaddy in the attic.'

'You got it!' Martha Claire said. 'Now give those fish to Granddaddy, and let's go pick those vegetables.'

'And some strawberries, too. Strawberries aren't vegetables. They're a fruit.'

'My, what a smart boy you are!' Martha Claire said, remembering another summer day when she had waited on the porch for Grayson and Iris to return from an early-morning fishing excursion. She looked at her husband, thinking to share her memories with him, but he was just standing there, staring down at the fish, a puzzled look on his face. 'Grayson, are you all right?'

He shook his head, as though to clear it, and looked at her with questioning eyes.

'Are you going to clean the fish?' she asked.

'The fish? Yes, I'll clean the fish,' he said gratefully, and followed her and Gabe round the back.

THE PARTY WAS CISSY'S IDEA. She insisted that Stewart's Dry Goods could not close its doors after more than eighty years without a bit of fanfare. She decorated the walls with old snapshots she'd had blown up to poster size—of Grayson's grandparents standing behind their cash register, of his parents behind the same cash register, of Martha Claire and Grayson in his army uniform standing in front of the store. She'd also had posters made from some of the old newspaper ads—shoes for two dollars and fifty cents, men's socks for a quarter. And she'd borrowed the picture of Buddy in his A&M football uniform from Gabe's bedroom.

A steady stream of people came all day. The punch and cookies ran out in the first hour. Cissy rushed off to get more. Then she went to the nursing home to fetch Reverend Huxley, and ended up making several trips back and forth when other residents wanted to come. The store was a part of their memories.

When the last of their guests had finally taken their leave, the family took down the posters and folded the tablecloth. Martha Claire cried as she locked the door. Wal-Mart finally had put them out of business. She hated Wal-Mart and had vowed she would never set foot in the ugly, sprawling store that was ruining downtowns all over America, but she also felt a sense of relief. She didn't want to spend her days down here any more, and Grayson could no longer manage the store on his own. He would forget how to give change and sometimes got lost on the way home. She needed to look after him and Gabe now. The store had represented such a major part of her life. It became who she was—Martha Claire Stewart from the dry-goods store. Even so, they probably should have closed it when Grayson's father died. She should have let Grayson have a go at another sort of life. She told him that as they walked home.

Grayson didn't answer for a long time. They walked half a block before he said, 'I never was a good storekeeper, but maybe I wouldn't have been a good army officer, either. What I should have been was a teacher.'

'You could have had a fine military career,' Martha Claire said, taking his arm, 'but you would have been a good teacher, too. You could have taken students to all those places you never got to go.'

'Cissy wants to take me to Europe,' he said.

'She what?' Martha Claire said.

'She found a tour for veterans and their families.'

They walked along in silence, past the house where he had grown up, past the little house where they had lived as newlyweds. So, here they were, Martha Claire thought, two old people walking down the street towards what was left of their lives. So much time wasted, so many regrets. And such a sense of missing. She missed her parents and Granny Grace, but most of her missing was for Buddy and Iris, who should both still be a part of her life, along with Iris's daughter and any children Buddy might have had.

'You should go,' she told him as they turned into the white gate of their own home.

'To Europe?'

'Yes, you should go. Tell Cissy about the war. Tell her all the things you felt and learned. Someday she will tell her son.'

'I love Gabe,' he said.

'I know you do,' she said as they climbed the steps.

For years I had thought of taking my father to Europe. Then, when Gabe came along, I thought maybe I'd wait until he was old enough to go with us. I began to realise, however, that Daddy couldn't wait that long. He often forgot what he was about to do, stopping in his steps, a puzzled frown creasing his forehead.

So we made the trip, joining our fellow travellers in Rome—old men, some with old wives, others with sons and daughters. There was a pair of ageing brothers who had travelled together from Wisconsin. A middle-aged woman from Oklahoma had come alone, fulfilling a life-long promise to herself that she would visit the place where her father had died. In all, there were forty-five veterans, two dozen wives, twenty-one children and two grandchildren. The men moved with shuffling steps and apprehension in their eyes. They had come seeking to ease the grief they had carried all these years for fallen comrades, and the guilt of having lived into old age when others had died so young. A sometimes suffocating blanket of poignancy hung over our bus journey through Italy, Germany, Luxembourg and France.

Daddy couldn't remember yesterday's news, yet he recalled vividly his war years and recognised many of the places he had been: 'That little stream was red with blood when we waded across,' he would say. Or 'Over the crest of the next hill is the town where my sergeant got hit.'

It was the cemeteries, of course, that tore us all apart. Cemetery after cemetery. Seas of white headstones, each one representing a young man who didn't get to go home to the rest of his life.

When we were planning the trip, I had asked Daddy if there was anyone buried over there whose grave he wanted to visit, and he told me about Fenton Crutchfield, the young driver who had died in his arms. It was the first time I'd ever heard him speak the name of any of the men he had known and fought with over there. Fenton had grown up in an orphanage in Iowa and planned to marry a girl named Sally when he got back home.

I had done my homework and knew that Fenton Crutchfield was among the 10,000 servicemen buried in the American cemetery outside Lorraine. You can't imagine what it was like climbing down from that bus and looking out over 10,000 white headstones. My poor father was overwhelmed to the point of speechlessness. With a map sent to me by the American Battle Monuments Commission, I led him up and down the rows until we found Fenton's grave, where he would pay homage to the driver who had died in his arms and to all the other men he had known who died. For all those years he had carried that unbearable burden, of living while most of the men in his command had died. 'I would have died to save any one of them,' he told me.

He knelt in the grass and embraced the cross that marked young Fenton's grave and wept. I wept, too, of course. How could one not? I wept for the burden my father and all these men had carried with them into old age. I felt privileged to share my father's sorrow, but my mother should have been the one to make this journey with him. Maybe then she might have understood how hideously difficult the war years had been for him; how he might have sought refuge in a woman's soft arms, even if that woman was his wife's own sister. I myself fully forgave him; I would have forgiven any of the men on our bus just about anything. They had suffered for me and my son.

In Paris, with hugs and tears, we bade our travelling companions farewell and stayed on for four more days of sightseeing. Our last night we went to the top of the Eiffel Tower and looked down on what must be the most beautiful city in the world.

While I had forgiven my father, the sinner, I found it difficult to forgive my mother. I blamed her more for what had happened to our family than I blamed him—or Justine. Which wasn't fair. Technically Mama had done nothing wrong.

I remembered asking Mama about inviting Iris to my graduation from medical school. Mama said she wouldn't come if Iris did. 'What did Iris ever do to you?' I had demanded.

'She left.'

'But Justine was her mother. What did you expect Iris to do?'

'She should have told Justine that she belonged here in Columbus with you and me and Buddy,' Mama had replied, real anger in her voice. 'I was the one who raised her while her so-called mother went trekking all over the world. Iris was sixteen years old. She could have told Justine that she wouldn't leave us.'

I never told Mama that my medical education had been Iris's idea and that she had helped me financially. And I never told her that Justine had funded me to live in Tulsa until Gabe was born. I suppose I was afraid she might withdraw her love from me the way it had been withdrawn from them. Maybe being adopted had altered me more than I realised, but I needed Mama to love me, no matter how conditionally. I had lived my entire life seeking her approval.

I did a general internship at Texas Medical Center in Houston, then a three-year paediatric residency, also in Houston. My salary was pitifully small, but I sent my parents whatever I could. I had become my aunt Justine, sending cheques every month and sweeping in and out of my child's life. I missed Gabe terribly and called him several times a week, but I had made my choices. Someday I would make it up to him. When it came time to decide if I would continue my postgraduate training or enter private practice, I decided to go home to Columbus. I wanted to be with my son and didn't have the heart to take him away from my parents.

Martha Claire Stewart might not have given birth to me, but as surely as if she had, perhaps even more so, I was and always would be my mother's daughter.

GABE WAS FIVE when I bought the building where Doc Hadley had practised for almost fifty years and hung out my plaque—CECELIA C. STEWART, MD, FAMILY MEDICINE AND PAEDIATRICS. I hoped eventually to limit my practice to paediatrics, but I needed all the patients I could get. At that point I probably would have treated puppies and kittens. My parents had sold the building where the store had been. My father had a small pension from the shoe company and another from the National Guard. They got by. Getting by had become a way of life for us.

But that would change. I would never be rich, but I would earn a good living. The bank didn't hesitate to lend the money to buy a clinic to someone with MD after her name.

The decision to open a practice in Columbus had not been an easy one. I was offered a fellowship in paediatric urology, which probably would have led to a faculty appointment and the opportunity to practise and teach at a university medical centre. For months, every time I drove home, I rehearsed explaining this to my parents—that I wanted to buy a house in Houston for Gabe and me, that I loved the challenge of the medical centre, loved saving the lives of children who would have died if they hadn't received the level of medical care provided there. In

Columbus I would be the front line of medical defence, not the last resort; the general practitioner, not the specialist with residents following me from bedside to bedside, hanging on my every word.

In the five years following Gabe's birth, I had only one relationship—with a cardiology resident from Argentina. It was a safe relationship, since he was going back home, and I was absolutely certain that Gabe and I weren't going to move to Buenos Aires. I hoped also that I had the resolve not to move back to Columbus. But I didn't. My mother had always assumed that I would practise there, which would make her proud of me again. How could I turn my back on my parents and their dream of having me practise in Columbus, of having me and Gabe with them for the rest of their lives?

Iris said I was a fool. After I told her I'd bought Doc Hadley's clinic, we didn't talk for several months. Then finally she called to apologise. 'But it is such a waste,' she amended.

It was and wasn't. Duplicating Doc Hadley's life would not be a waste, and being a good daughter was its own reward. Being a good daughter had been my destiny all along. I would live a full, rich life in the town where I had been raised, the town where I would practise medicine and raise my child.

Martha Claire pulled an afghan over her legs and studied her needlepoint, then glanced over at Grayson dozing on the sofa, Puppy Dog curled at his feet. The two of them spent a lot of time on the sofa these days, an old man and an old dog dozing away what was left of their lives.

Martha Claire picked up the remote control and changed the channel from the football game Grayson had been watching to an old black-and-white movie. Movies had changed so, she thought. The old ones seemed overly melodramatic, but the stars had such style. Years ago she had thought about being an actress herself. That notion had ended the day Grayson marched up on a stage and sang 'When the Moon Comes Over the Mountain', and she realised that she loved him.

The memory made Martha Claire think of Gabe. She wasn't sure she approved of all the time he was spending with the Caldwell girl. But she and Grayson hadn't been much older than Gabe when they had pledged undying love to each other.

Martha Claire put down her needlework and went to the kitchen, where she poured some apple cider in the pot to warm. Cissy and Gabe would be home soon from the high-school band concert. Gabe had given up football in favour of the band, which was a wise move. He played the clarinet much better than he could catch a football.

Martha Claire put a blanket round Grayson's legs, then returned to her chair and tucked the afghan round her own legs. A freeze was expected tonight, the first of the winter.

On nights like this she wished for a fireplace so that she could pull her chair close and toast her toes. If she had allowed Grayson his military career, probably some of the houses they lived in would have had a fireplace. She thought of the stately officers' quarters at Fort Sam Houston, each with a chimney, even though it got no colder there than it did in Columbus.

No telling how many places they would have lived, moving from army post to army post. As life turned out, though, except for the few years she and Grayson lived in the rented house next door to his parents, Martha Claire had spent her entire life in the house her mother had inherited from her parents. There was a bronze plaque out front now, mounted next to the front door, stating that the house was a historic landmark.

If Grayson had stayed in the army, Martha Claire wondered if she would have kept the house for them to return to when he retired. That was hard to say. But one thing she did know—if they had not been living in Columbus, she never would have had the opportunity to raise three children. She wouldn't have had those years with Iris and wouldn't have been here for Doc Hadley to drop off two little waifs in need of a family. If she and Grayson had come back to this house to live out their years after retiring from a military career, they would be living here alone. So it didn't do one bit of good to wonder how things might have been. There was no going back.

Only last week she and Grayson had been watching a documentary about England on television, when suddenly there was a shot of the white cliffs of Dover. Martha Claire studied Grayson's face, but he showed no reaction. 'That was where you went with Justine after the war,' she told him.

'With Justine?' he asked with genuine puzzlement.

'You don't remember going there with her?'

He shook his head. 'I remember France. I remember the war.'

Martha Claire didn't know if she should laugh or weep. *He didn't remember Dover.*

Now, as she picked up her needlepoint, she wondered if he had also forgotten the aftermath. Should she ask him? Before she could decide, the front door burst open and Cissy and Gabe came rushing in, along with a blast of cold air. Grayson blinked himself awake.

'I've got some apple cider warming on the stove and some freshly baked oatmeal cookies,' Martha Claire said, ready to herd them towards the kitchen. 'I want to hear all about the evening.'

Gabe put his arms round his grandmother and rubbed her cheek with his cold nose. He was taller now than she was. He was not handsome, but pleasant-looking, the sort of person you knew by the look of him was kind and good. Not that he was perfect. Gabe had a real lazy streak. He put off mowing the grass until Martha Claire shamed him by getting out the mower and threatening to do it herself. But he was silly and happy and made her heart swell so that at times she thought it would pop right out of her chest. If only she could have loved Buddy the way she loved Gabe, maybe things could have turned out differently for him.

IT GOT EVEN COLDER in the night, but Grayson kept kicking off the covers. Martha Claire would pull the covers back up and rub his shoulders to soothe him. 'Where am I?' he asked at one point.

'Here with me,' she told him.

'Will you stay with me?'

'Always,' she promised.

'Thank you,' he said before drifting back into a fitful sleep.

Finally he stopped thrashing about, and Martha Claire felt herself settling into a few hours of real sleep.

Towards morning, when she woke and reached for her husband's warmth, she knew the instant she touched his flesh that he was dead. Gently, she held him in her arms and wept and said all those words she never told him in life. She was so sorry for all those wasted years, so sorry for the years she had banished him from his family, so sorry she hadn't let him manage Buddy. She stroked his hair and kissed his face. 'You were the handsomest boy in all of Texas,' she told him. 'And you were the best father those children could have had. I never told you that, and I should have.'

Finally Martha Claire heard Cissy stirring and knew it was time for her to relinquish her husband's body and tell Cissy that her father was dead. Carefully, as though she might wake him, she kissed his lips, told him she loved him, and went to Cissy's room.

The door was open. Cissy was sitting on the side of the bed, dialling the phone—the hospital, probably, to check on a patient. She looked at her mother's face and returned the receiver to its cradle. 'Your father is dead,' Martha Claire said, her voice catching.

Cissy looked at her with disbelief, then went rushing out of the room. Martha Claire followed and watched while Cissy knelt beside the bed, buried her face against her father's chest, and cried out loud. Her cries brought Gabe, who knelt with his mother and tried to comfort her, but he was crying too hard himself.

Grayson had been loved, Martha Claire thought proudly. Her husband had been a good man and he had been loved.

A PERSON'S PUNISHMENT for living so long was all these funerals, Martha Claire thought as they walked towards the church. Grandparents, parents, in-laws, friends. And Buddy. Buddy's funeral had been the saddest of all. Grayson wouldn't mind her thinking that. Grayson was seventy-four, and his time had come.

But, oh, how she would miss him. Never again would she be able to reach for his hand or kiss his lips. Every day she would think of something she wanted or needed to tell him, and all she would have was a gravestone in the cemetery. And memories. She had lots of those. Trouble was, so many of them were upsetting.

It was a cool, crisp day. She had insisted on walking the three blocks to church, as she always did. She was arm in arm with Cissy and Gabe and counted herself fortunate indeed to have them with her. Someday they would be doing this sad task for her. But not for a long time yet, she hoped. She wanted to live on, to see how Gabe turned out and know her great-grandchildren. And she still hoped that someday Cissy would fall in love and they could have a wedding in the rose garden. She would even invite Iris if Cissy wanted her to. *Iris.* Martha Claire wondered if she would come to the funeral. She was sure Cissy had called her. Martha Claire wanted Iris to be there. When she had appeared at Buddy's funeral, Martha Claire had been distant, then regretted it afterwards. If Iris came today, Martha Claire promised herself that she would not be distant. She would take her arm and march up the aisle with her. Was Iris waiting inside? She paused for a minute to take a deep breath.

'Are you all right, Mama?' Cissy asked.

Martha Claire grabbed Cissy's arm. 'Did Iris come?'

'I don't know,' Cissy said. 'She didn't say one way or the other, but her husband isn't well.'

It was hard to believe Cissy was forty-four. Her dark hair shone in the sunshine. There were a few grey hairs, but not many, and a few lines round her eyes, but not many of those, either. It was a dear face, always so full of concern for others. Martha Claire said, 'Do you know what your father's last words were? He said, "Thank you." And I want to pass that thankyou on to you and your son. Because of you and Gabe the last part of your father's life was full of love. I thank you for that. For the rest of my life I will thank you for that.' Then, with her Cissy on one arm and Gabe on the other, Martha Claire marched up the steps of the church to her husband's funeral, with a prayer. *Please, let Iris be there*.

She was.

Just as she had been when Buddy died, Iris was waiting in the vestibule. It took Martha Claire a couple of heartbeats more to realise that the older woman with her was Justine.

Before she could absorb this stunning event, Iris stepped forward, and Martha Claire opened her arms.

'I loved him so,' Iris said. 'He was like a father to me. I wish I could have seen him one last time.'

But because he *was* her father, Iris had not been allowed to see him one last time, Martha Claire thought.

'Oh, Martha Claire, I've missed you so,' Iris was saying through her tears, relief on her lovely face that she was not being rebuffed.

'And I have missed you,' Martha Claire managed to say, even though she was only a few feet away from her sister, Justine, who had betrayed her as no sister ever should. How dare she come here for Grayson's funeral! The old hate rose in Martha Claire's throat. She felt Cissy tense beside her. And Iris.

Justine stepped forward. 'I had to come. I needed to come back. Not because of Grayson, but because of you.'

Martha Claire had to be civilised. She could not make a scene at her husband's funeral. She nodded at Justine, then walked up the aisle to the front row, reserved for Grayson's family. His coffin was there. She had debated about whether to have it open. She was glad now she had said no. Justine would not be able to look on his face and remember the time when they had made love.

Paul Huxley, leaning on his son's arm, offered a eulogy for his old fishing buddy. 'Grayson Stewart was not a religious man, but he was a spiritual one,' the old minister said. 'He knew the name of every bird, knew the habits of God's small creatures. He told me once that he had no expectation for a hereafter. He had killed men in the war and didn't feel like he had sent them on their way to some great reward. "They were pretty damned dead," he said. But those of us who do believe in a hereafter would like to see Grayson there. I myself can't imagine a paradise that didn't have a fishing hole and two spare fishing poles for me and my dear, dear friend Grayson Stewart, who was, in spite of himself, a godly man.'

That was nice, Martha Claire thought. Such an unlikely friendship: a minister and an agnostic. But it had been a good one.

At the cemetery, as she watched Grayson's coffin being lowered into the ground, she wanted to cry out, to tell them to stop, that she had to touch him one more time and tell him that she did love him, that she forgave him completely. But it was too late.

THE AFTERNOON PASSED in a blur, with Justine and Iris the centre of attention. Finally, when the last of the mourners had told Martha Claire one more time what a good man Grayson had been, they were alone. Just the five of them. Two old sisters and two younger women who had been raised as sisters. And young Gabe, for whom his grandfather's funeral had been his first.

'Go,' she told her grandson. 'Go find your friends. Celebrate life.' He had looked to his mother, who nodded and smiled, and he rushed up the stairs to change his clothes.

Martha Claire had meant to go back to the cemetery alone, but at dusk all four women were in the car, with Cissy driving and Martha Claire beside her in the front seat.

The evening was crisp and still. The four women lined up in front of the fresh gravesite. Martha Claire began to sob first.

Suddenly, with a feeling of panic, she realised that Iris and Cissy were walking away, arm in arm, leaving their mothers alone.

'I don't want to be here with you,' Martha Claire told Justine.

'I know. I'm sorry I came, sorry I have upset you so. When Iris told me about Grayson, all I could think of was coming back here to you. I'd like to start over, Martha Claire, if you will let me.'

Shivering a bit, Martha Claire began walking, and Justine followed her. They walked among the tombstones that presided over the graves of their parents and grandparents, of friends and acquaintances. And Buddy.

'It still hurts so much,' Martha Claire said, with a hand on Buddy's tombstone. 'Grayson wanted to make Buddy leave, to make him grow up, and I wanted him to stay. Grayson blamed himself because he didn't stand up to me. I blamed myself because I didn't have the courage to do what was best for my son. And Cissy thought if she had done a better job of looking after her brother, he wouldn't have been driving drunk along that country road. Until Buddy died, I thought that finding out about you and Grayson was the worst thing that could happen to me. It wasn't.'

'Can you ever forgive me?' Justine asked.

'Not forgive so much as give up,' Martha Claire said. 'I am weary with hating you.'

'I'm not well,' Justine said. 'When the time comes, I'd like to come back here to die—and be buried here with Mama and Papa. And darling Buddy.'

'And Grayson,' Martha Claire reminded her.

'Yes, and Grayson.'

Martha Claire led the way back to Grayson's grave. Where did she go from here? Justine's and Grayson's betrayal had given her Iris. Because of Iris, she and Grayson had the need and the courage to adopt Cissy and Buddy. And in spite of the heartache children bring, they had defined her life. How does one unravel it all and come to terms? 'I could have forgiven Grayson and saved my family, but it became who I was—a woman betrayed. I became a very ugly person.' She paused, then asked, 'Are you really dying?'

'Yes, so it seems.'

Martha Claire sighed. 'Feels like all I do is bury people.'

'Then it's all right for me to come home?'

'You couldn't wait to leave Columbus. And now you want to come back. It doesn't make sense.'

'A part of me never really left. I thought of you always, Martha Claire. You are my roots. My sister. If there was only some way—'

'Hush up, will you,' Martha Claire barked. 'I have my sins, too. Every time you went off to some faraway place, I thought how nice it would be if the plane went down. Then I could have Iris all to myself. I couldn't stand it when you took her away. I prayed that you would die so that she would come back to us.'

As it turned out, my aunt Justine lived on for almost two years. Iris insisted it was because Mama refused to let her die. She had come home to Columbus at Christmastime, the month after Daddy died, and she never left. Iris and her daughter came to stay with us the last month or so. Strange how life can be, with sadness and happiness drawn in with the same breath.

My mama's house is still there. My son and his family live in it. I returned to Houston—not to a brilliant career as a university-based specialist, but I am with a medical group that looks after very sick kids. Mama lives with me. I have a beautiful yard because of her.

We drive to Columbus every Sunday, and she inspects the yard there. Gabe earned a degree in landscape architecture at Texas A&M and designs gardens all over the state. But the one in Columbus he keeps as it was. He doesn't dare change it.

I ran into Joe McCormack a few years ago at a medical conference. He practises in Lampasas, a widower now. We see each other once or twice a month and go on trips together. Joe doesn't know that Gabe is his son, and I don't plan to tell him.

To this day Iris doesn't know who her father is, and I will honour the promise I made to her mother. With the advent of the Internet and all the possibility for tracking down birth mothers, Gabe wanted to launch a search for mine. I told him no, he absolutely wasn't to do that.

Martha Claire Mayfield Stewart raised me, and I am her dutiful daughter. Every year on my birthday she tells me that the woman who gave me birth is thinking of me that day, and I know that if that woman is still alive, those words are probably true. On that day I think of her and thank her for giving me life.

But the other three hundred and sixty-four days of the year my allegiance is to the woman who had the courage to take me from the arms of a wise old country doctor who wasn't afraid to play God.

JUDITH HENRY WALL

'I wanted to write a book about for-giveness and what happens when it's not forthcoming,' says American author Judith Henry Wall of her thirteenth novel, *My Mother's Daughter*. In it, she explores the lives of two sisters whose contrasting experiences of motherhood mark the beginning of a rift that sets them at loggerheads for many years.

Judith Henry Wall's early novels, written some twenty years ago, when her children were small, were more frivolous in style. Having gained some initial experience in writing by producing magazine articles and children's stories, she turned her hand to Mills-and-Boon-style romances, learning the basic rules of the genre by studying examples in her local library. Before long, her passion-filled tales 'of the kind of men that women want to run away with' were being published on a regular basis.

But Judith Henry Wall had always been interested in deeper issues. While at university in Oklahoma studying for her Master's Degree, she became interested in feminism, joined protests in support of equal rights, and wrote a paper analysing the influence of the romance novel. It was no surprise, then, that in the early nineties her novels began to tackle subjects such as the way in which motherhood changes women's lives.

It is, above all, the quality of Judith Henry Wall's characterisation that marks her out from the mass of women's fiction writers. Characters, she says, are 'the mystical part of writing' in the way that they gradually flesh themselves out and become more real as the story evolves. 'Good charac-ters stay with you always,' she says. 'You may forget elements of a plot, but you never forget a good character.'

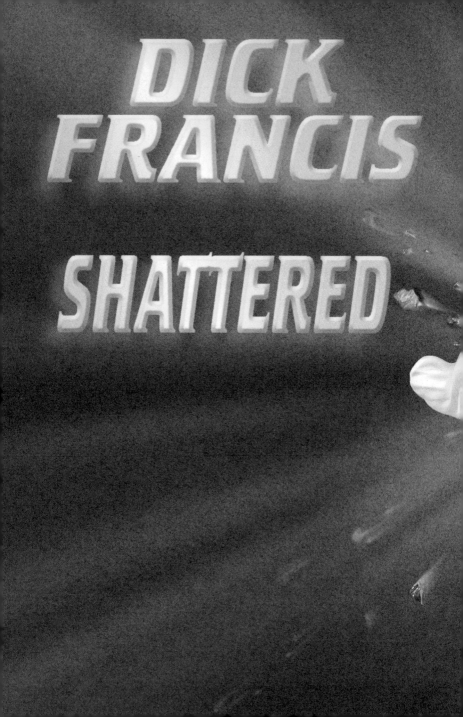

In his workshop, talented glass-blower Gerard Logan is only too familiar with the perils of working with glass at temperatures close to 1,800 degrees Fahrenheit.

But when he becomes embroiled in an investigation into his best friend's murder, he finds himself facing danger of a far more terrifying kind.

Chapter One ————

Four of us drove together to Cheltenham races on the day that Martin Stukely died there from a fall in a steeplechase.

It was December 31, the eve of the year 2000. A cold midwinter morning. The world approaching the threshold of the future.

Martin himself, taking his place behind the steering wheel of his BMW, set off before noon without premonition, collecting his three passengers from their Cotswold Hills bases on his way to his afternoon's work. A jockey of renown at thirty-four, he had confidence and a steady heart.

By the time he reached my sprawling house on the hillside above the elongated tourist-attracting village of Broadway, the air in his car swirled richly full of smoke from his favourite cigar, the Montecristo No. 2, his substitute for eating. He was spending longer and longer in a sauna each day but was all the same gradually losing the metabolic battle against weight. Genes had given him a well-balanced frame in general, and an Italian mother in particular had passed on a love of cooking, and vivacity.

He quarrelled incessantly with Bon-Bon, his rich, plump and talkative wife, and on the whole ignored his four small children, often frowning as he looked at them as if not sure exactly who they were. Nevertheless, his skill and courage and rapport with horses took him often into the winner's enclosure, and he drove to Cheltenham calmly discussing his mounts' chances that afternoon in two fast hurdle races and one longer steeplechase. Three miles of jumping fences brought out the controlled recklessness that made him great.

He picked me up last on that fateful Friday morning, as I lived nearest to Cheltenham's racecourse.

Already on board, and by his side, sat Priam Jones, the trainer whose horses he regularly rode. Priam was expert at self-aggrandisement but not quite as good at knowing when a horse had come to a performance peak. That day's steeplechaser, Tallahassee, was, according to my friend Martin on the telephone, as ready as he would ever be to carry off the day's gold trophy, but Priam Jones, smoothing his late-middle-age thinning white hair, told the horse's owner in a blasé voice that Tallahassee might still do better on softer ground. Lounging back beside me on the rear seat, that owner, Lloyd Baxter, listened without noticeable pleasure, and I thought Priam Jones would have done better to keep his premature apologies in reserve.

It was unusual for Martin to drive Tallahassee's owner and trainer anywhere. Normally he took other jockeys, or me alone, but Priam Jones from arrogance had just wrecked his own car in a stupid rash of flat tyres, thanks to his ignoring a deterrent no-parking set of rising teeth. The council's fault, he insisted. He would sue.

Priam had taken it for granted, Martin had told me crossly, that he—Martin—would do the driving. He would also chauffeur the horse's owner, who had flown down from the north of England for the Cheltenham meeting and was staying overnight with Priam.

I disliked Lloyd Baxter as thoroughly as he disliked me. Martin had begged me in advance to swamp the grumpy, dumpy millionaire owner with anaesthetising charm, in case Priam's fears materialised and the horse drew a blank. I saw Martin's face grinning at me in the rearview mirror as he listened to me lay it on. He had more than paid any debt he owed me by ferrying me about when he could, as I'd lost my driver's licence for a year through scorching at ninety-five miles an hour round the Oxford ring road (fourth ticket for speeding) to take him and his broken leg to see his point-of-death old retired gardener. The gardener's heart had then thumped away insecurely for six further weeks—one of life's little ironies. My loss of licence now had three months to run.

The friendship between Martin and myself, unlikely at first sight, had sprung fully grown in an instant four or more years ago. We had both been chosen for jury duty at the local crown court to hear a fairly simple case of domestic murder. In the jury room I had learned about the tyranny of weight that ruled a jockey's life. Though my life had nothing to do with horses, or his with the heat and chemistry of my own workdays, we shared, perhaps, an awareness of the physical ability that we each needed for success in our trade. Martin, in turn, had asked with polite curiosity, 'What do you do for a living?'

'I blow glass.'

'You do *what?*'

'I make things of glass. Vases, ornaments, goblets. That sort of thing.' I smiled at his look of astonishment. 'People do, you know. People have made things of glass for thousands of years.'

'Yes, but'—he considered—'you don't look like someone who makes ornaments. You look . . . well, tough.'

I was four years younger than he and three inches taller and probably equal in muscles.

'I've made horses,' I said mildly. 'Herds of them.'

'The Crystal Stud Cup?' he asked, identifying one of flat racing's more elaborate prizes. 'Did you make that?'

'Not that one, no.'

'Well, do you have a name? Like, say, Baccarat?'

I smiled lopsidedly. 'Not so glamorous. It's Gerard Logan.'

'Logan Glass.' He nodded, no longer surprised. 'You have a place on the High Street in Broadway, side by side with all those antique shops. I've seen it.'

I nodded. 'Sales and workshop.'

He hadn't seemed to take any special notice, but a week later he'd walked into my display gallery, spent an intense and silent hour there, asked if I'd personally made all the exhibits (mostly), and offered me a ride to the races. As time went by, we had become comfortably accustomed to each other's traits and faults.

That day at Cheltenham, Martin won the two-mile hurdle race by six lengths, then went into the changing room to put on Lloyd Baxter's colours of black and white chevrons, pink sleeves and cap. I watched owner, trainer and jockey in the parade ring as they took stock of Tallahassee walking purposefully around in the hands of his groom. The clear favourite, Tallahassee stood at odds of six to four with the bookmakers for the Coffee Forever Gold Trophy.

Lloyd Baxter (ignoring his trainer's misgivings) had put his money on the horse, and so had I.

It was at the last fence of all that Tallahassee uncharacteristically tangled his feet. Easily ahead by seven lengths, he lost his concentration, hit the roots of the unyielding birch, and turned a somersault over his rider, landing his whole half-ton mass upside-down and crushing the rib cage of the man beneath.

The horse fell at the peak of his forward-to-win acceleration and crashed down at thirty or more miles an hour. Winded, he lay across the jockey for inert moments, then rocked back and forward vigorously in his struggle to rise again to his feet.

The roar of welcome for a favourite racing home to win was hushed to a gasp. The actual winner passed the post without his due cheers, and a thousand pairs of binoculars focused on the unmoving black and white chevrons flat on the green December grass.

The racecourse doctor, though instantly attending him from his following car, realised that Martin Stukely was dying, as the sharp ends of broken ribs tore his lungs apart. A group of paramedics loaded Martin just alive into a waiting ambulance, and as the medical team set off to the hospital, they worked desperately with transfusions and oxygen. But quietly, before the journey ended, the jockey lost his race.

PRIAM, NOT NORMALLY a man of emotion, wept without shame as he later collected Martin's belongings, including his car keys, from the changing room. Accompanied by Lloyd Baxter, who looked annoyed rather than grief-stricken, Priam Jones offered to return me to Broadway before he went to see Bon-Bon, to give her comfort.

I asked if he would take me with him. He refused. Bon-Bon wanted Priam alone, he said. She had said so, devastated, on the telephone.

Lloyd Baxter, Priam added, would now also be off-loaded at Broadway. Priam had got him the last available room in the hotel there, the Wychwood Dragon. It was all arranged.

As Priam, shoulders drooping, and Baxter, glowering, set off towards the car park, Martin's valet hurried after me, calling my name. I stopped and turned towards him, and into my hands he thrust the lightweight racing saddle that, strapped firmly to Tallahassee's back, had helped to deal out damage and death.

The sight of Martin's empty saddle bleakly rammed into my consciousness the gritty message that its owner would never come back, and set me missing him painfully.

Eddie, the valet, was elderly, bald and in Martin's estimation hardworking and unable to do wrong. He turned to go back to the changing room but then stopped, fumbled in the deep front pocket of the apron of his trade, and produced a brown-paper-wrapped package.

'Someone gave this to Martin to give to you,' he said, 'but of course'—
he swallowed, his voice breaking—'Martin's gone.'

I asked, 'Who gave it to *him*?'

The valet didn't know. He was sure, though, that Martin himself
knew, because he had been joking about it being worth a million.

I took the package and, thanking him, put it into my raincoat
pocket, and we spent a mutual moment of sharp sadness for the gap
we already felt in our lives. He turned to hurry back to his chores in
the changing room, and I continued into the car park.

Priam's tears welled up again at the significance of the empty
saddle, and Lloyd Baxter shook his head with disapproval. Priam
recovered enough, however, to start Martin's car and drive it to
Broadway, where he dropped both me and Lloyd Baxter outside the
Wychwood Dragon. Then he departed in speechless gloom towards
Bon-Bon and her now fatherless brood.

Lloyd Baxter strode without pleasure into the hotel. He'd complained to Priam that his overnight bag was in Priam's house.
Priam's assertion that, after seeing Martin's family, he would ferry
the bag to the hotel, left Tallahassee's owner unmollified. The whole
afternoon had been a disaster, he'd grumbled.

My own glass business lay a few yards from the Wychwood
Dragon on the opposite side of the road. As I crossed over to the
gallery I wished that time could be reversed to yesterday, wished that
bright-eyed Martin would march through my door suggesting
improbable glass sculptures that in fact, when I made them, won
both commissions and kudos. He had become fascinated by the
process and never seemed to tire of watching whenever I mixed the
ingredients in the furnace.

The ready-made stuff, which came in 200-kilo drums, looked like
small opaque marbles, or large grey peas. I used it regularly, as it
came pure and clean, and melted without flaws, but I preferred to
mix the basic ingredients myself.

When Martin first watched me load the tank of the furnace with
a week's supply of the round grey pebbles, he repeated aloud the
listed ingredients. 'Eighty per cent of the mix is white silica sand
from the Dead Sea. Ten per cent is soda ash. Then add small specific
amounts of antimony, barium, calcium and arsenic per fifty pounds
of weight. If you want to colour the glass blue, use ground lapis
lazuli or cobalt. If you want yellow, use cadmium, which changes
with heat to orange and red, and I don't believe it.'

'That's soda crystal glass.' I nodded, smiling. 'I use it all the time. It's safe for eating or drinking from. Babies can lick it.'

He gazed at me in surprise. 'Isn't all glass safe to suck?'

'Well, no. You have to be exceedingly careful making things with lead. Lead crystal. Lovely stuff. But lead silicate is mega poisonous. In its raw state you have to keep it strictly separate from everything else and be terribly meticulous about locking it up.'

'What about cut lead crystal wineglasses?' he asked. 'I mean, Bon-Bon's mother gave us some.'

'Don't worry,' I told him with humour. 'If they haven't made you ill yet, they probably won't.'

'Thanks a bunch.'

I went in through my heavy gallery door of bevelled glass panes already feeling an emptiness where Martin had been. It wasn't as if I had no other friends; I had a pack of beer-and-wine cronies for whom fizzy water and sauna sweats were on their anathema lists. Two of those, Hickory and Irish, worked for me as assistants and apprentices, though Hickory was approximately my own age and Irish a good deal older. The desire to work with glass quite often struck late in life, as with Irish, who was forty, but sometimes, as with me, the fascination arrived like talking, too early to remember.

I had an uncle, eminent in the glass-blowing trade, who was also a brilliant flame worker. He could heat solid glass rods in the flame of a gas burner until he could twiddle them into a semblance of lace, and make angels and crinolines and steady, flat round bases for almost anything needing precision in a science laboratory.

Uncle Ron was amused at first that I should shadow him, but he finally took it seriously. He taught me whenever I could dodge school, and he died about the time that my inventiveness grew to match his. I was sixteen. In his will he left me his priceless notebooks, into which he'd detailed years of unique skill. I'd built a locked safe-like bookcase to keep them in and ever since had added my own notes on method and materials when I designed anything special. It stood always at the far end of the workshop between the stock shelves and a bank of four tall grey lockers, where my assistants and I kept our personal stuff.

It was he, my Uncle Ron, who drilled into me an embryonic business sense and an awareness that anything made by one glass-blower could in general be copied by another, which drastically lowered the asking price. During his last few years he succeeded in making uncopyable pieces, working out of my sight and then challenging me to detect and repeat his methods. Whenever I couldn't, he generously showed me how, and he laughed when I grew in ability and could beat him at his own game.

On the afternoon of Martin's death both the gallery and show-room were crowded with people looking for ways of remembering the advent of the historic millennium day. I had designed and made a whole multitude of small good-looking calendar-bearing dishes, and we had sold hundreds of them. I'd scratched my signature on the lot. Not yet, I thought, but by the year 2020, if I could achieve it, a signed Gerard Logan calendar dish of December 31, 1999, might be worth collecting.

The long gallery displayed the larger, unusual, one-off and more expensive pieces, each spotlit and available. The showroom was lined by many shelves holding smaller, attractive and less expensive orna-ments, which could reasonably be packed into a tourist suitcase. One side wall of the showroom rose only to waist height, so that over it one could see into the workshop beyond, where the furnace burned day and night and the little grey pebbles melted into soda crystal at a raised heat of 2,400 degrees Fahrenheit.

Hickory or Irish, or their colleague Pamela Jane, took turns to work as my assistant in the workshop. One of the other two gave a running commentary of the proceedings to the customers, and the third packed parcels and worked the till. Ideally, the four of us took the jobs in turn, but experienced glass-blowers were scarce, and my three assistants were still at the paperweight and penguin stage.

Christmas sales had been great but nothing like the New Year 2000. As everything sold in my place was guaranteed handmade (and mostly by me), the day I'd spent at the races had been my first respite away from the furnace for a month. I'd worked sometimes into the night, and always from eight onwards in the morning. The resulting exhaustion hadn't mattered, as I was physically fit.

Hickory, twirling colour into a glowing paperweight on the end of a slender five-foot-long steel rod called a punty iron, looked extremely relieved at my return from the races. Pamela Jane, smiling, earnest, thin and anxious, lost her place in her commentary and repeated instead, 'He's here. He's here . . .' and Irish stopped packing a cobalt-blue dolphin in white wrapping paper and sighed heavily, 'Thank God.' They relied on me too much, I thought.

I said, 'Hi, guys,' as usual and walked round into the workshop.

Stripping off jacket, tie and shirt, I gave the millennium-crazy shoppers a view of my working clothes, a designer-label white mesh singlet. Hickory finished his paperweight, spinning the punty iron down by his feet to cool the glass, being careful not to scorch his new bright trainers. I made, as a frivolity, a striped hollow blue-green and purple fish with fins. Light shone through it in rainbows.

The customers, though, wanted proof of that day's origin. Staying open much later than usual, I made endless dated bowls, plates and vases to please them, while Pamela Jane explained that they couldn't be collected until the next morning, New Year's Day, as they had to cool slowly overnight. No one seemed deterred.

Priam Jones called in fleetingly at one point. When he had been at Martin and Bon-Bon's house, he had found my raincoat lying on the back seat in the car. I thanked him with New Year fervour. He nodded, even smiled. His tears had dried.

When he'd gone, I went to hang up my raincoat in my locker. Something hard banged against my knee, and I remembered the package given to me by Eddie, the valet. I put it on a stock shelf at the rear of the workshop and went back to work.

I finally locked the door behind the last customer in time for Hickory, Irish and Pamela Jane to go to parties and for me to realise I hadn't yet opened the parcel Priam Jones had returned in my raincoat. The parcel that had come from Martin . . . He'd sat heavily on my shoulder all evening, a laughing lost spirit, urging me on.

Full of regrets, I locked the furnace against vandals and checked the heat of the annealing ovens, which were full of the newly made objects slowly cooling. The furnace, fuelled by propane gas under pressure from a fan, burned day and night at never less than 1,800 degrees Fahrenheit, hot enough to melt most metals. We were often asked if a memento like a wedding ring could be enclosed in a glass paperweight, but the answer was sorry, no. Liquid glass would melt gold—and human flesh—immediately. Molten glass, in fact, was pretty dangerous stuff.

I counted the day's takings and then enclosed them in a canvas bag ready to entrust to the night safe of the bank. Then I put on my discarded clothes and eventually took a closer look at my neglected parcel. The contents proved to be exactly what they felt like, an ordinary-looking videotape. The black casing bore no label of any sort, and there was no protective sleeve. A bit disappointed, I stacked it casually beside the money, but the sight of it reminded me that my videotape player was at my home and that fifteen minutes before midnight on a thousand years' eve wasn't the best time to phone for a taxi.

Plans for my own midnight, at a neighbourhood dance next door to my house, had disintegrated on Cheltenham racecourse. Maybe the Wychwood Dragon, I thought, not caring much, still had a broom closet to rent. I would beg a sandwich and a rug and sleep across the dark night into the new century, and early in the morning I would make an obituary for a jockey.

When I was ready to leave, someone tapped heavily on the glass-paned door. I unlocked it and faced an unexpected and unwanted visitor in Lloyd Baxter. He was carrying a bottle of Dom Pérignon and two of the Wychwood Dragon's best champagne glasses. The heavily disapproving expression, despite these pipes of peace, was still in place.

'Mr Logan,' he said formally, 'I know no one at all in this place except yourself, and don't say this isn't a time for rejoicing, as I agree with you in many ways, not only because Martin Stukely is dead but because the next century is likely to be even more bloody than the last. I therefore decided to spend the evening in my room—' He stopped abruptly.

I jerked my head for him to come in. 'I'll drink to Martin,' I said. I looked at my watch. Only nine minutes to ring-the-bells time and fireworks.

He looked relieved at my acquiescence. Loneliness still propelling him, he set the glasses on the table beside the till, ceremoniously popped the expensive cork, and unleashed the bubbles.

'Drink to whatever you like,' he said in depression. 'I suppose it was a bad idea, coming here.'

'No,' I said. Regardless of thrusts of raw, unprocessed grief, I found there was inescapable excitement after all in the sense of a new chance offered, a fresh beginning possible.

Five minutes to ring-the-bells. I drank Lloyd Baxter's champagne and still didn't like him. We'd been introduced two years earlier. I remembered that he'd had thick dark hair, but as his age had advanced from fifty the grey streaks had multiplied fast. He still had a powerful-looking brow and a no-nonsense jaw, but he had thickened around the neck and stomach. If he looked more like an industrialist than a landowner, it was because he'd sold his majority share in a shipping line to buy his racehorses and his acres.

He disapproved, he'd told me severely, of young men like myself who could take days off work whenever they cared to. I knew he considered me a hanger-on who sponged off Martin, regardless of Martin's insisting it was more likely the other way around. It seemed that when Baxter formed opinions he was slow to rearrange them.

Distantly, out in the cold night, bells pealed the all-important moment. Lloyd Baxter raised his glass to drink to some private goal, and I, following his gesture, hoped merely that I would see January 2001 in safety. I added with banal courtesy that I would drink to his health outside, if he'd forgive me my absence.

'Of course,' he said, his voice in a mumble.

Pulling open the gallery door, I walked out into the street still holding my golden drink and found that dozens of people had been moved by an almost supernatural instinct to breathe free new air under the stars. Nearby, a large group of people had linked arms and were swaying across the road singing 'Auld Lang Syne' with half the words missing. One or two cars crept along slowly, horns blaring, with enthusiastic youths yelling from open windows.

The man who sold antique books in the shop next to my gallery shook my hand vigorously, and with warm goodwill he wished me a happy new year. I smiled and thanked him. Smiling was easy. The village, a fairly friendly place at any time, greeted the new year and the neighbours with uncomplicated affection.

It was longer than I'd intended before I reluctantly decided I should return to my shop, my ready-for-the-bank canvas bag, and my unwelcome visitor, whose temper wouldn't have been improved by my absence. I pushed open the heavy door, preparing my apologies, and found that an entirely different sort of action was essential.

Lloyd Baxter lay face down, unconscious, on my showroom floor.

I knelt anxiously beside him and felt for a pulse in his neck. There was to my great relief a slow perceptible *thud-thud* under my fingers. A stroke, perhaps? A heart attack? I knew very little medicine.

What an appallingly awkward night, I thought, for anyone to need to call out the medics. I stood up and took a few paces to the table that held the till and all the business machines, including the telephone. I dialled the emergency services without much expectation, but even on such a New Year's Eve, it seemed, the paramedics would respond. It wasn't until I'd put down the receiver that I noticed the absence beside the till of the canvas bag with my takings.

I swore. I'd worked hard for every cent. I was depressed as well as furious. I began to wonder if Lloyd Baxter had done his best, if he'd been knocked out trying to defend my property against a thief.

The black unidentified videotape was gone as well. The wave of outrage common to anyone robbed of even minor objects shook me into a deeper anger. The tape's loss was a severe aggravation, even if not on the same level as the money.

I telephoned the police without exciting them in the least. They were psyched up for bombs, not paltry theft. They said they would send someone in the morning.

Lloyd Baxter stirred and moaned. I knelt beside him, removed his tie and rolled him onto his side so that he wasn't in danger of choking. The chill of the deep night seeped into my own body, let alone Baxter's, so I went and stood on the treadle that raised the trap door to the roaring furnace and let the heat flood into the workshop.

The ultraefficient men who arrived in the prompt ambulance took over expertly, examining their patient, making a preliminary diagnosis and wrapping him in a red warming blanket ready for transport. Baxter partially awoke. His gaze flickered woozily once across my face before his eyes closed again into a heavier sleep.

The paramedics had me provide them with as much as I knew (practically nothing) of Baxter's medical history. One of them listed the contents of his trouser pockets—a handkerchief, a bottle of pills and a hotel-room key.

I didn't even have to suggest that I should return the key to the hotel; the paramedics suggested it themselves. I rattled it into my own trousers without delay, thinking vaguely of sleeping in his bed, since the paramedics said he would be in the hospital all night.

'What's wrong with him?' I asked. 'Has he had a heart attack? Or a stroke? Has he been . . . well, attacked and knocked out?'

I told them about the money and the tape.

They shook their heads. The most senior of them discounted my guesses. In his opinion Lloyd Baxter had had an epileptic fit.

'A *fit*?' I asked blankly. 'He's seemed perfectly well all day.'

The medics nodded knowledgeably. The pill bottle's contents were listed as phenytoin, the preventative for epilepsy.

'Epilepsy'—the chief medic nodded—'and who'll bet that he was overdue with a dose? We have all the other symptoms here. Slow pulse and bluish lips. Alcohol.' He gestured to the depleted bottle of Dom. 'Late night without sleep. Then there's stress. Isn't he the one whose jockey was done for at the races today?'

Chapter Two

At the Wychwood Dragon Hotel no one questioned my takeover of Lloyd Baxter's room. In the morning I packed his belongings and arranged for the hotel to send them to the hospital. Then I walked down and across the road to the workshop, where Martin, though vivid in my mind, refused to fly as a statement in glass. Inspiration operated at its own good speed, and many a time I'd found that trying to force it didn't work.

The furnace roared in its firebox. I sat beside the stainless-steel table (called a marver) on which I should have been rolling eternity into balls of liquid glass, and thought only of Martin laughing and winning races, and of Martin's lost videotape. Where was that tape, what did it contain, and who thought it worth stealing?

These profitless thoughts were interrupted at nine o'clock by the doorbell and the appearance on the doorstep of a young woman in a vast sloppy sweater hanging round her knees. She wore a baseball cap over a shock of brassily dyed streaky hair. We stared at each other with interest, her brown eyes alive and curious.

I said politely, 'Good morning.'

'Yeah. Yeah.' She laughed. 'Happy new century and all that rubbish. Are you Gerard Logan?'

'Logan.' I nodded. 'And you?'

'Detective Constable Dodd.'

I blinked. 'Plain clothes?'

'You may laugh,' she said. 'You reported a theft at twelve thirty-two this morning. Can I come in?'

'Be my guest.'

She stepped into the gallery spotlights and glowed.

From habit I dramatised her in glass in my mind, an abstract essence as a conduit of feeling and light, exactly the instinctive process I'd tried in vain to summon up for Martin.

Oblivious, Detective Constable Dodd produced a card identifying her and adding a first name, Catherine. I answered her questions, but the police opinion was already firm. Too bad I'd left a bagful of money lying around, she said. What did I expect? And videotapes came by the dozen. No one would think twice about snapping one up.

'What was on it?' she asked, pencil poised over a note pad.

'I've no idea.' I explained how it had come to me originally in a brown-paper parcel.

'Pornography. Bound to be.' Her pronouncement was brisk, world-weary and convinced. 'Unidentified.' She shrugged. 'Would you know it from any other tape if you saw it again?'

'It hadn't any labels.'

My answers about the stolen money caused her eyebrows to rise over the amount, but she obviously thought I'd never again see the canvas bag or the mini-bonanza inside. I still had cheques and credit-card slips, but most of my tourist customers paid in cash.

I told her about Lloyd Baxter and his epileptic fit. 'Maybe he saw the thief.'

She frowned. 'Maybe he *was* the thief. Could he have faked the fit?'

'The paramedics didn't seem to think so.'

She wandered through the showroom looking at the clowns, sailing boats, fishes and horses. She picked up a haloed angel and disapproved of the price sticker. Her hair fell forward, framing her intent face, and I again clearly saw the bright analytical intelligence inside the sloppy hippie-type disguise. She was through and through a police officer, not primarily a come-hither female.

Replacing the angel, she folded her note pad and with body language announced that the investigation, despite its lack of results, was over. It was the go-to-work version of Constable Dodd that prepared to step into the street.

'Why the too-big sweater and the baseball cap?' I asked.

She flashed me an amused glance. 'You happened to have been robbed on my allotted beat. My assignment in Broadway is to spot the gang stealing cars in this area. Thanks for your time.'

She grinned with cheerfulness and shuffled off down the hill, pausing to talk to a homeless-looking layabout sitting in a shop doorway. A pity the hippie and the hobo hadn't been car-thief spotting at midnight, I thought vaguely.

I telephoned Bon-Bon. She wailed miserably into my ear. 'But, darling Gerard, *of course* I didn't tell Priam not to bring you with him. How could you believe it? You are the first person Martin would want to come here. Please, please come as soon as you can. The children are crying and everything's dreadful.' She drew a shaky breath. 'Priam is an old fool. He talked about the inconvenience of finding another jockey halfway through the season.'

'How long did he stay with you?' I asked.

'Ten to fifteen minutes, maybe. My mother descended on us while he was here, and you know what she's like. Priam was mostly in Martin's den, I think. He couldn't sit still. Said he had to be back for evening stables.' Bon-Bon's despair overflowed. 'Can't you *come?*'

'As soon as I've done one job and found transport. Say, about noon.'

'Oh yes, I forgot your bloody car. I'll come and fetch you.'

'No. Don't drive anywhere while you're so upset. At the worst we could persuade your mama to lend me Worthington and the Rolls.'

Bon-Bon's mother's versatile chauffeur raised his eyebrows frequently to heaven at Marigold's odd requirements, but he had been known to drive a roofless Land Rover at breakneck speed at night across stubble fields, headlights blazing in the dark, while his employer stood balancing behind him with a double-barrelled shotgun loosing off over his head at mesmerised rabbits. Martin said he'd been afraid to watch, but Worthington and Marigold had achieved a bag of forty and freed her land of a voracious pest. Worthington, bald and fifty, was more an adventure than a last resort.

On New Year's Day 2000 in England, the world in general came to a stop. People wanted to stay at home.

Logan Glass astounded the other residents of Broadway by opening its doors to the day-before's customers, who arrived to collect their overnight-cooled souvenirs. To my own astonishment two of my assistants, Pamela Jane and Irish, turned up, even though bleary-eyed, saying they couldn't leave me to pack the whole delivery job alone, so it was with speed and good humour that my new century began. I looked back later at the peace of that morning with a feeling of unreality that life could ever have been so safe and simple.

Pamela Jane, twittery, stick thin and wanly pretty, insisted on driving me to Bon-Bon's place. She left me in the driveway, then hurried back to the shop.

Martin and Bon-Bon had agreed at least on their house, an eighteenth-century gem that I admired every time I went there. A small van stood on the gravel, dark blue with a name painted on it in yellow: THOMPSON ELECTRONICS. Because I'd been working, I didn't remember that that day was a national holiday—definitely a moratorium for television repair vans.

Chaos was too weak a word to describe what I found inside the house. For a start, the front door was visibly ajar. Beginning to feel a slight unease, I stepped inside and shouted but without response, and a pace or two later I learned why.

Bon-Bon's mother, Marigold, frothy grey hair and floaty purple dress in disarray, lay unconscious on the stairs. Worthington, her chauffeur, sprawled like a drugged medieval guard dog at her feet.

The four children, out of sight, were uncannily quiet, and the door to Martin's den was closed on silence.

I opened this door immediately and found Bon-Bon there, lying full-length on the floor. I knelt to feel for a pulse in her neck, and I felt the living *ga-bump ga-bump* with a deep relief. Concentrating on Bon-Bon, I saw too late in peripheral sight a movement behind my right shoulder, a dark figure hiding behind the door.

I jerked halfway to standing but wasn't quick enough. I glimpsed a small metal gas cylinder, more or less like a fire extinguisher. But this cylinder wasn't red. It was orange. It hit my head. Martin's den turned grey, dark grey and black. A deep well of nothing.

I RETURNED SLOWLY to a gallery of watchers. The children's eyes looked huge with fright. I was lying on my back. Into the blank spaces of memory slowly crept the picture of an orange gas cylinder in the hands of a figure in a black head mask. I tried to stand up.

Bon-Bon said with great relief, 'Thank God you're all right. We've all been gassed, and we've all been sick since we woke up.'

I, for one, had a headache, not nausea.

Worthington, notwithstanding the muscular physique he painstakingly developed by regular visits to a punchbag gym, looked pale and shaky. He held each of the two youngest children by the hand, though, giving them what confidence he could. In their eyes he could do everything, and they were nearly right.

Bon-Bon had once mentioned that Worthington's top value to her mother was his understanding of bookmakers' methods, because, as Marigold herself disliked walking along between the rows of men shouting the odds, Worthington got her the best prices. A versatile and compulsive good guy was Worthington.

Only Marigold herself was now missing from the sick parade. Peeling myself off the floor, I asked about her. The eldest of the children, a boy called Daniel, said she was drunk. Snoring on the stairs, the elder girl said. So pragmatic, 2000-year children.

Bon-Bon's doctor promised he would look in, New Year's Day

notwithstanding. He asked if we'd informed the police of the attack.

It appeared that robbery had been the purpose of the mass anaesthesia. Three television sets with integral tape players were missing, together with dozens of tapes. Two laptop computers, with printers and racks of filing disks, were missing too.

Bon-Bon began crying quietly from the strain of it all, and it was Worthington, recovering and worth his weight in videotapes, who talked to the overburdened local police station. My constable, Catherine Dodd, he found, was attached to a different branch. Detectives, however, would arrive on the Stukely doorstep soon.

Not surprisingly, the Thompson Electronics van had gone.

Feeling queasy, I sat in Martin's black leather chair in his den, while Bon-Bon, on an opposite sofa, gave no complete answer to my repeated question, which was, 'What was on the tape that Martin meant to give me after the races, and where did it come from? That's to say, who gave it to Martin himself at Cheltenham?'

Bon-Bon studied me with wet eyes and blew her nose. She said, 'I know Martin wanted to tell you something yesterday, but he had those other men in the car and he wanted to talk to you without Priam listening, so he planned to take you home last, after the others.' Even in distress she looked porcelain pretty, the plumpness an asset in a curvy black wool suit.

'He trusted you,' she said finally.

'Mm.' I'd have been surprised if he hadn't.

'No, you don't understand.' Bon-Bon hesitated and went on slowly. 'He knew a secret. He wouldn't tell me what it was. He said I would fret. But he wanted to tell *someone*. I agreed you should be his back-up. Just in case. Oh dear . . . He had what he wanted you to know recorded onto a plain old-fashioned video tape, not onto a CD or a computer disk, because whoever was giving him information preferred it that way. I'm not sure why.'

'And he didn't say anything about what was on the tape?'

'He was awfully careful not to.'

I shook my head in frustration. The tape stolen from the glass showroom was surely the one with the secret on it. The one passed to Martin, then to Eddie the valet, and then to me. Yet if the Broadway thieves, or thief, had viewed it—and they'd had all night to do so—why were they needing to rob Martin's house as well?

Did the tape taken from the showroom actually contain Martin's secret? Perhaps not.

Was the second robbery carried out by a different thief, who didn't know about the first one? I had no answers, only guesses. Marigold at that point tottered into the den as if coming to pieces in all directions. I had been used to Marigold for the four years since Martin had presented me to his buxom mother-in-law, a magnified version of his pretty wife. Marigold could be endlessly witty or tiresomely belligerent, according to the gin level, but this time the effect of gas on alcohol seemed to have resulted in pity-me pathos.

The police turned up, and Bon-Bon's children described their attacker, right down to the laces on his shoes. He had stared with wide eyes through his black head mask while he'd pointed the orange cylinder at them and squirted a fierce mist, sweeping from face to face and knocking them out before they'd realised what was happening. Daniel described the black-masked man having something white tied over his face underneath. An elementary gas mask, I surmised. Something to prevent him from inhaling his own gas.

The gas had perhaps been exhausted by the time I arrived; a direct bang on the head had sufficed.

Scarcely had the police note books been folded away than Bon-Bon's doctor hurried in. It was the colour orange that slowed him into frowns and more thorough care. He and the police all listened to Daniel, brought out paper, and took notes. The doctor told the departing detectives to look for villains with access to the anaesthetic gas cyclopropane, which came in orange cylinders and wasn't much used because of being highly flammable and explosive.

Slowly, after thorough peerings into eyes and throats and careful stethoscope chest checks, each of the family was judged fit to go on living. Sweet Bon-Bon, when her house was finally free of official attention, told me she was utterly exhausted and needed help. Specifically she needed *my* help, and Martin would have asked for it.

So I stayed and looked after things, and because of that I saved myself at least another sore head, as thieves broke into my house on the hill that night and stole every videotape I owned.

ON MONDAY, after an early session in the workshop, I went to Cheltenham races (by taxi) to talk to Martin's valet, Eddie Payne.

Eddie was ready to help, he said, his gaze darting over my shoulder and back again to my face, but he couldn't. However hard he tried, he couldn't remember any more than he'd told me on Friday. I thought back to the moment of empathy between us, when we had each realised what we'd lost. That moment had gone.

The difference between Friday and Monday was a fierce-eyed woman approaching forty, now standing a pace or two behind me, a woman Eddie referred to as his daughter. He slid a second glance at her expressionlessly and said, almost too quietly for me to hear, '*She* knows the man who gave Martin the tape.'

The woman said sharply, 'What did you say, Dad? Speak up.'

'I said we'd miss Martin badly,' Eddie said, 'and I'm due back in the changing room. Tell Gerard—Mr Logan—what he wants to know, why don't you?' He walked away, apologetically saying as he went, 'Her name's Rose. She's a good girl, really.'

Rose, the good girl, gave me such a bitter flash of hate that I wondered what I'd ever done to annoy her, as I hadn't known of her existence until moments earlier. She was angularly bony and had mid-brown hair with frizzy sticking-out curls. Her skin was dry and freckled and, although her clothes looked too big for the thin body inside, there was about her an extraordinary air of magnetism.

'Er . . . Rose—' I started.

'Mrs Robins,' she interrupted abruptly.

I cleared my throat and tried again.

'Mrs Robins, then, could I buy you some coffee or a drink?'

'No, you could *not*.' She bit the words off with emphasis. 'You'd do better to mind your own business.'

'Mrs Robins, did you see who gave a brown-paper-wrapped parcel to Martin Stukely at Cheltenham races last Friday?'

Such a simple question. She primped her lips together tightly, swivelled on her heel and walked away.

After a short pause I trickled along in her wake as she made for the ranks of bookmakers' pitches in front of the Tattersalls stand. She stopped at a board announcing ARTHUR ROBINS, EST. 1894, and talked to an Elvis Presley lookalike with heavy black side whiskers. He was standing on a box, leaning down to take money from the public and dictating his transactions to a clerk, who was punching the bets into a computer.

Rose Robins, established long after 1894, had a fair amount to say to the Elvis lookalike. He frowned, listening, and I retreated. I might have strength and reasonable agility, but Rose's contact made my muscle power look the stuff of kindergartens.

Patiently I climbed the stands and waited while the Arthur Robins, Est. 1894 bookmakers—three of them—took bets on the final race of the afternoon and then packed up. I watched them walk towards the exit. As a group, they equalled an armoured tank.

From experience with Martin, I knew that jockeys' valets finished their work after most of the crowds had gone home. A valet was the man who helped the jockeys change rapidly between races. He also looked after and cleaned their gear, saddles, britches, boots and so on. Now, while Eddie packed up his hamper of saddles, kit and clothes for laundering, I waited with hope for him to reappear out of the changing room at the end of his day.

When he came out and saw me, he was at first alarmed and then resigned. 'I suppose,' he said, 'Rose wouldn't tell you.'

'No,' I agreed. 'So would you ask her something, for Martin's sake? Ask her if the tape Martin gave you was the one he thought it was.'

He took a few seconds to work it out.

'Do you mean,' he asked doubtfully, 'that my Rose thinks Martin had the wrong tape?'

'I think,' I confessed, 'that if Martin's tape ever surfaces after all the muddle and thieving, it'll be a matter of luck.'

He protested self-righteously that he'd given me Martin's tape in good faith. I insisted that I believed him. No more was said about Rose. Eddie, eyes down, mumbled a few words about seeing me at Martin's funeral, planned for Thursday. Then, in evident discomfort, he hurried away.

Rose Robins and her enmity added complexity to an already tangled situation. But I came to no satisfactory conclusion about the unexpected involvement of Eddie's scratchy daughter.

Meanwhile, still drifting in outer space was whatever confidential data Martin had meant to entrust to me. Unrealistically, I simply hoped that Martin's secret would remain forever hidden in uncharted orbit, and all of us could return to normal.

I caught a bus from the racecourse to Broadway. The bus wound its way from village to village, and it was after five thirty by the time I reached the doors of Logan Glass. My assistants told me that Bon-Bon had telephoned, saying she was begging me to go on organising her household in return for transport. Much to their amusement, the transport she sent was Marigold's Rolls.

I sat beside Worthington as he drove. In addition to being bald, fifty and kind to children, Worthington disliked the police force as a matter of principle, referred to marriage as bondage, and believed in the usefulness of being able to outkick any other muscleman in sight.

It wasn't so much as a chauffeur that I now valued Worthington at my elbow, but as a prospective bodyguard. The Elvis lookalike had radiated latent menace at an intensity that I hadn't met before and didn't like, and for a detonator there was fierce, thorny Rose. It was with her in mind that I casually asked Worthington if he'd ever placed a bet at the races with Arthur Robins, Est. 1894.

'For a start,' he said, 'the Robins family don't exist. That bunch of swindlers known as Arthur Robins are mostly Veritys and Webbers. There's never been a bona fide Arthur Robins. It's just a pretty name.'

Eyebrows raised in surprise, I asked, 'How do you know?'

'My old man was a bookmaker; he taught me the trade. You've got to be sharp at figures, though, to make a profit, and I never got quick enough. But Arthur Robins, that's the front name for some whizzers of speed merchants. Don't bet with them, that's my advice.'

'Did you know that Eddie Payne, Martin's valet, has a daughter Rose who says her last name is Robins and who's on cuddling terms with an Elvis Presley lookalike taking bets for Arthur Robins?'

Worthington sat straighter in his seat. 'No, I didn't know that.' He thought for a while. 'That Elvis fellow,' he said finally, 'that's Norman Osprey. You don't want to mix with *him.*'

'And Rose?'

Worthington shook his head. 'I don't know her. I'll ask around.'

ON WEDNESDAY, the day before Martin's funeral, a young woman on a motorbike—huge helmet, black leather jacket, matching trousers, heavy boots—steered into one of the parking spaces at the front of Logan Glass. Outside in the January chill she pulled off the helmet and shook free a cap of fair fine hair, then walked into the gallery and showroom as if she knew the way well.

I was putting the pre-annealing final touches to a vase, with Pamela Jane telling a group of American tourists how it was done, but there was something attention-claiming about the motorcyclist, and as soon as I thought of her in terms of glass, I knew her.

'Catherine Dodd,' I said.

'Most people don't recognise me.' She was amused, not piqued.

With interest I watched the tourists pack somewhat closer together as if to elbow out the stranger in threatening clothes.

Pamela Jane finished her spiel, and the tourists settled on their purchases. While Hickory wrapped the parcels and wrote out bills, I asked the motorcyclist if there were any news of my lost tape.

'I'm afraid,' said Detective Constable Dodd in plain—well, plainer—clothes, 'your tape is gone for good.'

I told her it held a secret.

'What secret?'

'I don't know. Martin Stukely told his wife he was giving me a secret on tape for safekeeping—that's a bit of a laugh.'

Catherine Dodd's detective mind trod the two paths I'd reluctantly followed myself. First, *someone* knew Martin's secret, and second, *someone*, and maybe not the same someone, could infer that the secret was known to me. Someone might suppose I'd watched that tape during the evening of Martin's death and for safety had wiped it off.

'If I'd had a tape player handy,' I said, 'I probably *would* have run that tape, and if I thought it awful, I *might* have wiped it off.'

'That's not what your friend Martin wanted.'

I said, 'If he'd been sure of what he wanted, he wouldn't have fiddled about with tapes, he would just have *told* me this precious secret.' I stopped abruptly. 'There are too many ifs. How about you coming out for a drink?'

'Can't. Sorry. I'm on duty.' She gave me a brilliant smile. 'I'll call in another day. And oh! There's just one loose end.' She produced a note book from inside her jacket. 'What are your assistants' names?'

'Pamela Jane Evans and John Irish and John Hickory. We leave off John for the men and use their last names, as it's easier.'

'And how long have they all worked for you?'

'Pamela Jane about a year, Irish and Hickory two to three months longer. They're all good guys, believe me.'

'I do believe you. This is just for the records. This is actually . . . er . . . what I dropped in for.'

I looked at her with a direct gaze. She all but blushed.

'I'd better go now,' she said.

With regret I walked with her as far as the door, where she paused to say goodbye, as she didn't want to be seen with me too familiarly out in the street. A tourist's broad back obscured my view of the departure of Detective Constable Dodd, and I surprised myself by minding about that quite a lot.

On Bon-Bon's telephone, later that night, I learned that Lloyd Baxter had deemed it correct to fly down for 'his jockey's last ride' (as he put it) but hadn't wanted to stay with Priam Jones, whom he was on the point of ditching as his trainer.

Priam also telephoned, meaning to talk to Bon-Bon but reaching me instead. I had been fielding commiserations for her whenever I was around. Marigold, Worthington and even the children had grown expert at thanks and tact. I thought how Martin would have grinned at the grade-A improvement in his family's social skills.

Priam blustered on a bit but was, I gathered, offering himself as an usher in the matter of seating at the funeral. Remembering his tears, I put him on the list, then asked him if, before he'd picked me up from my home on Friday morning, Martin had by any chance mentioned that he was expecting delivery of a tape at the races.

'You asked me that the day after he died,' Priam said impatiently. 'The answer is still yes. He said we wouldn't leave the racecourse until he'd collected some package or other to give to you. And I did give it to you, don't you remember? I brought it back to Broadway after you'd left it in your raincoat in Martin's car . . . Well, I'll see you tomorrow, Gerard. Give my regards to Bon-Bon.'

Also that evening, Eddie Payne went to his local Catholic church and confessed his past and future sins. He told me this with self-righteousness when I intercepted his condolences to Bon-Bon. He'd tried and tried to get someone else to do his racecourse work, he said, but he hadn't succeeded, and he'd have to miss the funeral, which grieved him sorely. I knew, however, that he could have more easily got stand-ins to free him to go to that particular funeral than if it had been for his own grandmother.

On the same evening (though I didn't learn of it until later), Eddie Payne's daughter, Rose, described to a small group of fascinated and ruthless knaves how to force Gerard Logan to tell them the secret he'd been given at Cheltenham races.

Chapter Three

On the first Thursday of January, the sixth day of the next thousand years, I, with Priam Jones and four senior jump jockeys, carried Martin into church in his coffin and later delivered him to his grave.

The sun shone on frosty trees. Bon-Bon looked ethereal, Marigold stayed sober, and the four children knocked with their knuckles on the coffin as if they could wake their father inside. Lloyd Baxter read a short but decent eulogy, and all the racing world, from the Stewards of the Jockey Club to the men who replaced the divots, crowded into the pews in church and packed the churchyard outside. Respects were paid. After the hundreds who had turned up for Martin had drunk and eaten and left, I sought Bon-Bon out to say goodbye.

'Stay with us one more night,' she said. 'You and Worthington have tamed the children. Let's have this one more night of peace.'

I agreed, and after midnight, when only I was awake, I sat in Martin's den, deep in regret. One had so few close friends in life. None to spare. I also thought of the videotape and whatever he'd had recorded on it. I had no idea what could have needed such complex safekeeping. Yet I did see that, much as I thought Bon-Bon a darling, she wasn't the most reticent person on earth. To Bon-Bon a secret would be safe until her next nice chat with her best friend.

It was time, I supposed, to make sure the outside doors were locked and to sleep away the last hours in Martin's house. A few weeks earlier I'd lent him a couple of books on ancient glass-making techniques and, as they were lying on the long table by the sofa, it seemed a good time to pick them up to take home without bothering Bon-Bon too much.

In the morning, saying goodbye, I mentioned I was taking the books. 'Fine,' Bon-Bon said vaguely. 'I wish you weren't going.'

Worthington drove me back to Broadway in Bon-Bon's runabout. 'I got a low-life investigator to ask about that woman, Rose,' he told me. 'He didn't get much further than you did. Eddie Payne thinks she saw who gave that damned tape to Martin, but I wouldn't rely on it. Eddie's afraid of his own daughter, if you ask me.'

I agreed with him on that, and we left it there.

My three assistants welcomed me back to a regular workday, and I taught Hickory—as I'd taught Pamela Jane before Christmas—how to collect a third gather of glass, so hot that it was red and semi-liquid and fell in a heavy teardrop shape that drooped towards the floor (and one's feet) if one didn't marver it fast enough on the steel table. Hickory knew how to press its lengthened tip into long heaps of dustlike colours before returning the revolving head into the furnace to keep the chunk of glass at working temperature. I showed him how to gather glass neatly on the end of a blowing iron before lifting it into the air ready to blow, and how to keep the resulting slightly ballooned shape constant.

Hickory watched the continuous process with anxious eyes.

'Practise handling three gathers,' I said. 'You can do two now easily.' A gather was the amount of molten glass that could be brought out of the tank at one time on the tip of the steel punty rod. A gather could be any size, according to the skill and strength of the glass-blower. Glass in bulk was very heavy and demanded muscle.

Owing to the space limitation of tourist suitcases, few pieces of Logan glass sold in the shop were of more than three gathers. Pamela Jane, to her sorrow, had never quite mastered the swing-upwards-and-blow technique. Irish, in spite of enthusiasm, would never be a top-rated glass-blower. Of Hickory, though, I had hopes. He had ease of movement and, most important, a lack of fear.

Glass-blowers were commonly arrogant people, chiefly because the skill was so difficult to learn. Hickory already showed signs of arrogance, but if he became a notable expert he would have to be forgiven. All day I watched my apprentice improve considerably, though there was a lot of swearing and a whole heap of shattered glass.

By five o'clock on this bleakly cold January afternoon I sent my three helpers home and with gloom did some long-overdue accounting work. The cash stolen on New Year's Eve left a depressing hole. It wasn't difficult, after a while, to lay aside the figures and pick up the books on ancient glass-making that I'd lent to Martin.

Flicking through the early pages in one of the books, I came across the picture of my favourite of all historic goblets, a glowing red cup, six and a half inches high, constructed around the year three hundred and something. It was made of lumps of glass held fast in an intricate gold cage (a technique from before blowing was invented). Absorbed with pleasure, I didn't notice at first a thin buff envelope held within the leaves.

The envelope was addressed by computer printer to Martin Stukely, Esq., Jockey. I had no qualms in taking out the single-page letter inside and reading it.

Dear Martin,
    You are right, it is the best way. I will take the tape, as you want, to Cheltenham races on New Year's Eve.
    This knowledge is dynamite. Take care of it.
                Victor Waltman Verity

The letter too was written on a computer, though the name given as signature had been printed in a different font. There was no address or telephone number on the letter itself, but faintly across the stamp on the envelope there was a round postmark. After long concentration with a magnifying glass, the point of origin seemed to me only XET around the top and EVO around the bottom. The date alone was easily readable: December 17. Less than a month ago.

There weren't many places in Great Britain with an *x* in their name, and I could think of nowhere else that fitted the available letters other than Exeter, Devon.

When I reached Directory Enquiries, I learned that there was indeed a Victor Verity in Exeter. But when I called, I spoke not to him but to his widow. Her dear Victor had passed away during the previous summer. Wrong Verity.

I tried Enquiries again.

'Very sorry,' said a prim voice, 'there is no other Victor or V. Verity in the Exeter telephone area, which covers most of Devon.'

'How about an unlisted number?'

'Sorry. I can't give you that information.'

Victor Waltman Verity was either unlisted or had mailed his letter far from home.

Cursing him lightly, I glanced with reluctance at the accounting work half done on my computer, and there, of course, lay the answer. Computers. Internet. The Internet might, among other miracles, put an address to a name.

I started a search for Verity in Devon, and the Internet, after surveying every fact obtainable in the public domain (such as the electoral registers), came up with a total of twenty-two Devon-based Veritys, but none of them any longer was Victor.

Dead end.

I tried Verity in Cornwall. Sixteen, but still no Victor.

Try Somerset, I thought. Not a Victor Verity in sight.

Before reaching to switch off, I skimmed down the list, and at the end of it noticed that at 19 Lorna Terrace, Taunton, Somerset, there lived a Mr *Waltman* Verity. Good enough to try, I thought.

Armed with the address, I tried Directory Enquiries again but ran up against the same polite barrier of virtual nonexistence. Unlisted.

Although the next day was Saturday and busier than usual in the showroom, my thoughts returned continuously to Taunton and Waltman Verity.

Taunton . . .

Having nothing else urgently filling my Sunday, I caught a westbound train the next morning and asked directions to Lorna Terrace.

The door of Number 19 was opened by a thin woman dressed in trousers, sweater and slippers, with a cigarette in one hand and big pink curlers in her hair. Thirty-something. Perhaps forty, I thought. Easy-going, with a resigned attitude to strangers on her doorstep.

'Mrs Verity?' I asked.

'Yeah. What is it?' She sucked smoke, unconcerned.

'Mrs Victor Waltman Verity?'

She laughed. 'I'm Mrs Waltman Verity. Victor's my son.' She shouted over her shoulder towards the inner depths of the narrow terrace house. 'Vic, someone to see you,' and while we waited, Mrs Verity looked me over thoroughly from hair to trainers and went on enjoying a private giggle.

Whatever I had expected Victor Waltman Verity to look like, it was nothing near the living thing. He must have been all of fifteen. He appeared quietly from along the narrow hallway and regarded me with curiosity mixed, I thought, with the possibility of alarm. He was as tall as his mother, with dark hair, pale grey eyes and an air of knowing himself to be as intelligent as any adult. His voice, when he spoke, was at the cracked stage between boy and man.

'What've you been up to, young Vic?' his mother asked, and to me she said, 'It's bloody cold out here. Want to come in?'

'Er,' I said. I was suffering more from the unexpected than the cold, but she waited for no answer and walked back past the boy until she was out of sight. I pulled the envelope sent to Martin out of a pocket and immediately set the alarm racing in young Victor.

'You weren't supposed to find me!' he exclaimed. Puzzlement set in. 'I mean, what do you want?'

'First, I'd like to accept your mother's invitation to get warm.'

He shrugged and said, 'The kitchen is warmest.'

He stretched to close the door behind me, then led the way along the hall to the heart of all such terrace houses, the space where life was lived. There was a central table with a patterned plastic cloth and four unmatched chairs. A television set stood aslant on a draining board otherwise stacked with unwashed dishes.

In spite of the disorganisation, there was bright new paint and nothing disturbingly sordid. I had an overall impression of yellow.

Mrs Verity sat in one of the chairs, rocking on its back legs and gulping smoke as if she lived on it.

She said pleasantly enough, 'We get all sorts of people here, what with Vic and his wretched Internet. We'll get a full-sized genie one of these days, I shouldn't wonder.' She gestured vaguely to one of the chairs, and I sat on it.

'I was a friend of Martin Stukely,' I explained, and I asked Vic what was on the videotape he had given Martin at Cheltenham.

'There wasn't a tape,' he said briefly. 'I didn't go to Cheltenham.'

I pulled his letter to Martin out of the envelope and gave it to him to read. He shrugged and handed it back when he'd reached the end.

'It was a game. I made up the tape.' He was nervous, all the same.

'What knowledge was it that was dynamite?'

'Look, none.' He grew impatient. 'I told you. I made it up.'

'Why did you send it to Martin Stukely?'

I was careful not to let the questions sound too aggressive but, in some way that I didn't understand, they raised all his defences and coloured his cheeks red.

His mother said to me, 'What's all this about a tape? Do you mean a *video*tape? Vic hasn't got any videotapes. We're going to get a new video machine any day now; then it will be different.'

I explained apologetically. 'Someone did give Martin a videotape at Cheltenham races. Martin gave it to Eddie Payne, his valet, to keep safe, and Eddie gave it to me, but it was stolen before I could see what was on it. Then all the videotapes in Martin Stukely's house and all the videotapes in my own house were stolen too.'

'I hope you're not suggesting that Vic stole anything, because I can promise you he wouldn't.' Mrs Verity had grasped one suggestion wrongly and hadn't listened clearly to the rest, so she too advanced to the edge of anger, and I did my best to retreat and placate, but her natural good humour had been dented. She stood up as a decisive signal that it was time I left.

I said amiably to young Victor, 'Call me,' and although he shook his head, I wrote my mobile number on the margin of a Sunday newspaper.

Then I stepped out of 19 Lorna Terrace and walked unhurriedly along the street, pondering two odd unanswered questions.

First, how did Victor happen to come to Martin's attention?

Second, why had neither mother nor son asked my name?

As I TURNED out of Lorna Terrace, I was conscious of not having done very well. I seem to have screwed up even what I thought I understood. I might be OK at glass but not excellent at Sherlock Holmes. Dim Dr Watson, that was me.

It grew dark, and it took me a long time to return to Broadway. Fishing out my keys, I plodded towards the gallery door. Sunday evening. No one about. Brilliant lights shining from Logan Glass.

I hadn't learned yet to beware shadows. Figures in black materialised from the entrance to the antique bookshop next door. I suppose there were four of them leaping about in the dark—an impression, not an accurate count. Four was profligate, anyway. Three, two, maybe only one could have done the job. I guessed they'd been waiting there for a long time and it hadn't improved their temper.

The attack consisted of multiple bashes and bangs and of being slammed against a lumpy bit of Cotswold stone wall.

Disorientated by the attack, I heard demands as if from a distance that I should disclose information that I knew I didn't have. I tried to tell them. They didn't listen.

All that was annoying enough, but it was their additional aim that lit my own inner protection furnace and put power into half-forgotten techniques of kick-boxing left over from my teens. A sharp, excited voice instructed over and over again, 'Break his wrists. Go on. *Break his wrists.*' And later, out of the dark, the same voice exulting, 'That got him.'

No, it bloody didn't. Yet pain screeched up my arm. My thoughts were blasphemy. Strong, whole and flexible wrists were as essential to a glass-blower as to a gymnast on the Olympic high rings.

Two of the black-clad figures waved baseball bats. One with heavily developed shoulders was recognisably Norman Osprey. One other had the bright idea of holding my fingers tightly together in a bunch against the wall before getting his colleague to aim just below them with the bat.

I hadn't been aware of how desperately one could fight when it was the real thing. My wrists didn't get broken, but my watch took a direct hit. There were lumps and bruises all over. A few cuts. But my fingers worked, and that was all that mattered.

Maybe the fracas would have ended with my taking a fresh hole in the ground beside Martin, but Broadway wasn't a ghost town; people walked their dogs in the evening, and it was a dog-walker who yelled at my attackers and, with three Dobermans barking and pulling at their leashes, got the shadowy figures to vanish.

'Gerard Logan!' The tall dog-walker, astounded, bending to look at me, knew me by sight, as I did him. 'Are you all right?'

No, I wasn't. I said, 'Yes,' as one does.

He stretched down to help me to my feet. 'Shall I call the police?' he asked, though he wasn't a police lover—far from it.

'Tom—thanks. But no police.'

'What was it all about?' He sounded relieved. 'Are you in trouble? That looked to me like pay-back business.'

'Muggers.'

Tom Pigeon, who knew a thing or two about the rocky sides of life, gave me a half-smile, half-disillusioned look, and shortened the leashes of his toothy life preservers. More bark than bite, he'd assured me once. I wasn't certain I believed it.

He himself looked as if he had no need to bark. Although not heavily built, he had unmistakable physical power and a close-cut dark pointed beard that added menace. He told me there was blood in my hair. I leaned gingerly against the lumpy wall. The dizzy world revolved. I couldn't remember ever feeling so pulverised, not even when I'd fallen to the bottom of the scrum in a viciously unfriendly school rugby match and had my collar bone broken.

Tom Pigeon opened the gallery door with my keys, and with his arm around my waist got me as far as the threshold. 'You'll be all right now, OK?'

I nodded. He more or less propped me against the door frame.

Tom Pigeon was known locally as the Backlash, chiefly on account of being as quick with his wits as his fists. He'd survived unharmed eighteen months inside for aggravated breaking and entering and had emerged as a toughened hotshot, to be spoken of in awe. Whatever his dusty reputation, he had definitely rescued me, and I felt extraordinarily honoured by the extent of his aid.

He waited until I could visibly control things and then stared shrewdly into my eyes. 'Get a pit bull,' he said.

I LOCKED THE DOOR against the violence outside. Pity I couldn't blot out the woes of battery as easily. Pity I felt so stupid. So furious. So dangerously mystified.

In the back reaches of the workshop there was running water for rinsing one's face and a relaxing chair for recovery of all kinds of balance. I sat and ached a lot.

At about ten thirty I fell asleep in the soft chair and half an hour later was awakened by the doorbell. Disorientated as I woke, I wavered upright and creaked out of the workshop to see who wanted what at such an hour.

Detective Constable Catherine Dodd smiled with relief when I let her in. She again wore motorcycle leathers. With deft speed, as before, she lifted off her helmet and shook her head to loosen her fair hair. 'We had reports from two separate Broadway residents,' she said, 'who saw you being attacked outside here. We had no complaint from you, so I said I would check on you on my way home.'

I made a noncommittal gesture.

She said, 'Gerard, I've seen other people in your state.'

'Poor them.'

'It's hardly funny. Why haven't you asked my colleagues for more help?'

'Because,' I said lightly, 'I don't know who or why, and every time I think I've learned something, I find I haven't. Your colleagues don't like uncertainty.'

She thought that over. 'Tell *me*, then,' she said.

'Someone wants something I haven't got. I don't know what it is. I don't know who wants it. How am I doing?'

'That makes no sense.'

I winced and turned it into a smile. 'It makes no sense, quite right.'

Constable Dodd frowned, faint lines crossing her clear skin. As it seemed to be question time, I said abruptly, 'Are you married?'

After a few seconds looking down at her ringless hands, she replied, 'Why do you ask?'

'You have the air of it.'

'He's dead.' She sat for a while without moving and then asked, 'And you?' in calm return.

'Not yet,' I said.

Silence could sometimes shout. She listened to what I would probably ask quite soon, and seemed relaxed and content.

The workshop was warmed as always by the furnace, even though the roaring fire was held in control for nights and Sundays by a large screen of heat-resistant material.

Looking at Catherine Dodd's face above the dark close-fitting leather, I most clearly now saw her in terms of glass, saw her in fact so vividly that the urge and desire to work couldn't be stifled. I stood up and unclipped the fireproof screen, put it to one side, and fixed instead the smaller flap, which opened to allow access to the tankful of molten glass.

With boringly painful movements I took off my jacket and shirt, leaving only normal working gear of bare arms and singlet.

'What are you doing?' She sounded alarmed.

'A portrait,' I said. 'Sit still.' I turned up the heat in the furnace and sorted out the punty blowing irons I would need, and fetched a workable amount of glass manganese powder, which would give me a black colour eventually .

'But your bruises,' she protested. 'Those marks. They're terrible.'

'I can't feel them.'

I felt nothing indeed except the rare sort of excitement that came with revelation. That Sunday night the concept of one detective darkly achieving insight into the sins of others, and then the possibility that good could rise above sin and fly, these drifting thoughts set up in me in effect a mental anaesthesia, leaving the flame of imagination to do its stuff. Sometimes in the disengagement from this sort of thing, the vision had shrunk to disappointment and ash, and when that happened, I would leave the no-good piece on the marver table and not transfer it to an annealing oven. After a while its unresolved internal strains would cause it to self-destruct, to come to pieces dramatically with a cracking noise, to splinter, to fragment . . . to shatter.

It could be for onlookers an unnerving experience to see an apparently solid object disintegrate for no visible reason. For me the splitting apart symbolised merely the fading and insufficiency of the original thought. On that particular Sunday I had no doubts or hesitation, and I gathered glass in muscle-straining amounts that even on ordinary days would have taxed my ability.

That night I made Catherine Dodd in three pieces that later I would join together. I made not a lifelike sculpture of her head but an abstract of her occupation—a soaring spread of wings, black and shining at the base, rising through a black, white and clear centre to a high-rising pinion with streaks of gold shining to the top.

The gold fascinated my subject. 'Is it real gold?'

'Iron pyrites. But real gold would melt the same way, only I used all I had a week ago.'

I gently held the fragile sculpture in layers of heatproof fibre and laid all three sections carefully in one of the six annealing ovens. Only then, with the sculpture safely cooling, could I hardly bear the strains in my own limbs and felt too like cracking apart myself.

Catherine stood up and took a while to speak. Eventually she asked what I would do with the finished flight of wings, and I, coming down to earth from invention, tried prosaically to say that I would probably make a pedestal for it and display it in the gallery.

We both stood looking at each other as if not knowing what else to say. I leaned forward and kissed her cheek, which with mutual small movements became mouth to mouth, with passion in there somewhere, acknowledged but not yet overflowing.

Arms around motorcycle leathers had practical drawbacks. My own physical aches put winces where they weren't wanted, and with rueful humour she disengaged herself.

'Maybe another time,' she said.

'Delete the maybe,' I said.

Chapter Four

All three of my assistants could let themselves in through the gallery with personal keys, and it was Pamela Jane alone whom I saw first when I returned to consciousness at about eight o'clock on Monday morning. After Catherine had gone, I'd simply flopped back into the big chair in the workshop and closed my eyes on a shuddering and protesting nervous system. Sleep had made things slightly worse.

Pamela Jane said, horrified, 'Honestly, you look as if you'd been hit by a steamroller. Have you been here all night?'

'Can you . . .' Even my voice felt rough. I cleared my throat and tried again. 'Pam . . . jug of tea?'

She scurried helpfully around, making the tea and unbolting the side door. By the advent of Irish, I was ignoring the worst of my creaking joints, and Hickory, arriving last, found me lifting the three wing sections of the night's work out of the ovens.

They couldn't help but notice that I found too much movement a bad idea, but I could have done without Hickory's cheerful assumption it was the aftermath of booze.

The first customer came. Life more or less returned to normal. If I concentrated on blowing glass, I could forget four black woolly masks with eyeholes.

Later in the morning Marigold's Rolls-Royce drew up outside with Worthington at the wheel, looking formal in his official cap.

Marigold herself, he reported through his rolled-down window, had gone shopping with Bon-Bon in Bon-Bon's car. Both ladies had given him the day off and the use of the car. He appreciated their generosity, he said solemnly, as he was going to take me to the races.

I looked back at him in indecision.

'I'm not going,' I said. 'And where am I not going?'

'Leicester. Jump racing. Eddie Payne will be there. Rose will be there. Norman Osprey will be there with his book. I thought you wanted to find out who gave the videotape to Martin.'

I didn't answer at once.

'Mind you,' he said, making allowances, 'I don't suppose you want another beating like you got last night, so stay here if you like, and I'll mooch around by myself.'

'Who told you about last night?'

'A little bird told me. A not-so-little bird. A Pigeon, in fact. It seems he thinks quite a bit of you. He phoned me at Bon-Bon's. He says to put it around that in future any hands laid on you are laid on him.'

I felt both grateful and surprised. I asked, 'How well do you know him?'

He answered obliquely. 'You know that gardener of Martin's that was dying? That you lost your licence for, speeding to get him there in time? That gardener was Tom Pigeon's dad. Are you coming to Leicester?'

'I guess so.' I went back inside, put on my outdoor clothes and told Irish, Hickory and Pamela Jane to keep on making paper-weights while I went to the races. They wished me luck.

I sat beside Worthington for the journey. We stopped to buy me a cheap watch and to pick up a racing newspaper. On the front page I read, among a dozen little snippets, that the Leicester Stewards would be hosts that day to Lloyd Baxter (owner of star jumper Tallahassee) to honour the memory of jockey Martin Stukely.

Well, well.

After a while I told Worthington in detail about my visit to Lorna Terrace, Taunton. He frowned when I said, 'Didn't you tell me that the bookmaking firm of Arthur Robins, established 1894, was now run by people named Webber and Verity?'

'And the mother and son in Taunton were Verity!' A pause. 'It must be a coincidence,' he said.

'I don't believe in coincidences like that.'

After a while Worthington said, 'Gerard, if you have any clear idea of what's going on, what is it? For instance, who were those attackers in black masks last night and what did they want?'

I said, 'I think it was one of them who squirted you with

cyclopropane and laid me out with the empty cylinder. I don't know who that was. I'm sure, though, that one of the black masks was the fragrant Rose.'

'I'm not saying she wasn't, but why?'

'Who else in the world would scream at Norman Osprey—or any-one else, but I'm pretty sure it was him—to break my wrists? Rose's voice is unmistakable. And there is the way she moves. And as for purpose, partly to put me out of business, wouldn't you say? And partly to make me give her what I haven't got. And also to stop me from doing what we're aiming to do today.'

Worthington said impulsively, 'Let's go home, then.'

'You just stay beside me, and we'll be fine.'

Worthington took me seriously and bodyguarded like a profes-sional. We confirmed one of the black-mask merchants for certain simply from his stunned reaction to my being there and on my feet. When he saw me, Norman Osprey stopped dead in the middle of set-ting up his stand, and Rose herself made the mistake of striding up to him at that moment, only to follow his disbelieving gaze and lose a good deal of her self-satisfaction. 'Bloody hell,' she said.

I said to them jointly, 'Tom Pigeon sends his regards.'

Neither of them looked overjoyed. Worthington murmured some-thing to me urgently about it not being advisable to poke a wasps' nest with a stick. He also put distance between himself and Arthur Robins, Est. 1894, and I followed.

'They don't know exactly what they're looking for,' I pointed out. 'If they knew, they would have asked for it by name last night.'

'They might have done that anyway if Tom Pigeon hadn't been walking his dogs.' Worthington steered us still farther away from Norman Osprey, looking back all the same to make certain we weren't being followed.

My impression of the events of barely fifteen hours earlier was that damage, as well as information, had been the purpose. But if Tom Pigeon hadn't arrived, and if it had been to save my wrist bones, and if I *could* have answered their questions, then would I?

Sore as I already felt all over, I couldn't imagine any piece of knowledge that Martin might have had that he thought was worth my virtual destruction, and I didn't like the probability that they—the black masks—wrongly believed that I did know what they wanted and that I was being merely stubborn in not telling them.

Martin, old pal, I thought, what the devil have you let me in for?

LLOYD BAXTER LUNCHED at Leicester with the Stewards. His self-regarding nature found this admirable invitation merely his due. He told me so when our paths crossed between parade ring and stands.

It was obvious that Baxter wasn't pleased to see me. I was sure he regretted the whole Broadway evening, but he concentrated hard on being civil, and it was churlish of me, I dare say, to suspect that it was because I knew of his epilepsy. Nowhere in print or chat had his condition been disclosed, and he may have been afraid that I would not only broadcast it but snigger.

Worthington melted from my side, and I walked with Baxter while he oozed compliments about the Stewards' lunch and discussed the worth of many trainers, excluding poor old Priam Jones.

I said, 'It wasn't his fault that Tallahassee fell at Cheltenham.'

I got an acid reply. 'He should have schooled him better.'

'Well,' I reasoned, 'that horse had proved he could jump. He'd already won several races.'

'I want a different trainer.' Lloyd Baxter spoke with obstinacy—a matter of instinct, I saw.

Along with lunch the Stewards had given Tallahassee's owner an entry ticket to their guests' viewing balcony. At the entrance, Lloyd Baxter was already apologising for shedding me, when one of the Stewards, following us, changed our course.

'Aren't you the glass man?' he boomed genially. 'My wife's your greatest fan. That splendid horse you did for her . . . You came to rig its spotlights, didn't you?'

I remembered the horse and the house with enough detail to be invited into the Stewards' guests' viewing balcony, not entirely to Lloyd Baxter's delight.

'This young man's a genius, according to my wife,' the Steward said to Baxter, ushering us in.

Lloyd Baxter's poor opinion of the Steward's wife's judgment was written plain on his heavy features, but perhaps it did eventually influence him because, after the cheering for the next winner had faded, Baxter surprised me by resting his hand lightly on my arm to indicate that I should stay and hear what he felt like telling me. He hesitated still, though, so I gave him every chance.

'I've often wondered,' I said mildly, 'if you saw who came into my showroom on New Year's Eve. I mean, I know you were ill, but before that, when I'd gone out into the street.'

After a long pause he faintly nodded. 'Someone came in. I

remember he asked for you and I said you were out. But I couldn't see him properly. My sight develops zigzags sometimes.'

'You surely have pills.'

'Of course I do!' He was irritated. 'But I'd forgotten to take them because of the terrible day it had been.'

I asked if in spite of the zigzag aura he could describe my unknown visitor.

'No,' he said. 'The next time I was properly awake, I was in hospital.' He paused while I regretted the cut-short sequence, and then with diffidence he added slowly, 'Thank you for your reticence. You could still cause me much embarrassment.'

'There's no point.'

Abruptly he said, 'The man who came was thin and had a white beard and was over fifty.'

The description sounded highly improbable for a thief, and he must have seen my doubt, because he added, to convince me, that the man reminded him chiefly of a university professor. A lecturer.

I asked, 'Did he say anything to you?'

Lloyd Baxter couldn't remember. 'If he spoke at all, I heard him only as a jumble. Quite often things seem wrong to me. They're a sort of warning. Often I can control them a little, or at least prepare, but on that evening it was happening too fast.'

He was being extraordinarily frank and trusting, I thought.

'That man with the whisker job,' I said. 'He must have seen the beginning at least of your . . . er, seizure. So why didn't he help you? Do you think he simply didn't know what to do, so ran away, or was it he who made off with the money in the canvas bag?'

'And the videotape,' Baxter said.

There was an abrupt breath-drawing silence. Then I asked, 'What videotape?'

Lloyd Baxter frowned. 'He asked for it.'

'So you gave it to him?'

'No. Yes. No. I don't know.'

It became clear that, however hard he tried, Lloyd Baxter's memory of that evening was a scrambled egg of order into chaos. It was just unlucky that his fit had struck at the wrong random moment.

When we parted we shook hands for the first time ever. I left him with the Stewards and found Worthington shivering and hungry outside. We smelt out some food and, while he polished off two full plates of steak-and-kidney pie (his and mine), I told him that we were now looking for a thin man, late middle age, white beard, who looked like a college lecturer.

'So how does this sit with you?' I asked. 'Suppose Mr White-Beard gives a tape to Martin, which Martin gives to Eddie Payne, who handed it on to me. Then when Martin died, Mr White-Beard decided to take his videotape back again, so he found out the tape would be with me in Broadway. He took it back, and on impulse he also whisked up the bag of money that I'd stupidly left lying around, and in consequence he cannot tell anyone that he has his tape back.'

'Because he would be confessing he'd stolen the cash?'

'Dead right.'

My bodyguard sighed and scraped his plate clean. 'So what happened next?' he said.

'I can only guess.'

'Go on, then. Guess. Because it wasn't some old guy that gassed us. Young Daniel described the trainers that the gas man wore, and nobody but a teenager would be seen dead in them.'

I disagreed. Eccentric white beards might wear anything. They might also make erotic tapes. They might also tell someone the tape was worth a fortune and that it was in Gerard Logan's hands. A few little lies. Diversionary tactics. Beat up Logan, make him ready to cough up the tape or, failing that, the information on it.

What had Martin been going to give me for safekeeping?

Did I any longer really want to know?

If I didn't know, I couldn't tell. But if they believed I knew and wouldn't tell . . .

Damn it, I thought. Not knowing was worse than knowing. So somehow or other, I decided, it wasn't enough to discover who took it. I had to find out what they expected as well as what they'd actually got.

We walked back to where the serried ranks of bookmakers were shouting their offers for the last race. Rose glared, rigid with hatred that gave my outraged skin goose bumps, but I asked again the question she had already refused to answer.

'Who gave a videotape to Martin Stukely at Cheltenham races?'

She answered this time that she didn't know.

I said, 'Do you mean you didn't see anyone give Martin a parcel or that you saw the transfer but didn't know the person's name?'

'Clever, aren't you,' Rose said sarcastically. 'Take your pick.'

Rose, I thought, wasn't going to be trapped by words. I guessed she had both seen the transfer and knew the transferer. Without much hope of being believed I said, 'I don't know where to look for the tape you want. I don't know who took it, and I don't know why. But I haven't got it.'

Rose curled her lip.

AS WE WALKED AWAY, Worthington sighed deeply with frustration. 'You'd think Norman Osprey would be the heavy in that outfit,' he said. 'He has the voice and the build for it. But did you see him looking at Rose? She's the boss. She calls the tune. My low-life investigator gave me a bell. He finds her very impressive, I'm afraid to say. She hates you. Have you noticed?'

I told him I had indeed noticed. 'But I don't know why.'

'You'd want a psychiatrist to explain it, but I'll tell you what I've learned. You're a man, you're strong, you look OK, you're successful at your job, and you're not afraid of her. I could go on, but that's for starters. Then she has you roughed up, doesn't she, and here you are looking as good as new, even if you aren't feeling it, and sticking the finger up in her face, more or less.'

I listened to Worthington's wisdom, but I said, 'I haven't done her any harm.'

'You threaten her. You're too much for her. So maybe she'll have you killed. Don't ignore what I'm telling you. There are people who really have killed for hate.'

Not to mention murders because of racism or religious prejudice, I thought, but it was hard to imagine it applying to oneself.

I expected that Rose would have told her father that I was at the races, but she hadn't. Worthington and I lay in wait for Eddie Payne outside the changing rooms after the last race. He looked from one to the other of us like a cornered horse. I soothingly said, 'Hi, Eddie. How's things?'

'I don't know anything I haven't told you,' he protested.

I thought if I cast him a few artificial flies, I might startle and hook an unexpected fish. 'Were you with Rose yesterday evening?' I asked the question casually, but he knew instantly what I meant.

'I didn't lay a finger on you,' he said quickly. 'It wasn't me.' He looked from me to Worthington and back again. 'Look,' he said wheedlingly, as if begging for forgiveness, 'they didn't give you a chance. I told Rose it wasn't fair . . .' He wavered to a stop.

With interest I asked, 'Do you mean that you wore a black mask

332

in Broadway yesterday evening?' and almost with incredulity saw in his face an expression of shame.

'Rose said we would just frighten you.' He stared at me with unhappy eyes. 'I tried to stop her, honest. I know it was *awful*. I went to confession first to ask forgiveness.'

'So there was you and Rose.' I said it matter-of-factly, though stunned beneath. 'And Norman Osprey, and who else? One of Norman Osprey's bookmaking clerks, was it?'

'No. Not them.' Horror suddenly closed his mouth. He had already admitted far too much.

I tried another fly. 'Do you know anyone who could lay their hands on anaesthetics?'

A blank.

'Or anyone with a white beard, known to Martin?'

He hesitated over that, but in the end shook his head.

I said, 'Do you yourself know anyone with a white beard who looks like a university lecturer?'

'No.' His reply was positive, his manner shifty.

'Was the brown-paper parcel you gave me at Cheltenham the self-same one that Martin gave you earlier in the day?'

'Yes.' He nodded this time with no need for thought. 'It was the same one. Rose was furious. She said we should have kept it ourselves and then there wouldn't have been all this fuss.'

'Did Rose know what was in it?'

'Only Martin knew for sure. I did more or less ask him. He just laughed and said the future of the world, but it was a joke, of course.'

Martin's joke sounded to me too real to be funny.

Eddie hadn't finished. 'A couple of weeks before Christmas,' he said, still amused, 'Martin and a few of the jockeys were talking about presents for their wives and girlfriends. Martin said that what he was giving Bon-Bon was a gold and glass antique necklace, but he was laughing, and he said he would have to get you to make him a much cheaper and modern copy. He said you had a videotape to tell you how. But he changed his mind because Bon-Bon told him she wanted new fur-lined boots.'

'He talked to you a lot,' I commented. 'More than most.'

Eddie didn't think so. 'He liked to chat with the boys,' he said.

Worthington, driving us home, summed up the day's haul of information. 'I'd say Martin and the white-bearded guy were serious with this tape. And somehow, through her father, Rose may have imagined that that tape showed how to make an antique necklace.'

I said doubtfully, 'It must be more than that.'

'Well, perhaps it says where the necklace can be found.'

'A treasure hunt?' I shook my head. 'There's only one valuable antique gold and glass necklace that I know of, and it's in a museum. It's priceless. About three thousand five hundred years old. It's called the Cretan Sunrise. I did make a copy of it, though, and I once lent it to Martin. I also made a videotape to explain the methods I used. I lent that to Martin too. Heaven knows where it is now.'

'What if there's another tape?' Worthington asked. 'Rose could have muddled them up.'

I thought it just as likely that it was Worthington and I who'd muddled everything up.

We arrived safely at Bon-Bon's house. As we scrunched to a halt on her gravel drive, Marigold came out of the front door to greet us.

'Bon-Bon doesn't need me any more,' she announced dramatically. 'Get out the maps, Worthington. We're going skiing.'

'Er . . . when?' her chauffeur asked, unsurprised.

'Tomorrow morning, of course. Fill up the petrol tanks. We'll call at Paris on the way. I need new clothes.'

Worthington looked more resigned than I felt. He murmured to me that the skiing trip would last less than ten days overall. She would tire of it quickly and come home.

Bon-Bon was taking the news of her mother's departure with well-hidden relief, and asked me with hope whether 'the upsetting videotape business' was now concluded. She wanted calm in her life, but I had no idea if she would get it. I didn't tell her about Rose or the distinct lack of calm that she represented.

I asked Bon-Bon about White Beard. She said she'd never seen or heard of him. When I explained who he was, she telephoned to Priam Jones, who—though his self-esteem was badly hurt by Lloyd Baxter's ditching of him—regretted he couldn't help.

Bon-Bon tried several more trainers, but thin, elderly, white-bearded owners of racehorses seemed not to exist. After she'd tired of it, she persuaded her mother to let Worthington take me where I wanted. I kissed her gratefully and chose to go straight home to my hillside house and flop.

Worthington liked skiing, he said as we drove away. He liked Paris. He liked Marigold. Sorry, he said, about leaving me with Rose. Good luck, he said cheerfully.

'I could throttle you,' I said.

While Worthington happily chuckled at the wheel, I switched on my mobile phone to call Irish at his home to find out how the day had gone in the shop, but, before I could dial, the message service called, and the disembodied voice of young Victor W. V. said in my ear, 'Send your email address to me at vicv@freenet.com.'

Holy hell, I thought, Victor had things to say. Flopping could wait. The only computer I owned that handled email was in the Broadway gallery. Worthington with resignation changed direction, at length stopping by my main glass door and insisting he come in with me, to check the place for black masks and other pests.

The place was empty. No Rose in wait. Worthington shook my hand, told me to look after myself and left lightheartedly.

Almost at once I missed the muscle man, missed him as a safety umbrella and as a source of a realistic view of life.

I roused my sleeping computer into action and sent an email message to Victor, with my address.

I expected to have to wait, but he replied immediately, which meant he had been sitting at his computer. 'Who are you?' he asked.

I typed and sent, 'Martin Stukely's friend.'

He asked, 'Name?' and I told him.

'How did you know Martin?' I asked.

'I've known him for ages, saw him often at the races with my granddad.'

I wrote, 'Why did you send that letter to him? How had you heard of any tape? Please tell me the truth.'

'I heard my aunt telling my mother.'

'How did your aunt know?'

'My aunt knows everything.'

I began to lose faith in his common sense, and I remembered him saying he was playing a game.

'What is your aunt's name?' I expected nothing much, certainly not the breathtaker that came back.

'My aunt's name is Rose. She keeps changing her last name. She's my mother's sister.' There was barely an interval before his next remark. 'I'd better log off now. She's just come!'

'Wait.' Stunned by that revelation, I rapidly typed, 'Do you know of a thin old man with a white beard?'

A long time after I'd settled for no answer, three words appeared.

'Dr Force. Goodbye.'

Chapter Five

To my considerable delight, Catherine Dodd again stood her motor-bike by my kerb and pulled off her helmet before walking across the pavement to the door I held open for her. It seemed natural to us both to kiss hello and for her to stand in front of the soaring flight of wings that I had barely finished lighting.

'It's tremendous.' She meant it. 'It's too good for Broadway.'

'Flattery will get you an awfully long way,' I assured her, and took her into the workshop, where it was warmest.

I showed her the print-out of my email conversation with Victor. When she'd read it she said, 'First of all, remind me, who is Victor?'

'The fifteen-year-old grandson of Eddie Payne, Martin Stukely's racecourse valet. Eddie gave me the videotape that was later stolen from here. Victor sent this letter to Martin.' I gave her the letter to read, which raised her eyebrows in doubt.

'You can't believe a word he says,' she commented.

'Victor said he was playing games,' I acknowledged. 'He's done what everyone does at some point—he's heard one thing and thought it meant another.'

I stopped to make us coffee, then continued. 'Start with a white-bearded man who looks like a university lecturer and might be called Dr Force. Suppose that this Dr Force has somehow got to know Martin. Dr Force has some information he wants to put into safe-keeping, so he takes it to Cheltenham races and gives it to Martin.'

'Crazy.' Catherine sighed. 'Why didn't he put it in a bank?'

'We'll have to ask him.'

'And you are crazy too. How do we find him?'

'It's you,' I pointed out, smiling, 'that is the police officer.'

'Well, I'll try.' She smiled back. 'And what then?'

'Then Dr Force went to the races as planned. He gave his tape to Martin. After Martin crashed, our Dr Force must have gone through a lot of doubt and worry, and I'd guess he stood around near the changing rooms wondering what to do. Then he saw Eddie Payne give the tape in its brown-paper parcel to me, and he knew it was the right tape, as he'd packed it himself.'

'So OK, Dr Force finds out who you are, takes himself here to

Broadway, and when you leave your door unlocked for a spell, he nips in and takes back his own tape.'

'Right.'

'And steals your cash on impulse.'

'Right.'

'So who squirted anaesthetic at the Stukelys and took their TVs, and who ransacked your own house and beat you up last night? And I don't really understand how this boy Victor got involved.'

'I can't answer everything, but think Rose. She is Eddie Payne's daughter and Victor's aunt. She is sharp-featured and sharp-tongued, and I think she's on the edge of criminal. She jumps to conclusions, and she's all the more dangerous for that. I'd guess it was she who stole all the videotapes in Bon-Bon's house and mine because they could possibly have been mixed up with the one I brought from the racecourse. I would think it likely that Rose chatters to her sister, Victor's mother, quite a lot, and I think it's fairly certain that Victor did overhear her when she said she knew of a tape worth a fortune.'

If only Martin had explained what he was doing! There was too much guesswork, and definitely too much Rose.

Sighing, Catherine gave me back Victor's print-out and stood up, saying with apparent reluctance, 'I have to go. I've promised to be with my parents tonight. I was wondering, though, that if you by any chance want to go to your house now, you—um—don't need a licence to ride pillion.'

I strapped on her spare helmet, clasped her close around her waist, and we set off. The bike had guts enough to take us up the hills without stuttering, and she was laughing when she stopped by the weedy entrance to my drive. I thanked her for the ride, and she roared off, still laughing.

There were no thorny briar Roses lying in wait this time. It seemed that the house gave back in peace the years the Logan family had prospered there, father, mother and two sons. I was the only one left, and, with its ten rooms still filled with sharp memories, I'd made no move to find a smaller or more suitable lair. One day, perhaps. Meanwhile the house felt like home in all senses: home to me, the home of all who'd lived there.

I walked deliberately through all the rooms thinking of Catherine, wondering if she would like the place.

The burglars who'd taken all my videotapes hadn't made a lot of mess. There had been television sets with video recorders in three rooms: in the kitchen and in each of the sitting rooms. There wasn't a single tape left anywhere that I could find. Out of my own room I'd lost a rather precious bunch of glass-blowing instruction tapes that I'd been commissioned to make for university courses. They mostly dealt with how to make scientific equipment for laboratories. I couldn't imagine those teaching tapes being the special target of any thief.

With the Rose-induced bruises growing gradually less sore, I slept safely behind bolted doors, and in the morning I walked downhill to Logan Glass, getting there before Irish, Hickory and Pamela Jane.

I made a fleet of little ornamental sailing ships and straightened out the worst of Hickory's growing hubris by giving him a sailing boat as an exercise, which resulted in a heap of sad lumps of stunted mast and mainsail that no breeze would ever fill.

Hickory's good looks and air of virility would always secure him jobs he couldn't do. In the first week of his company I'd learned more of his limitations than his skills, but every customer liked him, and he was a great salesman.

As Hickory's third try bit the dust amid commiserating murmurs from the rest of us, the telephone rang. It was Catherine.

'I've been a police officer all morning,' she said, 'and I've collected some news for you. I'll be along when I go off duty, at six o'clock.'

To fill in time, I emailed Victor, expecting to have to wait for a reply, as he should have been at school but, as before, he was ready.

He typed, 'Things have changed.'

'Tell me.'

There was a long gap of several minutes. Then, 'My dad's in jail. I hate her.'

I asked flatly, 'Who?'

'Auntie Rose, of course. She sneaked on Dad.' I waited. 'He hit Mum. Broke her nose and some ribs. He got sent down for a year. Will you go on talking to me?'

'Yes,' I sent back. 'Of course.'

After an even longer pause, he sent, 'Email me tomorrow.'

I replied fast, while he might still be online, 'Tell me about Dr Force.'

Either he'd disconnected or didn't want to reply. His silence lasted all day.

By six I'd managed to send my assistants all home, and by 6.23 Detective Constable Dodd was reading Victor Waltman Verity's troubles. 'Poor boy,' she said.

I said ruefully, 'As he hates his Aunt Rose for grassing on his pa, he might not tell me anything else himself. Sneaking appears to be a mortal sin in his book.'

'Mm.' She read the printed pages again, then cheerfully said, 'Well, whether or not you have Victor's help, your Dr Force is definitely on the map.' It pleased her to have found him. 'He's not a university lecturer, or not primarily, anyway. He is, believe it or not, a medical doctor. Licensed and all that.' She handed me an envelope with a grin. 'He was working in some research lab or other until recently. It's all in this envelope.'

'And is he fiftyish with a white beard?'

She laughed. 'His date of birth will be in the envelope. A white beard's expecting too much.'

Both of us at that point found that there were more absorbing facets to life than chasing obscure medics. I suggested food from the takeaway; she offered a pillion ride up the hill. We saw to both. I'd left the central heating on for comfort. Catherine wandered all over the house, smiling.

I still held the envelope of Dr Force's details, and I opened it then with hope, but it told me very few useful facts. His name was Adam Force, age fifty-six, and his qualifications came by the dozen.

I said blankly, 'Is that all?'

'That's all when it comes to facts. As to hearsay—well, according to a bunch of rumours, he's a brilliant researcher.'

I asked, 'Does Dr Force have an address?'

'Not in these notes,' she answered. 'In the *Who's Who* we used, it gives only the information provided by the people themselves. Tomorrow we'll catch him on the Internet.'

We ate the takeaway food, or a little of it, owing to a change of appetite, and I switched up the heating a little in my bedroom without any need for explanation.

She'd shed somewhere in her life whatever she had ever suffered in the way of shyness. The Catherine who came into my bed came with confidence along with modesty, an intoxicating combination. We both knew enough, anyway, to give to each other as much pleasure as we received, or at least enough to feel slumberous and fulfilled.

The speed of development of strong feelings for one another seemed to me to be not shocking but natural, and, if I thought about the future, it unequivocally included Catherine Dodd.

She went home before dawn, steady on two wheels. From my

doorway I watched her go into what was left of the night and quite fiercely wanted her to stay with me instead.

I walked restlessly downhill through the slow January dawn, reaching the workshop well before the others. The Internet, though, when I'd accessed it, proved less obliging about Adam Force than it had with Waltman Verity. Adam Force wasn't anywhere in sight.

Hickory arrived at that point, early and eager to take his latest effort at a sailing boat out of the annealing oven. Although he would get the transparent colours clearer with practice, it wasn't a bad effort, and I told him so. He wasn't pleased, however. He wanted unqualified praise. I caught on his face a fleeting expression of contempt for my lack of proper appreciation of his ability. There would be trouble ahead if he tackled really difficult stuff, I thought, but I would give him good references when he looked for a different teacher, as quite soon now he would.

Irish, more humble about his skills, and Pamela Jane, positively self-deprecating, came sweeping in together and gave the sailing boat the extravagant admiration Hickory thought it deserved.

We spent the day replacing the minaret-shaped scent bottles we'd sold at Christmas, working fast at eight pieces an hour, using blue, turquoise, pink, green, white and purple in turn and packing the finished articles in rows in the ovens to cool. Winter in the Cotswold Hills was the time to stock up for the summer tourists.

We worked flat out until six in the evening. Then with all six ovens packed, I sent my semi-exhausted crew home.

Every night that week Detective Constable Dodd slept in my arms in my bed, but she left before the general world awoke, and during that time no one managed to stick an address on Adam Force.

On Friday morning Catherine departed to a school friends' reunion, and at close of day Bon-Bon drove Martin's BMW, bursting at the seams with noisy children, to pick me up for the weekend.

'Actually,' Bon-Bon confessed as we detoured to my hill house for mundane clean shirts and socks, 'Worthington didn't like you being out here alone.'

'*Worthington* didn't?'

'No. He phoned from somewhere south of Paris and told me this place of yours out here is asking for trouble.'

'Worthington exaggerated,' I protested, but after we'd all unloaded at Bon-Bon's house, I used the evening there to invent a game for the children called 'Hunt the orange cylinder and the shoelaces'.

Bon-Bon protested. 'But they told everything they know to the police. They won't find anything useful.'

'And after that game,' I said, gently ignoring her, 'we'll play "Hunt the letters sent to Daddy by somebody called Force", and there are prizes for every treasure found, of course.'

They played until bedtime with enthusiasm, on account of the regular handouts of coins, and I laid out their final offerings all over Martin's desk in the den.

I had watched the children search uninhibitedly in places I might have left untouched, so their haul was in some ways spectacular. Perhaps most perplexing was the original of the letter Victor had sent a copy of to Martin. 'Dear Martin,' it said, and continued word for word as far as the signature, which didn't say Victor Waltman Verity in computer print, but was scrawled in real live handwriting: *Adam Force*.

'The kids found that letter in a secret drawer in Martin's desk,' Bon-Bon said. 'I didn't even know there was one.'

I told her the so-called secret drawer wasn't a secret at all, but was a built-in feature of the modern desk, designed to hold a laptop computer. I found the laptop drawer seething with interest. Apart from Force's letter to Martin, there was a photocopy of Martin's letter to Force, a not much longer affair than the brief reply. It ran:

Dear Adam Force,

I have now had time to consider the matter of your formulae and methods. Please will you go ahead and record these onto the videotape as you suggested and take it to Cheltenham races on New Year's Eve. Give it to me there, whenever you see me, except, obviously, not when I'm on my way out to race.

Yours ever,

Martin Stukely

Alone in the den after Bon-Bon and the children had gone to bed, I stared again not just at the letter but at its implications. Then I sorted through everything in the drawer. There were several old chequebooks with sums written on the stubs but quite often not dates or payees. Martin must have driven his accountant crazy.

Semi-miracles occasionally happen, though, and on one stub, dated November 1999 (no actual day), I came across the name *Force*. On the line below, there was the single word *BELLOWS*, and in the box for the amount being transferred out of the account there were three zeros, *000*, with no whole numbers and no decimal points.

The name Force appeared again on a memo pad. Martin's hand-written scrawl said: *Force, Bristol, Wednesday.*

I went back to the drawer. A loose-leaf notebook, the most methodically kept of Martin's untidy paperwork, listed the amounts he gave to Eddie Payne, his racecourse valet since June.

On the first page Martin had doodled the names of Eddie Payne, Rose Payne, Gina Verity and Victor. In a box in a corner, behind straight heavy bars, he'd written: *Waltman.* There were small sketches of Eddie in his apron, Gina in her curlers, Victor with his computer, and Rose . . . Rose had a halo of spikes.

Martin had known this family, I reflected. When he had received the letter from Victor, he would have known it was a fifteen-year-old's game. Looking back, I could see I hadn't asked the right questions, because I'd been starting from the wrong assumptions.

I lolled in Martin's chair, both mourning him and wishing that he could come back alive if only for five minutes.

My mobile phone, lying on the desk, gave out its brisk summons. Hoping it was Catherine, I switched it on. It wasn't Catherine.

Victor's cracked voice spoke hurriedly.

'Can you come to Taunton on Sunday? Please say you will catch the same train as before. I'm running out of money for this phone. Please say yes.'

I listened to the urgency, to the virtual panic.

I said, 'Yes, OK,' and the line went dead.

Chapter Six

Tom Pigeon strolled to my gallery door late on Saturday morning and invited me out for a beer. With his Dobermans tied to a bench outside the crowded pub, he drank deep on a pint and told me that I had more nerve than sense when it came to the Verity-Paynes.

'It was only a week ago tomorrow,' he said, 'that they hammered you until you could hardly stand.' He urged me to take him on board as bodyguard in Worthington's absence.

I reflected briefly on Tom's offer. His slightly piratical dark little pointed beard and his obvious physical strength turned heads our way. I might be of his age and height, but no one sidled away at my approach or found me an instinctive threat.

I wondered what my dear Constable Dodd would think of my allying myself to an ex-jail occupant with a nickname like the Backlash. I said regardless, 'Yes, if you'll do what I ask.'

'Just as long as it's legal,' he bargained. 'I'm not going back in the slammer.'

'It's legal,' I assured him. And when I caught the train the following morning, I had a new rear defender in the guard's van, accompanied by three of the most dangerous-looking black dogs that ever licked one's fingers.

Tom had wanted to drive. I shook my head. Suppose, I'd suggested, this is not an ambush, but just the frantic need of a worried boy. Give him a chance, I'd said.

We would compromise, though. We would hire a car with driver to follow us from Taunton station, to shadow us faithfully, to pick us up when we wanted and finally drive us to Broadway and home.

Victor himself was waiting on the Taunton platform. I'd travelled near the front of the train so as to be able to spot and to pass any little unwelcoming committee, but the boy seemed to be alone. Also, I thought, anxious. Also cold. Beyond that, an enigma.

Tom's dogs, travelling at the rear of the train, slithered down onto the platform. I reckoned, or anyway hoped, that Victor himself wouldn't know Tom or his dogs by sight, even though Rose and the rest of her family probably would, after their rout in Broadway.

Learning from the plain-clothes police, I wore a pale blue baseball cap at the currently with-it angle above a navy-blue track suit topped with a paler blue sleeveless padded jacket. Normal enough for many, but different from my usual grey trousers and white shirt.

I walked silently in my trainers to Victor's back and said quietly in his ear, 'Hello.'

He whirled round and took in my changed appearance with surprise, but chief of his emotions seemed to be straightforward relief that I was there at all.

'I was afraid you wouldn't come,' he said, shivering. 'Not when I heard them saying how they'd smashed you up proper. I don't know what to do. I want you to tell me what to do. They tell me lies.'

'First of all, we get off this windy platform,' I said. 'Then you tell me where your mother thinks you are.'

In front of the station, the driver I'd engaged was polishing a dark blue estate car. Tom Pigeon made contact with the driver and loaded the Dobermans into the rear.

Victor, not yet realising that the car and dogs had anything to do with him, answered my question and a dozen others. 'Mum thinks I'm at home. She's gone to see my dad in jail. It's visiting day. I listened to her and Auntie Rose planning how they're going to try again, after Mum sees Dad, to make you tell them where the tape is you had from Granddad Payne. They say it's worth millions. Auntie Rose says it's nonsense for you to say you don't know. Please tell her where it is or what's on it, because I can't bear the thought of her *making* you tell her.'

'Where is your Auntie Rose today?' I asked with an inward shudder. 'Did she visit your dad too?'

He shook his head. 'I don't know where she is.' He paused, and then said passionately, 'I wish I belonged to an ordinary family. I wrote to Martin once and begged to stay with him for a while, but he said they didn't have room.' His voice cracked. 'What can I do?'

It seemed clear that Victor's need for someone to advise him stretched very far back.

'Come for a ride?' I suggested with friendliness, and held open the car door behind the driver. 'I'll get you back home before you're missed, and before that we can talk about what you need.'

He hesitated only briefly, then climbed in. He had, after all, brought me there to help him, reaching out to someone he trusted, even though his family considered that person to be an enemy. Victor couldn't invent or act at this level of desperation.

I asked him if he knew where I could find Adam Force. The question caused a much longer hesitation and a shake of the head. He knew, I thought, but perhaps telling me came under the category of squealing.

Tom Pigeon sat beside the driver. Victor and I sat in the rear passenger seats with the dogs behind us, separated from us by a netting divider. The driver set off, heading through winding Somerset country roads towards the wide expanses of Exmoor. Even in the summer, I imagined, it would be a bare and daunting place. After a while the driver, taciturn from first to last, pulled off the road into a picnic area and pointed to a just perceptible path ahead, telling me it led onto moorland.

He would wait for us, he said, and we could take our time. He had brought a packed picnic lunch for all of us, as arranged.

Tom Pigeon's dogs disembarked and bounded free ecstatically, sniffing with unimaginable joy round heather roots in rich dark red earth. Tom himself stretched his arms and chest wide, filling his lungs with deep breaths of clean air, and set off fast along the track.

Under wide-open sky, Victor's face looked almost carefree, almost happy. He and I followed Tom, with Victor pouring out his devastating home life and difficulties, as I guessed he'd never done before.

'Mum's all right,' he said. 'So's Dad really, except when he comes home from the pub. Then if Mum or I get too near him, he belts us one.' He swallowed. 'No, I didn't mean to say that. But last time he broke her ribs and her nose. And when Auntie Rose saw it, she went to the cops, and it was funny, really, because other times I'd seen *her* hit my dad. She's got fists like a boxer when she gets going. She can deal it out until the poor buggers beg her to stop, and that's when she laughs at them. And then sometimes she'll *kiss* them.' He glanced at me anxiously, sideways, to see what I made of his aunt's behaviour.

We walked another length of track while I thought that possibly I'd got off fairly lightly at the hands of the black masks.

The ground widened into a broader flat area from which one could see distant views. Tom Pigeon stood out below us, his Dobermans zigzagging around him with unfettered joy.

After watching them for several moments, I gave life to an ear-splitting whistle, a skill taught me by my father and brother, who had both been able to accomplish the near-impossibility of summoning London taxis in the rain.

Tom turned towards me, waved acknowledgment, and began to return to where I stood. His dogs aimed towards me without a single degree of deviation.

'Wow,' Victor said, impressed. 'How do you do that?'

'Curl your tongue.' I showed him how, and I asked him again to tell me more about Dr Force. I needed to talk to him, I said.

'Who?'

'You know damn well who. Dr Adam Force. The man who wrote the letter you copied and sent to Martin.'

Victor, silenced, took a while to get going again.

In the end he said, 'Martin knew it was a game.'

'Yes, I'm sure he did,' I agreed. 'He knew you well, he knew Adam Force, and Adam Force knows you. You may know their secret, that one that was on the tape everyone's talking about.'

'No,' Victor said, 'I don't.'

'Don't lie,' I told him. 'You don't like liars.'

He said indignantly, 'I'm not lying. Martin knew what was on the tape, and so did Dr Force, of course. When I sent that letter to Martin, I was just pretending to be Dr Force. I often pretend to be other people. It's only a game.'

I asked him how he had obtained a copy of Dr Force's letter, which he had sent to Martin signed in his own name.

He didn't reply, but just shrugged his shoulders.

I asked him yet again if he knew where I could find his Dr Force, but he said dubiously that Martin had for sure written it somewhere.

Probably he had. Victor knew where, but he still wasn't telling that either. There had to be some way of making him want to tell.

Tom Pigeon and his three bouncing companions reached us at the viewing area, all clearly enjoying the day. 'That's some whistle,' Tom commented admiringly, so I did it again at maximum loudness, which stunned the dogs into pointing their muzzles in my direction, their noses twitching, their eyes alert.

Walking back towards the car, Victor did his best at a whistle that would equally affect the dogs, but they remained unimpressed.

Tom, Victor, the driver and I ate sandwiches inside the car, out of the wind, and afterwards sleep came easily to the other three. I left the car and walked back slowly along the track, sorting out Victor's muddling game of pretence. The absolutely first thing to do, I concluded, was to find Adam Force, and the path to him still lay with Victor. What I needed was to get him to trust me.

When there was movement around the car, I returned to tell the yawning passengers that it was time to leave if we were to get back to Lorna Terrace in advance of the time Victor was expecting his mum.

Tom walked off to find comfort behind bushes and jerked his head for me to go with him. Contingency planning was in his mind. The day had gone too smoothly. He wanted me to consider a few 'what ifs' with him. We did this, then returned to the car, where the driver was deep in esoteric chat with Victor about computers.

The contentment of the day on the moor evaporated as the estate car drew nearer to Lorna Terrace. Victor watched me anxiously.

The driver stopped the car where Tom Pigeon asked him, which was around the bend that kept him out of sight of Number 19. Victor and I disembarked, and I sympathised very much with the misery and hopelessness reappearing in the droop of his shoulders.

At the front door of Number 19, Victor produced a key from a pocket and let us in, leading me as before to the bright little kitchen. I had promised to stay as company until his mother came back, even though she might not like it.

The door from the kitchen to the back yard brought Victor to a standstill of puzzlement and unease.

He said, 'I'm sure I bolted the door before I went out.' He shrugged. 'Anyway, I know I bolted that gate from the back yard into the lane. Mum gets furious if I forget it.'

He opened the unbolted kitchen door and stepped out into a small high-walled square of back yard. Across the weeds and dead-looking grass a tall brown-painted gate was set into the high brick wall, and it was this gate that freshly upset Victor by not having its bolts, top and bottom, firmly slid into place.

'Bolt them now,' I said urgently, but Victor stood still in dismay, and, although understanding flashed like lightning through my mind, I couldn't get round Victor fast enough. The gate from the lane opened the moment I stepped towards it.

Rose had come into the back yard from the lane. Gina and the quasi-gorilla Norman Osprey marched out triumphantly from the house behind us. Both Rose and Osprey were armed with a cut-off section of garden hose. Rose's piece had a tap on it.

Victor at my side stood like a rock, not wanting to believe what he was seeing. When he spoke, the words addressed to his mother were a scramble of 'You've come back early.'

Rose prowled like a hunting lioness between me and the gate to the lane, swinging the heavy brass tap on the supple green hose, and almost licking her lips.

Gina, without curlers this time and pretty as a result, tried to justify the prospect ahead by whining to Victor that his caged father had told her to eff off, he wasn't in the mood for her silly chatter.

'And when we'd gone all that way!' Gina said. 'He's a mean brute. So Rose drove me home again. And you met that fellow, that one over there, that Rose says is stealing a million from us. How *can* you, young Vic? So Rose says this time she'll make him tell us what we want to know, but it's no thanks to you, Rose says.'

I heard only some of it. I watched Victor's face and saw with relief his strong alienation from Gina's smug voice. The more she said, the more he didn't like it. Teenage rebellion visibly grew.

The present and future scene unfolding here hadn't been exactly one of the 'what ifs' that Tom and I had imagined in the bushes, but now what if . . . if I could think it out fast enough . . . if I could use Victor's horrified reaction to his mother's outpouring . . . if I could put up with a bit of Rose's persuasion . . . then perhaps Victor would indeed feel like telling me what I was sure he knew. Perhaps the sight of Rose's cruelty in action would impel him to offer a gift in atonement. Maybe the prize was worth a bit of discomfort. So get on with it, I told myself.

Last Sunday, I thought, the black masks had jumped me unawares. It was different this Sunday. I could invite the assault head-on, and I did, at a run towards the gate to the lane, straight towards Rose and her swinging tap.

She was fast and ruthless and managed to connect twice before I caught her right arm and bent it up behind her, her face close to mine, her dry skin and freckles in sharp focus, hate and sudden pain drawing her lips back from her teeth. Gina, yelling blasphemy, tore at my ear to free her sister.

I caught a glimpse of Victor's horror an instant before Norman Osprey lashed out at me from behind with his own length of hose. Rose wrenched herself out of my grip, pushed Gina out of her way, and had another swing at me with her tap. I managed a circular kick-box that temporarily put the gorilla Norman face down on the grass, and in return I got another fearful clout from Rose along the jaw, which ripped open the skin.

Enough, I thought. Too much. Blood dripped everywhere. I used my only real weapon, the piercing whistle, for help, which Tom and I in the bushes had agreed meant 'Come at once'.

What if I whistle and he doesn't come?

I whistled again, louder, longer, calling not for a taxi in the rain, but quite likely for life without deformity. There was a vast crashing noise and Tom's voice roaring at his dogs, and then three snarling Doberman pinschers poured like a torrent out of the house's wide-opening kitchen door into the confined space of the back yard.

Tom carried an iron bar he'd borrowed from local town railings. Osprey backed away, his soft hose useless in opposition, his Sunday pleasure no longer one long laugh.

Rose, the quarry of the dogs, turned tail and ignominiously left the scene through the gate into the lane, pulling it shut behind her.

Gina screeched at Tom only once, his fierce physical closeness reducing her protests to nil. She was silent even when she discovered Tom's mode of entry had been to smash open her front door. She didn't try to stop her son when he ran past her along the passage from back yard to front. He called to me in the few steps before I reached the road.

Tom and the Dobermans were already out on the pavement on their way back to the car.

I stopped at once when Victor called me, and I waited. Either he would tell me or he wouldn't. Either the hose and tap had been worth it, or they hadn't. Pay-off time.

'Gerard . . .' He was out of breath, not from running but from what he'd seen in the yard. 'I can't bear all this. If you want to know, Dr Force lives in Lynton. Valley of the Rocks Road.'

'Thanks,' I said.

Victor unhappily watched me use tissues scrounged from his mother's kitchen to blot the blood on my face. I said, 'There's always email, don't forget.'

'How can you even speak to me?'

I grinned at him. 'I still have all my teeth.'

'Look out for Rose,' he warned anxiously. 'She never gives up.'

'Try to arrange to live with your grandfather,' I suggested. 'It would be safer than here.'

Some of his misery abated. I touched his shoulder in parting and walked along Lorna Terrace to where Tom Pigeon waited.

Tom looked at my battered face. 'You were a long time whistling.'

'Mm.' I smiled. 'Silly of me.'

'You delayed it on purpose!' he exclaimed in revelation. 'You let that harpy hit you.'

'You get what you pay for, on the whole,' I said.

'I SUPPOSE YOU walked into another black-masked door,' guessed Constable Dodd, horrified, although a doctor had stuck together the worst of the cuts with small adhesive strips.

'Rose didn't bother about a mask,' I said, putting together a spicy rice supper on Monday evening in my kitchen. 'Do you like garlic?'

'Not much. What are you planning to do about Rose Payne?'

I didn't answer directly. I said instead, 'Tomorrow I'm going to Lynton in Devon, and I'd rather she didn't know. It's a wise man as knows his enemies,' I asserted, 'and I do know our Rose.'

'But Rose Payne is only one person. There were four black masks.'

I nodded. 'Norman Osprey, bookmaker, he was number two, and Eddie Payne, Rose's father, he was number three and he's sorry for it, and all those three know I recognised them. One other—I think of him as number four—seemed familiar to me at the time, but I can't have been right. He was a clutcher setting me up for the others. He was behind me most of the time.'

Catherine listened in silence and seemed to be waiting.

Skidding now and then across a half-formed recollection went the so far unidentified figure. I remembered him most for the inhumanity he took to his task. It had been Norman Osprey who'd smashed my watch, but it had been Black Mask Four who'd bunched my fingers for him. For all Norman Osprey's awesome strength, in retrospect it was Black Mask Four who'd scared me most, and who now, eight days later, intruded fearsomely in my dreams, nightmares in which he intended to throw me into the liquid glass in the furnace.

That night, while Constable Dodd slept peacefully in my arms, it was she whom Black Mask Four threw to a burning death. I awoke sweating and cursing Rose Payne with words I'd rarely used before, and I felt more reluctant than ever to leave Catherine to the risks of her plain-clothes operation.

'Come back safe yourself this time,' Catherine said worriedly before zooming off in the dawn, and I, with every intention of carrying out her instructions, walked down the hill and did the day's work before my three helpers arrived.

I cheerfully left them practising dishes for the day while I walked out of the village for a mile to catch a bus, following Tom Pigeon's plan for an exit.

I felt, when I disembarked outside a busy newsagents in the next town and climbed into another prearranged car with driver—'Call me Jim'—that there could be no one on my tail.

Thanks to Tom's plan I arrived unmolested in Lynton on the north Devon coast. In the electoral register I found the full address of Dr Adam Force, in the Valley of the Rocks Road.

Disappointingly, there was no one home at the tall grey old building. A neighbour said he thought Dr Force visited patients in the Phoenix House nursing home on Tuesdays.

I thanked the man for his help. And could he describe Dr Force, so I would know him if I saw him?

'Oh yes,' I was told, 'you'd know him easily. He has very blue eyes and a short white beard, and he'll be wearing orange socks.'

I blinked.

'He can't see red or green,' he said. 'He's colour-blind.'

LEAVING MY DRIVER and his grey Rover outside the grounds, I took the quiet back way up a sloping road to the Phoenix House nursing home. The house spread wide in one central block with two long wings. The entrance hall looked like a hotel, but I saw no further into the nursing home's depths because of the two white-coated people leaning on the reception desk. One was female and the other grew a white beard and did indeed wear orange socks.

They glanced briefly my way as I arrived. 'Dr Force?' I tried, and White Beard satisfactorily answered, 'Yes?'

His fifty-six years sat elegantly on his shoulders, and his well-brushed hair, along with the beard, gave the sort of shape to his head that actors got paid for. Patients would trust him, I thought. His manner held authority. I was going to have difficulty jolting him the way I wanted.

Almost at once I saw, too, that the difficulty was not a matter of jolting him but of following the ins and outs of his mind. All through the time I was with him, I felt him swing from apparently genuine friendliness to evasion and stifled ill will. He was quick and he was clever, and, although most of the time I felt a warm liking for him, occasionally there was a quick flash of antipathy.

'Sir,' I said, giving seniority its due, 'I'm here on account of Martin Stukely.'

He put on a sorry-to-tell-you expression and told me that Martin Stukely was dead. At the same time there was a rigidity of shock on his facial muscles. I said I knew Martin Stukely was dead.

He asked with suspicion, 'Are you a journalist?'

'No. A glass-blower.' I added my name. 'Gerard Logan.'

His whole body stiffened. He absorbed the surprise and eventually pleasantly asked, 'What do you want?'

I said equally without threat, 'I'd quite like back the videotape you took from the Logan Glass showroom on New Year's Eve.'

'You would, would you?' He was ready for the question, and had no intention of complying. 'I don't know what you are talking about.'

Dr Force made a slow survey from head to foot of my deliberately conservative suit and tie, wondering if I had enough clout to cause him trouble. Apparently he gave himself an unwelcome answer, as he suggested that we discuss the situation in the open air.

He led the way to a path with close-growing evergreens crowding overhead, making it dark even in daylight.

Should he be aware of small damages to my face and so on, I said, it was as a result of Rose Payne being convinced that I either had his tape or that I knew what was on it. 'She believes that if she's unpleasant enough I'll give her the tape or the knowledge, neither of which I have.' I paused and said, 'What do you suggest?'

He said, 'Give this person anything. All tapes are alike.'

'She thinks your tape is worth a million. Is it?'

Force said what sounded like the truth. 'I don't know.'

'Martin Stukely,' I murmured without hostility, 'wrote a cheque for you with a lot of noughts on it.'

Force, very upset, said sharply, 'He promised never to say—'

'He didn't say. He left cheque stubs.'

I could almost feel him wondering, What else did Martin leave?

'Rose Payne,' I repeated, 'is convinced that I know where your videotape is and what's on it. Unless you find a way of getting her off my back, I may tell her what she's anxious to know.'

'Are you implying that I know this person, Rose, and that I am in some way responsible for your . . . er . . . injuries?'

I said cheerfully, 'Right both times.'

'That's nonsense.' His face was full of calculation, as if he weren't sure how to deal with an awkward situation, but wouldn't rule out using his own name, Force.

'All the same,' I said, 'you did take the tape from my shop, so please can you at least tell me where it is now?'

'Just suppose you are right and I have the tape. Perhaps I ran it through to record a sports programme from first to last. That tape might now show horse racing and nothing else.'

He had written to Martin that the knowledge on the tape was dynamite. No one would casually wipe out the dynamite if not sure he could bring it back. Nobody would do it *on purpose*, that was.

So I asked him, 'Did you obliterate it on purpose or by mistake?'

He laughed inside the beard. He said, 'I don't make mistakes.'

The frisson I felt was the recognition of a thoroughly human failing; for all his pleasant manner, the doctor thought he was God.

He stopped by a fallen fir trunk. 'Our business is completed. I have patients to see.' His voice was dismissive. 'I'm sure you'll find your own way down to the gate.' He started to walk back. To his obvious irritation I went with him.

'There are just a couple of things,' I said. 'How did you get to know Martin Stukely?'

He said calmly, 'That's none of your business.'

I said, 'Martin gave you a large chunk of money in return for the knowledge that you referred to as dynamite.'

'No, you're wrong.' He quickened his step a little. 'I want you to leave.'

'Did you know,' I persisted, 'that Lloyd Baxter, the man you abandoned to his epileptic fit in my showroom, is the owner of Tallahassee, the horse that killed Martin Stukely?'

He walked faster. I stayed close, accelerating. 'Did you know,' I asked, 'that in spite of the onset of an epileptic seizure, Lloyd Baxter was able to describe you down to the socks?'

'Stop it.'

'And of course you know Norman Osprey and Rose and Gina are as violent as they come.'

'No.' His voice was loud, and he coughed.

'And as for my money that you nicked with that tape . . .'

Adam Force quite suddenly stopped walking altogether, and in the stillness I could clearly hear his breath wheezing in his chest. He pulled from a pocket in his white coat the sort of inhaler I'd often seen used for asthma. He took two long puffs, breathing deeply while staring at me with complete dislike.

I was tempted to say 'Sorry', but he'd been the cause of my being subjected to both the black masks in Broadway and to a piece of hose in a Taunton back yard. So I let him wheeze and puff his way back to the reception area, where I checked him into a comfortable chair and went to find someone to pass him on to for safekeeping.

I heard his wheezy voice behind me demanding my return, but by then I'd hurried halfway down one of the wings of the building and seen no human being at all, whether nurse, patient, doctor, cleaner or flower arranger. In all the rooms that lined the corridor, there were beds, tray tables and armchairs, but no people.

There had to be someone somewhere, I thought, and through the closed door at the end of the wing I found a comparative beehive coming and going.

Twenty or more elderly men and women in thick white towelling bathrobes were contentedly taking part in comprehensive physical assessments, each test being brightly presented in play-school lettering, like YOUR BLOOD PRESSURE MEASURED HERE and WHERE DOES YOUR CHOLESTEROL STAND TODAY? An air of optimism prevailed.

My entrance brought to my side a nurse who'd been drawing curtains around a cubicle simply called UROLOGY. She said, 'Oh dear,' when I mentioned that the good Dr Force might be gasping his last. 'He often does have attacks when he has visitors,' the nurse confided. 'When you've gone, I expect he'll lie down and have a sleep.'

The good Dr Force was planning nothing of the sort. Registering annoyance like a steaming boiler, he wheezed to my side and pointed to a door labelled WAY OUT. I explained I'd only come to find help for his asthma, and he replied crossly that he didn't need it. He walked towards me with a syringe that was almost full of liquid. He jabbed the syringe towards me, and this time I thanked him for his attention and left.

In the forecourt outside, I found Jim, my driver, nervously pacing up and down beside his Rover. He held the door open for me, explaining that concern for my welfare had caused him to ignore my instruction to wait for me outside the grounds. I thanked him with true feeling.

I couldn't identify exactly what was wrong with Phoenix House and was little further enlightened when a large coach turned smoothly through the main entrance gate and came to a gentle halt. The name AVON PARADISE TOURS read black and white on lilac along the coach's sides. Below the name was an address in Clifton, Bristol.

I asked Jim to drive around Lynton for a while, because I wanted time to think before we left. I thought about the Adam Force who was colour-blind, asthmatic, volatile and changeable in nature, and who visited an obscure nursing home once a week. A minor practitioner, it seemed, though with a string of qualifications and a reputation for sparkling research. A man wasting his skills. A man who took a visitor outside to talk on a noticeably cold day and gave himself an asthmatic attack.

I thought of inconsequential things like coincidence and endurance and videotapes that were worth a million and could save the world. I also thought of the tape I had made, demonstrating step by step how I had copied a 3,500-year-old necklace worth a million.

Of course only the genuine antiquity in a museum had that value. The copy I'd made of 18-carat gold and coloured glass was in my bank, where I normally kept the instruction tape as well. I'd lent the tape to Martin and didn't care if he'd shown it to anyone else. But I dearly wished he had returned it before it disappeared, along with all the others from his den.

I thought perhaps Jim might not want to double the experience on the following day, but to my surprise he agreed.

'Tom Pigeon'll set his dogs on me if I don't,' he said.

I smiled and told him I prized my bodyguards.

Jim, short and stout, apologised for not being in the same class as Worthington and Tom at kick-boxing. 'But I can bash heads against walls,' he said.

I smiled and said that would do fine.

'So where do we go tomorrow?'

I said, 'How does Bristol grab you? A hospital area, best of all?'

He smiled broadly, transforming his face in one second from dour to delighted. He knew his way around Bristol and its hospitals. No problem. He'd driven an ambulance there one year, he said.

We shook hands on it, and I acquired bodyguard number three.

Chapter Seven

Bristol was wet with drizzle.

Quite reasonably Jim asked where we were going exactly. To find a phone book, I replied, and in the Yellow Pages I singled out Avon Paradise Tours. They advertised adventures throughout Cornwall, Devon and Somerset and all points to London. Jim drove us unerringly to their lilac headquarters.

Once they understood what I was asking, the women in the Avon Paradise Tours office were moderately helpful. On Tuesdays members of a Bristol area Health Clubs Association went on a scenic coach tour to the Phoenix House nursing home in Lynton for medical checkups and advice on healthy living. Dr Force, who ran the clinic, was paid jointly by the health clubs and Avon Paradise Tours. The office staff admitted they'd been told Dr Force had been 'let go' by the research lab he used to work for.

Which research lab? They didn't know. One of them said she'd heard he'd been working on illnesses of the lungs.

Another phone book—listing all things medical—had me trying all the remotely possible establishments, asking them via Paradise Tours' phone if they knew a Dr Force. Dr Force? Unknown, unknown, unknown.

I wondered what to try next.

Illnesses of the lungs.

Cheque stubs. A lot of noughts. The payee, *BELLOWS*. In Martin's handwriting. In capital letters. Lungs were bellows, of course.

There wasn't any listing for Bellows in the Bristol area.

My mind drifted. The Avon Paradise ladies began to fidget.

Bellows. Well, maybe, why not?

Abruptly I asked if I might borrow the office telephone again and spelt out *Bellows* in dial numbers, which resulted in 2355697. After maybe a dozen rings a brisk female voice hurriedly spoke. 'Yes? Who is that?'

'Could I speak to Dr Force, please,' I said.

A long silence ensued. I was about to call it a waste of time when another voice, deep and male, enquired if I were the person asking for Dr Force.

'Yes,' I said. 'Is he there?'

'Sorry. No. He left several weeks ago. May I have your name?'

I was beginning to learn caution. I said I would phone back very soon, and clicked off. To the Paradise ladies' curiosity I offered only profound thanks and left, taking Jim in tow.

'Where to?' he asked.

'A pub for lunch.'

'You're the sort of customer I can drive for all day.'

The pub had a payphone. When we were on the point of leaving, I dialled the number again and found the male voice answering me at once. He said, 'I've been talking to Avon Paradise Tours.'

I said, smiling, 'I thought you might. You probably have this phone booth's number in front of your eyes at the moment. To save time, why don't we meet? You suggest somewhere.'

I repeated to Jim the place suggested. Twenty minutes later he stopped the car in a no-waiting zone near the gate of a public park. Against the united teaching of Worthington, Tom Pigeon and Jim not to go anywhere unknown without one of them close, I got out of the car, waved Jim to drive on, and walked into the park.

The drizzly rain slowly stopped.

The instructions had been 'Turn left, proceed to statue', and by a prancing copper horse I met a tall, sensible-looking man who established to his satisfaction that I was the person he expected.

He spoke as if to himself. 'He's six feet tall, maybe an inch or two more. Brown hair. Dark eyes. Twenty-eight to thirty-four years, I'd say. Personable except for recent injury to right side of jaw.'

He was talking into a small microphone held in the palm of his hand. I let him see that I understood that he was describing me in case I attacked him in any fashion.

'He arrived in a grey Rover.' He repeated Jim's registration number and then described my clothes.

When he stopped, I said, 'He's a glass-blower named Gerard Logan and can be found at Logan Glass, Broadway, Worcestershire. And who are you?'

He was the voice on the telephone. He laughed at my dry tone and gave himself a name, George Lawson-Young, and a title, Professor of Respiratory Medicine. Even with modern technology he didn't know how I'd found him.

'Old-fashioned perseverance and guesswork,' I said. 'I'll tell you later in return for the real story on Adam Force.'

I liked the professor immediately, feeling none of the reservations that had troubled me with Force. My impression of goodwill and solid sense strengthened, so when he asked what my interest in Adam Force was, I told him straightforwardly about Martin's promise to keep safe Dr Force's tape.

'Martin wanted me to keep it for him instead,' I said. 'Force followed me to Broadway and took his tape back again.'

Out on the road, Jim in the grey Rover drove slowly by, his pale face through the window on watch on my behalf.

'I came with a bodyguard,' I said, waving to the road.

Professor Lawson-Young, amused, confessed he had only to yell down his microphone for assistance to arrive at once. He seemed as glad as I was that he would not have to use it. His tight muscles loosened. My own Worthington–Pigeon-driven alertness went to sleep.

The professor said, 'How did you cut your face so deeply?'

I said undramatically that I'd been in a fight, and when he asked what I'd been fighting about and with whom, his voice was full of the authority that he no doubt needed in his work.

'I wanted to find Dr Force, and in the course of doing that I collided with a water tap. It's unimportant. I learned how to find him, and I talked to him yesterday in Lynton.'

'Where in Lynton? In that new nursing home? He does good work there with the elderly, I'm told.'

'They seemed pretty happy, it's true.'

'So what's your takeaway opinion?'

I gave it without much hesitation. 'Force is utterly charming when he wants to be, and he's also a bit of a crook.'

'Only a bit?' The professor sighed. 'Adam Force was in charge here of a project aimed at abolishing snoring by using fine optical fibres and microlasers. But I don't want to bore you.'

My own interest, however, had awoken sharply, as in the past I'd designed and made glass equipment for that sort of enquiry. When I explained my involvement, the professor was astonished.

'We'd been experimenting with shining a microlaser down a fine optical fibre placed in the soft tissues of the throat,' he said. 'The microlaser gently warms the tissues, which stiffens them, and that stops a person from snoring. A reliable remedy would be invaluable for severe sufferers. Adam Force stole our data and sold it to a firm of marketers we had dealt with before. He produced the right paperwork. It was weeks before the theft was discovered, and really no one could believe it when we went to the marketers and they told us they had already bought the material and paid Adam Force for what we were now trying to sell them.'

'So you sacked him,' I commented.

'Well, we should have, but he was crucial to our research programme.' The professor, however, looked regretful, not enraged.

I said, 'Let me guess. You basically let him off. You didn't prosecute him because you all liked him so much.'

Lawson-Young ruefully nodded. 'Adam apologised more or less on his knees and agreed to pay the money back in instalments if we didn't take him to court.'

'And did he?'

'He paid on the dot for two months, and then we found he was trying to sell some even more secret information, and I mean *priceless* information in world terms. We are now certain that he is offering this work to the highest bidder. This is the information recorded on the tape Force took back from you, and it is this tape we have been praying you would find.'

I said with incredulity, 'But you didn't know that I existed.'

'We did know you existed. Our investigators have been very diligent. But we weren't sure you hadn't been indoctrinated by Adam, like your friend Stukely.'

'*Martin?*'

'Oh yes. Force can be utterly charming and persuasive, as you know. We think it likely he also swindled Stukely of a fairly large sum of money, saying it was for research. It is quite likely that Stukely had no idea that the contents of the tape had been stolen. He and Force met at a fundraising dinner for cancer research.'

I vaguely remembered Martin mentioning the dinner, but I hadn't paid much attention. It was typical of him to make friends in unexpected places. I had myself, after all, met him in a jury room.

After a while the professor said, 'We've searched absolutely everywhere for proof that Adam had in his possession material that belongs to the laboratory. We believe that he recorded every relevant detail onto the videotape, because one of our researchers saw him doing it, although of course Adam told him he was making routine notes. Adam himself entrusted a tape into the care of Martin Stukely at Cheltenham races. We learned from asking around that, when Stukely died, his changing-room valet passed the tape on to Stukely's friend, as previously planned.' He paused. 'So as you are the friend, will you tell us where to look for the tape? Better still, bring it to us yourself.'

I said simply, 'I can't. Force has the tape. But yesterday he told me he'd recorded a sports programme on top of your data and all that remained on the tape now was horse racing.'

'Oh God.'

I said, 'I don't know that I believe him.'

After a few moments the professor said, 'How often can you tell if someone's lying?'

'It depends who they are and what they're lying about.'

'Mm,' he said, smiling. 'Discard the lies and what you're left with is probably the truth.'

The professor shivered suddenly in the cold, damp wind, and my own thoughts had begun to congeal. I proposed that we find somewhere warmer if we had more to say, and the professor offered me a visit to his laboratory. His trust, however, didn't reach as far as stepping into my car, so he went in one that arrived smoothly from nowhere, and I followed with Jim.

The research laboratory occupied the ground floor of a fairly grand nineteenth-century town house with a pillared entrance porch. George Lawson-Young, very much the professor on his own turf, introduced me to his team of young research doctors. My ability to identify things like vacutaires, cell separators and tissue culture chambers, and the fact that the words *Logan Glass* were etched on their mini-pipettes, meant that when I asked what exactly had been stolen the second time by Adam Force, the professor finally told me what I'd needed to know all along.

'The videotape made and stolen by Adam Force showed the formation of a particular tissue culture and its ingredients. The tissue culture was of cancer cells of the commoner sorts of cancer, like that of the lung and the breast. Force's team was concerned with the development of genetic mutations that render the cancer cell lines more sensitive to common drugs. All common cancers may be curable once the mutated gene is implanted into people who already have the cancer. The tape probably also shows photographs of the chromatography of the different components of the cancer cells genetic constituents. It is very complicated. At first sight it looks like rubbish, except to the educated eye. It is, unfortunately, quite likely that anyone might override the DON'T RECORD ON TOP OF THIS tab.'

He lost me halfway through the technical details, but I at least understood that the tape that could save the world contained the cure for a host of cancers. I asked the professor, 'Is this for real?'

'It's a significant step forward,' he said.

I pondered. 'But is it worth millions?'

Sombrely, Lawson-Young said, 'We don't know.'

Adam Force had said the same thing. Not a lie, it seemed, but a statement that the process hadn't yet been extensively tested. The tape was a record of a possibility.

I said, 'But you do have back-ups of everything that's on that tape, don't you? Even if the tape itself now shows horse racing?'

Almost as if he were surrendering to an inevitable execution, the professor calmly stated the guillotine news. 'Before he left with the videotape, Adam destroyed all our at-present irreplaceable records. We *need* that tape, and I hope to God you're right that he's lying. It's two years' work. Others are working along these lines, and we would be beaten to the breakthrough.'

Into a short silence the telephone buzzed. George Lawson-Young picked up the receiver, listened, and mutely handed it to me. The caller was Jim in a high state of alarm. He said, 'That medic you saw yesterday, the one with the white beard?'

'Yes?'

'He's here in a car parked fifty yards up the road, and there's a big bruiser sitting next to him. He's got another car waiting but coming the other way. It's a classic squeeze set-up, with you in the middle. So what do you want me to do?'

'Where exactly are you?' I asked.

'Turn left out of the door you went in through. I'm parked four cars in front of White Beard, pointing towards the door. I'm on double yellow lines, and there's a traffic warden creeping about.'

'Stay where you are,' I said. 'Dr Force saw you and your car yesterday. It can't be helped.'

Jim's voice rose. 'White Beard's got out of his car. What shall I do? He's coming this way.'

'Jim,' I said flatly, 'don't panic. Don't look at Dr Force and don't open the window. Keep on talking to me, and if you have anything near you that you can read, read it aloud to me now.'

'Jeez.'

Lawson-Young's eyebrows were up by his hairline.

I said to him, 'Adam Force is in the road outside here, alarming my driver.' And I didn't mention the poisonous-looking syringe the doctor had seen me off with on our last encounter.

Jim's voice wobbled in my ear with the opening paragraphs of the Rover's instruction manual and then rose again an octave as he said, 'He's outside my window; he's rapping on it.'

'Keep on reading,' I told him.

I gave the receiver to the professor and asked him to continue listening, and I hurried out into the street. Adam Force, tapping hard on the window of the grey Rover, was clearly getting agitated at the lack of response from Jim.

I came up quietly behind Dr White Beard and, as I'd done to Victor at Taunton station, said, 'Hello,' at his shoulder.

Adam Force spun around in astonishment.

'Are you looking for me?' I asked.

Inside the car, Jim, in great agitation, was stabbing with his finger towards the lab's front door and the road beyond. Traffic in this secondary road was light, but one of the approaching cars, Jim was indicating to me, was ultra-bad news.

'Adam Force,' I said loudly, 'is too well known in this street.' I grabbed the charming doctor by the wrist, spun him around, and ended with him standing facing the oncoming car with his arm twisted up behind him, held in the strong grip resulting from years of manoeuvring heavy molten glass.

Force yelled, at first with pain and then, also, with bargaining surrender. 'You're hurting me. Don't do it. I'll tell you everything. Don't do it. God . . . Let me go, *please*.'

A small object fell from the hand I'd gripped. It lay in the gutter quite close to a storm-drain grating, and I'd have paid it no attention were it not for Force trying hard to kick it down through the grating into the sewer, to be forever lost.

The advancing car stopped at the sight of Adam Force's predicament, and the four cars behind it exercised their horns, the drivers impatient, not knowing what was going on.

'Everything,' I prompted Force from behind his ear.

'Rose,' he began, and then thought better of it. Rose would frighten anyone.

I jerked his arm fiercely to encourage him, and with some dismay I saw the big bruiser, Norman Osprey, lumbering out of his car. Over my shoulder I could see the second car of the classic squeeze moving towards me. I jerked my captive's arm yet again.

Imploring for release, he half said, half sobbed, desperately, 'I got the cyclopropane gas for Rose. I took it from the clinic's pharmacy. I can't see red from green, but I'm sure of orange. Now let me go.'

His 'everything' only confirmed what had already seemed likely, but I kept the pressure on just long enough for him to shriek out the answer I wanted to the question 'How come you know Rose?'

'Her sister Gina came with her mother-in-law to my clinic. I met Rose at Gina's house.'

Satisfied, I was faced with a fast, unharmed disengagement. The driver of the second car was hurriedly disembarking, and to my horror I saw it was Rose. Uninvolved cars made a constant cacophony.

Norman Osprey, a mountain on the move, charged towards us. Not seeing anything except straight ahead, he bumped violently into a traffic warden who was heading for Jim and his yellow lines infringement.

I shouted at Jim, 'Get the car out of here. I'll phone you.'

Jim suddenly proved his stunt-driving skills weren't a rumour. With not much more than two hand spans' clearance, he locked the wheels of his Rover and circled like a circus horse, bumping over the pavement and brushing me and my captive strongly out of the way with the rear wing. Then he slid round the corner and left the scene.

I let go of Force's wrist while at the same time shoving him heavily into the arms of Osprey.

In that disorganised few seconds I bent down, scooped up the small object Force had dropped, and *ran,* ran as if sprinting off the starting blocks on an athletic track. It was only the unexpectedness of my speed, I thought, that made the difference. I ran, dodging cars and irate drivers, swerving round Rose's grasp like a player evading a tackle in a rugby match.

The front door of the laboratory house swung open ahead of me, with George Lawson-Young beckoning me to safety. I ended breathless and laughing in his hall.

'I can't see what there is to laugh about,' he said, closing the door.

'Life's a tossup.'

'And today it came up heads?'

I *liked* the professor. I held out the small object I'd salvaged from the gutter, a sort of miniature syringe, and asked him with moderate urgency, 'Can you find out what this contains?'

He led the way back to that part of the laboratory that held the gas chromatograph, laid the syringe carefully in a dish, and asked one of his young doctors to identify its contents as soon as possible.

'It's insulin,' the young doctor said confidently ten minutes later. 'Plain ordinary insulin, as used by diabetics.'

'Insulin!' I exclaimed, disappointed. 'Is that all?'

The professor smiled indulgently. 'If you have diabetes, the amount of insulin in that syringe might send you into a permanent coma. If you *don't* have diabetes, there's enough to kill you.'

'To *kill?*'

'Yes, certainly.' Lawson-Young nodded. 'I can hardly believe it of Adam. We knew he'd steal, but to kill . . .' He shook his head.

The professor and I by that time were sitting on swivelling chairs in his office. He looked shattered. 'Do me a favour,' he begged. 'Start from the beginning.'

'I will phone my driver first.'

I used my mobile. When Jim answered his carphone, he sounded, first, relieved that I was free and talking to him and, second, anxious that he was going to be late for his wife's risotto and, third, worried about where he was going to find me safe and on my own. I was glad enough that he proposed to wait for me. The professor, taking my mobile, gave Jim pinpointing instructions for one hour's time, and suggested to me that I waste none of it.

'It's a tale of two tapes,' I tentatively began. 'One was filmed here and stolen by Adam Force. He persuaded Martin Stukely to keep it safe for him so that it couldn't be found.'

'We had obtained a search-and-seizure order from the court and had already started searching everywhere for it,' said Lawson-Young, 'including in Adam's own home, but we didn't ever think of it being in the care of a jockey.'

'That must be why he did it,' I said. 'But as I understand it, Martin thought Force's tape would be safer still with me, a friend who hasn't four inquisitive children.' And no talkative wife, I could have added. 'Martin received the tape from Force at Cheltenham,' I continued, 'and gave it to his valet while he went out to race.'

The professor nodded. 'Eddie the valet was one of the people that our investigators talked to. He said he didn't know anything about any stolen laboratory tape. He said he thought he was handling a tape that you yourself had made, which explained how to copy an ancient and priceless necklace.'

'That's the second tape,' I said. 'It's also missing.'

'Incidentally'—he smiled—'Eddie said he saw your copy of the necklace in the jockeys' changing room. He said it was stunning. Perhaps you will show it to me one day, when all this is over.'

I asked him what he would consider 'over', and his smile disappeared. 'When we find the tape of our work.'

He was aware, I supposed, that it was comparatively easy to make duplicates of videotapes. And that the knowledge recorded on them was like the contents of Pandora's box; once out, it couldn't be put back. The records of the cancer research might already be free in the world and would never again be under the professor's control. For him, perhaps, it was already over.

For me, I thought, it would be over when Rose and Adam Force left me alone. But abruptly, out of nowhere, the spectre of the fourth black mask floated into my consciousness. It wouldn't be over for me until his mask came off.

As casually as I could, I mentioned number four to the professor, fearing he would discount my belief, but instead he took it seriously.

'Add your number four into all equations,' he instructed, 'and what do you get in the way of answers? Do you get a reason for Force to want you dead? Do you get a reason for anyone to attack you? Think about it.'

I thought that that method must be what he used in nearly all research. If I added in an x factor, an unknown, into all I'd seen and heard and hadn't wholly understood, what would I get?

Before I could really learn the technique, one of the young doctors came to say that Adam Force was standing on the pavement opposite with a thin woman with brown hair—my friend Rose. Force would certainly have another man posted at the rear.

The professor said, 'So how do we get Mr Logan out of here?'

The brilliant researchers came up with several solutions. The idea

I followed came from a glowingly pretty female doctor, who gave me directions. 'Go up the stairs to the sixth floor. There's a door to the roof. Slide down the tiles to the parapet and crawl to the right behind it. Keep your head down. There are seven houses joined together. Go along behind their parapets until you come to the fire escape at the end. Go down it. I'll drive out and pick you up to meet your driver.'

I shook hands with George Lawson-Young. He gave me multiple contact numbers and said he would expect me to find the stolen tape. Deduction and intuition would do it.

I said, 'What a hope!'

'Our only hope,' he added soberly.

The author of my escape helped me slide down the gently sloping roof tiles to reach the parapet. To remain invisible, I sweated and trembled along on my stomach within the parapet's scanty cover. It was a long way down to the ground.

The seven houses seemed like fifty. The recent rain had drenched the roof and wet my clothes. But I found my way down, and my pretty saviour drove me, shivering, to my rendezvous with Jim.

I made a detour to talk to Bon-Bon on my way home and found her tears fewer. When I suggested a course of action, she willingly agreed.

By the time Jim decanted me yawning to my house, he and I were both very tired.

Catherine's transport stood on its frame outside the kitchen door. Inside the kitchen, when Jim had driven away, the warm welcoming smell of cooking seemed utterly natural.

'Sorry about this.' Catherine nodded at half-scrambled eggs. 'I didn't know when you'd be back, and I was hungry.'

She gave me a careful look, her eyebrows rising.

'I got a bit wet,' I said.

'Tell me later.' She cooked more eggs while I changed, and we ate in companionable peace.

I made coffee for us both and drank mine looking at her neat face, her blonde curving hair and her close-textured skin, and I wondered without confidence what I looked like to her.

Bit by bit, without exaggeration, I told her about my day.

She listened with horror as we sat together, squashed into one large chair. She felt right in my arms, curling there comfortably.

I told her about the professor and his x-factor method of research. 'So now,' I finished, 'I go over everything that anyone has said and done, add Black Mask Four into the picture, and see what I get.'

I realised with distaste that it meant I had to go back and remember every blow and listen again to every word of Rose's.

She'd shouted, 'Break his wrists . . .'

Catherine stirred in my arms and cuddled closer, and I discarded thoughts of Rose in favour of bed.

Chapter Eight

Catherine went off before dawn to her morning shift, and I walked down to Logan Glass. Although I arrived half an hour before the normal starting time, Hickory was there before me, obstinately trying again to make a perfect sailing boat. He'd put in red and blue streaks up the mast, and the whole thing looked lighter and more fun.

I congratulated him and got a scornful grunt in return, and I thought how quickly his sunny temperament could blow up a thunderstorm. To give Hickory his due, he handled semiliquid glass with a good deal of the panache he would need on the way to general recognition. I privately thought, though, that he would get stuck on 'pretty good' and never reach 'marvellous', and because he understood deep down where his limit lay, and knew I could do better, his present feeling of mild resentment needed patience and friendly laughter on my part if he were either to stay or to leave on good terms.

Irish and Pamela Jane arrived together, as they often did, and this time were arguing about a film they'd seen that had a bad glass-blower in it. They asked Hickory what he thought and embroiled him so intensely in the argument that with a bang his precious new sailing boat cracked apart into five or six pieces. It had been standing free on the marver table, the outer surface cooling more rapidly than the super-hot core. The stresses due to unequal rates of contraction had become too great for the fragile glass. The pieces had blown away from each other and lay on the floor.

All three of my helpers looked horrified. Hickory himself glanced at his watch and said bleakly, 'Three minutes, that's all it took. I was going to put it in the oven. Damn that stupid film.'

'Never mind,' I said, shrugging and looking at the sad bits. 'It happens.' It did happen to everyone. It happened to the best.

We worked conscientiously all morning, making swooping birds for mobiles, which always sold fast. Hickory, who could make neat little birds, recovered his good humour by the time Worthington drew up outside in Marigold's Rolls. Marigold herself, in a dramatic black-and-white-striped caftan, issued from her glossy car with mascara-laden eyelashes batting hugely up and down like a giraffe's. She had come, she announced, to present a proposal.

Worthington looked the more richly suntanned from the skiing trip. He had spent most of the time on the slopes, he said with satisfaction, while Marigold's wardrobe had swelled by three enormous suitcases. And a good time had clearly been had by both.

Marigold paraded up and down the brightly lit gallery as if she'd never been in there before, and halted finally in front of Catherine's wings to tell us all the reason for her visit. She said we were lucky to be in a studio that stood so high already in the world's estimation. She was going to give us all a huge jump forward in reputation because, 'Gerard'—she blew me a kiss—'is going to make a fabulous Marigold Knight Trophy, and I'm going to present it each year to the winner of a steeplechase run at Cheltenham on every New Year's Eve in memory of my son-in-law, Martin Stukely.' She spread her arms wide. 'What do you think of *that?*'

I didn't say, 'Over the top,' but I thought it.

'You see,' Marigold went on triumphantly, 'everyone benefits. People will flock to your door here.'

'I think it's a beautiful idea,' said Pamela Jane. The others, smiling, agreed. Even Worthington raised no security alarms.

Glass trophies were common in racing, and I was pleased to be commissioned to make one. I said, 'I could make a leaping horse with golden streaks. I could make it worthy of Cheltenham.'

Marigold, delighted, said she would consult the Cheltenham Race Trophy Committee immediately. The press should be alerted.

While she filled in the details to my excited team, Worthington drifted me with a gentle tug on the arm into the furnace end of the room and told me with the unhappiest of expressions that the underground fraternity of bookmakers were forecasting my destruction, if not death.

'Rose is still actively prowling round here, looking for vengeance. So you just look out, because I hear that someone in Broadway has binocs on you now, reporting every twitch you make straight back to Rose.'

'Binocs?'

'Binoculars. Race glasses. Seriously, Gerard, it's no joke.'

I promised to be careful.

Marigold had agreed earlier with her daughter to take me back to Bon-Bon's house, so she, Worthington and I made tracks to the Stukely gravel, arriving at the same moment as Priam Jones, who was carefully nursing his disgust towards Lloyd Baxter, who'd ordered his horses to be sent north to a training stable nearer his home.

Bon-Bon came out of the house in a welcoming mood, and I had no trouble, thanks to her manoeuvring it privately on my behalf, in talking to Priam Jones as if our meeting were accidental.

'Bon-Bon invited me to an early supper,' Priam announced with a touch of pomposity.

'How splendid!' I said warmly. 'Me too.'

Priam's face said he didn't care to have me there too, and things weren't improved from his point of view when Bon-Bon swept her mother into the house on a wardrobe expedition, and said over her departing shoulder, 'Gerard, pour Priam a drink, will you? I think there's everything in the cupboard.'

Bon-Bon's grief for Martin had settled in her like an anchor steadying a ship. She was more in charge of the children and had begun to cope more easily with managing her house. I'd asked her whether she could face inviting Priam to dinner, but I hadn't expected the skill with which she'd delivered him to me.

Priam and I made our way to Martin's den, where I acted, as instructed, as host and persuaded Priam with my very best flattery to tell me how his other horses had prospered, as I'd seen one of his winners praised in the newspapers.

Priam, his old boastfulness re-emerging, explained how no one but he could have brought those runners out at the right moment. At my invitation he relaxed on the sofa and sipped Scotch and water.

I sat in Martin's chair and fiddled with small objects on his desk. 'How well,' I asked conversationally, 'do you know Eddie Payne, Martin's old valet?'

Surprised, Priam answered, 'I don't know him intimately, but some days I give him the silks the jockeys will be wearing, so yes, I talk to Eddie then.'

'And Rose? Eddie Payne's daughter. Do you know her?'

'Why ever do you ask?' Priam's voice was mystified, but he hadn't answered the question.

I said with gratitude, 'You were so kind, Priam, on that wretched day of Martin's death, to take back to Broadway that tape I so stupidly left in my raincoat pocket in Martin's car, the one I'd been given in Cheltenham. I haven't thanked you properly again since then.' I paused and then added, as if one thought had nothing to do with the other, 'I've heard a crazy rumour that you swapped two tapes. That you took the one from my pocket and left another.'

'Rubbish!'

'I agree.' I smiled and nodded.

'Well, then'—he sounded relieved—'why mention it?'

'Because, of course, here in Martin's den you found tapes all over the place. Out of curiosity you may have slotted the tape I had left in the car into Martin's VCR and had a look at it, and maybe you found it so boring and unintelligible that you stuck the parcel shut again and took it back to me.'

'You're just guessing,' Priam complained.

'Oh, sure. Do I guess right?'

Priam didn't want to admit to his curiosity. I pointed out that it was to his advantage if it were known for a certainty what tape had vanished from Logan Glass.

He took my word for it and looked smug, but I upset him again profoundly by asking him who that evening, or early next morning, he had assured that the tape he'd delivered to Broadway had nothing to do with an antique necklace, whether worth a million or not.

I said without pressure, 'Was it Rose Payne?'

Priam's face stiffened. It was a question he didn't want to answer.

'If you say who,' I went on in the same undemanding tone, 'we can smother the rumours about you swapping any tapes.'

'There's never any harm in speaking the truth,' Priam protested, but of course he was wrong. The truth could hurt.

'Who?' I repeated.

'When Martin died,' he said, 'I drove his things back here, as you know, and then as my own car was in the dock having the . . . er . . . tyres replaced . . . well, Bon-Bon said I could take Martin's car. I drove it to my home and then back to Broadway, with Baxter's bag and your raincoat, and then I drove myself home again in it. In the morning Eddie Payne phoned.' Priam took a breath but seemed committed to finishing. 'Well, Eddie asked me then if I was sure the tape I'd taken back to your shop was without doubt the one he'd given you at Cheltenham, and I said I was absolutely certain, and as that was that, he rang off.'

Priam's tale had ended. He took a deep swallow of whisky.

It had taken such a lot of angst for Priam to answer a fairly simple question that I dug around in what I'd heard to see if Priam knew consequences that I didn't.

Could he have been Black Mask Four? Unknown factor x?

Eddie Payne had probably told Rose that the tape stolen from Logan Glass at the turnover of the new century had to do with a necklace. Rose had not necessarily believed him. Rose, knowing that such a necklace existed but not realising that the tape, if found, wasn't itself worth much and certainly not a million, may have hungered for it enough to anaesthetise everyone at Bon-Bon's house with cyclopropane and gather up every videotape in sight.

Thoughtfully I asked Priam, as if I'd forgotten I'd asked him before, 'How well do you know Rose Payne?'

'I've seen her around,' he replied.

'How well does she know Adam Force, would you say? Do you think Dr Force would be foolish enough to lend her a cylinder of gas from a nursing home he visits?'

Priam looked as shocked as if I'd run him through with swords, but unfortunately he didn't actually flag-wave any signs of guilt. He didn't feel guilty; almost no one did.

Bon-Bon's 'early supper' proved to be just that, slightly to Priam's disappointment. He preferred grandeur, but everyone sat around the big kitchen table—Marigold, Worthington, the children, Bon-Bon, me and Priam himself. I also acted as waiter, though Daniel, the eleven-year-old, carried empty dishes.

'Gerard,' he said, standing solidly in front of me between courses to gain my attention, 'who's Victor?'

I paid attention very fast. 'He's a boy. Tell me what you've heard.'

'He wants to tell you a secret.'

'When did he say that?'

Daniel said, 'He phoned here. Mummy was out in the garden, so I answered it. He said he was Victor and wanted to talk to you. I told him you were coming for supper, so he said to tell you he would try again if he could.'

I dug in my pocket and found some loose change. I was surprised I had any left after the coins they'd won several days earlier. Daniel whisked it away in a flash.

'That's disgraceful!' Marigold told me severely. 'You're teaching my grandson all sorts of bad habits.'

'It's a game,' I said. Daniel had done a good piece of work.

At seven thirty Marigold floated out to the Rolls and let Worthington drive off to her home. Priam Jones thanked Bon-Bon for her hospitality and bestowed a cool farewell nod to me.

Bon-Bon, going upstairs to read stories to the children, waved me to the den for the evening. Victor kept me waiting a long time. It was after eleven o'clock when the phone rang. The caller spoke with the familiar cracked voice of Taunton.

'Gerard? I'm in a public phone box. Mum thinks I'm in bed. She threw away your mobile number. I can't use the email—Auntie Rose has taken my computer. I'm absolutely sick of things. I want to see you. Tell me where. I'm running out of money.'

He was feeding small coins, I supposed, because he hadn't any others. I said, 'I'll come to Taunton. Same train, on Sunday.'

'No. Tomorrow. *Please,* tomorrow.'

I agreed, and the line went dead.

'YOU'RE RAVING MAD, that's what you are,' Tom Pigeon said at seven in the morning when I phoned him. 'Today's Friday. The boy should be in school.'

'That's probably why he was so insistent. He could skip school without his mother knowing.'

'You're not going,' Tom said positively, and then, a few seconds later, 'We'll get Jim to drive us. He's got an estate car for the dogs. Where are you?'

'At the Stukelys'. Can you pick me up here?'

'Last Sunday, five days ago,' Tom said with mock patience, 'dear Rose tore your face open with the tap end of a garden hose.'

'Mm,' I agreed.

'And the day before yesterday, I hear, you nearly got yourself killed.'

'Well . . .'

'How about staying at home?'

I smiled at the silly idea.

BY FRIDAY JIM'S WIFE had told him he should no longer drive for me. Our lateness on Wednesday had burned her risotto. However, my offer to pay him double was accepted, we shook hands on it, and Jim drove Tom, me and the dogs cheerfully to Taunton.

I'd spent part of the journey adding Victor into every event that Black Mask Four could have attended without disguise, and feeling

I was nowhere near as good as George Lawson-Young at this factor-*x* stuff, I couldn't make *x* fit Victor anywhere.

Jim parked outside the station and I found Victor in the waiting room, looking cold and anxious. 'What's the matter?' I asked.

'Auntie Rose has moved into our house.' He sounded desperate. 'I hate her. And Mum won't speak to me unless I do what Auntie Rose says. Mum's that scared of her. So where can I go? What can I do? I don't know anyone except you to ask, and that's a laugh really, considering your face.'

'Did you try your grandfather?'

Victor said hopelessly, 'He's scared of Auntie Rose too—' He interrupted himself. 'I'm really sorry about your face.'

'Forget it,' I said. 'Concentrate on Adam Force.'

'He's great,' Victor said without fervour, and then, with a frown, added, 'Everyone says so. He sometimes used my computer. That's how I got his letter. He thought he had deleted the file, but I found it in the cache memory.'

It explained a lot.

I asked, 'How long has he known your aunt?'

'About as long as he's known Mum. Months, that is. Mum went on a coach trip to his clinic, and he got hooked on her. He was a real cool guy, I thought. He came round for her when Dad was at work. So when Auntie Rose finds out, she goes round to the hotel where Dad's working and says if he comes home quick he'll catch them at it in Dad's own bed. So Dad goes round and Dr Force has gone by then, but Dad gives Mum a hell of a beating, breaking her nose and her ribs, and Auntie Rose goes round to the nick and tells on Dad. So they put him away for twelve months. Then, last Sunday,' he said miserably, 'Auntie Rose takes Adam Force off Mum, which I reckon she meant to do all along, and now he does what she tells him. It's queer, but I'd say she *hits* him most days, and I've seen them kissing after that.'

He spoke in puzzlement. Victor *couldn't* be Black Mask Four. The fourth attacker was lithe, like Victor. But Victor *couldn't* have bashed me about then and asked me for help now.

But what about Gina? Was she muscular enough? I didn't know for sure, and I decided, reluctantly, I would have to find out.

With a mental sigh I took Victor out of the station, and to his obvious pleasure reunited him with Tom and his three black canine companions. Victor played with the dogs, plainly in their good graces.

I said after a while, 'I'll go round to Victor's house, and if his mother's in I'll ask her if he can spend the weekend with us.'

Tom protested, 'I'll go.'

'We'll both go,' I said. We left Victor with Jim and, taking the dogs with us, knocked on the roughly repaired door of 19 Lorna Terrace.

Gina Verity came to our summons and failed to close her mended door against us fast enough. Tom's heavy shoe was quicker. In the five days since the previous Sunday, Gina had lost her looks and her confidence. She said helplessly, 'You'd better come in.'

Tom and the dogs stood on guard outside the house, because Gina didn't know when either her sister or Adam Force would return.

'I would like to invite Victor to stay for the weekend,' I said.

Gina lit cigarette from cigarette. 'All right,' she agreed in a dull sort of way. 'Pick him up from school. Better not let Rose find out. She wouldn't let him go with you.'

I stretched forward and lifted first her right hand and then her left, putting them down again gently. The muscles were flabby, with no tone. Too apathetic to complain, she merely said, 'What?'

I didn't reply. Black Mask Four, actively punching with strongly muscled arms, had not been Gina. The certainty was unarguable.

Time to go.

WHEN VICTOR AND I disembarked at Bon-Bon's house, she came out to meet us, with Daniel by her side. She, like me and also Tom, watched with fascination the flash of understanding between Victor, fifteen, and the four-years-younger Daniel. Those two discovered immediately that they spoke computer language with a depth that none of the rest of us could reach.

Bon-Bon, amused, said she would keep Victor for the night. Jim drove Tom, the dogs and myself back to Tom's house first, and then on to mine.

Catherine's motorcycle graced its customary spot outside the kitchen door, and she came out when she heard Jim's car arrive. There was no difficulty in interpreting her reaction to my return, and Jim drove away with a vast smile (and double cash), promising his service again 'day or night'.

Coming home to Catherine had become an event to look forward to. I'd never asked her to take me to see her own living space, and when I did that evening, she laughed and said, 'I'll take you there tomorrow. It's better by daylight.'

She asked me how my day had been, and I asked about hers. It was all very *married*, I thought, and we'd known each other for barely three weeks.

'Tell me about the police,' I said as we squashed companionably into one of the oversize chairs.

'What about them?'

'The priorities. For instance, on that New Year's Day, you in your plain clothes and the hobo lying on the doorstep, you were both there to frighten thieves off, weren't you, not to arrest them?'

She shifted in my arms. 'Not really,' she replied. 'We like to get our man.'

I knew better than to tease her. 'Tell me about your partner, the hobo.'

'He's not really a hobo,' she replied, smiling. 'His name is Paul Cratchet. Paul's a good detective. He's a big guy but misleadingly gentle. Many a villain has been surprised by his hand on their collar. He's known as Pernickety Paul at the station because he is so fussy over his reports.'

I enquired plainly, 'What events get most police attention?'

'Accidental deaths, and murder, of course. Any physical assault.'

'What about theft? Who would I go to if I found some stolen property?' I asked mildly.

'Are you talking about those old videotapes again?'

'Yup. Those old tapes.'

'Well, I did enquire about this. The tapes themselves are worth practically nothing. The information recorded on them is called intellectual property. It has very little priority in police thinking. How to make a copy of an antique necklace? You must be joking! Industrial secrets, even medical secrets? Too bad. No one is going to waste much police time looking for them.' She stopped as an entirely opposite thought struck her, then said, 'Does this dreadful Rose still believe you know where to find the tapes?'

'Don't worry about it.'

'But does she?' Catherine was insistent. 'Does she, Gerard?'

I told her, smiling, 'I now think she's had the necklace tape almost from the beginning and, if she has, she knows I haven't got it.' And Rose knows, I thought, that I could reproduce it any day.

'But the other one? The one stolen from the lab?'

'Yes.' I felt light-hearted. 'I could make a guess. Let's go to bed.'

I awoke first in the morning and lay for a while watching Catherine's calm, gentle breathing. At that moment it filled me with contentment, but would I feel the same in ten years? And would she? When she stirred and opened her eyes and smiled, ten years didn't matter. One lived *now*, and now went along as a constant companion, present and changing minute by minute. It was *now*, always, that mattered.

'What are you thinking about?' she asked.

'Same as you, I dare say.'

She smiled again and asked simply if I had plans for us on her free Saturday. Relaxed, I suggested a day at Logan Glass, and I accepted a pillion ride to get there.

I stripped down to a working singlet and helped Hickory, bringing a gather out of the tank when he needed it and holding the hot glass ready for his use. Hickory typically kept a running commentary for Catherine's sake, and flirted with her mildly. Seldom had I enjoyed a more frivolous start to the morning.

At a few minutes past noon the shop embraced first Bon-Bon and the two boys, Daniel and Victor, for whom glass-blowing had temporarily become a greater draw than email. Not long after them Marigold swooped in, batting the eyelashes, grinning at Hickory, smothering Daniel in a bright pink gold-smocked cloudlike dress, and telling Bon-Bon at the top of her voice that the Cheltenham Race Trophy Committee had decided unanimously to ask Gerard Logan to design and make a Martin Stukely memorial. A horse with golden streaks, rearing on a crystal ball, like the one in his book.

The book she was referring to was a record of the work I'd done over maybe twelve years, in the form of a series of glossy coloured eight-by-ten photographs.

'Can you make it today, darling Gerard?' Marigold enthused.

I had telephoned a jeweller, who had promised enough gold. But I needed time for thinking if it were to be a good job, and a good job was what I needed to do for Bon-Bon, for Marigold, for Cheltenham racecourse, and for Martin himself.

'I'll do them tomorrow,' I said. 'The crystal ball and the rearing horse. I'll do them on my own, alone except for one assistant. They will be ready on Monday for the gold to be added, and on Tuesday afternoon I'll join them together onto a plinth. By Wednesday the trophy will be finished.'

'Not until then?' Marigold protested.

'I want to get it right for you,' I said.

And also I wanted to give my enemies time.

Chapter Nine

Bon-Bon and Marigold left the boys in my care while they browsed the antiques shops.

In the workshop, Victor, utterly impressed, watched Hickory show off with two gathers of red-hot glass that he rolled competently in white powder and then coloured powder and tweaked into a small wavy-edged one-flower vase. Pamela Jane expertly assisted in snapping the vase off the punty iron, and Hickory lifted it into an annealing oven as if it were the Holy Grail.

Daniel, for whom the workshop was a familiar stamping ground, wanted me to go outside with him, and, seeing the stretched size of his eyes, I went casually but at once.

'What is it?' I asked.

'There's a shoe shop down the road,' he said.

'Yes, I know.'

'Come and look.'

He set off, and I followed. The shoe shop duly appeared on our left, and Daniel came to an abrupt halt by its window.

'See those trainers? Those at the back with green and white striped laces? The man with that gas, those are his laces.'

I stared disbelievingly at the shoes. They were large, with thick rubberlike soles, triangular white-flashed canvas sections, and threaded with fat bunched laces.

He said again, 'The man who gassed us wore those shoes.'

Away up the hill, Bon-Bon was beckoning Daniel to her car, to go home. Only the fact that she had already loaded Victor, having offered him another night's computer hacking, persuaded her son to join her. Presently, when Bon-Bon and Marigold had gone their separate ways, my little team began setting things straight, as it was now late Saturday afternoon, then departed with my blessing, leaving myself and Catherine to lock up.

I asked her whether, even though they would not be on duty the next day, she could persuade her hobo partner, Pernickety Paul, to walk up and down Broadway with her a couple of times. She naturally asked why.

'To mind my back,' I joked, and she said she thought he might come if she asked. I explained, before I kissed her, that she and the hobo might find handcuffs a good idea on the morrow.

'He always carries them,' Catherine said.

In the morning she said, 'All this walking up and down Broadway—is it because of the tapes?'

'Sort of.' I didn't mention life or death. One couldn't somehow.

All the same, I woke Tom Pigeon, who woke his dogs, who all growled (Tom included) that Sunday was a day of rest.

I phoned Jim. At my service all day, he said. His wife was going to church.

Worthington was already awake, he said, and had I noticed that Sundays weren't always healthy for Gerard Logan?

'Mm. What's Marigold doing today?'

'I've got the day free, if that's what you're asking. But why?'

I hesitated but replied, 'On account of fear.'

'Whose fear?'

'Mine.'

'Oh. You'll be alone in that workshop of yours, is that it? In that case, I'll be with you soon.'

'I won't exactly be alone. Catherine and her partner officer will be in the town, and Pamela Jane will be assisting me in the workshop.'

'Why not that bright young man, what's his name, Hickory?'

'Pamela Jane doesn't argue.'

Worthington's deep voice arrived as a chuckle. 'I'm on my way.'

I made one more call, this time to the home of Professor George Lawson-Young, apologising for the eight thirty wake-up.

'The hour doesn't matter,' he yawned, 'if you have good news.'

'It depends,' I said, and told him what he might expect.

'Well done,' he said.

'More to do.'

'I wouldn't miss it.' His smile came across the air. 'See you later.'

Catherine and her motorcycle took me to Logan Glass, where I arrived intentionally before Pamela Jane. I read the notes I'd made last time I'd tried my hand at a rearing horse. This one would take me about an hour to complete, if I made the whole trophy, including plinth and ball. At a little more than eighteen inches high, it would weigh a good deal, even without the added gold.

I had filled the tank with clear crystal and put ready at hand the punty irons I'd need, also the small tools for shaping muscles, legs and head. Tweezers too, essential always. I set the furnace to the necessary 1,800 degrees Fahrenheit.

While I waited for Pamela Jane to arrive, I thought about the wandering videotape that had raised so many savage feelings, and like curtains parting, the deductive faculty of Professor Lawson-Young continued to open vistas in my mind. I had at last added in his factor x, and the mask had dropped from Black Mask Four.

I reckoned that Rose and Adam Force should, if they had any sense at all, just leave the videotapes where they rested and save themselves the grief of prosecution. But thieves never had any sense.

I'd surrounded myself with as many bodyguards as I could muster that Sunday simply because neither Rose nor Adam Force had shown any sense of restraint so far, and because the making of the trophy horse left me wide open to any mayhem they might invent. I could have filled the workroom with a crowd of onlookers and been safe—safe for how long?

I knew now where the danger lay. However rash it might seem, I saw a confrontation as the quickest path to resolution.

If I were disastrously wrong, Professor Lawson-Young could say goodbye to his millions. The cancer breakthrough that would save the world would be published under someone else's name.

WHEN MY ENEMIES came, it wasn't just time, I found, that I had given them, as much as an opportunity to out-think me.

I was looking at the furnace and listening to its heart of flame when sounds behind me announced the arrival of Pamela Jane. She had entered through the side door, though usually she came in through the front.

'Mr Logan . . .' Her voice quavered high with fright and besides, she usually called me Gerard.

I turned at once to see how bad things were and found that in many unforeseen ways they were extremely bad indeed.

Pamela Jane, dressed for work in her usual white overalls, was coming to a standstill in the centre of the workshop. Her wrists were fastened in front of her by sticky brown packing tape. The charming Adam Force held a full syringe in one hand and with the other had dragged down a clutch of female overalls to reveal a patch of bare skin below the needle. Frightened, she began to cry.

A step behind Pamela Jane came Rose, her face a sneer. Strong, determined and full of spite, she held in a pincer grip the upper arm of Hickory. My bright assistant stood helplessly swaying, his eyes and mouth stuck out of action by strips of brown packing tape. The same tape had been used to bind his hands behind his back and to form a makeshift hobble between his ankles.

Roughly steadying Hickory's balance loomed Norman Osprey. Just inside the side door, keeping guard and shifting uncomfortably from foot to foot, was, of all people, Eddie Payne. He wouldn't meet my eyes. He took instructions steadfastly from Rose.

The actions of all four intruders had been whirlwind fast, and I had arranged little in any way of retaliation. All the bodyguards were simply to roam the street outside. Catherine and her hobo were to patrol their normal disjointed beat. Rose and her cohorts had somehow slid past them.

I was wearing, as usual, a white singlet that left my arms, neck and shoulders bare. The heat from the furnace roared almost unbearably beyond the trap door, if one weren't used to it. I put my foot and my weight sideways on the treadle, which duly opened the trap and let a huge gust of Sahara heat blow out over Norman Osprey's wool suit and reddening face. Furious, he made a snatch towards me, hurling me onto the trap door itself, but I sidestepped and tripped him, and unbalanced him onto his knees.

Rose yelled to Norman, 'Stop it. We don't want him damaged this time. You know bloody well we'll get nowhere if he can't talk.'

I watched as Rose tugged Hickory across to a chair. 'Now you sit there, buddy boy, and it will teach you not to put your nose in where it isn't wanted.' My blindfolded assistant tried hard to talk but produced only a throttled tenor protest.

'Now you,' Rose told me, 'will hand over everything I want. Or your friend here will get holes burned in him.'

Pamela Jane cried out, 'No, you can't!'

'Shut up, you silly bitch,' Rose acidly told her, 'or I'll spoil your silly looks instead.'

Rose stood on the treadle that raised the flap of the furnace, and Hickory shrank even deeper into his chair.

As if she could read his mind, she said in the same sharp tone, 'You, Hickory. You'd better pray that this boss of yours won't let you burn. I'm not fooling. This time he's going to give me what I want.'

She picked up one of the long punty irons and pushed it into the tank of molten glass. Somewhere, sometime, she had watched a glass-blower collect a gather from a tank. She withdrew the iron with a small blob of red-hot glass on the end of it and revolved the rod so that the glass didn't fall off.

Pamela Jane moaned at the sight, and all but fell onto the doctor's needle. I also heard the heavy wheeze of Adam Force's asthma.

'Gerard Logan,' Rose said to me with emphasis. 'This time you will do what I tell you. Now, at once.'

I'd seen Martin summon his mental vigour when going out to race on a difficult horse, and I'd seen actors breathe deeply in the wings when the play ahead dug deep into the psyche. I understood a good deal about courage in others and about the deficiencies in myself, but on that Sunday it was Rose's own mushrooming determination that pumped up in me the inner resources I needed.

I watched as she plunged the cooling small ball of glass into the tank and drew it out again, larger. She swung the iron around until the molten red-hot lump advanced to a too-close spot under Hickory's chin. He could feel the heat. He shrank frantically away and tried to scream behind the adhering tape.

'Look out!' I shouted automatically.

As if surprised, Rose swung the iron away from Hickory's face until he wasn't for the minute threatened.

'You see!' She sounded victorious. 'If you don't like him burned, you'll tell me where you've hidden the videotape I want.'

I said urgently, 'You'll disfigure Hickory if you're not careful. Glass burns are terrible. You can get a hand burned so badly that it needs amputating. An arm, a foot . . . You can smell flesh burning. You can lose your mouth, your nose.'

'Shut up,' Rose yelled at the top of her voice. 'Shut up!'

'You can burn out an eye,' I said. 'You can cauterise your guts.'

Pamela Jane, who lived with the danger, was affected least of all in spite of her fluttery manner, and it was big Norman Osprey who looked ready to vomit.

Rose looked at her red-hot iron. She glanced at Hickory and she looked at me. 'You came here this morning to make a trophy horse of glass and gold. I want the gold.'

Wow! I thought. Gold for the trophy hadn't been mentioned in Rose's hearing as far as I knew. I had ordered enough for the trophy and a little over for stock, but a quantity worth holding up the stage-coach for, it was not. Someone had misled Rose, or she had misunderstood, and her imagination had done the rest. Rose was still sure that one way or another I could make her rich.

Adam Force, his finger on the plunger of the syringe, applauded Rose with a smile.

If I could use this opportunity . . . I did need time now, and if I made the trophy horse, I could slow things nicely.

I said, 'The gold isn't here yet. I'm fed up with the delay.' The carefree but complaining tone I used nonplussed Rose into lowering the tip of the punty iron.

'If I don't get the trophy glass horse ready on time—' I stopped abruptly, as if I'd teetered on the brink of a monster mistake. 'Never mind,' I said as if nervously, and Rose demanded I finish the sentence. 'Well,' I said. 'Gold. I have to use it on the horse.'

Pamela Jane, to her eternal credit, dried her tears in mid-sniffle and in horrified disgust told me frankly across the workroom that I should be thinking of freeing Hickory, not making a trophy for Cheltenham races. 'How can you?' she exclaimed. 'It's despicable.'

'A car from the jewellers is bringing the gold,' I said.

Rose wavered and then demanded, 'When?'

I said I wouldn't tell her.

'Yes, you will,' she said, and advanced the hot iron in menace.

'Eleven o'clock,' I said hastily. A good lie. 'Let me make the horse,' I suggested, and I made it sound on the verge of pleading. 'Then I'll tell you where I think the tape might be, and then you must promise to set Hickory free as soon as you have the gold.'

Pamela Jane said helplessly, 'I don't believe this.'

She couldn't understand how easily I had crumbled. She couldn't see that her scorn was the measure of my success.

Rose looked at her watch, discovered she would have to wait an hour for the gold to arrive, and did the unwise calculation that she could afford to wait for it. 'Get on and make the trophy,' she instructed. 'When the gold comes, you'll sign for it in the normal way, or your Hickory's for the slow burn.'

She told Pamela Jane to sit in the soft chair. There, while Adam Force held his threatening needle at her neck, Norman Osprey taped her ankles together.

Pamela Jane glared at me and said she wouldn't be assisting me with the horse or ever again.

Rose consolidated this decision by telling her I'd always been a coward. I looked expressionlessly at Pamela Jane and saw the shade of doubt creep in, even as Rose poured on the disdain.

I hadn't meant to shape the trophy horse under the threat of

Rose's hand on the punty iron. I had in fact mobilised the bodyguards to prevent it, and they hadn't. Still, a confrontation with Rose
had been inevitable, and if it were to be *now*, then I'd need to think
a bit faster. I stood flat-footed, without drive.

Rose taunted, 'I thought you were supposed to be good at glass.'

'Too many people,' I complained.

She peremptorily ordered Norman Osprey and Eddie Payne to go
round the half-wall into the showroom, and with more politeness
shifted Adam Force round after them. All three leaned on the half-
wall, watching. Rose thrust another punty iron into the crucible—the
tank—holding now white-hot glass, and drew it out, a reasonably
sized gather.

'Go on,' she said. She hovered over Hickory's and Pamela Jane's
heads and threatened to melt off their ears if I gave her the slightest
cause. I was to tell her all the time what I proposed to do next. There
were to be no sudden moves on my part.

I informed Rose I would need to take four or five gathers from the
tank, and while she had her own lump of destruction close to
Pamela Jane's ear, I harvested enough glass to make a horse standing on his hind legs a foot high.

I told Rose that it was almost if not totally impossible to make a
horse of that size without an assistant, partly because the body of
the horse had to be kept at working heat after one had sculpted the
muscles of the neck and the upper legs, while one added pieces of
glass for each lower leg and foot, and others for the tail.

'Get on with it and don't whinge.' She was smiling to herself.

People in circuses could keep a dozen plates spinning in the air by
twiddling sticks under them. Making that rearing horse felt much
the same—keep the body and legs hot while you sculpted the head.
The result wouldn't have won in a preschool contest.

Rose was enjoying herself. The less I blocked and opposed her, the
more certain she grew that I was on the way to capitulation. Abruptly
I understood that victory to Rose was never complete without the
physical humiliation of a male adversary. Victory over Gerard Logan
wouldn't be sufficient for her unless it included her inflicting some
depth of burn.

I might shudder at such a prospect, but Rose wouldn't. I might use
plain muscle power in an all-out attempt to defeat her, but I
wouldn't try to wreak havoc of molten glass on Rose. Nor on anybody. I lacked the brutality.

Neither, though, could I desert my team and run.

With tweezers I pulled the horse's front legs up and its rear legs down and held the whole body on an iron within the furnace to keep it hot enough to mould.

There were still things I could do, I thought. Honourable exits. Exits that were more or less honourable, anyway.

I managed to juggle body and leg pieces into a headless racer. Exits, hell, I thought. Defeatism never got anyone anywhere.

I held two punty irons with difficulty and transferred enough glass from one to the other to attach and shape a mane, but it hadn't the elegance necessary for Cheltenham.

Worthington opened the gallery door and began to come in from the street. His eyes widened as fast as his comprehension as he spun a fast 180-degree turn and was on his way down the hill before Rose could decide which had priority—chasing Worthington or keeping me penned.

She stopped smiling, loaded her punty iron with a white-hot end of glass the size of a golf ball, and held it close to Hickory.

I did my best to make and fix a tail to my non-thoroughbred creation. The tail and two hind legs formed a triangle to support the rearing horse. It all balanced to perfection, but the finished object had no grace whatever. I stood it upright on the marver table.

In spite of the faults, Rose seemed impressed. Not impressed enough, however, to lower her guard or her punty iron beside Hickory's head. I glanced at the workshop clock. A minute—*tick tock, tick tock*—was a very long time.

I said, 'The gold will cover the hooves, mane and tail.'

Tick tock, tick tock.

Rose held a new white-hot gather near Hickory's head. 'How long,' she demanded, 'until that gold gets here?'

Two minutes. *Tick tock.*

'The gold,' I said, 'will come in small bars. It has to be melted.'

Hickory threw himself forward, trying to get out of his chair. Rose didn't move her punty iron fast enough to avoid him, and one of his ears did touch her waving white-hot blob of glass.

Under the parcel tape he couldn't scream. His body arched. Rose jumped back, but Hickory's ear sizzled and smelt of fried meat.

Three minutes. Eternity. *Tick tock.*

Hickory's horror, plain and agonising, had everyone staring. Rose should have gone to his help, but she didn't.

Three minutes, ten seconds since I stood the rearing horse on the marver table. Dangerous to wait any longer.

I picked up the big tweezers I'd used to form the horse's mane, and with them tore the parcel tape securing Pamela Jane's ankles. I pulled her up by her still tied wrists. I said to her urgently, '*Run*,' and she didn't, but hesitated, looking back to Hickory.

No time left. I lifted her up bodily and carried her. Rose ordered me to put her down. I didn't, but aimed into the showroom and shouted at the trio there leaning on the wall to get down behind it.

Rose came fast across the workshop after me and drove at me, holding her hot-glass-laden punty iron like a sword.

Half seeing her, half sensing the searing future, I twisted both myself and Pamela Jane roughly to let the iron miss us, like a bull-fighter, but Rose in fury dragged and stabbed and burned a long black slit through my white singlet.

No more time.

I lugged Pamela Jane around the half-wall to the showroom and threw her to the ground, and I fell on top of her to pin her down.

The rearing horse had stood unannealed at maximum heat on the marver table for three minutes forty seconds when it exploded.

Chapter Ten

The horse exploded into scorching fragments that flew like angry transparent wasps throughout the workshop and over the half-wall into the showroom beyond.

Adam Force, refusing to get down because it had been I who suggested it, had been hit twice, once in the upper arm and once, more seriously, across the top of the cheekbone below the eye, taking away a chunk of surface flesh. Half fainting from shock, the doctor had dropped his syringe. Blood reddened his sleeve.

It was the wreck of his good looks, I thought, that would in the end grieve him most. The speed and sharpness of the flying glass fragment had opened a furrow that was bound to leave a scar.

The trophy horse had split violently apart along the internal stress lines caused by the pulling and stretching as the glass cooled, the outer regions cooling faster than the inner core. The splinters had still been fiercely hot when they'd dug into the first thing they met.

Norman Osprey, kneeling in spite of his antipathy towards the source of good advice, had survived with his skin intact, if not his temper. Although slightly shaking, he still clung to the doctrine of 'Get Logan'. He rose from his knees and planted his gorilla shoulders close inside the gallery-to-street door, making an exit that way impossible. Eddie was still on his knees beside the wall. The valet looked as though he were begging an undeserved absolution.

Pamela Jane heaved herself from under me in a troubled dilemma as she couldn't decide whether to thank me for saving her or to revile me for leaving Hickory to take whatever razor-sharp damage came his way in the blast. Pamela Jane, of course, had understood the physics of stress and strain in superheated glass, and she would now be sure I'd intended to shatter the horse from the moment I'd started to make it.

When I stood up and looked over the half-wall to see what shape Rose and Hickory were in, I found Rose bleeding down one leg but still shaking with determined fury while she shoved a clean punty iron into the tank and drew out a second one already tipped with white-hot hate. Hickory, who had finally succeeded in flinging himself out of the chair altogether, lay face down on the smooth brick floor trying to rub the tape off his mouth.

Sharply aware that at some point somewhere Rose had succeeded in drawing a line of fire across my own lower back ribs, I felt I'd already had enough for one morning of the unequal combat.

Rose hadn't. Rose, it seemed, had energy in stock for a third world war. As she drew her loaded iron with speed from the fire, she told me that if I didn't get back at once into the workshop, the burn to Hickory's ear would be only the beginning.

I went round the half-wall. Hickory, hurting and helpless, was in no immediate danger from Rose, who advanced on me, holding the silvery-black five-foot-long punty iron loaded and ready to strike.

'Adam Force's videotape,' she said. 'Where is it?'

Short of breath from evading burns so long, I managed dry-mouthed to reply, 'He said he'd rerecorded it with horse races.'

'Rubbish.' Rose advanced towards me with the white-hot ball of glass inexorably leading the way. The ball, if one thrust it fiercely, would burn a path right through a body, searing and killing.

With at least some sort of plan I backed away from Rose and her deadly fire, cursing that I couldn't reach the five or six punty irons lying idle to one side, irons I could at least have used to fence with.

Rose began again to enjoy compelling me to retreat step by step. Backwards past the furnace, its trap door shut. Backwards across the workshop, faster as she increased her pace.

'The videotape,' she demanded. 'Where is it?'

At last, *at last*, I saw Worthington again outside the gallery door, Worthington this time flanked by Tom Pigeon, Jim, Catherine and her hobo partner, Pernickety Paul.

Norman Osprey, suddenly not liking the odds, stood back to let them in and dived fast around them out into the street. I had a last glimpse of him as he set off down the hill with Tom and his four-legged companions in pursuit.

The two plain-clothes officers, with Jim and Worthington, now filled the doorway. Furiously seeing the advent of my friends as her last chance to make me remember her for life, Rose rushed recklessly at my abdomen. I sidestepped and dodged yet again, and ran and swerved, and ended where I'd aimed for, beside the wide round pots of coloured powders on the stock shelves.

It was the white enamel I wanted. I snatched off the lid, grabbed a handful of the powder, and threw it at Rose's eyes.

The powder contained arsenic, and arsenic made eyes blur and go temporarily blind. Rose, her eyes streaming, went on sweeping around with her petrifying length of death-bearing punty iron.

Eddie seemingly rose from his prayers and walked around the half-wall pleading with her to be still. 'Rose, dear girl, it's over . . .'

But nothing would stop her. Blinded for a while she might be, but she lashed out with the killing iron at where she'd last seen me. Missing me didn't stop her from being more dangerous blundering about than if she could see me, and finally, disastrously, the unimaginably hot glass connected twice with living flesh.

There were screams chokingly cut off.

It was Eddie who, incredibly, she had hit first. She had seared the skin from her father's fingers as he held them in front of his face to defend himself. There were crashes of iron against walls and a fearful soft sizzling as the worst of all calamities happened.

Pamela Jane hysterically threw herself into my arms and hid her face, but it wasn't she who had burned. Across the workshop Catherine's partner, Pernickety Paul, folded to the ground and lay motionless, his limbs sprawling in the haphazardness of death.

Catherine stared in shock, disbelief and anger.

Adam Force came into the workshop to stand against the safe side of the wall, and he begged Rose to let someone—like himself—come to help her and her father, but she only changed direction towards his voice, lashing through the air in great sweeps of the punty iron.

Catherine, a police officer to the bone, called her station urgently for back-up, with Rose following the sound of her voice. Stifling human terror, she spoke tightly on her radio. 'Officer down,' she said. 'Red call. Officer in need of immediate assistance.'

She reported the address of Logan Glass and then added, with less formality and genuine emotion, 'Come at once. Dear God.'

She dodged Rose's rushing speed and with incredible bravery knelt down beside her silent hobo partner. The plain-clothes inhabitant of doorways, whose name to me had never been more than Pernickety Paul, would catch no more villains. He had taken a white-hot direct hit through his neck.

I disentangled myself from Pamela Jane and half ran across the room, away from Catherine, and called to Rose, 'I'm here, Rose. I'm over here, and you'll never catch me.'

Rose turned half circle my way and pivoted once more, when I jumped past her again and yelled at her. She turned again and again and finally began to tire enough with her blurring eyes for Worthington and Jim to reach my side and for Catherine to come up behind us and for the four of us to grab Rose and immobilise her still slashing punty-iron arm. I wrestled the iron a good safe way away from her, feeling the heat of it near my legs but not on my skin.

The police side of Catherine flowed in her like a strong tide. She found handcuffs and clicked them roughly onto Rose's wrists behind her back, the metal bands squeezed tight against her skin.

There was nothing about 'going quietly' in the arrest of Rose Payne. She kicked and thrashed even as an ambulance with paramedics and two cars full of bristling young police officers drew up outside the gallery. The officers fetched a blanket in which they rolled Rose like a baby in swaddling clothes and, with her struggling to the end, manhandled her out through the showroom door and into the back of one of the police cars.

Spitting fury, she was soon joined there by the burly Norman Osprey, whose muscles, Tom told me later, had been no match for three sets of canine fangs.

In the workshop I watched as Catherine, dry-eyed, brought another blanket in from a police car to cover the silence of Paul.

MORE POLICE ARRIVED. White overalls and grey plastic shoes were produced and soon the workshop took on the look of science fiction. One of the officers removed the tape from Pamela Jane's wrists, then took her personal details, while another, wearing surgical gloves, picked up the fallen syringe and placed it in a clear plastic bag.

I knelt beside Hickory. As humanely as possible, I pulled the tape from his eyes. It painfully came off with eyelashes attached. One of the young police officers stretched a hand down over my shoulder and simply ripped the strong tape off Hickory's mouth. He yelled, and went on yelling while the officer freed his taped-together wrists and legs. I brought the first-aid box from the stock shelves to put a dressing on Hickory's ear. The paramedics arrived and decided that he should go to the hospital along with Eddie, who was now deep in shock with hands that had already blistered badly.

Catherine stood by the ambulance watching Eddie being helped aboard. I told her other things she ought to know, extra things about Black Mask Four that had come to me during the night, that I hadn't mentioned in the dawn.

She said thoughtfully, 'Our superintendent is that man standing beside Paul. I think you'd better talk to him.'

She introduced me as the owner of the place, and I shook hands with Superintendent Shepherd of West Mercia police. Just then George Lawson-Young arrived. He asked me if I had worked out the identity of the fourth man who'd assaulted me two weeks ago.

'Yes,' I said, and told him how I had used his search-and-discard method to sort out truth from lies. But however flatly I said the name, it would cause consternation.

The professor made a slow visual inspection of the damage to the most familiar of faces turned his way. Adam Force, his facial bleeding now a trickle, looked as if he would prefer to evaporate rather than be in the same room as his one-time boss.

A spent Force, I thought ironically.

It was George Lawson-Young who related to the superintendent step by step how the data stolen from his laboratory had caused me so much pain and trouble.

'Adam Force,' he said, 'worked for me but jumped ship and stole our cancer research. We knew that he had stolen the information, had transferred it to a videotape, and had destroyed all other records of our research. We searched everywhere for it, even engaging private investigators after the police had shown little interest.'

Superintendent Shepherd flinched not at all, but continued listening intently.

'All our searches were in vain. We did not expect him to have entrusted the tape to the safekeeping of a jockey. Dr Force had passed it to Martin Stukely, but Stukely preferred to hand it on to his friend Gerard Logan here, away from the fingers of his own children. As perhaps you know, Martin Stukely was killed at Cheltenham races on New Year's Eve. But the tape had already begun its tortuous journey by then. Adam Force tried to steal it back. Tapes were stolen from here, from Gerard's home, and from the home of Martin Stukely.'

'Were we informed of those thefts?' asked the policeman.

'Yes,' I replied. 'An officer did come round the following morning, but there was more interest in the money stolen with the tape.'

'Did Dr Force steal the money as well?' asked the super.

'Yes,' I replied. 'But I think that was just an opportunist theft which he might have thought would somehow smoke-screen the removal of the tape.'

Dr Force listened dispassionately, his bloodied face giving away nothing.

'Anyway,' continued the professor, who did not welcome the interruption, 'somehow all the thefts failed to get back the tape they wanted, and Dr Force, with assistance from Rose Payne and others, has been trying here to coerce Mr Logan to reveal its whereabouts. He tells me he hasn't got it.'

'And have you?' asked the voice of authority.

'No,' I replied, 'but I think I know who has.'

They all looked at me expectantly. Adam Force, Lawson-Young, even Hickory, who had been listening with his good ear.

Into this tableau swept Marigold, floating in emerald silk with gold tassels and brushing aside the young constable who tried to stand in her way. In her wake came Bon-Bon, Victor, Daniel and the other children, like the tail of a kite.

Marigold demanded to see how her trophy was getting along but was brought up sharply by the sight of the blanket-covered form in the workshop. Bon-Bon, realising the enormity of the situation, swept her brood back through the door, leaving just her mother inside.

'Marigold, my dear,' I said wearily, 'there's been a disaster. Please go across the road to the hotel and wait for me there.'

'So who is Black Mask Four?' asked Lawson-Young into the silence when she had gone.

'Who?' said the superintendent. 'What are you talking about?'

The professor told him. 'Gerard was attacked by four people in black masks outside his shop here. Three of them were Rose Payne, her father Eddie Payne, and Norman Osprey. Gerard told me earlier today that he had worked out the identity of the fourth, so—' He turned to me and said, 'Who is it, and where is my research?'

'I don't think Black Mask Four has the tape,' I replied.

'What?' exclaimed the professor. His shoulders dropped; his expectations had been so high, and he took it now that I was leading him to another dead end.

I put him right. 'My fourth assailant, Black Mask Four, was just a hired help, and I'm not sure he even knew exactly what he was looking for.' But he knew, I thought, how to inflict maximum damage to my wrists. 'He is, however, a dab hand with anaesthetic gas.'

'Who is it, for God's sake?' The professor was finding it difficult to stifle his impatience, as was the superintendent, yet it wasn't the easiest disclosure I'd ever made. Still . . .

'Who was the fourth man, Hickory?' I asked my assistant.

He looked up from where he was kneeling on the floor, still holding a dressing to his ear.

'Why are you asking me?' he said.

'You bunched my fingers.'

'Of course I didn't.'

'I'm afraid you did,' I said. 'You held my hand against a wall ready for a baseball bat to smash my wrist.'

'You must be crazy. Why would I attack you? Why you of all people?'

It was a piercing question and one with a complex answer. I suspected that it had to do with my ability with glass-blowing and his comparative lack of it. Envy was a strong emotion, and I reckoned he wouldn't have needed a lot of persuasion to oppose me.

He still refused to admit it. 'You're crazy, you are,' he said, getting to his feet and turning away as if looking for some quick escape.

'The green and white laces,' I said.

He stopped dead and turned back.

I went on, 'You wore them here the day Martin Stukely was killed, and you wore them again the following day when you stole the tapes from his house, the day you hit me with the orange cylinder. Martin's eldest son, Daniel, saw the laces and told the police about them.'

Hickory advanced a step or two, his ear clearly hurting. His poise cracked. 'You're so bloody clever,' he said. 'I wish we *had* broken your wrists.'

The superintendent stopped leaning on the half-wall and stood up straight.

But Hickory had only just started. 'You and your fancy ways and your condescending comments about my work. I hate you and this workshop. I'm a damn good glass-blower, and I deserve more recognition.' He raised his chin and sneered. 'One day John Hickory will be a name worth knowing, and people will smash Logan glass to get to mine.'

Such a shame, I thought. He really did have some talent, but I suspected it would never develop as it should. Arrogance and a belief in skills he didn't have would smother those he did.

'And Rose?' I asked.

'Stupid bitch,' he said, holding his hand to his throbbing ear. 'Bloody mad she is. Tie you up, she said. Use you as a hostage, she said. Nothing about frying my bloody ear. Hope she rots in hell.'

I hoped she'd rot on earth.

'She promised me my own place,' Hickory said. 'Claimed she'd close you down. Her and that stupid father of hers.' He began to realise the hole he was digging for himself. 'They put me up to it. It was their fault, not mine.'

He looked wretchedly at the rapt faces around him.

'It wasn't my fault. It was their idea.'

No one believed him. It had been Hickory who had reported all to Rose. Hickory had had the 'binocs' in Broadway.

'So where is the tape?' asked George Lawson-Young.

'I don't know,' replied Hickory. 'Rose said that it must have been in Stukely's house or in Logan's, but I've sat through hours of bloody horse racing and glass-blowing, and I'm telling you, there was no tape of medical stuff.'

I believed him. Otherwise, I thought ruefully, I might have been saved a couple of beatings and Pernickety Paul would still be lying around in shop doorways.

A paramedic appeared and said that it was time to take Hickory to the hospital to dress his burn. The superintendent, roused into action, arrested Hickory and had him led off to the ambulance.

The super then turned his attention to Dr Force, who had listened in silence throughout. 'Well, Dr Force,' he said, in his officialese, 'can you enlighten us as to the whereabouts of a videotape containing medical research results stolen from the professor here?'

Force said nothing.

'Come on, Adam, tell us.' The professor, I saw, still had some vestige of friendship for the man.

Force looked at him with disdain and kept silent.

In his turn he too was arrested and taken away for wound stitching and fingerprinting.

IN TIME, THE GALLERY, showroom and workshop began to clear. The professor and I went over to the Wychwood Dragon. In the residents' sitting room Bon-Bon and her four sat tightly side by side on a sofa in descending height from the right. Marigold occupied a deep squashy armchair, while Worthington perched on its arm.

I took tea and was told that Pamela Jane, still badly shocked, had been given a pill and dispatched to bed upstairs.

Victor stood by the window. I joined him.

Without turning his head, he said, 'I suppose my Aunt Rose will be inside for a long time?'

'A very long time,' I said. Police killers didn't get early parole.

'Good,' he said. 'It might give me and Mum a chance.'

I turned and took Bon-Bon out into the hotel lobby. I needed her to do me a favour. Certainly, she said, and trotted off to the telephone box while I returned to the sitting room to finish my tea. Soon she returned with a smiling nod.

I thought about the events of the morning and wondered if there had been another way.

Punty irons in anyone's hands had to be swung around carefully. In Rose's hands a punty iron tipped with semiliquid glass had been literally a lethal weapon, and it had seemed to me that as it was me she was after, however weird and mistaken her beliefs, it was I who ought to stop her.

I'd tried to stop her with the shattering horse, and I hadn't succeeded. It had torn a hole in her lover, Dr Force, and stoked her anger. I'd thought then, if I could blind her, she would stop, so I'd thrown the powder. But blinding her had made her worse.

Paul had died.

If I hadn't tried to stop her, if I had surrendered at once . . . But, I reflected, searching for comfort, I couldn't have given her the tape she demanded, as I hadn't known where it was.

I'd done my best, and my best had killed.

THE ARRIVAL of my expected guest hurrying through the door brought me back to the present.

'Hello, Priam,' I said. 'It's so good of you to come.'

'I'm sorry?' he said, puzzled. 'I don't quite understand. Bon-Bon called me to say that she was with a potential racehorse owner and I should get down here pronto if I wanted the business.'

'That wasn't quite the truth. I asked Bon-Bon to make that call because I needed to talk to you about a videotape.'

'Not that videotape business again,' he said. 'I have told you already, I don't have any videotape.'

Daniel said distinctly, 'I know where there's a videotape.'

'*Shhhh*, darling,' said Bon-Bon.

'But I do know where a tape is,' Daniel persisted.

I had learned to take Daniel very seriously indeed.

I squatted down to his level on the sofa. 'Where is it, Daniel?'

'It's in Daddy's car,' he said. 'It's in the pocket on the back of Daddy's seat. I saw it there yesterday when Mummy brought us to your shop.'

Priam shuffled uneasily beside me.

I said to him, 'Why did you switch the tapes?'

'I told you—' he started.

'I know what you told me,' I interrupted. 'It was a lie.' Discard the lies, the professor had told me in Bristol, and I would be left with the truth. I asked again, 'Why did you switch the tapes?'

He shrugged his shoulders. 'I thought,' he said, 'that the tape Eddie Payne passed to you was one showing the hiding place of an antique necklace. Worth millions, I'd heard from someone. I found it in your raincoat that night, and I thought, with Martin dead, no one would know if I kept it.'

Half-truths and misconceptions had woven a path to death and destruction.

Priam went on. 'I took another tape from Martin's den, one with racing on it, and wrapped it in the paper and put it back in your rain-coat pocket, which I took back to your showroom on New Year's Eve. When I played the original tape at home that night, I discovered that it was all unintelligible mumbo jumbo with nothing about a necklace. So I just put it back in Martin's car when I drove it back to Bon-Bon's the next day.'

He looked around. 'No harm done. You have the tape back.'

No harm done. Oh God, how wrong he was.

IT WAS FOUR DAYS before the police would allow me back into Logan Glass. Marigold was waiting for me to start again on her trophy. Rose, Norman Osprey, Dr Force and Hickory had been remanded in custody, while Eddie had been remanded in hospital, his hands a mess. Rose did little else but scream abuse.

Catherine, cuddling in my arms every night, kept me up to date with the news from the police station.

Professor George Lawson-Young had been given the tape from Martin's car.

Dr Force had said a little but denied most. He had revealed, however, that Martin Stukely had been unaware that the information on the tape had been stolen. Indeed, Force had told Martin that he was protecting his research from others trying to steal it.

I was glad of that. Had I doubted it?

ON SUNDAY, one week after the mayhem, I set out again to make the trophy horse.

Dependable Irish had agreed to act as my assistant, and this time we had an audience of one. Catherine watched as I again readied my tools and stripped down to my singlet.

I stood on the treadle to lift the door to the furnace and let the heat flood into the room.

Catherine took off her coat.

'Hang it in my locker,' I said, tossing her the locker keys.

She walked to the far end of the workshop and opened a door on the tall grey cabinet.

'What's on this?' she said, holding up a videotape. 'It has a label: "How to make the Cretan Sunrise".'

I moved swiftly to her side. She had by mistake opened Hickory's locker, and there inside we found not just the necklace instruction tape but also, tucked into a brown paper bag, a pair of bright laces, green and white striped.

I laughed. 'A tale of three tapes, and one of them was under my nose all the time.'

'Three tapes?' she asked. 'Two were bad enough.'

'There were three,' I replied. 'The only really important tape was the one Force made from the stolen cancer research results. It's the tape that Rose and Dr Force have been trying so hard to find.'

'And the necklace tape?' Catherine asked. 'This one?'

I said, 'I had lent the necklace instruction tape to Martin, and it remained in his den at his house until Hickory stole it with all the others. Hickory kept it because, to him, the tape had some value. He thought he could make a copy of the necklace.'

'What's the third tape, then?' she asked.

'The tape,' I went on, 'that Priam took from Martin's den before Hickory's theft. He put it in my raincoat pocket, and it's that tape that Force stole at midnight on New Year's Eve thinking it was his cancer tape. I would have loved to see his face when he played it and found horse racing instead.'

I MADE THE TROPHY horse. With Irish's help I gathered the glass from the furnace and again formed the horse's body, its legs and tail. But this time I took time and care and applied the knowledge and talent both learned and inherited from my uncle Ron. I moulded a neck and head of an intelligent animal, prominent cheekbones and a firm mouth. I gave it a mane flowing as if in full gallop and then applied it seamlessly to the body.

I had started out to make a commercial work for Marigold and the Cheltenham Race Trophy Committee.

In the event, I made a memorial to a trusted and much missed friend. A memorial worthy of his skill and his courage.

The leaping horse stood finally on the marver table, and Irish and I lifted it quickly but carefully into one of the annealing ovens. There it would cool slowly and safely, allowing the strains and stresses to ease gradually. This one was not for shattering.

I WENT WITH CATHERINE to the funeral of Pernickety Paul. After the service it was a thoughtful and subdued police officer who mounted her motorcycle.

'I've been given leave for the rest of the day,' she said blankly, 'so where do you want to go now?'

I said, 'I haven't seen where you live, so how about now?'

She smiled with a touch of mischief and invited me to step aboard.

Her home was less than a one-minute motorcycle ride from the district police station, in a semidetached bungalow, and I knew within a blink that it wasn't the place for me.

Inside, the one-floor living space had been allied to *Alice's Adventures in Wonderland*, where a more than life-size March Hare and a same-size Mad Hatter sat at the kitchen table and stuffed a dormouse into a teapot. A white rabbit consulted a watch by the

bathroom door, and a red queen and a cook and a walrus and a carpenter danced a quadrille around the sitting room. The walls were
painted with rioting greenery and flowers.

Catherine laughed at my expression, a mixture no doubt of
amusement and horror.

'These people,' she said, 'came to me from a closing-down funfair
when I was six. I've always loved them. I know they're silly but
they're company.' She swallowed. 'They've helped me come to terms
with losing Paul. He liked them. They made him laugh. They're not
the same now, without him. I think I've been growing up.'

In keeping with the rest of the house, Catherine's bedroom was a
fantasy land of living playing cards painting rosebushes white and
pink against puffball clouds and vivid green leaves.

Brought to a standstill, I said weakly, 'Lovely.'

Catherine laughed. 'You hate it, I can see.'

'I can shut my eyes,' I said, and we pulled the curtains closed.

Later in the evening, when Detective Constable Dodd and her pillion rider climbed back on the saddle, it was to the big quiet house
on the hill that they went.

It was like coming familiarly home.

DICK FRANCIS

When Her Majesty Queen Elizabeth the Queen Mother was celebrating her centenary last year, Dick Francis was able to visit her in the royal box at Ascot to give her a special birthday present—a copy of *Shattered*, hot off the press, with a printed dedication to her inside the book.

The Queen Mother, of course, is one of Dick Francis's biggest fans. And Francis had great success as her jockey before he gave up racing in the 1950s to embark on his phenomenal writing career, which began in 1957 with the publication of his autobiography, *The Sport of Queens*, and which has now seen a string of best-selling novels, thirty-eight of them in all.

It was a visit to a glass-blower in the sunny Cayman Islands, where he has lived for many years, that gave him the idea for *Shattered*. Once Francis realised what a fascinating subject he had come across, his wife Mary, who had worked with him as chief researcher and editor on so many of his books, helped to find out the facts about glass-blowing for this one. Researching Francis's books over the years had led Mary to learn photography, flying and painting, becoming adept at all three. Sadly, *Shattered* was to be their final collaboration, because Mary died not long after the book was published. She was seventy-six years old.

'I couldn't have written the books without her,' Francis admits. Their books were very much a 'joint effort', he says, but 'she was quite happy for me to have all the credit'.

One of the most popular writers in the English-speaking world, Dick Francis has seen his huge success marked by numerous prizes and honours, and last year he was awarded the CBE.

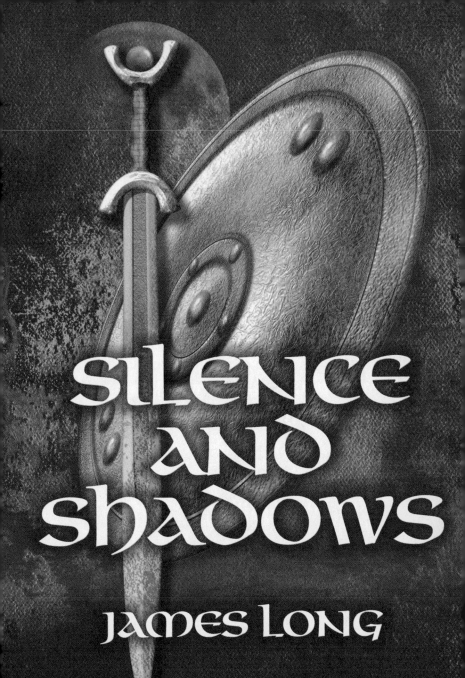

SILENCE
AND
SHADOWS

JAMES LONG

Time heals all, so they say.
But for one-time rock idol
Paddy Kane tragic memories
of the wife and son he has
lost just won't go away.

Returning to his old
passion for archaeology,
Paddy immerses himself in
the painstaking work of
unearthing an Anglo-Saxon
burial site, and in doing so
realises that it may hold the
key to escaping his past.

ONE

He was a tired traveller at the end of his tether, a gaunt shadowed man. He was as alone as it was possible to be and that was his choice. Wales was behind him. It was over for another year but he felt no better for it. Standing by the grave in the wet churchyard, he could hardly believe the person he had been, the man responsible for this headstone with its letters of accusation bitten into the slate.

On the last stage of his journey from the Welsh mountains, Patrick played mind games to keep awake. He ran through the list of the things he must not forget to pack. Tent, sleeping-bag, plate, mug, four-inch trowel. When that developed into its own soporific mantra, he wound down the window, let the damp air wash his face, and turned his attention to the signposts he passed. Village names contain rich pickings for archaeologists.

Archaeology. That was what he had studied, way back when life was simple. That was what he had returned to now. He had decided, in despair, it was easier to deal with those who were long dead.

The sign to the village of Fawler occupied him all the way from Charlbury to the walls of the Blenheim Palace estate. Fawler from 'faig-flor', the term the Anglo-Saxons had used for the mosaics scattered in the ruins left by the vanished Romans. Mosaics were very much on his mind. They were the reason time was tight, the reason he would have to pack in a hurry as soon as he got home.

Right on cue, the sign to Wytchlow flared white for a moment in his headlights and he checked his watch. Twenty past five and dawn was striping the sky to the east—four hours before he was due back here at Wytchlow again, ready to start.

On the very last stretch into Oxford, he blinked abruptly awake. Sleep was claiming him. He turned to his last resort, the radio, and as if there was an evil malignancy presiding over his affairs, a song was ending, a song from that shut-off past, a song he hated deeply.

'You can tell the truth to lovers but it's better when you lie.
A puppy's just for Christmas then you leave it out to DIE.'

'Nam Erewhon there with their infamous punk anthem, "Wedding Vows", requested by . . .'

Patrick's left fist hit the radio so hard that it split the OFF button and the tuning scale behind it into shards of plastic which fell onto the old Peugeot's filthy floor.

In the Cowley Road, a sodden pile of *Woman's Own* had been dumped on his front step—any secondhand value they might once have had washed out by the rain. Two feet away, a sign in the charity shop window scolded in vain: PLEASE DON'T LEAVE DONATED GOODS OUTSIDE. Patrick unlocked the door and the whole pile slumped into his hall so that he had to bulldoze it all back outside with his feet.

This place was not a home, it was just a space with nothing human in it to fight the short-let squalor. There was not enough left of him to turn it into a pleasant place and, anyway, he did not deserve to live in a pleasant place.

He slept for an hour on a harsh mattress that still smelt of some past tenant's spilt beer, then woke himself with a cold shower, not even trying the hot water because he was almost certain that the water heater wouldn't light. He threw what he needed into a bag. In that old life it would all have been there ready, washed and folded for him. Now he had to retrieve his clothes from corners.

There were two letters on the mat. One was an electricity bill, a final demand. The logo on the other envelope said 'Colonic Music' in gold over the silhouette of a broken purple guitar. He tore it open. Inside was a letter, addressed to him care of the company and now forwarded. It started: *Dear Paddy Kane, Can you settle a bet for my brother and me? He says that when you punched . . .*

Patrick crumpled it up, threw it in the bin where the rest of Paddy Kane belonged, and slammed the door of the flat behind him.

All the way out through the north Oxford traffic, retracing his earlier route, fears about the days ahead, his first real test in this new professional role, ballooned into his head. As a student, he had learned the techniques, the terminology, the minutiae. He had then immediately forgotten it all when he had shed the gown and put on the wild clothing of an ever more wild life. Now he was returning to archaeology. For the past two years he had buried himself in stuffy libraries, setting himself a course of intensive reading and picking up the strands of all he had forgotten. If he tried, he might get back to things that had once mattered.

All the money that had once poured through Patrick's fingers had been drunk, snorted and pissed away. The royalties still came in, unwelcome evidence that the songs he wished he'd never sung were still poisoning minds somewhere. Once in a while, he would use those cheques to fill a hole in his bank account. More often, they languished in a drawer until he found a good cause to send them to.

From now on, to sever that link, he intended to survive on a pay packet. He had found what looked like being a steady job with Paradigm Site Check, one of a new breed of companies operating on the profit-making edge of archaeology. His first assignment was one he hadn't been expecting and didn't really want, dumped in his lap by another man's bad luck.

'I know it's a bit early but it's a jolly good opportunity for you to show us what you can do,' John Hescroft had told him on the phone.

He knew straight away what that really meant. There was no time to find anyone else and they didn't want to spend the money. He'd expected to be, at best, number two on a series of digs while he found his feet. Trench supervisor was about his mark, not director. He knew this was beyond his knowledge and his capabilities.

'I'll see you have a good team,' said Hescroft.

A signpost said WYTCHLOW 1 MILE, and the road it pointed down was narrow, twisting between high, banked hedges and soft fields sprouting with an early fuzz of green. A steep rise led up through a dark filter of old woodland towards a clean skyline which showed no sign of the promised village. Then, round a sharp bend, the road was abruptly lined by stone cottages.

No sooner had Patrick registered the outskirts of Wytchlow than a woman burst out from a gateway into his path, looking back the way she'd come, oblivious of him, clearly upset.

He slammed to a complete halt as she banged into his door. She bounced off it and he stared horrified through his open window, shaking with shock, as she staggered to keep her balance. Behind her, blocking the gateway, a middle-aged man in a tweed jacket stood by a sign that said WYTCHLOW PRIMARY SCHOOL. His face was puckered up in distaste and his hand was held up, either warding her off or demanding silence. The woman turned, as if aware of the car for the first time, and bent to look in. Patrick was a foot away from her face.

When Patrick looked into her eyes he was overwhelmed. A flash flood of pure emotion swept through the dry watercourses of his soul. What he saw so shockingly was a perfect double, an identical twin of a girl now locked in his past, the girl with whom he had fallen instantly and completely in love at the age of eighteen.

What he saw first were the eyes—large and dark in a pale face, full lips parted in shock, showing pure white teeth. Her hair was tucked up out of sight under a woollen hat. He stared at her aghast for no more than two seconds. Then he wound up the window and drove away to safety.

He went only a couple of hundred yards, far enough to get out of sight round the corner, then stopped on the edge of a triangle of village green. He stopped to try to put this ambushing genie back in its bottle, but instead the genie just went on swelling in the fresh air.

It was not entirely true to say that this woman was Rachel's double. Someone in their thirties cannot look just like an eighteen-year-old. What this woman with the shining eyes looked exactly like was the Rachel who *would* have been, had her future been in the hands of a kinder lover.

TWO

The road into Wytchlow split and ran down two sides of the triangular village green, flanked by low stone houses, some thatched, some roofed with rough stone tiles. A whitewashed pub was the only building to break the run of warm Cotswold stone. On the third side of the triangle, beyond the war memorial, a field stretched up a gentle slope to an array of old barns along the skyline. The two roads ran off the far corners of the green, curving down past a church on the right and heading into higher ground on the left.

Driving on with part of his brain still locked into a baffled, looped replay of the sight of the woman's face, Patrick took the left-hand lane leading to the field at the far end of the village. As he drove into the tight little square of rough grass, he realised with a sinking heart that he was going to have to stamp his authority on events right away. Tents were going up all over the place, cars parked here and there among them. Only one tent was where it was meant to be, a tattered square marquee of patched canvas, standing beside a pair of mobile lavatories at the field's edge.

Patrick parked hard up against the fence and got out, clutching his clipboard. 'Come over here, everybody, please,' he shouted.

The person nearest to him glanced up for a moment and went back to his guy ropes. He was a crop-haired man with the battered air of a monk from some impoverished order. His forehead was angled back like an Easter Island statue, and round glasses filled his gaunt eye-sockets.

'A moment,' he said in a burred growl. 'I'll just be finishing this.'

'Oh no, you will not,' said Patrick, almost as vehemently as he felt, 'because if you do, you'll just have to take it straight down again.'

'Aren't you just the angry one today?' said the man.

The others were straggling towards him across the grass, a motley crew—a flock searching for a leader. Patrick scanned their faces as they approached, looking hopefully for one who might be the lieutenant he badly needed—the one who would fill the gaps when knowledge or confidence failed him.

The group formed a loose crescent round him. The only one who gave any impression that he had ever been in a field such as this before was a big, tough man of sixty or more—his grey hair bunched back in a ponytail. Across his barrel chest his black T-shirt said TERMINATE WITH EXTREME PREJUDICE, and his arms were covered in tattoos. When Patrick caught his eye, he gave a conspiratorial wink. It was a straw and Patrick grasped at it.

'Have you put your tent up yet?'

The tattooed man laughed and said, 'Not me, mate.'

'OK,' said Patrick to the group. 'Listen to me. I'm Patrick Kane. I'm the director of this dig and the first thing I have to tell you is that you're all going to have to take your tents down again.'

'And why would that be?' asked the Easter Island monk.

'Because you've put them up right over the top of the archaeology,' said Patrick evenly. They shuffled uncomfortably. 'We need the tents close together along the edge of the field over there by the catering tent. Put your cars next to mine at the far end.'

'Couldn't we just dig in between them?' asked a small woman whose blonde hair was much younger than her face and who had bright red lipstick distributed over her teeth as well as her lips. 'It's taken me absolutely ages to put my tent up. I've never camped before, you see.' Her polished, gilt-buckled shoes and white trousers made this explanation unnecessary and there was a guffaw from the tattooed man.

'What's your name?' asked Patrick, looking at his clipboard.

'Gaye,' she said, 'with an e.'

'The answer to your question, Gaye with an e,' said Patrick, 'is no, we can't dig round your tent. You need to move it so that we can start to mark out the trenches. Understood?'

She looked doubtfully towards the edge of the field. 'If that's the catering tent,' she said, 'it's awfully close to the toilets. I think Health and Safety might have something to say about that.'

Patrick ignored her. 'Right,' he continued, 'I've only been working for PSC for a short time so I'm sorry if there are some of you I *should* know and don't. Can I just ask which of you are PSC employees?'

Not a hand was raised.

I don't believe this, Patrick said to himself.

'So, hand up if you're a volunteer,' he said, and it seemed to him that every hand was raised. Just to check, he asked, 'Are there *any* professional archaeologists here?'

The tattooed man lifted a hand the size of a leg of pork. 'I am,' he said. 'Sort of.'

Patrick, feeling suddenly glad for very small mercies, found himself lacking the energy to discover what 'sort of' meant. 'Sorry, I don't know your name,' he said.

'No need to be sorry, Pat,' said the man. 'Be a bit amazing if you did, all things considered, being as how we never met before.'

'So what is it? And by the way, I'm Patrick, not Pat.'

'That's all right, Pat. I'm Dozer.' He was rolling a cigarette with one hand.

'That's another thing,' said Patrick. 'There's to be absolutely no smoking near any of the trenches once we've started.'

'Why is that?' said the monk. 'We are in the open air, after all.'

'What's your name?' asked Patrick, and the man reacted as if the question were a prelude to some sort of punishment.

'Aidan,' he said. 'I was only asking.'

'Tobacco ash mucks up carbon dating,' said Patrick. 'Is there anybody else who's not a volunteer?'

A pallid scarecrow of a boy in a bush hat put up his hand. 'I'm a student,' he said, 'Maxwell Muir. I'm doing this for my course. Fieldwork experience.'

'Right.'

'If we find things,' the boy went on, 'do we get to keep any of them?'

'How long have you been doing your course?' asked Patrick grimly.

'Since October,' said the boy with apparent pride.

'Then you shouldn't need to ask that. Now, the rest of you,' he said, 'how many of you have worked on a dig before?'

Only three.

'Let's see . . .' He looked at his clipboard in search of anything that might give hope. 'Are we all here? I'll just do a head count.'

It came out at sixteen. There were eighteen names on his list. He ran through it and they all answered except for R. Redhead and C. D. Corcoran.

He looked around at them again and found himself exhausted by the unfamiliar experience of speaking more than one sentence to more than one person. He strode away, reaching for his mobile phone. Halfway to the hedge he glanced back to see most of them straggling after him, and shooed them back like a herd of bullocks. He stopped at the corner of the field.

To the north, beyond the hedge, a field of short grass rose gradually over a rounded hill. On the skyline, a cloud shadow swept by and in the sunlight Patrick saw a man, sitting stock-still and hunched up, arms pulling his knees to his chest, staring down at them. Patrick stared back but the man made not the slightest acknowledgment.

The phone rang at the other end and Patrick was through to Hescroft.

'Patrick! How are things going out there? I'm planning to pop out and see you. Few things I want to discuss.'

'Such as?'

'TV,' said Hescroft, putting pleasure into the two syllables. 'Chance of a series if we play our cards right. Do us no end of good.'

'I've got enough on my plate with this dig for now,' Patrick said. 'I'm a bit concerned.'

'I don't think we need get too stirred up about this one, old boy. Pretty slender evidence to mount a Phase Two. Just do the minimum and let the poor bloody builder get on with it.'

That's all I need, thought Patrick grimly. A bent contract. Hescroft's got no interest in finding anything here that would stop the developer putting up his houses. Has he taken a backhander? Probably. John Hescroft was more businessman than archaeologist whatever his CV might say. The outcome of a dig like this could make a huge difference to the value of a building site.

'Is that why I've got such a crap team?' he asked.

'What's the problem, old boy?' Hescroft sounded shocked.

'The problem is that there's nobody here who knows one end of a trowel from the other. They're all volunteers.'

'Archaeology lives off volunteers.'

'Not if it's being done by a professional unit on a paid contract.'

Hescroft retreated. 'They're not *all* volunteers. You've got Phil there, haven't you? Big man. Ponytail, tattoos.'

'He said he was called Dozer.'

'That's him. Done thousands of digs. Knows it backwards.'

'Qualified?'

'School of *life*, old boy. You can't beat experience.'

'Are we paying him?'

'Sort of.'

That phrase again. 'What does that mean?'

Hescroft sounded uncomfortable. 'I'm getting his car fixed for him. It's tax-efficient.'

'Look, John,' said Patrick. 'How am I meant to do the recording? How do I do finds? How do I look after the trenches? I'm going to have to be everywhere at once. If this lot found Pompeii they'd dig right through it and out the other side.'

'Well, hold on there a minute. You've got CD.'

'Seedy?'

'C. D. Corcoran.'

'He's not here yet. Who is he?'

'Best in the business. Smart young Yank doing his doctorate. You'll like him. He takes this incredible bird with him everywhere.'

'Bird?' said Patrick, thinking the last thing he needed was another hanger-on, a girl in tow. Nothing hurt more than the sight of loving couples—nothing, that is, except loving couples with small sons.

Small sons, old enough to walk, young enough to hold hands. They didn't have to be black-haired, blue-eyed images of David. The way they walked, the way they trusted, was enough to pierce Patrick through and through.

He missed most of what Hescroft said next.

'. . . black bird. Great fun.'

Patrick was staring at the entrance to the field, at a man on a huge motorcycle now threading its way through the ruts, and at a black bird, clinging tightly to the rider's shoulder.

A KNOT OF PEOPLE converged round CD and the bird. The bike, a Harley-Davidson, was resting on its stand and CD was pumping the hand of Dozer, on whose shoulder the bird was now standing, cocking its head at each of them in turn.

''Ow long's it been, CD?' Dozer said. 'Where was it last, up the Orinoco?'

CD, a slight figure with thick pebble glasses and a mop of sandy hair, grinned and said with a soft American accent, 'That's right, you old rascal. The Aztec treasure.'

'Yeah, you owe me one for that,' said Dozer, and looked round at the rest. 'Pulled him out of the jaws of a crocodile, I did.'

'Well, yes,' agreed CD, 'but wait until I tell them how you got me *into* its jaws in the first place.'

'Can we save all this for later?' interrupted Patrick. He held out a hand to the American, but the bird hopped onto it instead, digging in its feet to the point of pain.

'I'm Patrick Kane,' he said, and a momentary flicker in CD's eyes alarmed him. 'Can you persuade your crow to go somewhere else?'

'No, no, no, no, no,' said CD. 'Lesson one, never call a raven a crow; they are very easily upset.' He looked at the bird. 'Edgar,' he said, 'come,' and the bird leapt and flapped onto his shoulder.

'That's not a raven or a crow. It's a jackdaw,' objected Gaye.

'I call him Edgar,' said CD, 'therefore he's a raven.'

'What does that mean?' said Gaye, baffled.

'Edgar Allan Poe,' said a smiling elderly man, whose hair was a mixture of grey and ginger. '"Quoth the Raven, 'Nevermore'." Yes?'

She still looked baffled.

'Can we go and talk?' Patrick said to CD, feeling irritation rising again. 'There's a lot to do and nobody much to do it.'

CD blinked amiably. 'That's cool,' he said.

'Just say the word, Pat,' said Dozer. 'I'll get stuck in. Want me to get these tents sorted?'

'Yes, that would help.' The words, 'It's Patrick, not Pat' formed and died on his lips. 'Come on, CD.'

They walked down the edge of the trees until they were alone.

'I've seen you before,' said the American, looking at him curiously.

'Around Oxford?' suggested Patrick, though he knew his recent seclusion made that unlikely.

Then CD stopped, snapped his fingers and said far too loudly, 'Paddy Kane! Sod this Patrick stuff. You're Paddy Kane. My hero. Where's the hair gone?'

'Be quiet,' said Patrick in a fury. 'Keep your voice down. I am *not*. I'm just doing a job here, like you are.'

CD took in the expression on the other man's face. 'OK, Patrick, if you say so,' he said. Then he shrugged. 'So tell me what we have here. A bunch of amateurs?'

'Barely even that,' said Patrick, suddenly anxious to smooth over what had just happened.

'No digger, no site hut, not enough shovels. That's Hescroft. Another contract stolen by undercutting the outfits with proper professional standards. The two of us are just desperate enough to take the job and compromise our immortal archaeological souls.'

That forced a wry grimace out of Patrick. 'The two of us' seemed a generous phrase, and he sensed the possibility of a real friend in this man. 'Why are *you* so desperate?' he said.

'Me? I have a loan to support. I owe the US Treasury more than most Third World countries for my studies. It's OK so long as I go on studying. I only have to pay it back when I get a real job.'

'So your loan just gets bigger and bigger?'

'I'm depending on that. One day it will get so big they'll decide it's a computer error.' CD looked at him. 'What about you? Been dropped in it, right? I guess you haven't done too much yet?'

It could have been a challenging moment with a different man but Patrick found himself letting the mask slip. 'No. I was expecting a gentler start.'

'OK, buddy. Don't sweat it. I can help here.'

'You should be the director, not me.'

CD laughed. 'You're staff. Hescroft has to pay you anyway. I'm freelance. He doesn't want to shell out Dig Director dollars to me. I'm here for the beer money.'

They talked until they saw the tents had been put in the proper places. Then Dozer walked over to them.

CD welcomed him with a grin. 'Three of us against the world, right, Dozer?'

'Yeah, just like that time in Siberia, mate. 'Ere, Pat, who's doing grub?'

Patrick looked at the clipboard. 'It doesn't say. All it says here is they've made arrangements.'

'Yeah, well, it's all in there,' said Dozer, nodding at the marquee. 'Boxes of this and that. There's gas rings there an' all. Just needs somebody to put it together. Anyway, there's something else you've got to worry about first. Trowels. Absence of.'

'How would it be if I give them the standard trowel lecture?' suggested CD, and Patrick agreed gratefully without the faintest idea what that was.

CD gathered the volunteers round him on the grass.

'OK, listen up,' he said. 'In a minute the director will be briefing you about the dig itself, but first off it falls to me to do a bit of the basic stuff. Hands up those of you who have a trowel with you?'

What they produced ranged from huge pointing trowels, still encrusted with old mortar, to tiny curved things of bent, coloured tin. CD held up his own. 'This is the only trowel to have. It's a four-inch WHS pointing trowel and nothing else will do.'

'And why do you say that?' said Aidan, the Easter Island monk.

'Because it has a forged blade and handle that are all of a piece,' replied CD equably.

'Eighteen quid they wanted for one of those,' said Aidan, scowling. 'I got mine at B&Q for three pounds ninety-nine.'

'This is not just a trowel,' replied CD. 'It is an extension of your arm and your arm is an extension of your brain. This is what tells you when you've found the finest of fine differences in the soil. Every little bit of information this blade meets goes on the fast track to intellectual processing. This is the blade that cannot lie.'

'And me thinking it was just a thing for shovelling dirt,' said Aidan.

'Soil, please,' said CD, 'never dirt. Soil has a million subtle varieties. You will form a deep bond with the soil. You will learn to taste it. Literally. When you find a piece of something that could be a pot or could be a rock, you will learn to put it in your mouth and see how it tastes because the mouth is the most sensitive organ.'

'That's disgusting,' said the blonde woman with the lipstick. 'I shan't be doing that.'

A frightened-looking, elderly woman at the back held up a very shiny trowel. 'I say,' she said, 'mine's a WHS but it's eight-inch not four. Will that do?'

'Well now, let's see,' CD said. 'In many parts of the world where you need something long enough to fend off the things that come out and bite that would do very well indeed. Here, I'm sorry to tell you, it is very definitely far too big.' CD opened a rucksack and started to bring out trowels. 'I guess I've got enough here to go round. Five pounds to hire one. Fifteen to buy.'

'They're old,' said Aidan. 'That's daylight robbery.'

'Yup,' agreed CD, 'I have a Harley-Davidson and a hungry raven to support. Gather round afterwards and shower money into my hands, but first we have to talk about mattocks.' He paused and looked around him. 'Today we will be deturfing. That is unglorified gardening. You will hate it. You will be using spades, shovels and mattocks to get rid of the topsoil and—'

Aidan raised a hand. 'I just wanted to ask, isn't it a bit easy to break things with a mattock?'

'That just about hits it on the head,' said CD. 'It is extremely easy to break things with a mattock. You might even say that breaking things is the whole point of a mattock, its *raison d'être*.'

'But we don't want to break things we might find, surely?'

'OK, time for one of CD's blinding insights, folks. Pay close attention here.' He cleared his throat. 'Most everything that's in the ground's been broken for a couple of thousand years already. Hit it with a mattock and you don't do it much more harm than history already did. Break nothing, find nothing. Get good with your mattock and know when to reach for your trowel. Anyway, it's only Roman crap we're looking for here. Far too easy. I'm an Anglo-Saxon man myself, stains in the soil. At this point I'll hand over to the director so he can tell you exactly why we're here.'

There was a moment of expectant silence before Patrick realised they were all looking at him. 'Um, there's a developer called . . .' He looked at his clipboard. '. . . Roger Little who has applied for planning permission to build houses on this site. There was some historical evidence of tesserae being picked up in the plough-soil here.' He saw that most of their faces were blank. 'That's pieces of Roman mosaic flooring. They've done a geophysical survey and there is evidence of a rectangular structure in the middle of the field. We have to find out whether there is anything important here before the building goes ahead. You can all have an hour off to get sorted out while we mark out the trenches, then we'll get stuck in.'

Patrick took CD and Dozer into the field with tapes, pegs and a mallet, and they marked out the first trench from the information in the geophysical print-out. While the other two were taping it, he walked away to the far corner to establish the line of the second trench and when he looked up he saw the watching man was up there on the hillside again.

As Patrick bent to push in a peg, his keen ears caught a shred of familiar words passing between CD and Dozer: '". . . Man's intended for deceiving—that's why Adam met the snake."'

He looked up at once, indignantly, and caught Dozer looking towards him, and CD guiltily looking away. Guessing at what had just passed between them, he felt a hot wash of betrayal.

When they came over to join him, his first instinct was to make an excuse and walk away, but he knew it had to be faced.

'Hey, Pat,' said Dozer, 'I thought—'

'No, me first,' Patrick said. 'I heard that and I can guess the rest. I want you to know that I just don't need it, right? You may think it's funny or something, but it's not.'

'I don't think it's funny,' said Dozer, 'and it ain't anything to be ashamed of, chum. You were one of the greats.'

'You wrote the words that made us all think,' said CD.

'No, no. You know nothing about it,' said Patrick. 'It's buried. It's in the past and I've got the right to leave it there. It has nothing to do with me now. I'm asking you both to keep it to yourselves.'

Dozer reached out and squeezed his shoulder. 'All right, Pat, whatever you say,' and Patrick was, for the first time, profoundly grateful he'd said Pat, fearing he might have said Paddy.

'Finish off this one, would you?' he said, looking at the trench and trying to keep his voice level. 'I'll go and see about the cooking.'

It was out of the frying pan into the fire. As he walked down towards the food tent, he could see there was someone inside. When he went through the flap, he collided for the second time with that scalding reminder of his past, the woman from the road.

PADDY KANE HAD WRITTEN 'Wedding Vows' in a drunken rage and almost immediately wished he hadn't. It became the single song for which his bawdy, violent band was best remembered and the main marker of the breakdown of his life. The story of how he wrote it became a punk rock legend in its own right.

This was the way it happened. Paddy Kane was delivered home one morning by a Colonic Music limo straight from Heathrow after a Frankfurt concert. He slammed in through the front door of his Georgian house near Marlow, furious that the crude nude figure he had sprayed on the front wall had been covered up in his absence. Rachel was too scared of him by this time to have it removed but she had compromised by concealing it behind a climbing rose.

Benny, the driver, was a Colonic Music faithful who could be relied on not to give away the story of the Marlow house, the house that didn't exist, or the wife and son, who didn't exist either. Benny was Paddy's confidant.

'What's up, Pat?' Benny said on the way back, because he alone in the company never called him Paddy. 'Bad gig?'

'I'm fucked,' the star said, and Benny knew what he meant.

They had dropped off Vic Bogart, Colonic's boss, first and Benny had heard every word he'd said. 'Paddy boy, the rags are sniffing round. We got to slide a little skirt into the picture, kid.'

'There's . . . there's Rache.' Paddy's voice had been slurred.

'Yeah, there's your contract too. I'm talking glamour here, not childhood sweetheart.'

When Bogart got out, Benny had taken a risk. 'You don't have to do what he says. Tell him to stuff himself. Make that little girl of yours happy. What is it stops you, Pat? On stage you're a demon. You come off and you let these old men push you around. You got to learn to handle them.'

There was a silence from the back. Benny was worried because he knew Bogart's plan. Paddy Kane was on the ragged edge. Booze him up, hand out the powder and he'd blow away Rachel all by himself. When she'd gone, the manner of her going could be a story—if it helped sell records. Benny didn't want that. He'd liked young Pat Kane when he'd first met him. Kane was intelligent, Kane was nice, Kane cared. Before they pushed the poison into him.

'You don't have to do it,' he said again as he held the limo door open. 'You're worth a cartload of money to them. Tell them to stuff themselves and they'll have to listen.'

It was too late. Paddy lurched in through the front door, ready to direct his vengeance in an entirely inappropriate direction.

He'd been enjoying student life and she'd just started teacher training, when he'd met Rachel at a dance. They'd both been far too young, two eighteen-year-olds who had married a year later in a vague haze of sweetness with circlets of daisies in their hair. Then in his final year of archaeology, playing in his student band at a town-centre pub, a scout had heard Patrick sing, and the lyrics he'd written, and had noticed the way, when Pat moved, every female eye followed. Pat had graduated with a contract already signed.

The money men of Colonic Music had seen how Pat's talent for words could be tuned to a new cutting edge. They'd started to channel him in their direction, and his slender reserves of wisdom and experience had not been enough to keep him straight. His music had changed to a harsher beat. Every big cheque had made it harder to say they were wrong. Rachel's invisibility had been part of the deal—a madness foisted on him that became madder still when David was born. Rachel had kept praying he would draw a line. When that seemed increasingly unlikely, she put her efforts into making a nest for their son, and the gulf between Rachel and Pat grew daily wider.

When Benny dropped him off in his wild, sleepless, fuelled-up state, Paddy had no idea that it was Monday and that, on Mondays, Rachel helped out at David's kindergarten. The house into which he staggered was silent and that wound him up even tighter. When shouting failed to produce any sign of Rachel, he took a thick black felt-tip pen and began to write all across the white kitchen wall, and what he wrote was the first and final draft of 'Wedding Vows'.

An hour later, as the alcohol loosened its hold, it started to dawn on him that this might be a mistake. Finding a pot of white paint in the garage, he covered the wall in obliterating emulsion.

When Rachel and David came home at lunchtime, he was quiet, somewhere deep inside himself. Rachel questioned him about the fresh paint but he wouldn't reply. She left him alone while David sat on his knee for much of the afternoon, content to be there even when his father fell asleep. Rachel put David to bed and later, when she had cooked supper, woke Paddy as one might approach an unexploded bomb.

It was halfway through a silent meal that she looked past his shadowed, staring eyes and saw dark shapes developing through the drying paint on the wall behind. She read the lyrics with growing anguish.

A wife is there for leaving. Marriage vows are made to break.
Man's intended for deceiving—that's why Adam met the snake.
Adultery's for adults, faithful's just for fools.
Monogamy's monotonous, even rulers break the rules.
You can tell the truth to lovers but it's better when you lie.
A puppy's just for Christmas then you leave it out to DIE.

Rachel's brother called in on his way to a party that evening, found his sister distraught and Paddy asleep, and copied the words down when Rachel wasn't looking, thinking—but not daring to say—that they were quite good. A girl he was trying to impress at the party that night took them out of his pocket when he fell asleep on her bed later and told the *Sun*. The newspaper printed every word of the song. The band's keyboard player wrote the music the very next morning and Paddy walked in late to a rehearsal studio to find his monster had taken living, breathing shape.

From that moment, Rachel lost her faith that Paddy would one day be Pat again—the Pat she had met and loved. He had stripped the surviving fragments of joy out of her so that what was left was no longer anything like the girl bride with the daisies in her hair.

Pat turned himself more and more into Paddy, a man with no need for responsibility, a man drawn not to sweet, quiet girls but to wild, fierce women who could match him drink for drink, drug for drug. Vic Bogart and his PR polished the legend of the wild man and his life on the road with the band. Paddy did not know then that there is a price for everything, and it was only when the bill came, on a sunny afternoon in Perugia, that he recoiled. He abruptly left the band, cut his extravagant, dyed hair, abandoned his extravagant, dyed life and became Patrick, puritan, isolated Patrick, and tried to get back to a worthwhile point in his life, to do some growing up.

IN THE CATERING TENT, the woman who had brought back memories of Rachel gave a little cry of shock as a tray was knocked out of her hands so that slices of cheese fell all over the grass.

'Oh, sorry,' she said, dropping to her knees and scooping up the cheese.

'I didn't know you were there,' Patrick said.

'Well, I was hoping you hadn't done it on purpose,' she said, giving him a quick grin. 'It's only grass. I don't suppose it matters.'

He stood there immobilised and tongue-tied.

'You can help me if you like,' she said. 'I don't want the boss to see me messing up the lunch before I've even got started.'

He knelt next to her and began to pick up the slices of Cheddar.

'I only told them I could do catering because I wanted to be on the dig. Have you met the director yet?'

'Who?' said Patrick, who had been lost in the sound of her voice without really taking in her words.

416

'The director.'

'Oh no. Well yes, I'm him.'

'You're . . .?' Horrified, she scrambled to her feet. 'Oh God, I'm sorry, I didn't realise. You must think I'm really stupid. I'm Bobby Redhead,' she said, holding out a hand.

'I'm er . . . I'm Patrick,' and he left out the Kane which seemed too dangerous in combination.

'Look, don't mind what I said, I *can* do the catering really.'

He didn't care in the slightest whether she could or couldn't.

'I saw you earlier, didn't I?' he said. 'I was in my car. You were having a row with somebody at the school.'

'Oh, was that you too? I'm sorry. I was a bit upset.'

Patrick tried to be professional. 'Do you have enough gas rings to do hot food in the evenings?' He looked around to break the gravitational pull of those eyes. 'They'll need a hot meal at the end of the day.'

'I thought I'd get it ready at home. Then I can bring it over and reheat it a bit.'

'How far away is home?'

She lifted the flap of the tent. 'Over there. Highbury Farm.'

Two fields away, a jumble of old stone buildings sat in a dip. A roof of lichened stone tiles branched and sprouted into dormers and cross-wings. Two barns formed the other edges of an open square and reinforced the message of the tractor in the yard. This was a working place.

'How much do you farm?'

'Not much—sixty acres.'

'This wasn't your field, was it?'

Her tone changed sharply. 'I wouldn't have sold it if it had been. It went with the old wood and the estate. I didn't even know it was up for sale when Little wriggled in and bought it.'

'You don't approve of this man Little, then?'

'I don't trust Roger Little and I certainly don't approve of Roger Little, no. The very best thing that could happen to Wytchlow right now would be for us to find something so important that he couldn't build his damned houses at all.'

'That doesn't happen too often, I'm afraid,' said Patrick.

'We can but hope.'

'Do you farm by yourself?'

'No, no. It's me and Joe.'

Well, of course there would be a Joe.

From outside the tent, a bass voice boomed, 'Oy, Pat.'

Patrick ducked back out to daylight and safety.

Dozer stood there jerking a thumb at a man standing talking to CD. 'Builder's 'ere,' he said.

Roger Little was a huge man with a pugnacious jaw and a Birmingham accent who looked elsewhere when he talked, as if he couldn't be bothered with you.

'You're not started yet, then?' were his first words.

'We've just marked out the trenches.'

'Look, time is money, right? Your man—what's he called? Heskin? He said this wouldn't take long.'

'That depends what we find. We're deturfing today and—'

'By hand? For Christ's sake, I'll get a machine up here.'

Normally, that would have been a welcome offer.

'No, thanks,' said Patrick. 'We can do it better by hand.'

Little stared around him at the diggers. 'This lot don't look like they've ever done a full day's work in their lives.'

CD laughed. 'Appearances can be deceptive.' With its head cocked on one side, the bird, perched on his shoulder, inspected the builder. 'You see Vera over there?' He pointed at the wispy woman who'd had the eight-inch trowel. 'She found tomb two eighteen in the Valley of the Kings. Dug it all by herself, shifted four hundred cubic metres of sand single-handed in eighteen days.' He stepped closer to Little and lowered his voice. Then there's Dozer here. Former President of the UK Hell's Angels. I've seen him lift a two-hundred-pound sarsen stone with one hand.'

'Pleased to meet you, Mr Small,' said Dozer, holding out a hand. Little gave a gasp as his own hand disappeared completely inside it, and seemed to decide not to argue about his name.

'Well, why don't I get a digger up here anyway?' he said. 'I'll have a man for you any time you want to use it.'

'Nah, just leave the keys. I'm trained,' said Dozer.

IN THE REMAINING TWO HOURS before lunch they cut the edges of one trench and took the turf off half of it. The team rapidly divided into the stalwarts and the complainers, led by Gaye, for whom nothing was ever right. She had some justification. The mattocks had splintery wooden handles, the spades had blunt blades, and out of ten wheelbarrows only two did not suffer from some combination of soft tyres, bent axles and missing bolts.

Then there was Maxwell, the student. Maxwell kept finding things. As every turf was hacked and levered out, Maxwell, scarlet eruptions scattered across an otherwise chalky face, would kneel to scan the exposed surface as if the rim of the Holy Grail might well be poking through it. Work in the immediate vicinity would then have to stop while he levered a small piece of stone from the earth and took it excitedly to show Patrick and CD. The first, second and third times, they took the trouble to look at his find closely, explain that it was natural and send him back to work with encouraging noises. The fourth time, CD held it up to the bird, which pecked at it and chattered.

'What do you reckon, Edgar?' said CD. 'Geology?'

Edgar lifted his tail and excreted.

'Yup,' said CD. 'Thought so. Geology.'

'What does that mean, geology?' said Maxwell.

'Rock,' said CD. 'Archaeology means things, geology means rock.'

The fifth time, CD took the proffered stone and without even looking at it, hurled it over the hedge.

'That could have been important,' protested Maxwell, aghast.

'Yup,' said CD. 'I guess we'll never know.'

By the time they broke for lunch, CD had managed to establish a position with the others that Patrick deeply envied, an air of effortless expertise that the humour helped. Dozer, too, had the attention and respect of the rest, but Patrick knew that he himself was far more of a mystery.

'Clear up your loose,' shouted CD when Patrick called lunch break.

'And what does that mean?' said Aidan, pushing his glasses firmly back into his eye-sockets with one finger as he straightened up.

'Get rid of the loose earth, put your tools on the ground, tip the barrows over to cover them.'

'Why don't we leave them where they are?' objected Aidan.

'OK,' said CD wearily, 'gather round for lesson two in CD's insights series.'

They all came towards him. He looked at them benevolently.

'You do it because I say so, and to get into practice for when it matters, because when you get down to the exciting stuff, if you leave the trench full of loose earth and it rains, then all you've got when you come back is mud, and we don't like mud because it washes the evidence all over the goddamn floor.'

'So we put the barrows over the tools to keep them dry?'

'No. You put the barrows over the tools because if you step on a mattock, I don't want to get sued.'

They sat on the grass outside the catering tent, eating doorstep sandwiches of cheese and pickle. The other diggers looked exhausted by their morning's work and seemed too reticent to join CD, Patrick and Dozer. Patrick knew he should be making the effort to get to know his crew but he couldn't summon up the energy. Instead, he sat in his own reverie while CD and Dozer spun ever more apocryphal tales to each other of their imaginary exploits together. Patrick watched Bobby as she moved in and out of the tent. Her dark woollen cap made her cheeks seem startlingly pale.

Gaye came over to him at a moment when he was miles away.

'You'll have to do something. We really can't be expected to put up with it,' she said, indignantly. 'They're revolting.'

'What are?'

'The . . . facilities. Those things.' She pointed at the loos. 'You can *see*.'

'What can you see?'

'Everything. It's all just . . . well, lying there. It's repulsive.'

'It's all right. That's how they work. They're full of special chemicals that neutralise it all. It's perfectly healthy. You don't have to look.'

CD put on a wolfish smile. 'I like looking in them,' he said. 'It's inspirational, it's ever-changing. The colours are fascinating. You wait until we have curry. Beef vindaloo is best. After that . . .'

Gaye had gone. She was replaced immediately by spotty Maxwell.

'I've been talking to the others,' he said. 'We all want to know when we're going to start *finding* things.'

'Really?' said CD. Edgar hopped off his shoulder and settled on Maxwell's head. Maxwell tried to bat the bird away but it dug its claws into the boy's scalp.

'Keep still and he won't hurt you,' said CD amiably. The jackdaw spread its wings for balance and stood there swaying like a heraldic crest on a knight's helmet. 'Now tell me, Maxwell,' CD went on, 'I guess you've seen the Indiana Jones movies.'

'Well, yes,' said Maxwell incautiously, 'I have, all of them.'

'And you just can't wait to find the secret chamber with the treasure in it.'

'Oh no, I know it's not going to be like that but I just—'

'Come with me.' CD stood up and the bird flew back to his shoulder. 'Over here, everybody. CD's insights number three.'

He led them to the plastic lavatories, with Gaye lagging well behind, and opened the door of the first of the pair.

'OK, Maxwell,' he said. 'Stick your head down there.'

'Where?' said the boy, appalled.

'Bottom left, down by the floor. Read me what it says.'

Patrick had tagged along to see what CD was up to. The stench was terrible.

Maxwell, crouched and twisted so that his head was distressingly close to the moulded plastic lavatory bowl, sounded as if he was gagging as he read the inscription: 'The Polyjohn Manufacturing Company, Wilmington, Indiana. US patent number seven five—'

'Stop right there. That's enough. You can come out now.'

Maxwell uncoiled himself rapidly.

'Listen up, everybody,' said CD. 'Patrick has asked me to tell you about *finds*.' Patrick hadn't done any such thing but was profoundly grateful that the American was sensitive to his authority. 'Finds are nice,' CD drawled. 'Finds are fun, but mostly finds are useful because finds help give us *dates*. Information is what we are looking for. If we find things we do not rush to dig them up. Oh no. We come and tell teacher and we are very, very careful to leave our find exactly where it is.'

Aidan cleared his throat. 'And perhaps you could tell us why exactly this young man had to stick his head down there so you could tell us that?'

CD laughed. 'Young Maxwell would like to be Harrison Ford and he's kinda hoping the Ark of the Covenant is round here somewhere. As you know, archaeology Indiana Jones-style is all about grabbing the treasure, escaping in a hail of bullets and to hell with recording the context.' He slapped the side of the blue plastic box. 'Well, this is the Indiana John, folks, and that's as close as you're ever going to get.' He looked at Patrick, and tapped his watch.

Patrick nodded. 'Back to work, folks. Tea break at three thirty.'

As they straggled off, Patrick heard Aidan grumbling to Maxwell. 'The thing that worries me is how he *knew* that name was down there.'

Because there is very little justice in life, it was Maxwell who made the big find later that afternoon.

THE YELL BROUGHT all the diggers rushing to the boy who had uttered it. It was too early for a find, they were still taking off the turf, but Maxwell had not followed the conventional, slow, patient ways of archaeology; Maxwell had dug his very own hole—a small square pit a foot and a half deep with coloured fragments gleaming at its bottom. Piled at the edge of the trench were what Maxwell had taken out of his pit, a small stack of dirty slabs.

Patrick pushed his way through the cluster of craning diggers. 'What's happened here?' he demanded.

'Mosaic tiles. You know, your tesser things. See? I've found a floor,' said Maxwell, pleased as punch and failing to pick up any warning from Patrick's tone.

Patrick looked at the hole and the pile beside it, unable to believe that one overgrown teenager could do so much damage.

CD and Dozer arrived at a run and gazed into Maxwell's hole.

'You took those out?' Patrick pointed at the dirty pile of slabs.

'Yup, and just look what was hiding under them.'

'You've removed a destruction layer, you little pillock. Roman roof tiles. You've dug right through the context. You've destroyed information. We need to know *how* this roof collapsed. You said you were an archaeology student, for God's sake. Haven't you learned *anything* yet?'

'I'm only a first year.' Maxwell blinked at him. 'I have found a floor, haven't I?'

It was true that at the bottom of that unforgivable hole there was a glint of rich colour, red and white and yellow, where a scatter of mosaic fragments poked through the moist earth.

'We told you. We're not here to find things. We're here to untangle the story of this place, slowly and carefully—not like a bloody bulldozer.' Patrick was on the verge of telling Maxwell to pack his tent when he saw a small, shining tear appear at the corner of the boy's eye. The part of him that could no longer bear to cause pain revolted. 'Oh, sod it,' he said. 'CD, give them a thorough lecture about contexts, will you?'

'OK,' said CD wearily. 'What is a context anyone?'

The older man with gingery grey hair answered. 'It's the position of a find on a site and its stratigraphic relationship to its immediate surroundings.'

CD blinked. 'I guess that's about the perfect textbook answer.'

Patrick reached for his list. 'I'm sorry, you are?'

'Peter Knight,' said the man.

'And you are Emeritus Professor of Archaeology at which university?' said CD.

Peter laughed. 'No such luck, I'm afraid. I've been a bit of a book-worm all my life. Lots of theory, not much practice. '

Aidan frowned. 'I have to say that explanation was as much use to me as a stepladder in a sandstorm.'

'OK. Well in plain language a context is a layer,' said CD. 'A layer of time. Suppose it's a ditch, then the surface of the ditch is a context. Supposing the ditch got itself filled in to halfway up, then that fill and anything that's in it is a context. When you're digging one context, whatever's sticking up out of the next one, even if it's the missing treasure of Eldorado, you don't disturb it until you've removed and recorded the whole of that context. Ever. Right?'

A rising growl made Patrick look towards the road. A large yellow digger crawled into view from behind the trees and turned to sway its way into the field. Roger Little walked in behind it with a proprietor-ial swagger. At that moment, Patrick caught a movement out of the corner of his eye. He saw the watcher was on the hill again, nearer now. For the first time, Patrick could make him out, a man of middle age, powerfully built—an outdoors man in a dun-coloured shirt and heavy, working trousers. As Little strode into view, the man on the hill made an abrupt lateral gesture with his arm, as if warding off something in disgust, and turned away.

'How are you getting on?' said Little as he arrived.

'Fine.'

'Waste of time. There's nothing here. Never was.'

A more experienced man might have kept quiet but Patrick found himself blessing young Maxwell for the first time that afternoon.

'There is. We've already found it. A Roman floor by the look of it.'

'Go on with you. Where?'

'There, see?'

Little looked into the hole for an uncomfortably long time.

'Funny way to dig a hole,' he said. 'Straight down like that. I thought you lot did things more carefully.'

'That's what we call a sondage,' said CD. 'Used for getting us a baseline resistivity check when the barometric pressure variation might invalidate the groundline reading.'

Little clearly had no idea what the American was talking about, but then nor did Patrick and nor did CD.

'So what happens next?' said the builder grumpily.

'We follow the lines of the geophysical survey,' Patrick told him. 'This shows up as a corner, so it looks like it confirms the indications that what we might have here is some kind of rectangular structure.'

Little squinted around the field. 'How far does it go?'

Patrick remembered the rough shape on the print-out. 'I'll pace it out,' he said.

He walked twenty paces diagonally towards the far hedge then turned at right angles and took twelve more. Little stood watching him as he completed the rectangle and came back.

'Could be worse. Maybe I could build round it. Leave it as a garden.' The builder sniffed and squinted up at the clouds. 'Best be off, I've got work to do. There's going to be a lot of rain.'

He was right. At half past four, an icy, drenching rain first washed the emerging layer of Roman roof tiles brilliantly clean, then filled the trench with an obliterating layer of muddy water.

The catering tent became a haven for the diggers as they huddled together at the rickety table inside, trying to avoid the dribbles leaking through the ancient canvas seams.

Gaye complained loudly. 'You can't expect us to sleep in the tents in this, surely? Isn't there a guesthouse or something?'

CD stuck his head out of the flap. 'Nothing wrong with this. Just a little local precipitation. That's all.'

Gaye's tent blew away at five o'clock, dragged across the grass by the rising wind. Dozer guffawed loudly at the sight, then looked at her stricken face and went out into the downpour to retrieve it and put in all the extra tent pegs that she had left out.

At five forty-five the old marquee gave up the struggle, letting water pour in simultaneously in a dozen new places at once. Patrick had no clear idea what to do, but then help came from an unexpected quarter. A van drove into the field entrance and its owner ran across to the diggers.

'I've got some dry sheds you can all sleep in at my yard,' said Roger Little. 'I suppose I'm responsible for you one way and another. Get your gear and pile in.'

There was a murmur of relief all round.

'OK,' Patrick said to Little. 'Thanks.'

They piled into the back of the van and were driven through the village to what had once been a farmyard. Only one barn survived and around it stood a cluster of small, square industrial units. Little unlocked one. It was large enough for all of them and blessedly dry.

'What are you doing about grub?' said Little.

'Bobby's cooking it. The woman from Highbury Farm.'

'Oh, her,' said Little. 'She's off her head, that woman. Tell you what: I'll get the grub brought over here, shall I? One of my blokes can pick you all up in the morning.'

'He's changed his attitude,' Patrick remarked to CD when the builder left them. 'I never expected any help from that quarter.'

CD gave him a delphic look. 'I guess,' he said. 'Anyway, I'm not too good on concrete, I might just walk back down there later on and sleep in that nice soft mud.'

But the American's intentions were fatally undermined by the dozen litre bottles of rough red wine that arrived unexpectedly with the food and allowed them all to sleep on that hard floor.

When Patrick woke the next morning, the shed looked like a refugee camp, an untidy sprawl of bodies, heads resting on shoulders of people who had been perfect strangers the day before. He remembered raucous singing late into the night and CD filling his plastic mug repeatedly for him in a vain attempt to get him to join in. When the party got to take-off point, horribly like old times, he had retreated into a corner, shunning the friendship and especially the songs.

His watch said 8.05. He wriggled out of his sleeping-bag and decided to walk to the field. He was halfway to the village when a beaten-up Land Rover passed him going fast the other way, braked, turned and came back to him. Bobby jumped out and his heart did a treacherous cartwheel.

'Get in,' Bobby said. 'You won't believe this. I'm so sorry. I should never have let it happen.'

'What? What's happened?'

She was on the verge of tears. 'Just get in.'

They were at the field in two minutes. The digger was standing in the middle of a sea of mud. Desecration had taken place. A huge rectangle of grass had been carved away to two feet or more below the surface, and Patrick knew with appalling certainty that the hole covered the whole area he had so obligingly paced out for Roger Little the day before.

'I slept through it,' Bobby said angrily.

'I'm an idiot,' said Patrick. 'Why didn't I stay with the tents?'

They stared at it in silence for a few moments.

'Shall we go and see him? I know where he lives,' said Bobby.

'You mean Little?'

'Of course I mean Little. Who else would I mean?'

'Well, what would I say?' He couldn't bear the way she was looking at him as if he had let her down. 'Yes,' he said. 'Sure. You bet.'

Little was coming out of his garage as they drove into his yard. He stopped and raised his eyebrows at the style of their arrival. Bobby was out of the Land Rover almost before it stopped, Patrick following her because he had no choice, propelled headlong into a confrontation for which he was not ready.

'What you've done is inexcusable,' said Bobby.

'What I've done?' said Little in mock astonishment.

'You know bloody well what I'm talking about.'

'I don't think I do and I don't like being addressed like that.'

'You dug up the field.'

'What, someone's dug it up, have they? You didn't leave the keys in the digger, did you? With all the kids around here? I hope they haven't done any damage.'

'Kids who cart all the earth away?' said Bobby. 'Do you know what you've destroyed?'

'You be careful what you say,' said Little. 'You could get sued for saying things like that.'

What happened next came as a complete surprise to Patrick, who felt himself taken over as if possessed by another voice, another body. Shaking with the effects of a flood of adrenaline born from fury, he moved in between Bobby and the builder, boring into Little's personal space and pushing him back towards his door with the force of his words and the ready-to-snap tension vividly evident in every fibre of his body.

'Listen to me, you,' he said. 'Who else stands to benefit from wiping out that site, eh? Who else knew exactly which bit to destroy? Do you think anybody's going to believe it wasn't you?' His voice was getting louder. 'You took us for suckers, didn't you? Getting us out of the way? Well, if you think you're going to get your planning permission now, you've got another think coming.'

They had reached the house, Little giving ground backwards all the way, and finally the builder turned quickly, opened his door and stepped inside.

'You can't talk to me like that,' he said through the closing gap. 'Get off my land.'

In the Land Rover, Bobby said, 'You were fantastic,' but all Patrick could do, instead of basking in the glow of her approval, was to sit there appalled by the knowledge that the old Paddy still lurked inside him, waiting for the slightest chance to get out.

THREE

In the pub that night, an ancient, wheezing stranger in a greasy cloth cap stuck his face close to Patrick's and opined that it wasn't Friday, jabbing him in the arm for emphasis and cackling with the mysterious humour of it. It was the fourth or fifth time that one of the locals had mentioned that it wasn't Friday, nodding as they did so towards the far end of the bar where a stool, a guitar and a mike stand were set up on a platform.

Every few seconds the door would open, letting in cold, wet air and cold, wet villagers who would also give their opinion that it wasn't Friday, and sometimes seek confirmation from the strangers huddled by the radiator in the corner. There had been no shortage of opinions expressed that day. By the time they all crowded into the pub that evening, Patrick felt he'd heard enough to last a lifetime.

Dozer's had been the most painful and the most straightforward.

'He'll get away with it, won't he? Must 'ave mates on the planning committee or he wouldn't have risked chucking his cash at that field in the first place. If we can't prove it was 'im, they'll just roll over and let him tickle their tummies.'

CD had blamed himself. 'That's why I planned to go back and sleep down there,' he said. 'I shouldn't have drunk that wine.'

Gaye was looking on the bright side. 'Does that mean we can all go home now?' she asked. 'I could certainly do with a good bath.'

Hescroft had been the worst, pre-empting Patrick by turning up at the field while Patrick had still been trying to get him on his mobile. Hescroft's opinions had been uncompromising. Patrick had shown an extraordinary lack of judgment in leaving the site to the mercy of hooligans. There was very little hope of taking any effective action against Little without hard evidence. Anyway, what made Patrick so sure it *was* Little? It could have been anyone. After all, they *had* left the key in the digger, which was a childish mistake. 'What do I do? Kenny Camden, the series producer, is coming to see me tomorrow,' Hescroft had said. 'What on earth am I going to tell him?'

'Tell him we didn't find anything. What do I do with all my diggers?'

Hescroft had looked round the despoiled field. 'You've still got to write a report. Have them dig two trenches out at right angles from that hole. Just to make sure there's really nothing left.'

The new trenches had turned up three tessera fragments and a quarter of a roof tile. It didn't amount to a lot. The only solid evidence they had of what had been there before was a single photo taken by CD of Maxwell's original hole. Morale had been so low by evening that there was little doubt, when it had started to drizzle, that the pub was the right place to go.

The Stag, halfway along the green, was a basic pub with lino on the floor and bright neon lights. Soon after the team had ordered their beers, there was a lot of background giggling going on at their expense. Whatever it was that made it not Friday clearly had something to do with them.

'What do we do now, Patrick?' asked Aidan.

'We finish those two trenches, then I guess—'

Suddenly the reason it wasn't Friday became clear with a loud guitar chord.

'Gawd Almighty,' said Dozer. 'Take a look at Eric Clapton over there.'

The man sitting on the guitar stool wore a cowboy hat and a bright red waistcoat. He strummed another chord or two then launched straight into a song, a simple variation on basic country-and-western hoe-down.

'They came up here to Wytchlow with their trowels all prepared,
To search for Roman ruins that the centuries might have spared.
They dug around all afternoon till it came on to pour
But they didn't like to get too wet so they all packed up at four.
A nice man offered shelter in a barn a mile away
And they slept there like a pile of logs until dawn of the next day.
When they went back to start again, they got a great big shock
Because while they'd all been sleeping, the digger ran amok.
They'd found the Roman pavement, but they didn't think too quick,
'Cos someone came there in the night and played a dirty trick.
When they saw what happened, they could not believe their eyes,
Next time they meet our Roger, they'll be a little more wise.'

The crowd roared its approval and the old man in the cloth cap reappeared to make sure Patrick had got the point. '"A *little* more wise", do you get it? Roger Little, eh?'

Patrick nodded wearily, realised that the whole bar was grinning in their direction, and waved in sheepish acknowledgment.

The door opened and Bobby walked in. It was safer to look away, but as she walked across the room she dragged his treacherous gaze after her. She was still wearing her working clothes and that old woollen hat. There was a chorus of greeting.

'How's the great struggle?' called a man in a Barbour jacket.

'We'll win,' she said.

'Bloody right,' said someone else.

'Always done it, always will,' said an old man with brown teeth.

For a few moments Patrick was distracted from the knowledge that was slowly forming in his head, the knowledge that he'd seen the singer before. If you took away the absurd hat and waistcoat, you had the middle-aged man who had been watching them from his position up on the hill. It wasn't only Little who had known what part of the field to dig up. This man had also been watching yesterday as Patrick had paced out the field.

He sought another glimpse of Bobby in the now-crowded bar but all he could see was the top of her hat.

As if he'd read Patrick's mind, Dozer said, 'Do you think she always wears that hat?'

'Scalp condition,' said CD. 'I had a girl once, she had a scalp condition all over. Had to wear a chemical warfare suit. Never did find out what she looked like.'

Bobby was down there at the far end, near the singer, who drained his glass and picked up his guitar again. The bar fell silent once more at the first sound of his fingers on the strings. This was a different sound, a gentle, skilful arpeggio contrasting greatly with the crude strumming of the first song.

> *'I sing you the song of the German Queen*
> *With her hair dark red and her eyes so green.*
> *I sing you the song of the way they cried*
> *On the dreadful day when the fair queen died.*
>
> *The eldest child of her father's line,*
> *A slender shoot from a sturdy vine,*
> *She kept his house from her early days*
> *Once her well-loved mother had passed away.'*

The pub audience listened in reverential silence but Patrick detected that they were a little puzzled. It seemed to him that the first rough song was more what they were used to than this quiet ballad.

'Her father wore the silver ring
From the German lands where he'd been a king
And, dreaming of what once had been,
He called the girl his German Queen.

There came a time in that gentle land
When their peace was marred by a roving band.
New arrived from the Saxon shore
With a grudge from home and an old, old score.

They climbed the hill on an autumn morn,
And the first light gleamed on the swords they'd drawn.
High on the hill, that glint was seen
By the chieftain's girl with her eyes so green.

She ran to the wall with the warning gong
And she made it sing its arousing song.
Her brothers leapt from their wives' warm arms
At the first loud cry of its harsh alarm.

They met the raiders, blade to blade
In a spray of blood by the old stockade.
Outnumbered by them five to one,
The fight was led by the oldest son.

At the moment when they saw him fall
And his soul took flight to the warriors' hall
The hills rang out to a chilling cry.
Their father saw the young prince die.'

Patrick slipped into a reverie, flashing back to the first time he'd ever been on a big stage, to the awesome, terrifying, thrilling moment of walking into a bombardment of howling applause. Rachel, worried, watching in the wings. Pat taking the first step towards being Paddy, tilted off-balance by the first taste of massive, uncritical adulation. He saw Rachel clearly in his mind's eye then, but it wasn't his mind's eye at all because this version of her was standing at the bar looking at the singer. Patrick stared at Bobby for an age, then she met his eye and frowned at the intensity of his gaze.

He blinked and broke the eye contact, and, as he became aware that he'd lost the thread of the song, he saw that the singer had got up and was coming towards him and his diggers, directing his song straight at them.

'Up on the hill on the sacred ground,
They dug a grave in the ancient mound.
They laid her there and in sorrow kneeled
Round that older tomb in the Bury Field.

Amber beads were round her head
And she sleeps there still on her wooden bed.
Her cloak secured with the royal jewel
That had marked the years of her father's rule.

Now leather and wood have turned to dust.
The iron brackets are dark brown rust.
The bed has lost its strength and weight
But the burden on it's no longer great.

The years and the plough have flattened the land
Which she saved with a stroke of her valiant hand.
Now silence and shadows mark the scene
Of the glorious grave of the German Queen.'

He bowed his head to the applause and Patrick was left utterly astonished at what he had just heard. A crude folk song, describing in detail something almost unknown except in the academic realms of archaeology—an Anglo-Saxon furnished bed burial. Was it just chance? What had he missed in the rest of the song?

Patrick looked across the table at the American. 'What did you make of that?'

'The chicken sword? Funny you should ask . . .'

'Chicken sword? What's a chicken sword? I meant the bed burial.'

'Well, I don't know much about—'

'Hang on. He's going. I've got to talk to him.'

The singer was making for the door. It took Patrick a moment or two to push through the crowd after him and, by the time he got out, the man was just a dark shape moving across the village green.

'Wait a minute,' called Patrick. 'Can I talk to you?'

The man didn't slow down and Patrick ran after him to catch up.

'I just want to know about that song you sang,' he said.

No response.

'I only want to know what it's called? Who wrote it?'

The man looked round at him and strode onwards.

'What's going on?' said Patrick angrily, trying to keep up. 'Why won't you talk to me? Was it you who dug up our field?'

At that the man swung round, made an emphatic gesture of rejection in complete silence, and pushed Patrick in the chest.

'Don't you bloody do that,' said Patrick, and grabbed the offending arm only to have his own arm seized from behind and wrenched away. He swung round to find himself confronting Bobby.

'Go home, Joe,' she told the singer. 'Go home. I'll sort him out.'

The man looked at her, grunted and walked off.

'That's Joe?' said Patrick, aghast. 'Your Joe?'

'Yes, that's Joe. What the bloody *hell* did you think you were doing, treating him like that?'

The anger in Bobby's voice was more than he could deal with. Now she didn't just look like Rachel, she sounded like her too.

'I didn't know that was Joe. I was only trying to talk to him.'

'You weren't. I saw you. You were pushing and grabbing at him.'

'I thought he was being pretty rude. He wouldn't answer.'

She laughed derisively. 'He *couldn't* answer, for God's sake. He doesn't talk. Don't say nobody in the pub told you!'

That made no sense. 'Come off it. I've just heard him singing.'

'Yes, he sings. He doesn't talk apart from that, can't get any words out. Even to me. He hasn't talked for years. There's no reason to go bullying him like that.' She was calming down a little.

'Bobby, I had no idea.' It was the first time he had said her name. He had to do it, to establish for himself who she was. 'I didn't know any of that. I wouldn't have gone chasing after him if they'd told me. Why is he like that?'

She made a noise of exasperation, the sound of someone who had been asked that question far too many times. 'I don't know. He talked when he was little then he just stopped.'

'And he doesn't talk to you, either?'

'He writes me notes.'

'I don't understand about the singing. How can he do that?'

'That's his way. He puts on his clothes and he's someone else. He's a performer, he's not Joe any more. Maybe he just needs to be somebody else. I know I should be able to explain it, but I can't. It's pretty hard to understand.'

'No it's not,' said Patrick, thinking just how much he knew about the lure of being somebody else on a big stage with the world looking on. In the dark, he could just see the shine of her wide eyes, turned on him. A door opened and closed somewhere behind him and the light from it showed him her face, framed in dark hair, the hat gone, and she was not Rachel because Rachel was blonde.

'I heard,' she said, 'that you used to sing.'

'Who have you been talking to? CD? Dozer?' Without wishing it, there was a harsh edge in his voice.

'No, no. It was one of the diggers, the guy with the round glasses.'

'Aidan?' Jesus. Did everybody know?

'Listen, Patrick, I didn't mean to upset you. It's none of my business.'

They were both silent as the echoes of discord died away.

'That song he was singing,' said Patrick, driven by the need to say something as well as by the need to know, '"The German Queen" and all that. Do you know it?'

'I've heard bits of it,' she said.

'Do you know where it comes from?'

'I think Dad taught it to him. Joe used to have a terrible stutter. Dad taught him old songs to help him talk but then, after Dad died, he stopped talking completely.'

'You and Joe were brought up together?'

'Of course we were.' He could see the pale disc of her face tilt as she put it on one side. 'He's my brother. Didn't you know that either?'

A younger sister protecting her damaged older brother. It began to make sense. She hadn't seemed like half of a couple.

'No, I didn't . . . Do you think he'll sing it again? In the pub?'

'I don't think so. He usually sings his own stuff. It's how he manages, see? All week he saves up all the things he wants to say and he makes them into songs. Just once in a while, when he's had his say, he'll sing one of Dad's old songs. You can't really ask him to do it. He's not very biddable, Joe. He sticks to his routines.'

'He didn't tonight. It's not Friday.'

'He sang tonight because of what's happened, because of you.'

'He was poking fun at us.'

'That was just his way. It wouldn't do to take your side openly against a villager. Think about it. His real message was that Little did it and that's what people will remember. Did you mind?'

'Yes.'

'I think he realised that. I think he sang the other song as a sort of present, to make up for it.'

'So it wasn't Joe who dug up the field?'

'Joe? Why on earth did you think it was Joe?'

'He was up there watching. I paced out the area we'd surveyed, the same bit that got dug up. Little was there, but Joe saw it too.'

'Listen to me. Joe would sooner cut his own arm off than damage anything from the past. He was beside himself when he heard what Little had done.'

'OK. I understand. Thank you for explaining. By the way, what was all that other stuff about? The business at the school?'

'Oh, that. I'll tell you sometime.'

'There might not be a sometime. We'll pack up soon, I expect.'

'Really? Damn. I've been looking forward to this dig.'

'We'll see how it goes tomorrow. Time I went back.' And because it was so very dark, Patrick added, 'Shall I see you home first?' and was discomfited when she burst out laughing.

She cut her laugh off with a hand over her mouth. 'I'm sorry. I didn't mean to be rude.'

The night hid his flush. 'I just meant it's very dark.'

'Yes, I know. I've lived here an awfully long time. I've managed all right so far.' Then, as if to take the sting out of her words, she went on, 'All the newcomers who move here start asking for streetlamps. We've managed to fight them off so far. One night, they look up and notice all the stars and after that it's all right. They get the point.'

He watched her as she strode away, then groped his way back to the field and crawled into his tent. Lying in his clammy sleeping-bag feeling miserable, he heard the diggers coming back from the pub, the diggers who, it seemed, all knew about Paddy Kane.

There was much to-ing and fro-ing and then a flickering glow through the walls of the tent as branches were fed into crackling flames. Next came unwelcome footsteps, close to his tent.

'Patrick, old bean. Are you awake?'

He pretended not to hear, but CD just cranked up the volume. 'Patrick. Yoohoo, Patrick.'

'What?'

'Are you awake?'

'I am now.'

'Come and join in the fun.'

'Not tonight, I'm tired.'

'Don't be a party-pooper. Guess what I've got in my pocket.'

'I don't know,' said Patrick wearily, who also didn't really care.

'Just a bottle of Glenboggy eight-hundred-year-old malt.'

'No, it's OK. Enjoy yourselves. I'm tired.'

'Hey, listen up. It's kind of like our last night. They'd like to see you. Gaye's got made up specially.'

'What?'

'Yeah, she got pissed and fell in the mud. Face first. She thinks it's funny. Hey, listen, Patrick, *I'd* like to see you. Come on out of there.'

So, reluctantly, Patrick joined the diggers round the fire.

'What did you want that singer bloke for, Pat?' asked Dozer. 'Saw you chase out after him.'

'That song. It was just something I wanted to know. But he's not a talker,' said Patrick.

'Yeah. They gave us the form in the pub,' said CD. 'Weird, eh? After he'd finished that song you said something about a bed.'

'Well, yes. I just had an idea that the song was about a bed burial.'

'Listen, my period's the Romans, not all this Saxon shit. You know the way it is on an Anglo-Saxon dig. You get really excited when the dirt changes colour 'cos maybe you've hit a hole. It's just like the song—silence and shadows. Give me something you can bounce a trowel off any day.'

'Hang on. Yesterday you said you hated all that Roman stuff.'

'That was yesterday. Whatever I'm doing, I like the opposite best.'

'You don't know about bed burials?' asked Patrick, feeling pleased that there was at least one area where he knew as much as the American. 'Have you read the Swallowcliffe report?'

'Nope. What's the gist?' CD passed Patrick the bottle.

He tried a small swig. A corrosive liquid seared his throat and kicked his brain from underneath. 'Jesus, what's that?' he said.

'You've not tried Glenboggy before?' said CD. 'Well, as they say in the traditional distilleries of the South Bronx, there's always a first time but there's not often a second time. You were saying?'

'I've got this thing about place names,' said Patrick, 'so I like this story. This guy Speake went back over the notes for a dig someone did years ago and never published. He put it all together from the finds and the dig notebook. Everything had been stacked away in dusty old boxes for heaven knows how long. It was a Bronze Age barrow down south of Stonehenge and in it they found an Anglo-Saxon woman, surrounded by all kinds of iron brackets. They realised she had been buried on a bed and they managed to work out what it had looked like. The way the song described it, the leather straps and stuff, that was pretty much the way it was.'

'So what's the business with the place names?'

'On the old charters, this burial mound was always called Posses Low. So everyone thought that someone called Poss had been buried there. Thing is, in among the finds were all kinds of bits of gold and silver and bronze, and when they put them together they realised they made up a really elaborate shoulder bag, a satchel. A pretty distinctive piece of kit. That's when they realised that *pusa* is the Old English for a bag and Posses Low might have literally meant the grave of the bag lady.'

'Nice,' said Dozer. 'Low as in Wytchlow.'

Patrick became aware that a silence had fallen and people were shuffling up towards their end of the circle to listen.

'What would the "Wytch" bit be?' someone said.

'Maybe a personal name.'

'You have to beware of creating a false tradition from the name of a place,' said Peter Knight. 'For people who couldn't read and write it was a bit tempting sometimes. They kept doing it in the *Anglo-Saxon Chronicle*, you know. They invented this man Port and his sons who landed at Portsmouth, when the name came from the Latin *portus*.'

'Well, anyway,' said Patrick lamely, 'it sounded to me like the song was about a real burial. But I expect it was all just chance.'

'I don't think so,' said CD. 'It wasn't just the bed, was it? There was the sword too. Could be there's an archaeologist out there writing songs. A whole new style, archo-rock.'

'I dig it,' said Dozer to a chorus of groans.

'I didn't hear the bit about the sword,' said Patrick. 'What was it?

Aidan, sitting in the lotus position straight on the wet grass with his round glasses reflecting flames, spoke in a lilting voice. '"The robber band, they turned and ran, before the wrath of a righteous man, leaving their dead where . . ." What was it now? ". . . where they'd been laid by the slashing edge of that chicken blade."'

'Hey, that's pretty impressive,' said CD. 'Can you do the rest of it?'

'That verse just stuck,' said Aidan.

'So what's this chicken blade, then?' said Dozer.

'You better all have some more Glenboggy,' said CD. 'The tale I am about to tell makes shaggy dogs look clean-shaven. It is *decidedly* far-fetched and there's nothing like Glenboggy to dull the critical faculties. I make it myself specifically for that purpose.'

'I bet it's not as far-fetched as that time you an' I got stuck in the Aztec tomb with the bats,' said Dozer.

'It comes close,' said CD, 'pretty close.' He looked at Patrick, owlish behind his pebble glasses. 'OK, here goes. Now it just happens that the first thesis I ever wrote for my doctorate was all about the evidence concerning sword manufacture in the Old Norse myths.'

All the diggers had squeezed in close to the fire, to hear better. Stifled chokes betrayed the course of CD's bottle.

'There's an Old Norse myth called Thiorik's Saga,' CD told them. 'It's the first detailed description of how they made old swords. A good smith would pick the right iron and twist bars of different grades together, so that when they were heated and hammered in the forging you'd get a really good blade. If a bad smith screwed up, the blade would bend halfway through a fight. Not good news for the guy holding the handle. Well, in the saga, there's this smith called Velent or Weland or Wayland, who promises to make his lord a really strong sword. So he makes this sword called Mimming, and when he finishes it he starts filing away at it. Nothing odd in that. Only thing is, Velent went right on filing until the blade was just a pile of shiny filings on the floor. He sweeps it up and mixes it with grain, OK? After that, he starves his chickens for three days and then he feeds them the mixture of filings and corn. Then guess what he does next.'

'Roasts them,' said Dozer.

'He collects their droppings. He collects the chicken shit, guys and gals, and he shapes it into a blade and he forges it all over again and there he has it, a nice shiny, hard sword. But he doesn't stop there. Oh no, you don't get into sagas by doing things the easy way. He did it *three times*. In the end, Velent has this amazing blade that's much smaller and as strong as hell, ready to give to his boss man.'

'Who goes out and kills lots of people with it?' suggested Maxwell.

'No, that would be just a little bit simple for your average Norse saga. What he then does is he makes an exact replica of the sword out of really crap metal and he gives *that* one to the king.'

'So what happened next?'

'No idea. I lost interest about there. I guess the king got killed and his kids sued Velent under the Sale of Goods Act.'

Aidan was in questioning mood. 'It's got to be a load of rubbish, right? I mean, you couldn't actually *make* a sword that way?'

'*Au contraire*,' said CD. 'What does chicken shit smell of? Ammonia. That's because it's full of nitrogen, and when you forge iron with nitrogen you get nitrides and that is just exactly what you want for a good strong blade.'

'So the chicken blade could be true?' said Dozer.

'Could be,' said CD.

FOUR

Patrick woke abruptly at just past six in the morning, when the tent collapsed on him, to find himself smothered in damp polyester and horizontal tent poles. He struggled out of his sleeping-bag and slithered out onto wet grass. His heart was racing because he knew it was impossible that his tent could collapse so suddenly and comprehensively without the intervention of some outside agency. These igloo-type tents didn't come apart easily.

He got out expecting to see a stray cow standing there, but there was no visible explanation. The rest of the campsite was silent and in good order. Perplexed, Patrick bent down to wrestle the poles back into place. There was a noise from behind him like stone striking stone, and only then did he look round, up at the hill behind their field, where Joe was now standing just the other side of the fence.

Patrick stared at him, frightened by the knowledge that Joe must have come to his tent and pulled his tent poles apart. Was this a punishment for his own aggression last night? He stared across at the older man. Then Joe lifted a hand in a summoning gesture.

Dressed only in the long T-shirt he'd slept in, Patrick found himself raising a hand in acknowledgment and pointing at his tent as if to explain he needed clothes. He groped inside for jeans, socks and boots, pulled them on and looked up to find that Joe was now well on his way up the hill.

Patrick wriggled through the fence, and the field beyond was rough pasture with tussocks of grass that tricked his feet as he climbed the gentle slope, so that he was forced to look down. But whenever he looked up again, he saw Joe standing waiting for him.

The rise of the hill was deceptive and the undulating shape of the land didn't reveal itself until Patrick had got to where he'd last seen Joe. He was on a gently domed plateau with fields and woodland to the west and the land falling away towards Oxford to the southeast. Joe stood a hundred yards away, facing him, stock-still, and when he was sure Patrick was looking at him, he pointed emphatically at the earth by his feet, then walked rapidly away.

Patrick fixed the spot with his eyes and, when Joe had disappeared out of sight into a copse of trees, walked slowly towards it. There was nothing remarkable to see, so he crouched and ran his fingers through the short grass. He had no idea what he was looking for.

Moving thirty paces to one side of the spot, he got down on the ground and did four slow press-ups, his head raised, staring at the place Joe had indicated. It was an old trick, shown to him on his very first student dig. The change in perspective as he lifted himself up and down, just a foot off the ground, gave him an exaggerated view of the small changes in the topography of the land ahead.

He suddenly knew what Joe had been pointing at. The very top of the hill rose just a fraction more steeply than the natural curve of the land, making a flattened dome maybe fifteen yards across. The evidence was slender, but after he'd looked carefully at it for several minutes he was convinced he was looking at a barrow, a Bronze Age burial mound, flattened by the slow erosion of wind and rain.

Patrick felt a sudden disappointment. A Bronze Age barrow was interesting enough. It did not square, however, with Anglo-Saxon bed burials. There had been an absurd hope at the back of his mind that Joe's song had meant that at the end of this mysterious journey there might be a clue to the last resting place of his German Queen. Instead there was something that predated it by over a thousand years.

He sat down on the top of the flattened barrow mound, wondering again why Joe had brought him to this spot. It was the first moment he'd had for reflection since this doomed dig began, and reflection wasn't something Patrick enjoyed. In the years since he had reformed his life, reflection had taken the shape of self-accusation more than anything else. But in the past two days, something had changed. He put it down to the fact that, despite himself, he was enjoying the company of these people: CD's nonchalant wit, Dozer's solidity, even Aidan and Maxwell. The truth was that he had started to become a real person again and the process was painful. For a moment his mind brought Bobby into the equation but Bobby was a dangerous diversion; Bobby took him back to a Rachel he still loved and couldn't blame for what had happened to David.

David would have run down this hillside. David, his dark, liquid hair flying behind him, would have jumped on his stocky legs and fallen over without minding, and rummaged in the earth for sticks and stones to produce as jewels. The earth was always full of treasure for David.

All this time Patrick had been fiddling, running his fingers through the soft soil of the molehill on which his right hand was resting. As his thoughts took this painful turn he toyed with one larger stone in his fingers like a worry bead.

Gradually, its cylindrical regularity forced itself through to the front of his mind and he opened his palm and looked down at it. Many an experienced eye has been misled by a freakishly regular piece of natural stone, but not many stones are shaped like cylinders with a tubular hole running through them. Patrick spat in his palm, rubbed the surface with his finger, and colour, bright yellow man-made colour, burst through its coating of grey soil dust. It was opaque yellow glass, decorated with thin red lines in a characteristic crossing-wave pattern, finely worked, beautiful—and datable.

Anglo-Saxon. Seventh century. He'd drawn Saxon beads by the hundred in his recent catching-up studies. This one was perfect—a bead you might easily find in a seventh-century burial. Joe's song had said something about beads, amber beads around her head. This wasn't amber but it did well as a substitute.

Patrick sat looking at the bead in his hand, not as an artefact heading for a glass case, but as a messenger, bursting out of the earth with a tale to tell.

He looked down the hill towards Wytchlow. 'Low' often meant a burial mound, 'low' from the old Saxon *hlaew*. Dozer had said last night that 'Wytch' could be a personal name, so this could be Wytch's low, the place where Wytch was buried. But there was the great forest of Wychwood too. The wood of the Hwicca? The double 'c' of Hwicca has a 'ch' sound. Something else was nagging at him, something he had read. It wouldn't come back.

The Hwicca were a mongrel race, without simple roots. Saxons from the north German coast and Angles from the southern Danish peninsula, they had been pushed out by rising sea levels in front and rising population behind, taking to their boats for a fresh start. What had they made of this alien landscape? He looked down towards the ruined field. The remains of Roman buildings would still have been a dominant presence, left behind as those who had organised Roman Britain fled for home. The Angles and the Saxons didn't use stone. They used up their creative energy more often in their possessions than in their housing. Post-holes for their houses, most of them little more than timber tents, were the only lasting evidence of their construction efforts. What could they have thought of the Romans' almost magical constructions? Civilisation crumbled fast in the 200 years between the Romans' departure and the burial of this bead. Four hundred years of occupation had taught the Britons how to enjoy the Roman way of life but not how to maintain it when the teachers had left.

Patrick knew that British and English were not synonyms then, far from it. English meant Angles, the Germanic incomers. British meant Britons, the Celtic people who'd been here long before the Romans came. The incoming 'English' and their neighbours the Saxons displaced the British by some unknown mixture of violence and integration. Archaeology showed, most fascinatingly of all, that quite suddenly, after AD 600, Anglo-Saxon attitudes changed. They began to annex the old Roman sites that they'd skirted for 150 years with new confidence, using the ruins as burial places for the most important among their dead. At the same time, they began to use much more ancient earthworks too, inserting their dead, cuckoo-like, into these old nests.

Then, in the middle of his thoughts, he remembered what was nagging him about the possible origin of the name of Wytchlow. Something he'd read, some dissertation on Oxfordshire place names, had suggested an older name for the village: 'Wytchamlow'. Wicham, in its various forms, was a name the Anglo-Saxons started using soon after their arrival, and it generally indicated a place associated with an old Roman site, often just by an old major Roman road.

Wytchamlow, the burial mound by the Roman ruins. It made sense. And who, he wondered, was the Saxon cuckoo in the old mound on which he was now sitting? Could it possibly be Joe's valiant German Queen on her wooden bed?

PATRICK HAD COME BACK down the hill with a secret in his pocket and a wild idea. He went straight into the catering tent where Bobby was serving solid porridge, and poured himself a mug of tea. She looked startlingly fresh against the frowsy queue of camping-crumpled diggers and she had a smile for everyone. She stared at Patrick curiously. Unsettled, he ran his fingers through his hair.

'Morning,' she said. 'How are you?'

'Good morning,' he answered, smiling. 'I've been up to the top of the hill. That is your field up there, isn't it?'

'Yes,' she said, 'and the field beyond.'

'Do you plough it?'

'No, it's just rough pasture really. There's hardly any soil.' She wondered why he looked so pleased. She had been wondering about him and the diggers' rumours of his past. This seemed a different Patrick who faced her now, a Patrick with someone there behind the eyes, someone who looked straight at you. They said he'd been a legend. Until this morning it had been hard to see how that could be. He looked fully alive for the first time since they'd met.

He left the tent as abruptly as he'd come. Well away from other ears, knowing the odds were stacked against him, he dialled Hescroft on the mobile phone.

'We're wrapping up this afternoon, John.'

'It's a big disappointment, Patrick. I don't need to tell you. All that effort and planning gone for nothing.'

'Well, there is one thing . . .'

'What's that?'

'I think I've found another site.'

'What do you mean?'

'A possible Saxon burial in a barrow just up the hill. Unknown, I'm sure.' He must be mad, he thought, to be inflating the slender evidence. Anyway why should Paradigm Site Check care? It was in it for the money, not for knowledge for its own sake.

There was silence, then a wholly unexpected response. 'Really? Now that's something else. Whose land is it?'

'Bobby's, the woman you hired to cook.'

'And you think it might be the real thing?'

'Well . . . too early to tell. But yes.'

'Would she let us dig?'

Us? 'I'm pretty sure she would.'

'I'll be out in an hour or so.'

Patrick ended the call in a state of pleasant bewilderment, astonished that Hescroft hadn't dismissed his idea out of hand. He was gazing up at the hill in thought when a hesitant voice behind him said, 'Patrick?', and he looked round to see Bobby there.

'Yes?'

'I didn't mean to disturb you. It looked like you were thinking. It's just I wanted to know how many more meals you'll need.'

When she talked, it wasn't so bad. She didn't sound like Rachel.

'I don't know yet,' he said, 'but it might depend on you.'

'How do you mean?'

'Joe led me up the hill this morning. Did you know there's a burial mound at the top, an old barrow? He pointed it out to me.'

'I can't think of anything up there that looks like a barrow.'

'You hardly notice it unless you know where to look. It's there right enough, and what's more, I found something too. Have a look.'

Patrick showed her the yellow glass cylinder and watched with pleasure as she turned it in her fingers, entranced by it.

'It's Anglo-Saxon,' he said, 'much more recent than the barrow. I think there must be a later burial there. I went on looking and found these.' He brought out of his pocket two short grey pieces of what could have been dry wood.

'Bones?' she said, taking one from him. 'Human toe bones.'

'Yes. How do you know?'

'Oh, I know some things. They're pretty distinctive.'

She gave it back. 'So when you say it might depend on me . . .?'

'I'd like to get my boss to agree to let us dig a trial trench up there, while we've got everyone together. You would have to give your agreement. It's your land.'

'Mine and Joe's—not just mine. He'd have to agree too.'

'I think he would. He showed me the place, after all.'

'I'll ask him if it's all right,' she said. 'He'll let me know one way or another if he doesn't agree.'

JOHN HESCROFT CAME in a huge black Toyota Land Cruiser with metallic red logos on the doors. Patrick read the words 'Belwether Productions, Film and TV', and began, belatedly, to smell a rat.

Hescroft had a wide public-relations smile on his face. 'Want you to meet Kenny, Patrick. Kenny Camden from Belwether. Kenny, this is our new young superstar, Patrick Kane.'

Kenny Camden smiled a tobacco-stained smile, long white hair flowing in the wind. 'Hi, Paddy. It's a great pleasure to meet you.'

'It's Patrick.'

Kenny gave a conspiratorial wink. 'OK. Patrick. Got it.'

'What about this new site?' said Hescroft. 'Give us the lowdown.'

'New site?' said CD, walking up. 'Hi, John.' Then he stuck his hand out to the TV producer. 'Hi, I'm CD, Mr C. D. Corcoran, if you want to be formal.'

'Kenny Camden. I read your piece on the Ridgeway hill-forts.'

'Wow, that makes three—you, me and my mother.'

'No, no, I was impressed,' said Camden smoothly. 'What do you think of this burial mound of Patrick's?'

Patrick saw that this was the point at which everything would fall to pieces. He hadn't even shown CD the bead.

'Too early to tell,' said CD, 'but you never know, do you? Better let Patrick talk you through it. I'll just listen. I'd love to hear it all over again.' He turned a beaming smile on Patrick, who blessed him from the bottom of his heart.

'There's a burial site at the top of this hill, an Anglo-Saxon burial inserted in an older barrow with a ring-ditch round it, possibly Bronze Age,' said Patrick, picking his words carefully. 'I was shown the place early this morning by someone who's lived here a long time. I found this in the soil.' He brought out the bead.

Hescroft whistled. 'Look at that! Typically Anglo-Saxon.'

'Ain't she a little beauty?' said CD, as if he had seen the bead before.

'Then there are these,' Patrick said, showing them the bones.

'Human,' said CD after the briefest of glances, 'definitely human.'

Hescroft and the producer exchanged significant looks.

'Well, now,' said Hescroft, 'Kenny wants to shoot a pilot to see if he can get one of the major TV companies interested in a series. We were going to suggest shooting the Roman dig until . . .'

'This is better,' said Kenny. 'We'll be in from the start.'

'There might be nothing there,' said Patrick faintly.

Kenny shrugged. 'It's only a couple of days' shooting to find out. It'll make a great show. I can see it now. The wild man of rock puts down his guitar and picks up a trowel.'

'What did you say?' Patrick swung round on Hescroft. 'What have you been telling him?'

'Nothing,' said Hescroft, astonished.

'Leave it out, Paddy,' said Kenny. 'He didn't tell me. He didn't have to. You've got a short memory. I shot your second video, remember?'

Of course he didn't. You just hired people to do things like that. They weren't people you noticed.

'OK,' said Camden, 'you've lost the hair but you're not hard to spot. You did the greatest disappearing act since Elvis. Everybody wants to know what happened to Paddy Kane and Nam Erewhon.'

'Nam what?' said Hescroft.

'Erewhon as in Samuel Butler's Utopian ideal, but more appropriately "Nowhere Man" backwards. They were the antidote to the Beatles. You really don't know who you've got here?' Kenny looked at Hescroft in surprise. The man who wrote "Wedding Vows". The man who—'

'That's my business,' interrupted Patrick. 'I don't want all that brought up. I just want to forget it, OK?'

'Not OK, no,' said Kenny. 'This show stands or falls on human interest, on you being in it. You haven't changed that much, chum. People are still going to notice you even if we don't tell them.'

'No way,' said Patrick. 'Absolutely no way.'

'John,' said the producer, 'let's you and I sit in the car and talk this through. Then we'll have a little talk with your boy here.'

Patrick stalked back down the field with CD.

The American cast around for something to say. 'Listen, it doesn't matter. He's just a TV tosser.'

Silence.

'Patrick, what difference does it make? Everybody here knows you used to be famous.'

'How do they know that? Because you told them?'

'No way. One of the other guys recognised you. Old Doze and I, we did our best. We . . .'

'You mean you two have been going around talking about me?'

'Hey, now that's enough, mister. Yeah, we did. We went around asking people to lay off you. Do you have a problem with that?'

'Yes. I'm not a freak show. I'm not there for people to tiptoe round me, gossiping when I can't hear.'

'The jury's out on that one. You're behaving like some kind of freak show.'

Patrick swung round on him, furious, then saw CD's eyes had nothing but concern in them.

He exhaled noisily. 'I'm sorry. Maybe I've got this a little out of perspective.'

'That's OK. Look, I don't know what you've been through but if you want to talk about it . . .'

Patrick had constructed his recent life around not talking about his past. The offer was kind but it hurt.

'CD, I know you mean well but there is nothing, absolutely nothing in my old life I want to talk about. I wish none of it had happened. I would dearly like it to be'—he was about to say 'buried' but the image of the graves in the Welsh churchyard punched him in the stomach—'forgotten.'

SITTING IN THE LAND CRUISER, Kenny Camden was spelling it out to John Hescroft. 'Now listen, John, you've got to talk to the boy. Make him understand. He knows about publicity.'

'What do I say to him? You heard him.'

'You say to him: you want to dig this barrow—you front the show. That's the price you pay, take it or leave it.'

'You mean you make it clear he was this . . . this rock star.'

The producer considered and grinned. 'You don't have to spell that out. Tell him we'll let him just be Patrick Kane, archaeologist.' The hell we will, he thought. This one is going to leak and then just watch the viewing figures.

So IN THE END Patrick, though he knew he was supping with the devil, had little choice. The song and the bead had got him and he could not leave the mound alone. The only way they could dig on the hill was if Kenny Camden would pay some of the bills.

When supper had been served in the catering tent, Patrick caught Bobby in the middle of clearing up and said, 'I need to talk to you about the barrow. When will you see Joe?'

'As soon as I get this lot back.' She indicated the stack of dirty pans. 'I'll come back over and tell you his reaction if you like. Probably not until about nine thirty.'

When she'd gone, Patrick called everybody together.

'You know this dig's over,' he told them, 'and I'm very sorry about the circumstances. Some of you, I know, are disappointed. Well, I don't want to raise your hopes too much but there's a possibility we could go straight on to another dig very close to here. I won't be able to tell you much more until tomorrow morning but think about it.'

He was about to let them go, then, on the spur of the moment, he decided there was after all something more to say. 'Also . . . I know that some of you have picked up the fact that I used to be, um . . . well, involved in the music business.' It would have been good to make some sort of joke out of it, but humour was unknown in the mental Siberia that made up this part of his life. 'That's something I've left behind, so please, if you don't mind, allow me just to be an archaeologist for the purposes of this dig.'

They all seemed to be looking at him very hard. Aidan nodded slowly and Gaye looked round at her neighbours with a disconcertingly conspiratorial expression on her face.

They all went to the pub but Patrick found it easy to resist their invitations to go too. He suspected that they needed a break without him, to discuss him in all probability, and he found he didn't really care what they said.

There were nearly two hours to kill before meeting Bobby, so he

walked down the lane into the centre of the village. At the far end
there was a village hall with lights on inside it. He stopped and
looked in. Two women were on their knees in the middle of the floor,
painting an old cart a glossy black. It had two wheels at the back, a
smaller one at the front and a long wooden handle to tow it along.
Inside was a seat of cracked and desiccated leather. A Victorian Bath
chair, he thought.

Patrick was inspecting this strange vehicle, when a hand grabbed
at his legs. He looked down in shock to see a small devil tugging at
his knees, cackling. It was half his height but its face was no child's.
It was dark and deformed, covered in disturbing, crawling shapes.

'No, stop that,' he said, alarmed. 'Leave me alone.'

A woman's voice from inside the hall yelled, 'Mikey!' and the creature rushed out of sight round the corner.

Patrick took a deep breath and walked away, heading back to the
camp, wondering just what he had seen.

Back at the marquee, he dragged one of the catering tables outside, set up a folding chair and lit a candle inside a jam jar.

He tried to draw the Anglo-Saxon bead on which his entire burial
theory rested and, as he dragged the jam jar closer to light his
sketchpad, the flame flared, sending a brief splash of red, green and
blue light out through the jar's lurid label and across the white sheet
of paper. Immediately, with a flood of pain, he was back in Italy.

In Perugia Cathedral, in limbo between his betrayal and the retri-
bution that immediately followed, he had watched a small boy playing on the solemn floor, entranced by the spangles of colour dashed
across the stone by the Italian sun through the stained glass. The
memory of that boy conjured David out of the darkness just as it
had at the time. David, brimming with trust and love and promise.

When Bobby came quietly back to the field, she saw in the candlelight that Patrick's cheeks were wet. Staring at his face, she wasn't
sure if he knew she was there. She waited until his head moved frac-
tionally towards her, then spoke softly. 'Hello, Patrick? I just came to
tell you that I told Joe what you said and he did a little dance.'

There was more silence, because Patrick was dragging himself
back from where he'd been and didn't yet trust himself to speak.

'You can start when you like,' she said to fill the gap. 'I suppose
you'll have to move all the tents out of here but there's a good flat
space at the top of the hill. I can move stuff with the tractor and
trailer if it would help. I'm sure we could manage if everyone—'

'"How beautifully blue the sky, the glass is rising very high. Continue fine I hope it may, and yet it rained but yesterday",' said Patrick.

'I think I'm missing something here,' she said cautiously.

His voice sounded normal to him now. 'Gilbert and Sullivan,' he said. 'It's a song the chorus sings to fill up an embarrassing silence. Is it *The Pirates of Penzance*? I can't remember.'

'You could ask Peter. He'd probably know. Was that what I was doing? Filling an embarrassing silence?'

'Weren't you?'

'I wasn't embarrassed. I just thought you needed a moment or two.'

'Yeah, I did. Thanks. Would you like a glass of wine?'

And so they sat there on opposite sides of a flimsy wooden table and the low yellow light lit one side of Bobby's face in a new and startling way so that Patrick saw just ivory curves and deep shadows. Her hair was tied back, dark in the candlelight, banishing Rachel.

He looked for safe ground. 'I saw something odd in the village. They were painting this old cart.'

'Ah. That's not just an old cart. That's the May Queen's carriage. It's May Day in nine days.'

'What happens on May Day?'

He knew at once that this might be safe ground for him but it wasn't for her. There was a note of bitterness in her voice when she replied. 'Normally something lovely. This year, maybe a revolution.' She sighed. 'There's a row going on in the village. It may sound a bit trivial to an outsider but it's one of those really divisive things.'

'Tell me.'

'There's a tradition here going back heaven knows how long. Everyone gets up at dawn on May Morning and we all go out into the meadow down by the river and pick the flowers while the dew is still on them. The children put the dew in little bottles for their mothers because if you put May Morning dew on your face, you lose your wrinkles. Did you know that?'

'I didn't.'

'After that, there's a big breakfast. Then we all decorate the cart with flowers and we push the May Queen round the village in it before the Maypole dancing.'

'So why the revolution?'

'There's a new head teacher and he's really into tests and league tables and all that. He says the May Day traditions have got to happen at the weekend this year, out of school time, because the

National Curriculum doesn't leave any room for it. I mean to say, what harm would a couple of hours do? He must be mad.'

'Isn't there anybody else you can go to? What about the governors?'

She shook her head. 'They're on his side. It's a Church of England primary school and we had a great vicar up to last year, but he's gone and now this awful old man has come in. He's straight out of Anthony Trollope, extraordinarily narrow-minded. He says it's a pagan festival and it's unchristian to celebrate it.'

'I suppose technically he's got a point.'

'Oh yes? Christmas was a pagan festival if you want to be purist. But really, what does that matter compared to the fact that this has been happening year in year out for as long as anyone can remember? There are old ladies of eighty who remember when they were May Queen. You should see their faces when the cart comes past their doors . . .' Her voice trailed off for a moment. 'Do you know why he really hates it? Because there's a lovely old carving that they put on the front of the cart. It's a sort of wooden mask with lots of little holes in. They push the stalks of the flowers into the holes so it comes to life. It's a face with two birds flying out of the mouth and a sort of beard made of leaves and fruits.'

'I've seen it,' said Patrick, remembering the little demon tugging at his knees. 'Is it a Green Man?'

'That's what the vicar says. He says it's pagan. Well, you get Green Man carvings in churches all over the place. He's just got some real beef against anything that's fun. I can't stand him.'

'What about the other school governors?'

'Guess who's the chairman?'

'I don't really know anyone round here except . . . Ah. Roger Little?'

'Precisely. He's only lived here three years. The vicar says it's good to have a businessman as chairman. I ask you.'

'So what are you going to do?'

'Mass disobedience. Most of the parents are on my side. They're going to take their kids out of school that morning and do it anyway. The head teacher says he'll suspend any child for a week who's not in school that day. It's absurd.'

'So that's what was happening when I nearly ran you over? But why are you so involved in this? Have you got children in the school?'

'Oh God. No, of course I haven't. I *was* a child. I did that procession every year I was in the school. I think it really matters. That bloody man's got no sense of the history of it.'

'Would it really make a difference if you did it a couple of days later?'

'Would you mind having Christmas the following Thursday?'

'I wouldn't really care,' he said.

'You haven't got kids?'

He breathed out sharply and his throat closed up on his words. He just shook his head.

She moved her head slightly to one side. Now the light spilled into her eyes and, dismayingly, the distancing hair lost in the darkness, she was the young Rachel looking at him again, concerned and close.

'I only know a bit about your band and your songs but you don't strike me as the sort of person who would do anything terrible. Why are you so harsh on yourself? What is this enormous price you've decided you have to pay?'

He tried to deflect her. 'You don't know I'm harsh on myself.'

'I have eyes and ears. I've rarely seen someone suffering as much as you are, Patrick. You've got a hair shirt on every second of the day. You jump down the throat of people who want to help you. It's like you're burning yourself to death from the inside. You can tell me to leave you alone but you can't tell me you're not suffering.'

He turned sharply to one side so that he didn't have to look at her. 'If I am, I deserve it.'

'What did you do to deserve it? Did you kill somebody?'

He jerked his head back to look straight at her and she was appalled to realise that in trying to suggest the worst impossibility she had hit on some sort of truth.

Something was changing in his eyes as the strict guardian inside him, his last line of defence, tried to slam the doors on her.

She reached out and clasped both his hands in hers. Startled and vulnerable, he gripped them tightly.

Behind them, Maxwell, unsteady after four pints of beer and coming back to his tent for more money, said, 'Well, look at you two then.'

THE NEXT DAY, on the way in to breakfast, Patrick got a knowing smile from Gaye and a smirk from Maxwell. He walked round the back of the food tent to collect himself. Two of the other diggers were sitting on the grass behind it, a rabbity man called Martin and the woman with the huge trowel, whom CD had labelled Vera. Patrick had no idea whether that was her real name. They were chatting and didn't see him coming.

'. . . holding hands. He saw them. That's what he said.'

Patrick stopped again and turned back. With nowhere left to go, he went into the tent. Bobby gave him a wide smile. 'Good morning. How are you today?'

There were half a dozen people inside the tent assembling their breakfast. Patrick felt as if every eye was upon him.

'Oh,' he said, 'I'm fine.' Then out of embarrassment he said, far too abruptly, 'Can we get your tractor and trailer over quite soon, do you think? We need to get this lot moved as soon as possible.'

'Er, well, yes,' she said, disconcerted.

'Thanks,' he said, helped himself to coffee and cornflakes, and went outside without meeting her eye again.

All that day he kept away from her. He told himself that he was there as a professional, as a leader, and a leader should not be the butt of gossip.

It was a busy day, but by late afternoon it was all done, and the new camp was a much nicer place to be than the old one. They were just over the brow of the hill, fifty yards beyond the barrow on a small, almost flat plateau. The diggers cut the turf back to make a big campfire a safe distance from the site.

The site itself was another matter. CD and Dozer had looked at it closely as Patrick showed them what he had seen and where he had found the bead. CD tried the same trick, doing press-ups, but he looked less than convinced.

'Jeez, I hope you're right. I'm not sure I can see it.'

Patrick was already feeling his neck was stuck out way too far when the TV crew arrived, eager to start shooting.

'Can't you do a bit of planning or something?' Kenny Camden said, clearly disappointed that they weren't ready to start. 'What about you guys walking round deciding where to put the trench?'

This was something Patrick had intended to do by himself, but now it worked well. CD was in a generous mood again, and contributed some thoughtful ideas phrased in such a way that it sounded as if he was agreeing with something Patrick had already said.

'You're absolutely right,' he said. 'We need to do it in quadrants. If we start a trench about *here*'—he scratched a mark on the ground—'and take it through to say *here*'—another mark—'we should catch the edge of the ditch and get into the centre of the mound.'

They pegged the trench out, took careful measurements and called it a day. Queuing up for supper, Patrick made sure he was in animated conversation with CD about the need to get some proper paperwork together. He avoided looking directly at Bobby.

That night nobody went to the pub. Dozer, putting dirty dishes in the car for Bobby, said, 'Come on back after. We'll have a few bottles round the fire.'

She smiled at him and said she might, but she didn't.

They'd used the tractor to bring in a load of wood from the farm, and round the blazing fire, fuelled by the wine, the diggers sang old Beatles songs, accompanied by CD on an improvised bongo made out of a catering tin of baked beans. Patrick almost enjoyed himself.

FIVE

By teatime on the first day of digging on the barrow, Patrick was getting sideways looks from the other diggers. Were his hopes unrealistic? He longed to see clear signs of a feature—a grave-shaped patch of different soil to prove that a later burial had taken place. What he saw, as he should have expected, was a horribly uniform surface of earth and small stones, and his doubts began to grow.

When Kenny Camden tried to get him to tell the camera what it was they were looking at, he couldn't put together any words that were halfway convincing. All they had found was an area of disturbance where rabbits had dug, and a couple of bullets.

Dozer twiddled one of the bullets between thumb and finger. 'Three-oh-three,' he said. 'World War Two, I reckon. Angle they were at, probably came from aircraft machine guns.'

Camden liked that and Dozer was encouraged to speculate on camera about the type of plane they might have been fired by.

'Spitfire, possibly,' he said, 'or a Hurricane.'

'Or someone out shooting foxes,' said Patrick under his breath.

'Always the romantic, eh, Dozer?' said CD.

'Hey, CD,' said Dozer, 'remember that time we were digging in Sumatra and I had to defuse that unexploded bomb?'

'No,' said CD, 'not Sumatra. That was Guadalcanal.'

'Saved your life, though, didn't I?'

'Yeah, that's another one I owe you.'

Maxwell had stopped trowelling and sat back on his heels as he

listened, goggle-eared, believing every word of it. Jack, the cameraman, smiled and switched off.

In the afternoon, just after the tea break, CD's bird made a
painfully clumsy landing on Patrick's knee as he sat on a stool, writing up the trench records, and Patrick's pen and notebook fell in the
grass. Edgar picked up the pen and flew off with it, landing on the
grass a few steps away.

'Sorry,' said CD, running up. 'I'll get it. Good ravens don't do that,
Edgar. Put it down.'

The jackdaw spread his wings, and disappeared into a large tree on
the edge of the wood below.

'OK,' said CD, 'leave it with me. I know which tree it is.'

He and Patrick were stopped in their tracks by a bellow from
Dozer. 'Over 'ere, you two.'

They walked back to the trench, where the other diggers were
gathering around Dozer, gazing at the earth intently. They made a
space for Patrick and CD.

Dozer, looking up at Patrick with an expression of proud ownership, said, 'Take a gander at this.' He was kneeling, and he put his
face close to the earth to blow the loose soil away.

Showing through it was a flattened, irregular disc of rusty iron.

'Shield boss?' Patrick said.

'Looks like it,' said Dozer. 'There's your Saxon.'

Patrick's relief was enormous. It was the central part of a wooden
shield and it increased to near certainty the chances that there had
been a burial here. Then the satisfaction was overshadowed by a
pang of regret. A shield meant a warrior. A warrior meant a man,
not a woman. Whatever they had found, it was not the grave of the
German Queen.

'Sorry, folks, I missed that,' said Jack, the cameraman. 'You couldn't
do it again, could you?'

'How do you mean, do it again?'

'Well . . . just maybe put a bit of earth back over it and sort of, discover it again. Just for the pictures.'

They had to do it three times before he was sure he'd got it right. It
went against everything Patrick had ever learned. You didn't mess
about with contexts, not for the camera, not for anything. He was
acutely uncomfortable and all the more so when they asked him to
describe to the camera what they were looking at.

'It's an iron shield boss, more or less shaped like a cone.' He pointed out its shape in the soil. 'There should be a flange around its base with holes where it was attached to the wooden part of the shield.'

'Paddy, give us a bit about what this means,' ordered Kenny Camden. 'You know, what it tells you about the burial.'

'Turn the camera off,' snapped Patrick, furious. Camden turned and nodded at Jack.

'OK. Get this. Do *not* call me Paddy. If you do that to me on film, I'm not letting anyone do any more digging until you're out of here, understand?'

'Hey, listen. Calm down. Nobody's going to hear my words,' said Camden. 'We cut those. It'll just be you talking, right?'

'Ah. Well, just don't call me that, right?' said Patrick, discomfited.

When he'd calmed down, Patrick did his best, greatly helped by some asides from CD about the complexities of shield bosses.

'The shield boss,' said Patrick on the third take, 'indicates the probability that this is indeed an Anglo-Saxon burial site. It's the right way up for a typical burial in which the shield might be laid flat, sometimes on the arm or across the chest. The design of these bosses developed steadily throughout the period, so it should help us date the burial fairly precisely. From what we can see of it so far, the shape looks as if it could be what's called a Group Six boss. That would date it from somewhere between the middle of the sixth century and the middle of the seventh.'

'Very good indeed,' said Camden.

'Nice one,' said Jack. 'I could do with a close-up.'

'Right,' said Camden. 'Can you just do that bit again.'

Patrick couldn't remember what he'd said so they had to play the tape to find out and he had to memorise his words. He was halfway through the fifth take when he ground to a halt.

'What's wrong now?' said Camden.

'Nothing,' said Patrick, looking intently at a small lump of soil. 'I think we've found bone.'

He pulled his trowel out of his back pocket and, with huge care, moved the soil out of the way, crumb by crumb, to expose unmistakable yellow-brown bone. The arm that had held the shield in battle still held it in death.

KENNY CAMDEN WAS delighted with the day's work when he and Jack drove off an hour later, leaving the diggers to put up a large square frame tent as a cover over the grave. At seventy-five miles an hour on the back road to Woodstock, Camden lit a cigar with both hands while he steered with his knees.

'Listen, Jacko,' he said, 'if we get another wobbly like that one, keep shooting, right? Even if he makes me agree to switch off, just pull out wide and keep the camera running. Act natural so he'll think it's off.'

'Mmm,' said Jack, who didn't much like being called Jacko either.

UNITED BY THE THRILL of having found something, eleven diggers gathered round the food tent that night in an extraordinarily cheerful mood. Six of the less enthusiastic volunteers had elected to quit when they moved to the new site and CD was missing. Sitting apart from the others, Patrick spun out the job of writing up the records. He was still on his guard with Bobby, feeling that any signs of friendliness he displayed could be misinterpreted, but he watched her when he thought no one was looking.

CD arrived as they were being handed bowls of a brown mixture that looked and smelt very like the previous day's stew. He was limping and dishevelled.

'Been in a fight?' said Dozer, looking hard at him.

'No,' he said, 'no, no, no. I walked into a door.'

'Dunno if you've noticed. This is the open air. It don't come fitted with doors.'

'Good point. Very good point. Couldn't have been a door then.'

'You've got a leaf in your hair. You been through a hedge?'

'Up a tree actually,' said CD, 'then down it again. Faster. Until I stopped. At the bottom.' He sat down and winced. 'Suddenly.'

'Not the tree where Edgar took my pen?' Patrick said. 'It wasn't anything special. You shouldn't have done it.'

'It's not just the pen,' said CD between gritted teeth. 'He took the keys to my Harley.'

'I'll sort it, mate,' said Dozer. 'Remember that time in Salisbury? I can crack a Harley lock in three seconds.'

'I'd rather you didn't,' said CD stiffly. 'That time, if you remember, you rode off on it too. I know exactly where my keys are. Believe me, that bird is in big, big trouble when he comes back.'

The meal was cleared away and nobody seemed inclined to move. It was a mellow evening. The diggers were sprawled on the grass. The wine had come out and CD and Dozer were telling old war stories.

'So there we were, miles from sodding anywhere,' Dozer was

saying, 'eight feet down in solid chalk, and this git sticks his head in the hole and says, "I say, my good men, this is han hancient monument. Hit his protected, don't you know?" So old CD here, he looks up at the geezer and says, "Bugger off. We're British Gas. We're looking for a leak." Worked like a charm.'

Patrick laughed, then caught a movement out of the corner of his eye and turned to find Bobby standing at his shoulder.

'Could I have a word with you?' she asked.

It seemed to him that silence had fallen. He suspected that they were all looking at him. 'Of course you can. What about?'

'Catering and things. I don't want to break up the party. Shall we talk somewhere else?'

'Right. Lead on.'

The last of the sun's glow slipped from the base of the western clouds as they left the circle. Bobby walked ahead of him to the gate where the farm track started, then waited for Patrick to catch up.

'Not here,' she said. 'Further away. Come to the house.'

Patrick walked down the hill after her in the deepening darkness. Ruts and potholes kept catching him out so that he fell further and further behind. Ahead, dark shapes of trees were fringed with light from the farmhouse beyond them and, as the track turned sharp left round a barn into the entrance to the yard, he saw Bobby waiting for him. Only then did he belatedly realise that she was really angry.

He walked slowly up to her. 'What's wrong?' he asked.

'What's wrong? I'll tell you exactly what's wrong,' she said. 'You seem to have singled me out specially for the cold-shoulder treatment and I must say I'm not quite sure what I've done to deserve it apart from listening to you last night. So what's going on?'

What could he say? That he'd let his guard down and she had slipped in under it? That he'd been embarrassed that others had seen his weakness? 'I . . . um, I made a bit of a fool of myself last night. When Maxwell came back and . . .'

'You mean he saw you upset and that's enough to make you think you have to be some kind of shitty, aloof bastard to me all day?'

'I didn't mean to—'

'You didn't mean to treat me like I wasn't there? Like I was some sort of scullery maid? What sort of person are you? Why do you have to be some great big macho iceberg all the time?'

'It's not that. Maxwell spread it around. I heard everybody talking this morning. They think . . . we've got something going.'

'Oh I see.' She nodded a couple of times. 'So because of that, you think it's all right to behave in this stupid way all day?'

He sat down on the edge of a stone trough and put his head in his hands. 'I'm sorry. I'm very, very sorry. You're right.'

She sat down next to him. 'What is wrong with you?' she said and the words sounded much less harsh. 'You stand out like a sore thumb. Just relax a bit. Stop putting yourself out in the cold.'

'I'm not very good at authority. I need to be in charge here. That's what I'm here for. It doesn't come naturally.'

'You don't do it that way. You can be yourself. If you're halfway reasonable with people, they'll respect you.'

'Oh God. Believe me, I can't be myself. That's one thing I'm trying very hard not to be.'

'What does that mean?'

'I don't think I can talk about it.'

'Patrick, I think you *have* to.'

Side by side, two feet apart, he could look straight ahead and not be disturbed by her face.

'I lost someone.'

'Well, yes. I know that.'

'How do you know?'

'I found out. You may have forgotten but you were quite famous. I looked you up on the Internet. There's pages and pages about you.'

'Are there?' He was genuinely astonished.

'Of course there are. Every song you ever did. Pictures of you on stage. Reams and reams of stuff about you quitting your band. It says you had a wife. It says no one knew until you quit.'

'When I quit,' he repeated softly, 'I didn't have a wife any more.'

As if she knew the shape but not the precise nature of the jagged tear in his soul, she skirted round the obvious question.

'Why didn't anyone know about her?'

'The record company didn't want them to. They want people like me to be an object of lust. I got married young. Rachel . . .' There, he'd said her name out loud. 'Rachel was too . . . I don't know. Normal? Not glamorous. Anyway, she got in the way, they said, so they told the world I was single. It was just plain dumb.'

'Did she mind?'

'I think she minded every single thing that happened to her from then on.'

'Patrick,' said Bobby. 'What happened in Perugia?'

'What do you know about Perugia?' He sensed her flinch away from him.

'All it says is that you quit your band in Perugia, after a concert. It says what happened was tied up with . . . well, I don't know. Something pretty bad. Was that when Rachel left you?'

He stood up. 'Enough. That's enough.'

'Patrick, I just want to help.'

'Look, Bobby, it doesn't help. I don't want to go there. You think this is good for me. I know what's safe and this isn't safe and it's me who has to live with it, not you. We've got a dig to do, thanks to Joe. That's all I'm going to think about.'

'All right,' she said helplessly.

'I've heard what you said and I'm sorry I upset you. I'll try to treat you exactly like I treat everybody else from now on.'

THE TRACK ROSE over the fold of the hill and, a hundred yards ahead, the campfire bloomed—black backs in front, orange flames and yellow faces beyond.

Patrick stopped at the field gate and stared towards the fire and wished from the bottom of his soul that he could turn the clock back and just be one of them, a normal person with a normal history of no great interest to anyone. He'd only been fooling himself by thinking he had managed to duck out of the spotlight for ever.

Perugia was his private hell, not another peg for public speculation, spread round the world by cybergossip.

In Perugia he had watched the little boy playing in the cathedral light. He had seen the boy's father sit down on a bench and watch the child, smiling in unhurried tolerance. Patrick, in an anguish of repentance for what he had done on stage the night before on world-wide television—and coming down from the effects of the chemical cocktails of the past twenty-four hours—had seen how a boy and his father should be. He had seen the little boy lost in his simple world. He had seen the boy's father respecting that world and giving him all the time he needed, centring his day on his child and not himself. In that moment, Patrick had vowed to be a better father to David and a better husband to Rachel.

Along the far wall had been a row of confessionals, open-fronted, priests sitting inside in full view. Patrick longed to confess but he had no God to confess to. He closed his eyes and made his confession to himself, but it came out with excuses attached. I've been selfish, he said to the listener inside his head . . . I needed the space. I've betrayed the people I care about most . . . but she's pushed me into it. She hasn't understood where I have to go.

Something about the place he was in stopped him, blocked his evasions and brought him closer to the inescapable truth that if he was to save anything from this, if he was to give David all he wanted to give him, then he had to leave the band. He had no choice but to walk out of the cathedral to where he had left the band's manager, Don Claypole, sitting at a restaurant table on the edge of the square.

He had headed for Don to tell him it was all over, finished. He didn't care if it cost him all the money he had. He would get Rachel back from the wasteland in which he had thrust her. For David's sake.

The scene was clear in Patrick's memory and always would be. His eyes protested at the bright lunchtime light. Coming up the steps towards him through the dazzle was a dark figure saying in Don Claypole's voice, 'Ah, Paddy, there you are,' and Patrick was saying back to him, 'Don, I've got something to tell you,' and the man replied, 'No, mate, I've got something to tell you first.'

He was pulled out of his memories by a figure coming towards him. 'Patrick? What are you doing out here? Did you sort things out with Bobby?'

'Er, yes.'

'Right.' CD leaned on the gate next to him and there was a long silence. 'Happy?' said the American in the end.

'God, what a question.'

'You want to hear what my mammy taught me?' He went on without waiting for an answer. 'She taught me not to leave my rocks near any hard places. Also to avoid animals with horns in case they turned out to be savage dilemmas. And to beat some other guy's back, not my own.'

Silence from Patrick, not trusting himself to reply.

'You've got to learn to zigzag. You got to know your snakes from your ladders. If you go one step forward and two steps back, you just say that's great, I'm waltzing, yeah?'

A small grunt came that could have been assent or amusement.

'OK,' said CD, 'that's good. You're in there somewhere. Now, let's talk about this.'

'It's late.' Everyone wanted to talk. Except him.

'It's only six o'clock on the East Coast. No need to panic. I'm only talking archaeology here. I guess that's allowed?' CD saw Patrick give a little nod. 'So, let's look at this guy we're digging up. He was born. He died. A thousand years later all we have left is the hard bits and a few knick-knacks. Maybe he was a happy guy. Maybe he was a sad old Saxon git. We sure as hell can't tell and he tasted the same to the worms. In the end it made no difference. The world still turns. You only get one chance and you might as well be happy. In the end, no one gives a shit.'

'I know it's silly, but I hoped it would be a woman,' said Patrick.

'Me too,' said CD. 'Maybe there's a woman there as well.'

'Unlikely. This one looks like it's dead centre in the barrow.'

'Well, dead, anyway. I did some digging in France,' said CD thoughtfully. 'Champagne-Ardenne. We found these incredible burials—men and women together. Some of them were holding hands. Some had their arms round each other. We all cried like babies. Dozer was there. Ex-President of the Hell's Angels and there he was, tears pouring down his face.'

'He really was a Hell's Angel? I thought that was just a story you made up for Roger Little.'

'No, no. He was the Boss, the toughest of the tough. Even back then, when he was still biking, he used to go on digs. Been digging since he was twelve. Two sides to his life.'

'We're not going to find another burial in the barrow.'

'I guess not. So much for our friend and his song about the German Queen. Shame. I would have liked to find the chicken blade.'

Patrick laughed.

'Hey, anyway, Patrick. We could do something for these diggers, you and I. Make it more real. Every night when the cameras have gone, we could do a bit of speculating round the campfire for fun, pin some humanity on those old bones.'

'I don't see why not.' Patrick looked up. The crowd round the fire was thinning out. His devils had left him and he felt drained and inexpressibly weary. 'Time for bed,' he said.

'OK,' agreed CD, content that his prime objective had been met. Bringing Patrick and his team together for a nightly session round the fire might help bridge the chasm between them. It might also help take away the pained, distracted vacancy in Patrick's eyes.

ONCE AGAIN IT WAS Dozer who made the next find, soon after they started in the morning. Kneeling on planks stretched across the trench, the huge man was gently teasing the grains of soil out from where the shield would have been, exposing the rib cage below. There, lying across two of the ribs, was a large circular object eight inches across. It was encrusted with dirt and corrosion, but at its edges intricately decorated metal gave away its origins, which were, quite clearly, much older than the shield.

Finding the disc brought work to a complete halt and took Kenny Camden to the point of rapture. For Patrick, the trouble started when Peter Knight looked at what they'd found and confirmed his fears.

'Look at the edge decoration,' Peter said. 'That's not Anglo-Saxon, is it? Roman, surely.'

CD agreed and after a quick conference between the two of them Patrick had to find something sensible to say for the camera.

'This is, um, definitely a bit of a surprise,' he said in the end. 'It's not at all the sort of thing you would expect to find with an Anglo-Saxon burial. It appears to be Roman . . .' After that he just trailed off into silence.

'What do you think it is?' Camden prompted, off camera.

'I haven't a clue. We'll have to get it cleaned before we know.'

'Look, Pad—Patrick, you've got to say *something* that makes a bit more sense than that. Viewers expect some sort of narrative. You can't just duck out.'

'But we *don't* have a clue. It's completely unexpected.'

'OK, well say so, but do it with a bit more force.'

Patrick had another go. 'This has come out of the blue. We don't know what it is yet. It needs a lot of cleaning but it's clearly highly decorated—some sort of plaque perhaps, apparently laid across the chest in the burial. The strangest thing of all is that it is very obviously not Anglo-Saxon. Our best guess at the moment is that it's Roman workmanship so what it's doing here, in the middle of this burial, is a complete mystery.'

'Very good,' said Camden. 'Just the ticket. How soon can we get it cleaned up?'

'Well, that's up to John Hescroft. That would be part of the post-exploration. When we've finished. If there's any money.'

'No, no, no. That won't do. I'll sort it out.' Camden started tapping numbers into his mobile phone, walking off towards his car. When he came back he had a triumphant grin on his face.

'Hescroft's fixed it. The lab is going to get stuck into it straight away. He said you'd know where to take it. I'm getting a good buzz out of this. We could be onto a good one.'

SIX

When the heavy Roman disc had been carefully lifted from the trench, Patrick took it into Oxford and saw it safely into the hands of the conservation specialists.

It was after five when he drove back into Wytchlow. Unwilling to dive straight back into the life of the dig, he took the right fork down the side of the village green and pulled into a small lay-by at the end of a pathway up to the church.

It proved to be old and simple, a mixture of Norman and Gothic. Inside it was full of spring flowers, sprays of white and yellow, and as Patrick looked at them a clear memory came back to him from the weeks immediately after Perugia. The weeks he had wandered through Britain's lonely places, seeking isolation, explanation and then finally, obliteration.

He'd escaped the press siege, had his head completely shaved, and had swapped his Mercedes for a small camper van. He'd headed north, driving into the night until he was deep into Northumberland. He went to sleep in a car park on the coast with no idea where he was. At seven, he looked out to find himself under the walls of Bamburgh Castle. He gazed out across the beach to where the waves were breaking on the Farne Islands and saw a place where he could make a grand, silent end of himself.

For the next two days it was as if he was counting down to that final moment, going over his entire life in detail, clearing the decks for that one-way swim that seemed the only remaining possibility.

What saved him was an extraordinary event on Holy Island.

He had waited at the landward end of the causeway until the tide's retreat let the first gleam of the road surface show through between the waves. Then he drove onto Holy Island, a low place of rough grass and sand dunes, a halfway halt between one world and another.

He left the camper and walked to Lindisfarne Castle on the seaward side where the waves exerted a hypnotic pull, roaring and frothing over the reefs. Last of all, he turned into the ruined priory.

Its miraculous archway, still arcing across from pillar to pillar where all the rest had fallen, came to him briefly as an omen, a signal that in all great ruins something precious may still sustain. The moment was immediately spoilt by the influx of a horde of tourists, a shrill army wrapped in bright plastic. To avoid them, he hurried into the tiny church that stood facing the priory ruins.

Inside, an old man in vicar's black smiled at him and, getting no response, left him to himself. Patrick sat on a pew. He could still find no God to talk to, no God to stop him, only his unbearable self and the trail of damage he had left. It seemed to him that he had committed a sin that was irredeemable, that the crucified Christ on the altar might well have died for sinners but not for sinners as bad as he.

Then, signalling the end of quiet thought, the entire group of sightseers, noisy as gulls and dripping wet, streamed into the narrow aisles. He got up and headed for the door. He reached the back of the church but got no further. A group of seven or eight teenagers burst in noisily, dressed in exuberant rags. In the lead was a girl with a face of fragile beauty and purposeful intent but her cohorts, all boys, had eyes that seemed to Paddy to be accustomed to trouble. As they made their way towards the altar, the vicar watched anxiously, prepared to try to stop them if they attempted to abscond with the candlesticks. But that was not their intention at all. They filed into the front pew and knelt to pray, then after a few seconds the girl stood up, framed by the white flowers in vases in the archway ahead of her. She held her hands out to each side and turned her face up towards the ceiling. The boys next to her got up and, as she let loose a long high note, they joined in, singing in harmony to some ancient unfamiliar tune, with words in a foreign language. It was a song of soaring power and at the end there were little noises of appreciation right through the church.

The girl turned and came back down the aisle, followed by the boys. The vicar put out a hand and stopped her.

'My dear,' he said, 'where are you from?'

'From the old eastern part of Germany,' she said.

'What you just did was very special,' said the old man. 'Would you tell me why you did it?'

'This is my brother,' she said, 'and these are my cousins, and since we were born we did not see each other until the Wall came down. I made a promise that if my brother and I could see our cousins, I would one day make . . . what is it? *Eine Wallfahrt.*'

'A pilgrimage?'

'Yes, I think so. I said I would come here and give thanks and that is what I have done.'

'Why here?'

'Oh. I had a postcard on my wall for all the years, a very old post-card of your church and your beautiful island. I always was thinking that it looked a good place for new beginnings.'

Paddy, seeking only an ending, left the church, striding out past the priory ruins to the rocks where the waves waited. He sat down to stare at the sea until the moment of certainty came, but what came instead was the German girl, following him in concern. She sat down beside him and asked him what it was that troubled him. While her brothers and cousins kept a distant watch, she listened with intense concentration as he unaccountably told her the whole story. Then, instead of anything banal, she nodded and said that, yes, the waves might be a perfectly good choice under such circumstances but it was hard to be sure because the future is not written yet and perhaps he had a lot to give in exchange for all that he had taken.

'You are right. You have done bad things. Better to throw away just that part of you, not the whole of you. And if you drown your-self here you will spoil my special place for me and I will never be able to look at my postcard again.'

Then she kissed him on the cheek and went back to her family while he sat on his rock and found that the impulse to self-destruction had now acquired a counterbalance. He walked along the seaward shore, taking a new interest in the shape and sound and smell of things. He was surprised when the Germans showed up that afternoon at the campsite near Berwick-upon-Tweed, but if he'd been watching in his mirror he would have seen their van shadowing him.

After that, by common agreement, they had continued in convoy for the next week, wandering through the Lammermuir Hills, spend-ing time walking, sitting and talking. The boys' English wasn't nearly as good as the girl's so she and Patrick spent most of that time talking together. She was called Beatriz, and she fanned the faint embers of his past enthusiasms, forcing him to dredge his memory for facts about the history of the land they were in. Eventually she found his true centre—archaeology.

'You care about these things,' she said. 'Maybe you should go back to take an interest in them. It will, I think, help you to heal. You have no god you recognise, so believe in something. Go on digging.'

They had all driven together back to Harwich and, when he waved them off as the ferry sailed away, he was back from the brink and set on the path that led him to this new life.

WHEN PATRICK RETURNED to the hilltop, by some TV-influenced miracle the site had acquired some of the trappings of a proper dig. A small hut had been delivered to protect the finds and a portable shower unit now stood next to the loos. Bobby served another variation on the theme of brown stew and mashed potatoes but they swallowed it with enthusiasm. Even Gaye ate it. Until now, she had been picking at the food then eating secret supplies in her tent.

Bobby sat down at the table opposite Patrick.

'You're eating with us tonight, then,' he said.

She raised her eyebrows and smiled. 'Looks like it. CD told us about the discussion session and I thought I'd like to be here.'

Temporarily, in the low light of early evening, she wasn't so like Rachel. The evening sun accentuated the planes of her face—more curved than Rachel's. Or perhaps, he thought, it's just that Bobby looks serene and Rachel never did.

'When are we starting?' she asked.

Everyone always thought he had a plan. He had no plans.

'I don't know. When we've cleared the table?'

They washed up using cold water from a newly erected standpipe and then they got the campfire going. Patrick found himself facing an expectant ring of faces. With his mind a complete blank, he looked for CD to rescue him, but the American sat there smiling amiably back at him with all the rest, his bird perched on his shoulder.

'OK,' Patrick said. 'Um, I thought we might, er . . . Well, we might go over what happened today and, well, you know, talk about it.'

Lame start, he thought.

'As you're all aware, we found an object this morning that doesn't quite make sense. We know this is an Anglo-Saxon burial.'

Aidan put up his hand. 'How do we know?' he said in his direct way.

'Well, we found the shield boss. It's typical of a particular period.'

'Yes, but now you've found something Roman so maybe it's the shield boss that shouldn't be there. Maybe someone buried the shield there later, on top of a Roman burial?'

'Well, the Romans didn't usually bury people in the middle of old barrows. That's definitely more of a Saxon thing.'

'What is this Roman thing anyway?' asked Gaye.

'It's too early to tell,' said Patrick. 'We'll have to—'

'You're always saying that,' cut in Maxwell. ' Too early to tell.'

CD smiled. 'That's the way it is, kid. You better learn those words. It's archaeologists' speak for I don't have any idea and I'm not going

to guess until I have to. Consider yourself privileged to be here
tonight for a rare event. This is guessing time. Tonight we can all
stick our necks out. Just don't hold it against us when we're wrong.'

'So let's hear your guess then,' said Gaye.

'OK,' said CD. 'It's more or less round. It's too big and heavy to be
a brooch and it looks too lumpy to be any kind of dish or plate. I
think it's most probably a clutch-plate for an early Roman Chevrolet.'

'Early Roman Chevrolets had automatic gearboxes,' said Peter. 'It
looks more like a Ford to me.' His face was deadpan and it was a
moment before the laughter started.

'Some kind of medallion, ain't it, Pat?' said Dozer. 'Something a
bit ceremonial. Looked kind of like that to me.'

'It's too . . .' started Patrick, and the rest of them joined in a
chorus, '. . . early to tell.'

They all burst out laughing and Patrick joined in. With delight,
CD watched his scheme starting to work.

'Supposing it is an Anglo-Saxon burial . . .' said Bobby's rich voice
from the growing darkness beyond the fire. 'And supposing this
other thing is Roman. He could have found it, couldn't he? Maybe he
just liked old things so they buried it with him.'

'I dunno,' said Dozer. 'They didn't 'ave time to go collecting then,
did they? Shelter and food and not getting a spear between the
shoulder blades, that's what they thought about mostly.'

'Bullshit, Doze,' said CD amiably. 'They made beautiful things,
those guys. Look at the Alfred jewel or the Kingston Down brooch.
They knew about beauty. Why couldn't they collect it? Maybe this
guy found it when he was digging up potatoes one day and thought,
Hey, cool. I'll keep that to be buried with.'

'They didn't 'ave potatoes, you dopey four-eyed git,' Dozer said.
'Thought you'd know that, you being a clever clogs with a college
education.'

'Oh right, so that invalidates my whole thesis, I guess. Potatoes,
turnips, whatever. Go sick him, Edgar.'

The jackdaw flapped onto Dozer's head.

'I give in,' said the big man. 'No call to start bringing in air support. Call your effing vulture off. 'Ere, Bobby. Can't your Joe sing us
another song? Tell us what's going on?'

'Joe sings when he wants to,' said Bobby. 'I can't tell him to. I don't
even know where he is tonight.' But she looked round and stared
into what was now full darkness on the hilltop.

'Of course the real question,' said CD, 'is why do we like all this old shit anyway? Who do we—? Whoa there, hang on just a minute. Was that a bottle I heard? The gentle slopping of some sublime liquid in a vessel of the clearest crystal? Is that the product of a far-off fermentation that I smell? I think it's singing to me. Come on, bottle. Come to daddy. Cast your Glenboggy on the waters as they say and it shall be returned threefold.'

Bottles emerged from the shadows. Wine began to circulate. Then Aidan said, 'Go on, then, what's the answer?'

'Answers? I don't have answers. I have enough trouble with the questions,' said CD. 'You know how it is: you pull a lump of Samian ware out of the ground and you're the first person to see it since some Roman matron smashed it in the year 300. That's half the thrill, but you look at it carefully because it might just be some kind of pattern nobody's ever seen before and then everyone will be saying "CD? Sure, isn't he the guy who first identified the Samian ware toothbrush steriliser?".'

'I can imagine that Anglo-Saxon finding his Roman clutch-plate,' said Patrick, speaking with no conscious effort from out of the reverie of thought CD had led him into. 'He wouldn't know where it came from, would he? He probably wouldn't even know how it was made. Maybe it seemed like magic.'

It was the first completely unforced sentence he had uttered in four years, but before that dawned on him a guitar chord came out of the darkness behind the fire and every head swivelled towards the sound.

'Come and join us,' CD called.

When the guitar sounded again, it was much easier to hear, but the person playing it was still all but invisible to them. When he started to sing, the voice was Joe's.

The tune was what they all wanted to hear—the song of the German Queen. This time, Joe started somewhere in the middle.

> *'A month went by while they mourned the son*
> *And marked the great deeds he had done*
> *By laying his shield across his chest*
> *As they put him in the grave to rest.*
>
> *That was when they came again*
> *In the storm-dark night, those murderous men,*
> *Feet wrapped in cloth and swords honed keen*
> *But they didn't allow for the German Queen.*

She stayed awake while her brothers slept.
Moon-shadows moved in the watch she kept
And when she heard a skittering stone,
She beat the gong with a great leg bone.

Three brothers only faced the foe
And they made their stand by the witch's low.
They stood surrounded, back to back,
Against the waves of the night attack.

Their sister raced to summon aid,
To bring the King with his chicken blade.
But the King's old legs brought him too late.
His last three sons had met their fate.

The King's hot blade was slaked in blood.
Six traitors lay in the red-striped mud.
Down that hill they bore their own
And buried them round their valley home.

The King turned to his daughter dear
And spoke to her of his dreadful fear.
"You, my Queen, are the only one
Left of my line. You must bear a son."'

Joe seemed to falter there, playing an extended instrumental passage, stopping and starting again as if uncertain where to pick up the tale. Then he came to a decision and launched into a new verse but it was clear he had jumped ahead in the story.

'At the village under the witch's low
The Queen and her children came to know
A time of peace, a time to mend,
A time they thought would never end.

She filled their home with the things she found
Given up by the riven ground,
Sharp axes chipped from ancient stone,
A stag's head carved from an old thigh bone.

When others shunned the Romans' stones
She dared inspect their resting bones
And there, when winter turned to spring
She found what proved her favourite thing.

What came to her from the deer-delved earth
As if the land had given birth
What she saw beneath the sod
Was the leafy brow of the woven god.'

There was another long pause. Eventually one of the diggers swung the beam of his powerful torch around the field but Joe was nowhere to be seen.

'What's a woven god?' said Aidan.

'I haven't a clue,' Patrick replied.

'I thought he said "Woden god",' said Maxwell. 'That would make more sense, wouldn't it? Wasn't there a god called Woden? Or maybe he said "wooden". A wooden god.'

'A hell of a story,' said Aidan.

'Come on,' Gaye said. 'It's obvious he knows we found something today and he's made it up. No offence, Bobby. But you don't want to start putting any faith into things like that.'

'Hang about, Gaye. You stop being the cynic,' said Dozer. 'That's my job. It's what I'm known for, good looks and cynicism.'

'And your slim figure, I suppose?' she scoffed.

'Even if Gaye's right,' said CD, 'he's a hell of a songwriter. Hears us talking and makes up a song to fit just like that.'

'Doesn't fit though, does it?' said Dozer. 'He's still going on about a her. What we've got here is a him.'

'Come on, Bobby,' said Maxwell. 'What's it all about?'

'Oh, don't ask me. He's my brother and he's a good man, but I don't know how his mind works. I'm sure that he always has the best of reasons for what he does. I think maybe it's some sort of parable.'

'What does that mean?'

'Well, I don't mean this to sound disloyal to him. What I mean is I don't suppose it's meant to be literally true. The axes and the stag's head in that last bit of the song, I know where they come from. They're on our mantelpiece at home.'

'There you are,' said Gaye.

'What sort of axes?' said CD.

'Old hand axes. My father used to collect old bits and pieces. People say he was a great one for seeing things. He'd walk the fields after ploughing and he'd bend down and pick up stuff.'

'Didn't you know him? You said "people say".'

'He died when I was pretty young. My mother and Joe ran the

farm after that. Joe was almost sixteen then. I was a bit of an after-thought. Then, when my mother died, I came in with Joe because he does need a bit of looking after. I mean he doesn't talk on the phone. That makes life a bit difficult.'

Patrick had been staring at Bobby, fascinated. 'So your father was a bit of an antiquarian?'

'Oh yes. The trouble is I often don't know what the things are.'

'You could take them to the museum.'

'There's not a lot of seconds left over in a struggling farmer's day for that sort of thing,' she said wryly. 'I know I'm taking time off to come up here but that counts as my first holiday for five years.'

'It's not exactly a holiday, is it?' said Patrick, feeling suddenly that they had all been taking her efforts rather for granted.

Dozer broke in. 'Someone's coming,' he said, and certainly a torch was probing in their direction from the track.

'Hello there. Are you the diggers?' called a querulous male voice.

'No, we're Diana Ross and the Supremes,' said Dozer.

'Yes, we are,' Patrick called back quickly.

The figure came up to the fire, shining the torch directly into Patrick's eyes. 'Are you the feller in charge?' said the new arrival.

'Yes. I'm Patrick Kane.'

'I'm the Reverend Augustus Templeton-Jones,' said the new arrival, finally switching off the torch.

'What can we do for you?'

'I heard that you might be in need of my services.'

'In what way?' asked Patrick, puzzled.

'You've found a body, I understand.'

So the news had got out already. One or two of the diggers had been down to the village shop. They must have told someone.

'We've found a possible burial, yes.'

'May I take it that you are going to observe proper procedures?'

'I'm not sure I know what you mean.'

'Oh, I'm sure you do, Mr Kane. As you will know, it is a require-ment that any Christian remains that are disinterred should be given proper Christian reburial, at the earliest suitable opportunity.'

'Reverend, er . . .' Patrick couldn't begin to remember his name. 'What we have here is almost certainly a pre-Christian burial. I'd say it's probably sixth- or seventh-century Anglo-Saxon and—'

'Augustine came to Kent in the year 597, young man. Correct me if I'm wrong but that was the sixth century.'

From the darkness, a voice, Peter Knight's, said, 'St Birinus didn't convert Cynegils of the Gewisse until around 639 and this would be on the fringe of the Gewisse's territory. There was, of course, the pagan reaction to Christianity during the reign of Æthelbert's son, Eadbald, to take into account.'

Someone clapped quietly.

'In any case,' said Patrick, 'this grave doesn't show the usual signs of Christianity. It's not orientated east–west. The evidence so far is that it's a pagan burial.'

'Well, that would suit some of my parishioners,' said the vicar with a sniff. 'I doubt you can be certain, however, and if there is any doubt then I shall insist on all the proper ceremonies being carried out.'

'Scuse me, governor,' put in Dozer. 'If it's not a Christian, is it all right if we just chuck the bones in a box?'

'That would be a matter entirely for you,' said the vicar.

'Suppose it's a Roman?'

'As I say, that would be a matter entirely for you.'

'But weren't most of the Romans Christians?'

'I think you're trying to trip me up,' said the vicar crossly, and turned on Patrick. 'Have you informed the Coroner's Office of your find? That is a requirement when you unearth human remains.'

'Well, I know it is in theory. In practice, they tend to get a bit annoyed if you ring them up about bodies that have been dead for over a thousand years.'

'I can see that none of you can be trusted to follow proper procedures,' said the vicar. 'I shall be keeping a very close eye on your activities. I bid you good night.' He turned away, switched on his torch and stumbled over a rabbit hole, to the barely suppressed delight of the diggers round the fire.

'Why is it that the words "total dickhead" somehow spring effortlessly to mind?' said CD when he'd gone.

'That's the man I told you about,' said Bobby. 'The one who's causing all the trouble at the school over the May Morning procession.'

'Would you like him killed?' said Dozer. 'I've got a mate does it on the side. He's a fancy cake chef the rest of the time.'

'No, thank you, Dozer. It's very kind.'

'He's right about the burials, you know,' said CD. 'If it's Christian, you have to do it right. I was doing all the post-ex on a dig last year. We hit the edge of the old paupers' burial ground in Saintsbrook. Two hundred and ten bodies. I went along to the crematorium and asked if they did a cheap deal for more than one body, but it still came to twenty grand.'

'What did you do?'

'Found a friendly vicar and put them all in a big hole when they were doing his drains.'

'So what's going to happen to our bloke here then?' asked Maxwell.

'There'll be tests to do. We look at his bones and decide what killed him and if he had any diseases, then they go in a box somewhere in case anybody wants to have another look at them later on.'

'Unless he's a Christian.'

'If he's a Christian, I'm a boiled egg,' said CD.

'I'd better go,' said Bobby. 'You don't want to be kept waiting for your breakfast in the morning.'

'Up the revolution,' said CD. 'Anything we can do to help, just say the word.'

She stood looking towards where Patrick and CD sat, and the light from the low fire painted her a new face. 'Thanks. Come and join the May Day march. It's next week.' Then she was gone.

'She's a great kid,' said CD. 'I didn't know farmers came with built-in beauty and culture. Maybe I should be a farmer. I could marry her and settle down.'

'Nah, she wouldn't 'ave you,' said Dozer. 'Anyone can tell she's only got eyes for one bloke.'

'Who's that then?'

'Me, of course,' said Dozer. 'You're too effing ugly.'

Before they all turned in for the night, someone started singing the inevitable campfire songs and CD noticed with satisfaction that Patrick sang along with them, though he kept his voice low.

EARLY THE NEXT DAY, Patrick dressed and crawled out of his tent into dew-laden grass. There was a gauze curtain across the land but the sun was already warm and a lark's song was sparkling down through the spring air. The mist would not last. He walked straight to the mound and found that someone had been there before him. A tin can sat on the grass next to the trench and in it was a bunch of wild flowers. He lifted the grave cover off carefully and the bones curved out of the earth, just the forearm and a few ribs so far.

A shadow fell across the earth. He twisted, startled, and an accusing ghost had climbed up out of the mist, staring at him.

Rachel reached out to touch his arm and said in a voice that was not Rachel's, 'Patrick. It's all right. It's me, Bobby. I just wanted to come up while it was still quiet. I didn't think anyone would be here.'

'We're not the first.' He pointed at the flowers. 'Was that Joe?'

'Maybe. I don't know. It's not like him.' She tilted her head. 'Do you think we'll uncover the rest of the body today?'

'You have to take things like this very slowly,' he said. 'Bones may look strong but they can crumble on you just like that. If the soil's too acid they get eaten away. It's quite dry and chalky here but it's not like that all the way through. There's a wet patch at the end of the other trench. I think maybe you've got a spring or something.'

'These bones look quite strong.'

'I hope so.'

'Thank you for last night,' she said. 'Will you go on doing the discussions?'

'Maybe. I will if Joe comes again. Those songs are extraordinary.'

'I'm glad you think so. He's not being a nuisance?'

'Anything that makes the Maxwells of this world think is not a nuisance.'

'Are you enjoying this dig, Patrick?'

'Enjoying it? I suppose I am. At least I'm starting to.'

'I'd better go and get the kettles on.'

She was gone and the mist was lifting. He looked after her and found he *was* enjoying it. For a man who fully expected never to enjoy anything, this came as a surprise.

CAMDEN AND HIS CAMERAMAN arrived two hours after the group started digging. Earlier, over breakfast, Dozer had got a metal detector out of his car and had run it over the spoil heap. 'Just checking,' he had said.

It buzzed and he dug around with his trowel until he found a small lump of earth with a metal edge showing.

'Well, that's a pity,' he said, bringing it back to the tent.

They all gathered round.

'Which of you threw it away, I wonder.'

'Why are you looking at me?' said Maxwell.

It might have been a pendant or a fragment of a brooch and seemed to have three short arms, one of them folded over where something had hit it. Describing it for the camera took half an hour.

'Could it be a cross?' Camden asked while Jack was filming.

'It's just possible. One of the arms could have been cut off. We won't know until it's been cleaned.' Patrick waited until he saw the camera switched off. 'Anyway, don't tell the vicar.'

He took Camden on one side. 'Look, if we have to keep stopping because you're not here when we find things, this could take years.'

'Paddy old son—'

'Patrick, please.'

'Patrick. Ease up. You know how it is with filming. Anyway, I'm the bearer of good news. I'm well on the way to getting proper money fixed up, a real budget for the pilot. If your boss agrees, we can both throw in a bit more, and then I can arrange things for you. More lab work. Whatever.'

'So long as you get what you want for the show?'

'We're going the same way, you and me. You want to find interesting things. So do I. If it needs a bit of cash to get them cleaned or whatever, we're up for it. That's all I'm saying.'

'Hescroft hasn't agreed to this yet, then?'

'Well, not yet, but you and I, we can persuade him, can't we?'

While this conversation was going on, CD had left the trench and strolled over, waiting politely for them to finish.

'Did you want something?' Camden said.

'Just a word with the boss,' CD said. 'Private matter.'

'Sounds interesting,' said Camden.

'Yes, it is. It's Maxwell. He's got terrible diarrhoea, so I was thinking, in case it spreads we should get a stool sample and send it off for analysis, so I need a jar and—'

'I'll leave you to it,' said Camden.

When he'd gone, Patrick looked at CD. 'What?' he said.

'Smoke screen. Well, more like riot gas really. Worked, didn't it? I need to tell you something and I didn't want him to hear until you had a chance to think about it. We've found more bones.'

'Yes?' said Patrick, thinking that was what you might expect when you were digging up a skeleton. 'So?'

'You'd better see for yourself.'

When Dozer saw the two of them walking back, he got out of the trench, beckoned Camden over to him, said something and then walked off with him towards the Land Cruiser where Jack was doing something to his equipment.

'He's running interference for us,' said CD. 'Good old Doze.'

They reached the mound.

'OK,' CD called, 'early coffee break. Cover up your loose.'

The diggers went without a backward glance and the hairs on the back of Patrick's neck began to prickle. Finds were usually announced immediately. These people had no idea that CD and Dozer had come across anything out of the way.

The cover was back over the skeleton and to start with CD left it in place. 'First off, let me walk you through the way it's gone. We've uncovered the side of the skull, all the rib cage and enough of the legs to be pretty sure the body is lying supine, with the arms crossed at the wrists over the pelvis. The skull's tilted to one side and we've exposed the top surface of the pelvis.'

'Sounds fine.'

'Well, it's not.' CD sounded rattled. 'Take a good look.'

He lifted the frame away carefully and Patrick stared down at what was now a recognisable skeleton, partly emerging from a bed of soil. At a quick glance there was nothing else to see.

'I don't see any extra bones,' he said. 'What do you mean?'

'You have to get down close.'

'OK.' Patrick knelt on the soil.

'Look just above the pelvis,' said CD.

When Patrick tuned his gaze, he saw two tiny bones, thinner than the thinnest part of a chicken's wishbone, rearing out of the earth.

'Oh, I see. Rodent?' said Patrick. 'Could be rabbit ribs.'

'Those bones are not from an animal. They're human.'

'Oh, come on. They're far too small. They're like a baby's . . .' Patrick's voice died away.

'They're exactly like a baby's,' said CD, 'because that's what they are. This warrior of ours was pregnant. Congratulations, young Patrick. Against all odds, we seem to have found the German Queen.'

Patrick stared at him, then back at the frail bones. Elation was quickly followed by a sense of something approaching horror. This was something unique in archaeological history. It meant that this was a huge dig, one that would have to be done just right. On the other hand, there was Joe's song . . . so much that couldn't be explained. Archaeology was science. Joe's song seemed more like magic. The two could not easily coexist.

'What do we do now, CD?'

'I guess we need a bit of time. Why don't we send them all off field-walking with the TV crew, then the three of us can have a think.'

That was what they did. The diggers went off across the hilltop in a long straggling line, searching for artefacts and signs of further human habitation. Maxwell accumulated a pocketful of oddly shaped stones. Gaye broke the buckle on her shoe. Aidan saved the day by finding a Tudor coin which had nothing at all to do with their dig but distracted everybody nicely. It bought enough time for Dozer, working with infinite care, to expose the eggshell fragments of a tiny human skull. They covered the skeleton as the diggers came back.

HESCROFT ARRIVED LATER and he, Camden and Patrick sat in the catering tent, while Bobby buttered bread.

Hescroft had the closed look he usually wore when money was at issue. 'We're faced with a tough decision, I fear, about where we go from here. Patrick, first of all, I should tell you that Kenny has made a suggestion about funding the rest of the dig which requires us to make a substantial contribution to costs. Now, that it isn't the sort of thing we usually do. We would perhaps have hoped that the television side of it might have covered a higher proportion of the total.' He looked at Kenny Camden, who was lighting a cigarette.

'Unfortunately—' Camden began.

'Unfortunately, you'll have to put that out,' said Bobby from behind him. 'This is a food preparation area.'

'I'm afraid she's right,' said Patrick.

Camden bent down reluctantly to stub the cigarette out in the grass.

'Could you give us a few minutes?' said Hescroft to Bobby.

'Not if you want lunch on time,' said Bobby.

'We have to discuss delicate matters.'

'Your choice. Go outside and I won't hear you. Stay inside and I'll try not to listen.'

They stayed inside.

'As I was saying,' said Camden, 'the reaction I'm getting, unfortunately, is that there isn't anything very earth-shattering about an Anglo-Saxon burial. You know very well how much TV archaeology there is these days. There's bone shows everywhere. It's in danger of being done to death. We're looking for something new. Personalities. Now you've got Dozer and CD, and they're both good on camera, but it's not enough to make anyone sit up and take notice, so there's a limit on what we can risk at this stage.'

'Well, I'm afraid I don't think my company can afford to fill the gap,' said Hescroft. 'It's a shame really.'

This is a set-up, Patrick thought with sudden certainty.

'I suppose it would be different if you could do the ex-rock star angle,' he said innocently.

Camden, who had been staring at the ground in the pose of someone who was reluctantly heading for a tough decision, lifted his head a little too sharply.

'Well, yes,' he said, 'it certainly would, but I thought that wasn't really an option.'

'It's not,' said Patrick, his suspicions confirmed.

'I don't know there's a lot else that can save it,' said Hescroft a little too eagerly. 'What a pity.'

'I have considered other angles,' said Camden.

Oh yes, I'm sure you have, thought Patrick. 'Such as?' he said.

Camden was clearly scratching around. 'Well, there's this strange business of the song,' he said.

'What song?' asked Hescroft.

'This guy, this old farm bloke, sings in the pub,' said Camden. 'He sang this song about a woman who was supposed to be buried up here. That's how your friend Patrick here found this grave. Didn't you know?'

'Is that right?' said Hescroft to Patrick, bewildered.

'Up to a point.' He looked at Camden. 'I didn't know you'd heard about it.'

'It doesn't work, though,' said Camden, 'not in TV terms.'

'You didn't tell me,' said Hescroft, glaring at Patrick. 'You could have had us all on a complete wild-goose chase. Have you any idea how much this sort of thing costs?'

Virtually nothing, the way you do it, thought Patrick. He felt like a poker player holding all four aces. 'The song by itself wouldn't have made me want to dig,' he said. 'Finding the bead convinced me.'

'Just as well,' said Camden, 'considering the song was about a woman. What you've got here is a man, after all.'

'Well, no,' said Patrick. 'It's not.'

Everything was suddenly completely clear. They were trying to present him with stark alternatives. Insist on privacy and have the dig cancelled, or agree to be ex-star Paddy Kane playing at archaeology and carry on. He decided to play his ace in the hole, the third option.

'It's not a man. It's a woman.'

Bobby gasped and Hescroft made a tutting sound. 'Come off it. How could you possibly know that for certain?' He held up a hand. 'I know what you're going to say. The shape of the skull, right? No pronounced brow ridges? Rounded upper margin to the orbit? It never gives you a definite answer. For God's sake, Patrick, there are no female Anglo-Saxon burials with weapons. It's adult males only.'

'I'm not going by her skeleton at all,' said Patrick. 'I'm going by someone else's skeleton.'

Hescroft made a derisive noise. 'How can someone else's skeleton tell you anything at all about this one?'

Bobby dropped the bowl of lettuce she was holding.

'It's the bones of her baby. She was pregnant.'

'A pregnant warrior woman?' said Camden. 'All right. Now we've got a show.'

'That's extraordinary,' said Hescroft. 'We'd better have a look.'

'We haven't told the diggers yet.'

'Why don't you tell them now?' said Camden. 'We'll shoot it.'

Patrick let them leave the tent first then turned to share the moment with Bobby—a brief, jubilant conspiracy.

They took the grave cover off and the diggers, realising something was in the air, gathered round. Hescroft knelt in the earth in his smart linen trousers and stared in absorption at the bones.

'No doubt about it,' he murmured. 'Absolutely extraordinary.'

Jack set up the camera and Patrick, forgetting entirely that it was there, told all of them what it was they had found, and for the first time his words came out with fire. When he finished, they all stood staring at the tiny skeleton in sombre silence.

The questions came that night when the TV men had gone.

'Is everyone here?' said Patrick, as they sat around the campfire.

'Gaye isn't,' said Dozer.

'Yes, I am,' she said, stepping into the firelight. 'Sorry, I dropped my lipstick down the loo.'

'Did you get it back?' asked Dozer.

'I decided no one needs lipstick *that* much,' she said primly.

'Blimey, Gaye, you're going native,' he said, and she joined in the roar of laughter.

CD lay back on the grass, staring at the first stars. 'I hope you guys all realise,' he said, 'that you've lucked in to a dig that's going to be in all the textbooks.'

'Facts first,' said Patrick. 'One female pregnant skeleton, with a shield across her chest. Plus, about six foot from the feet of the skeleton, Gaye has uncovered what looks like a section of a good sword blade. The metal must have been fantastic. It hasn't all corroded.'

'Nitrides,' said the American. 'Remember, it's the chicken blade.'

Patrick looked at him sharply.

'Joe sang it. That's good enough for me,' said CD. 'I believe it. In the evenings, anyway. Daytime, I turn back into a scientist.'

'Leaving that aside for the moment, there's what looks like the remains of a chatelaine.'

'Which is what exactly?' asked Aidan.

'It's usually a ring or a brooch that's also a sort of a toilet kit, with things hanging on it like tweezers and little picks.'

'The significance,' CD added, 'is that chatelaines only come with females, if anyone was still in any doubt.'

'Don't you find yourself wondering what she was called?' said Gaye. 'I'd really like to know.'

Everyone knew what she meant and that was the moment at which the woman in the grave started to become in their minds something much more than an assembly of old bones.

'So, we have an enormous question to answer,' said Patrick. 'Everything we know about the period tells us they were very hierarchical. Men fought, women didn't. The oldest son got the father's weapons.'

'The oldest son was dead,' said Bobby, 'so were the others. The song said so.'

'I don't remember anything about the oldest son?'

'Joe sang it in the pub, the first time,' said Aidan.

'Can you remember it?'

'I can,' said Bobby. 'There are one or two verses I know.'

She spoke them with a lilt that set the tune humming in their heads.

'They met the raiders, blade to blade
In a spray of blood by the old stockade.
Outnumbered by them five to one,
The fight was led by the oldest son.

At the moment when they saw him fall,
And his soul took flight to the warriors' hall,
The hills rang out to a chilling cry.
Their father saw the young prince die.

He burst on them, this vengeful lord
And he whirled the blade of the chicken sword.
They fell at his feet like stalks of corn
Harvested for his dear first-born.'

'We've got to avoid putting too much faith in the song,' said Patrick. 'What we do here is going to be under close scrutiny. If it appears that we're being led by the song we'll just look stupid.'

Bobby backed him up. 'My father taught Joe the song and I expect he got it from his father, I don't know for sure.'

'Surely,' said Aidan, 'he couldn't be singing it word for word the way he heard it. No one could do that.'

'I'm not so sure,' said Bobby. 'Joe's got an amazing memory and I sometimes hear him practising in his room. It's the only time I ever hear his voice in the house.'

Patrick caught a glimpse of how lonely life must be for her. 'I wish I'd listened more closely,' he said. 'What else have we missed?'

'I know a few more bits of it,' said Bobby. 'She tries to save her people from these raiders and they kill her brothers and then, in the end, she's killed too.'

'What surprises me,' said Vera, the wispy-haired woman with the huge trowel, who normally kept herself to herself, 'is that a woman would fight. She'd have been better off running away.'

'You don't know that. You have to hold your ground sometimes,' said Bobby. 'Haven't you ever felt angry enough to attack a man?'

'Oh no, I don't think I have,' said Vera rather primly.

'Well, I have,' said Gaye, looking meaningfully at Dozer.

'I would have picked up a sword if I'd had to,' Bobby went on. 'If someone threatened the people I loved. So would lots of women. You're not trying to tell me that wasn't true in those days too? Peter, what do you think?'

'Well, there's the precedent of Boudicca, Queen of the Iceni, an East Anglian tribe. She led a rebellion against the Romans in AD 60.'

'If she could take up arms and be that sort of queen, so could our lady here,' said Bobby.

'Maybe.' Peter sounded cautious. 'But Boudicca was a Celt. The Saxons seem to have been more male-dominated.'

The talk moved in circles until one o'clock, then a sharp chill descended and drove them to their tents.

Patrick couldn't sleep, and after half an hour he got up and took a torch over to the burial site. The sky was on fire with stars. He paused for a while outside the frame tent protecting the grave, then opened the zip. The woman showed white in the torchlight and he knelt beside the trench and stared at her. Only a week ago he had stood beside a grave in a Welsh churchyard.

David's bones would be more substantial than this never-to-be-born Saxon child but that was all David was now, just bones and a tear-pricking memory.

SEVEN

The waning moon showed Patrick his escape route from the open grave. He stumbled across the rough hilltop, seeing in his mind's eye the well-worn movie of the funeral. Rachel's father came at him yet again, yelling accusations through that frozen crowd of mourners. He saw one hand reach out for his neck and the other, clenched, pulling back for the blow. Eyes tight shut, he stopped to take sucking, sobbing breaths of air.

Then he heard footsteps.

Patrick opened his eyes. Out of the darkness, a man was coming for him, a real man in the same space that the memory of Rachel's father had occupied, rushing at him in the same way so that Patrick recoiled, horrified, yelled and put his arm across his face to ward off the blow.

No blow came this time. Joe stared at him with profound sorrow on his face. He looked into Patrick's eyes, then reached out a tentative hand and touched him with flat, coarse fingers on the centre of his forehead. It felt to Patrick like something you might do to a frightened animal, and it eased his breathing as Joe walked rapidly away down the track towards the farmhouse.

Patrick shivered and the memory of the funeral came back to claim him again. Rachel's father's punches hadn't hurt nearly as much as his words of denunciation. Patrick hadn't tried to defend himself. After the assault he had lain still on the ground. Not one person from Rachel's tribe stepped forward to help him to his feet. Patrick's cousins, the only members of his own meagre family present, faded away, too, and he was left to slink away out of their lives.

Again there were real footsteps in the Oxfordshire night. This time Bobby coalesced out of the blackness, running up the track towards him.

'Patrick? Joe woke me. He was worried. I could tell. What's wrong?'

He tried to drive her away with the brutal truth.

'I'm here because I'm not a nice man. Because that grave up there has made me remember something I did that no nice man would ever have done, OK? Do you want to hear about it?' He heard no reply. 'Do you?' he insisted savagely. 'Because if you don't, then go home.'

In the moonlight he saw her nod. Just as Joe could sing to his depersonalised pub audience, so Patrick found he could speak to this listener to whom the moon gave a third face, not the Rachel-face, nor the candlelit madonna, but something else, something inscrutable.

'I was on stage in Rome,' he said. 'It was part of the Debt Relief concert, all that African starvation stuff. Worldwide TV coverage. Do you know "Wedding Vows"? My very own bloody awful song?'

'Yes, I know it,' she said. 'I've heard it. Everybody's heard it.'

'Well, I wasn't going to sing it. I hated it before it was even released. But that night I'd had a bottle of tequila and God knows what else, and the organisers came in to say they didn't want it. Not in the spirit of the concert.'

'You sang it anyway?'

'Yes, I sang it but that wasn't the point. I dedicated it live to my wife Rachel. Live, in front of two hundred million people. I wasn't even supposed to have a wife. And I said I meant every single word of it.' He stared at her face, still impassive in the moon-gleam. 'I'm not a nice man.'

'What happened afterwards?' said Bobby. 'She left you, didn't she?'

'Oh, come on. You must know. You've been looking me up.'

'Not since I told you. You don't like people prying, do you? So I haven't pried. You can't have it both ways. Don't complain that I don't know.'

It was a moment when Patrick might very easily have poured it all out. He wanted to do just that. Then, standing on the edge of that vertiginous slope, knowing that to move even one more step meant demolishing the buttressing walls protecting him from the world, Patrick pulled back.

'I lost her,' he said. 'That's all.'

In the silence that followed, Bobby turned the silver mirror of her face slightly away. 'I don't mean this cruelly,' she said eventually, 'but you're not the only one. I've lost someone—a partner. I do speak that language.'

How could she say that, he thought with fury. She didn't even know what he was talking about. He meant death, not separation.

'A *partner*?' he said. 'I'm not talking about a partner. You can lose a partner. You can find another one. It just takes time. There are far worse things than that. There are things you can't replace.'

He might as well have slapped her, the way the impact of his words knocked her head back.

'I came here to try to help you,' she said. 'My mistake, maybe, but you can't bully me into thinking you're as bad as you say you are. I'll make up my own mind. I'm going back home because I don't think there's anything else useful I can say right now.'

She walked away, leaving him in his self-inflicted hell.

IT WAS THE MORNING after the concert, the morning after his brutal dedication. They were on the road again, leaving Rome, the phones in the tour bus ringing nonstop. Every rock journalist and gossip columnist in Britain was after the story of Paddy Kane's unsuspected little wife back home. The press were out for blood and plenty was promised by the way Paddy had revealed and reviled Rachel in the same instant. Every PR person on Colonic Music's payroll was frantically trying to put the genie back in the bottle.

The bus stopped for a lunch break in the ancient city of Perugia. There Paddy saw the boy playing in the bright spangles of light. When he came out and Claypole told him Rachel and David were both dead, it didn't seem, for a moment, that it could possibly be true.

He heard Claypole tell the outlines of what he knew. Rachel had never even made it down the drive of their house. Her car had hit the wall on the bend of the drive and ricocheted into the river. David was found drowned in the back seat next to an open bag, messily stuffed with the few things she had grabbed before rushing out of the house. Nobody knew exactly when it had happened.

Paddy knew. Paddy knew it had been within minutes of his song going out across the world's ether. He had run back into the cathedral, had walked blindly into a side chapel, the full, dreadful pity of it all crystallising in his head into a sharper and sharper pain, showing him that below all the surface scum of the past years he still loved Rachel. Far more acutely, he knew he loved David with his whole soul and that the future he had created held agony and guilt in huge and equal measure.

In the side chapel he saw an immense carved crucifix towering over him, dark and threatening. He turned his eyes quickly away and found himself looking up to where light burst through a stained-glass semicircle. The image in the glass was a wild, white-haired God in yellow robes whose eyes tore right through him and whose arm stretched down to point an accusing finger directly at him.

The band and its manager never saw Paddy Kane again.

After the funeral, Patrick had come to understand the full extent of what he had made Rachel suffer, but it was David's voice he would hear in the middle of the night, time and time again.

Now, before he went to sleep in his tent, Patrick wrote a note to Bobby and left it beside the gas ring. It just said, 'Thank you. I shouldn't have said that.'

Then he climbed into his sleeping-bag, looking out at the square shape covering the grave, trying to convince himself it was not his own past they had disturbed under the earth.

IT WAS HOT THE NEXT MORNING and what had been packed, moist earth deep below the topsoil had now dried out except in the patch of clay where Gaye had been digging. Dozer's shirt was damp with sweat across his back. He raised an eyebrow when Patrick came towards him, holding his trowel.

'Hello,' he said, 'funny how directors only get their 'ands dirty when you start finding the good stuff.'

'I'm going to give Gaye a hand with the sword,' Patrick said. He needed to lose himself in the painstaking work of digging. He needed distraction because David had come to him in the night, as he always did when Patrick let the memories out of their tight box. David, forever four years old, with Rachel's huge eyes in a face that was otherwise entirely Patrick's, had stood over him, soaking wet, and skipped back beyond his reach whenever he tried to touch him.

Patrick had woken searching for David, to find instead Bobby's disembodied arm, reaching in through the tent's door, offering a mug of coffee.

'Did you see my note?' he'd asked.

'That's why you get the coffee. One of the reasons, anyway.'

'I shouldn't have said any of that.'

'If you ask me, you should have said more.'

'Well, I shouldn't have said it like that.'

'No argument there. Anyway, there's a deputation to see you. The vicar and the head teacher. If you don't come soon I may have to take up Dozer's offer and hire his mate, the fancy cake chef.'

'The vicar? Where are they?'

'Sniffing around by the grave. On my land. Without asking.'

PULLING ON HIS CLOTHES, Patrick shot out into the sunlight and found the Reverend Augustus Templeton-Jones trying to undo the zip of the tent that protected the grave. A man in tweeds was standing behind him, the man Patrick had seen fending off Bobby at their first brief meeting.

'Leave that alone, please,' he called, irritated. 'That's a protected environment.' It sounded good and it stopped the vicar in his tracks.

'I do beg your pardon,' he said. He was bald on top with white side whiskers, and he didn't look sorry at all. In daylight, Patrick could see he had a sharply hooked nose that swept down in an unbroken curve from his forehead. The headmaster stood back, embarrassed.

'What can I do for you?'

'Word has reached me,' said the vicar, 'that you have made a further find. A crucifix, I believe. Is it true?'

'A crucifix? No, I'm afraid not.'

'Well, I apologise if I have been misinformed, but I understood that you had found a brooch in that form.'

'Look, the only brooch we have found is bent, broken and badly damaged. As far as we can see it's got three arms but—'

'If one arm was missing, that would make four. Four arms is a crucifix, young man.'

'At the moment, it's a broken brooch, that's all. Three arms. Ask me again in a month when it's been cleaned.'

'I also wanted to talk to you about another matter.' The vicar looked towards the tents. 'The woman who is doing your cooking, Miss Redhead.'

'What about her?'

'Just a word of warning. I understand that many people in this village have had problems with her attitude since her return. I'm afraid to say she has a reputation for causing trouble.'

Her return? Patrick wondered what he meant by that, but didn't want to discuss Bobby any more than he had to.

The head teacher broke his silence and his voice was peevish. 'As a case in point she is currently trying to get what you might call a civil disobedience campaign started among the parents in the village.'

'You're talking about the May Day parade? I don't quite understand your objection to it.'

The vicar stepped in quickly. 'It teaches the children a form of idolatry, Mr Kane. In effect they worship a graven image. Miss Redhead attempts to justify it in the name of tradition but this has every sign of a recent invention. It is directly against everything the Bible teaches us.'

'I thought Green Man images are found in carvings in quite a lot of churches?'

'Neglect of proper forms by long-dead wood carvers is greatly to be regretted. May I urge you to have as little to do with her as possible?'

'She is a valuable member of our team.'

'You will see the error of your ways.'

'That's right,' piped up the other man, 'you will. Good day to you.'

THE EXPOSED SECTION of the sword blade was six inches long and, brushing at the surface with a stiff paintbrush, Patrick was amazed at the condition. It was an even mid-brown colour, with nothing more than small surface irregularities caused by what seemed to be corrosion. He brushed harder and all at once could see regular markings.

'CD,' he called, 'you're the sword expert. Come and look at this.'

'What have you found, chicken feathers?'

'Patterning, maybe.'

CD took a large magnifying glass from one of the many zip pockets of his bulging waistcoat and stared at the blade for a long time in silence. Then he got to his feet as Patrick spoke.

'What do you think?'

'You were hoping this was pattern-welded, right?' said CD.

'Maybe.'

'What's pattern-welding?' said Aidan from the other trench.

'Get back to work, you son of a dog,' said CD. 'This is not for your ears.'

'Why not?' said Patrick. 'It's about time for another sword lecture. Especially when there's a real sword to talk about.'

CD gave him an inscrutable look. 'You may regret that,' he said. 'You may also want to leave off uncovering much more until dear Kenny and his merry men are here . . . well, his merry man anyway.' He bellowed at the others. 'All right, leave your trowels and come and soak up some wisdom, folks.'

The shout reached Bobby in the catering tent. Patrick saw her come out into the sunshine and stride towards them and he realised how glad he was that she didn't seem to bear grudges. He turned his gaze quickly back to CD.

'The boss here wants me to tell you all about pattern-welding,' said CD. 'Pattern-welding in sword blades produces interesting curvy herringbone sort of effects in the metal. Mostly it came from the way they put the blades together to get the right strength. Now, for our current state of knowledge, we are indebted to a man named Anstee, who didn't believe all the complicated theoretical garbage the sword experts were writing so he went and made one himself. He twisted together different bits of iron, a sort of club sandwich of flat strips and square bars and then he—'

'Fed them to the chickens?' suggested Maxwell.

'Well now, smarty-pants,' said CD, 'no, he didn't, *but* he did heat them up in a special paste, which if I recall rightly was made up of honey, flour, olive oil, milk and . . . guess what.'

'Ostrich droppings, chicken poo, elephant dung?'

'No, no, no. Pigeon shit,' said CD triumphantly. 'Anyway to cut a long story short, Anstee forged it all together and, lo and behold, he'd made a beautiful patterned sword.'

'And that's what we've got here, is it?' said Aidan.

'No,' said CD, 'I'm afraid not.'

'So why have you been telling us all about it?' said Aidan.

'I was asked to talk about pattern-welded sword blades.'

'But this isn't one?' said Patrick. 'I thought I saw a pattern.'

'Maybe you did,' said CD, smiling in delight.

'Well, how do you know it isn't pattern-welding?'

'Because when you try to weld wood, all it does is catch fire.'

'Wood? It looks like rusty iron.'

'I grant you that, but it's not. It's wood. Fragile as hell now but very hard once. I guess it's only there at all thanks to that spring.'

'Why's that?' said Aidan.

'Anaerobic conditions. No oxygen. That means the organisms that would normally destroy the wood can't survive. We'll have to be very, very careful because this is special. We've got to keep it wet.'

'Why's it so special? If it isn't a sword, what is it?'

'Did I say it wasn't a sword? Did I?'

There were scattered replies of 'No' and 'You didn't', except for Dozer who said, 'I can never understand a bloody word you say anyway.'

'My guess is it's a sword all right, but it's a little wooden one, kinda like a half-scale model,' CD went on.

'What use is a wooden sword?'

'You thought you could see a pattern,' said CD to Patrick.

'Yes. What was it? The grain?'

'Some of it, sure. But the rest is much, much better.' CD proffered his magnifying glass. 'Runes. I can see two of them pretty clearly and so I'll make a prediction.' He turned to the others. 'Important professional waiver here, guys and gals. Archaeologists don't make predictions because it's always too early . . .' he paused expectantly.

'. . . to tell,' they replied as one.

'Notwithstanding that,' he said, '—by the way, do you dig the truly English polysyllables?—notwithstanding that, I predict that when we uncover the rest of this, one end will be burnt. The only other wooden sword like this one I've come across—and if anyone's interested I do have copies of the appendix to my second doctoral thesis available at just nine dollars and ninety-nine cents—had a runic inscription that ran something like "return messenger", which fits the fact that it was burnt.'

Patrick remembered. 'Burnt arrows were a summons for help. It meant someone was in extreme danger. The other wooden sword came from Germany, didn't it?'

'Frisia,' said CD, 'on the coast.' He waved vaguely. 'Holland, is it? Dutchland, Deutschland, what's the difference?'

'There speaks a citizen of the country that was too busy to join in the first half of the big match,' said Dozer, sourly.

'Ah, come on, Doze,' said CD. 'We're all Germans really if you go back far enough.'

Patrick took the magnifier and knelt over the exposed part of the sword. It was drying out fast, to reveal a worm trail of lighter-coloured earth, embedded in the grooves. He made out a vertical line, with two parallel diagonals sloping down from its right—the 'æ' rune of Old English. The other shape eluded him. He couldn't be sure if it was the M shape that spelt 'e' or had the two extra lines of the 'd' rune.

'So what's with these runes anyway?' asked Maxwell.

'We'll talk about that this evening,' said Patrick. 'This is an amazing find and we need to protect it. It's out in the open air now and that's the worst possible thing.'

'Cover it up again,' said CD, and Patrick scooped wet clay from each side of the exposed wood, patting it gently into place over the sword to seal it from the air. Patrick called Hescroft and a conservation specialist from the Pitt-Rivers Museum in Oxford was on her way to them in minutes.

Hescroft also alerted the TV crew so the rest of Patrick's day was taken up satisfying them as much as superintending the painstaking removal of the wooden sword. When the last of the soil was carefully removed from the sword's pointed tip the black marks of old scorching were clear to see.

The specialist was a forthright Danish woman.

'Get that camera out of the way,' she snapped. 'You shouldn't have left it uncovered *at all*. Do you know how fragile this is? There is no time to lose. Bloody archaeologists.'

'So what do we do?'

'You do nothing. You stand still and watch. I take it out as a block. Slice down and under it, three inches at least below it so we support it from under and lift it like that.'

She did it under their anxious eyes, sliding a thin sheet of plywood beneath it. When it was safely on the grass, she wrapped the entire block tightly in clingwrap.

'I take it back now for proper treatment,' she said. 'Soak it in polyethylene glycol. Wax soluble in water. Gives it strength, or maybe I'll freeze-dry it. We'll see about that.'

When she'd gone and the camera had left them alone, Patrick found himself standing next to an unexpectedly thoughtful CD.

'What is it?' Patrick asked.

CD shrugged and Edgar, perched on his shoulder, fluttered indignantly. 'Hard to say. First he was a he, then she was a she, with a little one. Now there's this. Her distress call. I guess she's not just bones any more.'

'What do you make of the sword? Did she send it? Did she get it from someone else?'

'Speculation,' said CD. 'I only speculate after sundown.'

'It's six o'clock,' said Patrick.

'Sundown's a-comin',' said CD squinting at the sky. 'Just another couple of hours to get the Glenboggy in.'

'My turn,' said Patrick.

Patrick got in his car and drove down to the Stag. As he slowed down to turn into the pub car park, he noticed a little knot of people on the village green and saw with surprise that Kenny Camden and Jack were there with the camera. They seemed to be interviewing a group of people. He parked the car and walked over. Camden didn't see Patrick coming up behind him.

'So you agree with the vicar?' Camden said. 'If the woman does turn out to be Christian, you think she should be decently reburied?'

'Well, I do,' said a large woman. 'That would be the decent thing.'

Patrick cleared his throat loudly and Camden swung round.

'A word in your ear,' said Patrick coldly.

'I won't be a minute,' said Camden to the group, and glanced at Jack, nodding slightly. Patrick led him into the centre of the triangular green, aware that the whole group was staring after them.

'Who said you could do this?' he demanded. 'I had an earful from the vicar this morning. I wondered how he knew about the brooch. I didn't realise you were going around egging everybody on.'

'I've got a programme to make,' said Camden. 'I don't tell you about archaeology, you don't tell me about TV, OK?'

'No, not OK at all. We've got the security of the site to think about. You're prejudicing the whole dig.'

'To be frank, I think you're being a bit precious, Paddy.'

'Do *not* call me Paddy. I've told you enough times.'

'Oh, come off it,' said Camden to goad him. 'Big deal—Paddy, Pat, so what? I can't help it. It's the way I think of you.'

Patrick's fingers clenched into a fist and he fought to get back under control. 'Yes, that's the whole trouble. Time you stopped. I understand you have a job to do but you don't have to do it this way. I'm not here to be used and I'm pissed off with this. I'll do the job, but leave me alone, understand?'

'Understood,' said Camden soothingly. 'We'll stay out of your hair if you just play ball a little.'

As Patrick stalked across to the pub, Camden strolled back to Jack and the camera. 'You did get that, didn't you?' he said.

'Yes,' said Jack, rather regretting that he had. 'You won't hear much of it because I couldn't get that close but you'll see all the arm-waving and that. He was pretty worked up.'

'That's my boy,' said Camden.

SUPPER WAS STEW ON PASTA, though Bobby called it tagliatelle giardiniera. It didn't matter. Six litres of the Stag's cheapest red wine chased the taste away, and it seemed the diggers could hardly wait for darkness and the campfire chat.

'Do you think Joe's coming tonight?' Dozer asked Bobby.

'He's here already,' she said, nodding into the gloom, and there was her brother, standing motionless on the fringe of the firelight.

'No gitbox?' said Dozer.

'What?'

'As his official translator,' said CD, 'I can reveal that meant "The man in question has not come bearing his stringed instrument for making mellifluous music, namely his guitar.'"

'Come and join us, mate,' called Dozer, but there was no sign Joe had even heard.

'He'll come if he wants to,' said Bobby.

'No songs tonight, then,' Gaye said.

'Who knows?' Bobby said, smiling.

'So what do we think?' said Patrick, when they'd all settled down round the fire. 'It's after sundown, CD, and your jackdaw's tucked up. You're allowed to speculate now.'

'Raven,' said the American. 'All in good time. Let's lay out the facts. We have a pregnant Anglo-Saxon woman, probably seventh century, buried with a shield, and close by we have a half-size wooden sword burnt at one end and inscribed with runes. Both of these are very, very, very unusual. She is also accompanied by grave goods typical of female burials, plus we now think there is a real metal sword in the grave beside the skeleton.'

'We do?' said Patrick, startled.

'Sorry, forgot to tell you. It's too early, et cetera. Just a sign of something blade-like so far. While you were fetching the booze. Speaking of which, you seem to be clutching a bottle under your arm which I have not yet been introduced to.'

'It's Teacher's. They didn't have any rotgut.'

'I'll manage. So, speculate away, folks.'

'I bet she sent the sword for help at the last minute,' Gaye said, 'and they didn't come in time so she had to defend her children herself. Then when they did come, it was too late, so they buried the sword with her.'

'You think she had other children?' Maxwell was curious.

'Of course she did,' said Gaye. 'If she was pregnant she would have run and hid. Anything to defend her unborn baby. She would only have fought if she had other children to protect.'

'Is that right?'

'I think it is,' said Bobby. 'I've seen that.'

'Where?' said Patrick, surprised.

'Oh . . . that's a sidetrack.'

She was looking into the fire. Feeling his gaze on her, she glanced sideways at him, making a little face as if to dismiss the remark.

That he had been staring at the silhouette of her face for far too long was not noticed, because something else had grabbed everybody's attention. Joe was coming to join them round their fire.

He sat down on a log between Aidan and Gaye, looking at each of them in turn, meeting their eyes. There was a moment of silence then, holding out the whisky bottle, CD said, 'Nice to see you, pal. We'd been hoping you'd join us.'

Joe, dressed in a green army-surplus sweater and patched cord trousers, took the bottle, lifted it to his lips and passed it on. Patrick could see no trace of a family resemblance to Bobby. Her brother had a square, weather-beaten face, his grey hair was short and curly, and under bushy eyebrows his bright, pale eyes darted from side to side.

As they stared at him, he took a breath and sang three descending notes softly, 'Ah, ah, ah.' Then he looked at them enquiringly and sang the same three notes again. He stood up and held out both hands, palms up, in front of him, nodding at them.

Bobby sang the notes back at him, accurately, and he beamed with pleasure.

'Our turn, folks,' said Bobby. 'He wants us to sing the notes.'

It was ragged at first and Joe kept signing for them to start again. After five false starts, they sounded reasonably good. At that point, Joe made a chopping, cut-off sign with his hand and held up two fingers. This time he sang six notes, starting low and soaring up only to descend again. They'd got the idea now and it only took three tries to get it right. He confused them briefly by holding up one finger, but Bobby said it meant they should do the first one again and he nodded, beaming. One finger for the first, two fingers for the second. They did them one after the other until he was satisfied, then he held up three fingers.

'Blimey, how much more is there?' said Dozer. 'If we're doing Handel's *Messiah* in bite-size chunks, we're going to be here all night.'

They learned the third and fourth sections quickly. Then Joe beckoned them all to their feet with upward sweeps of his arms.

'I guess it's show time,' said CD, echoing Patrick's thoughts.

Joe walked off into the darkness and they followed as he led them up the gentle slope of the hilltop. They stopped in front of the frame tent protecting the woman and her child, and Joe went to it, holding one corner pole and looking towards Patrick.

'You want us to move it?' Patrick asked, and he saw Joe give another of his sharp downward nods. 'OK,' he said. 'Give us a hand to get the pegs out,' and the diggers moved the big tent carefully so that the grave lay bare.

Joe took a step closer to the grave and knelt as if in prayer. Then he got back to his feet, turned to the group and held up a single finger. He hummed the first note for a moment as a guide, looked round to check they were all ready and brought his finger sweeping down.

There was no hanging back in their response. All day the grave had been cluttered with the jarring gadgets of modern times. Now the night had brought back simplicity and they were just fourteen living souls on a hilltop honouring the dead with an ancient tune. The last note ended and they looked to Joe for guidance.

In the silence he half sang, half chanted:

> 'The boda came to Abbandun at evening bell,
> Brought by the child with sunset head.
> We left our looms to answer it as black night fell,
> That blood call on the summoning sword.'

An involuntary shiver ran through Patrick's body. Joe's pronunciation was precise and oddly foreign. 'Night' sounded almost like the German 'nicht' and 'blood' was 'bloode'. Intent on what he was doing, Joe held up a hand again and, carried along by the rhythm, they all knew that the second part followed. The notes they sang took on a beauty beyond anything they had sung before and, when it ended, Joe went on:

> 'The mother river broke its banks that heartless night
> And slowed our feet in beds of mud
> When we climbed to your shattered hall at dawn's first light
> You'd taken ship on seas of blood.'

This time, they needed no prompting at all, coming in unison into the third part.

> 'Your husband's kin, who failed to pay the sword-blade debt
> Now stand before you with bowed head.
> We came too late to help in time of need and yet
> We vow we'll keep your daughter fed.'

They all stood in stunned silence, Patrick staring up into the heavens. Those stars aren't really there at all, he thought, although I can see them. What I see is just a message from where they were a thousand years or a thousand millennia ago, from where they were when this woman was laid in the ground.

He pulled his gaze back to the earth. Joe was gone and the rest of them were looking at each other as if shocked by what they'd done. After a long moment, Patrick went over to the covering tent. CD and Dozer helped him walk it back into its place, then they all moved back to the fire and settled into their places around it.

CD produced the bottle of Scotch and it made the rounds. Then the American said, 'Before you ask, Aidan, Abbandun is the old Anglo-Saxon name for Abingdon, which is, I would say, four hours' hard march away in the times before there were roads.'

'Thank you,' said Aidan nodding. 'I hadn't yet thought of asking that. I *was* going to ask about the unfamiliar word there at the start. Sounded like boder.'

'It means nothing to me. Peter? No?'

'It was clear what the sense was,' said Maxwell, almost indignantly. 'The boder was the summons, wasn't it?'

CD shrugged. 'This is beyond my humble knowledge.'

Dozer nodded slowly. 'What gets me,' he said, 'is that I'm the king of the cynics but all the time I was listening to him, I was quite sure he wasn't just making it up.'

'It was special,' said Gaye. 'In fact, I think it was more . . . more wonderfully disturbing than anything else in my life. Last time the grave was open, they were laying her in it. I'd really like to think those words were more or less what they were saying then.'

That's quite a speech, thought Patrick, coming from Gaye who'd only seemed to feel strongly about hygiene when she first arrived.

'You can't say those were the same words, can you?' objected Maxwell. 'What he said tonight, that was modern English.'

'Oh, it's not so very different,' said Peter. 'The Old English words just got added to, a bit of French and a bit of Danish here and there. If you just take the time to learn to pronounce Old English, the mystery disappears. It wouldn't be hard to put together an Old English sentence that you'd understand with no trouble at all.'

'Boda, with an a,' said CD, who clearly hadn't been listening. 'Idiot. Maxwell, I owe you an apology. B, O, D, A—berkano, othila, dagaz, ansuz.'

'Bless you,' said Dozer, 'that's a nasty cold.'

'Names from the runic alphabet. I told you about the goddamn Frisian sword. That's half of what's written on it. The second word, boda. Wait. Do not move.' He leapt to his feet, ran to his tent and came back with a heavy book and a torch.

'Bedtime reading,' he said, 'and you get to give your pecs a work-out at the same time. Bosworth and Toller's *Anglo-Saxon Dictionary*. Boda, boda, boda, yup. Masculine noun, meaning "messenger, ambassador, herald", et cetera.'

'A summons to help,' said Maxwell. 'I told you.'

'So if the runes on *our* sword say boda, that would be pretty strong support for the song,' said Aidan.

'Runic characters,' said CD. 'Just to be really purist, runes were the sacred stones they were cut into. But yes, I guess it would.'

'What are these runes about anyway?' said Aidan. 'I thought that was comic-book stuff. Hobbits and wizards.'

'Ask Peter, the one-man database,' said CD. 'He knows everything.'

'An early system of lettering,' said Peter, chuckling, 'made up of straight lines, probably because the letters were incised into stone or wood and it's easier to do straight lines if you're using a knife. The alphabet is called the futhark, just like we say ABC, because that's what the first six letters spelt.' He turned to Aidan. 'Before you ask, I know futhark has seven letters, but the third one is a combined "th" sound. Runic words were used not for communication but for symbolic pur-poses,' he went on. 'You might put a name on a valuable object to label it as yours but more likely to give it a certain power. There were those poor Britons, used to Roman culture—history, poetry and plays—and in come these crude foreigners whose entire literary heritage adds up to a row of grunts carved on a rock. They have to wait another six hundred years before there's anything else worth reading.'

There was a scatter of appreciative laughter, then a silence.

Gaye said it for all of them. 'I don't really care where that song came from. It's true enough for me. That's a burial over there, not just a dig. She was as alive as we are, that woman. If Joe's songs are the best way to remember that, then that's good enough for me.'

There was a bit of whispering in the darkness then Maxwell went off to his tent and came back holding something behind him. Aidan encouraged him onwards but the boy was reluctant. In the end Aidan took the guitar Maxwell was carrying and came over to Patrick.

'Now, Mr Director,' he said, 'we have a favour to ask.'

Patrick looked at the guitar, appalled. 'What?'

'We know you have a fine voice, having heard it tonight, and we know you're an archaeologist through and through these days, which is all that matters. Some of us have the idea that you might also be rather good on one of these things and we wondered whether you might be persuaded to give it a shot, among friends. Just some tuneful old things that we'd all know. It would be a kindness.'

So, astonishing himself, Patrick reached out and took the instrument, feeling with a shock of familiarity the swell of it against his thigh. He suddenly realised, as his fingers touched the strings, how long it was since he had last played a guitar for pleasure. It was an old cheap acoustic with nylon strings and it was out of tune. He spent much longer than was strictly necessary getting it right. Then without thinking about it, he found a reggae beat and launched into 'Redemption Song'. He hadn't played anything plainly tuneful since before Nam Erewhon, but his subconscious brought the words and the chords back as if the years in between hadn't happened at all. When a log-falling leap of firelight made him look up, he saw a circle of underworld, flame-painted faces all looking at him.

'C'mon, Pat, give us something we can dance to,' called Dozer. 'Me and Gaye want to rock and roll.'

'I do *not*,' said Gaye.

Patrick did his best with 'Blue Suede Shoes'. Dozer got to his feet, trying to pull Gaye with him but she wouldn't, then Bobby smiled and jumped up and she and Dozer went into a dance as if they'd rehearsed it a hundred times. Patrick repeated the verses he could remember over and over again just to watch the two of them, until Dozer dropped exhausted and Bobby danced on.

He played her to a whirling finale and, not wanting her to stop, slowed into a song that came out of his subconscious. Only when some of them joined in, did he realise what it was he was playing. '*I'm a young man, growing up in the world . . .*'

He willed her to stop dancing before the chorus came: '*If you want to know, how she makes love, just look at the way she dances.*' Perhaps Bobby recognised the tune too because she sat down suddenly and, in the firelight, he realised that her cheeks were wet with tears. She turned her gaze away into the flames but after a while, knowing his gaze was on her, she stared straight back at him, her eyes still shining, then got up and walked off.

The rest were intent on him and few saw her go. He could do or say nothing to stop her, halfway through his song. He brought it to a premature halt at the end of the next verse and rested.

They clapped him and they wouldn't let him stop. By the time Patrick had been through all he could remember from Dire Straits to Dylan, exhaustion settled on them. He was happier than he'd been for as long as he could remember. As he handed the guitar back to Maxwell, the boy said, 'That was just great. Famous you, singing just for us,' and he didn't even mind that.

Before he crawled into his tent, he looked down the hill at the farm and wondered what had caused Bobby's sudden flight.

EIGHT

If there was a single moment that explained how Pat became Paddy it was that first time he went out on stage with the band when the darkness beyond the lights erupted with three thousand voices. In that moment of utter astonishment he found that he could play them like an instrument—a whirl of his arm doubled the volume, a flick of his head brought in the girls' screaming trebles. Fear disappeared and utter confidence in his mastery of this audience flooded through him. He had what they wanted and he played their hunger. They responded with ecstasy and total, uncritical adulation and Pat was washed away by it.

Now, waking to the unfamiliar tingle that the guitar strings had left in his fingertips, Patrick was back on that stage again for a moment and the future was not yet written. In the next second, the nylon-filtered green light brought him back to a hard today, and he felt another unguarded morning pang for David and Rachel. People had told him you got over it but he wasn't even sure you ever got used to it.

He steeled himself to crawl outside, then went to the marquee for breakfast. He felt raw and open. Last night Bobby had danced like an angel and he had watched like a slave. She's the cook, he told himself. I'm the director. I will go in and be polite and that will be it. She was busy frying eggs and hardly had time to look round when he said good morning. He took slices of bread and a scoop of marmalade, poured coffee and went outside to sit on the grass where CD and Dozer were already eating their food. It was a fine morning and, for the first time since they had arrived, there was no dew.

'Take a look at that,' said CD. 'They're early.' He pointed with his knife to where Camden's car was coming into sight through the gate.

'Maybe we won't mention last night,' said Patrick.

'My thoughts exactly. You go and occupy them for a minute or two and I might just spread the word round the gang.'

'I'll go,' said Dozer.

'No, no,' said CD. 'We merely want to delay him, not frighten him to death.'

The Toyota's tailgate was open and Camden was standing bent over, busy with papers in the back compartment, when Patrick walked up. Jack was sorting through his camera gear on the bonnet.

'Good morning,' said Patrick. 'You're bright and early.'

He took Camden by surprise. The man stood up sharply, cracked his head on the roof, yelped and dropped the cardboard file he was holding. As Patrick went to pick it up for him, he found himself staring, transfixed by a photocopy that had slid out of the folder. It was a page from a tabloid newspaper. He stared at the old headline: MAD PADDY BROKE MY CAMERA SAYS OUR SNAPPER. Anger rose in him that Camden should have such a thing in his files.

He heard Kenny Camden say, 'Whoops.' Then he tore the sheet into small pieces, and stuffed them into his pocket.

'Before you start,' said Camden, 'I forgot that was still there.'

'Why was it there in the first place?'

'Because I was finding out about you. I did my research. That's what you have to do when you're putting a programme together. I didn't know all this would be so sensitive for you. OK?'

'What else have you got in there?' said Patrick, pointing at the folder. 'I want to see it.'

'No, come on. It's private stuff.' Camden glanced round at Jack, to see that the cameraman now had his gear ready and it seemed to be casually pointing in their direction. 'Look, Patrick, I know you've had a rough time but I don't really know why. Maybe if you just told me a bit more, I could avoid treading on your toes.'

'Or you could jump on them harder.'

Camden decided to go for it. 'I know you lost your family. Car crash, wasn't it? No one could blame you for that.'

'You know nothing,' said Patrick. 'Nothing at all, and stop bloody prying into my affairs.'

'Look, I can see that maybe it's tough for you here. A grave with a mother and child.'

'That is nothing to do with it,' said Patrick, stung by the fact that it had everything to do with it. 'You shoot your stuff but stay off that. This is just a dig, nothing more. I'm going to work now.'

'Whatever you say. We'll be down in a minute.'

Camden watched Patrick walk away. 'Did you get all that, Jack?'

'No.'

'What do you mean, no? Do you mean you missed it all?'

'I had no idea you wanted me to shoot that. Sounded private to me.'

'Get this, you dickhead. *Nothing* is private where he comes in, OK?'

THE DIGGERS, ENJOYING their usual leisurely start to the day, were spread around the grass outside the marquee when Patrick arrived.

'Come on,' he barked. 'Let's get on with it.'

'It's only twenty past eight,' said CD.

Patrick turned to him. 'If I say it's time to start, it's time to start.' The words were out of his mouth before he could stop them.

'Easy, boss,' said Dozer. 'What's the matter? Hurricane expected?'

'No, sorry, guys. I had a punch-up with Camden.' Patrick made a big effort to smile and cancel out what he'd said, but it wasn't a complete success.

The diggers worked in a baffled silence until the day's first find gave them a common interest again.

'Take a look at *this*,' said CD.

Four small coins lay next to the woman's shoulder blade.

Though CD hadn't raised his voice at all, the antennae of the other diggers had started twitching and the usual ring quickly formed round the grave trench. Jack arrived with the camera.

Maxwell beat Aidan to the question. 'What are they?'

'Itett,' said CD.

'What's that?'

'Short for "it's too early to tell". But they could be sceattas, maybe?' The word sounded like 'shatters'.

'What are *they*?'

'Saxon silver coins,' said Peter promptly, 'usually cast in clay moulds, then stamped. But I'd say it's a bit early for them. Until the eighth century they're usually only found to the southeast of here.'

'Do you promise that you're not going to suddenly turn out to be somebody I should have heard of?' CD asked him.

'I'm afraid not,' said Peter. 'I *am* a bit of a coin specialist, though.'

'So what else might they be?' said Maxwell.

Peter bent to pick one of them up but stopped himself in time and turned to CD. 'May I?'

'Give me a minute to get it on the record sheet. Couple of photos.'

CD busied himself with the camera and the paperwork, then he gently loosened the top coin. 'OK, here you go.'

Peter rubbed at the surface. 'It's been pierced,' he said. 'There's a small hole near the rim. May I borrow your magnifying glass?'

CD passed it over and the older man inspected the coin carefully.

'All right,' he said. 'It's one of the type called radiates. Do you see there? There's a crown that radiates round the emperor's head? Looks like an antonianus to me. These coins are Roman. They could be as old as the third century.'

'So what are they doing here?'

'My guess is someone made them into a necklace. Look at the holes. You sometimes see them as pendants.'

'Well, dear lady,' said CD, looking down at the bones. 'Full of surprises ain't you? You just love those old Roman things.' He turned back to the others. 'You realise maybe we're looking at the first archaeologist here, folks? Hell, this stuff was three, four hundred years old when she was born. That's like me digging up a coin from the Stuarts. Pretty damned exciting, I'd call that.'

In the afternoon, Dozer found two pieces of shaped bone which he pronounced to be gaming counters. He went on trowelling away, and later exposed a flat slate. Wiping off the dirt, he discovered the incised straight lines of a superb gaming board. That stopped everything for quite some time, Kenny Camden wanting to know what the game was and even Peter not having an answer.

They were into the bottom four or five inches of the grave now, and the finds were coming thick and fast.

'Hey, look what's here. I think I've struck iron,' said CD.

In the next few minutes he uncovered several heavily rusted iron cleats, oblong plates in pairs, with the remains of rivets at each end.

'It's the bed,' said Patrick. 'Her wooden bed. Just like in the song. There were cleats like that at Swallowcliffe. They held the planks together. And look, there's an eyelet. Cords went through those and held up a latticework support for the mattress.'

'"She lies there still on her wooden bed",' said CD. 'Oh, hi, Jack.'

Patrick whirled round and saw the cameraman with dismay. Jack, noticing that Camden was nowhere in the immediate vicinity, put a finger to his lips and winked.

The American uncovered more and more of the fragile remains of the bed, but it was Dozer who exclaimed next. 'I've found glass!' That brought the crowd round.

'Can you get it out quite quickly?' said Camden, reappearing. 'I've got to be in Oxford for a budget meeting at five.'

'No, he can't,' said Patrick shortly. 'This dig is not going to be prejudiced by your timetable.'

'Hey, hang on. This meeting's in your interests.'

'In what way?'

'We're discussing putting in the cash to do a facial reconstruction on the skull. Wouldn't you like to see that?'

Yes, thought Patrick, more than anything. 'No,' he said. 'It's old hat, isn't it? They're always doing that on TV.'

'We've got the chance of going a bit further,' retorted Camden, stung. 'That's what I have to go and talk about.'

By mutual, silent consent, Patrick, CD and Dozer went very slowly, making a meal of every aspect of the recording. What was emerging from the soil was an intricate beaker of pale blue-green glass, the conical cup part ornamented by two tiers of curving glass arches. When the top half had been exposed and Camden had taken Jack and his camera away, Patrick called everyone over to see it. Bobby, who had been down at the farm cooking a curry that Dozer had already labelled Indian stew, was walking back up the hill, and Patrick waited until she joined them.

'Quite a day,' he said. 'We'll try to draw some conclusions tonight, but I just want to bring you all up to date on what we've found. We now know that she was indeed buried on a wooden bed and the latest thing to show up is a wonderful piece of glass, this clawed beaker.' As a joke, he called across, 'Peter, I don't suppose you know anything about clawed beakers, do you?'

It didn't occur to Peter for one moment to take it as a joke. 'A bit,' he said. 'They're Saxon copies of a Roman style of beaker but if you look at those curved supports running up from the base, the Saxon version is much cruder. The Roman ones often have dolphin shapes where the Saxons just used plain arcs of glass.'

'Thank you,' said Patrick. 'Now, these beakers are very often found in pairs, so with a bit of luck we might even find its twin tomorrow.'

Bobby had crouched down by the edge of the trench and was staring at the beaker.

'That's it for now,' Patrick said. 'Clear up your loose and get yourselves cleaned up. After supper we'll have the fireside chat again.'

An hour later, showered and changed into slightly cleaner jeans, Patrick was sitting outside his tent, brooding on the day.

A voice, Bobby's, broke in. 'Would you like a glass of wine?'

'I would. Thank you.' He took the glass she held out.

'You're not very observant, are you?' she said.

It was the sort of thing Rachel used to say in their early days when she'd had her hair done or bought new clothes. He stared at Bobby. Not her hair—she wore the same concealing woollen hat. Not her clothes. 'What have I missed?' he said cautiously. She was watching him like a hawk. He raised the glass to his lips and she raised her eyebrows. He realised the lip of the glass was very thick and the stem was an intricate and bulky affair. He looked at what he was holding—it was the clawed beaker from the grave.

He stared at it, bewildered. 'What have you done? You haven't taken it out? Don't you realise—'

She was shaking her head. 'It's still there,' she said. 'Just don't raise your hopes when you go looking for the matching one. You're already holding it.'

'This is the other one? How can it be? I mustn't drink *wine* out of it,' Patrick said, holding the beaker as carefully as possible.

'Why not?' she replied. 'That's what I've been doing for years. We've had it in the house ever since I can remember. I suppose it's something Dad found in a rabbit hole. I thought it was maybe Victorian or something until I saw the one in the grave.' She giggled. 'It's even been in the dishwasher.'

'You must have realised it was special, surely?'

Bobby shrugged. 'The house is stacked with Dad's stuff, everything he ever found. Joe spends a lot of time looking at it. You'll have to come and see it all.'

'Definitely. When shall I come?'

'After supper? No, that won't do. After the fireside chat.'

Patrick imagined the two of them walking off together into the dark and the whispering that would start all over again. He could suggest CD came too but he didn't want to. He wanted the chance to look at this stuff all by himself first, whatever it was.

'Fine,' he said, 'after the fireside chat.'

The curry didn't hold anyone's attention for very long.

'Undercooked British root vegetable vindaloo,' pronounced CD when he was sure Bobby couldn't hear. 'Executed with a certain panache or maybe it was potash, I couldn't be certain.'

Round the fire, Aidan spoke first. 'Our lady there—don't you think she was a bit of a sport? That gaming board stuff. She was competitive, I think—someone who'd give the boys a run for their money. I like a woman like that.'

Patrick sat in the dark listening, thinking of the women he'd turned to when life became exciting. Women who egged him on, who played pool, who drove aggressively and evoked a powerful response. He was astonished by how foreign all that felt now. That was not the nature of the woman of Wytchlow, this brave soul whose values were straightforward matters of life, death and loyalty, whose vitality had reached out to touch them all from the grave.

'Aidan's right,' said Maxwell. 'She's like Zelda. A real warrior woman. I bet she was beautiful.'

'Who on earth is Zelda?' said Gaye.

'Don't you know Zelda? The video game?'

'No, I most certainly do not.'

'I didn't say she was like that,' said Aidan, affronted. 'She was a good woman, wasn't she? Not some kind of a cartoon. I just meant she enjoyed a laugh or they wouldn't have put the game in there. I agree with old Maxwell though, I bet she was a beauty.'

'We might find out,' Patrick said cautiously. 'Kenny Camden's talking about doing a facial reconstruction.'

'Does that take a long time?'

'Not if we get her skull out in one piece.'

'Take her head off?' said Gaye aghast. 'That's horrible. I was thinking we'd, well . . . we'd keep her together. Treat her properly. I'm starting to see what that vicar means. While her bones are lying there, she's still a person, isn't she? Are we really going to take them apart?'

'We have to take the bones out of the grave. They need proper examination. They come out one at a time.'

To change the subject, Dozer turned to Bobby. 'Any chance of seeing your bro tonight, love?'

'I don't think so,' she said. 'He was loading up his backpack when I left. That usually means he's going to be off somewhere all night.'

'Where does he go?'

'I haven't a clue. He's always back by morning to start work.'

'Shame that. I was looking forward to another surprise.' Dozer spoke for them all.

The talk seemed to run out of steam after that.

'Might go down the pub,' said Dozer.

'Good plan,' said CD. 'Who's coming?'

Everyone was, except Patrick and Bobby.

'I might come later,' Patrick said. 'I've got a few things to do.'

Bobby took the dirty dishes down the hill in the Land Rover. When the others had all gone to the village, Patrick walked down after her, telling himself his anticipation was all about her father's finds.

As he came round the corner towards the gate, Patrick saw the tail-lights of a car swinging into the road. Bobby was standing in the yard looking furious.

'What's the matter?' he said.

'Roger bloody Little, our so-called Chairman of Governors.'

'Your friend and mine. What did he want?'

She waved the letter she was holding. 'He's given me notice that they're applying for a court injunction to stop us taking the children out of school for May Day. It's just vindictive, that's all.'

'You can fight it, can't you? There must be a hearing of some sort. You can give your side.'

'Oh sure. Just imagine how that will be. Me and a few of the mothers against three pillars of society? Can you imagine any judge taking the slightest notice of us? I haven't got any evidence.' He realised she was on the edge of tears.

'I'll help you. In any way I can.'

She shook her head. 'Come on in. Sorry, that wasn't much of a welcome. Would you like another glass of wine?'

'Out of an ordinary glass?' he said to try to make her laugh.

'I can probably run to plastic if you're happier with it.'

She led him through to a big kitchen with an old Aga and a huge table covered in cracked Formica. He followed her into another room almost filled by a rug-covered sofa and two old brown armchairs.

'Have a look. I'll get the wine.'

The walls were completely lined with shelving on which sat a hotchpotch of dusty objects. Patrick stood in front of them, staring. He picked up a tiny pottery oil lamp with a hand grip at one side, clearly Roman. Next to the lamp was half a medieval floor-tile, inlaid with a fleur-de-lis pattern.

'It's not great wine, I'm afraid,' said Bobby, coming back in with two glasses.

'I'm sure it's fine,' Patrick said, taking a sip and discovering she was right. He was staring at two small bronze pyramids, an inch or so across, decorated with some sort of filigree work. He picked one of them up. 'Look at these,' he said. 'They're Saxon. Part of a scabbard, I think. Where did they come from?'

'I haven't a clue.' She was preoccupied. 'Have you any idea what happens if you break an injunction?'

'We could ask Peter,' he said, and won a smile out of her. 'I think it's pretty serious stuff if you do because it's contempt of court. Don't go *that* far, will you? It's not worth it.'

'You don't know that. I keep wondering what *she* would have done.'

'Our woman in the grave?'

'Yes. I'm pretty sure she wouldn't have let them stop her.'

'I'm sure she wouldn't, but you're not going to take your sword to the vicar, are you?'

'Just give me the chance! Anyway, that's not why you're here. What do you think of our collection?'

'Extraordinary. You should get a professional to have a look at it.'

'I have. You're here. Joe wouldn't want lots of strangers going over this stuff, but I know he approves of you.'

'What makes you think he approves of me?'

'I just know it.' She looked at him, so full of crackling life that he felt a spark would jump across if he stretched out a hand. 'My mum used to say Joe had appointed himself guardian of Dad's treasures. I once broke a little bowl and he got so upset.'

'Was it something special?'

'I don't know. He mended it. It's here somewhere.'

She searched the shelves. Standing with her back to Patrick, her figure and her way of holding herself seemed to him so like Rachel that he longed to get up and put his arms round her and bury his face in her neck.

She turned round and raised her eyebrows at whatever it was she saw in his face. 'Is something wrong?' she said.

He took a step and his arms came out to her and he saw her eyes widen. He stopped then and looked down at the bowl and took that instead. 'Late medieval,' he said in a voice he didn't recognise.

'Um . . . is it? You can see where Joe mended it. It's the only time he's ever been cross with me. He was Dad's boy.'

'What happened to your mum?'

'She died three years ago. That's when I had to come back and help Joe run the farm. He couldn't do it on his own.'

'Come back? Where from?'

'A long way away and another world completely.'

'What were you doing?'

She shut off abruptly. 'It's not the right time for life stories.'

'I didn't mean to—'

'You don't want to talk about yours. I don't want to talk about mine. Isn't that fair?'

'I suppose so.' All at once, he could feel how it hurt to be shut out. 'I know I've probably been fairly unreasonable to you.'

'I have to admit it is hard when you suddenly treat me like your worst enemy. Can you tell me why you do that?'

'Oh dear,' he said. 'There's something I find very difficult to tell you, something that would explain it.'

He looked at the shelves, searching for the right words to start. His gaze fell on a photo of a man in some kind of tunic, smiling at the camera. 'Who's this?' he said, picking it up.

She took it out of his grasp. 'You tell me this difficult thing of yours, in full, with nothing left out, and if I think you've told me enough I'll decide whether to answer that question.'

'All right,' he said, but he still didn't know if he could do it. 'The thing is . . .'

She stood waiting.

'The reason I have behaved rather, well . . . oddly towards you is that I find just looking at you really disturbing. You look so like Rachel that I keep getting you muddled up.'

'I look like your wife?'

'*Exactly* like her. Well, exactly like she would have looked by now if I had treated her better. If I hadn't drained everything that mattered out of her.'

She was shaking her head. 'So what does that mean? I'm a painful reminder? Are you saying you can't bear to look at me, or what?'

'No, not that. You just take me straight back to the last time life was good, to the time when I was in love with Rachel. Every time I look at you, for a moment it's like life's given me another chance and then I realise it hasn't.'

She turned her face away. 'That's a heavy responsibility to put on me, Patrick. I'm not her and I'm nothing to do with your guilt.' She frowned. 'Actually, what you've just said pisses me off a bit. I've been quite glad that I seemed to be someone you felt you could talk to. I wanted to see if I could help. I thought we had some sort of point of contact. Now it seems we don't. I've looked at you when you've been looking at me and there's been something between us. Now you're saying it's all just an accident caused by the shape of my nose or something. That's not very flattering.'

He almost said there was much more to it than that, but reason once again overcame his emotion.

'I'm sorry if I've managed to upset you again.'

'Part of your problem,' she said, 'might just be that you think you're the only person in the world who has been through it. Well, I don't feel like telling you about this—' she waved the photo at him— 'because I don't suppose it can possibly match up to what's happened to you, not for a moment.'

'I'd like to hear about him,' Patrick said quietly.

'Well, I'll just give you the headlines. He's . . .' Her voice caught. 'He was somebody I was in love with. He got sick. I couldn't save him. He died. Right? Is that enough for now? One death for me, two deaths for you. You lead two to one.'

'Bobby, I am so—'

'No, no, no. Let's not get into who's sorrier than who. Let's just call it quits and get some sleep. You know the way out.'

He was halfway across the yard with his heart in his boots when he heard an upper window open.

'Patrick,' she called.

He turned and she was silhouetted in a dormer window.

Now her voice was softer and hesitant. 'I just wanted to say you should keep an eye open tonight. There's been too much talk around the village, a few hotheads talking about all the stuff you're supposed to have found. I'd be happier if I knew you were watching out.'

She wants the night to end on a different note, he thought. He felt grateful. 'OK, I'll listen out. Sleep well.'

Of course, after that, it was hard to sleep. The others disturbed him coming back from the pub and he lay on his back wishing he'd found words that might have gone down better. It was hard when he knew he mustn't let her think he was attracted to her. That wouldn't be fair. It wasn't her he was attracted to, it was just a ghost. Such thoughts became intolerable, and he decided to get out of the tent and walk round the hilltop.

The remains of the moon shone through fringes of cloud. In that tricky light, the square silhouette of the grave cover seemed to be moving against the sky. He walked towards it and saw it *was* moving.

As fast and as quietly as he could he approached the trench. Now he could see the cover stood to one side of it and close by there were two figures rushing towards each other. He heard the sound of a fist landing on flesh, a cry and then another blow.

'Stop,' he shouted, then both of the figures were running away and he was racing after them. He caught the nearer one easily, tripped the man with his leg and fell on top of him.

'Get off me,' said a woman's voice.

'Bobby? Oh shit. Sorry. Did he hurt you?'

'Not nearly as much as you did.'

Torchlights were coming from the tents now.

'Who's that?' shouted Dozer.

'Me, Patrick,' he shouted back. 'There was a guy trying to nick stuff. He's run off towards the village.'

'Right, I'll 'ead 'im off at the pass,' shouted Dozer. 'Come on, CD, you ride shotgun.' He lumbered towards his car with CD in pursuit.

'I heard two blows.'

'You did,' she said, sounding pleased with herself. 'The first one was me punching him in the eye. It wouldn't surprise me if Roger Little doesn't keep his face well out of sight for a few days.'

'It was Little? Really? Why would he be up here?'

'Because he's a greedy man who wants a bit of everything and it's probably been driving him mad wondering what we might be finding.'

'But why were you up here? You asked *me* to listen out.'

'I don't think you really believed me, did you?'

'I suppose you're right. You usually are about most things,' said Patrick. 'Well, you can go home and get some proper sleep now. I'll move my tent up here in the morning.'

'And the rest of tonight?'

He looked at the grave cover. 'If we put this back over it, there's enough room for me to sleep inside. I'll get my sleeping-bag.'

NINE

Patrick woke to find the ground drumming against his ear. The earth was telegraphing solid footfalls coming at him in the darkness. He was disorientated, aware immediately that he was in an unfamiliar place, then he recognised that he and the German Queen had been sleeping side by side. He sat up, holding his breath. The footsteps were coming from the far side of the hill.

A pale shadow was now looming up against the tent fabric and he felt he was only moments away from violence or horror.

The footsteps stopped, the shadow collapsed to half its height as if kneeling, and a man's voice began to sing quietly outside.

'There came the time of the old King's death
And he blessed her with his final breath.
He gave his sword to be handed down
For the boy who would one day wear his crown.

They buried him at the battle stone,
And the news went out that he had gone.
Far to the east, the traitors heard
Of the end of the King with the chicken sword.

The Queen again grew big with child
As it turned to winter, calm and mild.
She woke one night from a warning dream
And heard the watchman's dying scream.

Her husband left their bed so warm
And summoned men to brave the storm.
She dressed herself in a warrior's cloak
And the chicken sword from the wall she took.

Two hours they fought on that bloody hill
And the chicken sword's blade drank its fill.
They stood their ground in the Bury Field,
Outnumbered, they refused to yield.

Three to two they stood at last
On the burying place from a distant past.
There she fought like a bear for her children's life
And for one unborn in the midst of strife.

The traitors struck a mortal blow
That felled her lord on the witch's low.
She whirled the blade like an iron fan
And two more fell to join her man.

Right to the end on the blood-soaked grass,
She would not let those traitors pass.
Just one more faced her, towering tall,
The villains' leader, worst of all.

He cut her down with a coward's blow
Struck from behind and it laid her low.
They found her there, still holding tight
To the chicken sword in its final fight.'

Joe, back from his wanderings and unaware that he was overheard, was paying a visit to the German Queen. When the singing ended, Patrick wondered whether Joe would open the flap and, if he did, whether he would be embarrassed to find he had an audience.

Then Joe spoke. 'I've come to say I'm sorry, Queen,' he said, and Patrick, astonished, strained to listen, knowing it was far too late to reveal his presence. When he thought no one alive could hear him, Joe, it seemed, could find words.

'The thing is, I don't know if I need to or not. I brought them here, it's true, and they've disturbed you, but they know that you're special because I've made sure they know your story. Anyway, I can't help thinking that what was really you has gone into this whole hilltop now. They've disturbed your bones but bones weren't what you laughed with and loved with and fought with. They were just . . . the easel on which your picture was drawn. Oh yes, my dad told me what his dad told him—that you were really something. He said that when you died it must have been like a punch in the guts for all those who loved you, a punch that takes the wind out of you when you know that you shouldn't have taken all those moments for granted and that now there is just the bitter ache of the lonely future. That's why they put you up here, where they could look up at your mound every day from where they lived. Anyway, my lady, I think those other parts that were really you have gone into the ground here and they've helped make a million blades of grass and a great sprawl of flowers every year and those have seeded and spread and carried you across all the hills so I hope you don't mind what's happened too much.'

Then he walked off. When Patrick had heard the last of his foot-steps, he unzipped the tent flap and looked out. On the grass in front of him was a bunch of spring flowers in a jar. He went back inside, holding them, moved by what he'd heard and, looking down at the skeletons in the grave, put the flowers at the head of the trench.

He stared at her and tried to imagine her and of course he failed. Instead, Joe's words came back to him: "a punch that takes the wind out of you"; "the bitter ache of the lonely future".

Loss, when it came to Patrick in Perugia, had a shape to it, a long balloon inflating upwards from his stomach through his chest cavity, driving a prickling blizzard of tears ahead of it. It had a sound too, a shout that burst out of him, as loud as he could make it, but never loud enough to drain the pain.

'I wasn't any good as a father,' he said out loud to the woman in the grave. 'I meant to be a good father. I was going to be better. I was ready to change. I was going back to say "I'm sorry" to them both. Poor Rachel. I broke her. There was no excuse for that.'

He stood there in silence for a while, staring at the skeleton.

Next to her lay the sword, her father's great sword. Seeing the first light of dawn through the tent covering and knowing there would be no more sleep that night, he went to get his trowel. In the next two hours he excavated the last part of the sword, the hand-guard. There were swirling patterns of silver inlaid along the edges of a broad iron guard, a thick bar across the top of the blade.

The tang of the blade passed through the hole in the guard and, at the other end of the hand-grip, was clenched tightly into the pommel, a smaller bar with faint decoration just visible. The scabbard fittings he'd seen at Bobby's house could have gone with this sword.

'CD's got to see this before I do any more,' said Patrick out loud.

'CD's snoring in his tent,' said Bobby behind him.

Patrick spun round. 'Hello. How embarrassing, to be caught talking to our friend here.'

'It would have been rude not to,' said Bobby.

'Yes.' Should he tell her of the astonishing visit from her brother? He looked at her and saw the purple swelling on her cheek.

'Let me have a look at that,' he said. He took a step towards her, reached out his hand and felt it gently. 'Does it hurt?'

'Only when you press it,' she said, and he pulled his hand away sharply. 'Joke,' she added. 'Anyway, I came to say it was my turn to apologise. It was just a bad day yesterday, that's all.'

'There's no need. It was very brave of you to go for our intruder.'

'Well, I'd better go and get the food on.'

'Bobby. Wait a minute.' He'd reached a decision. 'Joe was here this morning. He scared the hell out of me until I realised it was him. The thing is, he didn't know I was inside here and I heard him. He spoke. He was kneeling outside and talking to her completely normally. He was apologising for the fact that we're disturbing her.'

'Did he speak for long?' she said incredulously.

'Well, yes. He said some very beautiful things. He said her bones were just an easel on which her body had been painted and that the grass and flowers were her real remains. You're crying.'

'I can't help it. I know he does do that. I've sometimes heard him when he thinks I'm asleep. I only *wish* he could talk to me.' She blinked the tears away. 'No, I'm glad. I always knew there was a lot going on in his mind. Did he find out you were here?'

'No. I think he'd be horrified if he knew I'd heard. Bobby, that reminds me. The night they got me singing, why were you crying?'

'Oh, it's complicated.'

'Try me.'

'Well, first my heart was in my mouth because I could see you had started to sing something that was painful for you. Then you stopped and played that other stuff and I suddenly saw the real Patrick. You just lost yourself in the music and it was beautiful.'

'And that made you cry?'

'Almost. Not quite. No, it was something you sang. It just happened to be a very painful song for me.'

'Do you want to tell me?'

'No, some other time. I've got breakfast to do. Play for us again before this is all over, won't you?'

'Only if you tell me what songs I mustn't sing.'

'No, we can't lead our lives that way. We just have to learn to hear them differently.'

A CONVOY OF CARS brought Hescroft, Camden, Jack and an unfamiliar iron-haired woman just as the diggers were ready to start work.

'This is Celia Longworth,' said Hescroft. 'She's our bone person. Got a few things to chat about in a minute or two.'

Patrick brought them up-to-date about the sword. 'It's a very fine weapon, according to CD. He says there's one almost identical to it in the Ashmolean and two in the British Museum.'

They collected the American and went up the hill to look at it, and when she saw it Celia Longworth gave a cry of excitement.

'Yes!' she said. 'My goodness me, you're quite right. It is very, very like the earlier of the Abingdon swords. The blade's in even better condition. What superb metal they must have used.'

Hescroft had other things on his mind.

'Patrick,' he said, 'Kenny here has some good news. He's picked up serious coproduction money from US Cable and Northern TV. We've got the green light to go from development into production and, what's more, we've got a budget that buys a few tricks.'

'What it means, Pat,' said Kenny Camden, 'is that we can do something pretty serious about your bones. You tell him, Celia.'

She looked at him with a knowing expression that said she was a professional and that she shared his clear distaste at the bullshit. 'Well, Patrick, of course you'll be familiar with facial reconstruction, building up muscle layers over the skull and working out the main dimensions through computer scanning programs.'

'Yes, I've seen them.'

'We've just gone one stage further in my unit. We've started analysing muscle attachment markings and joint articulation in the skeleton itself and we're finding we can get very realistic animation.'

CD whistled. 'You can make her walk around realistically?'

'What does that mean you have to do to our skeleton?' asked Patrick nervously.

'We just put all the bones through a three-D scanner. May I see the skeleton? I'll need to assess whether it's practical.'

They moved the tent for her. It felt oddly disturbing to see someone who wasn't directly involved going down into the trench.

'Bone preservation's very good,' Celia Longworth said after a long inspection. 'Everything's here except some toe bones on one foot. The foetus is amazingly intact apart from the skull. I'd say this is the ideal candidate. When can we lift it?'

'This morning, I suppose,' Patrick said. He hated the idea of putting her bit by bit into a box. 'Everything's exposed now except the lower part of the skull. That shouldn't take long. One thing, though,' he added. 'We all feel we would like to bury her and the child properly afterwards, up here, where she belongs.'

'Yes, that's right,' said CD, who hadn't heard a word of this before. 'We all feel very strongly that would be the right thing to do.'

'Sounds pretty good to me,' said Kenny Camden. 'A touching ending, I'd say.'

Later that morning, Patrick lifted the bones, carefully and with a heavy heart, one by one into the padded boxes they had labelled and prepared. Lifting the baby's crushed skull, a piece at a time with tweezers, was the worst of it and no one who was watching made a sound while he did it. When he finally wriggled his fingers delicately underneath the mother's skull to lift it, he felt the gap in the bone that explained why they had laid her with her head on one side: so that the terrible injury that had killed her would be hidden.

'SHE DIED FROM A VIOLENT downward blow to the left side of her head,' said Patrick that night round the campfire.

Joe was sitting in earshot but a little outside the circle.

'Would it have been . . . quick?' asked Gaye.

'I would have thought so,' said Patrick, because he'd asked himself the same question as he'd held the skull.

'What's Celia Longworth done with the skeletons?' Gaye asked. 'It really doesn't feel at all right, not having them here.'

There was a general murmur of agreement.

'I asked her from all of us if she would take special care,' Patrick said. 'She's laid them out, side by side on the examination table.'

'So what happens now?' said Dozer. 'Clean up and fill in?'

'No, it's a bit more than that. Camden wants to keep us all here for two or three days more while the labs do their work. So he can have us responding to it all on camera, I suppose. There's the message sword and the real sword to be cleaned and all the other small finds. Then there's this reconstruction and DNA testing they're going to do on the skeleton.'

There was something else Patrick couldn't bring himself to tell them about, revealed to him that afternoon.

'I'VE GOT A BIT of a dilemma you can help me out with, Pat,' Camden had said in a quiet corner of the Oxford lab. 'Let's get a cuppa and talk it through.'

Patrick smelt another attempt at a set-up.

They got plastic cups of not-quite tea from a machine in the hallway and Patrick sat down by the window. Outside, the traffic was stationary on the Cowley Road. His flat was less than a mile away and the thought that he would soon be spending his nights in it alone filled him with despair. He knew all at once that he'd become very fond of his bunch of diggers.

Camden perched on the windowsill. 'You know the way it is with networks,' he said as if Patrick was an old colleague. 'We've got the Yanks and the Aussies in it now and they both want human interest, you understand?'

'You still want to do the rock star angle, right?' said Patrick wearily.

'No, no,' said Camden with an expression that said he was astonished that Patrick could ever have thought such a thing. 'It would have been great, sure, but I've had to respect your wishes. No, I've been looking around for a different human interest line and I think

I've found something that's nearly as good. Well, three things really.'

'Oh? What are they?'

'OK. First there's the vicar and all this business of giving the bodies a Christian burial. You wouldn't have any objections to making that part of the film, would you? We'd have to film a bit of a ding-dong between the two of you.'

To Patrick it seemed a relatively small price to pay for his continued anonymity.

'No, I don't think I'd mind that.'

'So far so good. Then that leads on to this business about the vicar and the headmaster and the chick who's cooking for you.'

'The May Day parade? How could that fit in?'

'Oh, you know, village traditions. We'll find a way. While you're waking up the past on top of the hill, the headmaster's trying to put it to bed down in the village, something like that.'

'That would be up to Bobby. I don't know she'd want to do it.'

'Well, it's not her decision; it's a story; it's out there; it's public property. They're in court the day after tomorrow, aren't they? But leave that for now. It's her brother I really want.'

Her brother? Oh no. 'Why's that?'

'Now that's a *really* powerful story line. Anonymous archaeologist, down on his luck, listens to a song sung in a pub by the local weirdo and lo and behold, it all turns out to be true. You dig up the woman, you dig up the sword. Bingo, I've got a story the Yanks will love. The German Queen comes out of the grave. It's brilliant. It'll be great TV. Thing is, I need you to persuade the bloke to sing it again. We could use it as a soundtrack.'

Bobby will flip her lid, Patrick thought. She'll think I put them up to this to get myself out of the trap the TV man had sprung. 'There's something else you could do instead,' he suggested in desperation. 'This local builder, Little—the guy who wrecked the first site—why not bring him into it? Bobby caught someone trying to nick stuff from the trench last night. She's sure it was Little.'

'Oh please. You must know a bit about the laws of libel. You got any proof at all that it was him who did the damage? A local issue, that's not going to play too well in Peoria.'

'Where?'

'Just an expression. Cleveland, Wollongong, wherever. What do they care about a builder and a few square yards of flooring? A mute farmer with a direct line to history, now that's something else.'

That was when Celia Longworth came looking for them.

'You wanted my first impressions,' she said. 'She was in the prime of life. Maybe twenty-five. Quite tall, about five foot nine, and in good health. No sign of infections, breaks or disease on the bones.'

'And the wound?' asked Patrick.

'It looks like a single blow but I'll have a better idea when we've done a full examination. I'll let you know.'

After that, Patrick went to his flat to get another pair of jeans. There was only one letter on the mat, a royalty cheque, revealing the unwelcome news that two of Nam Erewhon's albums had taken on a new lease of life in the Far East. He left it on the kitchen table. He'd decide later what charity to send it to.

'IF ANYBODY'S DYING TO LEAVE, they can,' said Patrick that evening around the campfire, 'but Hescroft's agreed that we should widen the trench to check for anything we've missed.'

'And what might be the point of this DNA testing stuff?' said Aidan.

'It doesn't really help the archaeology,' said Patrick, 'but apparently it's the sort of stuff that makes good TV. The idea is you might find descendants.'

'So are they going to test us?' said Dozer.

'Not much point testing you,' said CD. 'You've clearly got no human ancestry whatsoever.'

'So there could be people still living in Wytchlow who are the great-great-great-times-a-hundred-grandsons of our Queen?' said Maxwell.

Peter cleared his throat and a reverent hush fell. 'It does have to be mitochrondial DNA,' he said. 'That means it comes down the mother's line. So there could be a man living in the village related to our Queen, but the ancestry would have to be through his mother and his mother's mother and so on.'

Maxwell turned to Peter. 'And it survives that long?'

'Oh, they've got DNA from Neanderthal man dating back over fifty thousand years.'

'Cool,' said Maxwell, 'but our Queen's baby died with her, surely? So how could she have any female descendants?'

'She might have had other kids before,' said Aidan.

'She *did* have others,' Gaye said indignantly. 'We know that, don't we? From Joe's song. You know, the one we all did by the grave.'

They turned to look at Joe, sitting outside the circle, and he, in that same half-chanting, half-singing style, repeated the opening lines:

'The boda came to Abbandun at evening bell, Brought by the child with sunset head.'

'It doesn't say it was her child,' said Aidan.

Joe nodded downwards, just once, and nobody felt like arguing.

'And what do you suppose those words mean, that sunset head thing?' said Aidan, to show willing.

'I'd like to think it means the child had hair like a sunset,' said Gaye. 'Wild hair, sticking out like rays of light, probably golden. That sounds more like a girl than a boy, so you see Peter's mito-whatever it was could easily have come down from her, couldn't it?'

'That's reading quite a lot into a single word,' said Peter.

'Well, I think I'm right,' said Gaye defiantly.

'That's my girl,' said Dozer. 'You tell 'em.'

'I'm not your girl and I never will be.'

'I'm proud of old Gaye here,' said Dozer. 'Do you know why?'

'Stop it,' she said. 'You promised you wouldn't tell anybody.'

'Dropped her hairbrush down the carzey this morning. Reached in and got it out. I found her giving it a wash.'

There was a round of applause and Gaye gave a shrug and a little smile. 'It's the only one I had,' she said.

'Sorts out the women from the girls, this kind of thing,' said Dozer. 'Here, speaking of women, where's Bobby? A campfire ain't a campfire without our Bobby.'

'She's down at the house. She said she'd be up soon,' said Gaye. 'I asked her to pick up some wine. It's on me tonight.'

There was a cheer which disturbed Edgar down in CD's tent. He cawed indignantly.

'You got your keys back from that tree yet?' Dozer asked CD.

'I'm borrowing a ladder tomorrow.'

'Look for my ring while you're up there,' said Gaye. 'He flew off with it this morning.'

'Raven burgers,' said CD. 'Imagine how tasty they would be.'

Bobby's old Land Rover groaned out of the twilight and she came over to Patrick. 'Special request,' she said. 'If I find you a guitar, will you play for us again?'

He found to his astonishment that something had changed. He could think of playing without any of the old associations being stirred in his mind. 'Only if it's not Maxwell's,' he said. 'My fingers are still recovering.'

'Wait a moment,' she said.

She walked back to the Land Rover and produced a padded guitar case. The instrument that came out of it shone deep golden brown and she passed it to Patrick. It was a classical jazz guitar, oozing handmade quality, and when he rippled his thumb across the strings, the sound they produced was exceptional.

'This is something else,' he said. Then he noticed the way Bobby was looking at him, and he knew that this was an emotional moment for her, a bridge of some sort she had decided to cross.

'Who made it?' he asked, trying to see if there was a label inside.

'Don't ask questions. Just go on. Play.'

So Patrick got them all singing, his own voice leading them like the Pied Piper, with Joe joining in with a deep bass. It was an evening spun from magic. When, at last, the wine was gone and the fire was dying down, Patrick walked back to the Land Rover with Bobby, and put the guitar back carefully inside.

'Thank you,' he said as she got in. 'It's got a story to it, hasn't it?'

She nodded.

'Would you tell me?'

'Why do you want to know?'

'Because I think you might want me to. Isn't that why you let me play it?'

'Perhaps,' she said. 'I don't know what I can say about it.'

'It's up to you.'

'I'm not sure I shut up the chicken house,' she said, looking away from him, down to the farm. 'I've got to go back and check.'

He thought that was the end of it but she turned back. 'Give me ten minutes. I'll meet you. Where the track takes you down to the yard, follow it on and there's a slope up into an old orchard above the vegetable garden. There's a sort of shelter with a bench in it.'

'HE CAME FROM QUEBEC, like the guitar,' she said without a word of preamble, when he found her sitting on the bench in the dark and sat down close to her. 'He was called Gilles and he worked with me and he died.' She was looking straight in front of her. A light in a window of the farmhouse showed him her profile.

'It was his guitar?'

'Yes, it was his guitar.'

'Why did you let me play it tonight?'

'Because you can play it nearly as well as he could but, more importantly, because this is all about attitudes to life.' She hesitated, then went on more forcefully. 'When something goes really wrong you have the choice, don't you? Leaving out suicide, you can either curl up inside your shell or you can go out and get on with it. What do you see when you look at me? I mean when you look at me—Bobby—not at some awful old memory.'

'I see someone who gets on with it, someone who all my diggers would happily go to jail for if the vicar got in her way.'

'When I look at you it seems to me that you're somewhere between the two, the curling up and the getting on with it. With a bit of a heave from your friends, you're just starting to come out of your shell, and I think it's time you started thinking about other people more.'

He was shocked. 'What do you mean?'

'I mean that nobody lives on this earth in a vacuum. You can be as miserable as you like by yourself but when you do it in company you take other people down with you. I don't think anyone has the right to be such a misery as you are. You've had the whole lot of them, CD, Dozer, everybody, tiptoeing round you for most of this dig, not sure whether you're going to fly off the handle or burst into tears on them.'

'God Almighty. I'm not that bad, am I?'

'And some. Well, you *were*, anyway. I have to admit there are slight signs of improvement.'

'Look, if I am that bad, I'm sorry, but I'm not sure I can always help it. You know why. I told you.'

'Your wife and son died. You said something you shouldn't have and *she* drove off the road. She did that, not you. It was a tragedy, but it's time to get it in proportion. You can't trail it around behind you for the rest of your life.'

'How did Gilles die?'

'We were working together. In the southern Sudan. There was a French-Canadian medical charity. Gilles was one of the doctors.'

'What were you doing, nursing?'

'Oh, sod off, Patrick.'

'What have I said now?'

'I was a doctor too.'

'I see.'

'That's why some of them round here think I'm a bit full of myself for a farmer's daughter. Anyway, we were cut off for a long time in a village, Gilles and me. There was a civil war going on all around us. We had a radio but a soldier put a pickaxe through it and we were running out of everything, and then Gilles got sick.'

She fell silent and Patrick prompted her gently. 'And you couldn't help him?'

'If I had a hospital lab, I could have done. If I could have found out what it was. All I had to go on was what I could see and I just couldn't tell for sure. He'd been on a trip out with one of the village men. When he came back he was confused and drowsy. The guy he was with thought maybe he'd fallen over. He had this bruise and swelling. I thought it was a subdural haematoma. Bleeding under the skull. But his pupils were different sizes and he had a fever. He shouldn't have had a fever. So maybe it was cerebral malaria, one of the few things I still had drugs for.'

'Did they work? The drugs?'

'No.' She sounded so sad, frightened. 'He just went on getting worse. I was going to fly him out on a supply plane. It didn't come on the day it was meant to. I waited all the next day. I was beside myself. All I could do was try to get liquids into him. In the early evening one of the village boys came running in and told me they could hear the plane. I went outside and we could see it, maybe half a mile off over some scrubland. Then I saw sparks flying up towards it like a firework and it veered away. Two or three seconds later I heard a burst of machine-gun fire from the scrub.'

'The plane was shot down?'

'No, it was just damaged, but it turned away.' She was speaking slowly. 'So then I knew I hadn't got any alternative. I thought it must be the haematoma after all, and there's only one thing to do with a haematoma. You have to drill a hole in the skull, to relieve the pressure of the bleeding. I drilled a hole in my lovely man's skull.' She sighed. 'There was no haematoma. Then before the plane finally came back five days later, he got meningitis because of what I did and . . . and he died.'

'Oh, Bobby.' His overpowering instinct was to put his arm round her, but she was far away with her dead lover and he could not. 'There wasn't anything else you could do, though, was there?'

'Do you think that helps?' she said grimly. 'Do you think when you love someone with all your heart and you're making plans to go back to Quebec together it helps to know that?'

'No. I'm so sorry.'

Her tone changed, became brisker. 'I didn't tell you so that you'd be sorry. The point of my little story is that life goes on. I got out a week later. I was back in Khartoum, then there was a call from Jean

Anderson down in the village telling me Mum was in hospital. So I came back and I was just in time to see her and then I realised I had to stay for Joe, so now that's what we do. We farm, day in, day out. When I heard about the dig, I thought: great, I'll have some fun. I didn't realise the dig director was going to come fitted with his own personal thundercloud. All the people who came on this dig, they all deserve something better, not just me.'

'Oh shit.' The weight of it hit him. 'I'd been living in my head for too long. This is the first time I've been out in public for ages. I'm doing better than I was, surely?'

'Most of the time. What was bugging you tonight when I arrived? I could see it in your face.'

'I had a difficult time with Camden. He wants me in his programme. Me, as Paddy Kane, punk rocker. Just to boost the ratings.'

'And you've told him to take a running jump.'

'It's not that simple. He says he needs a human-interest angle and if it's not me, he's threatening to use Joe.'

She sat up straight. 'Joe? How could he use Joe?'

'He's heard about the song and how we found the grave.'

'You told Camden that?'

'No, of course not. I didn't tell him. He says someone in the village told him.'

'If you've put him onto Joe to get him off your back I'll never forgive you, Patrick. Don't you dare off-load this onto Joe, OK? I hold you responsible. Good night.'

She got up and walked quickly to the house in the bitter darkness.

Soon after first light, CD was forty feet up an oak tree, roping himself carefully to the trunk, when he looked through a gap in the branches and saw Patrick in the far distance walking purposefully down towards the farm. The American had risen at the crack of dawn to get his tree-climbing out of the way before anyone else was up and about to laugh at him. He wondered briefly what Patrick was up to, but the tree and the problem of the final six feet to where Edgar had dropped his keys drove other thoughts away. He stretched out for the next handhold, hung precariously by his hands for a moment, and swung a foot onto a safe branch. Three feet left. Before he had fallen out of the tree the last time, he had made a note of the crook of a branch where Edgar had taken his finds. Now he could see that in that crook was an old bird's nest.

He climbed up a little further and lunged upwards with his fingers outstretched. The nest tumbled out of the crook of the branch and he watched it fall, shining objects spilling from it, into the thick leaf mould far below.

When he finally got down to ground level again, he saw his ignition keys lying on the ground and Patrick's pen near them. A bit of searching turned up Gaye's missing ring and he was about to go, pleased with his success, when he just caught the glint of something metallic, almost completely buried in the vegetation.

PATRICK THOUGHT ABOUT what Bobby had said for an hour or two before going to sleep, and when he woke up soon after dawn he went straight to the farm and sat quietly in the yard until he saw a light come on downstairs. Then he knocked on the door.

'Coffee's on the table,' called Bobby from inside.

He walked into the kitchen and she was standing at the Aga, with her back to him.

'Bobby?' he said, and she spun round, staring at him.

'I thought you were Joe. What are you doing here?' She turned back to stir a saucepan.

'I'm here to sort out a couple of things. First, you're right about me wallowing in it. You've made me look at myself. I needed it. Second, I want to say you don't need to worry about Joe. I've decided to tell Camden that so long as he stays completely away from Joe, I'll do it the way he wants. He can have his punk rocker. I've just realised there's no reason it should matter any more.'

'Thank you,' she said. 'Now go. I'm doing Joe's porridge. I'll be up at the camp in fifteen minutes.'

WHEN KENNY CAMDEN'S Toyota appeared after breakfast, Jack was at the wheel and there was no sign of Camden.

'Morning,' Patrick said. 'Where's your boss?'

'Please,' said Jack, grimacing. 'I'm a hungry freelance trying to keep my standards up. I prefer to think of him as my pay cheque. Look, I'm out of line here, but watch him. He's not a nice man.'

'Thanks. I'd sort of guessed. Where is he?'

'Down on the village green. They're setting up the DNA testing.'

Patrick walked off, leaving CD to deal with the trench.

There was a white tent on the green and Camden was standing outside it, talking to the villagers.

'We'll be ready to start at about one o'clock,' Patrick heard him saying. 'Get all your friends to come too. We'll stay open until about seven.' He turned round. 'Morning, Pat. What can I do for you?'

Patrick took him aside. 'I've changed my mind,' he said. 'You can bring me into your programme any way you like.'

'Ha,' said Camden, 'There's still a performer in there, eh? Well, thanks for that, Pat, but no need really. Truth is, I've gone off the idea. Let's face it. Four years is a long time. People have short memories. Sure, I was keen on it to start with but then I thought a bit and, well, it's old hat, isn't it? I think this farmer guy is a really good story.'

'Joe won't do it.'

'It's not for him to choose. We've already got shots of him.'

'What shots?' said Patrick with a sinking heart.

'You know the way he hangs around the fringes of the dig. I got Jack to watch out for that. It's great. I've managed to put together a few bits and pieces of the song from people who were there, too.'

'I think you're making a mistake.'

'Maybe,' said Camden cheerfully. 'See you back on the hill.'

Patrick couldn't bring himself to tell Bobby what had happened. He spent the rest of the day avoiding her, sitting in his car, writing up the paperwork while the diggers found nothing but two possible Bronze Age potsherds in the barrow ring-ditch.

As suppertime approached, it dawned on him that there was no sign of anything happening in the food tent. He went over and found the diggers inspecting three heaped trays of sandwiches.

'Bobby said she hoped we wouldn't mind,' CD explained. 'She's got some meeting about her protest thing. I said it would be OK.'

'You coming down to the pub?' said Dozer, turning to Patrick. 'Joe's doing another special apparently. Anyway, we're all going to get our DNA done just for a lark. CD's having his changed for something better, like a cockroach.'

'Hey, respect where respect is due, man. Remember, you're looking at a highly successful primate with amazing tree-climbing abilities.'

'You've got your keys back from wherever Edgar took them?' Patrick asked.

'Yup, plus your pen.' He reached into his pocket, 'Gaye's ring and one more thing I am very embarrassed to show you.'

'What?'

CD took out something that glittered dull silver.

'An Anglo-Saxon silver coin, namely one sceatta, almost certainly late seventh century.'

'Which would probably have been extremely useful dating evidence,' said Patrick, 'if we had the remotest idea where on the site it had come from, instead of finding it in a bloody jackdaw's hideaway.'

'He's confined to my tent until we're off the site,' said CD.

THERE WAS A LONG LINE of late arrivals at the DNA tent but the tests were quick. Each person was handed a tiny brush on a stick. It was a simple process. All they had to do was scrub the inside of their cheek, then the brush was put in a sterile bag and labelled.

The pub was packed and the first thing Patrick saw was a large group of women clustered around Bobby. She saw him come in and beckoned to him. He couldn't get right up to her, but she craned her head towards him and said, 'What's going on? They're saying you asked Joe to sing tonight.'

'No, I didn't. I haven't seen him.'

'I heard you sent him a note.' She was frowning.

One of the others turned to her and said, 'Bobby, we all think it should be you who speaks in court,' and she shrugged at Patrick and went back into the conversation.

Joe came into the bar, dressed in his hat and his red waistcoat, and a little cheer ran through the crowd. He sang a song about May Day that was savagely witty at the expense of the head teacher and the vicar. There was a service hatch to the kitchen set in the wall opposite Joe's microphone and Patrick noticed one of the flaps was half open. As the song came to an end, the tip of a camera lens came into view. He knew then that Jack was filming and that the note to Joe must have come from Camden in Patrick's name.

Joe started the introduction to another song and Patrick realised it was the song of the German Queen. He did not want the camera to have it. He started to get to his feet but Joe stopped playing abruptly and marched across to the hatch himself. He reached in, trying to grab the camera. Everybody in the bar started talking at once and there were muffled noises from the other side of the hatch. Joe slammed the hatch shut, turned round and strode out of the pub door.

Patrick saw Bobby rise; the look she gave him was one of pure hatred. He ducked out of the door into darkness. He would pursue Joe. But just outside the porch a hand shot out and grabbed Patrick's wrist, and Joe, who had been standing waiting for him, set off round the corner to the car park, towing him along.

'I didn't send that note,' Patrick said, and Joe turned his head, gave an unexpected grin and put a finger to his lips to silence him. Then he led Patrick round to the far side of Camden's big four-wheel drive, parked next to the pub dustbins. He knelt down, fiddled with the valve cap and Patrick heard the hiss of escaping air. Joe obviously knew who the real culprit was. He then went round to the windscreen and wrote, in mirror writing on the dirt, *CHECK YOUR TYRES*. Then he slapped Patrick on the back, indicated both of them in turn and mimed walking with his fingers.

'You want us to go for a walk?' Patrick asked.

The other man nodded and set off into the darkness.

It was soon obvious it was to be no mere stroll. Joe's long stride took them rapidly through the churchyard, over a stile and down the side of the field beyond. They took an old overgrown pathway down through the wood to the lower ground by the river and climbed another stile onto a signposted path. They walked fast for an hour and a half without ever taking to a road.

Joe climbed a wall and on the far side stretched his hand out to stop Patrick from blundering into a barbed-wire fence, hidden by darkness and foliage. The wood ahead looked impenetrably gloomy and Patrick said, a little nervously, 'Where are we going?' but Joe had already gone on into the wood on a narrow twisting track.

After many minutes they came to a bank and climbed down it to a wider track, surfaced with gravel and rough stones. The track curved and ran downhill for a hundred yards, and then in the darkness, rising above them, Patrick made out dim cliffs of rock and guessed they had arrived at a quarry.

Joe took him to the far end of it, picking his way between piles of old tyres and mounds of rubble, then crouched down, took a little torch out of his pocket and shone it on the ground, waving to Patrick to come and look. What they were looking at was the edge of a huge pile of earth. Small fragments of colour glinted in the torch-light, Roman tesserae, tumbled into the heap of soil that had been dragged there from Little's field. All they amounted to now was use-less builder's rubble.

'My God, what a waste,' Patrick said, turning to Joe. 'Have you been out searching for this every night?'

He got a single emphatic nod.

'Well done, Joe. We need to come and check through this lot. It won't do much good, though. We'll never prove it was him, will we?'

Joe nodded two or three times.

'We will? How? You've got proof?'

Joe shone the torch on himself and passed it to Patrick like that, then, smiling, he held out his hands as in a game of charades, making the symbols for book, film and play in quick succession.

Patrick laughed. 'You're going to act it?'

There was a quick nod.

'Two words. First word?'

Joe brought his two hands close together.

'Small? Something like small?' Joe was encouraging him. 'Oh, got it. Little? Yes. Second word?'

Joe stuck his arms out, tilting and making a droning noise.

'Aeroplane?'

Joe egged him on, then mimed, with a flat hand, something curving down to a horizontal halt.

'Aeroplane landing? Yes? Yes. Landing. Shorter than landing. Land? OK, land. That's it? Little land. What? Little's land? He owns this place? You're kidding.'

Joe mimed somebody taking aim with a gun and firing.

'He keeps it for shooting? And you knew that so you came and searched? Oh, bloody well done, mate. We'll get him now.'

It was one o'clock in the morning before they were back in the village and Patrick, completely exhausted, waved good night to Joe.

CD woke him in the morning. 'Hate to wake you but we've got a tiny little rebellion on our hands.'

'I found where Little dumped the stuff. Joe showed me.'

'Good, good. There's something more important than that going on. Or, rather, not going on.'

'Like what?'

'Like breakfast.'

A NOTE WAS PINNED to the flap of the marquee. It said: *Milk and bread inside. Make your own breakfast. I've had to go. Pub will do lunch if you tell them you're coming. Maybe supper. B.*

'This is all about me,' said Patrick, reading it ruefully.

'Yeah, I know. She was pretty angry last night after you guys went out. She had a go at Camden too,' said CD. 'It was not nice to hear.'

'I'll go down and see her.'

'I wouldn't go in without back-up, the way she sounded,' said CD. 'Take Dozer. Well, no. Normally that would be a good plan but he's otherwise occupied.' CD turned and stared at Dozer's tent.

'How?'

As if in answer, the zip opened and a face looked out, but it wasn't Dozer. Seeing them staring, it vanished again.

'Gaye? Was that Gaye?' said Patrick. 'No, it couldn't have been.'

'Believe it, baby. It's that end of the dig, last days of Rome atmosphere. They decided last night they were made for each other. In different factories maybe, but there you go.'

'I've got to go down and sort this out with Bobby. She thinks I tricked Joe into being filmed.'

But at the farmhouse there was just another note on the door. It said: *Louisa. I've gone to the Citizens' Advice Bureau. The hearing's at ten thirty at Oxford court. See you there. B.*

Patrick's mobile rang as he read it.

'Patrick. It's John Hescroft. Look, Kenny Camden asked me to give you a call. Can we meet at the conservation lab in twenty minutes? They've got some of your stuff from the trench cleaned up ready for the cameras and Jack's going to shoot some pictures. I thought it was a good chance for us to fly the PSC corporate flag a bit.'

Patrick almost laughed. He'd known Hescroft would pop up when the hard work was done and try to get his face on the programme. 'OK,' he said. 'I need to talk to Camden anyway, but listen, John. There's something else. Last night we found the soil that was stripped from the Roman site dumped on a bit of private land belonging to Roger Little. Can you tell the council?'

'Oh, that's a dead duck, surely?'

'No, it isn't. Will you tell them or will I?'

'It's very embarrassing, Patrick. I see him at the golf club.'

'You've got a conflict of interests?'

'Oh, no. No, no. Nothing like that. Talk about it later, old boy. I'll see you at the laboratory.'

Kenny Camden and Jack were waiting with the camera gear in the foyer of the lab. Patrick walked right up close to Camden.

'I'd like to know what you think you were doing last night?'

'Well, I had an excellent meal at the Luna Caprese, then—'

'In the pub.'

'We were filming, Pat. Perfectly within our rights. We had the landlady's permission.'

'You didn't have Joe's permission.'

'Didn't need it. He was performing on her premises under her licence. That puts her in charge.'

Patrick had no idea whether he was right or not. 'Well, I'm not having this. It's dishonest. You sent Joe the note, didn't you? You pretended it was me asking him to sing?'

'I might ask *you* who let down my tyre?'

At that moment, John Hescroft came in, spraying a foam of oblivious false bonhomie on the flames.

'Morning, old boy. Hello, Jack.' He looked at each of them in turn, frowning. 'Is there a problem?' he asked.

'Forget it,' said Patrick. 'What happened with the council?'

'I left a message. We'll have to see. If you've really got proof they might go for a prosecution.'

'Will it affect the planning permission?'

'Separate issue, I would have thought. Not really my bailiwick, nor yours, come to think of it. Perhaps we'd better stick to the job in hand. Paul McGovern should be expecting us. Let's give him a shout.'

McGovern, a ponderous man, came out to meet them and led them into a side room where various familiar objects were laid out on a table, dominated by the sword.

'We've finished all the cleaning,' he said.

Patrick leaned over the sword, studying it intently.

'This is very fine,' said Hescroft, joining him, 'very fine indeed.'

Patrick ran through a mental check list. The coins were there and the shield boss . . . The heavy disc of Roman work was missing.

'There's something else,' he said.

'I was saving that for last,' McGovern said. 'I think you'll like this. It's cleaned up very nicely.'

He lifted a plastic cover and an astonishing sight was revealed. What Patrick had only seen as an encrusted lump was now a disc of bronze, with an intricately cast man's face at its centre, perforated with holes at intervals all across it. Patrick knew this face already—the face of a man with a beard made up of leaves and fruit, and with two birds flying out of his mouth, a face later carved in wood and central to a tradition kept alive down the years to the present day. A tradition that was about to be put through the processes of modern law.

'Um, I need to borrow this for an hour or two.'

'What for?' demanded Camden, as Patrick picked it up. 'Where are you going? We need you. We need to get pictures of that.'

'I'll be back. Phone me on the mobile when you finish here. I'll join you.' Then he was gone.

'What was that about?' said Camden. 'Can anyone tell me why—' He snapped his fingers. 'Bloody hell, I know what it is. It's Joe's sister. It's about her court case this morning, I bet. Come on, Jack. We'll shoot this later. First things first.'

By that time, Patrick was already starting his engine. He drove into Oxford as fast as the traffic would allow. It took far too long to find a parking space and further agonising minutes to find out where Bobby's hearing was taking place. When he finally walked into the courtroom, it was already well under way.

A barrister in wig and gown was addressing the judge. His every syllable sounded expensive. '. . . in accordance with that. It is therefore the contention of the governors of the school in seeking this injunction that the parade is not in fact an old tradition at all and that there is no record which can be produced in evidence of any such tradition going back before the Second World War.'

Patrick couldn't spot Bobby to start with, then he realised she was the woman in unfamiliar smart clothes and a hat like a turban, who was sitting at the front of the court. He started scribbling her a note. But it was too late to get it to her. She was already standing up.

'In the village, we know it's been going for years and years,' she said, 'since time immemorial.' It sounded vague and he knew instantly that it wouldn't wash. What could he do?

In a corner, at the back of the chamber, was a large whiteboard and felt-tip pen. He went to it and wrote in big block letters, *BOBBY, CALL ME AS A WITNESS*. Bobby didn't turn round. The judge was now looking at him over his glasses.

'Miss Redhead,' said the judge, 'a young man at the back of the court appears to be attempting to attract your attention.'

Bobby twisted round and finally took in Patrick and his message.

'Do you know what this is about?' the judge asked her.

'No, Your Honour, I don't,' said Bobby. 'The, er . . . the young man is an archaeologist.'

Patrick saw the vicar, the head teacher and Roger Little, complete with a bruise just under his eye, frowning.

'He is perhaps an expert on local history?' suggested the judge.

'Perhaps,' said Bobby vaguely. 'I don't, well, I'm not sure . . .'

'May I suggest you call him as an expert witness? You do seem a little, well, undersupported,' said the judge kindly, so she did.

Patrick went to sit in the witness box and she stared at him, unable to tell what he could be doing there.

'You are Patrick Kane,' she said, 'an archaeologist who has been digging on an Anglo-Saxon burial site in the village of Wytchlow?'

'Yes, I am.'

'And . . .' There was a long silence, and he tried to get her to notice the bronze disc he was holding but her eyes were fixed above it, staring at his face. 'And,' she said decisively, 'what question would you like me to ask you?'

'I'd like you to ask me about the disc-shaped Roman artefact that we discovered buried in the Anglo-Saxon grave.'

'Mr Kane,' she said, 'would you tell us about the, er . . . the disc-shaped Roman thing?'

He held it up and she finally focused on it and her eyes widened.

'Yes,' he said, 'as you have no doubt already told the court, the May Day procession centres on the parade round the village of an old Bath chair carrying a very distinctive wooden mask in the shape of a Green Man face with two birds flying out of the mouth. The issue seems to be whether this has or has not been a long tradition. While we were digging in the Anglo-Saxon grave at Wytchlow, we discovered this Roman object buried with the body. The object was obscured by an encrustation of dirt, but I have just collected it from the laboratories where it has been cleaned. It is possible to date it with a high degree of confidence to the third or fourth century.'

He looked across at the vicar, who had his mouth tightly shut, then turned to the judge. 'It is virtually identical to the wooden mask used in the parade. I would infer, Your Honour, that there must be a very ancient tradition based around this particular facial form.'

IN THE CORRIDOR OUTSIDE, Patrick expected Bobby to be grateful for his Lone Ranger act, riding to her rescue at the last moment, but her anger ran deep.

'I suppose you think that was clever, crashing in like that,' she said. 'And I suppose you think it makes up for your truly disgusting behaviour over Joe. Well, it doesn't.' She walked off towards the WAY OUT sign.

Patrick went to follow her but his phone rang. Two of the Wytchlow mothers who had been in the court stood there looking at him with sheeplike admiration. At least he'd pleased somebody. Hescroft's voice in his ear said, 'Where are you?'

'In town.'

'Look, do pull yourself together. There's a change of plan. Kenny and Jack had to shoot off. Will you nip along to Celia Longworth at the computer place? She was expecting all of us. Can you give her a message? Camden wants her to bring the face reconstruction stuff out to Wytchlow on a laptop this afternoon so we can film all the village people looking at it.'

'Where is it?' Patrick said wearily.

'Thirteen, Mortlake Street,' said Hescroft. 'Get your skates on.' He hung up.

'Do you know where Mortlake Street is?' Patrick asked the two women.

'I think it's off the Iffley Road,' said one. 'Just after a pub.'

ON THE WAY, Patrick hissed at the windscreen all the things that he wished he'd said to Bobby. 'You ask your brother who got him to sing. He'll tell you. Somehow. You go off like a bloody firework all the time. Well, I've had it. Go back to your bloody farming and leave me alone. I'm glad the dig's nearly over. You're so ungrateful. You've got your bloody parade and that's down to me. How could I do it any other way? You think you're so brave about life and I'm so spineless. Well, you don't know me at all. Get out of my bloody way.'

He blew his horn at a cyclist who'd done nothing worse than travel on roughly the same bit of tarmac.

Then he thought instead of the other woman, the German Queen. She was so much easier to understand. He could safely let himself feel things for her that were far too powerful to be turned on anyone alive. She was a brave, straightforward woman, and he let himself love the idea of her. She had commanded love. That was what the tributes they'd piled round her said. And in a few minutes he would see her face. The impact of that hit him. He knew that it was all he needed—the sight of her face—to complete what he knew about her from the song and from the feel of her bones in the soil.

At 13 Mortlake Street, Celia Longworth took him to an upstairs room where three tables were crammed with a mass of monitors, keyboards and cabling. A young man was working at one of them. His hair was streaked blond and he had two silver rings in one ear.

'This is Nick,' said Celia. 'He's my right-hand man. Nick, this is Patrick. He's come to see his Saxon woman.'

'Great,' said the youth, then he did a double take. 'Patrick?'

'Yes, that's right,' Patrick said firmly.

But Nick kept staring at him. 'I know you, don't I?'

'Someone's party, maybe?' said Patrick. 'Do you know Alice?'

'Yeah, Alice. Was it there?'

It seemed to work. Patrick filed that one away for future use.

'This is where we do the clever stuff,' Celia explained. 'Now, do you know how all this works?'

'Vaguely.'

'The skull gives the face about ninety-five per cent of its shape, of course, but it's the other five per cent that matters, and that comes from the soft tissue, the muscle and the flesh. That's what's tough to get just right. Get the soft tissue wrong and you wouldn't recognise your own mother. Can you put up the skull, Nick?'

On a huge monitor, the familiar scanned-in skull of the woman from Wytchlow came up, slowly revolving, to reveal the great jagged hole across one side.

'There's our starting point. We'll just fix the damage.'

Keys clicked and the skull healed over.

'In the old days, the big problems were the mouth, the nose and the ears. No one could be sure of any of that. Now we've learned how to work most of it out from looking really closely at how the muscles attach. The marks on the skull tell us which way they pulled and how strongly.'

She was an enthusiast lost in the wonders of her world. All Patrick wanted to see was the outcome.

'If the teeth are still there, the outer edge of the canines gives you the width of the mouth and that also tells you exactly how the eyes were set because it's the same as the width between the inner edges of the iris. The general shape of the nose is quite easy. Do you want me to explain that?'

'No, I've got the general idea.'

'OK. Nick, give me the average face.'

On the screen a flattened mask appeared and wrapped itself over the skull. It looked like a shop-window dummy.

'Right, that's using average soft-tissue depths superimposed on the skull. Now the clever bit with this software is that we've built in different average values for various ethnic groups and that makes it much more accurate. So now we'll try with Saxon averages.'

'How do you get Saxon averages?'

'By going to Saxony,' she said, as if it ought to be obvious.

The face that formed on the screen, after Nick had added some brown hair, was blandly beautiful, but it didn't look at all like someone who would have picked up her father's sword.

'She doesn't look the hero type,' Patrick said, and Celia laughed. 'Of course she might have been the result of intermarriage,' he went on. 'Her mother could easily have been a Briton. We have no real idea.'

'I could do you a bit of Celt,' said Nick, and got busy on the keyboard, calling up menus onto his screen. 'I'll try sixty-forty Celt and Saxon, yes? What about a bit of heroic red hair for the full Celtic experience?'

'OK.'

It took a little while to process, the screen flickering as a new face emerged. This one took Patrick's breath away. The song had come to life before his eyes.

'Oh yes,' he said. 'Oh yes, that's her. That's definitely her.'

He felt absurdly happy, absurdly hopeful. This was the woman so valiant that she had been given the privilege of a warrior's burial. They had retrieved her from oblivion.

'How about that?' said Nick. 'Isn't she just something?'

'That's sixty-forty, is it, Nick?' said Celia. 'Try it forty-sixty.'

'No,' said Patrick vehemently. He couldn't bear to lose her.

'OK,' said Celia. 'Now, do you want to see her walk?'

The wonderful woman on the screen moved down a stylised country lane and began to walk towards them with a swinging, athletic stride. Was that a suggested bulge of pregnancy? It was extremely lifelike and Patrick gazed at her, lost in love. Nick pressed another button and she began to run with her hair flowing out behind her.

'Did you see how she threw her weight forward when she ran?' said Nick proudly. 'It's all from the joint and muscle marking analysis.'

'Now the really clever bit,' Celia added, 'is that we've managed to analyse the force and the direction of the blow that caused the damage to the skull. It was probably a single-edged weapon struck downwards and from behind, something like this.'

Then, before Patrick could prepare himself for it in any way, the woman appeared again, but this time she was being overtaken by a huge man with a blade raised behind him, a blade that slashed down into the side of her head as she came close. It was intensely realistic.

Patrick cried out as the German Queen collapsed. He found his eyes flooding with tears.

'No,' he said, choked, and lunged for the door.

'Are you all right,' Celia called out, but he ran down the stairs and out onto the pavement, overflowing with illogical grief.

He heard someone shout his name and there, coming down the pavement towards him, was Bobby. She broke into a run and a gust of wind took away her turban, releasing the hair he had never seen before in daylight, a cascade of deep red curls that tumbled around her lively, living face. She was so like the picture he had just seen on the screen that he searched the pavement behind her, heart pounding, looking for the giant swordsman.

She stopped in front of him and looked at him quizzically. 'What's happened to you?'

'Everything.' He hugged her.

'Wow. What's this for?' she gasped.

'For being alive,' he said, and kissed her hard.

She went tense for a moment, then kissed him back. When she broke away, breathing hard, she looked at him wonderingly and said, 'Jack told me it wasn't you.'

'How did you find me?'

'You asked Louisa where thirteen Mortlake Street was. Patrick, I need you. Jack says they're going back to Wytchlow to corner Joe. Jack can't stand Camden. He says Camden gave Joe a note this morning saying that if he didn't do the song, they'd do all the stuff about you instead. He thinks Joe's going to agree to sing.'

'Well, let's go and stop him, shall we?'

In the car, he looked sideways at her.

'I can't believe I haven't seen your hair properly before,' he said. 'Why do you always wear that horrible cap?'

'That's just a farmer thing,' she said dismissively, trying to scoop it all up and put the turban back on. It got out of control and she let it all tumble down again. 'Well, actually, can you imagine what it's like to be called Redhead and have hair like this?'

'Rather wonderful I should say.' He could hardly drag his eyes away.

'Watch the road. Does this thing go any faster? You look nice when you smile.'

'I'll do it more often.' He took her hand.

'Don't you need to change gear or anything?'

'Only sometimes.'

'What on earth happened inside that building? Was it the DNA results? Why did you come rushing out like that?'

'It was the face reconstruction. You'll see it later on. Forget the DNA. It takes ages. I'll tell you something, though.' He looked at her and a warm glow of certainty about the future flooded his body. 'There's not much point in waiting for it. I know the results already.'

He wouldn't tell her any more.

As they tore into Bobby's farmyard they were greeted by an unexpected scene. A grinning Joe, was walking into the house carrying a guitar, but he turned when he heard them approach and waved cheerfully. Kenny Camden, looking like he'd lost his wallet, was scrawling something on a clipboard while Jack, whistling aimlessly, folded his tripod.

'They've done it,' said Bobby. 'We're too late.'

They got out of the car and Jack winked at them.

'What's happened?' demanded Bobby.

'I've just wasted the last hour, that's what's happened,' said Camden. 'I suppose everyone thought it was very funny.'

'Do you want to see it?' said Jack. 'I can run it back through the viewfinder.'

'Yeah, that's right, let them have their laugh,' said Camden, and he climbed inside his car.

Jack ran the videotape back for them. Bobby and Patrick shared the headphones, their cheeks touching.

The camera showed Joe in the yard, washing off his boots with a hosepipe.

'Mr Redhead?' said Camden's voice.

Joe looked up and smiled.

'Could we have a word?' said Camden. 'Actually, I understand it's difficult to have a word because you don't speak at all.'

Joe looked surprised, shrugged, then said perfectly clearly, if a little slowly, 'Well, whoever could have told you that, I wonder?'

Camden, out of shot, seemed to have been struck dumb, and Joe waited, then asked politely, 'Was there anything else?'

Camden said, 'Er . . . there was a song you sang in the pub. The one about the German Queen. Would you sing it for us?'

'Oh well, you see I make them up as I go along. Can't say I remember that one. I have got one song I can do for you.'

'Er . . . all right,' said Camden.

'Wait a minute.'

There was a long pause while Joe disappeared into the house. The camera stayed on and they could hear Camden, off-mike, say, 'I think someone's been pulling my plonker.'

Joe came back with his guitar, tuned up and launched into a basic folk melody.

'There's a man they call Little who lives in this village,
And all that he's good for is plunder and pillage.
When they came to dig up what the Romans had left
He saw a threat to his profits so he turned to theft.

For the past it is yours and the past it is mine
And the man that destroys it is naught but a swine.
He brought lorries and bulldozers late in the night
And he wrecked the old villa as he dug up that site.

He'll make a small fortune as he sells off each house
That won't change the fact that he's simply a louse
For the past it is yours and the past it is mine
And the man that destroys it is naught but a swine.'

'Did you like that?' said Joe to the camera. There was no reply.

Jack stopped the film. 'That's it,' he said. 'Deeply satisfying.'

Patrick followed Bobby into the kitchen where Joe was standing by the Aga, waiting for the kettle to boil.

Bobby hugged him. 'You old bastard. How did you do that? Come on, say something to me.'

But Joe just smiled and put a finger to his lips. Then he took Bobby's hand, led her over to Patrick and wrapped Patrick's hand round hers. He kissed Bobby on the forehead and left the room.

'Ah,' said Bobby, 'that's odd. I seem to have just been . . . well . . . *given* to you, I suppose. Not even gift-wrapped.'

'The wrapping's perfect,' said Patrick, running his fingers through her hair and pulling her gently towards him.

THE NEXT MORNING, Patrick woke in a soft bed with his arms wrapped round Bobby. She was smiling into his eyes with a hint of wonder and he knew his penance was over.

'Hello,' he said. 'It wasn't a dream, then?'

She kissed him. 'Time to get up,' she said. 'It's May Morning.'

They walked out into the freshest day of Patrick's life and took the lane to the meadow by the river. There were families converging on it from every direction, small children running ahead to pick flowers out of the hedges. Bobby took a small bottle from her pocket and together they knelt down to gather dew from the grass.

They joined the children in gathering armfuls of flowers then trooped back from the field to decorate the cart.

It was then that Patrick remembered the priceless bronze object he had left in the car the day before. 'Would your wooden man mind if his ancestor took his place round the village this year?'

'Why don't they both come?'

So they wove the flower stems into the holes in the face of the bronze man and then, with the May Queen crowned, Patrick and Bobby took their place in the procession.

FIVE MONTHS LATER, the diggers gathered on the hilltop to bury the German Queen and her child again, laying the bones out tenderly just as they had found them. After a series of heated debates in Oxford, they had given up hope of reburying most of the grave goods with her, but Bobby insisted when it came to the Green Man mask. 'I know how she felt about it,' she said. The mask was carefully copied and the original face went quietly back into the grave.

Jack arrived by himself, with no camera, and asked if he might join them. They buried the bones with enormous care, sieving the heap of fine soil down over them, then they rolled the turf carefully back into place over the grave and laid flowers down.

The tents blossomed again in their old places and, with the campfire blazing and wine bottles being passed round, it was what they all wanted, a re-creation of past times, except now, as Dozer said, lying with his arm round Gaye, it seemed a whole lot nicer.

They talked for a while about the amazing moment when they had first seen the reconstruction.

'I was sure they were going to find your DNA was the same as hers,' said Gaye to Bobby. 'They must have got it wrong.'

'Not necessarily,' said Peter. 'It could go all the way down the line to Bobby's grandmother, then if it came down her father's side instead of her mother's it wouldn't show up, see?'

'Well, we all know who she's descended from, don't we?' said Gaye, and Patrick agreed.

'What did you think of the programme?' said Jack diffidently.

'Could have been worse,' said CD. 'I was glad to see Camden let old Patrick here off lightly. All it really said was that you used to be a rock singer and now you weren't.'

'Funny that,' said Jack. 'Bit of a technical problem with some of the videotapes. I don't suppose I'll be working for him again.'

'Well, it's past history now,' said Patrick.

'Can you tell us what happened about Roger Little?' asked Aidan. 'I couldn't help noticing there hasn't been any building on the field.'

'The Woodland Renewal Trust bought it,' said Bobby.

'So did he not get his planning permission then?'

'Yes, he did. Then he sold up. It's all a bit of a mystery.'

'No, it's not,' said Dozer, too far away for Patrick to kick him into silence. 'I made him an offer he couldn't refuse.'

'What with?' said Bobby in amazement. 'I didn't know that.'

'Spare royalties some pop star had hanging around, weren't it, Pat? Mind you, I got it for a rock-bottom price, having all that evidence of Roman flooring. He saw my point of view quite quickly, really. I was quite reasonable.'

'Where's Joe gone?' asked Maxwell. 'I didn't see him go.'

'He was here,' said Bobby. 'I think he went down to the barn. Have you seen it? He's made a great job of it. Patrick and I said he didn't have to move out just for us but you can't argue with him.'

'Well, you could, but it might be a bit one-sided,' said Dozer. 'Here he is.'

Joe walked up out of the darkness with two guitars and gave one to Patrick. They made space for him in the circle.

'There's only one song I want to hear tonight,' said Bobby, resting her head on Patrick's shoulder, and there under the stars, the two guitars met in perfect understanding, and Joe sang the whole story to its sweet finale.

JAMES LONG

How does a BBC economics correspondent and one-time student of car design end up writing a novel about Anglo-Saxon relics? James Long can't fully explain this surprising contrast of interests, but does remember a key turning point in his career, marked by John Birt's arrival at the BBC—'Let's just say there was a certain incompatibility about our approaches'. So, in 1988, after many years spent covering business and political stories around the globe, he cut loose and with Will Hutton, a friend who later became editor of the *Observer*, set up an independent TV channel showing European business programmes. When it went 'spectacularly bankrupt' after two years, he found himself free to do what he'd always wanted to do—write novels.

James Long's first four books were political thrillers, but with the publication in 1988 of *Ferney*, a novel about a woman reunited with a lover from a past life, he turned his hand to a far more romantic kind of story. *Silence and Shadows*, in fact, stemmed from a conversation he had with a friend, a retired archaeologist who lived in the Oxfordshire area where the novel is set. 'He was amazing. You could go field-walking with him and every so often he'd kick a lump of earth and pick up a bronze brooch or a piece of Roman tile. He'd been on a dig once where they'd found a female burial. Because of worries about grave robbers, he had to move his camp bed over the grave and sleep there at night, literally inches above the skeleton. In the course of the dig, he felt that he'd formed a bond with the unknown woman that was stronger, in some ways, than many human relationships he'd had.'

James Long lives in Devon with his wife and three children. He wishes now that he'd studied archaeology while at university. 'I got to take part in a dig in the course of researching *Silence and Shadows* and it was just fantastic. I'll be doing it again.'